32

FICTION RESERVE

The John O'Hara Omnibus

The John O'Hara Omnibus

ℜℜ

Ravette London

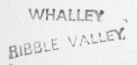

Contents

Pal
Joey

Contents

CHAPTER 1

Pal Joey

Dear Pal Ted:

Well at last I am getting around to knocking off a line or two to let you know how much I apprisiate it you sending me that wire on opening nite. Dont think because I didnt answer before I didnt apprisiate it because that is far from the case. But I guess you know that because if you knew when I was opening you surely must be aware how busy Ive been ever since opening nite. I figure you read in *Variety* what date I was opening in which case I figure you have seen the write ups since then telling how busy Ive been and believe me its no exagerton.

Well maybe it seems a long time since opening nite and in a way it does to me too. It will only be five weeks this coming Friday but it seems longer considering all that has happened to your old pal Joey. Its hard to believe that under two months ago Joey was strictly from hunger as they say but I was. The last time I saw you (August) remember the panic was on. I figured things would begin to break a little better around August but no. A couple spots where I figured I would fit in didnt open at all on acct of bankroll trouble and that was why I left town and came out this way. I figured you live in a small town in Michigan and you can stay away from the hot spots because there arent any and that way you save money. I was correct but I sure didnt figure the panic would stay on as long as it did. I finely sold the jalloppy and hocked my diamond ring the minute I heard there would be a chance down this way. I never was in Ohio before but maybe I will never be any place else. At least I like it enough to remain here the remainder of my life but of course if NBC is listening in Im only kidding.

Well I heard about this spot through a little mouse I got to know up in Michigan. She told me about this spot as it is her home town altho spending her vacation every year in Michigan. I was to a party one nite (private) and they finely got me to sing a few numbers for them and the mouse couldn't take her eyes off me. She sat over in one corner of the room not paying any attenton to the dope she was with until finely it got so even he noticed it and began making cracks but loud. I burned but went on singing and playing but he got too loud and I had to stop in the middle of a number and I said right at him if he didnt like it why didnt he try himself. Perhaps he could do better. The others at the party got sore at him and told him to pipe down but that only made him madder and the others told me to go ahead and not pay any attenton to him. So I did. Then when I got finished with a few more numbers I looked around and the heel wasnt there but the mouse was. She didnt give me a hand but I could tell she was more impressed than some that were beating their paws off. So I went over to her and told her I was sorry if it embarrassed her me calling attenton to her dope boyfriend but she said he wasnt a boyfriend. I said well I figured that. I said she looked as if she could do better than him and she said 'you for instance' and I said well yes. We laughed and got along fine and I took her home. She was staying with her grandmother and grand-father, two respectible old married people that lived there all their life. They were too damn respectible for me. They watched her like a hawk and one oclock was the latest she could be out. That to me is the dumbest way to treat that kind of a mouse. If its going to happen it can happen before nine oclock and if it isnt going to happen it isnt going to no matter if you stay out till nine oclock the next morning. But whats the use of being old if you cant be dumb? So anyway Nan told me about this spot down here and knew the asst mgr of the hotel where the spot is and she said she would give me a send in and if I didnt hold them up for too much of the ready she was sure I could get the job. I sing and play every afternoon in the cocktail bar and at night I relieve the band in the ballroom. Anyway I figured I would have to freshen up the old wardrobe so I had to get rid of the jalloppy and hock my diamond ring. I made the trip to Ohio with Nan in her own jalloppy which isn't exactly a jalloppy I might add. Its a 37 Plymouth conv coop. It took us three days to go from Mich. to Ohio but Ill thank you not to ask any questons about my private life.

This asst mgr auditioned me when we finely arrived and I knew right away I was in because he asked me for a couple of old numbers like Everybody Step and Swanee and a Jerry Kern medley and he was a Carmichael fan. Everything he asked me for I gave him and of course I put up a nice appearance being sunburned and a white coat from the proseeds of selling the jalloppy and hocking the ring. I rehearsed with the band altho Collins the leader hates my guts and finely I talked this asst mgr into letting me do a single irregardless of the band and he did.

Well you might say I ran the opening nite. I m.c'd and they had a couple kids from a local dancing school doing tap, one of them not bad altho no serious competition for Ginger Rogers. They were only on for the first week. They also had another mouse who was with the band, living with the drummer. She tried to be like Maxine. Well she wasnt even colored, thats how much like Maxine she was. The local 400 turned out for the opening nite and inside a week I was besieged with offers to entertain at private parties which I do nearly every Sunday as the bar and ballroom are not open Sunday or at least I do not work. In additon to the job at the hotel and the private parties you probably have read about the radio job. I went on sustaining the first week and by the end of the second week I got myself a nice little commercial. I am on just before the local station hooks up with NBC Blue Network five nites a week but I dont think you can catch me in New York. Not yet! My sponsor is the Acme Credit Jewellery Compay but I only have eight more weeks to go with them then I am free to negosiate with a better sponsor. Still Im not complaining. Your old pal Joey is doing all right for himself. I get a due bill at the hotel and what they pay me in additon aint hay. I also have the radio spot and the private parties. I went for a second hand Lasalle coop and I am thinking of joining the country club. I go there all the time with some of the local 400 so I figure I might as well join but will wait till I make sure I am going to stay here. I get my picture in the paper and write ups so much that I dont even bother to put them in my scrap book any more. The crowd at the club are always ribbing me about it and accuse me of having the reporters on my payroll but I just tell them no, not the reporters, the editors. I am a little sore at one of the papers because the local Winchell links my name constantly with the name of a very sweet kid that I go to the club and play golf with. Not that it isnt true. We see each other all the time and she comes to the hotel practically every nite with a party and when Im through for the nite we usely take a ride out to a late spot out in the country. Her father is president of the second largest bank.

It is the oldest. The biggest bank was formally two banks but they merged. Her name is Jean Spencer and a sweeter kid never lived. I really go for her. But this local Winchell took a personal dislike to me and made a couple cracks about us. One was 'That personality boy at a downtown hotel has aired the femme that got him the job and is now trying to move into society.' Me trying to move in to society! Society moved in on me is more like it. Jean was burned because she was afraid her father might see the item and when I meet her father I dont want him to have the wrong impression. I think the colyumist got the item from my ex-friend Nan. I didnt see much of her when I was rehearsing and the afternoon of opening nite she called up and said she wanted to come but what the hell could I do? Ask for a big table when they were getting $5 a head cover charge? I was glad enough to get the job without asking too many favors. Then a week or so later she called up and asked me could I let her have $50. I asked her what for and she hung up. Well if she didnt even want to do me the curtesy to tell me what for I wasnt going to follow her around begging her to take it. But I gave it a few days thought and decided to let her have it but when I phoned her they said she quit her job and left town. I understand from Schall the asst mgr that she sold her Plymouth and went to N.Y. Her name is Nan Hennessey so if you run into her anywhere youll know her. She could be worse, that is worse on the eye, a little dumb tho.

Well pally, they will be billing me for stealing all their writing paper if I dont quit this. Just to show you I dont forget I inclose $30. Ill let you have the rest as soon as possible. Any time I can help you out the same way just let me know and you can count on me. I guess you kissed that fifty goodbye but that isnt the way I do things. But I guess you know that, hey pal?

All the best from
PAL JOEY

CHAPTER 2

Ex-Pal

Dear Friend Ted:

That is if I can call you friend after the last two weeks for it is a hard thing to do considering. I do not know if you realise what has happen to me oweing to your lack of consideraton. Maybe it is not lack of consideration. Maybe it is on purpose. Well if it is on purpose all I have to say is maybe you are the one that will be the loser and not me as I was going to do certan things for you but now it does not look like I will be able to do them.

Let us rehearse the whole thing briefley. I wrote to you on the 26 or 7 of last month telling you how I was getting along and inclosing $30 and telling you all the news out here about me getting this radio job and singing in the hotel. Also telling you I was going around with a girl in the local 400 who had a father a banker et cetra. Then I also made the unfortunate error of telling you to look up a certan mouse if you happen to come across her. Which you did and mentoned my name. Well theres the rub. Oweing to your lack of consideraton (mentoning my name) there is hell to pay and I will tell you why. Maybe you know why. Maybe you knew damn well what you were doing and maybe not but anyhow I will tell you just in case.

The way I get it you meet this mouse and right off you shoot off your face about I wrote you and told you to look her up and she gets the wrong impression because as I understand it she thinks you think all you have to do is menton my name and you are in. Then she gets sore as hell and decides to get even with me. Well here I am 1000 miles from N.Y. and doing OK with my radio job and singing at the hotel and with this kid that has a father a banker and out of the blue everything goes haywire. You knew damn well the mouse I told you about was from this town because I remember distintly telling you all about her in my letter of the 26 or 7. I

remember distintly telling you she was no tramp and you only drew
your own conclusons and not from anything I told you. So here I
am doing OK with a car and two good jobs and this society kid
going for me and what happens. This is what happens. I do not
know what because it is too earley to say.

First of all the asst mgr of the hotel where I am singing he comes
to me and says 'Joey I just rec'd informaton that is not doing you
any good around this town and I want you to level with me and
tell me if it is true.' What? I said. What informaton? 'Well I do not
exactly know how to put it man to man. We are both men of the
world but this is what I have reference to, meaning that a certain
mouse from this town had to leave town on acc't of you and is now
in N.Y. and instead of helping her you are writing letters to pals
in N.Y. and shooting off your face about what a don Juan you are.
That dont do you any good personally and I will state frankly that
while we are highly pleased with your singing and drawing power
as a personality here at the hotel however we have to look at it
from all the angels and once it gets around that you are the kind
of chap that writes letters to his pals in N.Y. mentoning his fatal
attracton to the ladies why some nite some guy is just going to get
his load on and you are singing and a guy will walk up and take a
poke at you while you are singing. Think it over' he said. Well this
asst mgr is a pal of mine and I have the deepest respect for him
and I went on & did a couple numbers and after I went to him
and got him to tell me all about it. In detail.

So you call yourself a pal. Well that mouse I told you to look up
knew this asst mgr in fact I think I told you she introduce me to
him. I can see it all clearly. You met her and moved in and then
you told her I told you all about her and the little trip we took on
the way down from Michigan. As if that wasnt enough the next
thing you do you have to destroy the only fine decent thing that
has happen to me since coming to this jerk town, namely Jean. Jean
is the girl that has a father a banker and it was only a queston of
time before I was to meet the family and from there it was only a
queston of time before things came to the definitely serious stage,
but boy you certanly louse that up. I was to accompany Jean to a
private party last Tues. nite and she would pick me up at the hotel
after I did a couple numbers and go to this party. Usully when she
picks me up she is with another couple but last Tues. when the
doorman sent in word she was there she was alone in her Packard

conv coop. I thought nothing of it till I notice she was not driving
in the directon of this private party and also not opening her trap
but just driving and I called her attenton to the fact. 'No. We are
not going to Dwight and Connie Reynolds party this evening' she
said. I thought maybe it was called off and said so but she said no
it was not called off but she wanted to talk with me. Then out it
came. Thanks to you she gets this annonamous letter from that
mouse I told you about saying to look out for me that I was a guy
that would move in on her and then shoot off my face about it all
over. I ask her if I could see the letter and she said she tore it up
and I said did she look at the postmark. 'Was it postmark N. Y.?'
I said. She said no, here, but of course that mouse would send it
to some girl friend here and get it postmark here. Well Jean & I
had quite a scene much as I dislike scenes and no am't of persuason
on my part would convince her it was the work of a lousy bitch
that all she was was jealous. 'To think that I was on the vurge of
inviting you to Sunday dinner next Sunday' she said. That shows
how things stood between she & I, but so that is all loused up too.

Well I was frantic. I had come to care deeply for Jean. She lives
in a very different world than you and I. Her father is this banker
and very conservative and not use to having his daughter going
around with chaps that sing in a hotel even if it is one of the
principle hotels in the mid west. I go out with all the best people
here the 400 but not the older crowd & just on the vurge of going
to Jeans house for Sunday dinner she gets this annonamous letter
sticking the shiv in my back. Thanks to you. Well I thought for a
minute maybe the mouse came home & sent the letter herself and
I gave her a buzz Wed. afternoon and a dame's voice answered
and when she said who was it I told her and it turned out to be
the sister of the one that is causeing all the trouble. When I told
her who I was she called me everything she could think of till I
thought if anybody was listening in they would think they were
overhearing some bag and that she probably is because you got to
be a bag to know some of the things she called me. She also made
threats and said one of these nites she was coming down to the
hotel when I was doing a number and would personally spit in my
eye and knock me the hell off the stand. Then I told her what I
thought of her *and* her sister and if she ever showed her face around
the hotel I would knock her teeth down her throat. Woman or no
woman. I shut her up the bitch. I said she and her fine feathered

sister. Well I said if she wanted to know anything about her sister ask anybody that was in Michigan last summer and she would find out what I meant. So if you see the mouse again you can tell her. I dont give a damn if I lose my job here at the hotel or the radio spot. I dont have to take that stuff from any mouse or her sister. As for you my ex-pal you know what you can do and also you can sing for the $20 I owe you. I am making a little trip to N.Y. in the near future and we will have a little talk and you can explain your positon, altho the way I feel now if I saw you now your positon would be horizontle. I might as well tell you I am going to the gym 3 or 4 times a week and not that I need it because I always could slap you around when ever I wanted to.

You know what you can do.

Your EX-PAL JOEY

CHAPTER 3

How I Am Now in Chi

Pal Ted:

Well, pally, I have come to the concluson that old pals are best and never put too much faith in new acquaintances or you will end up two away from the 9 ball. When I tell you that you are getting it straight from head-quarters, because I know. I have been thinking it over and the true test of friendship is if you can weather such things as for instance you and I, meaning like differences of opinon over a mouse or the dough department and things on that order. You and I certanly have had our differences of opinon over the above yet here I am when I think it over and give the matter mature consideraton I think of you as a friend and I always hope you will consider me a friend if you have the ill fortune of ever getting in a spot in which I found myself recently. Then you can count on me altho' hoping the occason does not arise. (God forbid.)

Well I recall telling you about a little mouse one of the local 400 that her father was president of the bank (largest in town). This mouse Jean by name use to come every night to the hotel to hear me sing and it got so it was embarrasing owing to the fact that those lugs in the band would begin to kid me about it. They would say that mouse has got it for Joey but bad. She would come there and sit and just look at me and when she would get up to dance and I would sing she would just stand there in front of me with her escort and it became so that it was obvious and altho' I pride myself on being equal to such situatons (having had the experience before) it use to disconcert me more than I can say. However she arranged an introducton and I use to take her out especially when I was singing at private parties of the local 400. In a short time she use to stop for me at the hotel damn near every evening and I came to care for her as she was different than the usual ones that make a fool of themselves over a singer or entertainer. We were reaching the stage where it was you might say only a queston of time before Joey and Jean would veil up and perhaps I would consider giving up this life. Not that I ever intended doing that but she use to discuss it with me. She often use to ask me if I thought my life interesting and was it fun and how did I happen to get in it and of course that was her subtle way of getting me to consider probably going into the banking game with her father after we got married.

Well of course she was nineteen years old and one for the book as far as looks, figure, personality is concerned and also had plenty of scratch, being the bank presidents daughter. I went to work and bought a couple new arrangements in fact she gave me one for Xmas last Xmas. I happen to say one night I needed a couple new arrangements and she asked me how much they were and I told her my guy charged $50. She also gave me a set of studs and cuff links to wear with my tails that must have set her back the price of four arrangements. It was her favorite song at the time, the arangement she gave me. It was You go to my Head. I had an old arrangement of it from last summer but never had any call for it but she use to like it before she met me and so I got out the old arrangement and of course did not spoil it for her by saying it was one I had last summer and never had any call for. However I used the 50 to give her a Xmas present, a sport watch.

Then around the end of January they were having this ball in honor of the President (Roosevelt) to get up a fund that they would give for this infantile paralasys. Very white of them as they sit around all year and say what a heel he is and on his birthday they give him this ball and it is a club called the Junior League that she belonged to had charge of getting the talent and all that like publicity etc. So of course I gladly donated my services as I was going anyway having planned to escort Jean to the ball. The ball was in the ballroom of the hotel but I was going to escort her from her house. Then at the very last minute I said to her what should we do that evening until it was time to go to the ball (11.30 or 12) and she said she was going to a dinner party at these friends of hers named Fenton. I said it was a fine time to tell me that and said I consider it a fine thing to go to the Fenton's for dinner knowing that they were one of the few that took a snobbish attitude in connecton with me. I told her she could take it or leave it and if she went to their house for dinner she could count me out on the subject of escorting her to the ball. I was plenty burned and she

said she never understood I was taking her anyway and of course
she was right. I took it for granted and didnt bother to ask her until
the last minute and then I said well I will just stop for you at the
Fenton's about 11.30 and that will save you the trouble of coming
to the ball alone or with another couple. Imagine my surprise to
learn that she already had an escort, Jerry Towle a young dope
that does nothing but fly his own plane and scaring farmer's horses
and always in some kind of jam with the law but his old man has
plenty of scratch and gets him out of it. I said you go with Towle
and let him take you every other place from now on and I said and
dont bother to come to the hotel any more but stay away and our
date for the next night was off.

Well we had a quarrel about that and it ended up I didn't go to
the Fenton's and when I was singing that night at the ball she
made Towle dance her up and request Go to my Head but I said
very politely I only had the newer numbers and did not sing Go to
my Head this year. Did she burn? I didnt even dance with her and
I only sat with the boys in the band all night and then went up to
my room after I did my numbers and called up some hustler and
took her to a hamburger joint where the 400 go every night after
dances and hoped Jean and Towle would come in but they never
did so I gave the hustler 5 bucks for her time and sent her home
in a taxi.

Well the next night I am singing and in she comes but I never
give her a tumble but she gets her load on I notice and about one
a.m. a note comes over by waiter and she wants me to meet her
but she is with this party and I am burned so I dont answer the
note. I just tell the waiter no reply and when I finish my last
number I screw and go around the corner to have a cup of coffee
and there she is, followed me. I do not want to make a scene then
and there and she has her load on and will not go back and rejoin
her party so I send around and get my car out of the garage hoping
to take her for a ride and sober her up but oh no. Instead we go
for a ride and altho' it was freezing and we did not have a coat
either of us we are out for about an hour and always fighting and
it began to get late and I knew the grill at the hotel would be
putting the chairs up on the tables so I ignored her and turned
around and went back. No sign of her party. They have gone. That
means I have to take her home and she lives out in the suburbs
and by the time we get there somebody has called her up to see if

she got home and woke up the old man and he is waiting for her in a dressing gown. She is still plastered the little lush and her old man asks what the meaning of this is and who am I and bringing his daughter home in this conditon. Then I tell him who I am and he says Oh, he has heard about me and has always wanted to meet me and without any warning brings one up from the floor and I stop it with my chin, as dirty a punch as I ever saw. I got up but had the presence of mind so that I did not let him have one but said I dont want any part of his daughter, the lush. Keep her home or he would be a grandfather one of these days without a son in law. I think he would have got a gun but I was out of there before he had the chance.

Well the next a.m. about 10 the phone rings and it is the manager, my boss. He wants me down in his office so I go and he hears all about it only an exageraton of what really happened. To make a long story short I am out. I say what about my contract and he says read your contract and then I remember he had the right to fire me if I get out of line and he gives me the rest of the week (pay) and an extra week and says he advised me to lam out of there as I insulted the most powerful man in the whole town as I will soon find out. I find out alright. I call up this ad agency that pays me for singing on the local radio staton where my sponsor is this credit jewelry company. They were just about to call me. I am out. The mouse's old man only owns the God damn staton. I go to a lawyer but he wont take my case as he says I havent any case. Even if I had he would think twice about bucking this mouse's old man. So there I am holding an empty bag with my wardrobe and a car only about half paid for and all told about a little over 300 in my kick. So I go back to the hotel and start in packing (about 5 in the afternoon this is) and a messenger comes and brings me a note from Jean. She is sorry about it and did not want to cause me all this trouble and would do anything to make or mend. Her old man had her at the doctor's or she would have got in touch with me sooner and will I call her at this number, a girl friend of hers. They are going to take her to some place in N. Carolina the next day and she has to see me. I do not have to worry as the dr. says she is okay, but she would not be able to stand it going away like this with me feeling this way all over a little thing like a misunderstanding over the Fenton's dinner and she heard her old man threaten to get me bounced out of town etc and she is desperate because she loves me. Well I thought it over and what a fine chance I had to show her old man who was the most powerful man in town as far as his own family are concerned. All I had to do was pick up Jean and drive over the state line and inside of two hours he would have a son in law alright. I am sitting there debating within myself as to whether I will call her or not and the door opens. 'You know me,' he says. Towle. 'I see you are packing. Good. There is a 9 oclock for Chicago and an 8.30 for N.Y. and I would suggest the 8.30 but I leave the choice entirely up to you,' he says. 'I think I will sit around and take you to the train.' I ignore him but go on packing and when I finish up I send down and have room service bring me up a steak sandwich with French fries, a cup of coffee and a piece of pie and I eat it there with him sitting there. I had to pay cash for it as room service will not let me sign. Then I lit a butt and smoke it calmly and then I phone the railroad and order a lower on the 9 oclock for Chi. I can see he is burned but that is what I intend. Then the phone rings and he answers it and says he is not here but has just left and then he says 'Dont be a damn fool Jean this is Jerry and yes he is here but you are not going to see him if I can help it and you may not speak to him as I am acting on your fathers orders.' Then he hangs up. He is a big lug. Over 200.

Well I phone the garage and tell them to put my car into dead storage and take out the battry and then it is time to go to the train and he goes with me. When we get there I tell him he can have the pleasure of paying the taxi and he says it is a pleasure alright and I said I thought it would be and also a pleasure for me. When I go to get my ticket he even pays for the ticket, tips the porter, etc. I did not lose my sense of humor. I said 'By the way I have nothing to read on the train' and he buys me papers and magazines. I see the humor in it and I also say I always have chewing-gum on trains so he buys me some gum. But he does not see the humor for when the train is ready to pull out I reach out my hand and say it was a pleasure to have him come down and see me off, him of all people and just then he hauls off and slaps my hand, burned like I never saw anybody burned.

Well the train pulled out and that is the story of how I am now in Chi. I am singing for coffee & cakes at a crib on Cottage Grove Ave. here. It isnt much of a spot but they say it is lucky as four or five singers and musicians who worked here went from here to big

things and I am hoping. Well give my best to Artie and Fred and
Chink and Mort. Tell Mort congratulations as I hear he is starting
up a new band and I would be willing to work for scale. Tell Fred
when he comes out to look me up as I plug his last two numbers
every nite. Well Ted all the best and I don't have to say I think
your solo in Jeepers Creepers is as good as Vanuti. I am glad a pal
is having such good luck and I mean that sincerely as ever. Will
write soon again.

PAL JOEY

CHAPTER 4

Bow Wow

Dear Friend Ted:

Well pal I had to sit down the minute I came home just returning from a furniture store around the corner from where I am living. Having just heard what you did to Hong Kong Blues. Well if I was ever proud of a friend I am proud of you alright. To say it is a wonderful recording is to say the least. I happen to drop in at this store as I do every week to hear the new recordings. You know me, Ted. Strictly larceny when it comes to listening to those arrangements but I cant afford to buy any new arrangements of my own right now so I have to get them from recordings and take the best of this one and that one. The joint where I am singing and m.c-ing in is satisfied with my work and it keeps me in coffee & cakes but not much more. As a pal of mine said the other night Chicago is alright if you like Chicago altho I would rather be back in N.Y. or even go to Frisco for the other Fair. I have had one or two propositons in regards to Frisco but nothing attractive. That is to make it worth while going all the way out there and then maybe getting stuck where I dont know anybody. I dont know what to do so for the moment am sticking here getting my coffee & cakes and building up a local following. They have a place out on the North side that has made me one or two offers but I will stay down in this territory until I get a propositon from some place in the Loop dist. I figure I ought to go good in a place like the Chez Paris, tops here, or maybe one of the hotels. Downey always goes good here altho his stuff is of course different than mine. Well enough of my problems. I only wanted to conveigh my congratulatons on the new recordings and for a young band. Who have you got on the guitar? If I didn't know McDonough was dead I would say it was him. I also thought I recognised Fud but I guess he is still with Tommy so guess I am an error.

Well I guess you wonder what I do with my spare moments out
in this bailwick. Write letters is one thing. Just think a year ago
you were the one crying the blues and less than a year ago I was
doing alright with the Packard etc. And now you are up there and
there will be no stopping you and believe me you have the ardent
wishes of success from all your pals. I am getting by in this crib in
Chi. but guess I have learned my lesson and am a changed man.
All because of a dog.

Well this is the first time I wrote since I bo't Skippy the name
of my dog and it is wonderful what they can do. They give you the
courge to continue when things look bad. I use to hear Al White
on the subject of man's best friend the dog and use to laugh myself
sick when White would rib the love and affecton of a man and a
dog but he is wrong. There is something to it. It worked in my case
as when I came out here I didnt have any job and took the first
thing that came along and took the attitude that the world was a
pretty sorry place to live in and it effected my work. I would get
up to do a number and I took the attitude that I hated all the
people there and I guess it showed because Lang (no relaton to
Eddie) the owner of this spot gave me a call. He said get more of
a pleasing personality in it or pack. It put the fear of God in me as
I wasnt there long enough to build up a following and had not
stashed any dough away. Also no prospects or propositons from
other spots and of course this joint dont spend any dough advertising and the press agent gets no pay but only a certan am't of
drinks on the cuff so you can imagine how hard he works. So I
gave the matter my mature consideraton and then that week I was
out getting my breakfast around 4 one afternoon and right near
where I eat is this pet & dog shop. I never had any interest in dogs
and never considered owning one and thought they were a nuisance
especially in towns. But I saw this mouse standing there bent over
and talking to one of the dogs in the window of the shop. She was
about twenty and I didn't care if she had a face out of the Zoo but
spring was in the air and this mouse had a shape that you dont see
only on the second Tuesday of every week and when you do see a
shape like that you have to do something about it. So I stopped
and feined an interest in the dog kingdom and cased the mouse and
got a look at her kisser. Well it fitted in with the rest of the body.
Not pretty but cute. She had personality in her face I could see
that. She didn't see me because she was so crazy about this one

dog that had his nose up against the window and she was talking
to it before she noticed me and then got sort of embarassed when
she saw me. But by that time I was looking at the dog and smiling
at him and leaned over and started talking and the first name I
could think of came to my head and I said hello Skippy boy. And
the mouse looked at me and said is that his name, Skippy? I said
I didnt know I only pretend it was. I said I pass by here every day
and got to love him so much that I had to give him a name like
the name of an airdale dog I used to have when I was a kid. Oh
so I love dogs, she wanted to know and I said yes. Then she said
why didnt I buy this puppy and I said for the same reason why I
didnt buy a Dusenburg, money. Well the effect it had on her was
wonderful. I could see tears in her eyes and she said it was a shame
that anybody that love dogs so much had to be deprived of them
because of the finances where so many people that didnt really love
them had them and didnt treat them properly. Yes, I said, that is
true. I said I was saving up so I could buy Skippy and there was
a sign in the window that said $30. That part was the truth, that
is, I didnt have any $30 to buy any dogs with. I began telling her
about Skippy the airdale that I didnt have when I was a kid and
pretty soon got to believing it myself, all about how my heart was
broken when poor little Skippy was crushed beneath the wheels of
a 10 ton truck. I said my family were well to do people in those
days and wished to buy me another dog but I said to them no dog
would take the place of Skippy and never would until one day I
happen to be going by this shop and my eye caught this little
puppy's and something about him reminded me of Skippy and she
said yes, he was a little like an airdale. Well I didnt know a airdale
from a hole in the ground and didnt know what the hell this mut
was in the window and so I said it wasnt the breed, I said, it was
just something in this puppy's expresson that reminded me of my
old Skippy. She was touched. She said she never would of taken
me for somebody that loved dogs so much and I said you dont
know much about dogs then, Miss I said dogs have strange tastes
in people and only a dog knows who he likes. By this time Skippy
was laying down and I said he is tired and I said I had to go and
get my breakfast. I said this is the only time of the day that I can
see Skippy as they take them out of the window soon. Just a guess
but I didnt seem to remember seeing the dogs in the window late
in the afternoon and the mouse said 'Did I hear correctly when you

said you were going to have breakfast?' And I said yes, I am one
of those unusual people that their days are upside down. I said you
are probably the kind that would be having tea now but I am
having breakfast. That made her laugh and so I took advantage of
that and said why not have tea with me if she didnt mind sitting
at a counter for it? As I said before I had cased this mouse and she
was pretty but I knew she was no society debutante. Probably a
stenog out of work but very cute. So she said she often ate at
counters and went with me. I was right and she was a stenog
looking for work. She went with me to this one-arm where I eat
and she had a tomato on rye and a coffee and I had eggs and coffee
and we started talking and it turned out she was from some little
town in Illinois, not Peoria but some place like it. Her name was
Betty Hardiman and lived with her married sister and her husband
and only came to Chi a month before. I told her my people lost all
their money in the crash and I had to leave Princeton college and
go to work but the only work I was suited for was singing with a
band or in a night club and then she said she recognised my name
from passing the club on her way to the L. She said she thought
people that worked in clubs got plenty of money and I said it
depends on what club and then when it came time to pay the check
she said she would pay her own and insisted and said let me
consider that her contributon to buying Skippy.

Well I said I hoped she would come around to the club some
time with her boy friend and I would sing any number she would
request and she said her boy friend didnt live in Chi but went to
college at the Illinois U. at Champaign. I said well she should come
some time with her sister and her husband and Betty said her bro.
in-law never went to night clubs and I said I guess it was pretty
dreary for a young girl living like that and she said it was becoming
that way altho it was better than home. She said she loved Chi,
just going around the Loop and watching the people's faces on the
L trains, but would like to see some more of the fun but her boy
friend was working his way thru the Illinois U. and didnt get to
Chi only two or three times a year. Well I said this is very pleasant
but I had to go and rehearse a couple numbers at the club and got
her phone number and said I would like to take her out some night
if I got a night off and she said she tho't it would be alright.

Well I saw her a couple times but only in the day time. We use
to meet at the dog shop. We would go to the one-arm and then I

would have to leave her but one afternoon she borrowed her bro. in-law's car and drove out to the country and I gave her a little going over but not too much as I could tell the time was not ripe. I was even surprised I could neck her at all on acc't of this boy friend at the Illinois U. but I guess it was the first time a pass was made at her since the last time she saw the college boy and I guess she needed a little work-out. Well that night I hit a crap game for about eighty clams and two days later I met Betty and told her and she said now I could buy Skippy and I said no, unfortunately the flea-bag where I was living did not permit dogs. I said that was just my luck. Then I said I have an idea. I said how about if I buy him for her and she could keep him and on conditon that she would let me see him and she said she would love to but would have to ask her sister as they only had an apartment. I met the sister by that time and I knew she went for me but had not met the bro. in-law. She asked the sister but the sister said no, Betty couldn't have a dog in the ap't because it was too small, much as she would love to have a dog. So then I went to my landlady and asked her if I could have a dog and she said sure so then I went to Betty and told her I had a deal with my landlady that if I paid more rent I could keep the dog so Betty was overjoyed and I bo't Skippy. The landlady has a kid about ten or eleven and he takes care of Skippy for me. Takes him for his walks and washes him and the landlady thinks I am a fine young fellow but why shouldnt she when her kid has the use of a $30 dog for nothing. I often have fun with the mut too and pat him and I often think if it wasn't for Skippy I never would of met Betty. Her sister and bro. in-law are going away the week-end after next and we will have the ap't all to ourselves. It's about time but I had to be patient as she said she wanted to be sure first, but a man with such a love and affecton for dogs was a man you could trust. Well, pal, all the best and keep your eyes open for any spots you hear for me. I would rather be around N. Y. this summer as it gets hot as hell out here in summer but if you hear anything like a good spot with a band touring or some summer hotel in Mass. or Maine dont forget your pal. I have no contract here as they never heard of a contract at a crib like this so can leave at a moment's notice. Of course it will be worth sticking around a month or so if you get what I mean. Bow wow.

PAL JOEY

CHAPTER 5

Avast and Belay

Friend Ted:

Well, chum, still in Chi, doing alright and have my notices to prove it like one critic that I hardly know at all that works on a throwaway that they distribute at hotels etc. but is far the best writer on the nite life and he goes on to say I am the smoothest and most urbane singer of sophisticated melodies this town has seen in many a moon, and it was not a case of me taking an ad to get the write-up as the 1st I knew of it was when somebody showed it to me. 'What is he your cousin?' said one of the lightweights in the band as he ignore the band and just gave them a menton in passing and devoted all his write-up to me. I only menton this now because I have in mind an idea that I want to discuss with you in this letter.

Well, chum, this is the idea I have been taking under consideraton and the pro's & con's ever since around the beginning of Sept. but more so lately owing to a conversaton I had with another chap recently. You would not know the name if I told you but his name is Charley Goas. Charley is a man around 40 odd yrs of age and a mind like a steel trap and knows all the angles. He is still alive today but use to be a big accountaint for Capone or one of the big mobs out here like Capone or perhaps it was Bugs Moran or Deeny O'bannon or Collosimo. I never asked him that as he was not a mob guy himself but just did their accountaincy for them and I would not know that only I happen to ask somebody what he did and they told me. I think he owns a piece of the room where I sing in now but I am not suppose to know that and do not pipe. Well he took a liking to me and drops in every nite and we struck up an aquantainceship and I guess he more or less considers me like a kid bro. as he often gives me advice like on more than 1 occason he saw me looking at a mouse and when I looked at him he smiled and without me saying anything he said to me, 'That's for you, eh?

O.K. sonny boy if you want to end up on crutches.' So that shows how he took an interest in me and I apprisiate it and therefore when he offered me some other advise I also took it or am starting to take it by giving you this idea I have in my mind.

This is the set-up. Charley was telling me one nite how it looked like a sure thing there was going to be a war. Next day, they declare war, and there was a rumor around that the room would fold because business stank but I happen to know that Charley told the backers they shouldnt be silly. They were ahead enough so they could take a few bad nites and if business didnt pick up why then fold but dont fold until they saw if business was going to stay stinking or perhaps get better. Charley was right. We kept open and business is better than ever.

So all during this I got a chance to talk to Charley about the war and he got to remenissing about in the last war. I do not know for a fact if he was in the army or navy as with Charley you leave Charley do the talking and never ask questions. However he asked me what my plans were and I said I did not give it much tho't as I did not think we would be in it and time enough when we got in. 'Don't be silly,' said Charley. 'We will be in it before the horses stop running at Hialeah.' This came as rather a surprise to me but before I had the opportunity to discuss it with him he said pick your spots now and do not be a sucker and get drafted. Then they can put you where they want to but if you pick yr. spot now you can stay in it and he said 'Not this bunch of plumbers but do you have a contact with a guy with a good band' and I said 'yes' and mentoned you as one of my eldest friends and he said he heard of you and said flattering things about you on the air and said he never met you but caught you & the band somewhere and got the impresson you have a wonderful personality and I agreed with him extremely. Well he said I was a fool if I did not make some kind of a propositon with you like get you to join the navy. Wait a minute now and read it all before you think I am going wacky. He said if a jig band by the name of Jim Europe (probably his professional name) during 1917 could be a big success in Paris why not a fellow like you, a name band known from coast to coast on the air and by records. He said there was this jig name Jim Europe had a band and they just about ran Paris in the war and after it until somebody took a shot at Mr. Europe and that ended him. All those Parisienns went for the band too which is a handy thing in a

war. Acc. to Charley they even made this jig a lieutenant in the
U.S.A. and he was a regular officer with a snappy uniform and
white guys had to salute him owing to him being an officer. Well
if they did that they ought to do it for you. He said take for instant
Sousa, John Phillips Sousa and I remember him, the march king.
My old lady used to never tire of Sousa on the phonograph until
in desperaton I broke the damn records and my old man belted me
for it as he also use to listen to them altho he did not know a note
of music but was a son of a bitch for finding the nearest bar if you
pardon the gag. Well Sousa had this big corny band all brass and
what did they do but make him a kind of an admiral. Stars &
Stripes For-ever and Shine Little Glow-worm was the kind of stuff
he played so you can write your own ticket with your repretory. He
didnt play good but played loud and so my 1st suggeston is get
more brass and gradually expand the size of the band and if I were
you I would give the boot to that rum-pot you have now and get
yourself a real press agent that could get yr. picture in the Life
magazine and maybe it would be a good idea to get navy uniforms
and also get up a few routines like Waring use to have. Drills, only
learn to march instead of those routines with cocktail shakers etc.
that Waring use to have. All this is my idea not Charley's as he
only contributed the original tho't and I put my brain to work on
what you could do if I called yr. attenton to it.

I am not trying to tell you how to run yr. band as you do alright
without me and once in a while when I tho't to myself Ted ought
to do this or that I refrained from telling you as it is your band not
mine. However this war stuff is an angle you may not of thought
of.

I am only scratching the surface with these suggestons and have
many more that are on the same order but better and these randam
notes now are just suggestons or hints but ought to get yr. mind
running in that directon. We could do big things and at the same
time be patriotic doing it. As I understand it we ought to figure on
just the regular pay which is of course naturlly way below scale as
when you are working for Uncle Sam he never heard of scale but
would pay $30 a month to the ones with the rank of private and
only cigarette money to a leader like yourself but of course I guess
it would be understood with the army or navy that you could do
jobs and records and of course a big patriotic band would get all
the cream if you start soon enough. I have a slogan 'put your band

on the bandwagon' before the others get hep. I say we all the time
because I take for granted you would get me a pardon out of this
joint Chicago if you decide a good idea. If you wanted to put me
on the pay-roll now I could give this joint notice just by saying why
dont you guys go take a flying etc. and take a powder out of here
that day and be in N.Y. the next. A wire will do the trick Ted boy.
I will level with you. I get an honest yard here and was only saying
that for laughs when I told you I got $150 the way we all exagerate
in this business. You could go on working while I talk to the Army
and Navy guys and whichever offers us the best propositon you can
be sure I will take that one. Then when war is declared we are in
uniform and ready to go that nite. Maybe by that time you would
consider me such a good mgr. that you would have me for your
peace-time mgr. even before we get in the war. I would find out in
advance (from Charley) when we are getting in the war and would
book you into some big Bway spot in time so that nite when war
is declared we would be there in our uniforms. Think of the flash,
as they use to say in vaudeville days. The 1st Swing Band in
Uniform! It would be plastered all over the papers and with the
right handling I see you shaking hands with the President at the
White House, him congratulating you for being the 1st band in
kahki, altho I hope the navy gives us the better propositon as for
a band the navy has better toggery.

Well think it over Ted because Charley says the time is getting
short. Charley says before the hay-burners stop running at Hialeah.
John Phillips Sousa was an old man so they had to make him an
admiral but admiral sounds too old for you so if we decide the navy
offers us the better propositon you could be a Commander. I could
be a Leutenant Commander. One thing I will add to the informaton
above which is this. I am only kidding about telling these Chicago
guys where to head in and this is why. It is because Charley says
during the last war they had anywhere from 10 to 50,000 sailors in
Chi. believe it or not. They had a training camp here for sailors
and that was as close as they got to getting their head shot off. If
they got their head shot off it would be in a crap game amongst
themselves or in a riding academy on the South Side. I am more
in favor of the navy but of course will take the better propositon.
'So get the band aboard the bandwagon' Ted and I am ready the
moment you give the downbeat. Charley said a band like this no
doubt would be booked for liberty bond engagements when they

start selling liberty bonds to the people. I tho't of an angle there and asked Charley 'Suppose we are booked into a town to sell these liberty bonds for the government do we get our percent. of the gross' but Charley said not with Mr. Whiskers at the gate, nobody cuts in on Mr. Whiskers. But it just shows I was looking out for our interest. Also Charley may be wrong. He can be. He thinks his wife doesnt like me and boy he is so wrong.

Well Commander, avast and belay and all that sort of thing.

Your pal
JOEY

P.S.: I also want to warn you Vallee was in the navy in the last war and may have a good in there so we have to work fast so he wont crab our act.

CHAPTER 6

Joey on Herta

Dear Pal Ted:

Well Pal I suppose you did not hear that yrs. truly the undersigned and to-wit has manage to build up a following so that they are borrowing the money wherewith to enlarge the joint and take care of the bigger and higher class clintele which followed on the heels of when I put over 'Waiter with the Water'? But it is good news that you are banging them right over every where you go. I hear nothing but the best reports of you and the band and it is no secret that when you played the Palomar in Los Angeles, for a fairly recent band you broke the house record. Maybe you did not break the Goodman or Artie Shaw record but they made their record with an establish band and of course you went in there with scarcely if any radio build-up and still did terrific business. I am sure you glorify in your success and believe me when I say nothing could make me happier than you being right up there where you belong and am sure will not change in regard to your old pals. Might like to know later developments on how I am doing. Well here goes.

I told you the details and how I got creamed out of the hotel spot in Ohio & came here and made this connecton. For a while I was from hunger but suddenly clicked as it were over night. With me it was one of those things, just one of those crazy things. One nite singing a lung out for dopes that wouldn't know it if I was Toscanini, Al Rinker, or Brooks John or myself. All they cared about was if I sang Deep Purple 75 times a nite and they were satisfied. Female lushes that they would stand right under me while their escorts were giving them a little going over and I and the band were not suppose to see it. Oh no, just dumb, is what we were. I use to stand up there giving the Deep Purple and all the time the tho't kept cropping up in my mind 'I only wish I had a water pistol, an old fashion water pistol such as we played with as

a child and wouldn't I like to squirt you right in the eye with it
Madam right in the mist of your memory Madam.' But one nite I
happen to get a small slice of Phil Harris broadcasting from Los
Angeles and happen to tune in when he was polishing off Hold
Tight. I said this can not be the guy that formerly I use to consider
a road company Richman but it was. I knew there would be no
trouble at all so I polished off his Hold Tight and practicly over
nite I was the one man attracton of this joint. Then I caught Harris
again one nite doing Fishes and from then on I and the joint were
but set. The owner (only fronting for one of the many mobs they
still got left here in Chi) gave me a quick hist in pay and began to
talking contract but no said I. No contract now. Let's wait?
(Meaning maybe some advertising agency might grab me off and
did not want to be stuck with any contract.) So I let on like I was
very happy at this joint & the only reason I was saying no contract
was because I was coresponding with my agent in N.Y. and my
hands were tied until hearing from him. That is a laugh, my agent.
After they tied a can to my tail in Ohio there wasnt an agent in
the U.S. that would give me a tumble. However that is neither here
nor there but is a sample. So they put my name outside in lights
and I was in but good.

Well I started out to tell you a little experience I had which just
goes to show you how the leaches fasten upon a person practicly
before they have time to turn on the lights that spell out his name.
This one nite after I began clicking there was this large party given
by a bowling club consisting of people in the neighborhood that
belong to this neighborhood bowling club and met some nite every
wk. in order to indulge themselves in their silly pastime and this
nite was the nite when they had their annual get-together for the
purpose of the distributon of the awards & prizes and of course
they had about 40 or more there, men & women. Well the press
agent of this joint said to me it would make a nice gesture if I would
make a few reference to this club when I introduced my numbers
and dedicate some numbers to them. He kept talking about cagling.
The only Cagle I ever heard of was a football player that use to
play for West Point years ago but Cagling is also the name for
bowling so I made a few wise cracks about Cagling that the p. a.
gave me and I also put one of my own in about Keg-lined beer
cans altho why I should give a plug to Bernie's exsponsor I do not
know only that it occurred to me at the time. It went over big and

they liked me and soon were standing around asking for request no's.

I happen to notice in the sea of faces this one kisser that stood out in the crowd. About 21 and naturally blonde hair and complected and most likely a Swede I tho't. So then when they all insisted that I join them I naturally obliged them and this mouse named Herta Gersdorf was the one I gradually sat next to. One word led to another and it turned out she would like to be a singer and so to make a nice gesture to the club and for good will etc. I said I have an announcement to make and Miss Herta Gersdorf will sing. She pretend to be surprised but did not fool me as I knew she was working on me to do that very thing, so I brought her up to the mike and asked her what she wanted to sing and what key but she did not know what key, only the name of the song. Three guesses. Day in Day Out. I encouraged her and got her started and to my amazement she turned out to have a voice not of course a trained voice and had no experence in singing in public but I detected possibilities in the voice and began to think to myself I had a find. Well she got a big hand of course being a member of the cagle club and they did not detect the rough edges and amateur touches or if they did they forgave her owing to her youth and lack of experence singing in public. So I helped her with an encore and of course I made a lot of friends for the joint and also increased my own following by the gesture. Well I talked to her and inquired did she ever consider doing it professionally (singing I mean) and she said she always use to dream of it but knew there was no chance. So I said I would gladly help her and got her phone no. and she said she would have to ask her parents and the next day or 2 days later she called me up and said they would like it if she could take lessons from me but could not afford to pay anything and I said that would be o.k. So for a week I went to her house every nite when she got home from stenogging in the real estate office where she worked and showed her a few things then after the 1st wk. I brought her to the joint and late every afternoon I would show her some mike technique and the difference between singing in front of a mike & without it. She was a dumb little mouse but willing to learn. So all the time I was thinking this was going to be my favorite dish but at the time did not do anything about it as I was being taken care of but too good by a dame that had a little dress shop in the neighborhood. Anyway I never made a pitch with Herta. I was afraid it would Herta. So what I did was find out she was 21 and looked up an old agreement I had with an agent the 1st time I ever had an agent and copied it down and she signed it making me her agent in case she clicked. Therefore I went to the 'owner' of the joint and said I had this mouse and told him she was popular and had a voice which I was training and of course the 1st thing that heel did was he said he wanted to warn me to watch my step and dont get any bad reputaton in the neighborhood for fooling around with the neighborhood kids or there would be hell to pay and the patrons would stop coming in imagine! I said to him he could let me worry about my conduct, morals, etc and he said Oh if there was any worrying to do I better do it which sounded pretty sinistre but he was not throwing any scare into me for I replied to him let us pass over that phase of it and get down to business, did he or did he not want this mouse she being under contract to me in a strictly business legitamite deal and showed him the contract. I said acting as artists representative for the girl I wanted $35 a wk. for her services and we dickered until he came up to 25 and then I said its a deal so I swung the job for her. It was about time something like that happen to me after all the hard luck I been having and also it was about time Herta was getting around to paying something on acc't as she never paid me a nickel for my instructon and lessons and rehearsals and my time, etc, and her parents never offer to pay anything either so it was a lucky thing for her I got her the job as it enabled her to pay me back $25 a wk. for the instructon & time and lessons etc. and I was able to continue giving her lessons while she worked. I shamed her mother into getting up $30 for an evening dress. I took one look at the dress they picked out for her and said to them 'May I inquire if you think Herta is singing for a choir?' I did not want to lose my temper therefore the gag. The kid was built on the order of Babs whatever her name was that worked with the band when you use to play horn with Joe and here they were trying to make her wear a dress for a convent of sisters. So I entered into the situaton and informed them that I would take care of the clothes dept. and out of my own pocket advanced her $9.50 so she could pour herself into a $39.50 no. that showed everything but her scar where she had the appendisetis if she ever had it (some spelling I admit). Also advanced her $5 to get her hair fixed up and fingernails etc. Well I put her over but big and she only fumbled one no. a little and I

tho't at the time after the 1st nite she was going to be grateful as
she seemed grateful at the time. I was of course going on with the
instructon etc. and let her have for nothing a couple arrangements
I was thinking of polishing off for myself. Also featured her in my
own duets and also gave her a swell break when I would introduce
her nos. I would introduce her as my protege Herta (I dropped her
last name but only used Herta like Hildegard the singer that doesn't
say her last name either because it is some name from Milwaukee
or some place.) It went over. But little did I know.

Low & behold one nite before she went on she said to me she
had to be good that nite because her boss & his wife would be there
that nite. I said what boss, forgetting. She meant the boss at the
real estate office where she stennoged. I forgot she was still working
there. So I gave her a big intro. and also gave her 2 more nos to
sing than usual so she could impress her boss. Well I tho't no more
of it till the next nite she was there early & said she wanted to talk
to me and I said o.k. and what she wanted to talk about was dough
and I tho't being innocent I tho't she wanted to pay me back the
sums I advance to her but oh no. She said her boss asked her how
much she was getting and she told him our arrangement about me
coaching her etc. So the heel went to the 'owner' of the joint because
he (Herta's boss) handled the real estate deal on the property and
knew Lang, the 'owner'. He found out Lang was giving me the 25
for Herta and so he wanted to know why I didn't give her the 25
and put ideas in her head that she should get the 25 less $2.50 for
my commission. $2.50!!! my commission for teaching her everything
she ever knew. Anyway I told her I said I had a little matter of a
contract and that stopped her but the next nite who should come
in but Martin the name of her boss and Lang was also there, just
before the joint opened for the nite. I do not wish to bore you with
the details but dont let anybody tell you they got rid of the muscle
boys in Chi. because we argued pro & con and finally I got mad
and said I have a contract with Herta and Martin said let me see
it & I showed it to him and right before my two eyes he slowly tore
it up. He turn to Lang and said 'I guess everything is satisfactory
now?' and Lang laughed. I saw I was licked as those gorills do not
care anything about law and what was the use of me a stranger
trying to do anything. Then I said 'Mr. Martin just what is yr.
angle?' Meaning what, he replied. I said 'Oh nothing but I sure do
admire yr. nerve.' Oh my nerve is o.k. he said. I have nothing to

fear from a punk crooner like you. I said with a smile 'Go ahead and insult me as much as you care to, Mr. Martin, but I was not referring to that. All I was referring to was yr. nerve the way you bro't your wife here to hear the little girl friend the office wife sing.' With that he burned and came at me but I had a bottle in my hand under the table all the time he was talking & anyway Lang stopped him. Not because Lang likes me any more than Martin but a couple people came in while we were sitting there and the joint use to have a reputaton for 3 shootings they had there a couple years ago and Lang was told to keep his nose clean by the cops if he wanted to operate in that neighborhood as they did not want more complaints. 'Oh well he is not worth brusing my knuckles on' said Martin and I laughed in his face and he went out.

Well Martin has something on Lang o.k. because I found out from the cashier that Herta is getting 50 now. The nerve of this Martin, he still brings his wife to the joint and Herta often goes & sits with Mrs. M. and she is old enough to be her mother, so I guess it is one of those things where a woman would rather have her husband chasing around after young girls just as long as he don't get a divorce. You cant tell me any different. I see it all too clear why I could not move in on Herta. These 'innocent' ones are the ones alright. If I was a little more innocent maybe I would be right up there getting 2 grand a wk. etc.

Well Ted, give my love to everybody in 802 except about 5000 heels that all think that all they need is just a little 8 piece combinaton and they would have the best little band etc. etc. Drop me a line but be careful who you give my address to.

                                                    PAL JOEY

CHAPTER 7

Joey on the Cake Line

Friend Ted:

Well Xmas is coming and the geese are getting fat, please put a penny in the blind man's hat as the old saying use to go but not that I am asking you to put a penny in my hat or am not a blind man either as far as that is concerned. I never saw the day wherein no matter how much moola I had I could not use some more but I am saving you for a big touch in case I want to start my own band in competition with you (who knows I may be kidding on the level and that would be quite irony if it ever happened?) I do not know why it is that I sound like everything was sharp and I was right up there because if you want the truth and the whole truth and nothing but the truth your pal Joey is on the cake line. That is my way of putting it that I am on the bread line only I am still a little better off. You get what I have reference to about cake & bread. It was a famous historical topper when Josephine, the wife of Napoleon was informed that the poor people did not have any bread to eat and she said 'Why dont they eat some cake if they havent any bread.' Very good considering what they did was lop off her conk for saying it. Well I got my head lopped off too but not for making any crack. I went to the club one nite to give with the vocal chorus and add some class to the joint with my new midnite blue tails only there was no club there. That is the place was burn to the ground. 10,000 nite clubs in this country but I guessed they repealed the law of averages because they had to pick the one I was in to have a fire. I notice I never get that kind of odds when I go to the track. But who is complaning. I know one lug is complaning but will come to him later. So this nite I went there and all there was was ropes and fire hoses with ice hanging down and the joint stank worse than ever because you burn some rugs and pour some water on it and the water freezes to ice and

you have some stink. Believe you me. Well there was nobody around
but some firemen and a cop I know and the cop pointed to the
joint and said to me 'The hottest nite spot in Chicago' and I asked
him what caused it and he said kiddingly 'I guess some sparks from
your singing.' I have enough on him to crucify him but he lets me
park anywhere so I did not report him. It seems I did not read the
afternoon papers when I got up that afternoon and did not know
there was this fire. Well I finally got in touch with the 'owners' and
they said act of God and fire etc. wash up a contract automatically
and I said to them to wait a minute I did not have a contract. I
didnt either and I did not want them babies to think they had me
under contract because another spot was making me offers but they
did not understand what I meant but tho't I was going to try to
hold them up for my week as it was only a Tues. So they said 'Joey
you are the 1st one to come here and did not try to make some
trouble for us and with us you are a right guy altho it is a pleasant
surprise, even if we would of had a contract we would not had to
pay you because of fire and act of God but let us repeat you are a
right guy and any time we open up again we hire you before we
even hire a waiter.' So I saw what they were thinking I meant when
I said I did not have a contract. They were thinking I was giving
them a break so I said 'Well what the hell, I said. I do not pretend
I am some kind of a patsy but you fellows always put it on the line
for me every pay day and gave me good billing so I did not want
to come here only to offer you my sympathy and if I had some
moola put away I would even lend you some or any part of it to
open up again'. One of them looked at the other and looked at me
and then at the other and said 'Well, I have seen everything' and
then he stood up and shook hands and said 'As you know we are
only the front men here as the backers do not wish to appear but
as long as we are in this business one guy will always have a job
and it is you Joey. How are you fixed?' So I said well you saw that
new midnite blue tailcoat I just bo't I said that it was not paid for
only partly, just the down payment. I said you know how it is in
this business a guy has to have a front and I would hate to lose
that and they realised it and said they would give me my week
right away and reached in his pocket and pealed off 5 20s, my week.
I tho't I might as well give it to them but good so I said not if they
couldnt spare it and they said that was alright. Then Solly the one
fellow said he had been thinking it over and he had a little propo-

siton for me and it was this. He said for me to keep going around
to the good spots every nite and make contacts until they opened
up again and then when they did I would still be a big attracton
because people would not get the chance to forget me and get myself
some publicity as much as possible and he would leave that to me.
I started to say what would I use for moola and he said to me 'I
anticipate yr. queston. We in this business hate each others guts
but we all have to co-operate with one another and all I have to
do is call the boys that run the other joints and tell them I would
apprisiate it providing they would not slap a couvert on you and I
personally will give you 50 a wk to pay yr expenses, how does that
look to you?' Well you know how it look to me. Getting paid for
what I would do anyway so I shook on it and so that is what I am
doing and do not have to worry about another job but am ruining
the vocal chords smoking too much in joints and only singing once
in a while when some m.c. says 'I see we have another celebrity in
our mist' and introduces me and I give. So that is why I am on
the cake line not the bread line.

But will have to tell you a funny story like I hinted above
regarding one fellow that is complaning. I did menton how I bo't
this tailor-made tailcoat but only pd. the down payment. It is
midnite blue and it fits me like a sword holder fits a sword. About
a wk, before the joint burned down I got delivery on this tailcoat
and had to con the tailor into letting me have it for only the down
payment. All told it was to cost me $100. I put down 25 down
payment. But I said to him how can I pay you if you dont leave
me wear it and I lose my job. So when they had the fire I went to
him and said he could have it back as I could not pay for it and
he yelled bloody murder and I walked out on him and said go
ahead sue because you cannot garnishy my salary as I have no
salary and anyway I am bankrupted. Im not but how does he know.
So he had to take it back then I got a guy in the band with the
same build I have and he went in to the same fellow and said he
was thinking of having a tails made and the tailor did not know it
was a friend of mine and he said 'I have just the thing for you. A
customer did not call for this' proving he was a crook. My pal said
well he wanted one more conservative not blue but the tailor said
'I will tell you what I will do I will let you have it for $65 the latest
thing.' My friend said he was not thinking of paying that kind of
money and anyway he could get a ready made for 40. So the tailor

came down to 45 and my pal said okay. He took it. So I gave my
pal a fin for his acting ability and so all told I got my tailcoat for
a total of 75. They always overcharge you anyway those tailors
because they figure on losing dough when they give credit and bad
debts etc. So I just paid him what the damn thing was worth altho
on me it is very becoming as they say in that gag.

I guess you got my Xmas card. A funny thing. I ordered two
kinds this Xmas, the kind I sent you and also the conservative ones
with very formal Greetings of the Season and a stage coach & four
and my name engraved on it. They were for the Onawentsia crowd
friends but 'accidentally' I got one of the ones I sent you in the
envelope with the stage coach ones and now I understand the whole
town is talking about the amusing cards. Everybody wanted to
know who posed for it. Nobody did as the fellow that drew it copied
it out of *Esquire* but I just look wise when anybody says they think
it was so and so or this one or that. It certanly got me plenty
publicity.

Well Merry Christmas, as the saying goes. Guess I will have to
go to bed for 24 hrs so I dont have to stop hating my fellow men.
But that does not go for you, Ted. The best.

PAL JOEY

CHAPTER 8

The Erloff

Friend Ted:

In my prevous communicaton I informed you how I guess it was some critic of singing set fire to the joint I was singing in and I was out of a job. I am only kidding about the place being set fire by a music critic because what I hear the singing in Chicago does not have any high standards to acheive (sneeze when you say that Pal). They tell me it is been going on for years but I only just heard about the singers here, how what you do is get some guy that his idea of music is when he heard them sticking the little pigs in their throat down at the stock yards, which is plenty loud and plenty high (especially high at the stock yards if you get what I referring to and hold yr. nose at that gag). That is their idea of music and the 1st thing you know they are knocking themselves out indevouring to sign some baby that sings loud and high and sign her up to sing opera. At but all the moola a week anybody can spend not excepting I. Had I but known of this at an earlier age I would of made the nessary preparatons and arrangements and wd. be a soprano now at plenty moola a wk. instead of being somewhere between Frankie Parker outdoors on a rainy nite and the Groaner giving an imitaton of a cry of joy or scared of a mouse.

I told you I had this deal with my ex-boss, 50 a wk to go around the other joints and make an appearance so the public wd not forget me until my boss opened up again. Well I had this little mouse, a very nice little spivot that belong to the college crowd at the Northwestern U. I think you played a job there two yrs ago at a 'prom' so you know about it. They have some nice mice out there and she was one. I had her out this nite and over came a chap I say hello to occasonally, and he is a member of the Saddle & Cycle Club. Alright I am kidding you and this is 1939 or 1940 (I have not got it straight yet) and they do not have any club name the

Saddle & Cycle only they do!!! 1940! Anyway this is a rich playboy
type of a chap and kind of an Ed. Arnold type. He does all the
talking so I do not have to tell him any lies and when he saw me
and this mouse he said to join him as they are going slumming.
Slumming was what he said and slumming was what he meant.
From one of the top rooms in Chi we go bang to a joint that is a
joint. The mouse with me is strictly no cigar and the daughter of
a small town banker in Indiana and have a summer home up in
Mich. and I am thinking of next summer when I take her out. So
she is not the one I would of pick to go with me to a joint like the
one we went. But she said she wanted to go and when I said yes
her guess was as good as mine where we were heading. Strictly a
bruhaha. But Sat. nite! This guy that took us is wellknown or else
I would of turned around the minute we got there. In we go. Wide
open like a movie of a mining camp town. An ugly old hag of an
Irish lady is yelling for help altho using the words of I Want the
Waiter with the Water and accompanied by maybe her uncle or
maybe her son, a man that should of been in bed hrs ago. I am not
kidding. He thumped out the bass and drank his beer at the same
time and it was not on purpose.I mean it was not a gay 90 gag.
They were leveling. So pretty soon our party got seated at our table
and this little old guy came over and I tho't here is an old guy and
in a minute he is going to take out a piece of rope and ask the
gentlemen to tie him up and inside of 2 mins. he will be free. That
was what he looked like. But when he came over to our table Preston
stood up and shook hands with him and introduced everybody to
him and told him to sit down which he did. Well his name was
Paddy Dunlin and all he is is the owner of the joint. Not only of
this particular joint but about 50 other ones. I do not wish to get
ahead of my story but in plain words the old corpse has girls
anywhere from two bits to whatever you want to pay for. And the
face of a saint as they say. Anyway he sat down next to me and
had a beer on Preston and when the other members of our party
got up to dance, he looked me over and then he whispered to me
'What about the erloff.' I said what a couple times. I finally caught
on that he was asking me what about the little mouse. Oh, nothing,
I said. 'Slumming' he said. Then he said 'What do you think of the
erloff' and this time I did not say what but watched him. He made
a gesture with his head and his expresson and that meant he was
asking me what did I think of the joint. I stalled to think of some-

thing and he had to go away to answer the phone and Preston came back to the table and gave me some facts on the old guy. He said I was not in Chi long enough to know about him. He said the old guy was over 70 and was running joints from the time he was 21 yrs of age. There was a story around that when they had that bank holiday one of the railroad cos had to come to the old guy for cash. He had over 2 million in cash. Hotels, railroads, all the respectable big cos had to come to him for cash. He said (Preston) how for yrs every morning the sisters came around and collected choice meats like steaks & chops etc. that was left over from the nite before, and took it away and gave it to the poor. Also poatoes and salad and red beets etc. Also butter and bread. The works. Every single morning. He was always good for a roof on a church just as long as it was Catholic. He buried thousands of people that would of been buried in the potter's field if he did not get up the dough. Charity after charity. But then they gave an order that nobody was to take any more from the old guy. It made him sad and he almost began hitting the sauce, but his elderly wife would not allow him in the house with booze on his breath so he just did not drink.

I listened attentively because Preston was paying for the party but if you want the truth I was bore to death with Preston and with his old charachter. That was what Preston called him a fascinating old charachter. To me he was a dirty old man with a lot of moola. I was even thinking rapid calculation how much it would cost to take my little mouse out to her sororty house by taxi instead of waiting till Preston decide to take us home and just then the old man returned from his phone call. He must of got a big order from some Amer. Leg. conventon because he was smiling when he sat down with us.

The old dame got up again and began horse-whipping. The Lamp is Low. Dunlin said to me 'How do you like the erloff' and I said fine. Great I said. 'Right' he said. 'She is been with me fifteen yrs.' And I thought to myself yes and you must of looked her over a long long time before hiring her too. Her and the band been with me 15 yrs he said. I said that was wonderful these days to have such loyalty going on but to myself I tho't yes you all stick together to keep warm like old cows out on the range during a blizzard. I had a look at the band. He had them hid behind some palms but there was one old guy playing cornet that looked as if he was worried for fear that the Confederates wd catch him for being a

deserter. 'The erloff, they like the erloff' said Dunlin. Everything
was erloff with this decrept old bore and I was thinking to myself
2 million cash or no 2 million cash, old man or no old man, he is
driving me nuts so I am going to break a 5 dollar bill over some
hack driver's head and take my little mouse home in a taxi but I
am glad I didn't because just then the old man says to me 'Of
course in the Loop you got a different erloff Joey.' I said what?
'The erloff, he said. They like noise here and that's the way I like
it. You would just as well come wearing a shell if you ever took a
job in a spot like this, that is how big an egg you would lay. But
the class people that go to the rooms you been working in like
hardly any noise at all.' Well he called me Joey and I was figuring
all the while he tho't I was a Cycle Club boy but no. He made me
the minute he saw me, as the detectives say. He said he understood
I was a sock the last 2 rooms I worked and right out in front of the
little mouse he said 100 awk was not enough for a handsome young
chap that could put over a ballad and have the women with their
tongue hanging out. 'Don't worry, he said when you open up again
you will be getting one five o. You also have a nice personality for
that kind of a room.' I said I certanly would apprisiate him giving
me a plug with the owners and he looked at me and said 'Are you
kidding? *I* own that joint.' Then he got up and walked away and
I was too surprise to think for a minute and tho't I plumbered it
but we have opened up again in another room and I am getting
one five o. The erloff Pal.

Always your
PAL JOEY

CHAPTER 9

Even the Greeks

Friend Ted:

I don't think I will be able to take it out here much more. In the 1st place it is because you never saw cold weather until you spent a winter in Chi. I do not mean weather like you have to chop the alcohol before putting it in the radator of the car. I mean weather that is so cold that the other day this pan handler came up to me and braced me and said I look as if I had a warm heart and I gave him a two-bit piece because if it wasnt for him would not of known I was alive or frozen to death. That has how it has been here in Chi. Maybe that explains some of the pecular actons of many of the inhabintants. Illinois is a state of suspended animaton and the people live in hibernaton from Oct. to whenever it ever gets warmer. I do not know and hope I am not here long enough to find out. I am merely telling you this in case you ever decide to take a job to spend the winter in Chi and I am not there to stop you at the point of a gun.

Well if you think I am trying to infer that I have been running up against some of the pecularities of the local natives you will only be 100% correct. The club opened up again after the fire as you no doubt read here or there like in the *Variety* or the *Down Beat*. We got off to good business but that was to be expect it. It wd of surprised me had it been otherwise so only menton it in passing. What I want to tell you is about the pecular local people and this one case. Two wacks if ever I saw one and they are Nick the prop. of the Olympia rest. and Pete that works for him in the kitchen. The Olympia is on my way home when I am on my way home if you know what I mean.

I just as soon never go home but a man has to have his rest so when I go home ever since I have been living where I now am I use to stop in at the Olymp. for a coffee and raison cake before going to bed. I got to be a regular customer there and Nick would expect me to come in around 3, 4 in the morning so as to relive the monotony with a wise crack or two and I guess Nick was very grateful to me because one nite I heard somebody out in the kitchen yell 'right' and a minute or two later out through the hole in the wall bet. kitchen and rest. a plate slid and on the plate was some food. Nick was just about going to throw it in the garbage and then he noticed me and he said 'could you use a ham omlet?' I said sure. So he gave me the ham omlet, or what ever it was. I asked him what was wrong with it but he said nothing was wrong and go ahead and eat it if I preferred to. So I ate it and it was as good a ham omlet as I ever ate.

A nite or so after I went in Nick's again and was having a cup of coffee and once more I head somebody out in the kitchen yell 'right' and a couple minutes later out came a jelly omlet and once more Nick looked at me and said could I eat a jelly omlet and I said I could force one and he assured me that there was nothing phony about it but go ahead and eat it and it was as good a jelly omlet as any jelly omlet I ever ate.

Then I went in the next nite and ordered a coffee and waited but Nick didn't offer me anything. Then the nite after that I went in and sure enough somebody out in the kitchen yelled 'right' and in a minute or so out came a beautiful club sandwich. Nick asked me again could I use a club sandwich and I said I tho't maybe I could and it was a tasty club sandwich which I enjoyed to the hilt. So that was the way it went. Some nites hungry and not wishing to throw away a dollar I wd go to Nick's hoping to get an omlet or tasty sandwich but no cigar. I wd not get a thing. Other nites I wd go in and get like a small steak one nite. But I began to notice one thing. The only times I got a free meal it was when the fellow out in the kitchen suddenly yelled out 'right'. Nobody wd order anything but he wd yell it and then in a minute or two something very tasy wd come through the opening. So naturally I wd wait around hoping this fellow in the kitchen wd yell 'right' because if he did that meant I wd get a free meal. So all the time naturally I was helping Nick relive the monotony by chatting about this and that and one night the usual thing. The fellow yelled, out came liver & bacon and Nick just looked at me and at the liver & bacon and I said sure. Then my curosity got the better of me and I asked him. I said 'Nick what's with the free food? Explain.' So he said eat my liver and bacon and he wd explain the entire mystery. So I ate it and then he said to look out in the kitchen and I wd see a husky well built man about 50 yrs of age sweeping up or polishing pots and pans. That is Pete, said Nick. 'Pete use to be the best short order cook I ever ran across in all my experience in this business. But one day Pete's wife ran away with a wrestler and took their three little ones with them and Pete began hitting the sauce and got into a fight and somebody hit him over the conk with a bung starter and he was never the same after that. But Nick knew Pete as boys in the old country and Nick made up his mind that Pete wd always have a job as long as he owned a rest. So Nick had to hire another cook and gave Pete the job sweeping up. But every once in a while while sweeping up Pete wd think he heard Nick order something like a ham omlet or small steak or one of the other dishes that Pete was good at and he wd put down his broom and go and cook the omlet or whatever he tho't he hears. Oh and I forgot to say in there that when he wd think he wd hear Nick ordering he wd yell out 'right' and then start cooking it. I said to Nick that must run into money. Yes, it does, said Nick but that is okay and anyway you are here to eat the stuff so I do not have to throw it away.

Well that is all about Nick and Pete and I do not know which one is wackiest either Nick for keeping Pete or Pete himself. You can make up your mind as I have my own idea. But that is the way they are in this town. Even the Greeks.

Your

PAL JOEY

CHAPTER 10

Joey and the Calcutta Club

Pal Ted:

Well, Chum, the poor man's Bing Crosby is still making with the throat here in Chi. But if the present good fortune keeps up I ought to be getting the New York break pretty soon. The trouble is up to now the good fortune has been keeping so far up it is up in the stratuspere out of sight. But never out of mind, kiddy. Never out of mind. N.Y. is where I belong N.Y. or Hollywood or will settle for both. However have been off the bread line and working steady but you do not see me on the caviare line yet and was always a one to have the ambiton to starve to death within reach of caviare if you get what I mean. If I have to starve to death it would be this way, namely, have about 5 lbs. of caviare and filet mignon & champagne etc. but me too God damn lazy to reach for it. Maybe to make it perfect I would be firsting my attentons on like Hedy La Marr instead of just plain lazy and would be so busy would forget to eat. That is the manner in which I would prefer to starve to death.

Well, speaking of the charming opposite sex I have a little spot of annecdotes (I dote on annecdotes) to tell you which may amuse the chappies around Lebuses and give them all my best excepting those that I would not say I would not spit on them as I can hardly wait to spit on them. Well this is the story and not only a story but also a good thing to keep in mind in case you get in the same situaton some time yourself.

Shortly after I got started working here, a little mouse came in one nite with a party of six and naturally began asking for request nos. and in that way I got acquainted and also thru knowing one of the guys on the party. It was not a spending party, strictly cufferoo. The guy is a fellow named Quinn on one of the local papers here in Chi. and covers nite clubs, etc. and signs his initials

L.Q. to reviews he gives the spots here & there but mostly in the Loop etc. So Quinn asked me to join them and I did and this mouse with them named Jean Benedict looks like 10000 other dames on the line of some Bway show except when she opens her trap she has an accent that is so British even Sir Nevile Chamberlin would not be able to understand her. I knew she was strictly U.S.A. by appearance but the accent is so good I think what is the angle. What gives, I asked her, altho not in so many words. I inquired how she happen to have the accent and she said a lot of people inquire of her the same thing and it is easily explained. She is half American and her father is British. Well she sounded so refined I wanted to say a few one syllable words to her to note the effect to see if she would know what I meant. Well I did not, not that nite. About three nites later. The 1st nite all she did was say why didn't I call her up at her flat and drop in for a gin and 'it'. I said the 'it' was o.k. with me if we were both talking about the same thing and she put on the act as if not getting 'it' and then said priceless. Oh, how wrong she was when she said priceless but am getting ahead of my story.

Well on acc't of a certan other obligaton which I mentoned in my previous letter I could not give my full attenton to Miss Benedict but will just say in passing if I would of given her any more attenton at the rate I was going I would now not be cutting paper dolls. Oh no. I would not be able to lift a paper doll. However let me suffice it to say that I moved in & during the course of our more dull conversatons I accertain that Miss Benedict is living with this other mouse whom I do not meet. They are sharing this flat. Also she tells me her dear mother and dear papa are in dear old London. I never asked her that. All I asked her was did she live alone, etc. and now I recall it she certanly did jump at the chance to explain about the old man and the mother. I should of known that the English have more reserve about personal affairs but I guess I had good reason to forget all about reserve in connecton with Miss B. Anyway she gave me the routine about father & mother being in London that day and two days later when 'love dropped in for tea' meaning me, she kept standing by the window and looking out and when I would say anything to her she would act like as if she did not hear me and then I finally said pardon me but remember me I am yr. pal Joey, the fellow that just came in about 15 mins. ago and didn't we meet at the club etc. She said 'I apologise' but she was upset and maybe it would be better if I did not stay but went out to a picture that day as she was not herself. I must say the girl is an actress because I honestly tho't I squeezed it out of her that her check from her old man was late and she said no doubt because of the way things have been in dear old London. She said she always got her check of $300 by the 7th of the month, sometimes earlier depending on how soon the boats arrived from London. But here it was the 10 or 11 of the month and no check and no letter either. The check always came with a letter and she worried about if they sent her father off on some misson for the gov't and it was so important he was not allowed to let her know he was even going away. He was some important fellow in the office that runs India and maybe they sent him there. It was not only the money but what if it was an important dangerous misson? What about her mother, I inquired? Well, she said that was where she swore me to secrecy and told me that her mother was an American but also had a lot to do with India, also some kind of an agent but American in name only so as to keep her passport. Well of course all this went on for a half an hr. and eventually I was a sucker for the touch. I admit it. I let her have $75.

Well I gave her my oath I would not tell about her people being sort of spies against India but even so would not of told anybody about it as I did not want it to get around that I went for a $75 touch as you get the reputaton of being a soft touch like that and pretty soon girls from all over the country are waiting at yr. dressing room and also I had this 'other obligaton' if *she* heard I was putting out 75 here and there she would take back her car and maybe even get me the bounceroo from this spot. So I kept quiet but one nite soon after I happen to see Quinn and went over to thank him for a nice menton and he started out by asking me how was Miss Benedict. I played dumb and he said, 'Oh, I tho't you were in. I took for granted you were in and how did you happen to miss that as I was given to understand that you are a young man that moved right in.' Well imagine. I burned and said 'Listen, wise guy not only am I in but the nite you bro't her here she slipped me her phone no. with you sitting at the table,' I could of cut my throat when I realised what I said, insulting the guy after he gave me the good notice but instead he did not get sore. On the contrary he replied, 'Ah, then perhaps you will join our little club. What did she take you for?' I said for nothing. And he said 'Oh, you can

level with me, do you mean to say she did not put the touch on
you for a little, like a yard?' So I admitted it and then he told me.
It seems that I was a member of quite a club, and a paid up
member too. Miss B. took Quinn for 50 and another guy for 50 and
another for 75 and one guy for around 300, a middle aged fellow
that sold religous articles to churches and did not want any trouble.
So Quinn said we ought to form a club called the Calcutta Club
after the town over in India. Well I saw the humor of it but I would
of liked to give Miss B. a kick in the stomach if she came along at
the time.

Well I put it down to experence and tho't no more of it till about
two wks. later Quinn came in and told me he had a propositon,
not his but Miss B's. It seems what she did was take our India
money and move out and get a more expensive flat by herself
without the girl friend and after she moved in she was there about
two weeks and met some guy from Milwaukee that tho't she was
right and so much so that this guy was already talking wedding
bells even before he moved in. She had him thinking it made her
sick to see a woman smoke and she never went out to nite spots
but always had a good book around. How she picked him up I
don't know but he was going for everything. He had no suspicons
aroused because at the time she was absolutely staying away from
the spots. Well she only had two wks. to go she told Quinn before
the rent was due and that meant only two wks. to work on the
prospect from Milwaukee, so the propositon she put to Quinn was
if we would stake her to the next month's rent and she felt sure
that was all she would need. He asked me what I tho't of it and he
said frankly he had no $50 to throw away but he would rather
throw the 50 away on a chance of getting the 100 back and he
advised me to do the same. He won me over but I told him on one
conditon, namely, how did we know there was this sucker from
Milwaukee and so it was agreed that if she could produce him and
convince us then we would put up the ready. So that was how it
was and a nite or two later she came in the club and him with her
and I took one quick gander at him and was convinced but to make
sure I stopped at the table suddenly like I just recognised him and
said, 'I beg yr. pardon but havent we met. I am sure I met you in
Milwaukee last yr.' and the way he got red and said no I knew he
was from Milwaukee and I also knew something Miss B. did not
know as smart as she was, namely, he was dumb but not that dumb

that he would marry her, but was willing to put up the rent etc.
Well that was o.k. She pretend to go to the little girls rm. and I
had a talk with her and told her I was in favor of the propositon
and would tell the other members of the club I was and she would
have the front money. But I also told her that Mr. Milwaukee was
not going to marry her if I knew human nature and she said to me,
'Joey, darling, I could almost like you for being so intelligent, if for
nothing else.' She said 'I told Quinn that Chubby (the nickname
for the Milwaukee guy) did not move in but he did move in but
Quinn is a dope and I had to tell him a good story. What I want
the front money for is so Chubby will get expensive ideas and not
get the idea that he is only going for coffee and cakes dough.' Then
she gave me a little kiss on the cheek and said 'that will have to be
all for the present but we shall see what we shall see.' So the boys
all got their dough back last wk. including me but I got mine in
three 50 dollar bills inclosed in a gold clip with a watch on it. You
have to admire a girl like that from Buffalo, N.Y. where she is from.
That is how English she is. She has relatons in Canada. Anyway
she is a very smart little operator and I predict great things for her.
She got me putting on a little wt. as Chubby likes caviare and she
always keeps some in the frigidair for him but all we singers put
on wt. like Caruso, McCormick, Crosby, etc.

Yrs.
PAL JOEY

CHAPTER 11

Joey and Mavis

Friend Ted:

I do not wish this to constitute a regular letter as am only setting down my tho'ts at random more or less as they come to me sitting here casually after dinner while Mavis is at the movies with the kids. Perhaps a few words about Mavis would not be a miss as I have had so many things happening to me since writing you before that I did not get the opportunity to inform you regarding Mavis who has bro't such changes into my life that I can not believe it myself when I stop to think of it.

It happened one nite (from the picture of the same name) and I just finished a set and was outside on the sidewalk in front of the joint filling up my lungs with Gods air & some of my own cigarette smoke instead of 50 others people's and was talking to the doorman Sailor Bob a punchy stumble-bum that after 20 yrs learned how to open the door of that new inventon the auto but did not catch on how to close it. I use to go out and stand there & leave him pay me a few compliments on my voice as he tho't himself a great hand as a singer. He could not of been a worse fighter than a singer otherwise he would of been worm meat 20 yrs ago or more and none of this would of happened. He apprisiated my singing I will say that for him altho always asking why didnt I sing like Oh you beautiful doll which you are too young to remember and so am I but the story I hear is that when the Titanic went down (a ship) people sang it or hummed a couple bars and then said the hell with this and jumped the hell off the boat so they would not have to finish singing it. I do not know that for sure but only base that on hearsay based on a weak moment when I allowed the Sailor to sing it for me one nite. I tho't why does this happen to me, everything happens to me. I tho't I was the poor man's good Samaratan to listen to that but was glad later as one nite I was on on my way

out and some guy that had suspicons of me & his wife was waiting
for me and I was doing some very fast talking when out of the
corner of my eye I saw the Sailor and yelled to him and I must say
that what the Sailor can not do with his fist he does not have to do
as he does it with the boot. I have seen some dirty fighting in my
travels with the socialites and polo players I grew up with but
nothing to compare with the Sailor who is a pleasure to watch work
if you care for that sort of thing and I do especially when he is
working on somebody that a minute ago was going to stick their
fist down my throat. Anyway the guy had the wrong party as it
was not me but the drummer in the band. I had her sister and it
was not even the right nite he was referring to.

Well as I started in to say this one nite I went out and the Sailor
was on duty and I was more less fronting for him, that is on
smoking. He was not allow to smoke on duty but it was o. k. for
me to so I would say 'I will light one for you Sailor' and if the mgr.
came out the Sailor would hand it to me and would not get caught
smoking on duty. Then this 1937 La Salle sedan came up and four
got out, two couples. The fellow driving asked if it would be o. k.
to park here and the Sailor working for a tip stalled and said not
as a rule but in this case etc. so the fellow driving gave him a buck
and they went inside. I do not know how I happen to miss Mavis
but I did not see her until I had to go in again and polish off some
more dittys and they had a table ringside, and I went over and
asked them if they had any request nos. and Mavis asked for two
requests but did not have both of them only the Beguin no. The
other was an oldy like My Buddy which they were singing during
the civil war. I know it but forgot the lyrics. She looked around 32
or 33, inclined to take on a little weight but I also like them zoftick
as some goose in the band says. They asked me to sit down with
them and join them in a drink but I could not have a drink on the
job but we got into conversaton and in the course of the conversaton
she happen to menton that when she saw me outside talking to the
doorman she tho't perhaps I was there waiting for a date instead
of working in the joint and she meant it as a compliment as she
said this spot was new to her and she did not like to go to strange
spots but thinking I was the type customer the joint got she figured
it was o.k. I said I considered her a very wise person and I was
not kidding because all the time I kept looking at her I kept adding
up how much she had on her was worth. At least a two-caret

diamond ring on the engagement finger and also a diamond bracelet
and a gold cigarette case with inside it (not outside) her three
initials in diamonds M.W.K. (for Mavis Williams Ketchell but did
not find that out till later). The people with her were in their 40s.
Well I always make it a point to leave a table while they still want
me to stay (always leave them laughing) so I moved away and
merely said I hope they would come again etc. I could not figure
out any way how to get her phone no. without asking for one on
the chin. I had some preminiton that I could move in if I played
it right but was also not sure. I could not figure if maybe one of
the two guys bo't those diamonds or if she had her own dough or
if she was a wealthy young divorcee or young widow or what the
hell? She was so cagey that all I knew about her was all she wanted
to let me know. Even so I had that preminiton that once I got alone
with her I would let her do the talking and maybe she would talk
herself into it.

Well I went out again for a smoke and of course asked the Sailor
who own the La Salle but he never saw it before and I could not
get any clue but just then fate fell into my hands. At first I tho't
my luck ran out because here they were all coming out, Mavis &
the other three. The one fellow backed up the sedan and the others
got in and then when they were all in the other dame decided she
wanted to sit in back with 'Harry' and Mavis got out and the other
dame got in the back and sat with Harry and Mavis started to get
in front with the other guy and just when she was sitting down the
Sailor must of decided that the important thing was on the seat
because just then he slammed the door and got her right foot. She
let out one 'Jesus H. Christ' and then I saw her face and she was
biting her lower lip in pain. Trying to keep from crying I guess but
very couragous. Then when she had a look at her foot she passed
out and I damn near did too. The Sailor put everything in that
slam and it would take your appetite away to describe her foot. I
saw it all happen.

Well plenty of excitement. The mgr. came out and the Sailor was
non compass mentis and did not know what to do and the other
dame was screaming like she was the one that had the door slammed
on her own foot instead of Mavis. They finally got a dr. and they
took Mavis to a hospital. One of the guys in the car took my name
etc. and all I could think of was that fixed it fine as far as Mavis
coming back to the joint for a while or maybe ever. The way her

foot looked it would be lucky if she did not lose the foot. But it was not as bad as I tho't and a day or two later a guy came around to my place and asked me a lot of questons about how it happened. He was from the ins. co. he said and I tho't he meant the ins. co. that Mavis was insured by but no, he was from the one that covered the joint for accidents like that. I told him a story that should of got Mavis $1,000,000. The next wk. I got the bounceroo from the joint. It seems that they settled with Mavis for around $1100 but if I would of had a different story ready maybe they could of got away without settling for anything. I still dont know all the angles and do not give a damn. I told the mgr. if I knew what kind of a story he wanted me to tell maybe I would of told a different one but he said it was just too bad but they did settle. I was out and also the Sailor.

But I guess the Sailor can always get himself a spot in some gym but there I was with only about $85 in my poke and no job. So I was desperate and almost wired you to put the touch on you but at the last moment got this idea and decided to call on Mavis at the hosp. I did so and much to my pleasant surprise was told to go right up to room whatever it was. She was surrounded with flowers and was glad to see me instead of giving me the brush which was what I was afraid of. She had her foot in a plaster cast and first she made me feel at home and then said for me to take a pencil and write my name on the cast as she understood I saw the whole thing and must of told the truth about how it happened otherwise they would not of settled so quickly. 'Yes,' I said. 'I was too truthful for my own good, Mrs. Ketchell, as they discharged me because I was ready to go to court and tell the truth that the doorman was to blame for the unfortunate accident.' She tho't a minute and said she wished she knew that at the time before settling, however she asked me to sign my autograph on the cast and I did.

Well we chatted and she asked me to come and see her again and I said I would be happy to as I would have plenty of time and she said that was perfect because most of her friends worked in the day time and she did not have many woman friends in Chicago that could come and call on her and it was such a bore in the hospital alone. So I started going there every day and soon she told me the story of her life and how she was so happy with her two children and husband but one day he came home and shot himself and the ins. co. had to pay double because that was in the clause and she could not bear to live in the small town where her home was because it was too full of memories so she came to Chi. Her husband was 20 yrs. older than she and she was hardly more than a girl when she got married but even so was happy with him as he did every thing in the world for her. Well I can tell you one thing in the world he did not do for her because I am no 20 years older than she is and no old guy 50-some years old did everything in the world for her. They could attach a wire to here and I bet she could light up a city of 50,000 populaton the way they did with some ship out on the Coast. After she got out of the hospital she got me to take a room near where she has an apartment for herself & the two kids. She knows a guy that is going to back a new joint in the Loop dist. and when the thing is ready I am practically set to open there and meanwhile we go out about every nite. I caught her in a few lies but this is on the level and I think she has something on the guy that is backing the new spot as one nite we were on our way in a place and he was standing there waiting and she said to him, 'How nice to see you, Tom' and introduced me and said I was just the singer for the new spot and he began to stall and she said not to bore her but just make an appointment with me and he said 'Oh, is it that way?' and she replied 'Why, Tom darling, just what do you mean?' and laughed and he said o.k. and I see him next Tues. I sure would hate to let her get anything on me.

Well she ought to be back soon and I want to put this in the envelope and seal it up and when she sees I was writing to a guy and not some dame it should make her a happy girl. Age 37 if I can believe her drivers license.

I wonder what the poor people are doing?

Regards
PAL JOEY

CHAPTER 12

A New Career

Friend Ted:

By the business we are doing these nites one wd never be let to suspect that there is a world conflagraton going on but nevertheless such is the case. The rope is up every nite of the wk except Monday and then such is the kind of lug I am working for that he wants to put the rope up and hang himself from it because one nite of the wk maybe four tables do not get occupied by people buying wine. This is the same guy that I recall distintly six months ago if 4 tables did happen to be occupied he wd spend $40 phoning his girl on the road with some band that business was terrific. Now when he gets a bad nite he thinks it is brutal.

I guess you are wondering why I am giving you these physical details. Well I do not blame you because why should you give a good God damn about some crib in Chicago even if I do happen to be working there. Of course I always give a damn if it is you and I understand you are going to be booked into the N.Y. Paramount in a couple wks and whoever's record is tops I hope you break it and am sure you will. But of course why you should care if we do 8000 or 800 except that I have a little propositon that may arouse yr interest and it is this.

I will tell you all about it and how I happen to have my interest aroused. It is owing to those Monday nites. My boss is known by the name Harry Bonbon which is a mob nickname he got from the mobsters not because of him liking chocolate bon-bon candy but his name was Burnhaum and they had a mobster with an impedima in his speech and the closest he could come to the name was Bonbon. That is one vertion. However that is as good as any and I just wanted to tell you his name Harry Bonbon. So these Monday nites he just sits there chewing on the end of his cigar (personally I wish he would chew on the lit end but no such luck) and he counts the empties and then I see him looking around and he will call a headwaiter and point to some lights and say 'Save that' and the headwaiter will have to go out and turn off the light. He keeps doing that until by the time it gets to be 12 or half past the place is like a black out over France. It is a very handy thing for the out of town spenders that have some local mouse out for the first time and want to find out if she has a wooden leg. It also is a very fine thing in favor of the light finger gentery and I told Harry one Monday I said in case he was interested over there was a bump man I use to see out at the track some times and I said maybe he is now working alone but it will be a fine thing for the joint in case he happens to bump into one of the socialites and the socialites lose a handsome wallet stuffed with a liberal supply of folding. 'Jesus! said Harry, I never tho't of that and ordered the lights turned on. Of course he has only been in this business since around 1885 and should know by this time that any time the socialites go out they leave there folding money at home or most of it. My experence with socialites is they go to a spot with the expectaton of throwing away up to $3 if it is a party of 2 or 4.

Well that is just an illustration of what I mean about Monday nite and how Harry worries. If it is not the lights it is go easy on the ice or use napkins instead of fresh table clothes. Or go easy on the air conditoning or no fresh packs of matches but use the old packs with one match in them or else he is got the cashier going nuts because he wants a report every 15 min. So of course I also noticed another thing more important than the above. I happen to notice him one nite looking at me. He did not say anything. He merely looked. But the way he looked was the way the head man looks on one of those artic expeditons after nobody had anything to eat for a wk. They are going around barefooted because they have used up their moccassins for scoff. Maybe one of the chaps has knawed off a nice juicey thumb. But the head man is looking at me. I am the fat one (I did not put on any wt but this is just an illustraton). I am say the radio operator and got fat sitting around on the way North and the head man thinks and thinks and pretty soon he has no doubts about if he is going to eat me. All he is wondering is will I take much salt. Sunday nite they can have me for cold cuts. That is the way Harry is looking at me. Does he give a damn if I am the only one that can operate the radio and notify civilizaton? No. He is thinking I wd make a nice roast. The same with Harry. Is he thinking about the mice that come in because I work here? No. All he is thinking is how if I was not on the payroll it wd be the same as getting his electricity free.

Well I am a great student of human nature and always prided myself on reading characters, so I know Harry wd break my contract in a minute. If I was not willing to break my contract then he wd get a couple of hoods and I wd be in a taxi accident and maybe break my knee cap. I will break a contract any day in preference to my knee cap. So I sound out a couple other sports but they say I want too much money. I got desparate. I even went to one lug and said I wd sing and run the floor show and also take pictures. I did not have any kodak but anybody can take pictures but even so they said no and I wd not come down in price more than $25 a wk.

Well, that is an angle, I asked myself. Then because I always use to make my Easter duty and did a lot of people favors I got my reward. They had this busboy named Pablo that use to fix me up a sandwich once in a while and I befriended him by overhearing a tip on a horse at Arlington and it paid I think around $18.40 and Pablo was on it for a fin. So he always recalled that and one nite after Harry gave me the explorer look I was having a sandwich and I guess I was unable to disguise my feelings because Pablo ask me what was the matter and I just said nothing at all really. Just blue. And he tho't it was some mouse but I said any time a mouse made me feel that way he should let me know. I did not wish to worry Pablo and did not inform him why I was worried as I knew Pablo would worry too because even if he did not know it his job was also in danger and I wanted the poor chap to have his happiness. Well he took away the dishes etc. and you know how those people are and how nothing gets them down for long. They bounce right back because they are primitive and not very close to civilizaton jike jigs. So a minute after he was so sympatico Pablo was humming away a tune. Well I was smoking and thinking and suddenly this tune gradually began creeping into my thot's. It grew on me. Finally I asked him I said what was the name of it and he smiled and said it did not have any name. I said was it perhaps some Mexican folks' song and he said oh, yes, it was six or seven Mexican folks's songs all in one. He said it was one of his own, which he made up out of a lot of songs from his native land, Mexico. 'Sing it again,' I said. He was very pleased and sang it all through for me. Well I jumped up and as soon as the band finish the set I went over to the piano and one fingered it and wrote it out on the back of a menu card. But that was not necessary because on the way home I remembered it and the next afternoon when I woke up I remembered it.

Well you know how I am. Like Berlin. I can fake a tune in one key so the next couple days I was down at the joint in the afternoon playing it on the piano till I had it all mastered and not any too soon I might ad. Because the last afternoon I turned around and saw the guitar player in the band standing there. 'How long of you been here, I said. He said he just got there and I did not know whether to believe him or not as he wd steal my tune as quick as look at me but I did not want to let on it was important so I just said play a few and he was like any ham musican and started in and played Muddy Waters. I wanted to test him to see if he wd play my tune but he didn't.

Well now I have something in case Harry the explorer decides to cut me up but the hell of it is I cant trust any of these bastards and that is where you come in. I know there is no larceny in you Ted boy so what I am going to do is go to a music store and get one of those recording machines and play the tune and cut a wax of it. I will cut a couple and send one to you so that if you lose it or anything I will still have one and anyway that will show that it was my idea. Then when I send it to you you play it over and see if you think it has possibilites and if so maybe you can get Johnny Mercer or somebody to write some lyrics for it. I will guarantee to let you play if first over the air and who knows but perhaps that is not a new career for me, that of song writer. I have a lot of ideas along this line and only need a little encouragement. My tune can be played as either a rumba or conga, fox trot or waltz. If I could get a good Ascap rating this year I would quit this business in a minute and stop worrying about Harry the explorer. So look in the mail any day now for a record. Be sure and tell your secretary that anything from me is to go to you without opening it.

As always,
PAL JOEY

CHAPTER 13

A Bit of a Shock

Friend Ned:

Well Ted it may come like a bolt out of the blue sky me calling you Ned after all these years of you and I being mutual pals but why I called you Ned is because I wanted to prepare you for a surprise just like I got one about 2 wks ago. I had this little surprise around 2 weeks ago that I guess I certanly had it coming to me. In the ordinary course events a surprise comes from where you the least expect it and which is precisely what happened in my case. But dont worry as I do not intend to continue calling you Ned as you are Ted to me and the same old Ted and the same old pal Joey.

I menton above how where you least expect it etc. That goes double in spades and cards whatever that means. By double I mean in the 1st place *where*. The second place should be *how* and the third pl. *who*. Well where was a new crib where they had me rehearsing for a new show. I dreamed up a little comedy patter and a few stories like Joe E. Lewis and his little story about his cousin and the hot ferryboat but I guess I shouldnt of attempted that in Chicago as Chi. is where Joe E. got his start but that was just an error on my part and tho't they would of forgot the story by this late date. So anyway these gorills come and ask me to work for them in this new room they have, it being in the Loop dist. So being idle at the time I gave my consent before either one of us had time to change our mind. They tell me to come around Thurs. and I do.

How is the story.

Who is the mouse in the story.

Therefore we have where, how and who.

So I am rehearsing and they have a line consisting of six mice and only one of them you wd take to a building excavaton, or else take all six of them there and throw five of them in where it is deepest. It is the kind of a line where they all do challenge dances to make it look like they were all good hoofers or anyway make it seem like they had a line of 16 mice. The mobbers who run the joint have a relapse and decided to spend a small sum on advertising and that is how this Melba comes into my life. Melba works on one of these Chi. papers and there is very little doing in the clubs in the summer and so when the papers get a buck from club ads they like to play ball. So they decide to give us a little free publicity and send Melba around to get an interview with nobody else but yr. pal Joey. It is for the Sunday paper.

Well we are rehearsing and I am doing a patter with the kids in the line where they come up to me one by one and ask me what I want for Xmas and it is all the double entender. But it is the way I play it that is funny. I do not know exactly who to compare myself with but for illustraton Maurice Chevalier. I am having trouble with one of the mice because she is mugging even in rehearsal and as far as I could make out is doing her impresson of Kate Hepburn and any minute will go into her impresson of L. Barrymore. A poor man's Shiela Barret. In there punching and trying to crab *my* act. So I gave up in disgust and went over and sat down till Duilio, the boss came over and asked me why and I said I was all in favor of giving a fugitive from Maj. Bowes a little helpful push but wd be God damned if I wd play straight for them when it is my own act. I said you people have gone out and spent money advertising that I was going to open as master of ceremonies and then some mouse getting $23 a wk comes along and you might as well not have me there as it is a waste of money. Get her to get her brother or old man free, I said and you won't have to pay me. Duilio agreed and said 'Well I guess you are tired and why don't you take 15 minutes and during that time I will tell her and so I sat down and was having a quiet powder when in came something. I was tired and only raised my eyes when she came in but I tho't to myself Lesbo. I looked at her and tho't well so this is the kind of a joint I picked and did not know it. I tho't I could peg a joint like that from 2 mi. away and always did before but here I tho't I am all set to be m.c. in a crib where the Lesbos even come and watch the dress rehearsals. I am trying to give you the first impresson of this something. She is wearing this suit that you or I wd turn down because of being too masculine. Her hair is cut crew cut like the college blood. She is got on a pair of shoes without any heels and a pr. of glasses that make her look like she lost something but gave up the hope that she will ever find it. Then standing behind her is a little fat guy and when I first saw him I tho't now what the hell do these two do together. Then I got another look when she moved towards me and I saw he had a camera and I almost bursted out laughing. 'They are going to make some postcards for their private collection, I tho't. Then the dame came closer to me and I was just about to cover my face with my hands and scream but then Duilio came over and said hello to her and shook hands and you wd think she was Mrs. Marshall Fields the way he bowed and cowtow to her. 'What is this?' I said to myself, because Duilio is not double gaited as far as I knew but before I had a chance to do any more thinking he came over and introduced her to me and she gave me a slight brush and said okay let's sit over here and talk and she only had about a half an hour she said. Then Duilio menton that Miss so and so was the one that ran the night club dep't on some paper and gave me a punch in the ribs to con her into a good story.

Well we sat down and she ordered a double Scotch and water on the side and started out saying 'What is a nice boy like you doing in a place like this?' Oh, a wise guy, I tho't. So I tho't I wd be a wise guy with her so I said it was okay if she wanted to look down on my job but I said some people have too much pride to go on relief and since I was able to entertain people with a few songs and stories I wd rather do that in preference to being just a bum. Oh, she said, you have pride and I said I was born with it. I said I had to quit college because the family lost our fortune and she wanted to know what college and I told her Dartmouth University. There I made a mistake. She said you never went to any Dartmouth and I said I ought to know and she said yes you ought to know they call it Dartmouth College and not Dartmouth u. I said when I was there we preferred to call it Dartmouth u. and she said yes, when you were there it probably was a university but you were never there yet. So she said let it pass and tell me about that family fortune that the family lost. Was it well up in 3 figures? I said I was not brought up to boast about the am't of how much we had but if she wanted to know something when daddy blew his brains out in 1929 all the papers called him the millionaire sportsman and very sarcastically I said and of course the papers are always right. I said what did I know about how much he use to have? All I know was he left mother penniless. Sad, she said. Very sad. I said no not any more because mother was contented on the few pittances I was able to provide her and did not care any more about our fortune. I said may I ask where she went to college and she said she went to Mount Holy Oak. I said see the diff. bet. you and I. I said you bring up a place that I never heard of but I did not go ahead and deny there was any such place. I said the country is full of these small Catholic girls schools like Mount Holy Oak and I only had the greatest respect for them being a Catholic myself on mother's side. Okay, she said.

I thought I made my impresson by putting her in her place but the more the fool I. I wasn't satisfied with the crap I handed her but had to put it on thicker and all this time she stopped asking me questons but just listened, me thinking she was taking it all in and that I had her spellbound with my stories about polo and yacting and our huge estate. Then all of a sudden she held up her hand like a traffic cop and said you can stop now before you run down. It is been fascinating and thank you but she did not have time for any more. I said what did she mean and she said 'Pally I never heard so much crap in such a short time in my life. Such a fertle imaginaton it is a pity to be wasted in a nite club. I will write my own story but it wont be as good as yrs. 'Okay Moe, she said to the fat little camera man and he came over and then she called one of the mice and said something to her and the two of them went to the dressing room and about 5 min. later she came back but I did not know her. What she did was undergo a complete transformaton and took off her cloths and got into panties and brasserie that belong to one of the mice and took off her glasses and for the 1st time in many wks I forgot about Lana Turner. Yes that is how good this Melba was. Gams and a pair of maracas that will haunt me in my dreams and what is more when she got makeup on she was even pretty. I did not get the point but she said come on (to me) and put her arm in mine and posed like she was doing some kind of a dance step with me. She said Girl reporter at nite club rehearsal with new m. c. sensaton. Girl reporter lives life of nite club entertainers. She had me all over the place smiling and posing like we were dancing together. She said it was all pictures for the Sunday paper. Well I was a willing subject because anything to get my hands on her. All the time Moe kept taking pictures. Then she stopped and went back and got into her rags and by the time she dressed and shoed and glassed again I recovered my

composer. To think of this going around Chicago and never
anybody knowing about it because of the disguise. I said I hope
she wd come to the opening but she said she wd not be found dead
in a nite club and got over that yrs ago so I said well I did not
blame her because it was a shallow life &c. and said I wd like to
talk to her some time about it and she burst out laughing and said
dont waste yr time. You just got a little bit of a shock I am aware
but you just saw as much as you will ever see so get rid of such
ideas because among other things my husband use to play football
at Dartmouth U. as you call it. He is also satisfactory in every other
way and I must be running along. Its been nice knowing you &c.
So how do you like that? It is like the primitive savages that make
their women wear viels right here in the 2d biggest city in the
country. But I learned one thing to never judge a book by its cover
and the only trouble is when I walk along the street I am always
passing up the pretty mice and going on the make for the tired ones
dressed like girl scout masters.

                                                        PAL JOEY

CHAPTER 14

Reminiss?

Friend Ted:

I was only thinking the other day how it is every once in a while I get home late at nite and as the old no. use to have it I climb the stair and nobody is there but me and my shadow and how because of our kind of an occupaton it is too late to call anybody but something for a fin or a deuce who will come up and entertain you. But not good enough. I guess what you do you stand there leading one of the Naton's No. 1 name Bands all nite and see Betty there all nite and wd. not apprisiate any but the best and the same with me. Here I am in Chi and some nice mice are in Chi and know a lot of the best and wd. not be contented with any but the best. That is what happens to the both of us. I give with the vocals and wolf around in a nite club and see the best and it is not good enough if I can call up the highest paid bag in Chi and get it for ½. Mostly at that time of the nite I want it for free and with love too at that.

Thence I look around my tine nook of an apt. and see how I have a buck here & there hid in under the rug or a doz. Charvette ties from some souvenier of a romatic ideal. But feel sorry for my self all the same except when I happened to think I am also a man with a few good friends in this world and of them all there is none more highly prized than you Ted. Yes, I mean it. Some have the opinon that Joey, yr old pal Joey is a chap that if he did not have another breath of the body it wd be okay with them and they may be right. All of my life I did things that I wished I did not do because of hurting people like in Cincinatti that time we ganged that poor unfortunate mouse that you and I and also Kell went around with it in a sling for the best part of a yr. I recall that very distintly because of still getting bills from that quack in Pittsburg and if I were you Ted wd pay that little tab as he is getting nasty with me but you have a Name Band. Also the time when that lug in Pa. coal regons was trying to pay us off in the dark and was it you slugged him or me and we got in the bus and were in Maryland before he opened up his eyes. I wished I could reminiss about the time at the Penn State College which was some Prom and we took $50 off some College boy that wanted to have some summer job and we said we wd fix him with Waring. Well we had some great old times together you & I and I guess that is why when I get home some nites alone and wd. rather sit down and write to my friend Ted than waste my time on the phone winning some high paid bageroo.

That is exactly how the situaton is tonite and am sitting here and wish we had a jug of that corn stuff they gave us at the Virgina University and could talk it over and reminiss. I guess one time when we had a lot of fun was the time when we had the Battle of Music vs a college band the Barbury Coast Band from Dartmouth U. They said they were from Barbury Coast because of some reason I forget. But from Dartmouth U. I guess that was pretty nearly the 1st time I moved in on a society deb down at Webster Hall in the village but it burn down. I seem to have recalled that we made the college boys play all nite or any way 2 hrs straight meanwhile you and I and Pete and Noodles and Chick moved in on the society debs. We were all kids then and tho't how it was tough to move in on a society deb and I guess we tho't we wd all end up with a Jordan roadster in those days. I said I was from Princeton, I remember that much. I did not even know if Princeton was in Phila.

Well friendship is a great thing especially in our occupaton where we never get home at a decent hr. I seem to have recall that one time we were booked in the old Ballaban & Katz Publix or I guess you were not along that time but it was just after you went with Goldkette and I went along with the band and Sparky Bosch took his wife along for some un-known reason that I will never be able to understand. Mike Shortridge was suppose to be ahead of the band then but doubling back and our best interest at heart till one nite we played the 1st show and went out and it was this town Chi. where I now am and we went out to pollute the lungs with fresh air and the shock of it or something he ate put Sparky right on the pavement, out like a light. They had to get somebody to take him home as we were on again in 5 mins. But by the time he got back to the flea bag where we were staying he felt okay but did not feel so okay when he went up to his room and discovered that Mike

Shortridge and his little 2 wks old bride were in the kip and did not want to be interrupted by Sparky or any body else. I am sorry you missed that as Mike was around 50 yrs of age and Sparky around 21 but Sparky was always a fresh punk and Mike use to be a football star at Georga Teck. Sparky played a lot of horn in his day but he never got a lip like he got from Mike. Mike is a kind of a guy that you dont interrupt him when he is in the kip with a little 2 wks old bride even if it is yr bride.

Do you ever think about the old days? I do. I read the thing in the *Down Beat* about you about how at 30 you are still an old timer but maybe they meant two timer or double timer or back timer (only kidding Ted). I give them the same thing myself only they do not ask me. I mean *Down Beat* does not ask me. But in Chi. they do not recall I was here when Isham was still here at the College Inn. I even wear a little rug up front but so does the Grooner and Freddie Astare. I can level with them and tell them I do not know what they mean by the Loop because I wd rather forget most of the times I was here before. Jack Jenney and Carl Kress and Manny Klein go right thru town and never give me a bell and I guess they think they are hot stuff by so doing. But if you want to know the truth I wish they wd never look me up or give me a bell as the Chi people are of the opinon I am a kid from the Princeton college and if they see me around with Klein and Kress and Jenney and like Freeman and them these Chi. people know a lot about band guys and wd wonder how I knew them so well. I cultivated young Bobby Hackett so as I wd look younger when Hackett went thru here with Horace Heidt. Christ I knew Bix. I read all this stuff about Bix and how wonderful he was and all I remember about Bix was the article I saw in the Life mag. where Bud said he did not wash his feet. Well I never saw Hackett with his shoes off but for my dough he is a bare footed coal miner if that is the way Bix got to play good cornet.

Friend Ted I was just thinking of a bad wk in Pa. every summer for a couple summers. Do you remember Lakewood, Lakeside, Berwick, Schulkill Park, Reading, Mealey's in Allentown, Bach's in Reading, the Island nr. Harrisburg, Maher's in Shenadoh, Rocky Glen nr. Scranton, and Manila Grove near Tamaqua? Boy I could go on with them and so could you. I wish we had a chance to reminiss some nite even tho you are the leader of the Naton's No. 1 band. Not that I am not doing okay in Chi. because I am. I often think to myself that what if I turned out to be a Channcey Morehouse and a Dave Tough? That wd mean I was a really good drummer but not the lug that does not know a flammadiddle from a high hat. I put on such a good act here in Chi. that I kid myself and think I do not remember how to play Jazz Me. Jack Gallagher could sing it good and he only had one arm. I have both my arms so there is not any reason why I never sang it as equally as good. Do you recall the look of a surprise on Frank Trumbaur's kisser the nite I picked up an E flat and gave a slight job on Farewell Blues and he did not know I could play sax but also did not know that was the only thing I could play and the wart stood out as if he wanted to stab me with it. I ruined the reed that nite but always did not when I picked up an E flat alto but when I put it down. I guess this country is full of sax players that b't new reeds on acc't of me playing one chorus of Farewell Blues. Well you take a sax player and I will take a left handed pitcher. Put them all together they spell dixie.

Methinks I will not turn this missile over to the Post as it is just reminissing from here to Atlantic City but I had a lot of fun out of writing a letter to my friend Ted without putting the arm on him for a couple of bucks. Ted the only all around honest decent guy I ever knew except for one or two instants that if some mouse was not mixed up in it wd not of happened. Ted you are a great guy and should of been a priest the way yr mother said. Ted old friend am waiting for a bageroo for free and could go on writing to you and reminissing from here to Atlantic City Steel Pier 10wks guaranteed but methinks the bageroo is got her finger wedged in my doorbell. Will leave her wait a minute or two and teach her a good lesson not to get her fing. wedged in a gentleman's door bell at this hour of the night. If it is the one I called up she wd not miss a finger because she lost everything else when the boys came back with Gen. Dewey in the Span. American War.

Ted old friend how the hell are you and how does it feel to be rich?

Will bet you put yr dough into an insurance innuity and send the rest home to yr mother. I never saw you even pick up a tab for 4 mocha java coffees you cheap larceny jerk if there ever was one. I know you gave me the X X or otherwise I wd be making those so called wise cracks with Robin Burns every Thurs. and wd have my own stable of horses. It is a good thing I only write you letters instead of getting a hinge at yr holy kisser so I could hang a blooper on it. Friend Ted I am speaking to you and will tear this up but always was

Yr
EX PAL JOEY
(Hate yr guts)

Hope
of
Heaven

Contents

CHAPTER 1

Hope of Heaven

Maybe I am not the man to tell this story, but if I don't tell it no one else will, so here goes.

I was sitting in my office in the Studio one warm day last September. My feet were up on the desk, and I was admiring my new $35 shoes, and my $7.50 socks, and thinking how nice it would be to go out and get in my $2200 car and go for a ride. But that was out of the question. I was too far behind in my work, and they were beginning to turn on the heat. So I had to stay there and read the *Hollywood Reporter* and *Variety* and try to get my mind off the sound of the dynamo or the generator or whatever it was that made that sound. That sound never let up, and if you let yourself listen to it it had the effect of the dentist's drill, or the bastinado. That sound is in every studio that I've ever worked in, and I never have been able to determine just what it is. Some say it's a dynamo; some say it's the ventilating system; others say it's just water in the pipe-lines. Whatever it is, it's always near the writers' offices.

The door between my office and my secretary's was open, and I heard the phone ring. I looked up. My secretary.

'A Mr. Miller wants to speak to you,' she said.

'What Mr. Miller?'

'A Mr. Don Miller—'

'What Mr. Don Miller? I know five Don Millers.'

'If you'll give me a chance I'll tell you,' she said.

'Are you still sore at me?'

'He says he's from Gibbsville. He says he's a friend of your brother's.'

'Don Miller,' I said. 'He didn't say which brother he's a friend of?'

'No. I didn't ask him. He just said to tell you he was a friend of

your brother's, and he came from your home town. That's Gibbsville, isn't it?'

'Right. Okay, put him on.' I picked up the phone. 'Hello.'

'Mr. Malloy?'

'That's right.'

'My name is Don Miller. I'm a friend of Pat, your brother?'
There certainly was a question in his voice.

'Yes, I have one.'

'Well, I wasn't sure. I mean, I wanted to be sure I had the right
Malloy.'

'Very common name,' I said. 'How *is* Pat?'

'Oh, he was fine the last I saw him. Uh—I don't exactly come
from Gibbsville, Mr. Malloy.'

'Oh, no?'

'No. I'm from Swedish Haven—'

'Well—four miles.'

'That's right. Three and a half since they put the new road in. I
guess you weren't home since they put the new road in.'

'Nope. Two years since I've been home. How're things?'

'Oh, I guess all right. Uh—are you busy all day, Mr. Malloy?'

'Well, sort of,' I said. Aw-haw, I thought; a touch.

'Well, how about to-morrow then? Are you busy to-morrow? I
wanted to talk to you. I'm really a friend of Pat's, and I don't want
to borrow any money, but I don't know anybody out here and I
wanted some advice on something. I knew you were out here
working, but I didn't know what studio till yesterday. I saw in the
paper where you were working on some picture so I decided to call
you.'

'Well, I tell you,' I said, 'why don't you come around to the
Studio around four o'clock. Do you know where it is?'

'Oh, sure.'

'Okay. I'll leave word at the gate so they'll let you in, and if you
have any trouble just have the cop phone me. Is that all right with
you?'

'Oh, that'll be fine. Thank you very much. I'll be there promptly.'

'See you then,' I said, and hung up. 'Miss *Wendell!*' She appeared.
'Yes?'

'Come here, dear?'

'Definitely no. Is that all you wanted?'

'It seems like quite a lot,' I said.

'Well then, I'm going to lunch, *eef* you don't mind.'

'Will you phone the gateman and tell him I'm expecting a Mr. Don Miller at four o'clock, and he's to let him in.'

When I came back from lunch I busied myself for a while with Miss Wendell—Rose. It was no cigar; she was in one of her moods. I had kept her waiting an hour and a half in the Vine Street Derby the night before. She hated the Vine Street Derby because she said it was always full of Warner Brothers gangster types, and she had had to wait alone. So I told her I was sorry, and then the story editor sent for me and when I finally got back to my office it was six-thirty and she had gone home. On my way out I remembered Miller and I asked the gateman if there had been a Mr. Don Miller to see me, and he said no; no one had asked for me since three o'clock, which was when this gateman went on duty. During the next few days I wondered about Miller, but I had other things on my mind. For one thing, the Studio let me go. They had decided to shelve the story I was working on, as they were unable to borrow Jean Arthur. So a month or so passed and I thought very little about Miller.

Then one night I was having dinner at a South Sea Island kind of restaurant, off Hollywood Boulevard. The girl with me was Peggy Henderson. Although she was only twenty-one or—two, Peggy and I were old friends. Sometimes I was in love with her, and sometimes she was in love with me; but never at the same time, as the saying goes. At this point neither of us was in love with the other. As a matter of fact she apparently was in love with a boy her own age, named Herbert, about whom she was very mysterious. For a long time she wouldn't introduce me to him or tell me anything about him, except that he was not in pictures and he was not a Californian. He was Jewish, she said. 'Well, that's hardly a novelty in your life,'' I said. 'All your best friends are Jews. Except me.'

'You're more Jewish than any Jew I know,' she said.

I made her try to explain that, and she was explaining it when someone said: 'Mr. Malloy?'

I looked up. 'Yes.'

'I'm Don Miller,' he said.

'Oh, you are?' I said. I do not like strangers who introduce themselves when I am having dinner with a girl.

'Well, you don't have to get high-hat about it,' he said.

'Oh, I'm not so sure,' I said. 'What do you want?'

'I only wanted to apologize for not keeping that engagement, but if you're gunna get high-hat, skip it.'

'Oh, sit down,' I said. 'Miss Henderson, this is Mr. Miller. Will you have a drink?'

'No, thanks,' he said. He bowed to Peggy. Nodded is a better word, although he kept looking at her. She looked at him the way she always looked at anyone new. She was always friendly, and she always studied new people.

'Have a drink, for Christ's sake. Don't sulk.'

He smiled. 'All right, thanks, I'll have a rye and soda.'

'Mr. Miller is from my home town,' I said.

'Gibbsville!' said Peggy.

'You're wonderful,' I said. 'He's a friend of my brother's. One of them. By the way, how did you know me? Don't tell me I look like Pat. Or don't tell Pat.'

'No, nothing like that. Although I do see the family resemblance. No, I was sitting at the bar when you came in, and I heard the bartender call you Mr. Malloy, so I asked him if you were James Malloy. He didn't know, but the proprietor said yes, you were James Malloy.'

'Mm. Well, what happened the other day?' I said.

'The other day? You mean a month ago? I called you since then but they said you weren't there any more.'

'Well, that still doesn't answer my question,' I said.

'Aw, I just couldn't get there that day.'

'But why?'

'Why be so insistent, Jim? If he doesn't want to tell you,' said Peggy.

'I'd rather tell you some other time,' he said.

'All right,' I said. 'I suppose you don't need that advice any more?'

'Huh.' He got a vague look in his eyes.

'Skip it,' I said. 'Drink up. Peggy?'

'I'm not ready for another one,' she said.

'Waiter. A Tahitian Punch for Miss Henderson. A rye and soda for the gentleman, and I'll have a Scotch and soda.'

Miller sat with us and got a little tight and insisted on buying some drinks. Presently Peggy excused herself and when she left the table Miller said: 'Where can I get in touch with you?'

I was staying at an apartment hotel.

'Can I call you there to-morrow?' he said.

'Sure. But not before noon.'

'Did you tell Pat you heard from me?'

'No,' I said, 'I never write home. Hardly ever. Why? Don't you want me to?'

'No. I wanta ask you a favour. Don't tell anybody you saw me.'

Peggy came back to the table during the silence that followed his request, but I guess he understood that I would not tell anyone I had seen him, because right away he said: 'Are you in the movies, Miss Henderson?'

'Oh, no. I work in a bookstore.'

'Oh, do you? Where?'

'On Wilshire Boulevard.'

'What's the name of it?'

'He's moving right in,' I said.

Peggy laughed. 'The Avon Bookshop. It's in Beverly Hills. Why, are you a great reader, Mr. Miller?'

'Me? I haven't read a book since Christ knows when,' he said.

From then on he relaxed and we had a good evening.

The morning after we saw Don Miller I drove Peggy to the bookstore. Peggy did not have a car. Her kid brother, who went to the University of California at Los Angeles, had an old jalopy; a Durant Six roadster. She seldom drove it, although she paid most of the bills for it. How she managed so well I never will know. Her mother was dead, and she had not seen her father in years. Once in a great while she would hear from him, from Mexico, Texas, Montana, South America, Chicago. Never from New York or Europe or the Orient. Looking at Peggy and Keith, her brother, and having known their mother, and knowing as much and as little as I did about her father's life, I had my own picture of what Mr. Henderson was like. From him I imagine Keith got his height and leanness and casual, contemptuous good looks. Peggy looked so much like pictures of her mother as a girl that there couldn't have been very much of her father in Peggy's appearance. About the only thing Peggy got from him, as far as I could make out, was her independence, of which she had a complete set. Once in a great while Peggy would get a letter, forwarded, addressed to a house in which she had not lived for four years. The letter would be from Mexico City, Houston, Missoula, Quito, Clark Street, and it would be written on hotel stationery or on the stationery of some club, and in it would be a money order for as little as fifty dollars or as much as five hundred. 'Dear Kids—' it always began. I remember one time Peggy showed me a letter from New Orleans and she asked me what I thought he was doing. Well, it was hard to say. Chicago and Missoula spoiled my theory that he was in the oil business. The money order from New Orleans was for five hundred, which led me to suspect that Henderson might be mixed up in gun-running, because in that racket they pay off good, and in gold, but I did not say so at the time.

There was a peculiar reason why I did not say so. Aside from not wanting to take away any of her pleasure at the mere fact of getting five hundred dollars all at once, there was a reason that would have been more important. Peggy was politically almost as far left as she could go, and she might have been afraid her father was running guns for the wrong revolutionaries. There was nothing transitory about her beliefs, and nothing new. Her conviction began in high school; the things she learned in the intervening years were really only additional information that made for stronger conviction, until now she had become a symbol to me. Whenever I read silly stuff about Reds I would think of Peggy, and not of Mike Gold. Just as, whenever I read silly stuff about Catholics I would think of my mother and not of Cardinal O'Connell. Feeling that way, it was a wonder Peggy and I did not get married, but it might as well be understood this early that she had something to say about that. We can get that over with now, so that it won't complicate things later.

On mornings like this, tooling my beautiful Buick out to the bookstore, with the car working fine and Peggy looking sweet and a good big breakfast inside us and the morning air and a cigarette and the pretty jail-bait on their way to high school and the sun and money in the bank and no hangover—I would reach over with my right hand and pull Peggy to me. (That was another good thing about her: there was none of that 'Somebody'll *see* us.') 'Do you love me?' I would say.

'No.'

'Well, then, why don't you marry me?'

'I don't like you.'

"Well, why don't you marry me? God damn it, we oughta get married. I think you do love me.'

'What if I do! Suppose I did? I'd never marry you or anyone like you.'

'We're friends, aren't we?'

'Yes, and that's all. Just because I *sleep* with you? Listen we've had that out before—'

'Mm.'

'Oh, now you're going to spoil it with your lousy puns and I'll be disagreeable at the shop. Why do you have to—why can't you just accept our relationship—and don't look hurt, and sulk. You know damn well, James Malloy, damn well you know it, if I said I would marry you you'd want to get out of it. If I said all right, you and I'll meet at two o'clock this afternoon and file intention to get married, I'll bet you'd be at the Vendome, drunk. Trying to get out of it.'

'That's a lie, and you know it.'

'It's the truth and *you* know it.'

I always stopped the car about a block away from the bookstore. 'All right. You're right. You're omniscient. You're Havelock Ellis. You're Dorothy Parker. You're Dorothy Thompson. You're Dorothy Dix. You're—whoever knows all about men and women and class-angling, and ideology, and human relations. Oh, you're so God damn smart. Why don't *you* face a fact or two? For instance, why don't you admit you're in love with this Herbert guy?'

'Because—why should I let you put words in my mouth? You object to my uh, omniscience. Well, I object to yours.'

'All right, all right, all *right!*' I said.

'Major Bowes.'

'That's corny,' I said. 'Well, then, listen, how about this? Suppose you don't love me. Suppose you don't even love this Herbert—'

'Why do you keep calling him this Herbert? Just call him Herbert. I'll get the idea. I'll know who you mean.'

'Okay. Herbert. Suppose you don't love either one of us, this me, or that Herbert. All right. Now, I don't know what goes on between you two, but I think I can guess.'

'No, you can't.'

'Yes, I can. And I'll surprise you. My guess is, you're not having an affair with Herbert. Right?'

'Well, yes. You're right. As far as you go you're right. But only as far as you go. Listen to me, Jim. For a so-called intelligent man you don't seem to realise one important thing about me. I don't

say you give the matter much thought. I have a strong suspicion
that when I'm not with you you don't give *me* much thought. But
anyway, what you don't realise is, even if I'm not sleeping with
Herbert, he's much much closer to me than you are. Except when
you are actually sleeping with me. Why *can't* you realise that? I like
you. I do like you. And, I like to sleep with you. But you've made
me so mad this morning I'm going to tell you something. I'd rather
marry Herbert, and not sleep with anybody, than marry you.'

'Mm,' I said. 'Well, that about finishes that.' I looked straight
ahead. I was hurt, because she never had said anything as strong
as this. We had had substantially the same kind of discussion many
times before, usually under approximately the same circumstances,
but this was the first time she had been blunt. And I guess honest.
I punched the steering wheel with both fists. It was a 'safety'
steering wheel that yielded a little to the punches, as it was supposed
to yield to your body if you were in a collision. For a second I
forgot her in my misery, and then I felt her looking at me. She
reached over and put her hand on my knee.

'Hello,' she said.

'Hello,' I said.

'I'm sorry.'

'No, you're not. You're sorry you made me feel this way, but
you're not sorry you said what you did.'

She did not deny this.

'Peggy. I have a feeling this isn't the time to bring this up, but
I have one more proposition. You're the most realistic person I
know. I don't mean that in any way but honestly. It isn't flattering,
and it isn't unflattering. But you are. You're like Coolidge or somebody. I mean materialistic. Face facts. Good business head. That
kind of thing. Well now, how about this? I would like to live with
you. I have fun with you. I sort of love you. You have fun with me.
You sort of love me. And even though we don't think the same
way, or at least you think your way to things, for instance your
leftist stuff, and I feel my way. But we arrive about the same place.
Isn't that true?'

'More or less.'

'It is true. I haven't got a good thinking brain, but I have sound
emotions. You can give me the party line on the Scottsboro boys
or the Mooney case as though some God damn Jesuit worked it out
for you. On the other hand, I know almost right away, without

thinking, without using words like activise and ideology and dialectical materialism and all that crap, I am on the right side. That is, the leftist side. Isn't that true?'

'Yes, that's true.'

'Well, what difference does it make how we get there as long as we get to the same place?'

'Oh, a lot of difference. Emotions aren't trustworthy.'

'Did you ever hear of the false syllogism?'

'I don't depend on syllogisms.'

I lit a cigarette. I put the lighter back into the socket on the dash. 'Well, anyway. We've got so damn far away from my proposition. You concede most of what I say. You're realistic. I'm emotional. You like me. I like you. Now then. You concede these things?'

'Sure. Go on, or you'll get lost again.'

'Well, why don't you marry me on this basis. I make a lot of money out here. You make twenty-two-fifty a week at the shop. You get an occasional pourboire from your old man, which you can't depend on. Keith keeps you broke, and probably when he gets out of college he'll get a job as filling-station attendant. Your grandfather—'

'Oh, we don't count on him.'

'Well, you see what I mean. Marry me for my money. Marry me for economic independence. To do the things you want to do. As far as I'm concerned, it's a damn good bargain, so you don't have to worry about that angle.' I turned and faced her. 'Well, what do you think?'

'James. Dear James. I'll be late for work. I *am* late.'

'Well, for Christ's sake, give me some kind of an answer, or at least comment. Don't be so God damn patronising and superior. Dear James. Dear James my ass.'

She put out her finger and drew imaginary circles counter-clockwise on the crystal of the dash clock. 'Uh, in the first place, you hate working for pictures, so as a realist I have to take that into consideration. How do I know you'll stick it out another year? Even one more year? I don't, and you don't. So therefore I'd be taking that risk. In the second place, you said something about Keith. I'm not worried about Keith. He doesn't take much money. He practically earns his way through school. In fact, I'd say he does earn his way through. You know, he's a good athlete, and that's a great help. And then you mentioned something about my salary.

Well, we don't live on my salary. We have some money from my mother's insurance. Enough to pay the rent and electricity and little debts, and the money I get from my father may not seem like much to you, but honestly, it does always come just when we seem to need it. I don't know why, but it just does. The little bluebird, or God, or something. And, one other thing besides. More or less covering the whole financial aspect. You talk about financial independence.'

'Economic independence.'

'Well—'

'No, not well. *Economic* sounds more like the kind of thing *you'd* say.'

'Okay. But I wanted to tell you my theory. My theory is this. I haven't got the party line on it, Smartie, but it's this way. The only way, to secure economic independence, is to be independent of—is to be economically independent. In other words, I'll put it this way. It's a curious thing, but the more money you have, the less independent of money you are, is my theory. In other words, the very rich are the least independent of money, that is to say, independent of economic or financial problems. The very rich are just not economically or financially independent.'

'Well, now, I don't know about that,' I said. 'As far as it goes it sounds all right, but I imagine it's specious or Utopian. I don't mean Utopian Sinclair Utopian.'

'Ooh!' she said. 'And you talk about corny.'

'Right off the elbow. But we gotta have money. We gotta have wampum, or, or scrip. Kale. Mazuma. Spinach. Cabbage. Gelt. Uh—or amperes or volts or bushels. You know why paper money is? Or credit? Because it's too damn much trouble to be lugging gold all over the place—'

'Yes, I know, dear, and besides, there isn't that much gold. Yes, I know all that. Probably better than you do.'

'That's right. Do you love me?'

'Yes, now I do. And I'll tell you something else that ought to make you feel better, or at least restore your masculine pride. Herbert has offered me almost the same proposition, and I've turned it down. Except that with Herbert there wouldn't be any sex. Herbert—now don't you ever repeat this—Herbert has T.B. A spot. He just loves me. And without working he has more money than I'll ever need. Does that make you feel better?'

'In a way, yes, in a way, no. Doesn't make any difference. You know what I'd like to do?'

'I think so. You want to go back to the hotel, or to my house. Is that it?'

'Yes. You take the day off. We'll go to the beach, or the hotel, or your place, or San Luis Obispo, or the desert or anywhere. Let's go on a trip?'

'I'd like to. Honestly I would, but I'm not going to marry you or Herbert or anybody, so I need my job. Now I have to go. I'm a worker.'

'Arise, ye prisoners of starva-tion!'

'The first woman that comes in and wants to buy *Gone with the Wind* I'm going to sell her *The Coming Struggle for Power*—'

'Show her Strachey's picture.'

'All right. I will.'

'What if it's a man?'

'Men don't buy books in the morning,' she said.

'Mm. And women don't buy enough of them.'

'Right.' she said. 'Well, I have to go now. Oh, my.'

'If you change your mind.'

'I can't, Jim. I wish I could. What are you doing to-night, around ten o'clock?'

'No plans. Why?'

'I'm going to an anti-Fascist meeting. It ought to be over about nine-thirty. Do you want to meet me somewhere?'

We made the date and I sat in the car with my right arm stretched across the top of the seat. She was carrying her hat and she was wearing a sharkskin suit, not new, but one I liked. She always walked as though she were going some place. I liked her walk. I had nothing to do. When she turned the corner I got out of the car and went to a shop and bought some over-priced ties and then I went down Wilshire to Vine Street and Hollywood and bothered my agent, who had all the New York papers. I phoned the hotel and they said a Mr. Don Miller had called and left a number. I called him. He wanted to see me, so I said I'd take him to lunch, twelve-thirty.

It was a boring meal, up to the moment when Miller said he never drank coffee except in the morning.

He was there first, sitting on a tube-and-leather chair in the front of the restaurant, which was one of those modern eating places, all tin foil and black cloth and marble. He stood up. He was wearing an inexpensive Glen plaid jacket, cheap grey flannel slacks, imitation suede shoes, a dark brown polo shirt, and the conventional Hollywood neckerchief. His hair was cut short, but not 'crew cut', and he was taller than he had seemed before. Everything about him seemed newer than his sunburn, and he was a very handsome young man.

It was a very boring meal, because his attitude seemed to say, 'All right, get it up. Say something. Start the conversation. What have you got to say for yourself?'—which was not quite the case. After all, he had called me, not I him. Several times, during silences, I wanted to say the hell with it and get up and leave. There were at least two hundred other people in Hollywood I'd rather have lunched with.

He was a good six feet tall, with the kind of athletic build that is athletic, but one look at his face and you knew that this was no athlete. Probably he could do handstands on a beach. Possibly he could dive well. Maybe he had played high-school basketball or had picked up some golf or tennis. He undoubtedly was strong, but in a way that I was not afraid of. He had long fingers, with long wide nails that had been buffed to a nice shine. I bet myself that he played the piano, a sort of fraternity-house piano; competent, unimaginative piano; improvising-sounding, but someone else's improvisation. I could all but hear him, playing something like 'Easy To Love', which at that time was brand new. Slow, not in any steady tempo, and all chords. That's what those hands were for—at least that was one of the reasons and explanations for them. I also could easily imagine them going to work on a girl. It is not often that I notice a man's hands, but I had to notice his, because by the time his steak arrived I had taken a thorough dislike to him, and that was the reason why I sized him up so carefully. It is often a good thing to look a man over carefully when you start out with such an active dislike of him, and all during the meal I had a far-off notion that a casual word or a spilt glass of water might have us swinging at each other. Well, I kept telling myself, this was one decision I was pretty sure I could get.

We talked about what we were going to eat, and then what we were eating, and about a couple of dolls who sat across the room and the doll situation in Hollywood. There was no specific talk; it was all general, even when we talked about the food. I mean he didn't say his steak was good or bad; he said it was funny how in California the highest praise you could bestow on a steak was to say that it was 'New York Cut'. 'Yeah, that is funny,' I said. After a while the conversation settled down to a tempo: three or four mouthfuls of food, and some remark about movie extras and how some of them were easy to sleep with and some of them very difficult. Neither of us took dessert. One large coffee for me.

He didn't like my Luckies. He had Camels, which he took out of his shirt pocket. He reached in, surrounded the pack with his hand, slapped two fingers of his left hand on the top of the pack (noisily, and much harder than was necessary) until two cigarettes popped up. He extracted one and put it in his mouth. He scratched a match and held it to the cigarette and cocked his head far over to one side and took a deep inhale. Enough smoke to fill a bicycle tyre came out of his mouth and he blew out the match. Whenever you see a man go through all this you are looking at a man who has had plenty of time on his hands.

I could hardly look at him. I decided to shock him.

'What's on your mind, Miller?'

Some of his cockiness went away and he took another quick drag on his cigarette. He looked down at the cigarette, which he was rubbing against the ash tray. 'Plenty,' he said. 'But I don't know—I'll be frank with you. I don't know if I want to talk about it.'

'You mean to me or just to anybody?'

'Anybody, I guess. Yes, anybody. I might as well tell you this. No, God damn it, I don't know what the hell. Jesus, I don't know anything. God damn it.'

I waited. I watched him crush the cigarette.

'You don't like me, do you?' he said.

'I don't know,' I said. 'Why? What makes you think that?'

'You gave me that impression. I guess you think I'm a fresh guy. Well, I am. I always was, I guess.'

I waited again.

'You know, I used to know you,' he said.

'Did you? When?'

'Remember when you used to come down to Swedish Haven and write up the football games? You were working on the *Leader*.'

'I remember, yes.'

'You wrote me up in a game and you spelt my name wrong. The only time you ever wrote me up.'

'Miller? For Christ's sake, how could I spell that wrong?'

'It's not my name.'

'Oh,' I said. 'Oh-h-h.' Three notes. 'What is your name?'

'That's the God damn trouble.'

'You mean you don't want to tell me?'

'I don't want to tell anybody. Do you know anything about me? I mean, did you hear anything from Pat, to-day? This morning?'

'Nope. I'm not even sure Pat can write.'

'Pat's all right. He used to be a good friend of mine. He's a good guy. We used to go out and get cockeyed together.'

'You know, if you don't like Pat you don't have to say you do. I don't like him, so don't let that worry you. What's the matter? Are the cops looking for you, or what?'

'Mr. Malloy, I'll lay my cards on the table. Do you remember the Reverend Schumacher?'

'Sure. Pastor of the uh, Lutheran Church?'

'Reformed. That's the one. That's my father. He's dead, but that's the one you mean.'

'A bald-headed man, a little heavy, about medium height. He was a Phi Beta Kappa.'

'That's the one.'

'Sure, I knew him. I liked him. I didn't know him very well, but I remember he wasn't a Kluxer. I think he was a patient of my father's at one time.' I could see he wasn't listening much to this. Another silence.

'Some fresh coffee, sir?'

'Yes, I'll have some. Do you want a drink? One of your rye and sodas?' I said.

'No. No, thanks.'

'Just some more coffee,' I said. I lit a cigarette. 'Well, listen, Schumacher—by the way, how did I spell your name?'

'S, h, u, m, a, c, h, e, r.'

'That was a typographical error. I knew how to spell your old man's name, so I'd know how to spell yours. Anyway, you're in some kind of a jam, and you have some idea I can help you. That's right so far, isn't it?'

'Yes. I'm in a jam. I don't know why I phoned you in the first place. I had to talk to somebody, then when the time came, like the time I was to come to your office over in the Studio, I couldn't make myself go over. It's the same way now. I phoned you to-day because I wanted to talk about it.'

'What kind of a jam is it? Money? A dame?'

'Well—money. Oh, what the hell, I might as well tell you.'

'Whenever you're ready. I don't have to tell you I won't repeat it.'

'Oh, that don't worry me.' He smiled. 'You know something? I remember one time Pokey Armbruster, when he was coaching S. H. High, he was worried the night before the Gibbsville High game because he remembered how you knew all our plays, and your brother Pat was playing on Gibbsville High. Remember that one play from a place kick formation where the guy holding the ball—'

'Sure. It was an old Lafayette play.'

'Well, that was the one we beat Gibbsville on. So from then on, when Pokey realised how you didn't tell them the play, we all trusted you. Not that *I* ever had anything to trust you with, but all the same.'

I let him talk on, because some of my antagonism was disappearing. He was letting himself go and was becoming a frightened kid who had to talk to somebody.

'It seems funny, sitting here in Hollywood, talking about S. H. High and all that stuff.' He lit another cigarette, but not with all the motions he had gone through with the other. He took a sip of water, and a quick look at me. He watched the waiter pour my coffee, and when the waiter had gone he began: 'When my old man died, for a while I lived with my aunt in Swedish Haven. She was my mother's sister and she was a strict old maid, so when I'd come in late at night she'd bawl me out the next morning, also because I didn't have a job. The only money I had was from my old man's lodge insurance, about enough to pay for the funeral and a little over. I had a Ford coop and I used to go around with the fellas and sometimes lend the car out for a couple dollars, and when we'd go out on a double date I'd supply the car and the other fella'd buy the gas and I had a girl, she was stenographer for old Mossbacher, at the shirt factory, and he kept her. Old Mossbacher, he must be sixty-some years old, but I don't know. She'd never tell me much about him, but she was always good for ten bucks a week and a couple times we took trips. She used to get sore when I razzed her about Mossie. I used to say to her, "Don't tell me old Mossie gives you the works." And she'd get sore.

'Well, so anyway I was just about breaking even. I played a pretty good game of pool and I put up a good appearance because I had these clothes I bought when I was at State. I went to State for a year and a half after I got out of High, but I flunked out. I don't know. I got so I didn't give a God damn. So I used to pick up a couple bucks shilling at Jimmy's pool-room. That's new since you were there. But after a while the whole thing got on my nerves. I used to look at these muggs that used to come in the pool-room and I used to think, "What the hell am I doing wasting my time with them?" Their idea of something hot was to be a brakeman on the railroad and have a regular run. They used to drive me nuts. And this dame got on my nerves. I felt sorry for her in a way, but I wasn't responsible. Mossie'd keep her at the office after everybody went home and after he went home she'd call me up at my aunt's place and my aunt knew who she was and she'd raise hell. Those old maids, you know they always know when there's something funny going on. I had a friend of mine had a dose and my aunt, I swear she knew he had it before I did, even if I did see him every day. And this kid I was travelling around with, my aunt used to raise hell about her, and the kid, she'd call me up after Mossie'd leave. She'd have to see me right away. So I'd go over and pick her up and she'd make me drive right out the Valley, without any supper, and I'd give her a jump in the car. Well, that part of it was all right, but I began to get worried—you know, I used to kid her about Mossie, but these times when he'd been at her. I remember in Psychology reading about some of these old guys and I thought it was a lot of crap. Oh, I'm no kid. But this stuff I used to read, I used to think those old English colonels and Chinks—but not Americans. Not old Mossie. You know, guys with whips or pushing pigeon's eyes out. This kid used to be nuts, absolutely screwy after he got through with her. She earned her pay, all right. Anyway I got worried, because she'd cry and she was the hottest little babe I ever knew and I had some premonition I was getting into something. You know. Maybe she'd commit suicide, or Mossie'd do something to her and she'd die, and Mossie knew about us. I'd see him on the street and he'd look at me with this dirty look in his eye and say, "Good *eve*-ning, Harold, good *eve*-ning,' and give me

a sort of, you know, look. So I thought it was about time I got the
hell out of there.

'There were no jobs, of course. It was all right with my aunt if
I loafed around the pool-room all day and wasted my time, but
take a WPA job or something like that? Oh, no. We were too good
for that. I had to get out of town, so I went to see a fella that knew
Asa Merritt, the Congressman, and I got a letter to Merritt and I
went to Washington. I sold my car and my aunt gave me fifty bucks
and I went to Washington. I knew a guy there, he was a Beta,
which I was, and he flunked out the same time I did. I stayed with
him. His parents were over in Europe.

'Well, it took me a couple of days to get to see Merritt and he
stalled me but he said he knew my old man and since I was in
Washington anyway, I should stick around and maybe he could
find something for me.

'Well, one afternoon I was walking along F Street and I kicked
this thing, I thought it was a wallet. It looked like a wallet, and I
picked it up and then I thought it was a chequebook. But do you
know what it was? It was a book of these traveller's cheques. A
whole book of them, not one of them torn out. Brand new. I stuck
the damn thing in my pocket, thinking sort of in the back of my
head that I'd turn it in at some bank and probly get a reward for
it. You know why? Because it was for five thousand dollars. Five G's.
There were ten cheques, each made out for five hundred dollars. A
lot of money, you know.

'So the next day I had to go see Merritt, and this time the son
of a bitch finally got around to telling me the truth. He said,
"Harold, I'm very sorry to tell you, but I can't seem to be able to
find anything for you." He was polite and all like that, because he
probly was afraid he was losing a vote, and you know, like what if
I went back home and said Congressman Merritt was high-hat? It
might hurt him politically. But irregardless he didn't have any job
for me.

'That was one thing. Then when I went home that day, late in
the afternoon, back to this guy's apartment that I was staying at,
Joe said to me, he told me his mother and father were coming back
from Europe the following Monday and he had to go to New York
to meet them and I'd have to get out of the apartment. We had to
get a coloured fella to clean the place up after the way we left it.
Joe said why not go to New York with him, maybe I could find a

job there. Fat chance, I thought, and anyway I didn't have more than about ten bucks and being stuck in New York on ten bucks!

'Swell luck I was having all of a sudden. Then I got this idea. I remembered about this book of traveller's cheques. I didn't say anything to Joe about it, but I told him I'd let him know the next day in regard to New York.

'I went to my room and I got out this book of cheques and I looked at it and looked at it. I never saw one before, so I studied it carefully and the idea came to me, when I was a kid I used to be able to sign my old man's name to excuses when I bagged school. I was pretty good at it. Right now I could sign the old man's name and if you knew his signature you'd think it was all right. So I sat down at a desk and I began writing out, Donald R. Miller, Donald R. Miller, copying it over and over again, oh, a couple hundred times. This chequebook was in the name of Donald R. Miller, and there was his signature right there in the book, ten times, so I studied it, the different ways he wrote it himself, and by the time I went to bed that night I could write Donald R. Miller better than my own name.

'Well, to make a long story short, I went to New York with Joe, my friend, only I went to a different hotel, a better one, and I told Joe I was registering under the name of Donald R. Miller. I gave him some phony reason like I was afraid I'd run into somebody or something. I put up a good front. I had these clothes and a couple good suitcases and I looked the part. I even went out and called up the hotel and left messages for myself. Please call Mr. Gump at the University Club. Call So and So at the Bankers' Trust Company. Mrs. J. Archibald Smith would like you to come to dinner Thursday. Every day I'd have a lot of messages. Maybe the clerks didn't read them, but maybe they did. And I was there about three days and I got dressed up every night and when I'd go out I'd say to the clerk, if there were any messages for me I'd be at such and such a number, and then I'd go right out and call myself up. I had those guys thinking I was the most important guy in New York. They probly thought I was some rich man's son from Washington, D.C. I registered from Washington.

'Well, the third day, or rather night, I got all duked up and went out and ate a sandwich at some joint over on Third Avenue and went to a movie till around ha' past eleven and then I came back and I asked the clerk, I said I wanted to cash a traveller's cheque.

I said it was pretty big and he didn't have to give me all the money all at once. I only wanted fifty bucks, I told him. So that made it look all right and he gave me a hundred. I signed that thing, boy, every minute I expected to have some cop thump me on the shoulder, but I guess they probly compared my signature with the one on the register and it looked the same. They had three signatures. The one when I registered, the one on the cheque, and the one I signed right then when I cashed the cheque.

'They gave me the rest of the dough the next day and I stayed there the rest of the week. I even gave a party right there in the hotel when Joe's mother and father came back. We got two nice babes, respectable, and the party set me back around seventy dollars. Joe sort of wondered, but I let him guess. Jesus, Malloy, I'm giving you all the chance in the world to get me thrown in the clink.'

'Sure you are,' I said.

'Well, I'm taking that chance.'

'You certainly are.'

'I guess if I tried to move in on your girl you wouldn't let me get very far.'

'Well, then, don't try,' I said. 'But go on with your story. Didn't they ever catch up with you?'

'Never did. It was a funny thing. To get money I had to spend money. I went out and bought a new outfit, new bags, packed up, took a taxi to the Penn Station, checked the bags, came back a while later and got them, and registered at another hotel. I stayed at two hotels at the same time. I used the cash I got from one hotel to set me up at the second one and then I cashed another cheque at the second hotel. In about two weeks' time I had over a thousand bucks cash, so I decided it was time to blow. All this time I was always expecting some flatfoot to be waiting for me, but I got so I didn't care. I was living the way I always wanted to. There was a little dame at the place where they sold tickets to the shows, in the hotel. I'd go there and buy two tickets to a show and only use one. She got to know me, so I took her out and she was all right, and through her I got to know some others. Oh, I did another little thing, just to make it all look on the up and up. I'd call Joe in Washington every couple days, just in case they checked up on the bill, I'd have these Washington calls. I was wishing I could have stayed there till I spent the whole five grand, but I had other plans.

I wanted to get the cash and blow, which I did. When I was sure
of having a thousand bucks all clear, and my bills paid, I checked
out of the two hotels and I came out here.

'I been out here ever since. This place reminds me of those
Western stories I used to read, where they don't ask you your name
or where you came from or anything. I'm as much Donald Miller
as I am anybody. I have a car and a licence in the name of Miller,
and for a laugh, I even told them at this place where I'm living, I
said I was trying to get in the movies under the name of Don Mills,
but my real name was Miller, but if any calls came for Don Mills,
that was me. Oh, I've had a lot of laughs.'

'But still you're worried. Why?'

'Wouldn't you be? What if they begin catching up with me? I
can't understand why they haven't. This Miller guy, he must be a
crook or something, or else why doesn't he report losing five thousand bucks? That's the only answer I can think of. He must of been
a crook.' He took out a cigarette but did not light it. He held it in
his thumbs and forefingers, fingering it as though he were rolling a
cigarette. 'Anyhow, it'd make a good story for you, wouldn't it?'

'I'd like to know the ending of it,' I said.

'*You* would? What about *me*?'

'Uh, to get back to why you're telling me all this, you said you
were in a jam. What kind of a jam? I mean, is it anything new
besides your, uh, criminal record? You know, these banks and
insurance companies are tough. If they ever do catch up with you
they'll put you in that gaol-house and throw the key away. My
advice is, if you care anything about it, my advice is to be satisfied
with what dough you have and try to get a legitimate job, under
your real name. You could buy in on a hot dog stand or something
like that.'

'Me run a hot dog stand after the way I've lived! Say, that's the
God damn trouble. Supposing I did buy a hot dog stand and went
honest? Supposing I made enough dough to pay them back? That's
just when they would catch up with me. Just when I was going
honest. No, the hell with that. I considered going under my real
name, but this hot dog stand idea stinks.'

'Anyway, you're not in any immediate jam, other than what
you've been in the past six months or so?'

'No.'

'Then what are your plans? What's it all about? Why did you tell me all this?'

'Well, I had to tell you. I had to tell somebody. It may sound as if I was bragging, and I guess maybe I was, but I been thinking, I got away with this so far, why not use my brains to get into something honest, but where there was a lot of dough.'

'Oh, I guess that's where I come in. Do you want to be a writer?'

'Don't kid me. Me write? Listen, when I write Donald R. Miller on a cheque or anything else that's about it!'

'You're certainly one of the highest-paid writers I know.'

'No, that writing, that's not for me. I haven't a big enough of a vocabulary, and I'm a lousy speller. No, what I want is some job that pays a good salary and I don't have to work too hard or get dirty. And I don't want to start from the bottom.'

'It's too bad you're not a writer,' I said. 'Well, I'm sure I don't know what the hell I can do for you. Right now I'm not working myself. You have no ideas about what you want to do? No special training or anything like that?'

'Huh. If you call playing a good game of pool, or I can drive a car better than most guys. I'm a good dancer and I have plenty of clothes.'

'You'd make a good dress extra. You know what that is?'

'One of those guys that has a full dress, long tails? Sure, I know about them. There's a couple of them living where I live. You can have that. No, I want a real job. I bet I could sell. Real estate, or cars. Cars I'd be good at. Good cars, like say a Packard or Duesenberg.'

'How old are you?'

'You want to know the truth?'

'Mm.'

'I'm twenty-two. I look older. I could pass for twenty-seven.' He made a fist and punched the palm of his left hand. 'Oh, Christ, Malloy. I don't know what I am, or anything. Here I started out to tell you about myself, and you listened, and I didn't tell you the truth. Not all of it, I left out some, and put in some. I'm gettin' so I don't know what's the truth and what isn't. I wasn't cut out for this stuff I'm doing. I'm no crook. I should of been a rich guy instead of a minister's son without any dough. I can fool people into thinking I'm rich, and all I need is a few bucks and clothes. I just sit around and look wise. When I'm doing it I get a great laugh out of it at the time, like with those cheques, but when I'm alone, God, I don't want to go to gaol. All I want is a good job and then I'd even pay back the money, providing I was sure I wouldn't get caught. When I used to make a living playing pool I was always honest. Oh, I used to lose a couple games on purpose and then make the bets bigger, but that's business.'

'That's what they call a loss-leader.'

'Sure. But anyway, I am honest. I'd like to sell a car that I wouldn't have to be ashamed of, maybe get the better of a guy on a trade, but that's business.' He took a deep breath.

'It's after three,' I said. 'Give me your phone number and if I hear of anything I'll give you a buzz. Where do you live?' He gave me the address and phone number, and I paid the bill. He stood up, and by that act alone he changed. He was cocky again.

'Well, thanks for the lunch, old man. Gimme a buzz.' He almost looked around to see if anyone was admiring him.

'Oke,' I said, and he left me.

The Hendersons lived in a little one-storey house in the general direction of the Observatory. It took at least half a dozen visits before you knew the way, because of the winding roads and the names of the roads. They would take a name, say, Orchard, and there would be Orchard Road, Orchard Lane, Orchard Place, Orchard Drive, all together, intersecting and merging. It took a lot out of you to get there, too, because they have changed the ratios of steering-gears so you have to whirl your wheel continually all the way up to the Hendersons'.

I had the privilege of walking in without ringing the doorbell, and anyway I wore leather soles, which could be heard on the short cement walk and the wooden porch.

'Anybody home? Oh, hello, Keith.'

'Hello, Jim.'

'Don't get up,' I said. 'Sit still.'

'Peggy isn't home yet.' He was stretched out on a davenport. He rested his book, a fat textbook, on his belly. 'What's new?'

'Nothing much.'

He sucked his teeth, a habit of his. 'Want a piece of pie? Millie baked a darn good pie to-night. Sweet potato pie.'

'No, thanks, I just had dinner and a couple of drinks.'

'I can get you a drink. Scotch? I think we have some Scotch.'

'No, thanks. How're things out at Westwood?'

'Oh, 'bout the same as usual.'

'Gonna make Phi Bete?'

'Me? Not a chance. Well, maybe. Accidentally. I won't try for it. I'm not altogether convinced of the, uh, uh, value of Phi Bete. I'm not so sure about it. There was a fellow in my fraternity last year, now he should have been Phi Bete. He was one of the most brilliant fellows I ever knew, really brilliant. Some of the nitwits that did make it, cats! They couldn't carry his books, this fellow. They weren't in the same league with him. But, he had some trouble with I don't know, English prof, or French. French I think. And, he just didn't get Phi Bete. Cats! I dunno.' He rubbed the back of his head, fast and like a groom curry-combing a horse. "Do you think it's worth while?'

'In a way. A negative way. If you make it, if you have a key, then you can throw it away in the bureau drawer and forget about it. If you haven't got it and you pan it, then people naturally think you're sour-grapes. I guess that's about all it's worth. Get it and forget about it.'

'Guess you're right. You've got something there. Yep. But I'm not going to try for it. If I get it, okey-doke. If I don't, well. What are you working on? Haven't seen you around for a while.'

'I'm working on my agent right now. Otherwise, nothing. They aren't doing that picture I was working on, so I'm looking for another job.'

'I guess you won't starve. I don't know what's keeping Peggy. Did you have a date with her?'

'She's at a meeting. Yeah, I had a date, but you never know about those meetings.'

'Do you think that's a good idea, those meetings? I'm against Fascism. My God. But what do you think of those meetings? I don't mean for Peggy now, but just generally speaking.'

'Oh, they don't do any harm. It's better than nothing. At least it shows the Fascists that we know they're having *their* meetings, and then also if it weren't for the meetings a lot of people would just forget about the whole thing.'

'That's true. Um-hm. True. I went to two of them with Peggy, but, cats! I don't know, Jim. Same kind of people get up and do the speechmaking there as at school. I mean the same type. Cheerleaders. What if there hadn't been a depression. I wonder if

Peggy'd be going to anti-Fascist meetings. Or if there'd be any meetings at all. I'm too young I guess. I don't know enough, and all I learn is what they teach me. I'll grow up, I guess.'

'You'll be all right, Keith. You're all right now. You can't have all the answers at your age. You can't at any age, no matter how long you live, so don't let it worry you. That's the difference between you and me. One of them. When I was about your age I thought I knew all the answers, but *you* know you *don't*. I guess this is Peggy. I wonder who's with her.'

'Hello. Hello, brother darling.'

'Peggy. Hello, Herbert.'

'Hello, Keith. Good evening, Mr. Malloy.'

'Hello,' I said. This spoiled my plans.

'James, I brought Herbert along because I knew you'd have your car, and Herbert has to go downtown and he'd have to take a bus. We can all go together, except Keith. You study.'

'I don't want to go,' said Keith. 'Or, maybe I do. I'll have to give the matter a little more mature consideration. Do I want to drive downtown, or don't I? What advantage is there to be gained? No novelty in it. I've been there. Charming company. True. But is it worth—'

'While he's giving the matter his mature consideration let's go. Let us know when we get back,' said Peggy. 'By the way, don't take that seriously, little man. I mean, don't wait up for us.'

'Little man. Lit-tle—man, eh?' Keith was more than six feet tall, and built on the lines we have been led to believe Lincoln's were. He very deliberately placed his book upon the table and very deliberately rose.

'Don't you dare! Don't you you touch me,' said Peggy.

'Lit-tle man. Lit-tle man,' he repeated. He suddenly changed his posture and manner. He bent forward and held out his arms like a bear or an ape, and let out a Tarzan yell. Peggy ran and we, Herbert and I, followed her.

The three of us sat in the front seat, Peggy in the middle. 'Where to, Herbert?'

'The Los Angeles Biltmore,' he said.

'See what's on the radio,' said Peggy.

'There's something wrong with it,' I said. I switched it on, but it was bad, mostly static. On the way we passed the house I had had the first time Peggy ever stayed with me. I looked down, and across my shoulder at her, but she was looking straight ahead. We were silent for blocks.

'Malloy, tell me, how much did you make out of your book. I mean, about how many copies did you sell?' said Herbert.

'Which one? There were two.'

'The—the popular one. The one about the policeman in Central Park.'

'Oh, thirty thousand copies, including the English sales. Figure about thirty cents a copy and you have the amount,' I said. He annoyed me.

'Mm. Nine thousand dollars. Imagine, a book of that kind making nine thousand. How long'd it take you to write it?'

'You mean in work-hours, or over how long a period of time on the calendar? And why? Are you writing one?'

'Oh, I've written several. Unpublished. I can't publish while I'm living off my family.'

'What kind of books do you write?'

'Well, one is an epic poem, something like *Buddenbrooks*, by Thomas Mann. You know Thomas Mann.'

'Not personally. Do you?'

'No. But I know his work very well. In German.'

'Are you, uh, writing this, uh, epic poem in German? I thought *Buddenbrooks* was prose.'

'Oh, it is. Of course. No, you see mine is *like Buddenbrooks*, a book about a family, you *know?*'

'Yes. Family. *I* know.'

'But mine's American. Jewish-American.'

'I see. The last time I talked to you you were doing something for two pianos.'

'Herbert doesn't play any more,' said Peggy.

'I've given up the piano, permanently. It takes too much out of me. I'm not good enough at it, and the effect of even good piano is too ephemeral. De Pachmann dies, where is his art? Lost. Lost until one of these radio geniuses can recapture sound floating through the ether. You've heard of that, how they're going to be able to tune in and get the Gettysberg Address and the Sermon on the Mount. What kind of a voice do you suppose Jesus Christ had, Peggy?'

'Beautiful, I'll bet.'

'Anyway soothing,' I said.

'Soothing? Soothing I'm *sure* is precisely the word. Soothing. Soft. Not exactly musical. Mildly hypnotic. The kind that the Hindu fakirs have when they induce mass hypnotism.'

'You sound a little as if you had something against Him,' I said.

'Oh, shut up,' said Peggy.

'All right,' I said.

'No, don't,' said Herbert. 'I want to find out about books, from an author. You see, Malloy, I'm writing a novel about Los Angeles, present-day Los Angeles. The Angelus Temple. This fellow that killed his wife with the box of rattlesnakes. The Neon signs. The health people. No movie stuff. I'm going to ignore the movies.'

'Who's your principal character? The fellow with the rattlesnakes?'

'No. In fact I may not even use him at all, but this town is full of people like him. It's a fantastic place, you know, Malloy. Fantastic. You know why? Because it's so incredibly ordinary.'

'Mm.'

'Fan*ta*stic. It's in a semi-tropical climate. It has a Spanish name, with religious Roman Catholic connotations. A rather large Mexican population and Oriental. The architecture, that is, I mean by that the Monterey house and the Mission stuff, is Mexican and Spanish and a little Moorish. And yet, Malloy, consider this: the really fantastic thing about it is that it's the crystallization of the ordinary, cheap ordinary American. The people. The politics. The cults. These Iowa people that come here and really assert themselves. They do what they wanted to do in Iowa but couldn't, for various and sundry reasons. The crazy clothes they all wanted to wear back in Iowa. And of course it's no city, except in population. Fantastically ordinary, cheap, commonplace. And I'm going to put it in a book, which is the reason why I've been plying you with questions about your books. I want my book to be a success, and I want to know what constitutes a successful book. Not a *succès d'estime*, but a financial success.'

'Any book that makes any money is a financial success. From the author's point of view, any book that makes more than the two-fifty or five-hundred advance royalty.'

'Well, of course I want mine to do better than that. Thank you very much, Malloy. I'm going to buy a car next week, and I hope I can repay this. Peggy, *au 'voir*. I had a pleasant evening. Thank you for my dinner. Now I go to face one of my capitalistic uncles, the bastard. Good night.'

'Your heart's not in it, but as long as your body is I guess I have no kick coming.'

'It's a nice body, so I'm told,' said Peggy.

'Who told you?'

'You did,' she said. 'Light one for me, will you, please?' She took the cigarette but put it out after a few puffs. She was not what you would call an ardent smoker. She dinched it in the ash tray and then she settled back, apparently getting herself comfortable for a lengthy contemplation of the ceiling; but in a little while she took her hands from in back of her neck and lay over on her side and put her left arm across my chest. 'I may marry you after all,' she said, into the corner of the pillow.

'Oh, no. Not me.'

'Yes, you,' she said.

'Although it's as good an offer as I've had to-day.'

'What is that? That's the last line of a dirty joke, isn't it?' She raised her head a little, angrily.

'I think so. But I don't know the joke.'

'I'm glad, because—oh, Jim. I'm depressed, depressed. Why don't I tell Herbert to go away or leave me alone? Why do I feel so awful about the Jews under Hitler? Do you think Keith is a virgin?'

'Very likely.'

'I wonder what he thinks about you and me,' she said.

'He probably knows exactly where we are this minute. He's no dope. I've known about two kids like him in my life. They have an intelligence that transcends sex, or at least it keeps them out of that kind of trouble. Then, when the time comes, they get a girl, and the girl seems to be very well satisfied in that department. At least the other two guys I knew have wives that *look* very well taken care of, and content, and wouldn't cheat for anything. What about Herbert. Have you stayed with him yet?'

'Nope. I told you he had T.B. Put your arms around me. What are you thinking?'

'Nothing. I guess I may be in the middle of a train of thought. I have a theory that you're always thinking, always, always, always thinking. Isn't it awful? Think of being thinking all the time. Your brain banging away on all lobes.'

'Well, that's what it's there for.' She took a deep breath and gave it voice as she exhaled. 'Hello.'

'Hello.'

'What's this?'

'Search me. I just happened to notice it there myself. Some kind of a growth, I imagine.'

'Maybe you ought to see a doctor about it.'

'I've seen enough doctors about that,' I said. She lay on her back, I lay on my back, and she held my hand and we looked at the now dark white ceiling, and I don't know about her, but I had the illusion of walking hand in hand.

'This is nice, but I've got to go home to-night,' she said. 'I think you're right about Keith. I think he does know you and I go to bed, but I have a theory about that. Keith's a funny boy. If I went to him and said, "Keith, I'm having an affair with Jim Malloy," he'd probably say he knew it, and from then on everything would be easy. I mean, I could stay out all night any time I wanted to, and he wouldn't hold anything against you. But I don't want to do that. I don't want to come right out with it, because the kind of relationship you and I have, it may break off any minute. Any day. You might fall madly in love with someone, or I might, and right after I'd told Keith, and then I'd have to tell him the same thing about someone else. Then he'd think his little sister is a tart. Which she isn't.'

'No. She isn't.'

'And he's going through enough right now without any additional worries about me. He likes you.'

'I like him.'

'I must go now,' she said.

'No.'

'Yes.'

'No, No, I said.'

'Ah, Jim. Jimmy.'

'That's right, my sweet.'

Then for a few weeks Peggy and I did not see each other, which meant that I did not see Keith or Herbert. Also I did not see Mr. Don Miller, but that did not seem like much of a loss. Don Miller was the kind of man that for the most part it is a fortunate thing not to have to make up your mind about. There are people whom you see and you react to in a certain way, a way unfavourable to them, from your own point of view. You see them, like at a party or a racetrack or on a train. You know them and you are on a first-name basis. Maybe you sit down and have a couple of drinks, talking about—well, just talking. If you ask this kind of acquaintance about a mutual acquaintance it invariably is a friend of *yours* whom he knows, and not a friend of *his* that you know. I don't know why this is so, because there are reasons why it should not be so. Maybe it is because in mentioning *your* friend, who knows him, you are subconsciously standing beside your friend, in a two-against-one alliance. You just plain don't like this Don Miller kind of guy, but the chances are about five to one that there never is an open break. You even give him credit for some good qualities, unimportant ones. I could and did readily concede, for instance, that Don Miller was a handsome young man. By the time this story was ended and I had seen him more frequently than I had at this point, I would have conceded that he dressed more like an Easterner than a Californian. I saw right away, the first time I met him on the Coast, that Miller was a guy who very probably could give me some trouble if we were both after the same girl. He also had a kind of courage that I never have had. I mean the kind of courage that made him become Don Miller and stick to it. Under the same circumstances I would have been satisfied with the reward; or I might even have merely dropped the book of traveller's cheques in a mailbox and let it go at that. The kind of courage that it takes to be a certain kind of phony is something I envy. In its way it's wonderful, the self-confidence of these guys. It's easy enough to go around being a jerk if your father happens to be President of the United States. But to make up your mind to be something, even if it is something you're not, and to be it, and to be successful at being it—well, maybe Joan Crawford did want to hire a brass band, but that's a long way from five shows a day at the Capitol, and she made it. I'll take Mike Romanoff, and you can have Brian Ahearn. (But the trouble with all this is that you can also take the Lunts, and I'll take George Burns and Gracie Allen.) So anyway—Don Miller.

As I say, for a few weeks I did not see Peggy and the others. I could have got seven-fifty at one studio, but my last job, my last

four jobs, had been paying me a thousand. Not that seven-fifty is
tin, but about this time they were getting ready to release an epic
that I helped with, on which I was getting screen credit, and I
knew the picture couldn't miss. That meant that as soon as the
picture was released I would be getting a thousand again, somewhere. I was four or five thousand dollars ahead, and I hadn't been
to New York for a year, so it was New York.

New York was wonderful. The wonderful dirty old Jersey meadows.
The wonderful Pulaski Skyway. Beautiful Vesey Street and the dear
sweet asafoetida warehouses. Bert Lahr doing his swing song in *The
Show Is On*. The shrunken-looking kids in tails, trying to show that
Twenty-One was an old story to them—but walking directly to the
kitchen when what they wanted was the men's room. Jack White
and Pat Harrington and Screwball and Jerry and Doctor R. E. Lee.
Sherman Billingsley making his million and not losing anything by
it. Charlie Lucas, a good man to have on your side. My charming
pals among the Swing Street taxidrivers. My waiter friends, Vincent
and Karl and Georgetti and Stone and Nick and Joe and Tony and
Fritz. . . . Some time I'm going to write a book about New York,
but this isn't it. In a little more than two weeks, maybe a little
more than three, I was back in California, having done no Christmas shopping. My agent met me at the airport, which meant that
he was proud of the deal he had made for me: a three months' hitch
at a thousand dollars a week. On the way in from the airport the
thing that kept depressing me was that for three or four or five days
I would not be able to see a New York paper that I had not already
read in New York.

There were some ugly bills waiting for me at the hotel. There
were some swatches from some tailors, reminding one that Palm
Springs was in full swing and that the same tailors who had the
pleasure of serving Mr. William Powell, Mr. Joel McCrea, Mr.
Robert Taylor, and their agents, would be pleased to meet one's
Palm Springs requirements. They would whip up a pair of whipcord
jodhpurs for a hundred dollars, and they begged leave to call attention to the midnight-blue evening tails, now the accepted thing.
Some excellent vintage wines had been included in the latest ship-
ment to arrive at Vedome. Spirit. Something new in supper club
entertainment was being offered at the Club Something on Sunset
Boulevard. Something new in night club entertainment was being

offered at another club on Melrose Avenue. On the other hand, one's perennial favourites wanted to take the liberty of reminding one that it was not too early to make one's New Year's reservations at the Chez Something. Signed: the perennial favourites. There were about a dozen untelegraphed telegrams, written by persons of originality and taste (*de gustibus non disputandum*), inviting one to cocktail parties at private houses, new artists' agencies, and an automobile salesroom. There was an embossed, stiff paper opportunity to have a party of four or six at a dinner in honour of some Catholic big shot (my name got me on a lot of Catholic sucker lists). All I had to do was get up twenty dollars a plate. Black Tie. There were about two dozen splendid opportunities to help The Cause, from Tehachape to Tallahassee. There was a letter from my mother, a reminder that my school endowment pledge was unpaid, a request to straighten out an illegibly signed cheque. There was a Dutch Kalendar from a swell girl in Surrey, who wanted to be in plenty of time for Boxing Day. There were a few telephone messages to be ignored. And there was a note from Peggy.

It read:

James: It was nice of you to write me from New York, you . . . A card or a telegram would have done (Heaven knows you send enough of them for no good reason). But this is not the kind of note I started out to write. Whenever you get back (some time this week, according to the *Hollywood Reporter*) please phone me, unless you arrive at an unearthly hour in the morning. As you may imagine, this is serious. Love, PEGGY
P.S. It is nothing to worry about from your point of view. P.

I read the note in my room. It was around lunch time, so I phoned Peggy at the shop. For the first time in our life I failed to recognize her voice. 'May I speak to Miss Henderson?'

'This is she. Is this you, Jim?'

Yes, sorry not to have recognised, etc. 'I just got in. Do you want to have lunch?'

'I always *do*. What kind of a New York expression is that: "Do you want to have lunch?" Of course I want to have lunch.'

'My but you're snippy. I think I'll go right out and paddle that little round—'

'Yes, Mr. Bronson. I'll be glad to order it for you.'

'I think I'll go right out and paddle those little round cheeks of yours, Miss Bronson. Would you like me to come out and paddle those little round cheeks of your? Please be a little more respectful—'

'Thank you. I'll call you back,' she said, and hung up. In a few minutes she phoned me. 'Listen, you fool, the boss came in the shop and he could listen in on the extension.'

'I'm sorry, I didn't know you had an extension.'

'Is that another dirty remark?' she said.

'My God! What a really filthy mind! And you talk about me. You ought to be reviewing pictures for the Legion of Decency. Do you want to have lunch, *with me?*'

'If I can keep from throwing up. You make me sick. I'll meet you at the Derby, the Beverly one. Twelve-thirty.'

It was only a short walk from her shop to the Derby. The boy parked my car in the lot across the street, and Peggy arrived by the time I got a table. That Derby is always so full of jabbering Beverly wives, pathetically dolled up as though for the Colony or Voisin, that it is a good place to talk privately, so long as you don't get caught in a lull. But some very funny things come out of those lulls. One time a woman was telling her companions a story, with her voice at the regular volume, and she got caught in a lull just as she was saying, ' . . . I took opium.' That was too bad, because she will spend the rest of her days telling people she never took opium.

Peggy was so pretty and sweet. She came in, took a quick look around and spotted me. It is easy to spot a man at lunch at that Derby. John, the head-waiter, brought her to the table.

'New coat,' I said.

'Twenty-five dollars, on the Boulevard. Plus tax. Do you like it?'

'It's the best-looking coat I ever saw. Twenty-five dollars.'

'Yes. That makes it easy for me to tell you what I have to tell you."

'What have you done? Married Herbert? Let's see your ring.'

'No. Nothing like that,' she said. 'After I wrote that note I tried to remember exactly what I said. It was a foolish note. Ill-considered. Inchoate.'

'Whee!'

'I was a little worried about the effect it might have on you. I couldn't remember whether it had a postscript or not. I intended to write one but I wasn't sure I had.'

'You did.'

'Did you—were you afraid I was pregnant when you read the note?'

'Not after I read the postcript. What do you want to eat or drink, or be merry?'

'I think I'll have a straight whisky. Rye. And a chicken salad, Russian dressing. Coffee with the salad. Melba toast.'

'Did you get that, Bobbie?' I asked the waitress.

'Yes, Mr. Malloy. And you'll have?'

'A *sour* whisky sour, not one of those banana splits. Corn beef hash without the egg, or *with* the egg. You know. Glass of some light beer.'

'Thank you,' said Bobbie.

'Okay. Well, what about the coat? Who gave you the coat, or how did you get it, or what's your story? So you won't talk, eh?'

'I'll talk,' she said, with a nice smile. She lit a cigarette, scorning my assistance, because she liked to fool with those pull-out matches. She seldom smoked. 'I got the coat from my father.'

'Oh. Another cheque? Where from? Where's he spending Christmas?'

'Right where he is now. Right here. Seventy-two-sixty-eight Orchard Terrace.'

'No!' I said. 'Your father's here?'

'He's here, all right. In the flesh. Not a moving picture. Not a pretty picture, either.'

'Peggy, what *is* this? Start from the beginning.' Somehow I always had thought of her father as about as real as a character in some of the more entertaining virility fiction in *The Saturday Evening Post*. Now and then there would be an Anton Otto Fischer illustration of a story that would make me think: that probably looks like Peggy's old man. Now my jealous first thought was: How does she know it's her father? It's so long since she's seen him. I was ashamed of that, but there it was.

'A week ago yesterday,' she said, 'Herbert brought me home from the shop. He has a new car, and not that this has anything to do with the story, but if T.B. doesn't get him first, his driving will. I'm frightened to death to drive with him, but he comes for me nearly every afternoon and it's impossible to tell him how frightened I am. Most likely you think he's insensitive and he is, to other people's feelings, but—I'm sorry.

'Herbert came up to the porch with me, and Millie heard us and she came out looking frightened and began whispering. "Miss Peggy, there's a man here says he's your father. He's been here most of the afternoon," she said, "and", she said, "I couldn't phone you because I was afraid. He sat right beside the phone and I couldn't phone." And she said she wouldn't give him my address, meaning the shop, and didn't know when I'd be back and so that was that. So I went in and this man stood up and took a long look at me and said, "Peggy, I'm your father." I knew he was, too, right away. He knew me, too. It's true, Jim. There were some vibrations, is the only way I can explain it.

'Well, it was very embarrassing. Herbert, for instance. He wouldn't have been much help, but he insisted on coming in with me in case there was some trouble, so I had to introduce him to this strange man. "This is Herbert Stern, Father," I said.'

'I never can remember Herbert's name,' I said. 'I'm not even sure I ever knew it before.'

'It was terribly embarrassing, but Herbert had sense enough to leave, and my father and I sat there for an hour or so. We had plenty to talk about, naturally, but we'd finish one topic and we'd both sit there trying to think of what would be the next topic. Really, Jim. Have you ever had your father that you haven't seen for I forget how many years suddenly return?'

'No, and I hope he doesnt. At least not on a dark night. Mine's been dead ten years or more.'

'So was mine, really. Just think of it. It's an idea for a shocking short story. What if I were on a train, and this man decided I was nice-looking and I thought he was, and I let him pick me up and—so on. And he *is* attractive.' She never used the word casually, but always as though she had carefully chosen it. 'Or at least was this day. He was, well, if you can imagine Keith as he will be in about fifteen or twenty years or longer than that, but looking much younger than his age.'

'What's he been doing all this time?'

'I'll come to that. We didn't really get into that the first few days he was back. That night Keith didn't come home until late and of course it would be the one night when he didn't call up and say he wasn't coming home to dinner. As a rule he's very considerate about those things. Then when he finally did come home—Oh, first my father wanted to take me out to dinner, to the best place in California, but I told Millie, she's darling, that we'd have dinner, my father and I, and to save something for Keith. Then after we had our dinner he wanted to know all about me and Keith. Then came the problem of where my father was going to sleep, That was embarrassing, but finally I had sense enough to ask him if he had his bags here or where, and he was stopping at the Hollywood Plaza, I think, and I insisted on his going to the hotel and getting his bags, but he refused and then he made a concession. He said he knew we probably weren't prepared for another person in the house that night, but he'd move over with us the next day, provided we had room. We have an extra room, so that was all right, although I'm glad he didn't stay the first night.

'Then he said he guessed I went to bed early on weekday nights, and he was saying good night when Keith arrived home. That was the worst part of that first day, because I could see Keith didn't take to him, immediately. He was surprised, and looked at my father as though he'd come from some other planet, and in a very short time I could see Keith didn't like him. Of course Keith didn't show it, but I knew. I was glad to get my father out of the house.

'After he'd gone Keith didn't go to bed. I could see he expected to have a discussion about my father. You know Keith can suddenly get older and very mature. He started to smoke his pipe and look at me, waiting for me to start, but when I didn't he said: "Well, what about him?" And I said *what* about him, and he said: "What are we going to do about him?" And I said I couldn't think of what we were going to do about him, and then Keith wanted to know, just as though it were taken for granted, he wanted to know how we were going to get rid of him. Did we have to be polite? I said of course we'd be polite, but may be my father's coming this way would change things entirely. Well, saying that was stirring up a hornets' nest. Keith was furious, as mad as I've ever seen him. "Change things! It certainly will change things. He isn't going to stay in this house. He's never been our father, except the biological fact. He's never had any responsibility about us." Meaning he'd never taken any. Keith said: "We're not going to have him settle down here now, just because of some whim of his, or because he's afraid he's getting old and now he wants a home. You and I have a nice home of our own, and to hell with him. If he's planning to make our home his home, then I'm getting out." Well, I never expected anything like this from Keith. In the first place I never realised that he thought anything about our home. It *has* been nice, but I never realised he appreciated it. I don't mean about gratitude, but in so far as being aware of what a nice home it was. I was touched, because we're a very undemonstrative brother and sister. I'm touched now, when I think of it.'

I pressed her hand. She went on.

' "Well," I said, "maybe we won't have any difficulty with him. Maybe he'll just stay a few days and he won't *be* any problem to us. Just control your feelings till we see what his plans are." Then he wanted to know how I felt about my father. I keep calling him my father. Notice?'

'Yes,' I said. 'What do you call him when you're with him?'

'I try to avoid calling him anything, but I've been calling him Father. Anyway, when Keith asked me how I felt about my father I had to admit I didn't know, principally because I hadn't had time to form any conclusions, but when I began to think it over, to give Keith some kind of answer, I realised I didn't feel one way or another about him. Then. I do now.' She stopped.

'And?' I said.

'I can't stand him. I wish he'd go away. If he doesn't go away soon and if your offer is still good, I'll marry you. Or I'll live with you without getting married. I've just got to get away.'

'The offer's still good. If you want to be tentative, come and live with me until he goes away. Or, if you want money. Why not take some of that larcenous dough of mine? I have a new contract, three months at a grand a week. At Metro.'

'I always said I wouldn't take any money from you, but this time I might. Thank you anyway, even if I don't, but I knew I could count on you, without your telling me. Not that that's what I wanted to see you about. Mainly I wanted to talk to somebody. I've talked a little to Karen, but she has her own troubles. Father lost his best advertising contract. Mother just out of the hospital. Kid sister raising hell in school.'

'Well, here I am,' I said. 'Whatever I can do, and any time. I'm going to take a house in Beverly, and there'll be more than enough room. And if Keith wants to come with me, now or any time, the house I'd like to have has a room in a sort of wing of its own, with a separate entrance and so forth. He could come and go as he pleased.'

'I'll tell him,' she said. 'I guess I ought to get back to the shop, and I haven't even begun to tell you. Are you going to be busy

about five-thirty? You could pick me up at the shop if you weren't.
I want to tell you the rest of it, and I need some sex, too.'

'Let's plan to have dinner. I'll get you a little tight and get you
out of this. You're in bad shape, aren't you, my sweet?'

'Am I. Pay the cheque and walk with me to the shop.'

In some respects Philip Henderson was an older Don Miller.
Another way of putting it would be to say that Philip Henderson
was what Don Miller might easily turn out to be if he continued
his career. There are so many men who live as Henderson had
lived. Their stories can never completely be told, for the reason that
it would take a detective with an unlimited expense account to
follow them through the years, and since nobody cares that much,
no detective is likely to get such an assignment. It would take a
resourceful agent to check back on the story as Henderson's kind
would tell it. There are so many lies in his version. Lies that he
comes to believe himself. There are gaps in time, too, that frequently
can be explained by gaol sentences. Henderson himself undoubtedly
had a criminal dossier or two, because there were two gaps of a
year or more in his story.

But this much we did come to know about him: he was born in
the 'nineties, in Buffalo, New York. His father was a railroader, a
divisional superintendent of maintenance of way, which is a good
railroading job. The Hendersons were old York State, dating back
to pre-Revolutionary times. Henderson took pride in mentioning
the fact to Peggy and Keith, and was unable to understand their
apathy when this historical information was forthcoming, as it
frequently was. Philip, an only son, was sent to Cornell after high
school. His college career was brief, and he soon was fond of saying
that he hoped Keith was getting more out of college than *he* had.
He was fond of saying, too, that he had carved his name in Cornell
history—on a table-top in a beer-drinking establishment in Ithaca.
He said he just got sick of college one day, and said the hell with
it and quit. I had heard the same thing said in about the same
vague way by boys who I knew had been kicked out of school for
petty thefts. It was rather hard to believe that he had been quite
as gay in college as he said he had been. No man earning the salary
of a superintendent of maintenance of way could have afforded such
a son. He probably was gay enough, but not in the financial league
that his stories put him.

After he quit college he came out to California to 'grow up
with the country'. Through Masonic and railroading friends of his
father's he got a railroad job in Los Angeles, which he used only
to get started. After he got the lay of the land and made a few
thousand friends he went into the real estate business. Everybody
in California was in the real estate business in those days. He did
well enough to convince a girl named Margaret Keith that she was
getting a good thing in him. Besides, she loved him. So they were
married.

When the United States entered the war Mr. and Mrs. Philip
Henderson had a large bungalow several miles east of Hollywood.
They also had a snappy car, a secondhand Mercer phaeton. Their
friends were Angelenos and a few young married people in the
Pasadena-Santa Barbara group, and now and then some of the
Navy. The Hendersons quickly went into great debt, which was
not lessened by the death of Mrs. Henderson's mother. They had
presumed that when that sad day came, they would be at least out
of debt, but it turned out that there was not much more left than
it cost to put the old lady's remains under the ground. It was a
disillusioning experience to young Philip Henderson. The least a
woman can do is to do something for her only grandchild (for at
that time Peggy was an infant).

The Navy first attracted Henderson when he decided to do his
bit for Uncle Sam. The uniforms, the cleanliness, the travel, the
social life that his Navy acquaintances led, all were selling-points.
But he had better luck getting into an army officers' training camp
and it was as a second lieutenant of infantry that he went to
France. After being shunted around here and there, always with the
unhappy prospect of being assigned to the A.E.F. in Siberia, he was
sent to France with a draft division, and he returned to California
without having been shot either by the Germans or by his own
men. He knew, of course, that in his absence he had become the
father of a son. Also he rightly guessed that a deliriously grateful
people had done nothing about his debts. A 'college man', a
successful realtor, a first lieutenant, a husband and father, he nevertheless was unable to command, as he put it, the kind of job he
considered commensurate with his qualifications. He did not starve;
a job selling real estate on straight commission, $50-a-week drawing
account, kept food in the house. But it was not the large bungalow
that he had left in 1917. That, like the Mercer and a lot of other

things, had gone. Indeed, it became a piece of property that in his new job he once was asked to handle, but for sentimental reasons he asked another salesman to take it over.

It must not be inferred, however, that Henderson was all sentiment. he was not mawkish. In his service days he had come to face facts, such as the biological one that a man has to have a woman every so often. With Henderson it was pretty often, especially among the volunteers, the Junior League types who were there to run errands and things like that for the officers. In every good-sized city there were lovely young things in Sam Browne belts and beautifully cut uniforms. It was entirely up to you how far they could be persuaded to make a lonely and handsome young officer comfortable in what might be his last days on earth. Then there were women in France, and on the way to demobilization there were women at home.

And Henderson found out that there had been changes in his own home. His wife had had her hands full with the children and with the family finances. The presence of the children prevented her taking a job. She could not have made out financially by hiring a nurse. A nurse who was good enough for babies would have taken all the salary the young and inexperienced wife could have earned. And in 1918 when the day came when she broke her last five-dollar bill, she went through a kind of terror that she never forgot. The next day she went to one of her rich Pasadena friends and borrowed a thousand dollars from him. He said he was glad to let her have it, and he meant it. He was married, and he had two children of his own and a mother who single-handed kept him out of the army, and he told Margaret that he felt it was the least he could do, etc. A few months later she had to go to him again, and again he gave her money; more than she had asked. Then the first thing they knew they were having an affair. She was grateful to him, and he got from her a sense of being needed. Twice, then, she had had to transfer her love away from her husband; once for her children, and the second time for her benefactor.

The first time Henderson asked her if she had remained faithful to him she told him about the man in Pasadena, without naming him. Henderson took it calmly, and without a cross-examination—she didn't care—he confessed that his own body had not been inviolate. Her confession did make it easier for him to get around as much as he liked, and then one day he did not come home. He wrote her from Chicago, saying he imagined that she guessed that there was nothing to her marriage, and he was good and God damn bored with the life of a husband. He said he imagined she would get along all right; the fellow in Pasadena now had a clear track. If she wanted to get a divorce, that was all right too. He had no great feeling about the children; he'd never known them, and to tell the truth he wasn't sure Keith was his child. . . .

The fellow in Pasadena was frightened when Margaret showed him the letter, but when she convinced him that there would be no fuss, that her husband did not know who he was, they resumed the affair; a pleasant relationship that continued for four years. It was convenient for him, and it was a financial life-saver for her. She was able to have a nurse for the children, which in turn enabled her to go to business college and take a job in a department store. She became secretary to the head buyer of ladies'-ready-to-wear, and then she worked into selling in the Paris Shop, a department that sold more expensive clothes. Margaret Henderson was prematurely grey, just a little on the stout side, and she was pretty in a way that women liked. That is, she looked as though she belonged where she was, a perfect saleswoman whom you would almost but not quite invite on a trip to Del Monte or the desert. She never bothered to divorce Henderson.

Henderson went only as far as Chicago with the woman who took him away from Los Angeles. She was on her way to New York a few days ahead of her husband. Together she and her husband were going abroad, and it was fun for her and Henderson to have the week on the train and in Chicago. She *was* a bit surprised when he said he wasn't going back to Los Angeles, and she suspected him of a form of blackmail when he borrowed some money from her, but she had had a good time, and it was an even chance that this would pay Henderson off. It did.

Now comes one of the gaps. Henderson's story as I have put it down was pieced together from conversations we had, he and I, and from things he told Peggy and Keith and that Peggy knew from her mother. It may have been presumptuous of me, but when Henderson turned up in California I made a point of seeing a lot of Peggy. I was nearer to her father's age and his kind of life than anyone Peggy knew, and I didn't want anything to happen to her, so I saw a lot of Henderson. But of that, more to come.

This first gap, which Henderson not only left entirely unex-

plained, but even ignored as though for two years he had lived on
air, may be traced to the Cook County (Henderson called it Crook
County) criminal records. I don't know. Maybe he was skipping
the gutter at that time and had jobs that were so lowly that he had
succeeded in forgetting them. Maybe he had been mixed up in one
of the many mobs that ran various localities in Chicago. He never
admitted that, but he did have a pretty good account of the death
of one of the greatest trumpet players in jazz, a youngster who
offended a mob guy and for punishment a couple of hoodlums
rammed him up with the neck of a beer bottle. The pain drove this
trumpet player crazy, his hair turned grey, and Henderson's story
was that this fellow became a hophead, dying of an overdose.
Henderson told it almost as though he had been there all the time,
and better than I'd ever heard it before.

He must have known some of the influential gangsters, because
he once picked up the silverware in a Sunset Boulevard night club
and told us to an odd penny how much it was worth. When we
asked him how he knew, he said he had had a job selling silverware
to restaurants, and he said something to me about I knew what
kind of restaurants. He wouldn't come out and say speakeasy; he
liked unnecessary intrigue as much as he liked the necessary kind
that must have been a large part of his life.

I had been wrong about the gun-running in New Orleans. He
explained that part of his odyssey: he had been associated with
Huey Long. He said, 'Huey had work for a man that didn't have
a Southern accent.' I imagined Huey had plenty of work for a man
who didn't have a Southern accent, although it might have been
awkward to use him, say, as a repeater at the polls. Henderson must
have been there more than a few weeks, because he pronounced
Pontchartrain and Louisiana and New Orleans the way they
pronounce them down there. He also was a bore about oysters
Rockefeller, and he knew somebody named Legendre. He admired
Huey. He said Huey knew as well as anyone else that the every-
man-a-king stuff was so much sheep-dip, but Henderson said he
sincerely believed that if Huey had reached the White House he
would have done a good job. He admired Huey in the same way a
faithful employee admires a paymaster who has been shot in a futile
attempt to protect the cash.

This story was given to us in short takes, as they say in the
newspaper business. One part he always left out was the woman's

angle. He would start a reminiscence about a wild party in Boston or Memphis or Dallas, and even when Peggy was not present he would tell it up to a certain point and we who were listening would have to supply the women. It never entered my head that there weren't always women in Henderson's life. I never failed to get (and never tried hard to avoid) the impression that Henderson always had a solvent women to turn to when he was not in the money. Somehow you would picture Henderson arriving at Atlanta or St. Paul on a train that got in around 10 p.m. He would take a taxi to the second-best hotel, walk up very pleased with himself to the clerk, register for a double room, and before unpacking he would be on the phone, fixing up a party for that night with a handsome brunette of thirty-six, whose alimony came regularly on the first or second of the month.

He had covered the country pretty well thoroughly from Denver east, and twice he had done it legitimately; once as a sort of promotion and publicity man for a tyre company that was sending a small fleet of gaudily painted cars on an advertising junket. Another time he was with the William Bradwell Smith Associates, which I knew of old. The William Bradwell Smith Associates put on drives, big and little. The biggest ones would be for the Community Chest of some of the largest cities. The smallest ones they handled were for hospitals and churches. The minimum 'quota' for the minimum drive was $500,000, and the William Bradwell Smith Associates, practical philanthropists, would take care of the whole drive for a guaranteed 5 per cent of the minimum, plus a bonus over the minimum for as much as the traffic would bear. The William Bradwell Smith Associates, up to 1929, could turn any town in the United States into a frenzy of giving. The mayor, the 'civic leaders', the clergy (sometimes excepting the Catholics), the press, the luncheon clubs—all would get into a lather. There would be a forty-foot 'thermometer' in the Public Square; stickers on cars; consommé-veal-ice-cream luncheons at a dollar a throw (in the Y.M.C.A. cafeteria or in the local branch of an hotel chain); prizes for the team captains (usually boarded cowhide luggage donated by an unregenerate harness dealer who was tired of looking at it); a daily Page One story headed M'NULTY LEADS CHEST DRIVE, and two days before the drive ended Captain or General or Doctor Somebody would announce that he would give an additional, an *additional* $5,000 if that amount were subscribed before the final dinner. And it would be subscribed, thereby putting Middletowne over the top and saving it from disgrace in the eyes of the William Bradwell Smith Associates. In the picture I had of Henderson and the alimonied brunette the William Bradwell Smith Associates played an important part. As a William Bradwell Smith Associate, Henderson would have met many of those handsome small-city women who campaign because they have nothing else to do. And of course when the Associates were running a drive for some college he must have made contact with many a co-ed alumna.

I could see Henderson in this, one of the more legitimate of his admitted enterprises during the 'twenties and 'thirties. He would have learned the ropes under a veteran Associate, then he would be put on his own. I could see him, even as I sat with him in Hollywood, getting up at one of those luncheons. He was not a short man, but he was not so towering tall that he would annoy the inevitable big shot who was bantam in size. Henderson, like as not, would stand up at the speakers' table. He would pick up a spoon and beat a tatto on two glasses of water—a tinkling sound that was much more friendly than the rap of a gavel. Lin-cling-a-ling-cling. Shuffling of chairs as team members and captains faced the speakers' table. A sharp short whistle as one eater signalled a waiter to get some more coffee. The crack of silver plate on heavy china as another eater snapped his spoon through a block of Neapolitan ice cream. Quantities of phlegm being pulled from its resting place in a hundred throats. Then—attention. All eyes, except those of the man bolting his ice cream, on Henderson.

Blue serge suit, two-button, ready-made, the coat open to give an occasional hint of Henderson's Sigma Nu pin under the upper left vest pocket. Soft white shirt with the collar kept in place by invisible tabs. Two-dollar small-figured tie. In front of him, on the table, a small pile of papers, which he arranged neatly until silence came. Then the surprise technique, which he would have figured out for himself. Instead of going immediately into his little talk he would call to the waiters in the back of the room. 'Would you mind closing that door, please?' A volunteer would get up from a table and nod to a waiter and repeat Henderson's request, and then the volunteer would sit down, feeling as though he had rescued a family of five and their dog from a dangerous surf. He would be rewarded with a beautiful smile by Henderson, and a quiet but audible 'Thank you.' Then Henderson would cock his head and look at a

far corner of the ceiling, causing the less alert ones to wonder what
he thought he heard. The wise ones were sure he was considering
how best to phrase to-day's good news. The man with the ice cream
would put down his spoon and light a cigar.

Then suddenly: 'This morning at the corner of Smithfield and
Wood . . .' And Henderson was off.

In the few weeks between the return of Philip Henderson and
the annual observance of the Birth of Christ, there were certain
developments and adjustments *chez* Henderson. Among them:

More money in the Henderson household. Apparently Henderson had
not come to Los Angeles broke. He first took Peggy on a shopping
trip. He was paying cash, and she thought she might as well take
what he offered. Outstanding household bills were paid, and Millie,
the coloured maid-of-all-work, was given a three-dollar raise to
eighteen dollars a week.

Less seen of Keith at home. He moved to his fraternity house so that
he could study later and still get enough sleep. That was his story.
The truth was that he had not changed his opinion of his father.
He urged Peggy to get everything out of Henderson that she could.
The night Henderson said he had worked for Huey Long, Keith
said: 'Did you ever work for Zioncheck?' But Henderson refused to
be insulted.

More seen of Herbert. Herbert had much the same protective
impulse as mine. He was always around, it seemed. When Henderson would mention some 'dirty Jew' in a story, and quickly
apologize to Herbert, Herbert would say: 'That's all right. I don't
like all of them myself. You aren't compelled to like people just
because of your being of the same blood.' Henderson didn't get
that.

No word of any kind from Don Miller. No word of any kind from
Don Miller.

A lot of drinking. The first party was the Saturday night after
Henderson began his visit. 'To-night's my night to howl,' he
announced at noon. Peggy usually worked Saturday afternoons, but
her boss had given her the afternoon off to make up for the evenings
she would have to work when the Christmas rush began, Beverly
Hills being a good book customer at Christmas. I brought Peggy
home after lunch that Saturday and Henderson made his announcement. Henderson gave Peggy fifty dollars. 'Go out and buy yourself
a slam-bang evening gown, and if that isn't enough, there's plenty

more where that came from.' Peggy said it was more than enough.
'Well, just in case, here's ten more for a manicure and hairdresser.
We're going places to-night. Oh, by the way, do you think you
could scare up a girl for me?' Peggy was obviously shocked, and he
said: 'Doesn't have to be somebody my age. Get one of *your* friends.'
Later she said she was *afraid* that that was what he meant. She
called her best friend, Karen Waner, who broke a date to come
with us.

Henderson looked well in what he called a 'Tuck'. He had chubby
cheeks, but no double chin, and his hair dried quickly and became
very light brown, making him look not much older than I. His eyes
were green. His teeth tight and even and all present from bicuspid
to bicuspid. The missing teeth went unnoticed except when he
laughed his heartiest.

When I arrived at the little house Henderson was shaking cocktails in a Coco-Malt shaker. It was a strange sight. In the many
times I had gone to that house I never had seen three persons in
evening dress all at once. Once in a great while Peggy and I would
put on evening clothes, but on those nights there would be Peggy
in an evening gown, waiting for me, and *only* Peggy and I. Now
there were three: Peggy, her father, and Karen Waner. My coming
made it four, and there were still more to come. Keith had found
it simply impossible to go along. I forget what excuse he offered;
something unflattering and final that had to do with college life.
And so at the last minute Peggy had asked Herbert to come and
bring a girl.

The Martinis were watery and had too much vermouth. No one
noticed it. Henderson had the floor, and did not sit down at any
time. He kept busy pouring cocktails and urging us to drink up.
Karen had made a very good impression on him, which was not
strange. Karen's father, a photographer, had a favourite subject,
and it was Karen. If I had been a photographer she would have
been mine, too. She was about two inches taller than Peggy and
this night she had on a blue and white dress; blue, with large white
flowers printed on it in just about the colouring of Wedgwood. In
a way it was a bad dress, so far as the colours went. It was a pattern
that did not show off her figure. But to make up for this lack it was
cut low enough in front to offer at least circumstantial evidence
proving that she had nothing on underneath. Her breasts were
large, and then you noticed that her thighs were large, but she had

good calves and ankles. She had one of the most exciting bodies I've ever seen, but even without that she would have been a knockout. She had a small head, heavily lidded brown eyes, small curling lips, and a short straight nose. She did not look older than Peggy. They didn't look as though their ages could be compared by the same standards. Peggy was definitely a young girl, about twenty years old. Karen was a young woman who happened to be the same age. She also made Henderson seem young, or at least inept.

Henderson was trying not to be too attentive to Karen, and wondering how much she knew about him and his return. But he was in a spot; Karen knew everything about him that Peggy could tell her, and always had. Karen loved Peggy, needed her, depended on her.

But Peggy was in a spot, too. Now that the party was a reality, she wanted it to go off well. She was pulling for everyone, and for the first time I saw her as a conventionally timid hostess. It certainly was a new side—Peggy, who could get up before a hundred persons and say what she was thinking about Tom Mooney or Harry Bridges, was being a conventional hostess.

'You a Californian, Miss Waner?' said Henderson.

'I was born out here, but my mother and father are from back East.'

'Whereabouts in the East?'

'Columbus, Ohio.'

'Oh, yes. I've been there,' he said. 'Yes, Columbus. I have some good friends there. But I guess you wouldn't know them. Have you been there?'

'No, I never have.'

'It's quite a place. Yes, I've been there several times. You ever been there, Mr. Malloy?'

'Just for a short time. I've driven through a couple of times. Stayed there overnight I think once.'

'At the Deshler?' he said.

'Some name like that,' I said.

'You know, you have some cousins living there, Peggy,' said Henderson. 'Your second cousins. I haven't seen them—well, before I came to California. I never looked them up.' This, he realized, was a slight mistake. 'Where you from, Malloy?'

'Gibbsville, Pennsylvania.'

'Gibbsville. No, I don't think I've ever been there. Pittsburgh. Philadelphia, of course. Just where is that in Pennsylvania? Is it near Pittsburgh?'

'No. Nearer Philadelphia. In the hard coal regions.'

'Oh, the *hard* coal regions. Miss Waner? Dividend?'

'Yes, please,' said Karen.

'Say, I wonder if you're related to the ballplayers named Waner?'

'I don't imagine so. I never heard of them.'

'You didn't? Play for Pittsburgh? I guess you're not a fan, then. In 1927, in the World Series. Peggy, how about you? Mr. Malloy?'

Herbert arrived along about this time. In tails, and with a very tall Jewish girl, taller than he. Instinctively I knew that Miss Harris—Joan was her first name—was going to be my problem. She had good conventional manners and probably was a distant cousin of Herbert's. She accepted a cocktail without a word and took a quick look around, which was all she needed, and then settled down. She gave her attention to anyone who was speaking, and in between she would stare at Karen. I was thinking up a plan to snub her when Karen stared back at her, and then Joan smiled and it was a nice smile. After that I liked her. But she didn't help much in conversation.

'Well,' said Herbert, after he told Henderson he didn't drink, 'how do you like California? Oh, I forgot you've been here before.'

Henderson gave three chuckles. 'Well, this *is* all pretty new to me. By George, they certainly have done some building in the last eighteen, twenty years. You live here, Miss Harris?'

'Just for the winter. My home is in New York.'

'Oh, is that so.'

'Mr. Henderson, Joan and I have a friend,' said Herbert. 'He'd like to join us later. Would you mind telling me where we'll be around half-past eleven, twelve?'

'Why didn't you bring him along? Call him up and tell him to join us now. Extra man. I hardly ever dance, the girls—'

'Thank you, but he has an engagement for the early part of the evening. Joan's going up to San Francisco to-morrow and he wanted to see her.'

'Well, I don't know. Peggy, where do you think we'll be around that time?'

'Ho-ho. Don't ask *me*' said Peggy.

'Why, of course I'll ask you, Peggy. What's the best place, after dinner? The Trocadero's about the only place I know of.'

'Well, in that case you better ask Jim to get us a table, Saturday night.'

'Will you do that, Mr Malloy?'

'Sure. Be glad to, but I don't think we'll have to. The head waiter's a friend of mine.'

'Well, whatever you say. Mr. Stern, you tell your friend it would be a pleasure if he'd join us at the Trocadero.'

'Tell him to ask for my table, Herbert,' I said.

'All right, but remember, Mr. Malloy, this is my party. I want that understood before we start. Huh?'

'Sure,' I said.

'Don't you think we'd better get started, Father?' said Peggy. 'Jim, we can all go in your car, can't we?'

'Sure,' I said.

'I'll take Joan in mine,' said Herbert. 'Both of us have to be home early.'

And so we went to Lamaze and had a good dinner and everybody got tight, everybody but Herbert. Some ate filet mignon and some ate squab. All had champagne. Everybody danced, including Herbert, who was grim and silent with Joan, and loquacious with Peggy. He didn't dance with Karen. Henderson danced with each girl in turn. It was quite a workout for me, and only less so for Henderson. An armful of Karen made me forget that platonic basis we were on, and after I danced with Joan I told myself that if I weren't being temporarily faithful to Peggy I would certainly investigate Miss Harris. She liked to dance that way. When people bumped us out of that position she would settle back into it. Watching her face whenever she danced with Henderson, I was reminded of an engineer and a locomotive; his head sticking out of the cab was Intelligence; but it was the locomotive that was doing the work.

You could say to Karen: 'Well, what about it, Karen?'

And she would say: 'Why ask, when you know the answer?'

'Well, you might change your mind.'

'I know. Let's go to bed together and see what happens. *That* old stuff.'

'I warn you. You're taking the wrong attitude. I'll never make you a big movie star when I get to be a producer.'

'You'll never make me, period,' she said. 'Besides, I'm no good. They all tell me that. A man like you, with all your experience, you'd want somebody to be very good. So. By the way, I hear you're out of the unemployed class.'

We often talked that way, and the thing was, that kind of talk was full of truth. I liked Karen, and the things I said I meant, but without any optimism. Peggy knew all about Karen, and what I knew about her Peggy had told me. Their good friendship had begun when they were together in high school. It had the little beginnings: Peggy thought Karen was the prettiest girl in school, and with her usual generosity, said so. Karen was a pretty but frightened freshman of a few days, and when she heard what Peggy said she remembered that she *was* pretty. With this renewal of confidence in herself she was able to go out of her way to make friends with Peggy, and in a month or so each knew what the other was doing every hour of the day. So it had continued. Peggy, in her way, needed Karen. Peggy was not a pretty freshman; whenever she wanted to she led her class, but she was a rather fat little thing. She had no beau. Then the boys began to see that if they were going to get to Karen, it had to be through Peggy, which was how Peggy became a non-virgin. It was hardly more than a technical knockout for the boy who accomplished Peggy's change of status. There were no ill effects; in fact, only a great curiosity and surprise that there were no effects at all. Peggy often said she waited for someone to notice the change in her, but no one ever did. Even the first boy didn't realize or believe that he was the first. She promptly told Karen, who more or less promptly determined to change her own status; but in Karens case there were effects. The first time was bad, and there was a frightened hated boy, and a frightened, miserable girl. Then for Peggy a good adolescent love with a good, slightly older boy, but for Karen the next time—a year or so later—was as bad as the first; she had to have an abortion.

They lived near each other, and after high school the friendship was even better than it had been. They didn't *have* to see each other every day, as was the case in school, but hardly ever did two consecutive days pass without their being together.

Henderson paid the bill and we moved down Sunset Boulevard to the Trocadero. John, the head waiter, whom I had known in New York night clubs, gave us a table in the second row from ringside.

More champagne, and more dancing. Henderson was duly impressed with the movie stars, and completely unimpressed with the directors, not one of whose names he recognized, so I gave up trying to point out local celebrities who were not actors. Fan magazine photographers, trade paper owners, agents, brothers and sisters of the stars, visiting musicians, producers, press agents, Los Angeles politicians, and a large and rather badly behaved group of Pasadena-Santa Barbara younger set meant nothing to him, and they were the people I spoke to. I didn't know any star there well enough to introduce Henderson. I said: 'Sometimes the stars sit downstairs in the bar, if you'd like to meet some. I might know someone downstairs. I'll take a look.'

'Oh, that's all right,' he said. 'I've met some of them. Not the present-day ones. Wally Reid. I used to know Wally. Norman Kerry. There was a well-built chap.'

'Well, I'll take a look.' I went downstairs to the bar, not to do Henderson any favour, but to take a look around for my agent, who I was fairly sure would be there. But on my way to the bar I saw good old Don Miller, sitting in a booth. I immediately recognized the girl with him, and so would have at least half the men in the room. She was one of the girls; a free-lance. Miller was paying his bill, and he saw me. 'Malloy, old boy. How the hell are you?'

'All right,' I said. 'Hello dear.'

'Huh. I didn't think you'd remember me,' said Dear.

'How could I forget you?' I said. She was all right, but sometimes a trouble-maker when she got drunk and remembered that she had been Miss Potter County Texas or something.

'Just paying my cheque,' said Miller. 'How about a quick one. You're all duked out. What's it, a party?'

'Mm-hmm. Upstairs.' I sat down. 'What's with you?'

'You mean Charlotte?'

'No, I don't mean Charlotte. I wouldn't refer to Charlotte that way, would I, dear?'

'I don't know how you'd refer to me and I'm sure it doesn't concern me in the least how you refer to me.'

'Oh, it's that way,' I said. 'Okay.'

'You shut up,' said Miller to Charlotte. 'This is my pal. My pal Malloy, huh, Malloy?'

'If you say so,' I said. 'Scotch and soda.'

'St. James, Mr. Malloy?' said the waiter.

'Yes. Oh, hello, Franz. Well, kid, you must be doing all right.'

'You mean Charlotte?' he asked.

'No, I don't mean Charlotte. That's twice I don't mean Charlotte. I mean the Troc and so forth. Where you living?'

'Same place.'

'Where are *you* living, dear?'

'I'm living in Honolulu, where do you think I'm living? Are you trying to pretend you don't know where I live? I suppose I'm not good enough for you in the Trocadero. Hunh. You don't have to take that attitude, *Mis*-ter Malloy.'

'I don't think she likes me,' I said. 'I think I'll have my drink at the bar. Give me a buzz, kid. I'll be at Metro from now on.'

'She's a little drunkie,' said Miller. 'I'll be seeing you.'

I picked up my highball and went to the bar, and Miller and Charlotte departed. I talked to the bartender while I drank my drink, forgot about my agent, and rejoined the party upstairs.

In my absence they had decided to go some place else, but agreed to wait ten more minutes for Herbert's friend. In those ten minutes I had a strange conversation with Henderson. It began when I explained to Peggy that I had met Miller downstairs: '*Don* Miller. You met him.' She remembered him.

'Don Miller? What Don Miller?' said Henderson, who I thought was busy with Karen's garter.

'You wouldn't know him,' I said. 'He's a kid—I beg your pardon. A young fellow from back East.'

'Where from? Washington, D.C.?' said Henderson. 'I knew a Don Miller there. What business is this fellow in?'

I didn't know whether to make up a whole new story to protect Miller, or to give Henderson some truth, or to stall. I stalled. 'I don't know just what business he *is* in.'

'How old a fellow is he?'

'Oh, I don't know.'

'About twenty-four,' said Peggy. 'Wouldn't you say?'

'Somewhere around there,' I said.

'What kind of a looking fellow is he?' said Henderson.

'Handsome. Tall, dark, and handsome,' said Peggy, giving a very bad imitation of Mae West.

'It couldn't be the fellow you know, Mr. Henderson,' I said.

'I don't think so either,' said Peggy. 'This boy is from Jim's home town.'

'Oh, Pennsylvania,' said Henderson.

'That's the name of the *state*,' I said. 'No, this couldn't be the same guy. Peggy, how about a jig?' We danced.

I was not satisfied that Henderson was satisfied. I realized that I must have seemed unnecessarily evasive. If Henderson knew the Donald Miller on whose traveller's cheques my Don Miller, or Schumacher, was living, he might also know about the cheques. It was too bad that I hadn't told Peggy the real story of Miller, but it seemed better now not to take a chance.

We waited about twenty minutes for Herbert's friend, and he did not show up, so Herbert took Joan home. She was in a bad temper on account of her dilatory friend. Karen and Peggy and Henderson and I went to a couple of other places, to see Jerry Bergen and Louis Prima, and then I took them to their homes.

When I got home I called Don Miller and after a long wait a sleepy voice said he didn't think Mr. Miller was home, because his key was in the box. I left a message, but I had no hope of its ever being delivered or even written down. Then I called Charlotte's number, but no answer. I re-read parts of Zola's *Germinal*, stopping every half-hour or so to telephone Charlotte. About five-thirty she answered.

'Charlotte, this is Jim Malloy. Is Miller there?'

'Oh, it's you. What do you think this—'

'This is important. If Miller's with you, I have to speak to him.'

'Go— Yourself,' she said. 'You can't high-hat—'

'Tell Miller it's about Washington,' I said.

'What'd he do, cross the Delaware?' she said, and hung up.

I tried to get her back, but she left the phone off the cradle. Of course there were two or three things I might have done—but there were reasons why I couldn't send her a telegram or go to her house, because I didn't know her last name, and I didn't know her address. She often had come to my house, but I had never been to hers. All I knew was that it was a three-or four-dollar taxi ride from a house I'd had in Beverly Hills, which wasn't much help. The best I could do was to send Miller a telegram to his house, which I did.

The next day I awakened five or six times with an inexplicable hangover; inexplicable in that I had not been drunk the night before. No blank periods; I remembered everywhere I had been, everyone I had spoken to, everything I had done. It may have been that I drank too much without getting stewed. Whatever it was, I had a hangover, and I awakened five or six times, dozed off again, changed my position in bed in the hope of getting rid of the throbbing headache. It was no use.

It was the middle of the afternoon. I sent down for a big orange juice and scrambled eggs and coffee and oatmeal and the Sunday papers. The eggs were not done the way I like them, but I put away the rest of the food and presently, after the usual natural functions, I felt well enough to tackle Miller on the phone. He was home.

'Say, what was the idea calling me at Charlotte's? I call that a pretty lousy—'

'Listen, you punk, I don't care what you call it. You listen to me. I think you're in a real jam. You better come on out here and I'll tell you about it.'

I read Louella and her daughter and W.R.'s editorial, and studied my favourite study, Ginger Rogers in colour, and second-guessed the eastern football scores, and got mad about the latest ex-Communist who was telling all, and won a bet with myself that my name would not be in a list at a party I'd gone to, and read the second-hand automobile classifieds (but no Alfa-Romeo for $450 cash) and saw a fairly good wisecrack I had made three years before attributed to a New York orchestra leader, and read the titles of the Sunday sermons, and tried to calculate how much I should make if I were a sports writer again and on the take. I thought, as I thought every day, of the Paramount writer who came home from the studio one day and saw his father reading the paper. 'What's in the paper, Dad?' he said.

'Huh,' snorted the old man. 'L. A. dog chases L. A. cat over L. A. fence.'

I thought of Ginger and wondered how many youths at Yale and Kenyon and Stanford and Texas Christian and St. Bonaventure's and Clemson and Magdalen and McGill and Bowlder and Yale-in-China were thinking of her at just that minute. And the next minute I was sending flowers to Peggy. I had the clerk say on the card: These are New York Cut. Then the phone rang and it was Miller. He came up.

'Sit down,' I said. 'Want some coffee? Get the glass out of the can.'

He got the glass from the bathroom and I filled it with coffee.

He drank some, put the glass on the desk and lit a cigarette. 'What's the jam I'm in?' he said.

'I *think* you're in one,' I said. 'Let me think how to begin this.

'Well, suppose I begin this way. I'll give you the worst part first. The facts. Then you can help me figure out if you're in a jam. Last night when I saw you at the Troc, one of the guys upstairs on the party I was on—when I came upstairs I happened to mention I saw you. I was with the Henderson girl. You met her with me that night at the South Seas.'

'Sure, I remember her. Nice little number.'

'Sure. Well, I mentioned your name, and immediately this guy wanted to know *what* Don Miller. From Washington?'

'Jesus!' said Miller.

'So I started to say I didn't know where you were from, but Peggy, the Henderson girl, she said you were from Pennsylvania. Then this guy wanted to know what business you were in. I said I didn't know. I said I didn't know you very well.'

'Who was the guy?'

'And I told him I didn't know how old you were, but she volunteered the information that you were around twenty-four or—five.'

'Who was he?'

'Just let me tell you the story, will you? Then he wanted to know what you looked like, and we gave him a sort of stall, but maybe not enough of a one. Peggy said you were tall, dark, and handsome, like Cary Grant in that Mae West picture.'

'Jesus.' He put his face in his long fingers and sat like a kibitzer or a condemned man. 'Well, who was this guy?'

'I don't know whether to tell you or not. I don't know whether it'll do you any good to tell you.'

'God damn it, sure it will, Malloy. Give me a break.'

'I'm giving you a break. These L.A. cops are tough, you know. I could just as easily be held as accessory after the fact or something, just sitting here talking to you. In my room, don't forget. All right, I'll tell you who it was. It's Peggy Henderson's father. He suddenly blew into town the other day.'

'Jesus!'

'They don't know much about him, she and her brother. He disappeared when the brother was a kid, about fifteen, twenty years ago, give or take a couple years. Since then he's been travelling around the country, practically every place but out here. Different jobs. Advertising. I sat in on one session with the guy, and he's told his kids a few things, but I don't think he's a cop. Still, he may be. Not a regular cop. Maybe some kind of a special dick. An investigator. One of those. Maybe he works for that American Express or American Bankers or whatever it is. The people that issued those cheques of yours.'

Miller took one hand from his face and made a fist and pounded the air. 'Oh, God.'

'What?' I said. 'The heat's on?'

'I guess so.'

'What are you going to do? What are your plans?'

'Screw out of here, that's the first thing,' he said.

'It might be a very good idea, but where, and how? Have you any dough?'

'Uh-huh. A couple hundred bucks. I owe a little, not more than fifty bucks. I don't know where to go though. Get a job on a ship, maybe.'

'How? You've never been to sea, you don't belong to any union, and I wouldn't advise you to do any scabbing out here. But how do you know this Henderson is after you? It might be just a false alarm, or maybe he does know this Don Miller, maybe he's an older guy. All you have to do is change your name again, quietly leave this part of the country and go back to Swedish Haven or wherever you please.'

'No, I got a hunch on this. This is it, all right. See, Malloy, they have my description everywhere I cashed one of those cheques, and another thing, my pal in Washington, they probly got a description from him, so they'll be looking for me at Swedish Haven. So I can't go there, and I can't be Schumacher again, either. And there's something else makes me think this is the right guy. I mean by that, makes me think he's a detective. God damn it!'

'What's that?'

'Well, you were pretty swell to me so I might as well let you in on it. I cashed another cheque.'

'Oh, you damn fool. What'd you do that for?'

'That bim I was with last night. Charlotte.'

'Why, you dope, you didn't have to—why, she's a—she isn't any two-buck whore, but you could have been on the free list.'

'Better'n that. She wanted to keep me. But I picked her up one night and I gave her this line of crap. I told her my old man was

a big-shot banker in New York and I was out here to learn the
business end of the movies. So I started in spending dough on her.
I *was* on the free list, that's true, but I would of done better just
giving her ten or twenty bucks every time. I spent that much on
her every time I went out with her.'

'Why?'

'I do' know. I liked her. Maybe she is a whore, but. Well, you
laid her. I had to have more dough, see? I put on this act, banker's
son and all that. I bought a new Ford. Aah.' At this point I thought
he was going to cry. 'I was only sore last night because I thought
you were trying to get her to come out, or you come down to her
place.'

'Nope,' I said. 'Last night was the first time I saw her since, oh,
last summer. Are you in love with her?'

'I don't know. I never exactly thought of it that way. That's
something I never was, in love with any girl. But she's all right.
She often says to me, 'We don't have to go out.' She says I probly
get a small salary and hardly any allowance and I don't have to
spend it on her. That's what she said after she saw the joint where
I live.'

'Can you tell her the truth? Is she in love with you?'

'She offered to give up hustling for me.'

'Maybe she'd be glad of the chance if she thought you could keep
her. What do you honestly think? Is she in love with you enough
so that you could trust her?'

'Well, it's so hard to say. Sometimes I think she is, but then I
don't know. The first night I was with her, I went crazy. I never
had anything like it. I thought, this dame must be nuts for me. She
tells me I'm the only guy she ever enjoyed it with. We'll be walking
along the street together or in a movie, and all of a sudden she'll
start in, only talking. The other night we went to the movies and
we no sooner got inside than she started in, did I like it last night,
did I want to do it that way with the dame in the picture. Till I
couldn't see straight.'

'I guess you must be all right in the hay,' I said.

'No, its her. And she's only from Texas, only a plain ordinary
American. Pretty, but, you know.'

'Sure. Well now, listen, anything to get off this subject or I'll be
sending down for the operator or somebody. Here's what I suggest.
You figure out whether you can trust this Charlotte or not. That's

entirely up to you. If you have any doubt about it, the hell with
her. Don't see her any more, because she can be trouble. I imagine
the cops know her, otherwise she wouldn't be able to operate even
if she didn't have a record. As far as I know she's honest, and has
no record. But they might be able to trace you through her, if
they're going to trace you. Now what you do, you get rid of that
car. Get out of that place where you're living and move to some
place 'way the hell away from here, like on the other side of Western
Avenue, or else go to Long Beach or any place, but don't stay
around Hollywood or Beverly or any of these places.

'Change your name, and get a job. Get some kind of job that
isn't a white collar job. Car-washer. Take any kind of dough, just
to get a job. You have enough to stake you for a while, and if you
need dough later I'll lend you some. Only don't get the idea that
I'm going to keep you. How're your eyes?'

'Good, I guess.'

'Well, go to some cheap jewellery store where they examine eyes
and they'll find something wrong with them. They always do.
Nobody has perfect eyes out here, and if one of these oculists saw
perfect eyes he'd think there was something wrong with them.
Get yourself a pair of glasses with steel rims, not tortoiseshell.
Tortoiseshell look phony sometimes.'

'Were you ever on the lam?'

'That's none of your business,' I said. 'I write for the movies,
and whether I was on the lam or not doesn't make any difference.
Another thing. You have to cultivate a new personality. Dress
differently. Get yourself a cheap suit that doesn't fit so well, a coat
that doesn't cover your arse. Did you pay cash for your car?'

'Yes,' he said. 'Traded the old one and the rest cash.'

'Sell it at a loss, to get rid of it quickly. Maybe you ought to get
a motor-cycle, second-hand. That would certainly be a new thing
in your personality. While I think of it, don't ever call me here. It's
safer to call me at the Studio. Let me know where you are, but
don't get in touch with me except when it's absolutely necessary.
Will you remember all this?'

'Yes.'

'Don't forget it. I want to tell you something. You know, this
may be a false alarm. But even if it is it'll be a good thing for you
to change your identity again. If it'll make you feel any better. I
was on the lam once, in New York, and I threw off the people that

were after me by pretending to leave New York, but all I did was move to another hotel a block away, by way of Grand Central. Well, I guess that's all I have to offer.'

'Well, Malloy, I sure appreciate your kindness. I—'

'Skip it. By the way, where did you cash this last cheque?'

'At some gambling joint. They knew Charlotte and she told them my old man was a banker. All—'

'What gambling joint? The Surf?'

'Yes,' he said. 'It's *some place*.'

'My boy,' I said, 'you want to get the hell out of this section as fast as you can. You're in the middle, between the law and the mob guys. Beat it, and good luck.'

He left, and I sat there in comfort, thinking about him and how I came to know him. The town he came from was a few miles from my home town, but it might as well have been a few states away, for all the mixing the people of the two towns did. As a reporter it was my job to know people like his father and all the other ministers, undertakers, cops, justices of the peace, politicians, station agents and other news sources. But this kid himself was not important enough to know, even though I had once written his name, wrong. Probably the only way he would ever get to be known outside of his home town was the way another townsman of his had become notorious. This other fellow was a sort of bush-league public enemy, who held up a dozen banks and filling stations before he was accidentally killed by a West Virginia deputy sheriff. The deputy didn't sound like the kind of minion of the law who goes around routing out public enemies. Anyway, this public enemy turned out to have been born in Swedish Haven, although he hadn't lived there from the age of two on. It gave us a good one-day story, and it made Swedish Haven feel that the eyes of the world were upon it, the way such towns feel when the local Elks take the lead from all the cities of that size in new members gained during the month of October, and get written up in the *Elks Magazine*. Or when the high school relay team wins its event at the Penn Relays. Or when some obscure housewife wins a Plymouth sedan for the very best last line to a prepared advertising limerick, and her name and address are announced over the radio.

And yet to me this kid was a sort of celebrity, the way anyone is who is wanted by the law. Sitting there in my room he was a frightened kid, the same age as one of my brothers, and he was about as unexciting a figure as there was in Los Angeles County. But the moment he left the room he began to be different. Already I was *remembering* him, not seeing him, and what I remembered was a figure that had passed, like a celebrity who has been pointed out to you just as he passed, so that you don't see his face but only his back. Miller was a tall young man, whose rounded shoulders contributed to the picture of a hunted man. All hunted men have rounded shoulders, in your mental picture of them. Sometimes they are turning their heads over a shoulder. I hoped Miller would get out of his own jam without any help from me, but that he would I neither doubted nor believed.

I put on a new brown double-breasted suit and a blue shirt and brown foulard tie and an old pair of brown Scotch grain brogues. I left the coat hanging until I had called Peggy and told her I would take her for a ride. She told me to come right over.

She was alone. She said her father had gone out to have a demonstration of a second-hand La Salle that he was thinking of buying. He had wanted her to come along, but she said she expected a call from me, which was nice of her, as I had not mentioned that I would call.

'Oh, I just used you as an excuse is all,' she said. 'I don't want you to think of me sitting all alone by the telephone.'

'Waiting for a ring, a ting—a-ling. Well, I'm glad you waited, and I'm glad I called.

'And I'm glad you sent me flowers. Why don't you do that oftener?'

'I don't know.'

'New York Cut,' she said. 'Oh! I just got it! You meant the steaks. Of course, of course, how stupid of me.'

'No,' I said. 'You're *used* to seeing it, and it's still new to me.'

'Why don't you send them oftener? I *know* why, of course.'

'Why?'

'Well,' she said, 'if you were in love with Karen I'll bet you'd send her flowers, all the time. Every day when Karen came home thered be a little box of flowers with some witty note.'

'Not a witty note every day. Flowers maybe, but—'

'Yes, you'd try anyway. But with me—I'm not a glamour girl like Karen. I'm not beautiful. Im a mere, oh, I don't know. Slightly pretty. Slightly intelligent. Pushover for you.'

'Now don't talk like that, Peggy.'

She laughed her fat little laugh that began low and went high and came back to low. 'All right. But I'm a woman. Remember that. And I like to receive flowers. I may not *like* flowers, but—'

'Oh. So you don't like flowers. That's what you're carping about.' I pretended to ignore her, and the first thing I knew I was ignoring her. There was a car ahead of us—we were driving out Wilshire by this time, with Malibu vaguely in my mind—and it was a convertible sedan like mine, with a low top so that I couldn't see who was in it. But the radio was on rather loud and it was playing something that I liked. It might have been the 'Toccata and Fugue', or it might have been the 'Three Oranges March', or it might have been 'Stack o' Lees Blues'. It was something I liked and did not expect to hear from a California car on a Sunday afternoon on Wilshire Boulevard. It was the kind of thing that I expected every Californian to turn off. I switched on my own radio and tried to find the station that the other car had.

'You hurt?' said Peggy.

'Shh!' I monkeyed with the radio. 'Trying to get something.'

'You'll get something. A sock on the head if you shush me.'

'Peggy, I'm trying to get the station that those people have. The Chrysler. The car like mine.'

'I thought this was a Buick.'

'It is. Please.' I couldn't find the station, and then I got a break in traffic and drew up alongside the Chrysler. In it were four people: two girls, two young men. 'What station have you got?' I said.

'I beg your pardon?' said the girl who was driving.

'I wanted to get that tune. What station are you tuned in on?'

They told me. It was one of those stations that broadcast nothing but phonograph records. I tuned in and it was what I wanted. Then the light changed. I was enjoying myself, and after I changed gears I reached over and took Peggy's hand. She took it away. 'Wasn't that rather obvious?'

'Can't I hold your hand?'

'You know what I mean. I've seen you practically sock somebody that just looked at me when I was with you, but you, you drive right up to a girl on Wilshire Boulevard. What nerve! If I'd been one of those men. . . .'

'Oh, balls!' The anger came first. Later I would be pleased that she was jealous. Now it was so unreasonable and so petty feminine that I wanted to hit her. 'You must be getting change of life or

something. I wanted to hear that music, and I thought the kind of
people that listened to that music wouldn't mind if I asked them.
I thought—well, what the hell.'

'Don't try to explain it. You simply saw a pretty girl and so you
picked a fight with me and *drove* the car fifty miles an hour through
traffic to catch up with her, and then you couldn't think of anything
better to say than, "I beg your pardon, but as one music-lover to
another I know I can't pick you up now, but if I see you again at
the Trocadero will you remember me because you're very pretty
and we have this mutual love of good music. Isn't it wonderful?
Two souls, brought together by our passion for Bach!" '

'Who writes your dialogue? And what an actress! Boy, when you
want to turn on the histrionics! I'll bet you wowed Hollywood High
in *Paolo and Francesca*, or *Green Stockings*.'

She burst out laughing, and she couldn't stop. 'Well?' I kept
saying. 'What was it? Come on, what did I say?' I soon was laughing
myself.

When she stopped laughing, she said: 'I was *in Green Stockings*.'
Then she put both hands on my shoulder and it was all right after
that. I kissed her and we were quiet. We turned off Wilshire and
drove slowly up Rodeo Drive and across Carmelita and up Roxbury
to Sunset and then back to Rodeo and down and around and
around, and I said 'Pick a house. Look for one around three-fifty
or five hundred. I'm going to rent a house, the hell with this hotel
life.'

'I wish you did have a house. I don't like where you live now. I
don't like anything about it. I'd rather live where I live. You could
have a house like ours and two servants for what you pay now, and
still save money. Too many people can see me going in and out of
your place. But I thought you had one picked out.'

'I did, but I want you to pick one *you* like.'

'If you live out here—well, the capitalists have got you at last. If
they didn't always have you.'

'Oh, yeah?' I said. 'I lived here before, remember." Then I drove
her around and pointed out houses that were owned or rented by
the leftists in the movie colony. She pointed out houses that were
owned by the reactionaries. 'Sure, sure,' I said. 'I concede all that.
My only point was that if the nice guys can live in these houses
and still be nice guys, why can't I? Couldn't you?'

'I'd always be thinking of how much I could save by living

somewhere else, and sending the difference to the Loyalists or the Scottsboro boys.'

'You better learn to like this part of town, because you're going to live out here.'

That afternoon we didn't do much more driving. I called up a movie writer I knew who had a house in Beverly, and he was going away and I borrowed his house. Late that night I told Peggy my suspicions of her father, and Miller's story, and she promised to find out what she could.

The next day I started my new job at Metro and the second day I was there I acted on an impulse, the overwhelming kind that I always got when I started a new job: the impulse to spend money in a big way. I left the studio that afternoon and drove over to a real estate agent I knew, picked out a house in Beverly for five hundred a month, had the agent hire a Negro couple, and the next day I moved in. I called for Peggy at the shop that day and behaved with all the mysteriousness I could summon. We drove in, stopped the car in the driveway, and I got out and said: Come on, get out.'

'What's this all about?'

'Get out.'

She got out and I picked her up and carried her to the door and rang the bell, and Jonas, the Negro, opened the door and I carried her in, to the amusement of Jonas, who then left. I kissed her hard before putting her down. 'I love you,' I said. The strange thing was that that was impulse too; I had no intention of saying it. I put my arms around her and kissed her again, long.

'Oh, Jim,' she said. 'This is the way to do it. Here, hold me here. Let me hold you. I want you. Where do we go?'

On the way upstairs we stopped again. She was two steps higher than I and I held her to me. 'It's like a first time, only better, isn't it?' she said.

'It is a first time, darling,' I said. 'Say it.'

'I love you. I always loved you. I'm so excited. let's stand here and think of what we're going to do. Let's talk about it. Do you know what I'm going to do to you?' She whispered.

'Let's do it now,' I said. I was getting superstitiously apprehensive. I was in a hurry to have the first time accomplished. She kissed my forehead and turned and began running up the remaining steps. She took things off as she ran; her jacket, her sweater. She turned around and looked at me only once. I never had been so excited in my life—and ten minutes before I had only intended to show her the house. There was something new in her eyes. She seemed younger, too, and with her hands she was discovering her own body while she watched me. 'Is it true about Chinese women?' she said.

'No.'

'How do you know?'

"Well, it isn't true about Japanese women. I do know that.'

'Oh, you do, eh? What about coloured women?'

'Don't know anything about them. What about you, is it true about you?'

'Stop talking and hurry up.'

'Yes,' I said. She was right; this was one time when we could do without the talking and joking that we always did. Later on, when she was finishing a cigarette, we did talk.

'How much does this place cost?'

'Five hundred.'

'Goodness! how long'd you take it for?'

'Three months.'

'Has it got a swimming pool?'

'No. What good would a swimming pool be this time of year? You must have been reading the ads, the Year Round Club ads.'

'You'll have to get a double bed. I don't like twin beds.'

'I think there is a double bed in one of the other bedrooms. In fact I know there is. But I like this room better than the one with the double bed.'

'I guess most people don't need as much room as we do. Otherwise twin beds wouldn't be so popular. The furniture is nice. Whose house is it?'

'I have to think. It's a strange name. A long German name. They aren't picture people. The husband came out here for Ford or General Motors, and I think he's been transferred. The rest of the house is nice, too. There's a pool table.'

'Is there a nursery? I may need one after this.'

'Oh, Peggy, you must know by this time I'm sterile.'

'You mustn't be. Don't you want children?'

'I do if you do. I have no great feeling about perpetuating the name. I have enough brothers to take care of that.'

'I wonder how I'd be as a mother.'

'Wonderful,' I said. 'I really mean that.'

'Why? What makes you think so?'

'You're sweet and kind and intelligent, and passionate. I think you have to be, to be a good mother. I don't know, your breasts are so good.'

'I used to hate them. I had them when I was fourteen, almost the same size as they are now. They are nice, aren't they? What do you like best about a girl's figure?'

'Her breasts.'

'Not here?'

'Sure, but breasts mostly. Are you psycho-analysing me?''

'No, not specially. Do you like Karen's?'

'*Do* I!'

'Did you ever lay Karen?'

'You know damn well I didn't.'

'Did you ever make a pass at her?'

'Often.'

'Do you want to lay her?'

'Do you want an honest answer?'

'If I asked her to, as a favour to me, she would, I think.'

'What would you say to her?'

'I'd say I had the curse or I was pregnant or whatever it happened to be, and I didn't want you to go around with other women and get a disease. Or I'd just *say* to her, Jim wants to sleep with you and I want him to have what he wants, she'd do it. I think she would.'

'I'm not so sure. Sometimes I think she doesn't like me.'

'Yes, she does. I think she'd like to sleep with you. She asked me one time how you were in bed. She's very curious about it. She never had an orgasm with a man. Something always goes wrong.'

'She'd never been in love,' I said. 'She'd be all right if she'd fall for some guy and have a long affair with him. She's a perfectly normal girl, and with the right guy.'

'That's the great difficulty. I think you might be the right guy.'

'Don't put ideas in my head. Your father certainly thinks—'

"He's horrible. He was trying to put his hand up her skirt all last Saturday night. He wanted me to ask her to spend the night with us, and I almost did but something stopped me. I wish he'd go away and never come back. I wish he'd never come here in the first place. Still, I guess I always would have been curious about him. Wanting to know what he looked like, and whether he was alive. Well, I know now.'

'By the way,' I said.

'I didn't find out anything. He carries a pistol. I found that out.'

'How?'

'I saw it in his back pocket when he was coming out of the bathroom.'

'Did he know you saw it?'

'No, I don't think he did. He didn't try to hide it, though.'

'Has he said how long he's going to stay?'

'No. I didn't know how to broach the subject. I know he'll be here till after Christmas.'

'Well, that's not very long. What does he do in the daytime?'

'Well, of course I'm never there, so I don't really know. He's home for lunch usually, Millie tells me. He gets up after I've gone to the shop and goes out and comes back with the Chicago and New York papers. Oh, yes. He buys racing papers. I imagine he must play the horses quite a lot.'

'Good God, you don't think he's going to be here for the whole Santa Anita meeting?'

'God forbid! But I wonder why he carries a pistol. Maybe he is a detective.'

'Well, let us be detectives. Does he get any phone calls at the house?'

'Not that I know of.'

'Mail?'

'Well, yes, but not at the house. General Delivery, I think.'

'Doesn't he ever try to explain what he's doing out here?' I said. 'I should think he'd feel that he had to say something about his plans.'

'No. He sometimes gives me the impression that he thinks this is his home. Our house. And he's the father, and we're the children. Goodness knows I never have any such feeling.'

'I guess we'll just have to wait and see,' I said. I turned over and we lightly kissed each other and felt our passion slowly coming on again. 'Ah, this is nice. This is what we're here for, isn't it?'

'Mm-hmm. Want me to stay all night?'

'Sure. It's a long time since we've done that.'

'After a while I'll call Millie and tell her I'm not coming home, and I'll fix it with Karen. I want to stay in your nice new house,

but let's sleep in the room with the double bed. Not now, but when
we go to bed to-night.'

'Anything you say. I'd like to christen every room in the house.'

'In one night? Not if I know you. Am I good for you, Jim?'

'Yes, you're good for me. Am I good for you?'

'Yes. Yes,' she said. 'Yes. Yes!'

I had a friend, not exactly a friend, but a fellow I had known
slightly in New York, although I had known him well by reputation.
He was a hard one to figure out. He did a little tap-dancing in the
Guinan days, and he was what we call around-Broadway. He had
been a press agent, hoofer, errand boy for gamblers, and more than
once I had seen him getting a nod from big-shot public enemies. I
seriously doubt whether he ever was convicted of major crime, or
even was accused of it. He was not hophead enough or ruthless
enough to be a torpedo. In fact, I am not even sure that he would
actually steal, although he often referred to himself as 'a larceny
guy like me.' This probably was his euphemism for chiseller. He
was a chiseller, all right, but I liked him. He had come to Hollywood
around 1930 or 1931, as a 'technical advisor' on a gangster picture.
He appeared in the picture, and in several subsequent ones. Then
he was an artists' representative for a while, and after that he sold
an original story, based on fact. 'I made a little,' he was always
saying, to cover his business activities.

He wrote and acted under the name of Jerry Luck, but everybody
called him Red; I don't know why, I telephoned him from the
studio that day after Peggy and I housewarmed. I made a date for
breakfast, or lunch. We met at the Beverly Derby. He had not gone
Hollywood in his clothes. He had on a one-button suit of Eleanor
Blue, black pointed shoes with Spanish heels to give him a little
extra height, soft white shirt that had been starched too much, and
a spotless, almost white hat. He was carrying one of those wrap-
around camel's-hair coats. When I got there, he said, 'Jim boy,'
without looking at me. 'Don't round now, but ain't that that Loretta
Young?'

'Mm—yes,' I said.

'That's for me,' he said. 'Where do we sit?'

We got a table. He carefully folded his coat, carefully laid down
his hat, and smoothing his suit coat over his hips, he sat down,
taking in the whole room slowly. He picked up the menu and read

it item by item, and then tossed it in front of him like a disgusted cardplayer. 'Frig dat,' he said. 'Hey! Miss!' he called the waitress.

She said hello to me, and gave him her attention. 'Yes, sir?'

'You wanna go in pictures?' he said.

'Sure,' she said.

'All right then, get this order and I and Mr. Malloy may have a part for you in our next picture. I want—' and he held out his hands like a man holding a water-melon. 'I want some of that brannis wit' the portis salad dressing on top wit' a little—Jim, what's the name of that sauce?'

'Escoffier?' I said.

'Escoffyer sauce. You know?'

'I'm sorry, sir, I didn't get it,' she said.

'She didn't get it,' he said. 'All right, once again. Now look. I want some of this brancovy portis like wit' the cullaba on *top! On top!* Usely you don't put it on top here, but that's the way I want it—'

'I'm sorry, sir—'

'You're sorry! Jesus Christ, she's sorry. What am I, talkin Greek or Saskatchewan or sumpn? Calla headwaiter. Calla captain.' The poor girl brought the captain.

'You the captain?'

'Yes, sir.'

'I'm S. J. Sterncliff from Gaumont British. Y'ever hear Gaumont British?'

'Oh, yes, sir,' said the captain.

'Well, that's who I am, the New York representative Gaumont British. Now this here is my first trip to Hollywood and I'm accustomed to the best, the best. I ask this young lady to bring me a brannis salad wit' the portis on top like wit' Escoffyer. You know.'

The captain looked at me and smiled sadly, and then at Red. 'Is this the double talk, sir?'

'Oh, a wise guy. Okay. Gimme a bacon and tomato on whole wheat toasted. Coffee. Wudda *you* eatin', Jim boy?'

I ordered corn beef hash. The captain and the girl left us.

'To what do I owe this honour, Kiddy?' said Red.

'A favour, Red,' I said. 'Do you know any private dicks?'

'Do I! You mean them gumshoe artists, Jim? Those hawkshaws? Those flatfoots, Jim?'

'Yes.'

'Indeed I do. They have shadowed and tailed me all over the lenth and breadth of this fair land. Are you levelling? Why do you ask?'

'I'm levelling. Did you ever know one by the name of Henderson?'

'Henderson. No, not by that name. Why?'

'How's your memory for faces?'

'The best, Jim. A second Al Smith. A *first* Al Smith. A veritable photographic memory, if you know what I mean, Jim.'

'I have a guy I want you to take a gander at.'

'You mean give him the double-O, Jim? The once-over? The up and down, Jim?'

'Yes.'

'Done, sir, done. You have my hand on it, and when a Luckman gives his hand, you better go right to Doctor Wharton, one flight up, leave this place as you find it. Is it you, or somebody else?'

'It's somebody else. A couple of other people, in fact,' I said.

'What can I do? You want me to look at this guy and see if I know him.'

'Right.'

'Where is he, Jim?'

'I'll find out right away, if I can.' I had a phone brought to the table, and called Peggy. She happened to be at the bookstore, and I told her to call her home and see if her father was there. I had a plan. She called me back and said he was there.

'If you're not doing anything for the next half-hour,' I said.

'All afternoon, Jim. Anything you say. Jesus, that Loretta Young. Who's that with her?' 'Eddie Sutherland. You know him.'

'Eddie Sutherland the director. No, I don't know him. He was at Paramount when I was there a couple times.'

'He's *still* there.' I said.

'All right, pallie, you don't have to put salt in the wound. Here she comes.'

'Hello, Eddie,' I said. 'Hello, Gretch. Gretch, this is Mr. Luck, Miss Young. Mr. Sutherland.' Red did a scramble like Benchley in *How to Behave*, and they passed on. Red grabbed my arm.

'Pardon the vice-like grip,' he said, 'but anything you want, Jim. Anything you want. Anything she wants, too. A ray of sunshine in a drab life. A merciful angel. A lady bountiful whose very smile.'

'I didn't know you cared, Red.'

'Cared! For the pal who introduced me to Loretta

Young—anything! Where is this Henderson? I will bring together the mains and the semi-mains and we will put the son of a bitch on the spot, Jim. We will rub him out. His number is up. We will *see* him. Jim. You know the sinister meaning of see, don't you?'

'Yes, dear,' I said.

'You sure you don't want me to stop for my chopper? My type-writer? My tommy-gun, Jim? We'll let him have it, the rat.'

'Just the double-O is all I want, Red,' I said. 'And the check, honey. Bobbie. Naomi. Betty. Ella. Check, please?'

My plan was simple. We would go to Peggy's house and pretend I had a date to meet her there. We would stay long enough for Red to get a good look at Henderson, and then retire. This we did.

Henderson was home. Millie came to the door and I motioned to her to let us in. 'Is Peggy home yet?' I said, pretty loud.

'No, Mist' Malloy, she ain't home yet. Won't *be* home before six I guess.'

'Yes, she was coming home. I was to meet her here.'

'Well, in that case I guess you better come in wait. Will you rest your hats?'

'Ah, Malloy,' said Henderson. 'This is quite a surprise.'

'I was supposed to meet Peggy here around two-thirty. Didn't she phone or anything?'

'Only to tell Millie what to have for dinner. About I'd say a half an hour ago.'

'This is Mr. Luck, Mr. Henderson.'

'Glad to meet you.'

'Glad to meet *you.*'

'It's funny she didn't call. She's usually pretty, uh, punctilious,' I said.

'Why don't you try calling her at the store?' said Henderson. 'Sit down, Mr. Lock?'

'Luck.'

'Luck. Anything in the name, eh?' said Henderson.

'Lots of it. All bad,' said Red.

I telephoned, putting on my act for Henderson's benefit. 'She says she forgot all about it,' I said. 'Well—'

We left. On the way down the hill in my car Red was biting his lower lip. 'We can go to the Bamboo Room and refresh your memory.'

'That won't do any good,' he said. 'Of course we can *go*. I'll buy you a powder.'

We sat down in the too-low chairs of the Bamboo Room.

'I'll tell you the God's honest truth,' said Red. 'I don't know.'

'Well, it was only a chance,' I said. 'One in a million.'

'No, it's better than that,' he said. 'When we first got there I was positive I never saw him before in my whole life but while you was at the phone I kept looking at that kisser and, I don't *know*. You don't know if he took on weight or something? He couldn't of taken on *much*, but maybe just enough.'

'Were you ever in Chicago?'

'A million times.'

'For any length of time?' I asked.

'A week, two weeks. Split weeks in the neighbourhood houses. I was to open in a club there once. I'm sorry, Jim. I'd like to straighten you out on this, but I honestly can't. I can't swear I ever saw him before, and I can't swear I didn't.'

'When you were around the clubs did you ever meet a guy that sold silverware, knives and forks?'

'No, I wouldn't have been around doorn that phase. Of course a guy like that would come back and spend a little if he sold the silverware to the club.'

'That's what I was thinking.'

'Yeah. But that's no clue. I just have to give up till I can go to work on the old memory.'

'Red. A personal question, and you don't have to answer it. Did you ever do time?'

'Yes,' he said. 'But he didn't. I'd bet on that.'

'Thanks, pal,' I said. 'You're pretty sure?'

'Well, you can always be wrong about that. You hear about these guys that take a powder from some chain gang and they go and live in Ohio or some place and veil up and live respectable lives for fifeen years and nobody the wiser. But most of the time it's like the clap. I can tell you in this room who had the clap. You did, didn't you?'

'Sure.'

'That guinzo over there. He had it. I had it, and I can tell just by lookin' at a guy. Usely I can wit' guys that did time, and I would say this Henderson never did. Jim, I'd like to be able to say

I made that guy the minute I laid eyes on him, but I can't say that. If I did I'd be telling you a lie. But one thing I will say.'

'What's that?'

'This much I will say. If I ever saw a wronggo, that Henderson is it.'

'I'll go with you on that,' I said.

So we sat and had a few powders and I got my load on and had to have Jonas come down in a taxi and take me home, as I never drive when I am a little stiff.

Christmas stank. Maybe it is because I am a sucker for Christmas, and this was my first in Hollywood. Always before I had gone East, or happened to be East. It doesn't have to be White for me to like it, but it ought to be reasonably cold, and there never ought to be palm-trees. Well, maybe palm-trees. I could easily have made a better day of it in the Gauguin country, me in torn shorts and the girls in sarongs or better, and all of us drinking out of coco-nuts. As it was I took the day off on Christmas Eve and went around buying presents, I bought Keith a twenty-five-dollar shockproof wrist-watch, I bought Karen a metal vanity case that looked like a radio set and weighed about two pounds, and cost eighty dollars. I bought Red a pigskin cigarette case for fifteen dollars. I sent Millie a telegraph money order for ten dollars because I was sure she'd never had one before. I gave Jonas and his wife two weeks' pay, and I bought toys for the children of people who have no part in this story. I was glad to get a tie from Don Miller, sent to the studio. And I put down four hundred dollars on a star sapphire ring for Peggy. I had everything sent, except the ring, and then I went to a party at the studio and then a cocktail party at somebody's house and then had Jonas drive me to the bookstore to pick up Peggy. She would have kept me waiting, but that was all right, because I went to the bar at the Beverly-Wiltshire and plied myself with Scotch and soda, humming the praises of 'Good King Wenceslaus' with a dash of 'Lord Jeffrey Amherst' and 'I'm Only a Mercersburg Boy', which was to make me homesick. I got very drunk and they asked me to leave. I went across the street to the Brown Derby and distributed largesse of five dollars to each waitress except my favourite to whom I gave 4.49 dollars. I told her if she was a good girl for the rest of the year I would give her the rest. I felt very good, but that was Christmas Eve.

Peggy was sitting in the car. I got in and took her hand and kissed it. 'I have whisky on my breath,' I said.

'On your *breath!*'

'I've tried Sen-Sen and cloves, but no good. Now this little hand, which I now kiss, kiss, indicating kiss on hand, have you got a kiss on hand, Miss? I'll take—anyway. This little hand which I now kiss, I now decorate like gilding the lily.' Then I put the ring on her thumb. 'It doesn't mean anything unless you want it to, so put it whatever finger your heart's desire.'

She took it off and looked at it and at me, and put it on the third finger of her left hand. 'I don't care,' she said. 'Even if you are drunk.' She put her arms around my neck and kissed me, and I started to cry because I loved her.

'I gotta cut this out,' I said. 'You like my house I bought for you?'

'You didn't buy it,' she said.

'All right, I didn't buy it. All right. Very well. I didn't buy the God damn thing. I guess I didn't buy it, eh? Jonas!'

'Yes, sir.'

'Have you got the deed of our house in your pocket? Do you happen to have it?'

'No, sir.'

'Hmm. Well, maybe you're right, then. I didn't buy it. But I will. If you like it, that is. Contingent on your liking it only. Otherwise—the hell with it. We'll go set fire to the God damn thing. Let's do it anyway. Only fooling. Firemen are all drunk on Christmas Eve, drunk and home with their wives and little children.'

'Will you take me home now?'

'Don't you want to go to our little home?'

'I want to go to my own little home. *Next* Christmas, we'll go to our little home, and we'll have little children like the firemen.'

'I can't have little children. Only big little children. We'll go to the Shelter and adopt two big little children and get a lot of publicity, like the movie stars. Wonderful kind movie stars, adopting poor little waifs. Waives? Waifs. We get our picture in the paper. Mr. and Mrs. James Malloy with the poor little kiddies they adopted out of the kindness of their hearts because Mr. and Mrs. Malloy are so big-hearted. Especially Mrs. Malloy. Darling, I hope

you don't mind being Mrs. Malloy? There's another one around
somewhere.'

'I know.'

'Do you mind?'

'Sure I mind, but what can I do about it?'

'Maybe she'll marry somebody and then she won't be Mrs.
Malloy. Maybe she'll marry the Duke of Windsor. At long last I'm
gonna say a few God damn words of my own, you sons of bitches.
Maybe she'll marry Oswald Mosley?'

'Who? Mrs. Simpson?'

'Mrs. Malloy. I'm a great lover of music, Peggy.'

'I know.'

'Adeste fideles, laeti triumphantes. Venite, venite in Beth-le-hem,
I used to be a boy tenor. At SS. Peter and Paul.'

'SS. Peter and Paul sounds more like a ship.'

'That reminds me. Jonas, you know where Miss Henderson lives?
Well, start tacking, Jonas. That's where we're going. Everybody's
talkin'. They hadda have something new. Tacking. I love all music,
Peggy. You know that, don't you?'

'Yes.'

'You know I love you, too, don't you, Peggy?'

'Yes.'

'Do you know that?'

'Yes, I guess so.'

'That's right. At least I love you as much as I can love anybody
that isn't James Malloy. I hate him.'

'I'm James Malloy, too.'

'What?'

'I said I'm James Malloy, too.'

'God knows I hope you mean what I think you do.'

'I do.'

'Kiss me.'

'All right.' She kissed me. 'I think I'd like to get a little tight,
too.'

'I don't blame you. I always get nervous when I'm sober and
someone's tight and I'm with them. But you gotta go some, my
sweet.'

We stopped at the Trocadero and there was hardly anyone there.
We had Lanson 1926. 'Drink up, sweet. You gotta go some. How
I love music. Frère Jacques, Cuernavaca, ach du lieber August. All

languages. A walking Berlitz. Berlitz sounds like you with that champagne, my sweet, or how you're gonna sound.' We drank a quart of champagne and Peggy began to get a little tight.

'Waiter!' I called. The waiter came.

'There's a drunken man,' I said.

'Where, sir?' he said.

'Here. Me,' I said.

'Yes, sir.'

'Oh, yeah? You wanna make sumpn of it? Where's Billy Wilkerson?'

'He isn't here, sir.'

'If this place is good enough for me it's good enough for him. Let's get outa here, Peggy.'

'All right. I'm willing. Woo-woo!' We left, both saying woo-woo quietly.

Jonas had the car parked on Sunset instead of on the parking lot, which was a good thing. We got in, and Peggy leaned forward. 'Jonas,' she said.

'Yes, Miss Henderson.'

'The stockings were hung by the chimney with care. Finish it.'

'In hopes that St. Nicholas soon would be there,' said Jonas.

'Woo-woo,' said Peggy.

'None of your lip,' I said. 'Yes. Some of your lip.'

'Here,' she said. 'Have some of my lip.'

'Merry Christmas, cried the warden, and the prisoners shouted balls.'

'Woo-woo. I drank that fast too champagne,' said Peggy. 'Woo-woo.'

'Whose little home shall we go to?' I said. 'Let's go to the Bide-a-Wee Home. The Ellin Speyer Home.'

'Let's go to the Wee Kirk o' the Heather. Who is Ellin Speyer?'

'Ellin Prince Speyer? You don't know her? You must be drunk, I'll take you home and put you to bed.'

'Aw, now you're hinting,' said Peggy. She tried to whistle.

'How're you ever gonna wet your whistle, when the whole darn world goes dry? You're too young for that. Sahara, we sympathise with you, Sahara, we'll soon be dry like you. You're far too young for that, too. How dark and still to-night, by the old distillery. I'm a different generation, Peggy. I'm too God damn old for you.'

'Woo-woo.'

'I am.'

'Woo-woo.'

'All you can think of is woo-woo.'

'Woo-woo.'

'Home, Jonas,' I said.

'Woo-woo. No. My home.'

'Stop at the Seven Seas, Jonas.' We drove to the Seven Seas, and we were the only people there. We had more champagne. The waiters stood around trying to smile, now and then slapping imaginary dust off the table-cloths. 'Are you my baby?'

'Yes.'

'Bore a hole, bore a hole—'

'Stop it! I've changed. I'm dignified now.'

'I like to think of old Bethlehem, to-night. Yes, I like to think of old Bethlehem. And old Allentown, and old Easton. And Catasauqua.'

'I don't.' Then suddenly: 'I've got to go home. Come on.'

Jonas drove us to her house. We sang on the way, and necked while we sang. She hummed 'Some Day I'll Find You', and I simply repeated, neeah-neeah, neeah-neeah. Outside her house she said: 'How do you like my new ring that some man gave me for Christmas?'

'Well—ostentatious. I hope he does right by you. Who is the guy? A girl doesn't get a ring like that for nothing.'

'He is my betrothed. I want you to be the first to know,' she said, 'Are you sure you want me to have it?'

'Well, temporarily. In about twenty years we'll wake up some day and realize it was only sex.'

'Come in for a minute,' she said.

We went in and Henderson was reading the paper. 'Oh, there you are. Malloy. Say, are you drunk? Peggy?'

'Not very. Just a little.'

'Now look here, Malloy. She's a young girl.'

'She's twenty-one,' I said.

'Twenty-one? That's young. How old are you? You must be thirty-five.'

'Oh, for Christ sake.'

'Did you wait supper?' said Peggy.

'I had mine, Keith just got home, too,' said Henderson.

'I'll go tell Millie I'm home.'

She staggered just a little and Henderson watched her. 'You wait,' she said to me.

Henderson stood there with the paper in his hand. 'Malloy, I want to have a talk with you.'

'Oh, for Christ sake.'

'Yes, for Christ sake. We might as well have this out now, unless you're too drunk.'

'I'm not too drunk but there's nothing to have out. You might as well get that straight.'

'Oh, no? Where was Peggy last night?'

'At Karen's. Why?'

'That's a lie. I happen to know she wasn't at Karen's.'

'Well, I happen to know she was. I took her there.'

'Yeah? What time?'

'After work. Why? Are you implying she was with me?'

'Implying nothing. This is the second time she said she was at Karen's, and the other time I *know* she was with you.'

'Listen, Henderson, it's a little late in the day for you to be coming around acting the stern parent.'

'That goes for me, too,' said Keith, in the doorway. He had a towel in his hand and was drying the inside of his ear.

'You. What kind of a brother *are* you? I guess you've known about this all along.'

'Thanks for the watch, Jim. Cats, it was swell. I didn't get you anything but I just couldn't.'

'Your money isn't wanted here, Malloy. I have enough to take care of my family.'

'Aw, why don't you shut up?' said Keith.

'Now you listen here—' said Henderson, taking a step towards Keith.

'I wouldn't if I were you,' I said. 'He'll knock your block off.'

'And you'd help him, I suppose.'

'Gladly. But he wouldn't need my help. Listen, Henderson, why don't you get wise to yourself? These kids have got along without you for a long time. If you want to be a father you have to be it in a different way.'

'I don't need any advice from you. I guess that's where they get their radical ideas from.'

Peggy came in, apparently having gone from the kitchen to the bathroom which she shared with Keith. 'I doused my face in cold water,' she said. 'Keith, look,' She held out the ring finger.

'Cats! What is that?'

'Star sapphire. See it, Father?'

Henderson looked down and frowned, then looked at her and at me. Peggy came to me and pulled my head down and kissed me.

'Jim! Congratulations,' said Keith, squeezing my hand. He kissed Peggy, and Henderson shook hands with me. 'I'm sorry,' he said, and then he held out his hand and kissed Peggy's forehead. I think it was the first time he had kissed her. Anyway, Peggy looked around at everybody, sat down on the sofa, and then quietly passed out. We all laughed and Keith went to the kitchen and got Millie to put her to bed. We had a few drinks and then I left as soon as I could and went to a Christmas-tree-trimming party out in Beverly, and Jonas got me home somehow.

I did not go back to the studio until the Tuesday morning after Christmas, and when I did my stenographer said someone had been calling me almost every hour in my absence. That Tuesday afternoon she said I was wanted on the phone, and she said she was quite sure it was the same person who had been calling. Wouldn't give his name. I told her to put him on.

'Malloy?'

'Yes.'

'This is that friend of Pat's. Don't mention my name if you recognize my voice.'

'Yes. I know who it is.'

'Will you do me another favour? This is a big one.'

'What is it?'

'You know that place where I used to live?'

'Yes. I think so.'

'That's all right, if you don't remember. I sent you a telegram with just the address.'

'Yeah.'

'Well, this is the favour. Will you go there and there's a fairy there that runs the switchboard. Blonde-haired. About my age. You go to him and ask him if there was anybody there looking for me. Then I'll phone you to-morrow and you tell me. I can't call there myself because they may have the wires tapped.'

'That sounds pretty melodramatic,' I said.

'Well, will you do it? I'm going nuts,' said Miller. 'If there was anybody looking for me find out what he looks like.'

'All right. I'll go this afternoon, late,' I said. 'By the way, thanks for the tie.'

'Don't say that,' he said. 'Throw it away or they may trace it.'

'Jesus,' I said. 'You've got it bad.'

That was all the conversation we had. In a few minutes the telegram came, and late that afternoon I went to the address he gave, a sort of hotel on Gower Street. They called it a bachelor's club. You went up three steps and to the left as you went in there was a door and a window on one side of the hall. That was the office. The switchboard was behind the window.

'May I help you?'

I looked down and there was this fairy with a sun-lamp tan and almost platinum blond, wavy hair. He was sitting on a low chair behind the switchboard and he had to hold his head back, chin up, to see me. With just a little narrower face I swear he would have made a swell ad for Tangee lipstick.

'I'm a friend of Mr. Miller's.'

'Oh, Donnie's? How is he? You're the second person asked for him to-day.'

'Well, that's what I came about. Could you tell me who else was looking for him?'

'The party didn't leave his name. Very mysterious. He wanted to know all about Donnie. Of course I couldn't tell him much.'

'Oh, I'll bet you could.'

'I *beg* your pardon?'

'Skip it. What about this guy? What'd he look like?'

'Well—he was about, ah, a man of forty, perhaps? Not quite your height? With a nice head of hair for his age? That is, not bald. Nice teeth?'

'How was he dressed?'

'Oh, very conservatively. Nothing flashy. The business man type, you know.'

'Yes. What did he say?'

'Oh, just how long since I saw Donnie, and what did he look like. Oh, yes. He asked me if I ever cashed any cheques for Donnie. Me cashing cheques! Oh, I know who you must be. I've been wracking my brains. Are you Mr. Malloy?'

'Yes.'

'I *thought* I recognized you from your picture. I loved your book. It was so true to life even if it was a fantasy. I mean I believed it all the time. I really did. I wish I had a copy here, I'd ask you to autograph it, but my friend went away and took it with him.'

'Why, the dirty thing,' I said. 'I'll send you one. What's your name?'

'Noel Sherman. Not Lowell Sherman. *Noel* Sherman.'

'As in Noel Coward?'

'Yes, but it really is my name. My middle name,' he said. 'Will you really send me an autographed copy?'

'Of course I will. Noel Sherman. It's a pretty name. Well, thanks very much.'

'Oh, notta tall, Mr. Malloy. Glad to oblige.' He stood up and I left.

The next day Miller phoned and I told him Henderson was getting warm. That was the last I ever heard from Don Miller.

For the next week I was as industrious as I could be under the circumstances, they being an average of two parties a day at my friend's houses. It just seemed as though all my married friends decided that the Christmas-New Year's period was the time to give parties, and I wanted them all to meet Peggy. Not many of them knew her, because they mostly patronised a bookstore in Hollywood, not the Beverly one where Peggy worked. The women were nice to Peggy, and of course the men were too. They all wanted to know when we were going to get married, to which Peggy's answer was that we hadn't made up our minds, but soon, she said. I went around glowing, because it was a new thing to me. I was proud of Peggy and glad people liked her. I felt much older than Peggy, which of course I was; but I felt younger myself than I had in years. Maybe ever. My other marriage had not been very good, and there had been no engagement. My first wife was rich and older than I and divorced, and her friends used to make me feel like a God damn Marchbanks, although I think I really loved her at the time. So it was all new to me, and it was fun, and I guess it was kind of fun for my friends, practically all of whom had settled down to their homes and work and children and some extra-marital dabbling. They were mostly newspaper men I had known in New York, and their first or second wives, and all the men wrote or produced pictures. There were only two movie actresses in the lot, and they knew their place and were always trying to improve themselves,

like reading books and going to concerts and buying Picassos and
publicly smuggling contributions to the I.L.D. I guess they were
all right. Anyway the week passed, and there was a lot of talk about
giving parties for Peggy. The parties never came off, because in the
second week of the new year Peggy's father killed Keith.

On the second Wednesday morning after New Year's Peggy had
gone to the shop early as it was her turn to open it. Every other
day she opened up, her boss doing it on the alternate days. When
she was leaving the house she called to Keith to snap out of it and
get to school, and he called back to her that he was taking a couple
of cuts to go down to Vermont Avenue to the dentist. Her father
was not up yet when she left. (She had given notice at the shop. I
wanted to get married right away. She told her boss, who always
had been nice to her, that she would look around for a good girl to
take her place. Now I wish she had quit right away.)

At about eleven-thirty that morning Millie telephoned her and
told her to come, that something terrible had happened. Millie did
not make much sense, and it took all of Peggy's pleading to get
Millie to tell her what kind of terrible thing, and then Millie told
her that her father had shot her brother.

I am trying to give the straight facts on this first.

Peggy told her boss what little she knew, and he closed the shop
and they got into his car and at the corner of Santa Monica and
Rodeo they saw a motor-cycle cop he knew, and the cop gave them
an escort out of Beverly, then they got another somewhere along
Sunset and were at Peggy's house in less than fifteen minutes.

There were two police cars outside the house, and a small group
of people. Peggy and her boss went in, and her father was sitting
in the living-room with his head in his hands, with two cops leaning
against a bookcase, their caps on the back of their heads, and
smoking. Henderson had no coat or vest on and his shirt was open.

Keith was not here. They had taken him to hospital.

Henderson looked up just once and said: 'Don't ask me anything,
Peggy. All I can say, it was an accident.'

Peggy's boss picked out a nice cop and he went with them to the
hospital. When they got there Keith was in the operating room,
and Peggy had to wait. While she was waiting Karen's mother
arrived at the hospital, and she waited with Peggy, and then before
they brought Keith out of the operating room Karen arrived too.

The doctor in charge said it would be 'some time' before Keith
came out of the ether. He lied, and said Keith had about an even
chance to live. He had lost a lot of blood, and there were internal
haemorrhages besides. Then Peggy told Karen to phone me, but I
was not in my office. I had gone to a projection room to watch a
picture being run off, and after that I had gone to kill some time
before lunch with Don McGinnis, a writer, whose office was
nowhere near mine. I went off the lot for lunch, and did not get
Karen's message until around three o'clock. I went straight to the
hospital, but I did not see Peggy until around six-fifteen, five
minutes after Keith died.

He recovered consciousness a little sooner than they expected.
He opened his eyes, and when he did he was as conscious as you
or I. A detective was there, and a doctor and two nurses and Peggy
and Mrs. Waner. He said hello, faintly, and then the detective
began to ask him questions, like. 'Who fired the shot?' and 'How'd
it happen?' The poor kid knew he had to save breath, so he told
the detective only two things: 'It was an accident,' and 'It was my
fault,' and then he said to Peggy: 'Right hand up, Peggy. My fault.'
Then he said hello to Karen and she started to cry, and a sort of
bored look came into his eyes and he made that noise in his throat
and died. Peggy looked at him for a minute and then she heard the
doctor say to the detective: 'Remarkable. Seven hours. Why do you
know, that bullet—' That was when she came out.

She came right to me as though she had known exactly where I
would be, and she took my arm. I thank God I had sense enough
not to say anything. Then I saw a cop coming out of the room and
I asked him if it would be all right for me to take Miss Henderson
home, and he asked the detective, who said he saw no reason why
not. Peggy's boss came up to her and said: 'Miss Henderson,
anything I can do. If you want money, or anything. I'd consider it
a privilege.'

'Thank you, Mr. Milton,' she said. 'I'll let you know.' Then she
pressed my arm and we walked to the elevator and went out and
got in my car.

I offered her a cigarette, and she took it, and the lighter wouldn't
work. I reached for matches, but she said she didn't really want to
smoke. She looked at me a couple of times. She wanted to tell from
the expression of my face how she was taking it, or how I thought
she was taking it. A cop came up and told me he'd have to give

me a ticket if we didn't move on, and I showed him an honorary detective's badge that I had borrowed from Don McGinnis. 'Well, don't stay too long,' he said. 'They blame me if this place ain't clear.'

'Let's drive to the top of the mountain,' Peggy said.

We drove up, high above the broken Hollywood land-sign, and she took off her hat and rested the back of her head on the leather seat. Her hands were in her lap. Her pretty legs were stretched out straight under the dash. I sat and looked at her, and I wanted to kiss her, but I didn't. It was so quiet that I could hear the tiny sound as she moistened her dry lips.

'How does it feel to be a Catholic?' she said.

'Sometimes good, sometimes bad.'

'Do Catholics believe that when you die your soul goes up in the sky? To heaven, if they go to heaven?'

'The poor people do. The educated ones believe that heaven is a state, a sort of metaphysical state. At least I think that's right.'

'The soul doesn't rise, up in the air?'

'No.'

She waited. 'That was one of the reasons why I wanted to come up here. If *you* believed that, about their going up in the air, you'd be close to him. I don't believe it, but if you did I wanted to be with you while you believed it. Now I can never be a Catholic. The only thing I ever wanted from the Catholic Church I can't have. One little thing. But I guess he'll be just as alive down there, home. Oh, God! Oh, Jesus! He will be, Jim!' Then she broke, and so did I.

She stopped crying before I did, and this time she lit a cigarette and told me all she knew, starting by saying: 'I have to be practical now. He said my father didn't do it on purpose, and I believe him. I wouldn't believe him, but now I remember how my father looked when I got home. I wouldn't have believed him, because he would have lied. That's the way he was. Look how soon it's the past tense. He was.' She puffed on her cigarette. 'What will they do?'

'They'll hold him, your father. Probably for manslaughter. I think probably involuntary manslaughter, if he has anything like an explanation. A lot depends on you, maybe a little on me, and a lot on Millie. If they knew Keith didn't like your father, he'd have a tough tough time. What do you want to do?'

'I want him to go away so I'll never see him again.'

'Well, then I guess—I wish we knew what Millie told the cops. We can take a chance of repudiating what Millie might say. Hysterical coloured woman saying anything in a crisis.' I thought a minute. 'I know one thing you can do.'

'What's that?'

'You can say you're going to get a lawyer for your father. I'll give you the money. Then when they ask around they'll find out how much you loved Keith, so they won't think—I have to be blunt, Peggy.'

'I know.'

'Well, they won't think you were, oh, relieved by Keith's death. See what I mean? You're the loving sister, but you're also the loving daughter, convinced that it was accidental. I know a hell of a good lawyer in Pasadena. He doesn't try criminal cases, but he'll know the best one to get. I'll call him right away as soon as we leave here. By that time they'll have taken your father downtown and booked him. They won't let him out on bail. At least for a while. Depends on what they decided to do. This is a good time of year, you know.'

'Why?'

'Well, no election going on or coming up. When there's an election coming up the D.A. tries to get as many convictions as he can to make him look good. If your father has a good defence, they're likely to figure on saving the expense of a trial. I'll do all I can.'

'I know you will,' she said. 'All I want is to get him away from here and never come back.'

I took my arm away from her and put my hands on the wheel. 'What about us? You're alone now. Let's get married as soon as we can.'

'There's no hurry, is there?' she said. 'Either way.'

'What do you mean, either way?'

'Well, I don't know. There's no hurry.'

We did it as we planned, and it came out as we wanted it to. I telephoned my Pasadena friend, and he made a good suggestion: not to get the local Leibowitz, but to get a less conspicuous but able lawyer for Henderson. The idea being that the Fallons and the Rogerses often get a case tried by the newspaper reporters before the suspect is indicted. People think the suspect is guilty because he hires the top lawyer.

They booked Henderson on suspicion of murder, but that was as far as it got. The detectives had to make a report that favoured Henderson, and the Coroner's jury report that followed gave a verdict of accidental death, and so the complaint deputy in the D.A.'s office refused to issue a complaint. The only worry, Millie, was out of the picture, because she was not in the house when the shooting occurred. She was five blocks away, at a market. Peggy, acting the loving daughter, was convincing. They asked me a few questions, but they didn't pay much attention to anything I said.

It was a one-day story in the papers, and not a very good one. The father was a private detective for a surety company, and had a permit for the .38 detective special, not in California, it was true, but in New York, where the Sullivan Law is tough about carrying revolvers. This information must have interested Don Miller, because there was a picture of Henderson on an inside page of the *Herald-Express*, and one enterprising reporter wrote that Henderson was in California in connection with some stolen traveller's cheques. This information cost Henderson his job.

He was realeased in less than a week after Keith was killed, and he aroused no suspicion by making preparations to leave. I never knew whether he made the decision unaided, or if Peggy told him to go away.

The day before he left he came out to see me at the studio.

I did not get up when the stenographer led him in. She knew who he was, and she could hardly take her eyes off him. For her benefit I was cordial to him, and then I got up and closed the door.

'Cigarette?' he said.

'I have some,' I said.

'I guess you know I lost my job,' he said.

'Peggy told me.'

'I'm going away,' he said.

'I know. When?'

'To-morrow. I'm going up to San Francisco. I figure it's better not to leave the state. I used to know a couple fellows in the Army. I might be able to get something up there.'

'Probably.'

'Malloy,' he said. 'you're making it tough for me. I guess I know what you think. You're thinking, here's a man that killed his own son, the brother of the girl I'm going to marry. I guess you wish

I'd get the hell out of here, the way Peggy can't stand the sight of me. Can anybody hear me?'

'Not if you don't talk too loud.'

'Malloy, I'm a young man, comparatively. Or I was. Now I'm an old man. I'm not looking for any sympathy. Most of my life I've been a louse, a bastard. Some of the time I had a good time, sometimes not. I was kicked out of college for something I didn't do. I have a letter somewhere to prove it. My own fraternity brothers thought I stole a gold watch and chain, and they asked me to hand in my pin. I did, and I was so surprised I didn't make any stink about it, so they believed I was guilty and I was kicked out. Then five or six months later they caught the guy that did it red-handed, and they wrote me a letter and sent me my pin. Here it is. But by that time I didn't give a God damn. I was one of those fellows, give a dog a bad name, and by that time I was living off a whore in Baghampton, New York.

'Well, I've been a lot of things in my time. I was indicted twice, money matters, but they could never make it stick, so I never did time. Then I've been in legitimate business several times and twice in my life I've had a credit rating of over a hundred thousand dollars. But I don't know, I knew a dame one time that was pretty good at fortune-telling. Palmistry. She looked at my hand and she said she wouldn't tell me what she saw. I'll bet she'd feel pleased with herself right now.

'Anyway, one thing, I've always been pretty good at sizing up people, and I became a private detective, because I can get to know people easily, and I never forget a face. And, I'm a good liar. Convincing. But you know I'm telling you the truth. For instance, I was within a week of catching up with your friend, Schumacher, alias Donald R. Miller. Now I have no job, which is a break for him. Probably for you, too, but that's not what I came to tell you about. You know what I came here for?'

'Money?'

'No. I'll take some if you give it to me, but I don't give a damn if you offer it to me or not. I came here, Malloy, because you're going to marry my daughter. As bad a father as I've been, she's my own flesh and blood and I'm proud of her. Maybe she wouldn't have been as good as she is if she'd had the kind of breaks she deserves. Her mother was—well, her mother was all right, too. 'What I came here for. The whole world knows I killed my own

son, but I'm the only one in the world knows how it happened. I'm
going to tell you so you can tell Peggy some time, whether you like
it or not. And it's the truth.

'The morning he was killed he came in my room and I was
getting dressed. I had my gun on the bureau and I was tying my
tie when he came in my room. He stood there and looked at me a
minute, and I said, "What is it, son?" And he called me a son of
a bitch or bastard or something, and I asked him what was the
matter? Then he yelled at me. "God damn you," he said, "if you
ever put a finger on Karen Waner again, I'll kill you."

'Well, I pretended I didn't know what he was talking about, but
I knew. The night before I had a date with this Waner kid. I met
her down there at Third and Rossmore. She came down there in a
taxi and she got in the car I had and we drove to Long Beach. We
had a lot of drinks. On the way back I lost my way, and it wasn't
any gag. I was lost. We ended up near the oil wells. Well, I made
a pass at her and I thought she liked it. Hell's bells, she was willing
to go out with me without letting anyone know it, and I figured
what I figured. What anybody'd figure under the circumstances. I
was her friend's father and she looked like the most beautiful
piece—well, anyway, the first thing I knew she was fighting me off.
I thought that was put on, but she kept it up so I started the car
and we came back to Hollywood. I guess I tore her dress.

'The next morning she must have been afraid Peggy'd find out
or something like that, because she called up and Keith took the
call, and what she told him I'll never know, but he must have sat
there a while, burning, and I guess he liked her more than he ever
let on. Be that as it may, he came in and the way I told you, called
me a bastard and I told him to calm down, and then he got up.
Well, at that very minute I happened to have my gun in my hand,
putting it in my hip pocket. It was a detective special, which is a
very dangerous thing to fool with. The next thing to hair trigger,
this was, and a .38. Short barrel. You probably know what they're
like.'

'Sure.'

'I had it in my hand, and I was looking at myself in the mirror,
when he grabbed my arm. The gun went off, and got him right
here. I don't see how it didn't kill him right away. Instantly. I'm
glad it didn't, though, because he knows what I said to him when
he fell to the floor. That's between him and me, but I think the kid

knew it was an accident. I sound like a heel to say it, but it was his own fault. He said so on his deathbed. I think for the first time he knew that no matter how much a louse I was, I wanted to change. But with a guy like me, the life I led, these changes don't come all of a sudden.' He stopped. 'Or *maybe* they do, Malloy. Maybe they do. In the last week I've changed. I don't know.

'Well, there it is, there's my story. You be good to Peggy, and some time the time may come when you can tell her what I just told you. I'll never bother you or her. I'm disgusted.'

I waited for him to say something more, but he didn't. He started to get up. He reached for his hat.

'Would five hundred bucks help you?' I said.

'One hundred bucks would help me.'

'I'll let you have five,' I said.

'You'll never get it back,' he said.

'I know,' I said. I started to write the cheque. 'Henderson, I think I believe you.'

'I don't *give* a damn any more. I've told you the truth.'

'I'll give you the address of my agent. If you get in a bad jam, I mean you're badly on the nut or something like that, you write me care of this guy, and I'll let you have some more. On one condition.'

'That I never bother Peggy. Don't worry. And thanks for the offer, but I'll never bother you, either. I don't think I will. If I do, don't send me any money. It'll only go for booze. That's what this is going for.'

He had half a load on now, but was carrying it well.

'Here's your five. The bank in Beverly will cash it right away. They may call me, but that'll only take a minute.'

'Thanks,' he said. 'Well, good luck.' He looked at me and half smiled. He picked up the cheque, which I had laid on the desk in front of him. 'You wouldn't even hand it to me, would you?'

'Nope.'

'Well, take care of Peggy,' he said. 'Good-bye, Mr. Malloy.' And he left.

Peggy stayed in the litte house for about a month after her father left, and during that time I saw her nearly every night. We went to the movies a few times, but one night on the way from the theatre to the car she said she couldn't help thinking that the way a shot sounded in the picture must have been the way the shot sounded when Keith was killed. After that we stayed away from the movies. Instead we would go for long rides, long conversationless rides to Pomona and Santa Barbara, or nearer places when we had less time. Then we formed another habit, that of going to a late spot that I knew of, where the fellows from the dance orchestras would meet after work and have jam sessions. Nobody knew Peggy. Nobody wanted to. The life of the place was the jam session, and non-musicians went there under sufferance. I kept my own liquor there, and it was a good place for us, because Peggy had been developing a fondness for brandy.

During that month or so I expected, and observed, changes in Peggy, just as anyone would have. Her drinking, for instance. It had become a serious matter with her, almost a job. She always had been one to take a drink, but she had given it a holiday spirit. Now she had become a drinker. Well, she was a healthy girl, and she could take it; never got mean or noisy. I drink too fast myself, but now she was taking drink for drink with me. I didn't like it, but I never said anything, because she would have tried to explain what neded no explaining.

Herbert often phoned her, but I don't think she saw him, unless he came to the shop (she wisely went back to work almost immediately). Otherwise she saw only Karen and me. One night as that first month was ending I suggested dinner at my house, and she said all right. It was the first time she had been there since Keith was killed. Jonas and his wife turned out a good dinner, and after dinner we sat in the library, a small room with sets of books and tennis trophies that had been left behind by the owner of the house. There was a Capehart in the room, and I put on some records and we sat and drank Courvoisier until about ten-thirty or so.

'Turn that thing down,' she said. 'Or turn it off altogether.' I turned it off.

When I came back to the sofa, she said: 'Jim, I know what you're going to say in a little while.'

'Do you?'

'Yes. I'm sorry, Jim,' she said, and held out her hand and I saw the star sapphire was in it.

'Oh,' I said. I stood up and walked to the other side of the room and sat on an uncomfortable straight chair. 'I don't suppose you'd have any reasons.'

'You know the reasons,' she said.

'Do I?' I said. 'Well, anyway, keep the ring.'

'No, you take it.'

'No. When I gave it to you I put it up to you where you wanted to wear it. It was a Christmas present. So you keep it.'

'All right. Thanks. You can always have it back. Do you want to take me home now?'

'Not unless you want to go.'

'I don't, but I thought you might want me to.'

'No,' I said. We had a lot more to drink, and then we had a messy scene that I am ashamed of, and she made me take her home. I telephoned her the following night, but she told me she had a date with Herbert. After that I called her twice, late at night, when I was drunk and afraid, but she would not see me, and the next time I felt like that I remembered Charlotte, whom I had not seen since the night she was with Miller. Charlotte is all right.

Then my contract was expiring at Metro and there was some talk of a play of mine being produced in New York, and I was getting ready to leave, so I went to the shop to say good-bye to Peggy. She was glad to see me. She started to smile when she saw me, and she kept smiling as she came up from the rear of the shop. 'I hear good news about you,' she said.

'About me?'

'The play. Congratulations. Is it the one I read last summer? Haven't they changed the title?'

'The title, and almost everything else,' I said.

'Not the main idea, I hope. Remember I said I thought there were too many characters. When are you leaving?'

'Tuesday or Wednesday.'

'Will you write to me?'

'What about, Peggy?'

'New York. The play. What you're doing.''

'That's the kind of letter I'd write to Karen or somebody like that.'

'You think I'm a heel, don't you?'

'No,' I said.

'If I wrote to you, will you—no. You write to me and tell me where you're staying. I wanted to talk to you, but I think a letter would be better.'

'Peggy, why don't you marry me and come with me? Are you in love?'

'I'd better write to you.'

'Will you kiss me good-bye?'

'Yes,' she said. 'Come to the back of the shop.' We went to the back of the shop and I knew from the way she kissed me that she was not in love with someone else. I had a feeling at the time that she probably had not even kissed anyone else. 'You must go now,' she said. 'Go on, Jim.' I knew from the way she said it that she meant it and could not be made to change her mind.

The next I heard from her was when she wrote to me in New York. Here is the letter:

Dear Jim:

I know now I never could have said what I have to say in a talk with you. The reason that I know it is that it is so hard to get started in a letter, without your distracting presence and equally distracting hands. With them I never could get started—if I ever do. (This makes the fifth attempt to-night.)

I love you, but as you have guessed and despite Francis Brett Young, love is not enough. It isn't even enough to know that not only do I love you, but that you also love me. I have known that since Christmas, but I did not entirely believe it until the day Keith died, when we went to the mountain. Since then, those first weeks, when you were kind and considerate and sensitive, I have wanted to do or say something to thank you, but when the time came at your house the same thing that kept me from telling you would not let me stay with you. The unreasonable aspect of that was that I wanted to stay with you, but here I am faced with the same suspicion, namely, that it wasn't only you I wanted to stay with. Almost anyone would have done. (Does this make any sense whatsoever?) Let me try again. Now don't go into a rage when I tell you this, but please read on and let me finish and then try to understand.

The trouble has been that you reminded me too much of my father, and at the same time you reminded me of Keith. I could not live with or sleep with that combination. All I wanted from you was the thing that you were giving me: peace, or silence in which to think. To return to your reminding me of my father, I do not mean physically (although your head is shaped like his). I refer to the way you *are*, the kind of life you have led, which in curious ways reminds me of my father. You are not his generation, but you are not mine, either. You both have the same attitude towards life, which in a phrase is 'To hell with it.' At a time when I needed stability in someone, you gave me stability, and for that I was and am grateful, but, dear Jim, that could not last forever. I am not blaming you, but I think I was right in not seeing you because your dutiful stability was apt to exhaust itself while I still needed it. In one sense, it did. The night we had dinner at your house, the stability was beginning to crack, too soon. One more week might have made the difference, but I will not swear to that.

As to you reminding me of Keith, that is true too, but for an altogether different reason. When you are gay, you seem as young as Keith (and sometimes when you are not gay). If we were married, or if we had been married these past two months, the resemblance or things you have in common with Keith would have been unbearable. What I really want to say is that I have known so few men intimately that when one of the three men I have known intimately in the past six months, kills the man I loved best in the world, the third man is unfortunately identified with the other two. I grew to know my father and to think he had a certain charm. Then he killed Keith, and that left you, and somehow I resented you. I begin to realize that I have been resenting all men. If Herbert were not a sort of 'cripple' as he calls himself. I could not stand him; but because of his poor health he is not a normal man, and another good thing about Herbert is that he will talk to anyone who will listen, which makes it very easy for me. He sits with me while I get tight, talking away, and never letting my glass become empty.

I have been sitting here since I finished the last paragraph, and I have come to the conclusion that it was a good thing to write this letter, despite the fact that it is not a good letter and does not say half what I wanted to say. But it is making me think, and it is about time I did some straight thinking. I think if you were with me this minute we should be closer than at any time since Keith died, but I also think it is better that you are in New York. When you come back I will still be at the shop. My salary has been increased, and the boss is talking about taking a trip to Europe, leaving me in charge. Perhaps I shall turn into an old-maid book-shop owner, an old maid with her memories. (But knowing myself, and knowing that inevitably you will return to Hollywood, I doubt

that.) Be nice to the New York girls, but not too nice. I want you
to be unattached when you come back here. Karen sends love and
so do I, and I don't know which kind she means or which kind I
mean. And write to me.

PEGGY.

My play was an inconspicuous success, and I stayed around New
York half the summer, and then they sold the play to the movies
for 60,000 dollars and I went back to Hollywood for Universal. All
I could think of on the plane was that I was going to see Peggy,
and how rich I was. I did not tell her exactly when I would arrive.
I had written her 'news' letters, and had had two news letters from
her. I arrived at the airport on a Sunday, just before noon, and I
telephoned her at home, at her new apartment, but there was no
answer. That night I saw her at the Troc, and she was with my
friend Don McGinnis and two other people, all very tight. The next
night I had a date with her, and she stayed with me, but never
after that. She has not made up her mind about me, or probably
anything else. She goes to the Trocadero often, but hardly ever
more than two or three times with the same man. I guess we are
all washed up. Karen thinks so.

CHAPTER 2

The Public Career of Mr. Seymour Harrisburg

Seymour M. Harrisburg put away the breakfast dishes and took off his wife's apron and hung it in the kitchen closet. He frowned at the clock, the face of which was an imitation dinner plate, and the hands of which were a knife and fork. He tiptoes to the bedroom, put on his vest, coat and hat, and with one glance at the vast figure of his wife, he went to the door of the apartment. Opening the door he looked down and saw, lying on the floor, the half-clad body of Leatrice Devlin, the chorus girl who lived in the adjoining apartment. Thus began the public career of Seymour M. Harrisburg.

Miss Devlin was quite dead, a fact which Mr. Harrisburg determined by placing his hand above her heart. His hand roved so that no mistake was possible. The body was clad in a lacy negligée, and part of Miss Devlin's jaw had been torn away by a bullet or bullets, but she had not been disfigured beyond recognition.

Mr. Harrisburg, observing that there was some blood on his hand, wanted to run away, but it was five flights down to the street in the automatic elevator. Then his clear conscience gave him courage and he returned to his apartment and telephoned for the police. He readily agreed not to touch anything and not to leave, and sat down to smoke a cigarette. He became frightened when he thought of what was lying on the other side of the door, and in desperation he went to the bedroom and shook his wife.

'Get the hell out of here,' said Mrs. Harrisburg.

'But, Ella,' said Mr. Harrisburg. 'The girl next door, the Devlin girl, she's been murdered.'

'Get out of here, you little kike, and leave me sleep.' Mrs. Harrisburg was a schicksa.

His repetition of the news finally convinced Mrs. Harrisburg, and

she sat up and ordered him to fetch her bathrobe. He explained
what he had come upon, and then, partly from his recollection of
what he had seen, and partly from the complicated emotion which
his wife's body had aroused, he became ill. He was in the bathroom
when the police arrived.

They questioned him at some length, frankly suspicious and
openly sceptical until the officer in charge finally said: 'Aw, puup,
we can't get anything out of this mugg. He didn't do it anyhow.'
Then as an afterthought: 'You sure you didn't hear anything like
shots? Automobile back-firing. Nothing like that? Now think!'

'No, I swear honest to God, I didn't hear a thing.'

Shortly after the officers completed the preliminary examination,
the medical examiner arrived and announced that the Devlin
woman had been dead at least four hours, placing her death at
about 3 a.m.

Mr. Harrisburg was taken to the police station, and submitted
to further questioning. He was permitted to telephone his place of
employment, the accounting department of a cinema-producing
corporation, to explain his absence. He was photographed by four
casual young men from the press. At a late hour in the afternoon
he was permitted to go home.

His wife, who also had been questioned by the police, had not
missed the point of the early questions which had been put to Mr.
Harrisburg. Obviously they had implied that there might have been
a liaison between her husband and Miss Devlin. She looked at him
again and again as he began to make dinner. To think that a hard-
boiled man like that cop could have believed for one minute that a
woman like Devlin would have anything to do with Seymour. . . .
But he had thought it. Mrs. Harrisburg wondered about Seymour.
She recalled that before their marriage he was one of the freshest
little heels she had known. Could it be possible that he had not
changed? 'Aah, nuts,' she finally said aloud. Devlin wouldn't have
let him get to first base. She ate the meal in silence, and after dinner
she busied herself with a bottle of gin, as was her post-prandial
custom.

Mr. Harrisburg, too, had noticed the trend of the official questions, and during the preparation of the meal he gave much specu-
lative thought to the late Miss Devlin. He wondered what would
have happened if he had tried to get somewhere with her. He had
seen two or three of the men she had entertained in her apartment,

and he felt that he did not have to take a back seat for any of them.
He deeply regretted the passing of Miss Devlin before he had had
an opportunity to get around to her.

At the office next morning, Mr. Harrisburg realised that the
power of the press had not been exaggerated. J.M. Slotkin, himself,
vice-president in charge of sales, spoke to Mr. Harrisburg in the
elevator. 'Quite a thing you had at your place yesterday,' said Mr.
Slotkin.

'Yes, it sure was,' said Mr. Harrisburg.

Later, after he had seated himself at his desk, Mr. Harrisburg
was informed that he was wanted in the office of Mr. Adams, head
of the accounting department.

'Quite a thing you had at your place yesterday,' said Mr. Adams.

'Yes, it sure was,' said Mr. Harrisburg. 'Geez, I'll never forget
it, reaching down and feeling her heart not beating. Her skin was
like ice. Honest, you don't know what it is to touch a woman's skin
and she's dead.' At Mr. Adams request Mr. Harrisburg described
in detail all that had taken place the preceding day.

'Well, you sure got in all the papers this morning, I noticed,' said
Mr. Adams. 'Pictures in every one of them.' This was inaccurate
but certainly Mr. Harrisburg's picture had been in five papers.

'Yes,' said Mr. Harrisburg, not knowing whether the company
applauded this type of publicity.

'Well, I guess it's only a question of time before they get the man
that did it. So any time you want time off to testify, why, only say
the word. I guess they'll want you down at headquarters, eh? And
you'll have to appear at the trial. I'll be only too glad to let you
have time off. Just so you keep me posted,' said Mr. Adams with
a smile.

Throughout the day Mr. Harrisburg could not help noticing how
frequently the stenographers found it necessary to go to the pencil
sharpener near his desk. They had read the papers, too, and they
had not missed the hints in two of the smaller-sized journals that
Mr. Harrisburg knew more than he had told the police. Hardly a
moment passed when Mr. Harrisburg could not have looked up
from his work and caught the eye of a young woman on himself.
At lunch time Mr. Harrisburg was permitted and urged to speak
of his experiences. The five men with whom he lunched almost
daily were respectfully attentive and curious. Mr. Harrisburg,
inspired, gave many details which he had not told the police.

The only unpleasant feature of the day was his meeting with Miss
Reba Gold. Miss Gold and Mr. Harrisburg for months had been
meeting after business hours in a dark speakeasy near the office,
and they met this day. After the drinks had been served and the
waiter had departed Mr. Harrisburg got up and moved to Miss
Gold's side of the booth. He put his arm around her waist and took
her chin in his hands and kissed her. She roughly moved away.
'Take your hands off me,' she said.

'Why, Reba, what's the matter?' said Mr. Harrisburg.

'What's the matter? You don't think I didn't get it what they
said in the papers this morning. You and that Devitt or whatever
her name is. Ain't I got eyes?'

'Geez, you don't mean to tell me you believe that stuff. You don't
mean to tell me that?'

'I certainly do. The papers don't print stuff like that it it ain't
true. You could sue them for liable if it wasn't true, and I don't
hear you saying you're going to sue them.'

'Aw, come on, don't be like that,' said Mr. Harrisburg. He
noticed that Miss Gold's heart was beating fast.

'Take your hands off me,' she said. 'I and you are all washed
up. It's bad enough you having a wife, without you should be mixed
up with a chorus girl. What am I, a dummy, I should let you get
away, with that?'

'Aw, don't be like that,' said Mr. Harrisburg. 'Let's have a drink
and then go to your place.'

'Not me. Now cut it out and leave me go. I and you are all
washed up, see?'

Miss Gold refused to be placated, and Mr. Harrisburg permitted
her, after a short struggle, to depart. When she had gone he ordered
another drink and sat alone with his thoughts of Miss Devlin, with
whose memory he rapidly was falling in love.

The next day he purchased a new suit of clothes. He had been
considering the purchase, but it now had become too important a
matter for further postponement. What with being photographed
and interviewed, and the likelihood of further appearances in the
press, he felt he owed it to himself to look his best. He agreed with
his wife that she likewise was entitled to sartorial protection against
the cruelty of the camera, and he permitted her to draw two hundred
dollars out of their joint savings account.

In the week that followed Mr. Harrisburg made several public and semi-public appearances at police headquarters and other official haunts. He was photographed each time, for the Devlin Mystery had few enough characters who could pose. The publicity increased Mr. Harrisburg's prestige at the office, Mr. Adams being especially kind and highly attentive each time Mr. Harrisburg returned to tell what line of questioning the authorities were pursuing. Miss Gold alone was not favourably impressed. She remained obdurate. But Mr. Harrisburg had found that Mr. Adams' secretary, who was blonde and a Gentile, was pleased to accompany Mr. Harrisburg to the speakeasy, and was not at all the upstage person she seemed to be in the office.

Then one day the police investigations began to have results. A Miss Curley, who had been one of the late Miss Devlin's intimates, admitted to the police that Miss Devlin had been annoyed by her former husband, one Scatelli, who had made threats against her life. according to Miss Curley. The night of the murder Miss Devlin had said over the telephone to Miss Curley: 'Joe's around again, damn him, and he wants me to go back and I told him nuts. He's coming up to-night.' Miss Curley explained that she had not spoken earlier in the case because Scatelli was a gangster and she was afraid of him. Scatelli was arrested in Bridgeport, Connecticut.

Mr. Harrisburg appeared before the Grand Jury, and it was after his appearance, when he was leaving the Grand Jury room with an assistant district attorney, that he first suspected that his news value had suffered as a result of Miss Curley's disclosures. For when he read the next day's newspapers he found only the barest mention of his name in one lone newspaper. Miss Curley, on the other hand, was all over the papers. Not only were there photographs of the young lady as she appeared after giving testimony, but the drama departments had resurrected several which showed Miss Curley holding a piece of black velvet in front of her fair white form, and several others in which she was draped in feathers. Scatelli's rogues' gallery likenesses received some space.

The baseball season had become interesting, and Mr. Harrisburg could not help noticing that at luncheon the following day his colleagues' sole comment on the Devlin murder was that they saw where the police got that guy that did it. The remainder of the conversation was devoted to satirical remarks about the Brooklyns. In the afternoon, after hours, Mr. Harrisburg waited for Mr. Adams' secretary, but she left with Mr. Adams. Miss Gold walked past him without so much as a how-do-you-do, the little slut. Passed him up cold.

Mr. Harrisburg did not feel that this state of affairs could continue, and when the case came to trial he was smartly clad and nodded a friendly nod to the cameramen. Their faces were blank in response, but Mr. Harrisburg knew that they would come around at the proper time. However, when he gave his testimony the attorney for the defendant caused mild laughter with his tripping up Mr. Harrisburg. Mr. Harrisburg, describing the finding of the body, declared that Miss Devlin's chest was like marble, it was so cold: and that he had taken away his hand and found the warm sticky blood on his fingers. The defence attorney suggested that Mr. Harrisburg was of more importance as a poet than as a witness, a suggestion with which the assistant district attorney secretly concurred. Getting down from the witness box Mr. Harrisburg looked hesitantly at the photographers, but they did not ask him to remain.

Mr. Harrisburg's press the following morning did not total more than forty agate lines, and of pictures of him there were none. There was something wrong, surely, and he was lost in pondering this phenomenon when he was summoned to Mr. Adams' office.

'Now listen, Harrisburg,' said Mr. Adams. 'I think we've been pretty generous about time off, considering the depression and all that. So I just wanted to remind you, this murder case is all through as far as you're concerned, and the less we hear about it from now on, why, the better. We have to get some work done around here, and I understand the men are getting pretty tired of hearing you talk and talk and talk about this all the time. I've even had complaints from some of the stenographers, so a word to the wise.'

Mr. Harrisburg was stunned. He stopped to talk to Mr. Adams' secretary, but all she had to say was: 'I'm busy, Seymour. But I want to tell you this: You want to watch your step.' She refused to meet him that afternoon, and by her tone she seemed to imply, 'any other afternoon.' At luncheon Mr. Harrisburg was still so amazed that one of his colleagues said: 'What's the matter, can't you talk about anything but that murder, Seymour? You ain't said a word.'

Nor was there an improvement in the days that followed. Even one impertinent office boy told Mr. Harrisburg pointedly that he was glad Scatelli was going to get the chair, because he was sick of hearing about the case. Mr. Harrisburg began to feel that the whole office staff was against him, and this so upset him that he made a mistake which cost the company two thousand dollars. 'I'm sorry, Harrisburg,' said Mr. Adams, 'I know its tough to get another job in times like these, but you're just no good to us since that murder, so you'll have to go.'

It was the next day, after he had passed the morning looking for another job, and the afternoon at a Broadway burlesque show, that Mr. Harrisburg came home and found a note tucked in his bankbook. The bankbook indicated that Mrs. Harrisburg had withdrawn all but ten dollars from their account, and the note told him that she had departed with a man whom she frequently entertained of an afternoon. 'I should have done this four years ago,' wrote Mrs. Harrisburg. Mr. Harrisburg went to the kitchen, and found that she had not even left him any gin.

CHAPTER 3

Sidesaddle

For perhaps twenty minutes the room had been all silence except for the efficient bustlings of the smiling maid and the clicks and snapping of his cigarette lighter. Then Josie's voice.

'Charles. Charl—? Oh, there you are. I was afraid you'd gone, without seeing me.'

'Nope. Just getting a load of this view,' he said. He turned from the window and reached out his hand.

'Aren't you going to kiss an old friend? And an old wife?' she said.

He kissed her. What the hell? The country was practically populated with men who wanted to kiss her. He kissed her again, this time full on the mouth, and he put his hand around her. She held it, or let him hold her, until an imaginary director might have called, 'We'll print that.'

'Sit you down,' she said. 'Do I look awful? Do you mind seeing me like this? You have often enough before. Her hair was tucked back over her ears, and if she had on any make-up (he suspected just a little) he was not able to tell where it began and ended.

'Well, when I knew you you didn't have—that.' He nodded down at her dressing gown, light-blue silk.

She smiled and made some sound through her nose that meant no. 'Nor this,' she said, indicating the Waldorf Towers; at least as much of it as they could see. 'Well, that's old stuff.'

'It's old stuff to *you*, Josie. They almost weren't going to let me up. I went to the desk and they gave me a card with a number on it, and I had to give it to the elevator operator. I almost went out and had a Wassermann.'

'Don't say things like that, Charlie.'

'Why not? That's what I felt like.'

'Well, the maid,' she said. 'What would you like to drink?'

'Oh, I don't know. What are you drinking?'

'Nothing before seven,' she said.

'What!'

'Do you *have* to say *what* that way?' she said. She gave him the well-known profile, and raised her voice slightly. 'Myrtle.'

'Yes, Miss Jefferson,' said the maid.

'Scotch-and-soda,' said Charlie.

'Scotch-and-soda for Mr. Evans, and I think a lemonade.'

'Did you just get up?' said Charlie.

'Just get up! I've been up since eight-thirty this morning. I went all the way downtown, thinking I was smart, to get my French visa, and I could have got in Radio City.'

'You could have got it through the travel agency, for that matter.'

'You would tell me that now.'

'Well, honey, I didn't have much chance to tell you before. I didn't know where you were till to-day.'

'It was in all the papers,' she said. 'But I don't suppose you read the movie columns. Oh, Charlie, let's not *quarrel*. I asked you to come here because I want a favour from you. That's being frank, isn't it?'

'Well, of course I knew—'

'Now, darling, don't say you knew, meaning you knew I wanted a favour or I wouldn't have called you. It's true in a way, but not the way that sounds. I mean I feel perfectly friendly. I don't believe in being a phony after you're divorced, but I'm not as mean as it sounds, and I'm at least frank.'

'All right. What is it you want? You know you'll get it, especially the way you look now. God damn it.'

She smiled in acceptance of the compliment. She watched Myrtle set down the drinks, and when Myrtle had departed she leaned forward. 'Charlie, have you still got that old sidesaddle?'

'What old sidesaddle?'

'That old sidesaddle of your mother's. Remember I used it the last time we went to Hartford.'

'Gee, I may have,' he said. 'Or at least it may still be in the stable at Hartford. Why? Don't tell me you want it?'

'I do want it. That's the favour.'

'That ought to be easy. That is, if it's still there, unless one of my sisters is using it. Let me think. I went home for Christmas. Nobody rode then. Last fall. Betsy. Come to think of it—I hardly ever go home, but it seems to me, I think Betsy rides side—I'm not sure—'

'Well, I am, and that's the whole point. Betsy rides sidesaddle. She rides both, but she prefers sidesaddle. I know it.'

'Mm. Then it's going to be tough, or at least it may be. You know, uh—well, Betsy hasn't got money to throw around on new saddles, and—'

'And Betsy hates me. Yes, I know.'

'Well, then why don't you buy one? My God, you can have one made, to fit you. That saddle was my mother's, and I must say, much as I loved my mother—'

'Don't look at me like some assistant director. I know I can have one made. I'll have one made, for Betsy. I'll give her the price of a new one, and a bridle, or a pair of boots.'

'Betsy's pretty tough,' he said. 'She never liked what you said about the family when—'

'Charlie, I know all about that. I'm sorry about it, and you know it was only publicity stuff. Now look here, I happen to want that saddle. *Everybody* has *new* things in Hollywood. I don't like new things. At least not new saddles and things like that. Can't you get it for me, darling?'

'You know I'd like to.'

'Do you want to know how much I want it? Before I left Hollywood Jack said to me, "If you see that ex-husband of yours while your there, I'll"—I don't know what he said. He hates you, just as much as Betsy hates me. He told me I could see anyone but you. He'd be furious, but I'm so dying to have that saddle that I had to take the chance. Please, Charlie. I'll give you the money and you can go over to that place over on Forty-sixth or wherever it is and pick out the best saddle they have, or have one made. I'll give you the money. I'll give you five hundred dollars. That ought to be enough. Then you can buy a saddle and bridle and one of those straps that goes round the horse's neck—'

'Martingale.'

'—and take it up to Hartford and bring back the other one. You can be back Sunday easily.'

'Betsy knows I haven't got that kind of money,' he said.

'Oh, tell her some story. Tell her the man ran into you on the street and wants your business again and made you this offer. Or tell her—*I* know. Tell her somebody ordered it and then didn't call for it, so you got it cheap. Please, will you do it for me, Charlie?'

He put down his glass. 'Josie, you really are a—'

She smiled. 'Don't say it, darling.' She put her arms around him and held him for a moment and then shut her eyes and kissed him. 'Then you can bring it here Sunday night. Jack doesn't get in till Monday morning.'

CHAPTER 4

Saffercisco

While Jack Grant is not the world's most famous movie actor, it can be truthfully said that he has been; and even to-day his name on the marquee of the Paramount in Palm Beach or the Majestic in Tamaqua, Pa., means box office. But it is not with his power as a draw that this little anecdote is concerned. Maybe it would be better to say that among his four or five wives (many persons are vague as to whether he ever actually was married to one of the ladies) are two of the, say, fifteen most popular movie actresses. And among those fifteen at least two more have been his mistress. That score more or less establishes the fact that Jack got around, and when he fell for Maude Hislip it was as much of a surprise to him as it was to anyone.

She came out to Hollywood on the crest. That is, she had been in one hit, one forced-run play, and several turkeys. Shortly after she came to Hollywood, she married Bobby Waterman, the writer. (He is the kind of writer whose name is inevitably followed by the appositional 'the writer.') They got veiled up and were together about two years when Jack met Maudie.

Well, he fell in love. He had met her at parties, but then suddenly one day he really saw her, and loved her dearly. He also liked Bobby Waterman. Jack thought it over and thought it over and talked with a friend (an old girl friend) about it, and he made up his mind that he had to marry Maudie. So he called her up and asked her if he might come to dinner the following Friday, and Maudie said she'd be delighted. What Jack wanted to do was to lay his cards on the table; say to Bobby, 'Bobby, I love Maudie and I want to marry her.' Open and above-board. Honest. Decent. Civilized. He could hardly wait till Friday. He consulted his old girl friend about what clothes to wear: whether to wear the tweed jacket and flannel slacks, or dinner coats, or tails. The girl friend said he would be wise to wear the tails; it was a momentous occasion, and besides he was at his handsomest in tails.

So that Friday Jack was dressed and ready at seven, and he had a couple of drinks and drove out to Santa Monica, arriving at Maudie and Bob's around eight o'clock. Bob was in riding breeches and coat, with a scarf around his neck, and he greeted Jack pleasurably and obviously sincerely. They had a drink together and a few more, and no sign of Maudie, but Jack didn't want to be hasty or gauche or anything like that, so he did not say anything. They had a lot of drinks, fast, and nine o'clock came and no sign of Maudie and no sign of dinner. And they were getting stewed. Jack read a lot, and they covered the world's literature, then they talked movie politics and exchanged funny stories about producers and things that had happened to them on location and all about horses and dogs, and Jack thought he never had met a more charming guy, and Bobby not only thought so, but in time came to the point of telling Jack so. 'I didn't know you were such a nice guy,' Bobby said. 'You know, I *like* you. I thought you were more or less of a heel at first, but you're all right. O.K. You ought to do this oftener—drop in for dinner.'

'Drop in?' said Jack. 'I didn't drop in. Wuddia mean drop in? Maude knew I was coming.'

'Did she? Didn't say anything to me about it. Oh, well, I don't care. Here you are, so let's have a powder, one more little powder, then we'll go in and graze. Wunnia say?'

'Sure, but what about Maude? Don't you think we oughta wait for Maudie?'

'Oh.' Bobby began to laugh quietly. He looked down into his drink and shook his head, signifying nothing. He kept it up until he exasperated Jack.

'What is this?' said Jack. 'Didn't Maudie expect me?'

'Don't think so. If she did, she didn't tell me, Jack.' Bobby cleared his throat and changed his tone. 'You know where she is, don't you? You don't mean to tell me that you don't *know* where Maudie *went*. Don't you know where Maudie is?'

'No, of course I don't. I had a dinner engagement right here in this house. Right *here*.' He made a gesture like an umpire indicating Strike One. 'Where is she?'

'Saffercisco.'

'Sa'Fra'cisco?'

'S-a-n Fran-*cis*co.'

'You mean on location, or what? A personal appearance?'

'No, no. No, no, no, no, no. Maudie is up in Saffercisco spending the weekend with Harry Lotterman, her director.'

'What do you mean?' said Jack.

'What do you mean, what do I mean? You know what I mean. She went away with Harry Lotterman for the weekend. Wunnia think I mean? Jack, you're not dumb. You're a big boy now. Wunnia mean, what do I mean? What kinda talk is that, Jack?'

'You mean to sit here and tell me your wife goes to Sa' Fra'cisco with a louse like that and you just sit here?'

Bobby looked at him a long time, wet his lips a couple of times, getting ready to talk, and then he gazed at his cigarette until he began to get cross-eyed. Then he said, 'Well, Jack I'll tell you. I wanna tell you something. Listen to me, Jack, while I tell you this. Maudie, the first time she did this I just couldn't stand it. It hurt me. It hurt me, Jack. And then the second time. That hurt me, too. Really did. Bu-u-ut then, you know you can only stand so much, Jack. Only so much. Then you begin to get used to it. I had to get used to it, Jack. And let me tell you something'—he leaned over and tapped Jack's knee—'Jack, old boy, you might as well get used to it, too.'

CHAPTER 5

Price's Always Open

The place where everybody would end up before going home was Price's. This was the second summer for Prices. Before that it had been a diner and an eyesore. The last man to run the diner had blown town owing everybody, and somehow or other had put a curse on the place. No one, not even the creditors, wanted to open up again, and time and the weather got at the diner and for two years it had stood there, the windows all smashed by passing schoolboys, the paint gone, and the diner itself sagging in the middle like an old work horse. Then last summer Mr. Price got his bonus and he went into the all-night-restaurant business.

The first thing he did was to get permission to tear down the diner and put up his own place. It was a corner plot, and he built his place twice as wide as the diner had been. The Village Fathers were only too glad to have Mr. Price build. In other times they would never have let the place go the way the diner had. The neatness of the village was always commented upon by new summer people, and bragged about by those who had been coming there for generations. But things being the way they were. . . . So Mr. Price built a sort of rustic place, which, while not in keeping with the rest of the village architecture, was clean and attractive in its way. All the signboards were simulated shingles, and the lettering has been described as quaint. Mr. Price frankly admitted he got his idea from a chain of places in New York. There was one neon sign that stayed on all night, and it said, simply, 'PRICE'S'. Nothing about what Price's was; everyone knew.

Mr. Price had one leg, having left the other somewhere in a dressing station back of Château-Thierry. He was not a cook but a house painter, and he had had to employ a couple of short-order cooks from New York and Boston. But Mr. Price was always there. Not that anyone ever wondered about it, but it might have been interesting to find out just when he slept. He was at his position near the cash register all night, and he certainly was there at noon when the chauffeurs and a few summer-hotel clerks and people like that would come in for lunch. As a matter of fact, he did not need much sleep. No day passed without his leg bothering him, and seeing people took his mind off his leg. Best of all, he liked late at night.

Saturday night there was always a dance at the yacht club. That was a very late crowd. The dances were supposed to stop at one, but if the stricter older members had gone home, the young people would keep the orchestra for another hour or two, and even after that they would hang around while one of the boys played the piano. The boy who played the piano was Jackie Girard.

They were a nice bunch of kids, practically all of them, and Mr. Price had known their fathers and mothers for years, or many of them. Sometimes the wife's family had been coming to this island for years and years; then she married the husband, a stranger, and the husband and wife would start coming here and keep coming. Sometimes it was the husband who was old summer people. Most of the present younger crowd had been coming here every summer for fifteen, twenty years. One or two of them had been born here. But Jackie Girard was Mr. Price's favourite. He was born here, and unlike the others, he lived here all year round.

Jackie had a strange life with the summer people, and it probably was that that made Mr. Price feel closer to him than to the others. The others were nice and respectful, and they always said *Mister* Price, just as Jackie did. But they were summer people, and the winters were long. Not that Jackie was here in the winter any more, but at least he came home several times in the winter. Jackie was at college at Holy Cross, and naturally his holidays were spent here.

The strange life that Jackie had apparently did not seem strange to him. He was not a member of the yacht club, naturally. Jackie's father was a carpenter, the best in the village; the best out of three, it's true, but head and shoulders above the other two. Henry Girard was a French Canuck and had been in the Twenty-sixth Division with Mr. Price, but never an intimate of Mr. Price's. Jackie had three sisters; one older, two younger. Jackie's mother played the organ in the Catholic church. The older sister was married and lived in Worcester, and the younger ones were in high school. Anyway, Jackie was not a member of the yacht club, but he was almost always sure of being invited to one of the dinners before the regular Saturday-night dance. He was one of the clerks at the hotel, and that, plus an occasional five or ten from his sister in Worcester, gave him just enough money to pay for gas and his incidental expenses. He could hold his end up. The only trouble was, except for Saturday and Sunday, he did not have much end to hold up.

There were gatherings, if not parties, practically every night of the week. Every Thursday, for instance, the large group of young people would split up into smaller groups, sometimes three, four, five, and after dinner they would go to the boxing matches. Jackie was not invited to these small dinner parties. He had been invited two or three times, but his mother had told him he had better not go. For herself, she wished he could have gone, but his father would not have approved. After Jackie had regretted the few invitations he got, the summer people figured it out that all he cared about was the yacht-club dances. He was the only town boy who was invited to yacht-club dances, and they figured that that was all he wanted. It did not take them long to decide that this was as it should be all round. They decided that Jackie would feel embarrassed at the smaller parties, but that he did not need to feel embarrassed at the club dances, because in a sense he was earning his way by playing such perfectly marvellous piano. But this was not the way Mr. Price saw it.

Almost every night but Saturday Jackie would drop in. Two nights a week he had been to the movies, which changed twice a week, but Mr. Price at first wondered what Jackie would do to kill time the other nights. Jackie would show up around eleven-thirty, and sit at the counter until some of the summer crowd began to arrive. They would yell at him, 'Hi, Jackie! Hi, keed! How's it, Jackie?' And Jackie would swing around on his stool, and they would yell at him to come on over and sit at a table with them. And he would sit at the table with whichever group arrived first. In the early part of the summer that did not mean any special group, because when the other groups would arrive, they would put all the tables together and form one party. Then there would be some bickering about the bill, and more than once Mr. Price saw Jackie grab the cheque for the whole party. It was not exactly a big cheque; you could not eat much more than forty cents' worth at Mr. Price's without making a pig of yourself, and the usual order was a cereal, half-milk-half-cream, and a cup of coffee; total, twenty cents. But you take fourteen of those orders and you have a day's pay for Jackie.

As the summer passed, however, the large group did break into well-defined smaller groups; one of six, several of four. By August there would be the same foursomes every night, and of these one included the Leech girl.

The Leeches were not old people, in the sense that some of them were. The Leeches belonged to the newcomers who first summered in this place in 1930 and 1931. They had come from one of the more famous resorts. Louise Leech was about twelve when her family first began to come to this place. But now she was eighteen or nineteen. She had a Buick convertible coupe. She was a New York girl, whereas most of the other boys and girls were not New Yorkers; they all went to the same schools and colleges, but they did not come from the same home towns. Some came from as far west as Denver, as Mr. Price knew from cashing their cheques. And even what few New York girls did come to this place were not New York friends of the Leeches. Mr. Leech was here only on week-ends and his wife was away most of the time, visiting friends who had not had to give up Narragansett. Louise herself was away a good deal of the time.

It was easy to see, the first summer Louise was grown up, that she was discontented. She did not quite fit in with the rest of the crowd, and she not only knew it but she was content not to make the best of it. Mr. Price could hear the others, the first summer he was in business, making remarks about Louise and her thinking she was too good for this place. And they had been saying something like it the early part of this summer, too. But after the Fourth of July, somewhere around there, they began to say better things about her. Mostly they said she really wasn't so bad when you got to know her. To which a few of the girls said, 'Who wants to?' And others said, 'She doesn't like us any better. We're still not good enough for her. But Sandy is.' Which did explain a lot.

Sandy—Sandy Hall—was from Chicago, but what with prep school and college and this place and vacation trips, he probably had not spent a hundred days in Chicago in the last seven years. In a bathing suit he was almost skinny, except for his shoulders; he looked cold, he was so thin. But Mr. Price had seen him in action one night when one of the Portuguese fishermen came in drunk and got profane in a different way from the way the summer people did. Sandy had got up and let the Portuguese have two fast hard punches in the face, and the fisherman went down and stayed down. Sandy looked at the man on the floor—it was hard to tell how long he looked at him—and suddenly he kicked him. The man was already out, and so there was no need to kick him, but the kick had several results. One was that Mr. Price brought a blackjack to work the next night. The other result was something Mr. Price noticed on Louise's face.

He had not had much time to take it all in, as he had had to leave the cash register to help the night counterman drag the fisherman out of the place. But he remembered the expression on the girl's face. It began to appear when the fisherman went down from the punches, and when Sandy kicked the man, it was all there. Mr. Price standing where he did, was the only one who caught it. He thought of it later as the way a girl would look the first time she saw Babe Ruth hit a home run, provided she cared about home runs. Or the way she would look if someone gave her a bucketful of diamonds. And other ways, that would come with experiences that Mr. Price was sure Louise never had had.

Sandy had not come with Louise that night, but Mr. Price noticed she went home with him. And after that night they were always together. They were part of a foursome of whom the other two were the dullest young people in the crowd. It took Mr. Price some time to determine why this was, but eventually he did figure it. The foursome would come into Price's, and Louise and Sandy would watch the others while they ordered; then Sandy would say he and Louise wanted the same, and from then on neither Sandy nor Louise would pay any attention to the other two. Stooges.

Another thing that Mr. Price noticed was that Jackie could not keep his eyes off Louise.

Along about the latter part of August, it was so obvious that one night Mr. Price kidded Jackie about it. It was one of the nights Jackie dropped in by himself, and Mr. Price said, 'Well, she isn't here yet.'

'Who isn't here?'

'The Leech girl.'

'Oh,' said Jackie. 'Why, did anybody say anything to you? Is that how you knew I liked her?'

'No. figured it out for myself. I have eyes.'

'You're a regular Walter Winchell. But don't say anything, Mr. Price.'

'What the hell would I say, and who to?'

'I'll be back,' said Jackie. He was gone for more than an hour, and when he returned the crowd was there. They all yelled as usual, but this time one of the girls added, 'Jackie's tight.' He was, rather. He had a somewhat silly grin on his face, and his nice teeth made a line from ear to ear. Several tables wanted him to join them and they were friendly about it. But he went to the table where sat Louise and Sandy and the others.

'Do you mind if I sit down?' he said.

'Do you mind?' said Sandy.

'No,' said Louise.

'Thank you. Thank you,' said Jackie. 'Go fights?'

'Mm-hmm,' said Sandy.

'Any good? Who won?'

'The nigger from New Bedford beat the townie,' said Sandy. 'Kicked the Jesus out of him.'

'Oh, uh townie. You mean Bobbie Lawless. He's nice guy. Za friend of mine. I used to go to high school—'

'He's yellow,' said Sandy.

'Certainly was,' said Louise.

'Nope. Not yellow. Not Bobbie. I used to go to high school with Bobbie. Plain same football team.'

'Where do you go to school now?' said Sandy.

'Holy Cross. We're gonna beat you this year.'

'What is Holy Cross?' said Louise.

Sandy laughed. Jackie looked at her with tired eyes.

'No, really, what is it?'

''Tsa college. It's where I go to college. Dint you ever hear of Holy Cross? Give another hoya and a choo-choo rah rah—'

'O.K.,' said Sandy.

'I'll sing if I wanta. I'll sing one of your songs. Oh hit the line for Harvard, for Harvard wins to-day—'

'Oh, go away,' said Sandy.

'Yes, for God's *sake*,' said Louise.

'Oh, very well, Miss Leech. Very well.' Jackie put his hands on the table to steady himself as he got to his feet, but he stared down into her eyes and for two seconds he was sober.

'Come on, Jackie, you're stewed.' Mr. Price had come around

from the cash register and had taken Jackie by the right arm. At that moment Sandy lashed out with a right-hand punch, and Jackie fell down. But he had hardly reached the floor before Mr. Price snapped his blackjack from his pocket and slapped it down on the front of Sandy's head. Sandy went down and there was blood.

'Anybody else?' said Mr. Price. By this time the night counterman had swung himself over the counter, and in his hand was a baseball bat, all nicked where it had been used for tamping down ice around milk cans. None of the summer crowd made a move; then Mr. Price spoke to two of the young men. 'Get your friend outa here, and get out, the whole goddam bunch of you.' He stood where he was, he and the counterman, and watched the girls picking up their wraps.

'Aren't you going to do anything?' Louise screamed. 'Chuck! Ted! all of you!'

"You get out or Ill throw you out," said Mr. Price. She left.

There were murmurs as well as the sounds of the cars starting. Thinking it over, Mr. Price agreed with himself that those would be the last sounds he ever expected to hear from the summer crowd.

CHAPTER 6

Hotel Kid

My first encounter with Raymond was about a week after I had arrived in the strange city. I was going down in the lift, thinking about death and love, when I felt my insides being pulled out as the car stopped at the eighth floor. The lift operator pulled the door open, and a boy of seven or eight stood in the doorway and said: 'Hey, Max, did you see my brother?'

'No,' said the operator.

The boy stared at the floor, meditating, and then he said: 'All right, Max. You can go. If you see him tell him I'm waitin' for him.'

The operator closed the door and we dropped slowly, the more slowly so he could turn and explain to me that 'That's Raymond. If you're gonna be here a while you'll get to know him all right. He's the craziest kid!'

'Yeah?' I said. 'Who is he?'

'Kid by the name of Raymond Miller. He lives here in the hotel. He's a little pest, and for a while there we usen't to stop at the eighth floor sometimes, because we knew it was Raymond, but Joe, one of the other operators, got in Dutch, so we have to stop now, regardless of whether we know it's Raymond or not.'

I saw Raymond for the second time under somewhat similar circumstances. This time he stopped the lift and asked for his brother, and then told Harry, the operator, that he could continue. 'Is that kid always looking for his brother?' I said.

The operator laughed. 'He ain't got a brother,' said Harry. 'That's a gag. You know. Like Gracie Allen on the radio, she's always talking about her lost brother, and this kid picked it up somewheres, I guess.'

A few days later the lift again stopped at the eighth floor, and this time a beautiful Jewess, about thirty years old, got on, and Max said: 'Good morning, Mrs. Miller.'

'Hello, Max,' she said. The car began the descent. 'Was Raymond pestering you again, or was it one of the other boys?" she said.

'It wasn't me,' said Max. "I guess it must of been one of the others. Why?'

'Well, he was swearing at you this morning. Not you personally, but just the whole damn bunch of elevator boys, as he said. So naturally I thought he must have got a little too fresh and somebody gave him a talking to. Don't hestiate to when he gets too fresh, and especially if he wants to go down to the lobby. I won't have him hanging around down there. He has plenty of room to play. . . .'

Late that same afternoon I had a date to meet someone in the lobby, and I was very early, so I was reading a paper, when I looked up, and there was Raymond, standing in front of me, apparently undecided between speaking to me, and, I suspect, punching my paper.

'Hello, there,' I said.

'Hello, Mr. Kelly,' he said, and smiled very broadly.

I knew what was expected of me, so I said: "Howd you know my name?'

'Asked,' he said. 'Asked Miss McNulty. She's the room clerk, Miss McNulty. The one over there." He pointed, and I looked over, and saw that Miss McNulty was looking our way and laughing. Raymond nodded at Miss McNulty, and them said to me: 'Do you like this hotel?'

'Yes, it's all right,' I said.

'Well, shake your head yes. Miss McNulty wants to know if you like it. She told me to ask you and if you said you did you were to shake your head yes.' I thought it was strange, but I obliged with a pretty vigorous shake. Raymond smiled *very* broadly then and nodded again at Miss McNulty, then he looked at me and laughed, and then he ran away.

It was some time later that I discovered what it was all about: Raymond had told Miss McNulty that I wanted to kiss her, and when she wanted him to tell how he knew that, he said he would prove it.

The next time I saw Raymond he stopped the lift and when he saw me he started to run. 'Hey, you,' I said. 'I want to talk to you.'

He came back and got on the lift. 'My mother doesn't allow me to go down to the lobby,' he said.

'That's all right,' I said. 'What was the idea of playing that trick on me the other day? I'm wise to you, Mr. Miller.'

'Are you gonna tell my mother?'

'No,' I said.

'Lemme off, Max,' said Raymond. Max stopped the car at the third floor and Raymond got off.

I suppose Raymond dodged me after that, because I did not see him for a week or so, and then he came over and sat with me in the lobby. 'Well,' I said. 'You're a stranger.'

"Huh?'

'I said you're quite a stranger. Where've you been keeping yourself?'

'Upstairs. I wasn't allowed to leave the floor without permission. My mother wouldn't let me.'

'Oh,' I said. 'What were you up to this time?'

'I didn't do anything,' he said.

'Come on,' I said.

'It wasn't me,' he said. 'It was another guy named Nathan Soskin. He comes up to play with me sometimes, and he put a pin in the elevator button and I got the blame for it. Somebody squealed and they said I did it. I get blamed for everthing. He was going to turn on the fire hose if I wouldn't of stopped him.'

'Well, you probably got away with a couple of things where nobody thought you did it.'

'Not many,' he said. 'Not many. I bet if somebody did turn on the fire hose I'd be blamed.'

'Well, you'd better not let any of your friends do it then.'

'Oh, I don't mean Nathan or them. I mean the drunks. Were you ever here when there was a convention?'

'Yes,' I said.

'Well, them. They do stuff like that. Boy—Some of the stuff they do! A man was killed here one time when I was seven. He got killed falling out the window but he was drunk.'

'How do you know?'

'How do *I* know? Told. All the bellboys said so, and Max and Harry and Joe and Mr. Hurley and Mr. Dupree and Lollie, the chambermaid. They all said the man was drunk. Boy, they do crazy stuff. When we lived in Chicago they turned on the fire hose. I was only a little kid then.'

'How old are you now? Eight?'

'Eight? Like fun. Nine, going on ten. You're from New York, aren't you?'

'Yes,' I said.

'That's a sucker town,' said Raymond. 'That's what my mother said. We're going there soon, maybe next week. My mother said there isn't any big money in this town so we're going to New York. I guess I'll see you if you go back there. My mother said it was just a hick town like all the rest, but they have big money there.'

'Well, I suppose that's true,' I said.

'I'd like to see the New York Giants sometime,' said Raymond. 'A friend of my mother's took me to see them one time when they were here. Do you *know* my mother?'

'Not to speak to,' I said. 'We've never met.'

'Oh,' said Raymond. 'Well, I guess I have to be going up. Mr. Hurley knows my mother to speak to. You can get him to make you acquainted. Well, so long.'

'So long,' I said.

CHAPTER 7

Of Thee I Sing, Baby

During the run of every successful revue, the press-agent, at some unimaginative point, gives in and writes one, two, or all of three formula stories. The first is the one about the girl who is not a chorus girl, really, but is only doing it for the fun; she is a member of the Knoxville, Tenn., Junior League. The second is the one about the sloe-eyed lady in the Living Picture number, who is a Phi Beta Kappa from the University of Winsconsin, and is taking an extension course, on Dante, at Columbia. The third story is about the girl who is going to renounce the show business and plans to enter a convent.

Grayce never has had that kind of publicity. The Junior League maintains no chapter in Maspeth, Queens, where Grayce's family resides. Grayce did not finish high school, so the press-agent cannot give her a Phi Beta key. And if Grayce ever mentioned going into a convent, it was this way: 'Heck, this town is as dead as Faust. I'm going to join a convent.' There is nothing about her, except her height and her figure, which separates her from possibly a thousand other girls who are eligible for the two hundred available jobs for chorus girls in the good productions.

In her seven years in the chorus, Grayce has been picked at about half the calls which she and a couple of hundred other girls have answered. This is a good average, but Grayce is a good type.

She is twenty-four years old, and looks that; no more, no less. She is tall for a girl: five feet seven. And right now when for the moment she is out of a job, she weighs a hundred and thirty-two. She talks about going to Madame Rasch's to take off the extra fifteen pounds which a beery idleness has put on. She hardly ever goes. She does not much care any more, because she wants to get in the dramatic end. It is estimated that the professional life of a chorine is ten years, but Grayce thinks that is three years too many.

Anyhow, it is so far as she is concerned. She takes after her father, who is as big as Faust. Two more chorus jobs, she says, and she will be washed up as a chorus girl. In fact, the only reason she says two more is that she misses the dressing-room. The gang in the dressing-room.

In her last show, Grayce never saw such a bunch of kids. There were eleven of them in the same dressing-room, and, counting herself, only three from New York. The rest were from California, and Pennsylvania, and places like that. There was even one from Europe: Germany. She was a German girl who came over here a couple of years ago and did not know a thing, but Grayce liked her and they even lived together for a while. The German girl was a good sport or she would not have fitted in with the crazy kids in the dressing-room. And they were as crazy as Faust. They had a song. They called it their fraternity song, and it was *so* dirty. 'Oh, was that song ever dirty!' says Grayce. The kids would sing it every night at eight or a little after, when they'd all get together before the show, and then again they would sing it while they were getting into their street clothes after the show. Grayce says in all her experience she never ran up against a bunch of kids that clicked the way they did. You'd come in the dressing-room with a new hat or a new dress, and they'd say: 'Where's you get that great big stinking hat?' or 'Where'd you get the great big stinking dress?' Or they'd say: 'Hey, take off the old dead brazeer' or 'Take off the old dead pair of stockings.' All the kids were popular, and there was some party every night, if you wanted to go to it. Of course, there was one snitch. There's always one snitch who runs and tells the stage-manager if one of the kids comes in tight; or if a girl is playing sick and doesn't want to go on, the snitch will always run and tell the stage-manager that the girl isn't really sick. But in the last show Grayce was in, the dances were so easy that even if you were tight or really sick you'd go on for the first number. If you go on for the first number, you get paid for the whole performance.

Nearing the end of the show's run, the girls were given two five-dollar cuts, which brought their salary down to forty dollars a week. Then they began to save money. All the kids began to save money frant-tically, because of the way show business is to-day. Grayce wasn't as worried as some of the girls, because she has a little money in the bank from a great big mad love affair with a certain producer. Not that she ever worked for him: she never got a job that way, or through a drag or anything like that. She was working in another show when she met this certain producer, and she fell in love with him and he fell in love with her, so they decided to have this great big mad love affair. He never gave her money, except for her rent and once in a while ten dollars for taxi fare, and some bonds. She says she could have had a great big stinking car at her disposal, but she didn't want it. She didn't want to get the name of being like that, and she and the certain producer never let on to anyone else that there was anything between them. She never even went to his calls, because she could get a job without doing that. So she considered herself lucky. The love affair was all washed up long ago, but she still has the money from the bonds, and doesn't have to be afraid she would have to get a job in one of the movie houses, the way she once did. Twenty-five a week in the movie houses, and four shows a day; five on Saturday, and Sunday, and on Friday, the day the new shows open, you have to be there at eight o'clock in the morning for rehearsals. Grayce wouldn't take one of those jobs again, not even if she had to. All she had done the time she did work for the movie house was to ride on a float. She was a show girl. But the hours! 'After playing five shows a day—oh, was I ever tired?'

Grayce's most devoted admirer is her mother. Her father, who is separated from her mother and works out of town, is as crazy as Faust; whenever he comes to town, he takes Grayce to expensive speakeasies and night clubs. He says: 'Now remember, you're my girl friend to-night,' and spends money like crazy—although if you ask him for twenty dollars for a new pair of shoes, he says he can't afford it. He's just crazy. When he and Grayce's mother were living together, he'd come home from trips—he was a salesman then—and her mother would find bills for jewellery in his pocket; jewellery he bought for other women. Her mother didn't say anything for a while; then, finally, one day she told him to get out and stay out, and he did. He's only about forty-two or three and sort of handsome. He has a wonderful position, but sometimes you'd think he didn't have a brain in his head. He's like a kid, but Grayce says she wouldn't want to have him around all the time, and she doesn't blame her mother.

Her mother lives with Grayce's kid brother and two sisters. Whenever Grayce is picked at a call, her mother gets all the papers every day during the run of the show. She cuts Grayce's pictures out of the papers and sends them to her for her scrapbook. One time she bought five copies of the *Red Book* because Grayce's picture was in it. She didn't know who to send the other copies to, so she still has four left.

Grayce is all that her mother wanted to be. Her mother's people were strict, from Providence, R.I., and the elder Grace—Grayce, at her mother's suggestion, has always spelled her name that way—was so afraid of her parents that she never even dared suggest that she might like to go on the stage. When Grayce was born, her mother was happy. All through Grayce's childhood, her mother took her to matinées in New York, and sent her to dancing school. If Grayce spent more than one year in a grade in school, it was hardly noticed; her father had other things on his mind, and her mother had other plans for Grayce: an off-to-Buffalo was more important than the sum of the squares of the other two sides. She learned all about back bends, pendulum bends, Greek turns, mazurkas, splits, assembles, time steps, and all the other forms of the Terpsichorean mélange, including the slang and the not-quite-right pronunciations of the French terms. She learned these things; and if she learned nothing else, no one cared; least of all her mother cared. To-day, Grayce wishes she knew a foreign language. 'But anyhow, what good would it do me?' she says. 'I never expect to go to Europe.'

She started to go to chorus calls when she was fifteen. Her mother took her out of school, and frequently accompanied her to the calls. But after a bit Grayce saw it wasn't helping her to have her mother along; and her mother realized it, too. And so Grayce went alone, and for two years she assimilated knowledge of Broadway. She learned about the man who makes girls stand on his desk and show their legs. She lent money to girls she didn't know. She was almost hired for a movie which was being made for the stag-smoker circuit, but an older girl warned her away. Even before she got her first job, she knew which of the men in the theatre had chronic 'hand trouble', and when, finally, she did get a job, she was well able to take care of herself. This confidence is her mainstay to-day; she will go out with almost any man. She never has got over her fear of gangsters, although she is addicted to the cliché that gangsters treat a girl a lot better, more like a lady, than some of those Park Avenue polo-players.

She likes parties, and drinks anything, but is in no danger of being a dipsomaniac. She suffers too badly from hangovers to become a drunkard, and she never yet has taken a drink in the morning to get over a hangover. She is probably one of the ten healthiest women in New York. When she isn't working in a show, she eats steak dinners, or even steak luncheons, when she gets up in time. She frequently walks all the way to Times Square from her apartment in the West Seventies, and she is a strong, enthusiastic swimmer. Like so many people in the show business, she is by way of being a Christian Scientist; but in Grayce's case the Science has had few occasions for a showdown. She just doesn't get sick. Her complexion is marvellous, thanks to her health, and to the daily use of cold cream—in or out of a show. She makes up her eyes only for the stage; outside of the theatre she is sparing in her use of cosmetics, because of her fear of make-up poisoning, which has been known to last for months and is a hideous condition. Her figure is still good enough to get her out of the chorus, every now and then, and into the exclusively decorative position of a show girl. When she was in her teens, in the early days of her dancing career, she was instructed always to wear a brassiere, and to do as little toework as she could get away with; hence her good figure after seven years in the chorus.

Grayce insists she means it when she says she wants to get married and have children. She says she would like to have ten children, if her husband could afford it. She would like them all to be boys, because boys are easier to handle, and they're not sneaks like girls. But sometimes Grayce says every woman ought to have a career; any career; just so it isn't home-making. Her own idea of a career would be to achieve the standing of, say, Lynn Fontanne. 'Look at her,' Grayce says. 'She's married, isn't she? It just goes to show.'

Whatever does happen to Grayce probably won't be important, even to herself. It is hard to imagine her bewailing her fate, unless she should marry a man who would beat her. But it is just as hard to imagine a man who would want to do that.

CHAPTER 8

In The Morning Sun

The door between the kitchen and the dining-room swung back and forth, wung-wung, wung-wung, behind Mrs. Demarest. She stopped, without seeming to stop, to straighten the centrepiece on the dining-room table, and continued through the dining-room to the side porch, which ran along that side of the house. Dining-room and library opened on to the side porch, and the porch itself opened, through screen doors, to the garden. The porch was cool, almost as cool as the interior of the house, but she went out through the screen door to where her son was sitting under the tree.

'My, but it's going to be warm,' she said. 'You can tell it already.'

'Mm,' said Sam. He did not take his eyes off his book. Sam was very clean in a clean white shirt and white flannel trousers. He wore no socks, and on his feet were rope-soled espadrilles, tied with strings around his ankles. Sam's face was brown, except for a small white line just in front of the ears, where he had not tanned. His ankles were white and sick, with just enough hair on the instep to make the white skin stand out. Mrs. Demarest would have known from the hair on his head that he had been reading quite a while, because he always ran his hand through his hair when he got interested in a book. Even as a boy he had done that.

Mrs. Demarest sat down and put on her spectacles. She knew she needed new ones; it took her eyes so long to get focussed on newsprint. But new glasses were a nuisance. All the trouble of it, and the doctor in the village, Dr. Fleischer, would talk your head off. She would wait until she got back to New York. In the short time it took her to focus her eyes on the newsprint, she decided to suggest to Sam that he ought not to go without socks, and then she decided not to say anything. A lot of harm could be done by letting him think she coddled him; besides, it was warm, very warm. She wondered how hot it was in New York. Nobody—hardly anybody could catch cold from not wearing socks on a day like this. It was going to be a scorcher. But better than being in New York.

There was nothing on the front page to interest Mrs. Demarest, and her stocks were all right, considering. She was glad that she had enough of this world's goods. Sam, sitting across the little table from her, did not have to work. He could live forever without working. Well, forever if the country did not have a revolution and turn Communistic. Sam would not have to work so long as she had money. And that was something to be thankful for. There he was, getting better now. The doctor said he was taking on weight in a healthy way and was in the best shape he'd been in in years, literally years. He was only twenty-seven, but his health had not been good since college. And then the mess about the divorce. Not as bad a mess as some divorces, but still any divorce is a mess. You can't get around that. Mrs. Demarest wondered if Sam ever thought of Christine. Oh, he must think of her; but she wondered if Sam ever—if he still loved her. He never said so. He never spoke of her. He didn't, as a matter of fact, ever say much about anything.

She laid her paper in her lap and tried to think back over conversations she had had with Sam in the last six months. She thought a long time and she discovered that since he had come back from Albuquerque he hardly ever said anything. He would say he was going some place for dinner, or had had a letter from someone in New York, or was going to take the Ford instead of the Packard. He never talked about himself, his inner self, or of anyone or anything that concerned his inner self. He would be irritated by what he called people's stupidity, or he would praise this or that person or thing, but it never got deep. She wondered if he had any depth. Depth.

She watched him turning the page of his book, and something else struck her: she discovered that Sam was through. Oh, that was ridiculous. He was not through. He was only a young man. It would be almost three years before he was thirty, and his best years were ahead of him. But were they? Mrs. Demarest could not quite let herself say that in all honesty she believed that Sam's best years were ahead of him. The truth, she was beginning to suspect, was that Sam had lived a life.

A life at twenty-seven? Surely not. Yet there, sitting across the little wicker table from her, was—aside from her own relationship—a person, a citizen, a young man who had lived a life.

If something happened to him—if he should die—he would die having lived a life, and who was to say it was not a complete life? He had been born, nursed, vaccinated, educated. He had fallen in love, married, been divorced, been very ill. That was enough life for anybody, more than many had. There you are, she thought, sitting in your flannel trousers and your nice white shirt, and you have been so many places—Russia, Egypt, New Mexico, California, the Panama Canal—and now you are back here with me, with no labels on you to show that you have seen so much of the world; and you are just a young man, twenty-seven years of age, who is wearing hardly any clothes and reading a book and smoking a cigarette. You have nothing on your arm or chest like a tattoo mark to show that you have been in love or that you have been married. At this moment, looking so tanned, you would have a hard time making anyone believe that you almost died six months ago. What are you? she wondered.

But she knew. He was her son, her own flesh and blood, and she loved him because he was her own flesh and blood, and also because he was anybody, because he was alive and handsome and breathing and able to spit out bits of tobacco that stuck on his lips. But she also knew that he had lived his life, enough life for anyone. He had been wild and bad, but now he was through. She knew this not sadly, but logically and sensibly. Later, she guessed, she would get this all mixed up with the mother-and-only-son feeling and she would not be able to think about it, but for the present she could think about it. She knew that Sam's life, the real living part of his life, was over, because she did not think of him as young or old or anything. If he were going to go on living a life, something inside her would have told her so and she would act differently towards him. As it was, she did not even think of him as a sick boy, someone to nurse and give your warmth to. Her instinct, she knew, was only to make him comfortable.

Ah, you, she thought. I am sturdy. And because I am sturdy I am young, so much younger than you. I am fifty years old and younger than you. I will go on and you are through. I wish it could be some other way, that you could have the years ahead, but you have no years ahead. You have lived too much, abused your body and done strange things to your mind, and done things to other people. I wonder what you did to your wife, she thought.

That was it, partly. Everyone who came in contact with him was affected by him. It never failed. People always remembered him, even people who had met him only once a long time ago. Even now he was always getting things like wedding invitations from people he had a hard time remembering. And now he was sitting in a chair, reading a book.

He looked up, resting his eyes for a minute, and he saw she was looking at him. She had to say something. 'Have you any plans for to-day?'

'No, I guess not,' he said. 'I was thinking I'd play some golf, but I guess I'll wait till late this afternoon and see how the weather is.'

'Too hot to play now,' she said.

'Are you doing anything?' he said.

'No. Mrs. Curtis is coming over after lunch. She said something about going up to the Mountain House, but I guess I won't. Too much trouble.'

'It'd be cool,' he said.

'Oh, the heat doesn't bother me much. I hardly ever mind the weather one way or another. When it's cold, I'm usually bundled up, and right now the house is just about perfect.' He wasn't paying much attention to her. She stood up. 'I think I'll go inside.'

'You just said you didn't mind the heat,' he said.

'Oh, it isn't the heat,' she said.

'It's the humidity?' he said.

'Oh, no,' she said. She walked slowly to the side porch.

She sat on the porch and tried to figure out what suddenly had made her leave him. She had not even given any reason for leaving, and when she was walking away she had felt his eyes on her, like the feeling you have when you leave a room and know people are talking about you. Oh, she had not dared stay there with him, thinking about his life. He was keen, and she was a little afraid of him. He might have looked at her again and discovered what she was thinking about.

She crossed her legs, almost gripping the arms of the chairs, and saying to herself: 'My boy.' But it did not thrill her to say it. It did not move her, want to make her laugh or shed a few tears, the kind you can swallow and want more of. And she did not feel the vague anger and satisfaction that you can derive from having classified a person, the superiority. She was angry with herself for saying 'My boy,' because it sounded insincere and sentimental. To think of Sam sitting there doing nothing made her nervous; she was hitting the heel of her right shoe on the grass mat, and her nerves were on edge. She stood up again and looked out at Sam. He was not reading, and he did not look as though he cared or knew whether there was anyone else in the world. When she first looked, he was leaning forward and his hands covered his forehead and temples and eyes, and then his head went back and his tired face faced the sky, and she could almost hear him saying it; 'Oh. Oh.' And his mother shivered, for there was nothing she could do.

CHAPTER 9

Can You Carry Me?

It was one of those Beverly Hills afternoons when a fire in the fireplace is a good idea. The beautiful blonde saw that right away, the moment she entered the room. 'Jesus!' she said, and hugged her bosom. She was wearing white gabardine slacks and a white gabardine blouse. Over the left bosom, stitched on the pocket, were her initials, not less than six inches high, but adding no warmth. The blouse had only half sleeves and it was unbuttoned almost to the belt of her slacks. 'Alice!' There was no answer. 'That dumb dinge,' she said.

She opened her mouth to yell again, but changed her mind. Instead she lifted a glass-and-chromium lamp that was on an end table, and set it on top of a portable push button.

Alice appeared.

'Light the fire, will you?'

'Yes, ma'am,' said Alice. 'It did get colder, din it, Miss B?' She bent down and lighted the gas, with which all Beverly Hills fires are started. Alice stood there until the logs had caught, and Miss B pushed her out of the way so that she could toast herself. She would warm her hands and then pass them over exposed portions of her body, and she was doing this when the doorbell rang. Alice went to answer the door, and Miss B jumped to the davenport.

Alice reappeared. 'It's Mr. Confelt. He said he—'

'But of course, don't keep him waiting, Alice.' She began to get off the sofa to greet Mr. Confelt, but reconsidered and slumped back, with her knees drawn up in front of her. When he came in she stuck out her left hand, which he took, pressed, and released. 'You're punctilious,' she said.

'Well, I try to be,' he said.

'Cigarettes there, in the white pig-skin box. Drinks, whatever you prefer. I'm going to have a dry sherry, but don't let that influence you.'

Mr. Confelt cackled. 'It has to be whisky or brandy to influence me.'

She smiled, and indicated the cut-glass decanters.

'Well, Miss B,' said Mr. Confelt.

'*Miss*-ter C,' she said.

'You're a-lookin' might fine, mighty fine.'

'Thenk yaw, Mr. C. I guess it must be because I—I know how to take it. I guess I have a tough hide.'

'Not from where I sit I wouldn't say so. Oh, you mean that piece Duval wrote.'

'The same,' said Miss B. 'The very, very same. I was under the impression I had a great in at your magazine, but not after I saw Miss Duval's little autobiography.'

'Well, I wouldn't exactly call it an autobiography—'

'Well, you know what I mean. The article she wrote about me. You know what I have reference to.' She reached for her sherry, raised it to her eyes, and drank it. 'Bottoms up.'

'Bottoms up, if I can make it,' said Mr. Confelt. He didn't quite, but he finished quickly. 'I think we owe you an explanation on that piece.'

The explanation took a good half-hour, and when it was concluded Mr. Confelt went from the explanation to two or three other cases of actors and actresses who had been distressed by Miss Duval's writings. This addendum continued until the last of the Scotch and the last of the sherry.

'Uh-huh,' said Miss B. 'Push that button over there will you?'

'What button?'

'That one on that table, it has a wire—oh, wouldn't you know. That damn Ethiopian, she—I bet she turned it off in the kitchen.'

'Oh, you mean this one, under the lamp.'

'*Alice!*'

Alice appeared. 'Yes, ma'am. More Scotch and sherry. Ice. You want more soda, Mr. Confelt.'

'Sure he does,' said Miss B. 'Well—uh—oh, yes. Well, what I was gonna do, I was gonna go to the Hays office and say look here, this Confelt's writers have got to be barred from the lot. All lots. All Confelt's writers. You remember a couple years ago, how these magazines, they got in plenty of trouble, Confelt, and you know it.

And you hadda show us what you were going to print beforehand.
You know that.'

'Yes, that's true.'

'Well, I was gonna do that, but then I talked to Rawson and he
advised me against it. Rawson said he advised me against it. He
said he wouldn't do it if he was me. I. So I took his advice. I didn't
go the Hays office.' She stopped and smiled to herself. 'Hello,
Confelt.'

'Hello, Miss B.'

'How're you feeling?'

'Top of the world. Never better.'

'Have a nice big drink,' said Miss B.

'Don't mind if I do,' he said. 'How about you?'

'No—all right. Sure. 'Cause I'm feeling good, too. I feel top of
the *world*.'

He poured her sherry and mixed a highball. She was still smiling
at him. 'So, I din go the Hays office.'

He smiled.

'*But!*' she said. 'You know what I *did* do, Connie my pigeon. *I*
went to my *lawyer*.'

'I—'

'And I said, "Joe, let's sue those sons of bitches for a million
dollars." So Joe said all right, and so that's what we're doing,
Connie. We're suing you for one million smackeroos. And I'm not
the only one. At least three other friends of mine are going to sue
you for a million smackeroos.' She smiled and raised her glass to
him.

'Now listen, Miss B, I know all that.'

'So you knew it? Well, you had a hell of a nerve then sticking
that pan of yours in this house. My house. What are you gonna do,
try and con me out of it? Well, guess again, pickle face. The stuff
you printed about me.'

'I wasn't here. Duval was running the magazine. I was in the
hospital. You know I'd never—'

'Sure. Sure. You'd never. Oh, no. Not much. Not much. You'd
never print those things about me. Only you did, see? And you're
gonna pay right through that pickle nose of yours.'

'You don't have to make personal remarks,' said Mr. Confelt.

'Oh? So I don't have to make personal remarks. Now the shoe
fits you you don't like it so much. You can call me a drunken bum,

practically, and all that stuff about the grips and the juicers and everybody and what a laugh they get from me when I get mad at something. Well, listen, you heel. My mother reads your goddam magazine. How do you think she felt when she read that stuff? What about the sisters?'

'What sisters? I didn't know you had a sister.'

'I haven't got a sister. I mean in school. The sisters that taught me. What if they saw your goddam—'

'Oh, nuns. Well, I don't think many nuns, uh—'

'Sure I mean nuns.' Miss B. had a tear or two in her eye. 'I was almost one myself, and now what would they think? I wanted to be one. I coulda been if I didn't have to go to work when I was fifteen. Fif-teen.'

The tears were now more numerous, and Miss B was sniffling. Mr. Confelt gave her a handkerchief, which she applied. He watched her, and there was only a slight involuntary motion of his fingers when she took the handkerchief down from her face and tucked it in the pocket of her blouse.

He clapped his hands. 'I've got it. Marvellous!' he said.

'What have you got?'

'See what you think of this. Now, don't get me wrong. I'll print a retraction if you want me to, but there's no story in a retraction. Miss B. *You've* given me the idea, marvellous. Listen and see what you think of this. I'll write a piece. I'll write it myself. About your childhood. How you went to this school and you were the favourite of all the nuns. Led all your classes. The most religious one in the whole school, without any question. High hopes. Then your father dies—'

'He was put in jail.'

'No. He died. He died, and some talent scout saw you in a school play and juut at the right moment, because right after your father's funeral, or right before he died, this mugg comes along and offers you a contract—'

'You mean Earl Carroll?'

'I *don't* mean Earl Carroll. I mean Max Reinhardt, or Gilbert Miller. I don't give a damn who it was right now. You get this offer when you're fifteen, and the only reason you take it is because your father's investment turned out—'

'My father didn't have any investments. Listen, Connie, I'm sure

I don't know what the hell you're talking about. But I do know
I'm sleepy. Can you carry me?'

'Why, sure, dear,' said Mr. Confelt.

CHAPTER 10

Lunch Tuesday

It was one of those good, characterless restaurants in the East Fifties, run by a former speakeasy proprietor. It was 1.25 and there was a fair-sized crowd for luncheon. Mrs. Flintridge was lighting a denicotinized cigarette—her second in twenty minutes. She was looking down at the flame when she heard a voice say, 'Darling, I'm terribly sorry.' Mrs. Flintridge shook the match and put it in the ashtray, heedless of the fact that the match burned on. 'Have you been here long?' the newcomer asked.

'Well, I had nothing to do, so I was on time for a change,' said Mrs. Flintridge.

'I'm terribly sorry, but I came in on the tube and had to stop at Macy's, and traffic really was something. What are you drinking? Is that a Daiquiri?' Mrs. Walton sat down.

'No, a Side Car,' said Mrs. Flintridge.

'Oh, brandy.' Then, 'Are you drinking *brandy*?'

'This is my second. I got home at four this morning, or at least I think it was four. It might have been later. We went to one of those parties at the club. Every time we do it, either Bud or I swears we'll never do it again during the week, but he's been pretty good lately and I thought a little binge—'

'I'll have a Side Car, please. Two Side Cars. You're ready for another, aren't you?'

'Oh—all right,' said Mrs. Flintridge.

'Well,' said Mrs. Walton, a little like a crier opening court. For the next few minutes the women talked about traffic and shopping and what they wanted to eat, and Mrs. Walton was persuaded to catch up with Mrs. Flintridge's quantity of Side Cars. They thought a little white wine with their luncheon, and then, because each had half a Side Car left, they thought no, no wine. Mrs. Flintridge said frankly no, she didn't like Mrs. Walton's hat. The hat was all right, but she thought the ribbons in the back were a little on the long side. Mrs. Walton said that was what she was afraid of, but she couldn't be sure. She'd have them shortened. Maybe taken off altogether. Mrs. Flintridge said not to take them off altogether, just shorten them. She also said she wished she could wear a hat like that, but that Mrs. Walton didn't look thirty, whereas she, Mrs. Flintridge, looked her thirty and probably more. Mrs. Walton told Mrs. Flintridge that she looked about twenty-eight, but had looked twenty-eight five years ago and would go on looking twenty-eight till after she was forty. That was better than looking younger and then all of a sudden, around thirty-two, looking older. At least that's what Mrs. Walton thought. They talked pleasantly that way, the talk of old friends who seldom saw each other any more. They came to the end of the meal and they thought a little crème de menthe, but Mrs. Walton didn't know how that would go on top of a Side Car, or a couple of Side Cars. Mrs. Flintridge said that was an exploded theory about mixing drinks. It all depended on the condition of your stomach. But of course she conceded that her own stomach wasn't in any too good condition to-day, what with last night, and she added, 'And I'll bet Bud—'

'Well, then a brandy. A brandy'd be all right. Waiter, two brandies, please. I mean two Courvoisiers.' Then, 'What are your plans for this afternoon? Is there one of those Actors' Fund matinees, do you suppose? That's the trouble with Tuesday. We can't go to a matinee unless they're having one of those Actors' Fund matinees. I wish I'd have thought of it when I called you. Then we could have made it Wednesday or Thursday. Shall I get a paper and see if there's a matinee?'

'All right,' said Mrs. Flintridge. 'But it wasn't you that called me. I called *you*. You *never* call *me*.'

'Oh, I *do*, Peggy, I do too. I called you the last time.'

'No, I called you,' said Mrs. Flintridge.

'Well, the time before.'

'The time before you didn't call me. That was when Bud and I met you and Harry on the train going to New Haven.'

'Oh, well, what difference does it make who calls who? Whom.'

The waiter brought the newspaper, and not only was there no matinee, but the feature picture at Radio City Music Hall wouldn't be going on again till nearly four o'clock, and there was nothing else they wanted to see. Then a man came in and stood at the bar, where they could see him. He was soaking wet. His derby hat was soaking wet; his light overcoat was soaking wet; and as he spoke to the proprietor, whom he obviously knew, he was laughing in the way people do when they have been caught in a sudden downpour. 'Look at that man,' said Mrs. Walton. 'It must be teeming. And me with a new hat, naturally. We might as well wait here as anywhere.'

'All right, let's,' said Mrs. Flintridge. 'I could do with another drink.'

'If I have another, I'll be tight. Oh, well.'

'We can ask the waiter to let us know when it stops raining,' said Mrs. Flintridge. 'I think I'll switch to Scotch. Brandy depresses me, and the rain.' She switched to Scotch, but Mrs. Walton stuck to brandy and soda. She said, 'I think I'll just have a little brandy and soda.' Their drinks were brought to them and they received them in different ways: Mrs. Walton looked at hers, not touching it right away, as though it were a surprise birthday cake in a night club; and Mrs. Flintridge, the moment the waiter combined the highball, picked it up and narrowed her eyes and took a good, long drink out of it. By this time they had reached the stage where a drink could interrupt any conversation. During the silence the proprietor came over to them. '*Mesdames*,' he said, and then, addressing Peggy Walton, 'Mrs. Walton, the gentleman at the bar, he asks if he may buy a drink. He sess he is a friend of Mr. Walton and has met you.'

'You're being picked up. I guess the hat's all right,' said Mrs. Flintridge.

'I'm sorry. I'll tell the gentleman. Please forgive me,' said the proprietor.

'Oh—he looks all right,' said Mrs. Walton. Somehow, in the shuffle, the man came over.

'Mrs. Walton, I didn't mean to be fresh, but I'm Arthur Luddy and I do know Harry very well, and I met you one night at the Stork Club. You were with—I forget his name.'

Peggy Walton interrupted his loss of memory to introduce Mrs. Flintridge.

'Oh,' said Mr. Luddy. 'How do you do?' He really made it a question. He sat down and had his drink brought from the bar.

'Is the Stork Club fun?' said Mrs. Flintridge. 'I've never been there, and even Bud, he's only been there once.'

'I hardly ever go,' said Peggy Walton. 'I don't like night clubs.'

'I don't as a rule, but I like the Stork,' said Mr. Luddy. 'You seemed to have been having a good time that night. Don't you remember at all? There's no reason why you should, but a fellow called Merle Stafford brought me over to your table to meet his partner.'

'Merle Stafford?' said Mrs. Flintridge.

'Yeah. Do you know him?'

Mrs. Flintridge picked up her drink and looked down into it and slowly raised her eyes to the terrified eyes of Peggy Walton. 'As a matter of fact, he's my husband's partner,' said Mrs. Flintridge.

'Well, then, huh huh, I guess you know him,' said Mr. Luddy, with right good humour. 'I don't know him very well. I just happened to run into him, and he was a little tight, and you know—'

'Mr. Luddy,' said Peggy Walton. 'Do you mind if would you mind getting the hell out of here?'

'Yes, please, Mr. Luddy, will you get the hell out of here?' said Mrs. Flintridge.

'Weh-heh-hell. Notta tall. You *asked* me to sit down. Sure I'll go.' said Mr. Luddy. He got up and looked from one woman to the other and went back to the bar, talking to himself. The women watched him paying his check and leaving with one more backward glance, and they watched the proprietor, who had not missed any of it, coming towards them.

'Ladies, I am very sorry. Was there something wrong?'

'It's all right. Please go away,' said Mrs. Flintridge.

They looked at each other, and Peggy Walton was suffering first of all the acute discomfort of being a little the drunker and knowing it, and wishing that of all times in her life this time she wasn't. She took a gulp of her drink and watched her hand as she put the glass down on the table.

'I tell you how it happened,' she said. 'Please let me. You were away somewhere and I was in town and I happened to run into Bud one afternoon. *You* know. And we—'

'Ah, what's the *use*, Peggy? I knew it was somebody. I just didn't know it was *you*, that's all.'

CHAPTER 11

Shave

'But I'd like to see you before I go back to New York,' said Adams.

'Do you have to go back this afternoon?' said Morris.

'I have to be there to-night. Some time to-night.'

'What time is it now?' said Morris.

Adams was holding the telephone with his left hand. He lowered the phone and looked at his wrist-watch. 'Twenty after. About twenty. Eighteen. I may be a little fast.'

'Well, the only trouble is—you could make it, I guess. But—do you remember how to get there?'

'I think so. Sure. It isn't hard.'

'Well, if you leave right away. But I'll tell you, Johnny, if you're not here by ten of three I'll have to leave. I won't be able to wait. This is the only day they'll let me see her.'

'I'll leave right away. I'll check out this minute, and I ought to be there before ten of three.'

Adams got a break with the traffic lights and the cops, and he was out of Boston in good time. Although he had not been to Morris's house in more than a year, and never had been there more than three times, he began remembering landmarks, and he arrived at Morris's a few minutes ahead of time. Morris, in the same kind of Brooks suit he had worn for fifteen years, was leaning against the front door, smoking a cigarette and with one hand in his trouser pocket. He threw the cigarette away and came down the short walk to the gate, where Adams stopped the car.

'Johnny, how are you?' said Morris. 'Fine. How are you, Willie?' They shook hands across the front door of the car.

'Christ, you didn't shave! Johnny, you can't see her looking like that.'

'Why, I didn't know I was going to see her. I only came out to say hello to you.'

'Not at all. You mean you didn't think she was allowed to see outsiders. Well, she can. A few. Now listen, go on in and shave. I want her to see you, but not that way.'

'I'm sorry. I'd have shaved if I'd known.'

Adams followed Morris to the bathroom, and while he was taking off his things Morris put a new blade in the razor and held it out when Adams had finished lathering his face. Morris sat on the edge of the tub, his hat on the back of his head. He was smoking another cigarette. He watched Adams for a minute of so.

'You've put on some weight,' he said.

'Look at these arms. Look at them. I'm *all* fat.' Adams, not interrupting his shave, raised his elbows to indicate his arms.

'Don't you play squash or anything?'

'*Do you?*'

'No, but I don't get fat. I guess I never will. All my family, both sides were all thin people, or at least not fat.' He flicked his cigarette ash on the floor. 'Betsy's lost a lot of weight.'

Adams did not know what to say to that. Then he said, 'I hear she's a lot better.'

'Where the hell'd you hear that? You didn't hear any such thing.'

'Yes I did. I heard it somewhere.'

'Well, she's worse if anything. Johnny, for Christ's sake, don't you *know* about her? She'll never be any better.' He flung the cigarette into the toilet. 'Listen, Johnny, about this afternoon. You have to take your cue from her. When you see her, use your intelligence. If she seems all right, normal, and she wants to talk about herself, let her. Encourage her. It'll shock you, the first time you hear her saying it. "Why hello, Johnny," she'll say, and then she'll say something about coming to see a nut. She always calls herself a nut. And this place she's staying at she calls her crazy-house. I asked the doctors—they have one good man there—I thought that was a hopeful sign, that she could—*you* know—talk about herself that way. Well, he's an honest guy, and said he honestly didn't think so. You remember how she used to be, she was always articulate, and for all I know *that* was part of *this*. That stuff is good for after shaving. Just use a little of it if you're not used to it, but it's pretty good. You look a hundred per cent better.'

'I feel better. I did a little drinking last night.' Adams put on his shirt. 'Well, now do you—shall I stick around, or shall I just say hello and then leave?'

'Depends on how she is to-day. You see, I only see her once a week. She's allowed to go for a ride with me, not more than an hour. This week I smashed up my car. I got drunk and drove smack into the garage wall.' He halted. 'I might as well tell you. I had a girl with me. Christ, I have to have *some*body, don't I?'

'Was she hurt?'

"Always the practical Johnny. No, she wasn't hurt and she's a good kid. She's a little Irish girl. She knows all about Betsy.'

'What does she do?'

'She's a stenographer. Secretary.'

'Well, just so you don't get yourself into a jam with her. How are you and the sauce?'

'What do you mean?'

'The sauce. Drinking.'

'You and your New York slang. Oh, I drink enough to keep from going stale. But I don't want you to worry about me. I'm not drinking enough to be declared incompetent. That, by the way, is the least Betsy will call herself. Incompetent. "We incompetents," she says. Would you like a drink now?'

'Don't you think we better get going? I've made you late enough already.'

'Your watch *was* fast. We have time for one quick one,' said Morris. 'I think you'd better have one anyway. You may need it. And I may need it, watching you.'

'Always the insulting Willie. You haven't changed at all.'

'Not me,' said Morris. 'No-ho. Not me.'

CHAPTER 12

Portistan on the Portis

One night not so long ago I was having dinner with a friend of mine, Jimmy Shott, who used to be a good foot-in-the-door reporter until he accepted a lucrative position in the advertising game. Jimmy took me to an Italian place in the West Forties, and the idea was I would meet Damon Runyon. Well, Damon did not show, but just after Jimmy and I sat down in came two prize-fight managers. One of them was an older man, around fifty, who looked not unlike an uncle of mine. His name, and also the name of my uncle, is Mike. The other manager was Hymie, and he right away began talking fighters, and was very proud of one of his boys, who had won the decision in a preliminary to the Joe Louis exhibition in which Max Baer was the third man in the ring. At one time I covered a great many fights and I long ago learned that all you have to do to get along with fight managers is to nod and keep nodding and put on a slightly sleepy look and occasionally ask either a very dumb or a very smart question (and they are interchangeable). This went on while Jimmy and I ate the ravioli, and then Jimmy interrupted Hymie and asked him to give the wop waiter some double-talk, which isn't pig-Latin, which isn't *anything*. Hymie smiled, very pleased, and called the waiter. He dug his fork in a piece of veal and turned it over and over, and said to the waiter, 'You portis on the portistan on the veal.'

'Sir?' said the waiter, bowing.

'Portis. Portis on the portistan on the veal portis, and the stamportis,' said Hymie, continuing to turn the veal over as though he had a sword with a red cape hanging from it, like a bull-fighter.

'I don't understn' sir,' said the waiter.

'God damn it! I said the portis on the portistan on the *veal* portis and the veal—call the head waiter!'

The head waiter already was on his way, and Hymie repeated.

The head waiter shooed the waiter away and said, 'Once again will you repeat it please?' Then Jimmy burst out laughing and the head waiter caught on and laughed too, but not heartily. He didn't altogether get it, because Hymie, who is thirty-five years old, has the expression you think you see in the pictures of cops whose widows received yesterday the Departmental Medal of Honour. 'Aah, what the hell,' said Hymie.

As we were getting ready to go, Hymie asked us if we should like to go to Newark to see some fights, and we said we should. He would only be a little while finishing his dinner and we waited. While we sat there smoking and drinking coffee he and I discovered that we had been in Hollywood at the same time, and of course we knew a lot of people in common. He knew bigger people than I did, and two of his pals—*but* the best—were an actor and a crooner. Every morning the crooner would call him and say: 'What do you hear from the mob, Hymie?' And Hymie would reply: 'The mains are coming to town. The semi-mains just took over Kansas City.' And the crooner would say: 'What do you hear from Louie the Lug, Hymie?' And Hymie would say: 'Louie the Lug? He's from the opposition. A wrong gee, Bing. A wrong gee. Strictly an opposition guy.' And then: 'We're gunna straighten him out, Bing. I sent for my iron-rod gun moll, and we're gunna straighten out Louie the Lug as soon as the mains get in town. The semi-mains just took over Kansas City.' This kind of conversation would go on every day, the crooner talking movie gangster slang to Hymie and Hymie replying in kind.

Hymie finished his dinner and said good night to Mike, who was leaving, and then the three of us went out and got in Hymie's car, being joined by Tony, a friend of Hymie's. We drove like hell through traffic and down the elevated highway to the entrance to the tunnel. Hymie paid the toll, handing the Port Authority cop a dollar, and as he got his change Hymie said, just above a whisper: 'Wuddia hippum the mob?'

The cop paid no attention, and Hymie half turned around and said to me: 'An opposition guy, John. We'll let the semi-mains take care of him. We'll get him straightened out.' By that time we had reached the cop who takes the toll tickets.

'What d'ya hear from the mob?' said Hymie slowly.

The cop looked at him and then at the rest of us and said: 'What mob?' but not liking it a bit.

Hymie gave the car the gas and we went down into the tunnel.

In New Jersey our troubles began the moment we left the Pulaski Skyway—the wrong way. We were in Newark, but not anywhere in Newark that we wanted to be. So every few blocks Hymie would stop and ask for directions. We were in a tough district, but that did not deter Hymie. After getting directions from boys hanging around poolrooms, from motormen and cops and women, Hymie would whisper to our informants: 'Wuddia hippum the mob?'

He always got an answer. The young men who you could tell were mob timber would say they hadn't heard anything for a couple of days, or give some answer which showed they were aware that there was a mob. The motormen would just laugh and not say anything, afraid to say the wrong thing. The same with the cops, except that they did not laugh. They were simply afraid to say the wrong thing (our car was black and shiny and new). Once we encountered a wise kid who wanted to give us some repartee, and Hymie said: 'Hey, *waaaaid* a minute, waid a *minute*, there, wise guy. A wronggo. An opposition guy. Maybe we better straighten 'im out.'

'Hymie, we gotta get to them *fights*,' said Tony.

'Yeah, but first we oughta spray this wise guy with hot lead, from our Thompson sub-machine-gun iron. This is a wise guy.' But we drove on.

Hymie was in the corner for two boys or maybe three, all of them his brother's fighters, his brother also being a manager in that neck of the woods. Hymie is a good man in a corner, and I remember his boy won in one fight, another fight his boy was robbed, and I forget the other. We were sitting in the second or third row, and between rounds Hymie would talk to his boy, but just as he was climbing down from the ring he would call over to us: 'Wuddia hippum the mob?' And we would point to the opposing fighter and yell out: 'An opposition guy!'

'A wronggo,' Hymie would say.

After the fights we went to the dressing-room while Hymie received. He also gave. He gave to the referee, who was on the take two ways. He slipped five bucks to one of the fight reporters (it is a pleasure to go out with someone like Hymie and find out which reporters, big or little, will accept cash gratuities). He picked Al Roth to beat Tony Canzoneri at the Garden (Canzoneri, of course,

won). He spent a little time with the best of the boys he had
seconded, trying, as he had done during the fight, to tell the boy
that in short he would have no hands left if he persisted in punching
Negroes in the head. After half an hour or so we left to continue
our entertainment.

Our hosts were a handsome young man who was introduced only
as Harry, and a man who looked like Warren Hymer, the movie
actor, and was called Blubber. Harry told us that the week before
he had organised the organ-grinders at two dollars a week per
grinder. They took us to a very attractive bar and Harry called to
the singer, Mabel or Melba, to come over and join us. 'Sit with
Hymie,' said Harry. She sat next to Hymie, and he began right
away:

'You uh portistan on the portis the joint?'

'Wha'?'

'Portistan. On the portis. Harry said you'd portis on the portistan
the joint. That's what he told me.'

'Liss-sunn,' said Melba.

'Go on,' said Harry. 'Answer him yes or no.'

'Well, if you say so,' said Melba.

'I said so,' said Harry.

'Well, then,' said Melba.

'Oh, I don't want it that way,' said Hymie. 'Listen, you, Melba
or whatever your name is, if you portistan the stanportis—'

'I *said* I *would* didn't I?' she said.

'Okay, then I buy you a corsadge. You be my gun moll.'

'Say, what is this?' said Melba.

'Sure. I buy you a corsadge and you put the shooting iron in it.'

'Do I have to?' she asked Harry.

'What he says,' said Harry.

'I tell you what I'll do for you,' said Hymie. 'I'll turn over my
beer racket to you. I gave it to my sister but I'll take it back from
her and give it to you if you'll be my gun moll. How'd you like to
be my gun moll?'

'She's too dumb,' said Harry. 'She don't know what you're talking
about. Let's eat. I want a steak. Who else wants a steak?'

The waiter came over (he didn't have to come very far) for our
order, and Hymie said: 'Listen, you donkey, Melba is going to be
my gun moll so I want a steak, but I want a small portis with a

portis on top, see? Then garnish it with a stanportis and a portis medium—'

'Medium well done, sir?' said the waiter.

'Hey, I don't even think you're listening. Now get this, A small steak with a portis, but Melba wants a portistan portis on the ubbadate stanportis *steak*, with*out* the prawn portis. And a cup of tea, on account of Melba's going to be my gun moll, aren't you, Stupid?'

'Ha ha,' she said.

'Oh, a wronggo,' said Hymie.

'What's that, a wronggo?' said Harry.

'You hear him? Say, what are we, in the provinces or something? You don't know what wronggo is? Wait till the mains hear that. The mains and the semi-mains. They just took over Bushwick from the opposition and what they're gonna do, they're gonna take over this territory next week.'

'No,' said Blubber.

'He's nuts,' said Harry. 'Don't pay no attention to him when he's like this.'

'That's what I thought,' said Melba.

'*Not* you,' said Harry. 'You're his gun moll.' At that Harry burst out laughing, the only time he laughed all night.

CHAPTER 13

The Cold House

The house in the country was cold, and Mrs. Carnavon sat with her hat on, her sealskin coat open, her bag in her lap, her left hand lying flat on the bag. The slight exertion—but not slight to her—of getting out of the car, stepping down, walking up the three steps of the porte-cochère, had left her breathing heavily, and the thumb of her right hand was beating against the forefinger. She had had a long nap in the car, coming up from New York. Driscoll drove so you could sleep. He had to; that was his job. She knew Driscoll, and how he would look in the mirror to see if she was asleep before he would increase his speed. Driscoll was so thoroughly trained in moderate speed that she often had had to feign sleep in order to get some place in a hurry. But to-day she had not had to feign sleep. Up at six-thirty, and now it was almost time for lunch. But first a rest, a little rest. The house was very cold. Mrs Carnavon rang for the maid.

'I didn't expect you till late afternoon,' said the maid. 'I'll build you a fire.'

'Never mind, Anna.'

'But it'll only *take a minute*, Ma'am. I kin—'

'No, never *mind*.'

'Well, but of course if you—'

'I won't change my mind. Is the phone connected? I mean here in the house.'

'No, only over the garage, where we are.'

'Then will you go out and telephone the Inn and tell Mr. McCall—ask him if I could have a chop and a baked potato. Or anything. Nothing much. Cup of tea.'

'I could fix you something.'

'Too much trouble to start a fire. No, just tell Mr. McCall, and find out how soon he can have it.'

'Of course he'll more than likely have to go out and buy it, and—'

'All right. He can go out and buy it.' Mrs. Carnavon hated to be short with Anna, but Anna had the hide of an elephant. She knew that Anna would not be hurt; she watched Anna leave the room and knew that Anna was thinking: 'The poor woman is all upset.'

She looked out of the window and saw Anna, with a very ugly shawl over her head and shoulders, looking rather pathetic, hurrying to the garage to telephone Mr. McCall. Mrs. Carnavon lit a cigarette. It steadied her a little. It steadied her body, her hands; there was no unsteadiness to the lump in her heart, the thing in her mind. She held the cigarette as high as her face, taking regular, deep inhales. She idly opened a china cigarette box on the table beside her, just tilting the lid. There were four cigarettes in the box. She took one out and it was as crisp as a twig. She broke it with her fingers. It was from last summer. A cigarette that her son could have smoked. She looked at it and saw that it was a cigarette that Harry would *not* have smoked; it was a brand he never had liked. But still, when he had a few drinks she had seen him smoking just that brand without noticing any difference. 'Mom, why do you have those things in the house? Everybody passes them up. They're really vile. They are. They're vile. I hate to tell you what they remind me of.' One time he had emptied all the available boxes of that brand. But she noticed that when some friends of his were at the house, they would ask Anna if there didn't happen to be some of that brand—'on the premises', one boy had said. She didn't remember much about the boy, but she remembered that strange expression.

Now that she was here—'I came up here for something,' she said aloud. Well, what? The cracked window-pane that she had noticed the first time one morning after Harry and his friends had been to a dance? Two decks of cards on the desk? The copy of *Life* magazine on the rack? (A Mr. Weir of Weirton was on the outside page.) The summer *Social Register*, with its warped cover curling up? She heard a screen door slam, an odd sound in this kind of weather, when the flies had died. It was Anna, of course. Anna's hands were cold; Mrs. Carnavon noticed them when Anna reached up to take off her shawl.

'He said he'd be glad to serve you in about three-quarters of an hour,' said Anna. 'I was right. He does have to go out and buy the chops. About three-quarters of an hour, he said. I think what he's doing, I think he wants to warm up the dining-room a little, too. You know, it was awful this winter for Mr. McCall. I don't believe he had more than two or three people there a week. A couple regulars, like salesmen, passing through, but overnight I don't believe he had more than two or three people. Just for lunch, the regulars. I don't think it paid him to keep open.'

'Anna, will you go upstairs in Mr. Harry's room, there's a picture in a silver frame—'

'Of Dr. Carnavon. I have it out in our room.'

'How dare you!'

'I'm sorry, Ma'am, I only meant to do the right thing. I didn't want anybody to steal—'

'You had no right to touch anything in that room. Go bring it to me!'

The tears came and Anna fled, and Mrs. Carnavon was weary of herself, flaring up at this miserable soul, who had no way of knowing that that room was not to be disturbed. No order had been given. Indeed, Mrs. Carnavon admitted that until now she had not thought of leaving that room the way it was, the way it had been all winter. It was part of her confusion, trying to find some reason for making this trip. Trying to find some excuse, she admitted, that would explain the trip to the servants, to Anna. And then, finally, finding the worst excuse of all: Anna would know she had not driven all this distance merely to take home a picture of a husband long dead. Weary, wearily, Mrs. Carnavon climbed the stairs to her son's room.

On the wall the same diamond-shaped plaque, with the clasped hands and the Greek letters; another wooden diamond, with the head of a wolf; a photograph of a baseball team, with names badly printed in white ink under the picture; a large bare spot where there had been a reproduction which he had liked well enough to take back to town. A magazine that he may have read. She opened it: ' . . . and it will become increasingly apparent that the forces of Fascism are labouring night and day . . . choice may have to be made sooner than you expect; but no matter when it comes, when it does come it will be sooner than you like. . . .' A young friend, an *old* friend, of Harry's had written that. An intense young man had come to see her a month or so ago; he had been abroad, he had just learned, he couldn't *believe* it. Why, he and Harry, for eight

years. . . . Eight years? What about twenty-four years? What was
eight years? Well, for one thing, it was eight years during which he
had seen Harry a good deal more than she had, like it or not.

Everything in this room would have to go. Those things, those
shields, those pictures, all that would have to go. She would send
them to the right people. Everything would have to go. She now
saw that in the back of her mind, as she was climbing the stairs,
had been some vague plan to lock this room and leave everything
as she found it; but now when she saw this she felt chilled and
disgusted. Let him be dead, but let him be dead! Let him be what
he was, and let it have ended with no awful sanctuary or crypt of
useless things. Oh, how useless were these things! 'I do not even
know what Upsilon means,' she whispered. 'These baseball players.
Do I want to see *them?*' She recoiled from the nearness of a danger,
the danger of keeping this room the way it was, and the lone, secret
visits she would have paid it, looking at things that had no meaning
to her. She could see clearly, like watching a motion picture of
herself, what she would have done, what she had been in terrible
danger of doing: next August, next September, a year from next
August and a year from next July, she would have come up here,
unlocked the door, come in this room and stood. She saw herself,
a woman in white, trying to squeeze out a tear at the sight of these
things of wood and brass and paper and glass—and all the while
distracted by the sounds of passing cars, the children next door, the
telephone downstairs, the whirring vacuum cleaner. And she even
knew the end of this motion picture: she would end by hating a
memory that she only knew how to love.

She walked out, leaving the door open, and went downstairs.
Anna was standing in the hall, with fear in her eyes. Mrs. Carnavon
looked at her watch. 'Tell Driscoll to bring the car around.'

'He's having a bite with us,' said Anna.

'Tell him to bring the *car* around!' said Mrs. Carnavon. 'I'm
going back by train.'

The train was quicker.

CHAPTER 14

Days

After the first few days there the habits of living in a new place began to form. Larkin would lean over and kiss his wife good-bye, get out of the car, go inside the station, buy his paper at the newsstand, walk through the station, and stand out there waiting for the train. He liked to get that much air anyway, and that was how he began to notice her.

She, he found, would come out of the large apartment house, the last building before you got to the station. She walked across the gravelled space and did not go inside the station at all, not even on rainy days. He had been in the town only a few weeks, and so he did not know whether she stayed inside the station when it was snowing, but from the beginning he was pretty sure she stayed outside, winter and summer.

She carried her paper under her arm. It seemed part of the general neatness of her gloved hands, her bag, her tailored clothes, the scarf at her throat, and even the way she held her head. The paper probably was the one she had delivered at her apartment, because he never saw her buy a paper at the news-stand. On that theory, one day in New York he lingered after everyone had got out of the train, and went back and picked up her paper, hoping it would have her name pencilled on top, the way some newsdealers do; but the only mark on the paper was 9-H, obviously the number of her apartment. He felt ashamed that day, and terrified that the conductor, who would have recognized him, would come in and see him at a seat so far forward of the one he always tried to get. He always, after the first week or so, tried to sit behind her so that if she turned her head he could see her profile. She seldom turned her head.

The other habits were merely habits, but there was one of which he was conscious: the habit of knowing all through breakfast and

before it that he would see her. In a way it was awful, to be so
excited about so little, but it made the mornings good, even some
bad Monday mornings after golf tournaments. The excitement
would be there until she appeared, then a sort of relief, and, in the
train, actual comfort. Yes, comfort, he told himself. The way he
wanted to be with her; sort of like being in the same comfortable
room, quietly reading, knowing she was there. But then once they
were in New York, once people began getting up in the car, it would
be different, a different kind of excitement that was not good, but
upset him. He knew her path to the subway, and on the way she
would pass tunnels that led to hotels. What if he could meet her
and then some morning they could take the train as they always
did, but this one morning she would turn in at one of those tunnels
and wait for him, and they could go to the hotel together?

He would wonder how he could get to meet her. It was too large
a suburb, too many people got on the train, for casual good mornings with people you hadn't met. There were two country clubs,
and he guessed she belonged to the smaller one, the one with a
nine-hole golf course. He sometimes thought of joining that club,
but he knew his wife would put her foot down. 'Two country clubs?'
she would say. 'What do you want to join that club for? Lot of
other things we could use the money for.' And there were, of course,
and pretty soon, when his son got home from prep school, the
expenses would climb. And anyway, he had no way of knowing she
even belonged to the smaller club. The apartment house in which
she lived had a lot of tennis-courts, and she probably played tennis.
He seldom went to the movies, and he never saw her there, but
what if he did? He had a better chance of getting to know her on
the train than at any damn movie, with his wife there with him.

He came home one afternoon and said, 'I think we ought to have
a man here. A chauffeur-gardener.'

'What for?'

'We need somebody like that, and they don't cost so much. He
could take me to the station in the morning in the big car and you
could use him to drive around, and of course, this fellow we have
now, he's only a part-time gardener and not so damn good, for that
matter.'

'I don't see what we need a full-time man for. It's only additional
expense.'

'Now listen, it wouldn't cost that much more, and we'd get a lot more out of him if we had a full-time man. When Teddy comes home and starts using the Ford all the time you'll be glad of a man to drive you in the big car. You know that yourself. I'm going to call up an agency tomorrow.'

'It's your money, but I think you're silly,' his wife had said. And so Larkin no longer was driven to the station by his wife. In a way, he told himself, he was doing it for her; he didn't want to stop kissing her good-bye, but he didn't want to be seen kissing her by the woman, whoever she was, that he loved.

Well, there it was, acknowledged at last; something he had known all along, more than likely from the first day, when seeing her appear from behind the corner of the station had had an effect on him like—a jolt. Now he began to listen to the words of songs about love, trying to discover a voice on the radio that would be just like a voice he never had heard. In a way he began to envy the people who got into messes in the papers, although that was the last thing he wanted for either of his two women—the one he was married to, and the one he loved. 'Mrs. Larkin and two detectives surprised her manufacturer husband at a morning tryst with an attractive brunette at a midtown hotel. The woman, Mrs. Larkin said, was attired in a flimsy négligée, and was about thirty years old. She said her husband had registered under the name of Lawrence. A property settlement . . . alimony . . . custody of their one son.' Hell, no! That wasn't the way Anna would do it; not the way he would have it.

Oh, no? Well, if he couldn't have it any other way, he would have it that way. When he went to the station the morning after he lay thinking these things he wanted to explain to her: 'If we can't have it that way, if you love me enough, let her go ahead and do as she pleases. I'll give her all the money she wants.' And then he had to laugh out loud at what he was thinking, and at that moment she turned, and there was a smile in her eyes. Two other men smiled, too, at him, this man standing alone and laughing out loud at some private joke. But *she* had smiled and it was beautiful. *She* was beautiful. And on the way in on the train he suddenly knew that now it was only a question of days. Days!

CHAPTER 15

Are We Leaving To-Morrow?

It was cool, quite cool, the way the weather is likely to be at an in-between resort when the Florida season is over but the Northern summer season has not yet begun. Every morning the tall young man and his young wife would come down the steps of the porch and go for their walk. They would go to the mounting block where the riders would start for the trails. The tall young man and his wife would stand not too close to the block, not speaking to anyone; just watching. But there might have been a little in his attitude, in his manner, of a man who felt that he was starting the riders, as though his presence there made their start official. He would stand there, hatless and tan, chin down almost to his chest, his hands dug deep in the pockets of his handsome tweed topcoat. His wife would stand beside him with her arm in his, and when she would speak to him she would put her face in front of him and look up. Almost always his answer would be a smile and a nod, or perhaps a single word that expressed all he wanted to put into words. They would watch the riders for a while, and then they would stroll over to the first tee of the men's golf course to watch the golfers start off. There it would be the same: not much talk, and the slightly superior manner or attitude. After they had watched their quota of golfers they would go back to the porch and she would go up to their rooms and a Negro bellboy would bring him his papers, the *Montreal Star* and the *New York Times*. He would sit there lazily looking at the papers, never so interested in a news item that he would not look up at every person who came in or went out of the hotel, or passed his chair on the porch. He watched every car come up the short, winding drive, watched the people get in and out, watched the car drive away; then when there was no human activity he would return to his paper, holding it rather far away, and on his face and in his eyes behind the gold-rimmed spectacles there was always the same suspicion of a smile.

He would go to his room before lunch, and they would come down together. After lunch, like most everyone else, they would retire, apparently for a nap, not to appear until the cocktail hour. They would be the first, usually, in the small, cheery bar, and until it was time to change for dinner he would have a highball glass, constantly refilled, in his hand. He drank slowly, sipping teaspoonfuls at a time. In that time she might drink two light highballs while he was drinking eight. She always seemed to have one of the magazines of large format in her lap, but at these times it was she who would look up, while he hardly turned his head.

Not long after they came she began to speak to people; to bow and pass the time of day. She was a pleasant, friendly little woman, not yet thirty. Her eyes were too pretty for the rest of her face; in sleep she must have been very plain indeed, and her skin was sensitive to the sun. She had good bones—lovely hands and feet—and when she was in sweater and skirt her figure always got a second look from the golfers and riders.

Their name was Campbell—Douglas Campbell, and Sheila. They were the youngest people over fifteen in the hotel. There were a few children, but most of the guests were forty or thereabouts. One afternoon the Campbells were in the bar and a woman came in and after hesitating at the entrance she said, 'Good afternoon, Mrs. Campbell. You didn't happen to see my husband?'

'No, I didn't,' said Mrs. Campbell.

The woman came closer slowly and put her hand on the back of a chair near them. 'I was afraid I'd missed him,' she said to no one; then suddenly she said, 'Do you mind if I sit with you while he comes?'

'No, not at all,' said Mrs. Campbell.

'Please do,' said Campbell. He got to his feet and stood very erect. He set his glass on the little table and put his hands behind his back.

'I'm sorry I don't remember your name,' said Mrs. Campbell.

'Mrs. Loomis.'

Mrs. Campbell introduced her husband, who said, 'Wouldn't you like a cocktail meanwhile?'

Mrs. Loomis thought a moment and said she would—a dry

Daiquiri. Then Campbell sat down, picking up his drink and beginning to sip.

'I think we were the first here, as usual,' said Mrs. Campbell, 'so we couldn't have missed Mr. Loomis.'

'Oh, it's all right. One of us is always late, but it isn't important. That's why I like it here. The general air of informality.' She smiled. 'I've never seen you here before. Is this your first year?'

'Our first year,' said Mrs. Campbell.

'From New York?'

'Montreal,' said Mrs. Campbell.

'Oh, Canadians. I met some awfully nice Canadians in Palm Beach this winter,' said Mrs. Loomis. She named them off, and Mrs. Campbell said they knew them, and he smiled and nodded. Then Mrs. Loomis tried to remember the names of some other people she knew in Montreal (they turned out to have been Toronto people), and Mr. Loomis arrived.

A white-haired man, a trifle heavy and about fifty, Mr. Loomis wore young men's clothes. He was brown and heavy lidded. He had good manners. It was he who corrected his wife about the people from Montreal who actually were from Toronto. That was the first time the Loomises and the Campbells had done more than speak in passing, and Mrs. Campbell was almost gay that afternoon.

The Campbells did not come down to dinner that evening, but they were out for their stroll the next morning. Mr. Loomis waved to them at the first tee, and they waved—*she* waved, Campbell nodded. They did not appear for cocktails that afternoon. For the next few days they took their stroll, but they had their meals in their room. The next time they came to the cocktail lounge they took a small table at the side of the bar, where there was room only for the table and two chairs. No one spoke to them, but that night was one of the nights when the hotel showed movies in the ballroom, and after the movie the Loomises fell in with them and insisted on buying them a drink, just a nightcap. That was the way it was.

Mr. Loomis brought out his cigar case and offered Mr. Campbell a cigar, which was declined, and gave the orders for drinks, 'Scotch, Scotch, Scotch, and a Cuba Libre.' Mrs. Loomis was having the Cuba Libre. As the waiter took the order Mr. Campbell said, 'And bring the bottle.'

There was a fraction of a second's incredulity in Mr. Loomis's face; incredulity, or more likely doubt that he had heard his own ears. But he said, 'Yes, bring the bottle.' Then they talked about the picture. It had been a terrible picture, they all agreed. The Loomises said it was too bad, too, because they had crossed with the star two years ago and she had seemed awfully nice, not at all what you'd expect a movie star to be like. They all agreed that the Mickey Mouse was good, although Mr. Loomis said he was getting a little tired of Mickey Mouse. Their drinks came, and Mrs. Loomis was somewhat apologetic about her drink, but ever since she had been in Cuba she'd developed a taste for rum, always rum. 'And before that gin,' said Mr. Loomis. Mr. Campbell's glass was empty and he called the waiter to bring some more ice and another Cuba Libre, and he replenished the highball glasses from the bottle of Scotch on the table.

'Now this was my idea,' said Mr. Loomis.

'Only the first one,' said Mr. Campbell. They let it go at that, and the ladies returned to the subject of the star of the picture, and soon Mr. Loomis joined in. They got all mixed up in the star's matrimonial record, which inevitably brought up the names of other movie stars and *their* matrimonial records. Mr. and Mrs. Loomis provided the statistics, and Mrs. Campbell would say yes or no as the statement or opinion required. Mr. Campbell sipped his drink wordlessly until the Loomises, who had been married a long time, became simultaneously aware of Mr. Campbell's silence, and they began directing their remarks at him. The Loomises were not satisfied with Mrs. Campbell's ready assents. They would address the first few words of a remark to the young wife, because she had been such a polite listener, but then they would turn to Mr. Campbell and most of what they had to say was said to him.

For a while he would smile and murmur 'Mm-hmm', more or less into his glass. Then it seemed after a few minutes that he could hardly wait for them to end an item or an anecdote. He began to nod before it was time to nod, and he would keep nodding, and he would say, 'Yes, yes, yes,' very rapidly. Presently, in the middle of an anecdote, his eyes, which had been growing brighter, became very bright. He put down his drink and leaned forward, one hand clasping and unclasping the other. 'And—yes—and—yes,' he kept saying, until Mrs. Loomis had finished her story. Then he leaned farther forward and stared at Mrs. Loomis, with that bright smile and with his breathing become short and fast.

'Can I tell you a story?' he said.

Mrs. Loomis beamed. 'Why, of course.'

Then Campbell told a story. It had in it a priest, female anatomy, improbable sitations, a cuckold, unprintable words, and no point.

Long before Campbell finished his story Loomis was frowning, glancing at his wife and at Campbell's wife, seeming to listen to Campbell but always glancing at the two women. Mrs. Loomis could not look away; Campbell was telling her the story, and he looked at no one else. While Mrs. Campbell, the moment the story was begun, picked up her drink, took a sip, and put the glass on the table and kept her eyes on it until Campbell signalled by his chuckling that the story was at an end.

He kept chuckling and looking at Mrs. Loomis after he had finished, and then he smiled at Loomis. 'Huh,' came from Loomis, and on his face a muscular smile. 'Well, dear,' he said. 'Think it's about time—'

'Yes,' said Mrs. Loomis. 'Thank you so much. Good night, Mrs. Campbell, and good night.' Campbell stood up, erect, bowing.

When they were entirely out of the room he sat down and crossed his legs. He lit a cigarette and resumed his drinking and stared at the opposite wall. She watched him. His eyes did not even move when he raised his glass to his mouth.

'Oh,' she said suddenly. 'I wonder if the man is still there at the travel desk. I forgot all about the tickets for to-morrow.'

'To-morrow? Are we leaving to-morrow?'

'Yes.'

He stood up and pulled the table out of her way, and when she had left he sat down to wait for her.

CHAPTER 16

Salute a Thoroughbred

Say, maybe you're right. It says here McDonough is going to put Divak in '*Ballast*, sea epic soon to be placed in production at West Coast studios.' Divak in *Ballast!*

I don't know what you call her. I know what I call her. She's a friend of yours, so if you want to stick up for Divak, I don't blame you. Friendship! I might as well be brutally frank with you, Laura. I'm only the same age as you, dear, but I've seen a lot more of this world. I've travelled and been around, and of course in my travelling around this place and that place I haven't spent every minute of the time just gadding about and having a good time. Oh, no. You get tired having a good time, and often-times when everybody else was out dancing or going to this, that, and the other thing, I often preferred to stay home, in my room, and read. Travel always means that to me. I love to read, Laura. If I'm in the right mood, there's nothing I'd rather do than take a nice hot bath and get into bed and lie there reading. Once I get in that mood, you couldn't get me to leave my bed, not if you had Clark Gable up on deck dying to meet me, and I like Clark Gable, but plenty.

But anyway, although we are the same age, with only a few months' difference between us in ages, Laura, you have to admit I have seen a lot and read a lot, and it's made me cynical, travelling around that way and reading the really good books, not trash that you don't get something from, Laura. That's why I'm cynical about friendship; my experience, both actual *and* mental, they've made me cynical about the copybook maxims that we are brought up to believe. These copybook maxims tend to make you put too high a price on friendship, with the result, oh, inevitably, they create the result that what you do is weaken your character instead of strengthen it. So don't think you are being a strong character defending Divak or being on her side in this. Because you're not, Laura. It's

really much more difficult, Laura, to come right out and condemn
a person like Divak and take the stand I'm taking and not let false
sentiment obscure the issue. It's much more difficult to do that way
than what you're doing defending a person, Divak or anyone else.
The minute you say anything disparagingly about another girl,
another woman, people are all too ready to fly up and criticise you
and say you do it because you must have something personal in it,
as if I had something personal against Divak. Do I have anything
personal against Divak? Do you think I have, Laura? You don't
think so, I'm sure, because you and I are close enough friends, so
you know, even if I never said it before, you know that in my heart
I have nothing but commiseration for that poor dumb Swede. What
I mean is, any woman that can stand living with McDonough, I
have nothing but commiseration for her.

And yet I don't know if perhaps she isn't just as well off. I don't
know but perhaps I'm wasting my commiseration, because I have
to admit—anybody has to admit it, I guess—if ever I saw anyone
suited to anyone else it's Divak is suited to McDonough. I'll give
him one thing, and that is he recognised almost from the very start
how high-strung I am. Not in the sense of excitable and flighty, like
Bertha, for instance. I don't mean that way high-strung. The best
example I can think of is how our temperaments, they used to clash
sometimes on any and every occasion. I would come home from
the studio really all pooped out, ready for a piping-hot tub and bed,
and sometimes McDonough would be there when I got there, and
sometimes he would come in after I arrived home. Well, he might
come home tired too, sometimes from work, directing a picture, and
sometimes from polo. I would be upstairs in my tub relaxing and
every nerve refreshing itself for those few precious minutes. All of
a sudden I'd hear him wandering around in riding boots and spurs,
looking for something or other, or just wanting someone to cross
his path so he could vent his spleen on whoever he happened to
run across. Well, a couple of times he came in while I was in the
tub, and he would just sit there and mutter things like 'How did
Bairnhardt do to-day, Bairnhardt?' That was his idea of funny, only
when you've heard it steen thousand times in two years, you begin
to catch on, and I wouldn't pay any attention to him. But finally
I had to issue instructions to my maid that Mr. McDonough was
not to be admitted to my bathroom while I was in the tub relaxing.
He just wouldn't respect my privacy otherwise, so I barred him

from my bathroom. I'm much too sensitive a person, is what I'm trying to say, to stand for invasions of privacy when I am tired and trying to recoup my strength.

We had some other clashes, some of them of a more violent nature and some just ordinary little clashes that take place, I suppose, whenever you throw together two people with temperaments. Not that mine was temperament in the accepted sense of the word, Laura. I'm not the kind to hold up a production and cost the company thousands of dollars while I get temperamental over something the script girl says or I don't like the grips' faces or I want to take a sock at my stand-in. But by nature I'm cursed with temperament, and of course that wild Irish bastard, he was born with temperament and never got over it. So naturally we had clashes. Then when he and I agreed to disagree, I remember how sweet he was, rather sweet and sad about it, when he said to me: 'My love,' he said, 'I salute a thoroughbred.' I don't know whether you know that line, Laura. 'My love, I salute a thoroughbred.' That was in *Strange Virgin*, the picture they released under the title of *Adorable Girl* when the Catholic Church made all that stink. One of the characters says to me, 'My love, I salute a thoroughbred,' and I say, 'Idiot!' Like that. 'Idiot!' And give a comradely, platonic, gentle smile, because the character that says that to me is only a minor character and he never gets to first base with me. So when McDonough says that to me, I came right back at him. 'Idiot!' I said, with a platonic, gentle, comradely smile. Of course I knew he would go right to Divak or someone of her type as soon as he saw I wanted to be free of him, and I was right. Straight to Divak.

Well, good luck to them both, I say. And mean it. I mean it like I've never meant anything in my life, really. They'll need it. Look at McDonough. Shortly after I left him, they made him a producer. Of course that sounds like a kind of promotion, but it's really only being kicked upstairs. You notice he doesn't direct any more pictures. That's it. He's a producer now, and the reason is he didn't have the imagination and fire to be a director, so they made him a producer. Oh, it makes me a little sad, because as an individual, as a person, McDonough lost something *fine* these last six months or so. I wouldn't be that conceited that I'd mean me when I say he lost something fine. I don't think of myself in that way. I just mean that something fine went out of his life and it makes me sad to see it gone. Three years ago, McDonough would no more have thought of putting that little tramp in a—oh, well, skip it. Let's just skip it.

CHAPTER 17

Sportsmanship

Jerry straightened his tie and brushed the sleeves of his coat, and went down the stairway where it said 'The Subway Arcade.' The sign was misleading only to strangers to that neighbourhood; there was no subway anywhere near, and it was no arcade.

It was early in the afternoon and there were not many people in the place. Jerry walked over to where a man with glasses, and a cigar in an imitation amber holder, was sitting quietly with a thin man, who also had a cigar.

'Hyuh, Frank,' said Jerry.

'Hyuh,' said the man with glasses.

'Well, how's every little thing?' said Jerry.

Frank looked around the place, a little too carefully and slowly. 'Why,' he said finally, 'It looks like every little thing is fine. How about it, Tom? Would you say every little thing was O.K.?'

'Me?' said Tom. 'Yes, I guess so. I guess every little thing is—No. No. I think I smell sumpn. Do you smell sumpn, Frank? I think I do.'

'Aw, you guys. I get it,' said Jerry. 'Still sore. I don't blame you.'

'Who? Me? Me sore?' said Frank. 'Why, no. Would you say I was sore, Tom? This stranger here says I'm sore. Oh, no, stranger. That's my usual way of looking. Of course you wouldn't have no way of knowing that, being a stranger. It's funny, though, speaking of looks. You look the dead spit of a guy I used to know, to my sorrow. A rat by the name of Jerry. Jerry—Jerry, uh, Daley. You remember that Jerry Daley rat I told you about one time? Remember him, Tom?'

'Oh, yes. Come to think of it,' said Tom, 'I recall now I did hear you speak of a heel by that name. I recall it now. I would have forgot all about the rat if you wouldn't of reminded me. What ever did happen to him? I heard he was drowned out City Island.'

'Oh, no,' said Frank. 'They sent him to Riker's Island, the party I mean.'

'All right. I get it. Still sore. Well, if that's the way you feel about it,' said Jerry. He lit a cigarette and turned away. 'I only come back to tell you, Frank, I wanted to tell you I'd be satisfied to work out the dough I owe you if you leave me have a job.'

'Hmm,' said Frank, taking the cigar out of his mouth. 'Hear that, Tom? The stranger is looking for work. Wants a job.'

'Well, waddia know about that? Wants a job. What doing, I wonder,' said Tom.

'Yeah. What doing? Cashier?' said Frank.

'Aw, what the hell's the use trying to talk to you guys? I came here with the best intention, but if that's your attitude, *so long.*'

'Guess he's not satisfied with the salary you offered, Frank,' said Tom.

Jerry was back on the stairway when Frank called him. 'Wait a minute.' Jerry returned. 'What's your proposition?' said Frank. Tom looked surprised.

'Give me the job as house-man. Twenty-five a week. Take out a ten a week for what I owe you. I'll come here in the mornings and clean up, and practise up my game, and then when I get my eye back, I'll shoot for the house—'

'Using house money, of course,' said Tom.

'Let him talk, Tom,' said Frank.

'Using house money. What else? And the house and I split what I make.' Jerry finished his proposition and his cigarette.

'How long id take you to get shooting again?' said Frank.

'That's pretty hard to say. Two weeks at least,' said Jerry.

Frank thought a minute while Tom watched him incredulously. Then he said, 'Well, I might take a chance on you, Daley. Tell you what I'll do. You're on the nut. All right. Here's my proposition: the next two weeks, you can sleep here and I'll give you money to eat on, but no pay. You practise up, and in two weeks I'll play you, say, a hundred points. If you're any good, I'll give you thirty bucks cash and credit you with twenty bucks against what you're in me for. Then you can use your thirty to play with. That oughta be enough to start on, if you're any good. I seen you go into many a game when you were shooting on your nerve and come out the winner, so thirty bucks oughta be plenty. *But* if you're no good at the end of two weeks, then I'll have to leave you go. I'll charge up twenty bucks against what you owe me, and you can go out in the wide, wide world and look for adventure, the way you did once before. Is that a deal?'

'Sure. What can I lose?' said Jerry.

'Sure, what can you lose? How long since you ate last?'

In two weeks Jerry had lost the tan colour of his face, and his hands were almost white again, but he looked healthier. Eating regularly was more important than the sun. The regulars who had known Jerry before he stole the hundred and forty dollars from Frank were glad to see him and made no cracks. They may have figured Frank for a real sucker, some of them, but some of the others said there were a lot of angles in a thing like that; nobody knew the whole story in a thing of that kind, and besides, Frank was no dope. It didn't look like it. Jerry was brushing off the tables, putting the cues in their right bins—the twenty-ounce cues into bins marked 20, the nineteen-ouncers in the 19 bins, and so on—and retipping cues, and cleaning garboons and filling them with water, and dusting everywhere. He caught on soon about the new regulars, who wanted what table, and what they usually played. For instance, every afternoon at three o'clock two guys in Tuxedos would come in and play two fifty-point games, and the rest of the afternoon, before they had to go and play in an orchestra, they would play rotation. Well, you had to keep an eye on them. They paid by the hour, of course, but if you didn't watch them, they would use the ivory cue ball to break with in the games of rotation, instead of using the composition ball, which did not cost as much as the ivory ball and stood the hard usage better. The ivory ball cost Frank around twenty bucks, and you can't afford to have an ivory ball slammed around on the break in a game of rotation. Things like that, little things—that was where an experienced house-man like Jerry could save Frank money.

Meanwhile he practised up and his game came back to him, so that at the end of the two weeks he could even do massé shots almost to his own satisfaction. He hardly ever left except to go out to a place, a Coffee Pot on Fordham Road, for his meals. Frank gave him a 'sayfitty' razor and a tube of no-brush-needed cream. He slept on the leather couch in front of the cigar counter.

He also observed that Frank was shooting just about the same kind of game he always shot—no better, and no worse. Jerry therefore was confident of beating Frank, and when the day came that ended the two weeks agreed upon, he reminded Frank of the date, and Frank said he would be in at noon the next day to play the hundred points.

Next day, Frank arrived a little after twelve. 'I brought my own referee,' said Frank. 'Shake hands with Jerry Daley,' he said, and did not add the name of the burly man, who might have been Italian, or even an octoroon. The man was dressed quietly, except for a fancy plaid cap. Frank addressed him as Doc, Jerry first thought, but then he realized that Frank, who was originally from Worcester, Massachusetts, was calling the man Dark.

Dark sat down on one of the high benches, and did not seem much interested in the game. He sat there smoking cigarettes, wetting them almost half-way down their length with his thick lips. He hardly looked at the game, and with two players like Frank and Jerry there wasn't much use for a referee. Jerry had Frank forty-four to twenty before Dark even looked up at the marker. 'Geez,' he said. 'Forty-four to twenty. This kid's good, eh?'

'Oh, yeah,' said Frank. 'I told you one of us was gonna get a good beating.'

'Maybe the both of you, huh?' said Dark, and showed that he could laugh. Then Jerry knew there was something wrong. He missed the next two times up, on purpose. 'There they are, Frank,' said Dark. Frank ran six or seven. 'Got a mistake in the score, there,' said Dark. He got up and took a twenty-two-ounce cue out of the bin, and reached up and slid the markers over so that the score was even.

'Hey,' said Jerry. 'What is it?'

'That's the right score, ain't it?' said Dark. 'Frank just run twenty-four balls. I see him, and I'm the referee. Neutral referee.'

'What is it, Frank? The works or something?' said Jerry.

'He's the referee,' said Frank. 'Gotta abide by his decision in all matters. Specially the scoring. You have to abide by the referee, specially on matters of scoring. You know that.'

'So it's the works,' said Jerry. 'O.K. I get it. Pick up the marbles.' He laid down his cue. 'What a sap I been. I thought this was on the up-and-up.'

'I hereby declare this game is forfeited. Frank wins the match. Congratulate the winner, why don't you, kid?'

'This means I'm out, I guess, eh, Frank?' said Jerry.

'Well, you know our agreement,' said Frank. 'We gotta abide by the decision of the referee, and he says you forfeited, so I guess you don't work here any more.'

'Congratulate the winner,' said Dark. 'Where's your sportsmanship, huh? Where's your sportsmanship?'

'Don't look like he has any,' said Frank, very sadly. 'Well, that's the way it goes.'

'Maybe we better teach him a little sportsmanship,' said Dark.

'All right by me,' said Frank. 'One thing I thought about Mr. Daley, I thought he'd be a good loser, but it don't look that way. It don't look that way one bit, so maybe you better teach him a little sportmanship. Only a little, though. Just give him a little bit of a lesson.'

Jerry reached for the cue that he had laid on the table, but as he did, Dark brought his own cue down on Jerry's hands. 'Shouldn't do that,' said Dark. 'You oughtn't to scream, either. Cops might hear you, and you don't want any cops. You don't want any part of the cops, wise guy.'

'You broke me hands, you broke me hands!' Jerry screamed. The pain was awful, and he was crying.

'Keep them out of other people's pockets,' said Frank. 'Beat it.'

CHAPTER 18

Dr. Wyeth's Son

There were many things that made Johnny Wyeth stand apart from the rest of our gang. For one thing, his accent. He had a Southern accent. He had come to our town only the winter before that summer, and his accent was unchanged, although he went to school with us and we all had at least traces of Pennsylvania Dutch inflections and sentence structure in our talk. But being with us did not change his accent, although being with him may have had its effect on ours. But besides his accent, there was his way of dressing that made him different from the rest of us. We all wore, in the summer, a sort of uniform for all but dress-up occasions. When we had to dress, we wore white duck knickerbockers and blue Norfolk jackets, but other times in the evening we wore khaki (we pronounced it 'kyky') knickerbockers and blue shirts and 'Scouts' shoes, which were ordinary brown high shoes except they had a cap on the toes. But Johnny, in the summer evenings, wore white linen suits and white buckskin Oxfords, which had the advantage of being noiseless when we played games like Run, Sheepie, Run, and a game which we simply called Chase. Then, Johnny was different from the rest of us because he wore glasses. He was crossed eyed, and to boys of that age being cross-eyed is not unattractive. At least in Johnny's case it gave him a wild look which I suppose caused us to credit him with a lot more daring than we all had.

Johnny's father, like mine, was a doctor, and I used to hear my father say that Dr Wyeth was the best diagnostician who had come to our town in years, but that 'it was to bad to drank'. This was a curious admission to come from my father, who was a total abstainer and a rabid dry. I knew Dr Wyeth drank, all right. Nights he used to come home and leave his car with the engine running, in front of the Markwith house, where the Wyeths lived. (They didn't own their home, as we all knew.) He would sit in the car for a few minutes and then get out and stagger in, and Johnny would leave us—we hung around Victoria Jones's porch—and go up and turn off the motor. I remember the switch, a shiny Bosch switch it was, and Johnny never would let us turn it; he had to do it himself.

There was one other thing that kept Johnny from being like us, and that was his language. He cursed and swore all the time. We were pretty clean of speech; the majority of us were Catholics and we had to tell it in confession when we used bad language, but Johnny was Presbyterian and he didn't care what he said. One of his favourite words was 'baster'. He did not know what it meant, and neither did we, but he said it was the worst thing you could call anybody, and he said his father had told him that if anyone ever called him that, to go right ahead and kill him, hit him with a rock or anything else. Johnny used it whenever he was extremely angry. The rest of the time he simply cursed and swore and used dirty words. The Holding twins, Gerald and Francis, in whose back yard we had our headquarters, in a dusty, dirt-smelling tool house, were the ones who most frequently told Johnny to cut out his language. But they had no effect on Johnny.

However, one afternoon that summer, late one afternoon, we were playing Million-Dollar Mystery in the Holdings' tool house. *The Million-Dollar Mystery* was the name of a movie serial which we were all following, and we would use the scenario of each episode to provide us with a game from Friday to Friday. It was quite late, almost supper time, and we were playing hard, and Gerald or Francis, I forget which, had an old, rusty Daisy air rifle, which he stuck in Johnny's stomach with too much force behind it, and Johnny let out a yell you could have heard up at the courthouse. 'God damn you! What's the idea you doing that?' And so on, with a lot of profanity.

'Oh, come on,' we all said. 'Don't get so sore about nothing. Quit swearing and put up your hands. He has you covered.'

'No, sir, I won't do anything of the kind,' said Johnny. 'This no-good baster ain't gonna do that to me.'

'Don't you call *me* that,' said the Holding twin.

'Oh, I won't eh? Who says I won't, you baster?' Johnny raised his voice and the argument went on, everybody getting in it one way or another, but always Johnny's voice and the words he said were more distinguishable than anything else. And then suddenly we looked around as the door of the tool shed opened, and there was Mr Holding. Mr Holding in bedroom slippers, spectacles with a little gold chain reaching back to one ear, necktie held against his shirt by a little gold pincher.

'Who's using that language in this yard? John Wyeth was that you?'

'What if it was? No baster ain't gonna hit me with any God-damn rifle.'

'Here, here! Stop that kind of talk this minute. Leave that yard or I'll take you by the ear. Leave this yard this minute, you young guttersnipe, using language like that. I'll show you—' He advanced towards Johnny, and Johnny moved back and grabbed an old garden rake.

'God damn you, don't you put a hand on me! I'll sure hit you with this, you put a finger on me.'

'Oh, *ho!* Like father, like son,' said Mr Holding. 'Well, we'll see who has the say about what goes on in this yard. Come on, you boys. Hurry up and go home. I'll settle with Johnny. Ought to know what to expect from his kind.'

'Go on, *get out!*' Johnny screamed, and called Mr Holding an old baster and a lot of others things which we did not make out, because we were out of the tool house. Mr Holding went right to the house, and standing in the area-way beside the house we could hear him on the telephone. 'Dr Wyeth? This is Holding, next door. Will you come over and get that son of yours out of my yard, or will I have to call the police? . . . Decent young boys . . . *my* sons hear talk like that . . . and keep him away from these boys or you'll hear from *all* the fathers in this neighbourhood. We're all getting fed up with the goings-on since you moved here.' We heard no more, because Mrs Holding told us to go home.

But that night after supper we met early at Victoria Jones's porch and we all waited for the Holding twins, and at seven or so they came down the street together. Right away we asked them about what had happened after we were sent home.

'Oh, did he get his!' said one Holding.

'Did he get his!' said the other.

'What happened?' we said.

'Papa called up Mr Wyeth and told him to come over and get Johnny or else he'd get the police and arrest him, and so pretty soon Mr Wyeth—'

'Doctor Wyeth,' I said.

'Aw, well, Doctor. He came over and got Johnny and took him out the back gate, and *then* you should of *heard* it. He had Johnny yelling and cursing. What he beat him with, it must of been at least a cane. He must of beat him with a cane for a half an hour.'

'More than once. A couple of times,' said the other Holding.

'Oh a couple of times at least. He was still giving it to him when we sat down for supper. The worst I ever heard anybody get beaten.'

We asked them more questions, but they did not know many more details, and after that Victoria Jones came out and sat on the porch and the other girls came one by one, and the argument was about whether Johnny deserved it. Johnny did not show up that night, but along about nine o'clock, when it was just getting dark, we saw Dr Wyeth drive up in his car and stop in front of his house, and this night he was the worst we'd ever seen him. He could hardly get out of the car. When he did finally get out and go in the house, none of us dared to go over and turn off the motor.

CHAPTER 19

Over the River

Mr Winfield's hat and coat and bag were in the hall of his flat, and when the man downstairs phoned to tell him the car was waiting, he was all ready. He went downstairs and said hello to Robert, the giant Negro chauffeur, and handed Robert the bag, and followed him out to the car. For the first time he knew that he and his granddaughters were not to make the trip alone, for there were two girls with Sheila, and she introduced them: 'Grandfather, I'd like to have you meet my friends. This is Helen Wales, and this is Kay Farnsworth. My grandfather, Mr Winfield.' The names meant nothing to Mr Winfield. What did mean something was that he was going to have to sit on the strapontin, or else sit outside with Robert, which was no good. Not that Robert wasn't all right, as chauffeurs go, but Robert was wearing a raccoon coat, and Mr Winfield had no raccoon coat. So it was sit outside and freeze or sit on the little seat inside.

Apparently it made no difference to Sheila. He got inside, and when he closed the door behind him, she said, 'I wonder what's keeping Robert?'

'He's strapping my bag on that thing in the back,' said Mr Winfield. Sheila obviously was not pleased by the delay, but in a minute of two they got under way, and Mr Winfield rather admired the way Sheila carried on her conversation with her two friends and at the same time routed and rerouted Robert so that they were out of the city in no time. To Mr Winfield it was pleasant and a little like old times to have the direction and the driving done for you. Not that he ever drove himself any more, but when he hired a car, he always had to tell the driver just where to turn and where to go straight. Sheila knew.

The girls were of an age, and the people they talked about were referred to by first names only. Ted, Bob, Gwen, Jean, Mary,

Liz. Listening with some care, Mr Winfield discovered that school acquaintances and boys whom they knew slightly were mentioned by their last names.

Sitting where he was, he could not watch the girls' faces, but he formed his opinions of the Misses Wales and Farnsworth. Miss Wales supplied ever other word when Sheila was talking. She was smallest of the three girls, and the peppy kind. Miss Farnsworth looked out of the window most of the time, and said hardly anything. Mr Winfield could see more of her face, and he found himself asking, 'I wonder if that child really likes anybody.' Well, that was one way to be. Make the world show *you*. You could get away with it, too, if you were as attractive as Miss Farnsworth. The miles streamed by and the weather got colder, and Mr Winfield listened and soon understood that he was not expected to contribute to the conversation.

'We stop here,' said Sheila. It was Danbury, and they came to a halt in front of the old hotel. 'Wouldn't you like to stop here, Grandfather?' He understood then that his daughter had told Sheila to stop here; obediently and with no dignity he got out. When he returned to the car, the three girls were finishing their cigarettes, and as he climbed back in the car, he noticed how Miss Farnsworth had been looking at him and continued to look at him, almost as though she were making a point of not helping him—although he wanted no help. He wasn't really an *old* man, an *old man*. Sixty-five.

The interior of the car was filled with cigarette smoke, and Miss Farnsworth asked Mr Winfield if he'd mind opening a window. He opened it. Then Sheila said one window didn't make any difference; open both windows, just long enough to let the smoke get out. 'My! That air feels good,' said Miss Wales. Then: 'But what about you, Mr Winfield? You're in a terrible draught there.' He replied, for the first use of his voice thus far, that he did not mind. And at that moment the girls thought they saw a car belonging to a boy they knew, and they were in Sheffield, just over the Massachusetts line, before Miss Farnsworth realised that the windows were open and creating a terrible draught. She realised it when the robe slipped off her leg, and she asked Mr Winfield if he would mind closing the window. But he was unable to get the crank started; his hands were so cold there was no strength in them. 'We'll be there soon,' said Sheila. Nevertheless, she closed the windows, not even acknowledging Mr Winfield's shamed apologies.

He had to be first out of the car when they arrived at the house
in Lenox, and it was then that he regretted having chosen the
strapontin. He started to get out of the car, but when his feet
touched the ground, the hard-packed frozen cinders of the driveway
flew up at him. His knees had no strength in them, and he stayed
there on the ground for a second or two, trying to smile it off.
Helpful Robert—almost too helpful; Mr Winfield wasn't that
old—jumped out of the car and put his hands in Mr Winfield's
armpits. The girls were frightened, but it seemed to Mr Winfield
that they kept looking towards the library window, as though they
were afraid Sheila's mother would be there and blaming them for
his fall. If they only knew. . . .

'You go on in, Grandfather, if you're sure you're all right,' said
Sheila. 'I have to tell Robert about the bags.'

'I'm all right,' said Mr Winfield. He went in, and hung up his
coat and hat in the clothes closet under the stairs. A telephone was
there, and in front of the telephone a yellow card of numbers
frequently called. Mr Winfield recognised only a few of the names,
but he guessed there was an altogether different crowd of people
coming up here these days. Fifteen years make a difference, even
in a place like Lenox. Yes, it was fifteen years since he had been
up here in the summer time. These trips, these annual trips for
Thanksgiving, you couldn't tell anything about the character of the
place from these trips. You never saw anybody but your own family
and, like to-day, their guests.

He went out to the darkened hall and Ula, the maid, jumped in
fright. 'Ugh. Oh. It's you, Mr Winfield. You like to scare me.'

'Hello, Ula. Glad to see you're still holding the fort. Where's Mrs
Day?'

'Upstairs, I think. . . . Here she is now,' said Ula.

His daughter came down the steps; her hand on the banister was
all he could see at first. 'Is that you, Father? I thought I heard the
car.'

'Hello, Mary,' he said. At the foot of the stairs they went through
the travesty of a kiss that both knew so well. He leaned forward so
that his head was above her shoulder. To Ula, a good Catholic, it
must have looked like the kiss of peace. '*Pax tibi*,' Mr Winfield felt
like saying, but he said, 'Where have you—'

'Father! You're freezing!' Mrs Day tried very hard to keep the
vexation out of her tone.

'It was a cold ride,' he said. 'This time of year. We had snow flurries between Danbury and Sheffield, but the girls enjoyed it.'

'You go right upstairs and have a bath, and I'll send up—what would you like? Tea? Chocolate? Coffee?'

He was amused. The obvious thing would be to offer him a drink, and it was so apparent that she was talking fast to avoid that. 'I think cocoa would be fine, but you'd better have a real drink for Sheila and her friends.'

'Now, why do you take that tone, Father? You could have a drink if you wanted it, but you're on the wagon, aren't you?'

'Still on it. Up there with the driver.'

'Well, and besides, liquor doesn't warm you up the same way something hot does. I'll send up some chocolate. I've put you in your old room, of course. You'll have to share the bathroom with one of Sheila's friends, but that's the best I could do. Sheila wasn't even sure she was coming till the very last minute.'

'I'll be all right. It sounds like—I didn't bring evening clothes.'

'We're not dressing.'

He went upstairs. His room, the room itself, was just about the same; but the furniture was rearranged, his favourite chair not where he liked it best, but it was a good house; you could tell it was being lived in, *this year*, to-day, tomorrow. Little touches, ash-trays, flowers. It seemed young and white, cool with a warm breath, comfortable—and absolutely strange to him and, more especially, he to it. Whatever of the past this house had held, it was gone now. He sat in the chair and lit a cigarette. In a wave, in a lump, in a gust, the old thoughts came to him. Most of the year they were in the back of his mind, but up here Mr Winfield held a sort of annual review of far-off, but never-out-of-sight regrets. This house, it used to be his until Mary's husband bought it. A good price, and in 1921 he certainly needed the money. He needed everything, and to-day he had an income from the money he got for this house, and that was about all. He remembered the day Mary's husband came to him and said, 'Mr Winfield, I hate to have to be the one to do this, but Mary—Mary doesn't—well, she thinks you weren't very nice to Mrs Winfield. I don't know anything about it myself, of course, but that's what Mary thinks. I expected, naturally, I thought you'd come and live with us now that Mrs Winfield has died, but—well, the point is, I know you've lost a lot of money, and also I happen to know about Mrs Winfield's will. So I'm prepared to make you a pretty good offer, strictly legitimate, based on current values, for the house in Lenox. I'll pay the delinquent taxes myself and give you a hundred and fifty thousand dollars for the house and grounds. That ought to be enough to pay off your debts and give you a fairly decent income. And, uh, I happen to have a friend who knows Mr Harding quite well. Fact, he sees the President informally one night a week, and I know he'd be only too glad, if you were interested. . . .'

He remembered how that had tempted him. Harding might have fixed it so he could go to London, where Enid Walter was. But even then it was too late. Enid had gone back to London because he didn't have the guts to divorce his wife, and the reason he wouldn't divorce his wife was that he wanted to 'protect' Mary, and Mary's standing, and Mary's husband's standing, and Mary's little daughter's standing; and now he was 'protecting' them all over again, by selling his house so that he would not become a family charge—protecting the very same people from the embarrassment of a poor relation. 'You can have the house,' he told Day. 'It's worth that much, but no more, and I'm grateful to you for not offering me more. About a political job, I think I might like to go to California this winter. I have some friends out there I haven't seen in years.' He had known that that was exactly what Mary and her husband wanted, so he'd gone.

There was a knock on the door. It was Ula with a tray. 'Why two cups, Ula?' he said.

'Oh. Di put two cups? So I did. I'm just so used to putting two cups.' She had left the door open behind her, and as she arranged the things on the marble-topped table he saw Sheila and the two girls, standing and moving in the hall.

'This is your room, Farnie,' said Sheila. 'You're down this way, Helen. Remember what I told you, Farnie. Come on, Helen.'

'Thank you, Ula,' he said. She went out and closed the door, and he stood for a moment, contemplating the chocolate, then poured out a cup and drank it. It made him a little thirsty, but it was good and warming, and Mary was right; it was better than a drink. He poured out another cup and nibbled on a biscuit. He had an idea: Miss Farnsworth might like some. He admired that girl. She had spunk. He bet she knew what she wanted, or seemed to, and no matter how unimportant were the things she wanted, they were the things she wanted, and not someone else. She could damn well thank the Lord, too, that she was young enough to have a whack at whatever she wanted, and not have to wait the way he had. That girl would make up her mind about a man or a fortune or a career, and by God she would attain whatever it was. If she found, as she surely would find, that nothing ever was enough, she'd at least find it out in time; and early disillusionment carried a compensatory philosophical attitude, which in a hard girl like this one would take nothing from her charm. Mr Winfield felt her charm, and began regarding her as the most interesting person he had met in many dull years. It would be fun to talk to her, to sound her out and see how far she had progressed towards, say, ambition or disillusionment. It would be fun to do, and it would be just plain nice of him, as former master of this house, to invite her to have a cup of cocoa with him. Good cocoa.

He made his choice between going out in the hall and knocking on her door, and knocking on her door to the bathroom. He decided on the second procedure because he didn't want anyone to see him knocking on her door. So he entered the bathroom and tapped on the door that led to her room. 'In a minute,' he thought he heard her say. But then he knew he must have been wrong. It sounded more like 'Come in.' He hated people who knocked on doors and had to be told two or three times to come in, and it would make a bad impression if he started the friendship that way.

He opened the door, and immediately he saw how right he had been in thinking she had said 'In a minute'. For Miss Farnsworth was standing in the middle of the room, standing there all but nude. Mr Winfield instantly knew that this was the end of any worthwhile life he had left. There was cold murder in the girl's eyes, and loathing and contempt and the promise of the thought his name for ever would evoke. She spoke to him: 'Get out of here, you dirty old man.'

He returned to his room and his chair. Slowly he took a cigarette out of his case, and did not light it. He did everything slowly. There was all the time in the world, too much of it, for him. He knew it would be hours before he would begin to hate himself. For a while he would just sit there and plan his own terror.

CHAPTER 20

Pleasure

The taxi-drivers in front of the Coffee Pot said, 'Hello, baby; hello, sweetheart; hi, kid; how you doin', baby; hey, what's your hurry, sweetheart?' She walked on. They kept it up until she turned her head slightly in their direction and called back at them, 'Nuts!' She turned the corner, and her heels felt as though they were biting into the sidewalk, the way they always felt when she was angry. Every time she passed the Coffee Pot, every time she came near the taxi-drivers, she had her mind made up that she was not going to say a word to them. 'I won't give them that satisfaction,' she would say to herself. And every time she snapped back at them, it made her angry. Some evenings she would be on her way home in a good humour; tired, all right, but with a good day's work behind her and that much more money earned. Then she would come to the Coffee Pot, and the same thing would happen over again, and she would get home full of hatred and with her feet hurting again.

Down the block she walked until she came to a house with a broken iron fence in front of the basement, and went up the stone steps and inside. She hesitated at the door, found it unlocked, climbed three flights of stairs, and entered her room. She walked with her hand in front of her in the dark until she touched the bulb in the light fixture. She turned the switch once and the light went on and off, then she turned it again and this time the light stayed on. She pulled down the shade in the single window, and undressed and hung up her clothes. She drank a glass of water and then filled the wash-basin and washed her stockings and hung them across the newspaper on top of the radiator. Then she opened the small package she had brought in with her, and laid a cinnamon bun on the table.

Five months since she had been really hungry. July, August, September, October, November. Almost five months, not quite, and

there had been plenty to eat every day. At the cafeteria where she
worked, first as dish-washer, but now as a clean-up girl, they
provided two meals a day, and her pay was sixteen dollars a week.
Now and then there was a dime for her. Her job as clean-up girl
consisted of wiping off tables, seeing to it that the people had water
to drink, keeping the chairs in their places. She wore a maid's
uniform and cap, black with white collar and apron and black-and-
white cap, and it looked all right. There was one mean-dispositioned
old guy who often left a dime for her, and sometimes there would
be people with kids whom she helped, and they would leave a dime.
Never more than a dime, but a dime covered the 'L' fare. When
they first gave her the job of clean-up girl, she thought of herself as
a sort of hostess, and finally one day she even said to the manager,
'I guess I'm a sort of a hostess on this job.'

'How do you mean?' he had said.

'Why, I make them comfortalbe. You know,' she said. 'Keep
their glasses full, and see that they have napkins and stuff.'

'Yeah?' he had said. 'Well, don't get that idea. You're still gettin'
dishwasher's scale, and any funny business and back you go.' It
was the first time she realised that the manager had sized her up.
He had sized her up the same way the hack-drivers had sized her
up. They just took one look at you, and they thought they knew all
about you. She knew she didn't look altogether American. Why
should she? Her mother was Polish, her father was Polish; so why
should she look American?

She opened the bureau drawer and took out the candy box in
which she always kept six or seven dollars. She figured that if a
sneak thief came in her room while she was at work, he would open
the bureau drawer first and take a look at the cheap rings and
necklaces and say the hell with that, and then he would open the
candy box and take the six or seven dollars and beat it. Now she
saw that the money was still there. She put it back in the drawer
and opened the door of the built-in closet. She took out two cheap
suitcases, and then she lifted a loose board in the floor and saw
that the little red-enamelled box was where she had left it. She
opened the box and counted the money: one hundred and twenty
dollars. Every week she made herself put five bucks in the box. Five
in the box, plus three she paid for the room, plus fifty cents a week
for the 'L', plus sixty cents a week cigarette money, plus fifty cents
a week on the winter coat and another half a buck on the suit, and

two bucks a week she sent her married sister—she wished she could account for the rest, but somehow she never could. She didn't really have to buy papers, because people were always leaving them in the cafeteria, and there were always enough to go around among the employees, but she kept on buying them because the man at the 'L' station was blind. And she went to the movies a couple of times a week. 'There ought to be two hundred and forty bucks there,' she said, 'Instead of a hundred and twenty, if I'd of saved ten bucks a week.' She closed the box, locked it, and put it back under the flooring. 'But what the hell, a person has to have some pleasure,' she said. And so saying, she lit a whole cigarette.

CHAPTER 21

Alone

Hague closed the door of his old room. That ought to keep them out. Something had made him do it, and he realised as he sat down that it must have been an instinct of defence, for even as a small boy he always had left the door open. He never closed it, neither did his mother nor his father nor his sister. When in those days he was unhappy or had been punished he did not go to his room; he went to his tent in the back yard, or to the attic, or to the stable-garage. Certainly they all would remember that the door always had been open, and they ought to have grace or tact or sense enough not to disturb him. Even his mother would understand that, no matter how strongly she was impelled to come to him. Now he could be alone for a few minutes.

He went through the motions of lighting a pipe. It was an old Dunhill and it was dated by the silver C that was inbedded in the bowl. He was a little ashamed of having been so collegiate. He had had many pipes since college. . . . Quite suddenly he began to cry. He had cried a lot in the past three days, but now he sought a reason for it, and he realised that it was because Nora's last gift to him had been a pipe. It was queer how he could feel like crying, and cry, and not know until the tears came why he was crying. He laid aside the pipe and employed his handkerchief. Then he thought: Oh, what the hell, I might as well cry—and having thought it he stopped crying.

Hague picked up a magazine. It was *The New Yorker*, which he always had vaguely resented. He tried to remember how Nora felt about it. He reflected now that if he were asked what Nora had liked in the way of reading matter of any kind he would not be able to answer. She bought many books and she seemed to have opinions on the more popular ones. But he felt rather than knew that her taste was good. His memory held no proof of it. In music it was different. He knew what she liked. He could not give the names, but he could recognise her favourite melodies. He could remember the names of her favourite dance tunes. One of them had been 'When Hearts Are Young'. That came from a show called *The Lady in Ermine*. He had taken Sue Colby to that show. If he had married Sue he now would be (all things being equal) the father of two children and the husband of a healthy girl. . . . But even healthy girls drown, and there was no use blaming Nora for drowning.

Well, he could be glad he hadn't been there when it happened. He had had enough of his mother's sympathy as it was, without having been on hand to provoke quiet, vicarious hysterics. That was unkind, but he knew perfectly well that his mother didn't give much of a rap for Nora herself; it was about the effect of her death upon him that his mother cared, and this he resented. He remembered what his mother said when he told her that he was going to marry Nora. 'All I want to be told, Herbert, is that you love her. People do marry girls older than themselves, and it turns out splendidly in some cases, but if there's the least doubt in your mind, I wish you'd wait a little longer.' He knew now that that was as close as his mother dared come to telling him not to marry Nora. Well, he had married her, God damn it, and he had been happy. He would go on being happy, too, in spite of his mother. He admitted that was a little vague, but he told himself that was what he meant.

His mother's shock and grief and the rest of the performance she was putting on were her way of making up to him for her tacit disapproval of Nora. Or else she was afraid that he had seen through the disapproval and wanted to make him believe it never had existed. Bah!

He guessed he ought to take a drink. . . .

That was another thing. He guessed he could get a leave of absence from the office, and it would be a good idea to take a trip somewhere and go on a mild bat. He'd get Phil Casey to go with him. Phil Casey certainly would be the person. Phil was the only other person in the world who had known he and Nora were living together before they were married. Phil was their closest friend. Hague suspected that Phil liked Nora so much because he was so fond of Hague, but he was good to Nora and wanted Hague to be good to her, too. He remembered a night when he had kissed a girl Phil had brought to their apartment. Phil threatened to punch his

nose. 'Not because I give a damn about that little monkey,' Casey
had said. 'But if you'd seen Nora's face, you'd know why.' Which
was Casey's way of showing that he knew Nora was the best thing
that ever happened to Hague. He wondered how Casey was taking
this. He'd bet Casey was good and drunk and showing his grief
more than Hague himself was. Yes, Casey was a swell guy and
would be good company on a bender—and immediately Hague
decided that the last person he wanted to see for the next six
months was Phil Casey. Anybody who had known him and Nora so
intimately (except for the doctor, Casey was the only other person
who knew Nora was pregnant) would be unbearable, and Casey,
the maudlin drunkard most of all. No, by God, he wouldn't sit in
a hotel room and drink brandy with Casey. Even if neither of them
ever mentioned Nora it would be unbearable, unbearable.

Who else was there? Not his sister. Louise was one of those people
who Know When to Stop; a good drinking companion, but she
knew when to stop. She wouldn't get so drunk as Hague wanted to
get, and besides he didn't really know her. She was almost his own
age but he had not seen much of her in the last couple of years.
Still . . . maybe that was a recommendation. At least she had had
honesty enough not to eulogise Nora. She hadn't known Nora,
really, so she might be a good one to go away with. She had her
own little unhappiness, too. She'd probably be glad of the chance
to get away from home for a month or two. That was it. They'd go
to Bermuda. It wouldn't cost much.

Nora had about twenty thousand dollars her father had left
her. . . . Oh, God!

Concentrate on a trip with Louise, that was the idea. And try to
put up with his mother until they went away. With that decision
Hague felt slightly more kindly towards his mother. She was a
stupid woman. In another time, five hundred years ago or whenever
it was women were more actively predatory (that wasn't the word,
exactly, but something like that), his mother would have been the
kind that would fight for her young. Now the best she could do was
to be overcautious about their marriages and meddlesome in their
lives. By God, she certainly had loused up Louise's, just because
Louise had wanted to marry a Catholic. He felt suddenly convinced
that Louise was not a virgin. He didn't know why he knew it, but
he knew it, all right. That small tarnished cup on his desk had been
given him for winning the junior boys' singles championship at

Camp Idlewild. Hague wondered if he ought to write to the Vassar alumnae magazine and tell them about Nora. Her mother and father were dead and somebody ought to do it.

He lit a cigarette and his mind was a blank. Then the cigarette began to taste like warm mist in his mouth and he began to cry. The cigarette tasted awful and he dinched it. There was a knock on the door. It was his mother. She looked older and somehow weaker. 'It's time, dear,' she said. God in heaven! *It's time, dear.* Why couldn't she say the whole thing? How he hated that dodging.

'You mean it's time for the service.'

Her lower lip quivered and she looked straight at him, hurt. 'Yes, dear,' she said. Then he knew that she saw he had been crying and he began to cry again. He put his arms around her, and he knew that in all the world there was nothing he wanted but to hold her like that. He didn't care what she said so long as she wept for him.

CHAPTER 22

Frankie

Frankie had bustled into the shop one afternoon when things were quiet. The usual rush of men who get their late shaves around noon had passed, and there were no haircuts in the shop. Frankie walked in and said: 'Who's the big shot here?' Dimello introduced himself, or rather said: 'I am the propri'tor,' and Frankie said he had noticed there were only four barbers but there were six chairs. 'I'm a first-class barber,' he said. 'You gimme a job, straight commission? I'll work union or scab; do' make any difference.'

'Do you drink?' Dimello asked.

'Wuddia got? . . . Oh, you mean do I get drunk? Well, I get drunk, but I never missed a day in my life from hangover. You do' needa worry about that. You just gimme a job and you'll be happy. I'm first-class.'

Dimello took him on and Frankie proved an efficient barber. He never seemed to talk to people without their enjoying it. That, of course, was because he knew when not to start a conversation. He made a lot of money for the shop and he wasn't there two weeks before he had a couple of regulars. He also had had a date with Betty, the manicurist.

Betty always had made it a rule never to go out with any of the barbers because she disliked Italians, but she liked Frankie's teeth. Besides, he pestered her to death until she said she would go out with him. He didn't know any girls in New York, he said, and he was getting lonesome, going to the moving pictures by himself. Betty hadn't been out with a man less than ten years older than herself in God knows how long, and she couldn't ever remember having been out with a kid ten years younger than she was. So she said she would go to the pictures with him. 'How naïve,' she told Marline, her room-mate. 'Isn't it naïve of me to be having a date with a kid twenty-five years old and going to the movies with him?'

Frankie came for her and he was something to impress Marline, all right, with a graceful powder-blue suit that buttoned once just below his chest, and a little white stone in his solid-blue tie, and a white shirt with a collar that had long starched points. He was a little short for Betty, but he had an air about him and nice manners. 'I'm pleased to meet you, Miss Burns,' he said to Marline. 'I heard a lot about you at the shop.' He showed his teeth. 'And it was all flattering.' Betty could see that Marline was impressed, all right. Maybe he was only a kid, but he was no mugg. Betty had a lone, favourite epigram which she now thought of: 'Guys with gold in their pockets would be swell if they didn't have a lot of gold in their mouth too.'

They went out and walked to Columbus Circle, at Frankie's suggestion. On the way over Frankie said: 'Got any special idea where you want to put on the feed bag?'

'No, no place special.'

'Oke. Because I was thinking about a Wop place I went to the other night where they got good wine. Me being a Wop I like good wine. Do you like wine? You're Irish, aren't you?'

'No, I'm half English and I have Spanish blood in me on my mother's side. But I like wine, all right.' The fact of the matter was that Betty was no longer so entranced with the novelty of a tame movie. They went to a speakeasy and had a lot of wine, and they both got a little tight. Frankie suggested getting a couple of bottles of wine and going back to Betty's apartment, but Betty knew that probably Marline's friend would be there, so she said no. Frankie took her home and she wouldn't let him come up, not even for a little while.

For the next couple of days he was polite and that was all. One day he said: 'How's Marline?'

'She's fine.'

'Does she ever ask about little Frankie?'

'Not that I can recall. She's innarested in a very dear gentleman friend.'

'Oh. Oh-ho-ho.' Frankie smiled. That night he called Marline, who had a date, but she mentioned the call to Betty. The next day at the shop Betty said: 'Listen, little boy, it ain't any of my concern, but just as a friend, if I were you I would lay off calling Marline.'

'She told you, eh?'

'We have no secrets from each other. She is my closest friend.

And I just wanna advise you that Marline is innarested in a very dear gentleman friend. In fact she's ingaged to be married.'

'So am I,' said Frankie, and laughed. He walked away, a few steps, and then he went back and said: 'Of course you ain't jealous by any chance, Betty?'

'Why, you little—!'

'I get it! I get it!' said Frankie.

After that he made Betty's life a hell. She would be at work on some old punk's nails or maybe trying to promote a date with one of the 'Garden mob', but Frankie never would let her get to first base. He would interrupt her conversations and look at the man with a we're-both-men look of understanding, and the prospective date would smile at Frankie and begin to kid Betty, but it wouldn't be the kind of kidding that leads to dates. The man would say slightly insulting things and laugh and glance around at Frankie, who would laugh too. God knows how many dates Frankie spoiled for Betty.

And when the shop was empty he would stand there, leaning against his chair, smoking a cigarette. He would look over at Betty, and not say a word for a few minutes; then he would say, 'Pull your dress down, sweetheart; this here is a dignified shop, eh, Mr Dimello?' Dimello, who liked Frankie, and liked Betty, too, would smile and mumble something that didn't matter. Frankie was always making cracks, always tormenting her. But the time that she wanted to kill him was when she came home at four o'clock in the morning and found him there with Marline.

From then on he stopped making cracks, but worse than the cracks were the looks he would give her. Always smiles. Betty wanted to give up her job. She compromised by not living with Marline any more. She got to hating the shop, which she once had liked, and even when she was working on a man's hands at some chair other than Frankie's, she wouldn't start a conversation, nor would she continue one that had been started. Her tips dwindled.

This went on for six or seven weeks. Then one day two large men with flat fat faces came in the shop. One of the barbers snapped to attention and indicated his chair, but the man who was in the lead didn't even take off his hat. He walked straight to Frankie's chair and said: 'Now no fuss, Jimmie. Finish the man's shave, becuss it's going to be the last you'll do for about ten years.'

Frankie turned around and grinned. 'Well, Murph, it took yuz long enough. How's every little thing in Phillie?'

Frankie finished the man's shave and then took off his own white coat. He went up to Dimello and whispered a few words, and Dimello reached in his pocket and gave Frankie a couple of twenties. Frankie shook hands with him and was just about to leave. He remembered Betty. 'How about a little good-bye kiss, sweetheart?'

Betty looked dumb for a second, and then said: 'Why not?' Frankie kissed her.

'Always give the ladies a break,' he said, and departed.

CHAPTER 23

The Gentleman in the Tan Suit

Robert, she supposed, was well dressed. Well dressed for San Francisco. He was not well dressed according to the standards Mary had had to adopt as Mr Monkton's secretary. In the years that she had been Mr Monkton's secretary Mary had had to learn about Charvet and Peel and those people. She knew how much it cost to have a pair of shoes sent back to Peel for rebuilding. She knew it cost two or three dollars more than the shoes Robert was wearing would cost new. Mr Monkton was one of the best-dressed men downtown, and one thing she had noticed about Mr Monkton's clothes was that no matter what he wore in the country (and she knew little enough about that), his city clothes were not the kind that would have to be pressed after a single wearing. That was the way Robert's clothes impressed her in the first few seconds. The suit was too light a tan, so light that she did not see how he could keep it clean after one ride in a taxi, and already it had wrinkles at the side of the knee and in the elbows that would not disappear into the cloth. She noticed that his shirt was only half a shade away from the tan of the suit; the tie was tan with white figures, the socks were silk, tan silk. The shoes were tan. The hat was tan, with only the beginning of finger marks where it was dented in the crown. Kay probably thought he dressed wonderfully. Mary thought it was awful.

Mary had come home and found him here. Not to her surprise; she knew they were coming, Kay and Robert. She had wondered a little about the young man's curiosity, what kind of curiosity would make him want to meet his wife's sister after he had been married a year, and make him want it so much that he would be willing to spend so much money. Mary had written in answer to Kay's letter, telling her that unless it was New York they wanted to see, why not save the money and she would come out to San Francisco when Mr Monkton went abroad in October. But Kay had replied that all their plans had been made—Robert had made them. His pay cut had been restored, his father had given them money for a new car which they did not need, and—this was something Mary supplied without any information from her younger sister—apparently they had not done any planning towards having a baby. The money was there, so Mary told them to come on.

Robert was alone in the apartment when Mary arrived there. He was sitting on the davenport, with one arm along the arm of the davenport, and the other arm along the back. It looked like a position that had just been assumed, but when Mary saw how many cigarettes had been smoked and noticed that there was no impression in any of the chairs or elsewhere in the davenport, she thought she had an idea what kind of young man her sister had married. She had seen many, many young men waiting for Mr Monkton, sitting in that same position, not insulted when Mr Monkton would go out with his hat on, ignoring them. They would wait in the reception-room for Mary and ask for another appointment, and another, if necessary, until Mr Monkton would keep an appointment, or talk to them in the elevator or somewhere. Young men who sat that way almost always got to see Mr Monkton. Usually that was as much as they did get, but Mary knew that they felt they had made a contact. And so Mary knew her sister had married a young man who knew how to wait. What they said about the men who made them wait was another matter; she had heard them more than once at Schrafft's and places like that, sometimes identifying Mr Monkton by name: 'Why, I waited for that bastard Monkton. . . .' Mary, when she wasn't too tired, delighted in passing close to young men whom she thus overheard, knowing they would recognise her and get the lump because they could not be sure she had not overheard them.

Robert turned his head when she let herself in the apartment. He did not stand until he had a look at her. He laughed and showed his teeth. Mary knew him for the kind of young man who would go to his dentist regularly just to be able to say (truthfully) that dentists would starve if everybody had teeth like his. His teeth were so good and so obviously good all the way back that there was no suspense to watching them. She wondered if he ever bit Kay.

'You're Mary, I'll bet,' he said.

'Yes,' she said. 'And Robert. How are you, Robert? I'm so glad to see you.' She struck the same note on glad and see, which took the curse off the sentence.

'I'm glad to see you, too, Mary,' he said.

She wondered whether there was any special reason, the way he said it. They shook hands a long time, and his not kissing her right away was something in his favour.

'Do I kiss my sister-in-law?' he said.

'Mm-hmm.' She extended her cheek.

He was a little embarrassed after kissing her. 'That's the first girl outside of Kay I've kissed since God knows when. Anyway two years is a conservative estimate.'

What did he want? Did he want her to relay that to Kay, or was he lying, or was he trying to boast about his fidelity? 'Well, that's pretty good for 1935,' she said.

'Good, hell, it's perfect,' he said. 'Kay will be here any minute. She's supposed to be here now, but I guess she had to stop and buy something, is my guess.'

'How about a cocktail?'

'Not for me, thanks,' he said. 'If you want one.'

'We'll wait till Kay gets here, then,' she said.

'I only drink beer except on state occasions. Not that this—'

'Well, I should think'

'Well, you know, like football games or sumpn. Kay likes a cocktail, though. You bet. She makes about the only decent cocktail I ever drank. She's going to be awfully glad to see you. Gee, five years. I guess she was only eighteen when you saw her last time.'

'You understand about my not going home for the wedding, don't you, Robert?'

'Sure. I said to Kay, I said, "Listen, a job's a job these days. You can't expect your sister to just up and—" '

'Oh. Did you have to explain? I mean apologise for me?'

'Well, frankly, you know. It's a year ago now, so it's all over and done with, but yes, in a way. I didn't have to—you wouldn't call it apologise, but Kay couldn't get it through her head that you couldn't just up and go, right in the middle of winter. I said to her, "Listen," I said, "this Mr Monkton" —your boss—"I happen to know he's a big shot, and secretary to him probably means a twenty-four-hour-a-day job." She got it finally. Hell, your aunt and uncle, they were swell.' He stopped abruptly and sat down. He looked up at Mary. 'You know what?'

'What?'

'You know what suddenly occurred to me—oh, after we were married. I don't know how to put this.'

'You can say anything to me.'

'Well, I didn't realise till after we were married why she wanted you to be there.' He shook his head. 'You know, Kay didn't know a god-damn thing. You know?'

'Oh.' She sat beside him. 'I thought girls to-day—I suppose I've been living in New York such a long time.'

'Not Kay. And your aunt never told her anything.'

'But twenty-two years old.'

'That's what I thought.'

'Oh, I should have gone home. How about now?'

He smiled. 'Okay now. Yes, she's all right now. We've been married a year, you know.' He stood up. 'Well, I guess this is a hell of a way to talk the first ten minutes I meet my wife's sister. But that was the only thing—I admit I sort of held it against you myself, but I don't any more.'

'I *couldn't* be so thoughtless.'

'*It's* all right,' he said. 'Honestly, there's nothing to worry about any more. See, it's all *right* now, so I thought Kay and I—it'd be a good idea for her to come East and see you, now that everything's all right.'

Mary looked at him and burst into tears.

CHAPTER 24

Most Gorgeous Thing

I don't think I could ever go back to the stage. You're constituted different than I am, Lucille. I have to have more and more time to myself. You know my new contract? Five pictures a year and permission to do one outside picture for another company. That way I have more lezzure time to myself to do what I like. What about you? You used to be a great reader, but I don't see how you do it any more with eight performances a week, and I think of the reading you did in Hollywood. I wouldn't of missed *Goodbye, Mr Chips!* for anything, but where would I get time to read if I had a play on Broadway? Oh, I'm committed to Hollywood. Definitely. Still, in your case. I was saying just before I left. When I mentioned that I was going to New York, I said I was going to see you and we all said the same thing. I know how you hated it out there, and naturally, the way they treated you. But I said, 'Now that Lucille is in a hit, watch them try and get her, but I'll bet they won't get her for any lousy seven-fifty *this* time.' You hold out for fifteen hundred, darling. You can get it. I believe Eddie MacIllaney. Oh, you never knew him, did you? He admired your work from ten years ago. I didn't know him when you were out there, and now, poor Eddie! He shot himself just before I left, but he said you could get fifteen hundred easily, and *ought* to get five *thousand!* . . .

Do you really want to hear about him? Well, there isn't so much. He was crazy. Towards the end I was his only friend left in the world, but even so I have to admit he was crazy. Nobody knew why he committed suicide. He had a job. I got him a job at the studio because I didn't want to see him lose his self-respect. About a year ago I got him this job. It only paid forty dollars a week, but it was something. It was a sort of a writing job. I never even knew if he could write, except poetry a long time ago, but on his say-so I got him this job. It's a kind of a job that I don't know how to

explain it. You see, when they have a classic, that there isn't any
copyright to it, what they do is to register with the Academy. The
company says we want to produce, say, *Uncle Tom's Cabin* or, uh,
Macbeth, and that means they register it with the Academy, and
then they have to put somebody to work on it, otherwise some other
company is liable to go ahead with it and produce it. So what they
do is they get somebody like Eddie and pay him forty dollars a
week to write a treatment or something, just to be working on it.
Of course they never use anything he writes, but it's some kind of
a technicality. You know what a screwy place it is. Anything can
happen there, and usually *does!* But that's what Eddie did. I got
him the job because I felt sorry for him and I didn't want him to
lose his self-respect.

People used to wonder why I was so nice to him, but he was
grateful, even if he did have funny ways of showing it sometimes.
I guess if he hadn't been around forty-five they would have torn
my reputation to pieces, but nobody ever thought of Eddie that
way. I used to call him up any time I felt like it, four in the morning,
and I'd tell him to whip over and cheer me up when I was blue or
depressed. He'd come over, and would we get plastered, but he
never took advantage of it except once. One night I came home
from a party by myself, I mean I came home without an escort,
only a married couple, and I wasn't a bit sleepy, so I called Eddie
Mac and he came over and we started drinking out in the kitchen,
just the two of us, and the first thing I knew Eddie had his arms
around me and kissing my neck and God knows what all he wasn't
doing, and saying to me, 'You're the most gorgeous thing that
ever came to this ill-fated town,' meaning Hollywood. Imagine! Of
course, naturally, I've had to handle a situation like that before.
Well, whenever I've had to deal with a situation like that I've
always considered the man, and I knew the best way to deal with
Eddie Mac was to talk to him sensibly and reason with him. I said
to him, 'Don't you think you're making a mistake, Eddie?' I said.
'Aren't we being a little foolish? In the first place,' I said, 'I have
no feelings like that for you. Couldn't have.' I told him how I felt
about him, the difference in our ages and how he was twenty-one,
old enough to vote at least, when I was born, or maybe not even
that. 'Let's forget all about it,' I said, and I convinced him that it
wouldn't do him any good if I did have an affair with him. He'd
lose his job and everything, so even if I felt that way about him it

was better for *him* if I didn't give in. He was very depressed and all, but he finally saw it my way, and the only unpleasant thing about it was I caught his cold. We went in my pool without any clothes on later, but I'd done that before without catching cold, so I must have got it from him.

He was laid up for a while with a touch of pneumonia after that and couldn't go to work, but to show him I forgave him I went to bat for him at the studio and made them keep him on salary till he got better. Then, after he was up and around, I called him up one night and he came over and it was just like old times. He was the only man I felt really safe with. I like to get good and plastered every three or four months, and it's nice to know you can get somebody to drink with you that you can forget everything and not have to worry the next day about what did I do and all that. You remember how *you* used to worry, Lucille. I told him that, about how you used to worry. We were talking about you, and he was so impressed because you and I were friends, and he said it was nice of me to show the human side of you, because he'd always thought of you as some kind of a cold idol, like. But anyway—uh—oh, yes, when he was sick. No, I did tell you that. It was when he got better, and this night he came over and we had our first good binge, and that was the last time I saw him alive or at all. I can't bear to look at a dead person, so I never saw him again after that night. He went home, and then a few days later a man came to my house and he said he was Eddie's doctor and I thought he came about the bill, so I said send him in, and he came in and I said was there any trouble about the bill, because if there was I'd pay it, and he said well, it wasn't that exactly. He said he was perfectly willing to let the bill ride, because he went to college with Eddie, but he said what he wanted to talk about (and I knew it was something screwy), he wanted to ask me if I would help Eddie in a more important way, and I answered him by saying I'd probably done more for Eddie than a lot of people he went to college with, and this bird said yes, but would I do more, and I said that depends. I thought it was going to be some kind of a shake. Well, what he wanted, he wanted me to make Eddie go on the wagon. He said if Eddie drank any more he'd probably keel over and die. Well, what's that got to do with me, I said. Was I responsible for a man old enough to be my father? Did I start him drinking, I said. Didn't Eddie ever hear of liquor before me? I was furious at Eddie and this punk doctor.

I called my butler, and right in front of this person I gave orders that if Mr MacIllaney phoned I wasn't in, no matter what circumstances. 'You'll regret this meddlesome tactics,' I said, and then I said if that concluded his visit, I was busy and he walked out, and I'll bet he went right back and made up some story to Eddie, because Eddie phoned that night, but I wouldn't talk to him. I wanted to prove to this doctor that Eddie drank of his own accord and not because I made him. So of course people came over and told me how they saw Eddie plastered all over the place, and then one morning I picked up the papers and big headlines about him committing suicide one afternoon in his office at the studio, otherwise they wouldn't of made such a fuss about it, because Eddie wasn't well known. But people that think I'm cold and aloof, they should of seen me when I read about Eddie doing the Dutch. I couldn't sleep for a week without taking something. He might have bored you, Lucille, but I wish you could of known him slightly. Poor thing, he loved the theatre and New York. He was always going to write a play for me.

Oh, before I forget it. Are you going to El Morocco Saturday? I'll get Arthur to get someone for you if you want to.

CHAPTER 25

It Must Have Been Spring

It must have been one of the very first days of spring. I was wearing my boots and my new corduroy habit, and carrying my spurs in my pocket. I always carried my spurs on the way to the stable, because it was eight squares from home to the stable, and I usually had to pass a group of newsboys on the way, and when I wore the spurs they would yell at me, even my friends among them. The spurs seemed to make a difference. The newsboys were used to seeing me in riding breeches and boots or leather puttees, but when I wore the spurs they always seemed to notice it, and they would yell 'Cowboy crazy!' and once I got in a fight about it and got a tooth knocked out. It was not only because I hated what they called me. I hated their ignorance; I could not stop and explain to them that I was not cowboy-crazy, that I rode an English saddle and posted to the trot. I could not explain to a bunch of newsboys that Julia was a five-gaited mare, a full sister to Golden Firefly, and that she herself could have been shown if she hadn't had a blanket scald.

This day that I remember, which must have been one of the very first days of spring, becomes clearer in my memory. I remember the sounds: the woop-woop of my new breeches each time I took a step, and the clop sound of the draught horses' hooves in the thawed ground of the streets. The draught horses were pulling wagon-loads of coal from the near-by mines up the hill, and when they got half-way up the driver would give them a rest; there would be a ratchety noise as he pulled on the brake, and then the sound of the breast chains and trace chains loosening up while the horses rested. Then presently the loud slap of the brake handle against the iron guard, and the driver yelling 'Gee opp!' and then the clop sound again as the horses' hooves sank into the sloppy roadway.

My father's office was on the way to the stable, and we must have been at peace that day. Oh, I know we were, because I remember it was the first time I wore the new breeches and jacket. They had come from Philadelphia that day. At school, which was across the street from our house, I had looked out the window and there was Wanamaker's truck in front of our house, and I knew that The Things had come. Probably crates and burlap rolls containing furniture and rugs and other things that did not concern me; but also a box in which I knew would be my breeches and jacket. I went home for dinner, at noon, but there was no time for me to try on the new things until after school. Then I did hurry home and changed, because I thought I might find my father in his office if I hurried, although it would be after office hours, and I wanted him to see me in the new things.

Now, I guess my mother had telephoned him to wait, but then I only knew that when I got within two squares of the office he came out and stood on the porch. He was standing with his legs spread apart, with his hands dug deep in his hip pockets and the skirt of his tweed coat stuck out behind like a sparrow's tail. He was wearing a grey soft hat with a black ribbon and with white piping around the edge of the brim. He was talking across the street to Mr George McRoberts, the lawyer, and his teeth gleamed under his black moustache. He glanced in my direction and saw me and nodded, and put one foot up on the porch seat and went on talking until I got there.

I moved towards him, as always, with my eyes cast down, and I felt my riding crop getting sticky in my hand and I changed my grip on it and held the bone handle. I never could tell anything by my father's nod, whether he was pleased with me or otherwise. As I approached him, I had no way of telling whether he was pleased with me for something or annoyed because someone might have told him they had seen me smoking. I had a package of Melachrinos in my pocket, and I wanted to throw them in the Johnstons' garden, but it was too late now; I was in plain sight. He would wait until I got there, even though he might only nod again when I did, as he sometimes did.

I stood at the foot of the porch. 'Hello,' I said.

He did not answer me for a few seconds. Then he said, 'Come up here till I have a look at you.'

I went up on the porch. He looked at my boots. 'Well,' he said. 'Did you polish them?'

'No. I had Mike do it. I charged it. It was a quarter, but you said—'

'I know. Well, you look all right. How are the breeches? You don't want to get them too tight across the knee or they'll hurt you.'

I raised my knees to show him that the breeches felt all right.

'Mm-hmm,' he said. And then, 'Good Lord!' He took off his hat and laid it on the porch seat, and then began to tie my stock over again. I never did learn to tie it the way he wanted it, the way it should have been. Now I was terribly afraid, because he could always smell smoke—he didn't smoke himself —and I remembered I had had a cigarette at recess. But he finished tying the stock and then drew away and commenced to smile.

He called across the street to Mr McRoberts. 'Well, George. How does he look?'

'Like a million, Doctor. Regular English country squire, eh?'

'English, hell!'

'Going horseback riding?' said Mr McRoberts to me.

'Yes,' I said.

'Wonderful exercise. How about you, Doctor? You ought to be going, too.'

'Me? I'm a working man. I'm going to trephine a man at four-thirty. No, this is the horseman in my family. Best horseman in Eastern Pennsylvania,' said my father. He turned to me. 'Where to this afternoon? See that the mare's hooves are clean and see if that nigger is bedding her the way I told him. Give her a good five-mile exercise out to Indian Run and then back the Old Road. All right.'

I started to go. I went down the porch steps and we both said good-bye, and then, when I was a few steps away, he called to me to wait.

'You look fine,' he said. 'You really look like something. Here.' He gave me a five dollar bill. 'Save it. Give it to your mother to put in the bank for you.'

'Thank you,' I said, and turned away, because suddenly I was crying. I went up the street to the stable with my head bent down, because I could let the tears roll right out of my eyes and down to the ground without putting my hand up to my face. I knew he was still looking.

CHAPTER 26

I Could Have Had a Yacht

'What do you do?' I said to him. 'Do you just sit around and drink coffee all night long till daylight?' He looked at me kind of funny, the most amazing look, and I thought he didn't understand me. 'Is that all you do?' I said, and repeated my question. 'Don't you ever do anything but sit around and drink coffee all night?' I said. I said, 'I should think the waiters'd get sick and tired of looking at you, drinking coffee. What *is* it?' I said.

'Darling,' he said, looking at me just as dead pan as I don't know what. 'Darling, you mustn't worry so about me,' he said. Well, I told him, I said I wasn't worrying about him. God forbid. Me worry about some ordinary piano-player? I guess he is like Terry said. He has to put everything on a personal basis, right away. There I'd only been with him, I mean been in his *company*, just that one night, and I asked him a casual question and he wants to build up a great big love affair out of it or something. At least that's the impression I gathered by his remark, otherwise why would he say like that, 'Darling, don't worry so about me?' I wasn't worrying about him, I was only trying to make casual repartee so's the both of us wouldn't sit there like two mummies. I wasn't worrying about him. I wasn't even thinking about him when I said it if he wanted to know the truth, but naturally when you're with a man like that, sitting in Dave's or any place, and he doesn't carry on a conversation, naturally you try to make conversation by finding out if you have interests in common that the two of you can talk about, because otherwise you just *sit* there and it looks terrible to see two people sitting in a restunt the man drinking one cup of coffee after the other and smoking these cigars and not saying anything. Right away he wants to put everything on a personal basis and I practically had to tell him I just wasn't interested.

Like he said to me on the way home in the taxi. He was sitting there with a cigar in his mouth and not even condescending to hold up his end of the conversation except yes or no once in a while, and then this all of a sudden he said, 'Say, Toots, you have a nice pair of gams.' 'Oh,' I said. 'I have a nice pair of gams.' I said to him, 'Aren't you old eagle eye, though? You been to the show three nights in succession, if one is to believe your story,' I said, 'and,' I said, 'just now you notice I have nice legs. Where were you looking if you're just finding that out?' I said. I said, 'Mr Carroll thinks so, too, and so do a lot of other people that I'd take their word for it sooner than I would yours. Where were you looking all this time?' 'Not at your legs,' he said.

You know I asked a lot of other musicians about him. I asked them if they knew this fellow, and they all did. As a rule I wouldn't even spit on a musician. You know what they did to a friend of mine, don't you? Priscilla Wortman. She was with a unit that played, you know, the movie houses around. Boston, Chicago, Baltimore. You know. One of those units. So Priscilla, every town she went to—first of all I ought to tell you. The show opened in Pittsburgh, the unit did, and played there a week, and Priscilla had a great big mad love affair with a trumpet-player there. But gave! Then the unit played I think Boston, and so on. Well, every town they went to, always one of the musicians would make a big play for Priscilla, and after they were on the road a month or so, Priscilla began to notice that it was always a trumpet-player that made a play for her. Always a trumpet-player. Well, so when they played Chicago they were held over a couple of weeks in the same theatre, and Priscilla went out with this trumpet-player in the theatre, and she kind of fell for him, about this much. And one night he got a little drunkie and he told her plenty. He got sore at her for something and he told her plenty, right before a room full of people. Explained why trumpet-players always took her out. You know what? This guy in Pittsburgh, or wherever it was, he wrote on the music: 'For a good time get the brunette third from the right in the military number.' And of course every town the unit went to the trumpet-player in that town would see this note on the music, and he'd make a play for Priscilla. And by the time the unit reached Chicago the trumpet-players in all the towns had put okay and the name of the town on the music, to show that they all agreed with the original one. So when they went to Detroit and the trumpet-player there asked her to go out with him you bet Priscilla told him what she thought of him and all trumpet-players in general. If it'd of been me I'd have made them get new music, but Priscilla isn't equipped with much up here.

So even since I heard that story I wouldn't even spit on a musician, but I had to find out about this Jack. I wanted to know if they ever heard of him, *and*, they all did. Some of them even stuck up for him. He wrote 'Blue Moon'. . . . No? Well, it had Blue in the title. I guess it wasn't 'Blue Moon.' Blue something. Who wrote the 'Rhapsody in Blue?' I know it wasn't this Jack, but the one he wrote is *like* the 'Rhapsody in Blue,' so he must be very well known in those circles. Not that that impresses me. You have to be more than a musician to impress me. I could have had a yacht, so it takes more than a musician to impress me, but I must admit I like his attitude. He said to me the other night—oh, I see him. I see him two or three times a week. I didn't see him Tuesday of this week, so it isn't every night. But I was gunna say, the other night he said to me, 'Darling,' he said, 'don't talk. Just don't talk,' he said, 'just be beautiful.' And that's a nice compliment, you know. We have things in common, I can see that, but if he only wouldn't make these crypty remarks all the time.

CHAPTER 27

Olive

Miss Bishop had been the hotel's guest six months without having put in or received a call worth listening in on. Within a month of Miss Bishop's checking in, Olive, the day operator, knew all the regulars, out-going and incoming: the hairdresser in East Forty-seventh Street, the bank downtown, the dry-cleaner, the drugstore, and the Jersey City number. The Jersey City number Olive came to know as Miss Bishop's aunt; a stingy old woman, Olive thought. When Miss Bishop put in a call for the Jersey City number, the call would last ten minutes and sometimes more, but when the aunt's voice asked for Miss Bishop the call stayed within three minutes.

It was always the same. The call would come in at nine or thereabouts, just after Miss Bishop had asked for a waiter to take away the breakfast things: 'Olive, will you send someone up please for the breakfast dishes?' An hour later Miss Bishop would appear at the desk and cash a small cheque, usually ten dollars. Then she would sit and wait for her aunt, who might arrive five minutes later, or might keep Miss Bishop waiting a couple of hours. When the old woman arrived Miss Bishop would go out with her and be gone until three in the afternoon, returning with a few small packages. She would stop at the news-stand and Charlie would hand her the *Sun*, and she would sit reading it in the chair she preferred, in a corner of the small lobby. She would be reading five or ten minutes and Colonel Browder would join her.

Colonel Browder was easily thirty years older than Miss Bishop, but they got along very well together. Miss Bishop never smoked unless Colonel Browder was with her—at least not in the lobby or any of the public part of the hotel. As far as Olive knew, Miss Bishop may have smoked her head off in her room. She must have done something in her room, she spent so much time there.

The Colonel and Miss Bishop were the only guests in the hotel to take tea, and it was understood that the tea and cinnamon toast were to be put on the Colonel's monthly bill without its being presented to him each afternoon.

It was easy to see that the Colonel welcomed the arrival of Miss Bishop at the hotel. When she first came he had been a widower three months and everyone had got used to not having Mrs. Browder around. Her absence made a difference: there was no one to go around complaining of dusty chairs and frequently non-existent cockroaches in the corner nearest the dining-room. For a while the hotel staff missed Mrs. Browder because it was so pleasant without her bellyaching around; and then when the staff had become accustomed to her not being there the Colonel began to miss her. He went around, as Semple, the day clerk, said, like a chicken with its head cut off. When Mrs. Browder died everyone said it was a good thing for the Colonel, and he seemed to think so at first, but that was because he had things to do the first few weeks after her death. When those things had been attended to was when he began to go around like a chicken with its head cut off. Then Miss Bishop arrived and Mr. McLoughlin, the manager, introduced the Colonel to her and they became friends.

The Colonel had given up his parlour-bedroom-bath when Mrs. Browder passed on, and at the time of the change Olive thought to herself that it didn't make much difference in her young life; the only time the Colonel ever used his phone was to ask for the correct time by her clock, and not by the Meridian number. The Colonel sometimes told Olive the telephone was a waste as far as he was concerned. Too much telephoning. People ought to walk more and use their legs. He said it was just as easy to walk a block or two for whatever you wanted as to telephone. Olive did not reply that she thought he was crazy, which was her first thought, or that she knew he used the nickel coin-box in the rear of the dining-room. With these old babies that lived in the hotel you had to keep a civil tongue in your head.

But after Miss Bishop and the Colonel had pretty well established their tea-time as one of the customs of the hotel Olive began to notice that the Colonel was using his phone, and for outside calls. The little matters that took him either on short walks or to the nickel coin-box, he was beginning to take care of from his room, with calls which cost him a dime apiece. Olive thought about this

a long time before she saw what it meant—that the Colonel liked
to stay around the hotel as much as possible, or rather to leave it
as little as possible; and the reason he did not use the five-cent pay
station was that he did not want Miss Bishop to see him chiselling.
This, and the standing order for tea, which was fifteen dollars a
month extra on his bill, convinced Olive that the old boy was going
for Bishop. And she was at least thirty years his junior. Bishop was
around thirty-six, giving her a break, and the Colonel was what
you might call a well-preserved seventy.

When Olive noticed the Colonel taking an interest in Miss Bishop
she began to watch for something big to happen, and then when
nothing big happened she kept her eye open for little things. The
Colonel always gave Olive five dollars for Christmas—five for her,
and five apiece for the other operators, which was the biggest
present the operators got. But this did not make Olive warm up to
the Colonel. Without doing anything to show it, the Colonel
managed to give the impression that he thought talking to telephone
operators was beneath him. You could see it in other things: he
would talk to Henry, the head waiter, by the hour, or to Tommy
Bond, the night clerk. But he would not waste much time with
McLoughlin and he hardly ever said a word to any of the bellboys.
In other words, a snob. Tommy Bond had gone to a school named
Andover and a year to Yale College before the depression got him;
Henry (who was not so snobbish that he would not reach for Olive
whenever he got a chance), he would listen while the Colonel talked
about the wines which he seldom bought. Olive knew McLoughlin
noticed it, too. 'As long as they pay their bills that's all I'm innarested in. I don't care if they think I'm dirt under their feet as long
as they get it up the first of the month,' McLoughlin would say.
Olive did not feel the same way about it. Other people thought she
was plenty all right. Tommy Bond thought so. Tommy Bond would
be getting ready to leave when Olive came to work in the morning,
and he always had a few words to say of a kidding nature, not too
personal, but Olive knew by the way a man looked at you how he
felt about you. She knew Tommy preferred her to Bishop, for
instance.

But even that was not satisfactory to Olive. She wondered why
it had not occurred to her before, but thinking about how Tommy
liked her, she resented it. She resented being liked by the men
around the place and not by the women—Miss Bishop now, and

Mrs. Browder before. Sex got into it when it was a case of a kid like
Tommy Bond liking you. A kid like Tommy liked you irregardless.
Telephone operator or society débutante, when a kid like Tommy
liked you he didn't care who you were, because what made the
difference was sex. Whereas with the Colonel, sex did not enter into
the consideration. With Miss Bishop the same. She was a woman,
so there was no sex to confuse the issue. Therefore, when Bishop
and the Colonel did not like her, that meant it was because they
were snobbish about her. What the hell right did they have to be
snobbish about her? She was as good as they were any day. She
earned her own living and she had good morals.

In regard to her likes and her dislikes, Olive never did anything
about them until something happened that made her express
approval or disapproval, hatred or love. If she liked someone she
did not do anything about it until the name of the party came up
in a way that led to Olive's coming right out and saying she
liked So-and-so; and if underneath she hated someone, it stayed
underneath until the occasion when she would get on record as
hating them. The occasion when she expressed her feelings about
the Colonel and Miss Bishop came fairly soon after she had made
up her mind about them.

Melba, the relief operator, came on one afternoon as Olive was
quitting for the day, and she made some crack about the Colonel
and Miss Bishop. The crack was something unimportant, like: 'Mm.
The young love birds are having their tea.' It was unusual because
Melba seldom said anything about the guests, but this day she must
have got out of the wrong side of the bed or something.

Olive looked over to the corner of the lobby where the two were
conversing. 'Yeah,' said Olive. 'What is that, anyway? That Bishop.
And him. It's enough to make you sick to your stomach, watching
them.'

'Why, what do they do?' said Melba, who was a little surprised
that a casual remark had such affect on Olive.

'What do they do?' said Olive. 'Any minute I expect him to give
her the business.'

'Why, he's too *old*. Isn't he?'

'Too old? He isn't too old to look right through a person worse
than any of the bellhops. Didn't you ever notice it?'

'In a way I did,' said Melba, who had noticed no such thing,
but was not going to tell Olive so.

'Just because he has one foot in the grave don't mean *any*thing,' said Olive.

Having thus committed herself, Olive never let up on Miss Bishop and the Colonel. Every time she had a chance she said something against them, always against them as a unit. 'Those two,' it was. It began to tell in her attitude towards them, and she was curt to Miss Bishop one day over the phone, so much so that Miss Bishop said, 'Look here, Olive, don't you talk to me that way.'

'If you have any complaints to make you complain to Mr. McLoughlin,' said Olive.

'Well, if you're not careful I will,' said Miss Bishop.

'Go ahead and see if I care,' said Olive. 'You or Colonel Browder.'

'What about Colonel Browder? What are you talking about?'

'I guess you know,' said Olive, and pulled out the cord, disconnecting Miss Bishop. Miss Bishop signalled her to come back, but she made her wait. When she plugged in again and connected Miss Bishop the latter said, 'Is this Olive?'

'Yes. Who do you think?'

'Either you apologise or I'll report you to Mr. McLoughlin. I won't have your nasty little insinuations. You're impertinent.'

'Go ahead and report me. I don't care.'

Miss Bishop did not report Olive, but the next day Olive learned that when the month was up Miss Bishop was leaving the hotel. The day after that she learned, by listening to a conversation, that Miss Bishop was going to live with her aunt in Jersey City temporarily until she found another place. 'If you come over here you might as well stay,' said the aunt. 'I don't see why I should go on paying rent for two places.'

In what was left of the month Olive was a little afraid Bishop might go to McLoughlin and snitch on her, but not really afraid. People like Bishop did not get you fired; they were the ones that were afraid, afraid you would get even with them for having you fired.

After Bishop left, Olive looked for some difference on the part of the Colonel. She thought he might be rude to her. But no; his attitude towards her did not change. He didn't notice her. She did hear him tell Semple that for the time being he would go on having tea served, as he expected Miss Bishop to drop in now and then. But she never did.

CHAPTER 28

Ice Cream

People standing in front of shops and hotels watched with dull, exhausted interest Harry's progress up the street. They gave him about the same perfunctory attention that their ears gave to the elevated trains half a block away, on Sixth Avenue. Harry was carrying something in a paper bag, holding the bag in front of him and walking as fast as he could, in short, quick steps. It was just too awful that anybody should be in such a hurry on a night as hot as this. There were blots of perspiration on his light-blue 'polo' shirt, but he looked cool—or at least not hot. His shirt was open at the neck and had half-sleeves. He wore suspenders and he had on a wrist-watch that had square metal links instead of a strap.

He turned in at one of the hotels and went up a flight of stairs to a street-front room. Inside lay a big mound of a woman, on the bed. Her face was made up, even to the blue eye-shadow; but her lip rouge, obviously put on in the same style she had used when her face was much smaller, did not make her face look smaller now. Her fingers and breasts were small, but the flesh rolled down on the backs of her hands and over her ankles, and under the black négligée she was huge in the hips and abdomen and thighs. She was smoking a cigarette, and two independent curls of smoke came out of her nostrils and hung in the air in front of her face. She waved the smoke away as Harry came in.

'No more strawberry,' he said. 'They ran out of it, so I got burnt almond.'

'Burnt almond! Burnt—almond! Why didn't you get plain vanilla, then? Burnt almond!'

'All right,' said Harry. 'Just eat the chocolate, then, if you don't want the burnt almond. I wasn't going to call you up and waste a nickel at the drugstore to find out what kind of ice cream you wanted.'

'You could of thought a minute, and if you had any sense you'd of remembered about my cavity. I can't eat burnt almond with this cavity. It has nuts in it, you dope.'

'Yah. You and your cavity. I don't see why you don't go and have it filled. It sure would be worth it to me if you'd get it filled. What would you do if you were going to have a kid, if you're that afraid of a little thing like going to the dentist? My God!' He dished out some ice cream, putting half in one saucer, half in another.

'No fears,' she said. 'Anyway, who ever heard of going to the dentist for a baby? I'm sure I didn't. What's the dentist got to do with that, I'd like to ask?'

'Either you're pretty dumb or else is this your idea of a gag, because if it's your idea of a gag, you're my idea of dumb. Not that you ain't anyway.'

'Oh, skip it. Skip it, and pass me that stuff. You took long enough getting it, till I thought there for a minute I better send little Oscar out to look for you and see if he could find you, didn't I, Oscar-Woscar?' A little dog on the floor held up its head and then lowered it again.

'Well,' said Harry, sitting down to his share of the ice cream, 'I was delayed on account of I happened to run into a friend of yours over near the B.-M.T. entrance.'

'Who?' she said.

'Wuddia mean, who? You don't have that many friends that you can't guess who.'

'Oh, come on. Not in this heat. Who did you see, a friend of mine?'

'Well, if you must know, it was—oh, I don't know if I ought to tell you. I might enkindle the light of love all over again.' He put a heaping spoonful of ice cream in his mouth and drew the spoon out slowly, levelling it off.

'What do you mean by that, may I ask? You mean you saw some beautiful doll, I guess. Some beautiful little doll from Shreveport, Louisiana, that had a father that owned a bank, and she wanted you to run away with her when you were with Whiteman. Don't give me that again, for God's sake.'

'Did I say anything about a doll? Did I? I said a friend of yours, didn't I? I didn't say anything about any friend of mine. This one's no friend of mine, the party I saw.'

'Well then, for the sixtieth time, who was it?'

'It was none other than Lank Long.'

'Lank! My husband? Where'd you see him? Are you—what are you giving me, Harry? Is this a rib, or what?'

'I'm only trying to tell you. I ran into Lank Long. Your first husband, by the way. Not your husband. You're married to me now. Remember? Remember marrying me? Anyway, I was coming out of the drugstore and I saw this piece of humanity standing near the B.-M.T. entrance. He had a fiddle under his arm, but that didn't make me think anything. You never can tell who's going to turn out to be a fiddle-player, so I was getting ready to walk by him when he turned and recognised me. We said hello, me very you-know, giving him the cold eye and so on, and right off the reel he asked about you—'

'Wud he have to say about me?'

'—and he said he heard I married you and I said yes, and to change the subject I asked him what he was doing and he said he was kind of waiting around, hoping to see Tommy or Jimmy Corsey, I forget which he said, and I didn't pay much attention. He's such a liar, and in addition to that I wasn't innarested in his doings, but only to make conversation I asked him that question. Well, he said he was going to make a record with a couple of the boys, and I said that's funny, I thought they would be using Benuti if they were looking for a fiddle-player. Naw, he said. Not Benuti, he said. Benuti's all washed up, he said. No good any more. "Is that so?" I said. I said I seemed to hear Benuti was doing all right, but Mr. Long said no, Benuti was all washed up.'

'Then what? How did he look?'

'Looked all right. Looked in the money, in fact, and I guessed he noticed me sizing him up and studying him, because right away he explained how he happened to have this swell outfit. He had a pair of sport shoes and tan coat and flannel trousers, like I had when I was with Lopez, and so your Mr. Long, said he happened to have the outfit from when he was working with Fiorito out in Chicago. Fiorito out in Chicago, for God's sake! Telling me where Fiorito is. Me, one of Ted's best friends. He has the nerve to tell me whereabouts Fiorito is and gives me this about getting an outfit working with Ted, when I know Ted wouldn't give him work without me hearing about it. Well, I guess he could see I was thinking, because that was when he had the nerve to try and put the touch on me.'

'Asked you for money?"

'Asked me for money is right. He saw me looking him over, and then he said, "Harry, I'll come clean with you. Right now," he said, "I'm on the nut. I need a five-dollar bill, because when I meet these fellows I want to take them over to the Onyx and buy them anyway a round of drinks." Yeah, I thought. And what about the tab you owe at the Onyx? He owes plenty there for over a year. So I let him have it, plenty. "Listen here, you heel," I said. "If you're trying to put the arm on me for dough just because I happen to have taken your wife away from you when you weren't *man* enough to hold her, if that's what you have in mind, you better forget it," I said, "because when Betty gave you the air and came and lived with me, did I bother to collect the thirty-seven bucks you owed me?" I said. I said, "Now you're back in town, I think what I'll do is get a judgment out against you for that thirty-seven bucks. I can use thirty-seven bucks, and as for lending you any more—huh," I said.

'What did he say to that? Was he sore when you said it about how I gave him up for you? I bet that burned him up.'

'Well, I suppose it did, but he couldn't let on, because he was trying to make a touch. Anyway, I knew all the time he didn't have any dough, and that about getting a judgment out against him, how could I? I have nothing to prove he owes me a nickel. But of course he's too stupid to figure that out. So he said all he had was a few clothes and his fiddle. If that's the same fiddle he used to have, I told him, why, Bob Motherwell would be willing to give him a hundred-dollar note for it. I said, "Go sell the fiddle to Bob and pay me what you owe me. But if you don't get it up, cash on the line, inside of twenty-four hours, I'll get a judgment and take the fiddle away and sell it myself." Well, did he crawfish on that! Sure, he'd positively have the money for me. Where could he get in touch with Bob? Where was I staying? So forth and so on.'

'Then what?'

'Then I walked away. But I guess that's the last I'll hear of Mr. Long, the maestro. Either he'll sell Bob the fiddle and beat it out of town, or else beat it without selling the fiddle and try to get a job with some band on the road. And you know what chance of getting a job on the road anybody has. But I got rid of him.

'He's getting what he deserves. But imagine all the dough he used to have, and now he hasn't even the price of a meal, most likely. He used to have a La Salle automobile, and a trunkful of clothes to wear and all the money a person would need, and now the poor dope—starving for lack of food.'

'What the hell? Who wants to eat in this weather?'

'Who wants to eat? Maybe you don't,' she said, 'but you ought to see the justice I could do to some more of that ice cream. But not that burnt almond.'

CHAPTER 29

Brother

There were a lot of voices; there was one authorised voice singing 'I'm Putting All My Eggs in One Bas-ket'; there was a fine jazz orchestra wasting its arrangements on three hundred and fifty unheeding persons; seltzer bottles squawked their bottom drops into highball glasses. At the moment there was no conversation at one table, around which were seated four persons, three ugly men and a pretty girl. The girl was sitting so she could see the dancers, and the men were characteristically looking over their shoulders at the dancers, at people at other tables, at people entering the place. This was Hollywood.

'Hello.'

The four persons glanced at one tall, thin young man, pale of face, blond of hair, and garbed in a gun-club-check jacket and dark-blue flannel slacks. Around his neck a silk scarf.

'Hello, Leonard,' said the pretty girl.

'Can I sit down with you?' said Leonard.

'Sit down,' said one of the men.

'How's Ruthie?' said the pretty girl.

'Fine,' said Leonard.

'Yeah, how's Ruthie?' said one of the men.

'She's fine,' said Leonard.

'How's your mother?' said another of the men.

'Fine. I just left her,' said Leonard.

'Have a drink, Leonard?' said the third man.

'I'll have a beer,' said Leonard. 'I'll pay for it, though.'

'Naah,' said the first man. 'Waiter, give him a beer.'

'I'm only drinking beer,' said Leonard.

'Fattening,' said one of the men.

'He can use it,' said another.

'Yes,' said Leonard. 'I want to put on some weight.'

'Where's Ruthie to-night?' said a man.

'I don't know. I thought she'd be here.'

'That's for me, that Ruthie,' said another man.

'Yeah, I go for that. I'm glad she's not my sister.'

They all laughed.

'I bet Leonard's glad she's *his* sister,' said a man. The men laughed.

'Shut up, wise guy,' said the pretty girl. 'All of you.'

'They can't kid me,' said Leonard. 'I got plenty of that even before I came out here. Where I used to work they'd always try to kid me about me being Ruthie's brother. They used to call me that, Mr. Ruth Rugby.'

'Where'd she ever get that name, Rugby?'

'Rogowicz,' said Leonard. 'Rugby is a school in England, also a game.'

'I heard of the game,' said a man.

'Well, what's with you, Leonard?'

'How do you mean what's with me?' said Leonard.

'You gettin' much?'

'Oh, shut up, you guys,' said the pretty girl. 'Leonard's a nice kid. Leave him alone.'

'Oh, they can't kid me,' said Leonard. 'I got a letter from a friend of mine back in New York. Monday. He said I suppose you're right in there with those chorus girls for Ruthie's next picture. I wouldn't do that. Wouldn't that be a smart thing if Ruthie's brother got mixed up with some chorine?'

'Cho*rine*, is it?' said a man. 'Say. The gaberoo.'

'He knows from nothin',' said another man.

'Don't pay any attention to them, Leonard. Did they start shooting yet on Ruthie's new picture?'

'Yes. Yesterday. I'm glad,' said Leonard.

'What the hell, she gets paid anyway,' said a man.

'I'll slap your face, Louis Harrow,' said the pretty girl. 'Why are you glad, Leonard?'

'Oh, gives me more to do. I get tired of doing nothing. When she's working at the studio I drive her to work every morning. I do it for something to do.'

'Why don't you go to college?' U.C.L.A. *That's* a big college,' said the girl.

'Well, I don't know. I never finished high school,' said Leonard.

'They hadda burn down the school to get him outa the freshman class,' said a man.

'Oh, geezes. With Cantor they'll have you next,' said another.

'Why don't you go home, wise guy?' said the girl.

'Some people haven't got anything else to do but make cracks. Agents,' said Leonard.

'Who ast you to sit here if you don't like it?' said the man.

'Parasites that live on their ten per cent that they didn't earn,' said Leonard.

'Don't answer him, Leonard. Don't give him that much satisfaction,' said the pretty girl.

'Go out and call up Ruthie,' said another man.

'I would, only I don't know where she is,' said Leonard.

'I could tell you,' said another man.

The others snickered.

'You only think you could,' said Leonard. 'I went by there and her car isn't there.'

'Oh, he knows,' said a man.

'Dirty, evil-minded bastards, all of you,' said the pretty girl. 'Don't mind them, Leonard.'

'Certain people try to get somewhere and they don't, so they get sore. You know, Peggy,' said Leonard.

'She knows, all right,' said a man. 'Nobody's sore at Peggy.'

'Wade a minute,' said another man.

'Oh, all right,' said the man who had made the crack.

'Well,' said the man who had resented the crack.

'Of course it's all right what she calls me because I want to rib this punk. Sure. I'm a bastard because I rib Leonard.'

'He's right,' said Peggy's defender. 'You oughtn't of called him that.'

'Then what right does he have to say things like that about Leonard's sister?' said Peggy.

'It ain't for you to insult your friends, though. Nobody ast Leonard to come to this table. Not even you. So don't call your friends names like that. I don't like it. You owe Louis an apology.'

'I'll owe it to him,' said Peggy. 'I guess you better go sit with some other people, Leonard.'

'I was just going to,' said Leonard. 'Good night, Peggy.'

'Good night, Leonard,' said Peggy.

'Gi' my regards to Ruthie,' said a man.

'She wouldn't even know your name,' said Leonard, going.

'That's what *you* think,' said the man. 'I have a notion to give him a punch on the nose. Punk.'

They watched Leonard. A few people spoke to him, with that expression in which there is full recognition, achieved without a nod and with only an almost imperceptible movement of the lips. It so uncompromisingly means, Don't sit down. Then he was gone out of sight.

CHAPTER 30

By Way of Yonkers

The man lay on the counterpane on the three-quarter-size iron bed. He lay with his hands clasped behind his head, and his feet were crossed. Every once in a while he would move, to rub his beard, to draw his leg up. The room was not cold enough to make it worth while to put a blanket over his legs, but it was not warm enough to lie perfectly still and be altogether comfortable. The man was wearing a pair of grey trousers, brown shoes, and a white shirt with brown stripes. The shirt was open at the collar. His belt was loosened but not unbuckled. He lay there with his eyes open, contemplating the picture of the frightened young princes in the Tower. 'I'll bet they got it,' he said aloud.

Without taking the other hand from behind his head, without moving his head or anything but his right arm, the man reached over, groped only a little, and got his right hand on an alarm clock which was on a small high table beside the bed. He lifted the clock high, at arm's length, and held it in a position so that he could tell what time it was without even moving his eyes. In that way the clock went into the same focus as the two little princes in the Tower. At that moment there were three knocks on the door and the man quickly replaced the clock as a woman's voice said, 'Knock, knock, who's there?' It was a voice kidding itself, and not unlike the telephone operator saying, 'Grand Hotel good *morning*.'

'Come in,' said the man.

The door was opened and a girl came in. She had on a black cloth coat, gunmetal stockings, black patent-leather pumps, and a Cossack hat. She had a neat, short nose with jigsaw nostrils and her eyes were bright and black and probably the long eyelashes were basically her own. She was a little taller than short, and in a few years she would be fat.

'Am I very late?' she said, still in the Grand Hotel operator voice.

'You must have come by way of Yonkers,' he said.

'I didn't have time to tell you when I called you. I wasn't home then. I was out and I called back to see if there were any messages and of course I recognised your number. I called you from a drugstore.'

'How d'you do?' he asked.

'Oh—' she said it very high. Then: 'All right. Fi-nancially. But do we have to talk about it? You and me?' She began taking off her hat and coat. He did not get up off the bed. She went to a closet and hung her coat on a thin wire hanger and put her hat on the shelf, to reach which she had to stand on tiptoe. She ruffled her hair with fan-spread fingers.

'Do you want a drink?' he said.

'I don't know. I don't guess I do. I'm gettin' tired of liquor. I don't know, lately I sort of lost the taste for it. I go to a bar or some place and I, I don't exactly *want* a drink, but I go there through sheer force of habit or something. And then the bartender says what will I have, and I think and think. I say to myself, "Will I have a *cock*tail?" No. "How about a *brandy*?" No. "A Stinger?" No. "Gin? Beer? Highball?" No. Then I finally end up with a Scotch-and-soda and it's all I can do to finish it. I don't know what it is with me. I used to love to drink, anything.'

'You're almost ready for straight liquor,' he said. 'You better look out.'

'Oh, I'm not afraid of liquor. Gambling, that's the only thing I gotta fear. Especially now. I had a horse come in yesterday. Of course I didn't get track odds because like a goddam fool I just didn't insure the bet and this bookie I deal with, he *knows* I always insure my bets as a rule but this time I had a real hot tip from one of my regulars, a party that gets a lot of tips but always tells me to lay off the horses and won't ever tell me a thing. But the night before last, he said to me to play this horse, on the nose, but if I bet more than twenty dollars I was to spread it around and not give it all to the same bookie. Well, I only had twenty bucks to spare, so I went to my regular *bookie* and just gave him the money and said on the nose and I didn't insure it. Bott I guess I can't complain.'

'You must be in the chips,' the man said.

'I would be, but I have some dental work. Look. See this tooth? Perfectly good. Or you'd think so. Well, don't call me later in the week because I gotta have that out. And up here, you can't even see them, but I have about three or four cavities, and my dentist is terribly dear.' She laughed a little.

'What's funny?'

'You'll die. He's a nice Jew, about I'd say around thirty-four-five, and whenever I go to him I know he's dying to make a pass at me. Of course he doesn't know anything about me, and he's *very nice.* I went there through a friend of mine I used to know, a very wealthy party, and you know how when you go to a dentist or a doctor they say who sent you, and I gave the name of this wealthy party because he *told* me to, so this dentist, much as he'd like to move right in, I imagine he's afraid to on account of this other party.' She put her hand on his ankle and began rubbing it, slowly. 'What's with you?' she said. 'I missed you. I was wondering what happened to you, you didn't call.'

'I've been broke,' he said.

'*That's* all right,' she said. '*Don't* ever let that stop you from calling. My God, we're old friends by this time.'

'*I* know, but.'

'Listen, I'm not worried about you sticking me. And what I just told you, about only having twenty bucks to spare. I said to *spare.* I save a certain amount each week and I stick to it. I make myself do it. If I have a bad week, I still manage to save that certain amount. It's the only way. But for you, well, that's different, honestly it is, Bill. Look. New shoes, new dress, and that coat, I only have it 'bout two months and you know what it cost me? Enough to pay the rent on this dump I'll bet for—four tens are forty—two months at least. I buy good things when I buy them. But I also save my money, a certain amount each week. It's positively the only way.' Her words came back to her and she was suddenly embarrassed by the sentimental note. 'You said you *been* broke. Does that mean you aren't broke now?'

'That's right.'

'Job?'

'Mm-hmm. I guess I won't see you again for quite a while.'

'Going out of town?' she said.

'Milwaukee, Wisconsin,' he said.

'What doing, or shouldn't I ask?'

'It's all right. Selling beer. During pro'bition I used to have a lot of connections out that way and the other day I ran into an old pal of mine. He was just in town for a couple days and I happened to run *into* him. I did him a couple good turns in the old days and now he's right up there. He took one look at me and said, "Now, listen, level with me. You're strictly from hunger, ain't you?" And I stalled, but he knew. Then he wanted to know if I was in any kind of a jam and I told him no, I just didn't seem to be able to make a connection in this town. So to make a long story short, we went out and got drunk together—'

'Why didn't you call me?'

'I never called you when I was drunk *yet*," the man said, suddenly angry. Then: 'Anyway, I'm to meet him at his hotel to-morrow and we'll probably take the train together the next day or the day after. Didn't you notice the new suit and stuff when you hung up your coat?'

'I didn't notice,' she said. She crossed her legs.

'He gay me an advance. He said a lot of the same boys are in the business out there and won't take any time at all before I'm back where I was in 28. Of course maybe not as *much* dough as before, but practically no risks to speak of. I wish it wasn't so late. You and I could go out and celebrate. We can go over to this place over on Fifty-fifth Street.'

'I don't want to go anywhere,' she said. 'Any chance you being back in town soon?'

'Well, not right away, honey. First I have to build up my connections again.'

'Well, I don't have to tell you, I'm glad for you. It's about time you got a good break.' She resumed rubbing his ankle. He put his hand on the top of her head.

'Yeah? You're as good a break as I ever got.'

'Ah, Christ, Bill,' she said, and fell face down in tears.

CHAPTER 31

My Girls

For some reason—oh, why? oh, why anything?—Mrs. Cole had made herself sit with her back to the windows. She knew it was partly because she did not want to see the roadster coming up the street. But why not? Well, some day a hundred years from now she might be able to answer that question. Now it made no difference. The reason made no difference in the world. All she knew was that she had made herself sit so that she could not see the street, and thus it was that the first she knew Jane was home was when she heard the gravel crunching in the drive. Then the sound of the racing engine, which Jane always made before switching off the ignition. Then the screen door, and two heeltaps on the hardwood floor before Jane's feet reached the hall rug. All sounds that filled Mrs. Cole with the mysterious fear that is like the fear just before going into the doctor's inner office.

'Jane,' she said.

'Hello,' Jane called from the hall.

'Jane, will you come here? Please? I want to talk to you.'

'In a minute.'

'No, now, please.'

'Mother, I'd really *like* to go upstairs, *eef* you don't mind.'

'All right, but please—'

'All *right!*' said Jane. 'What difference can two *minutes...*' Her voice died down.

Mrs. Cole waited, and then there were Jane's deliberate footsteps on the stairs, and then she was standing in the room, for a fraction of a second deciding which chair to sit in. 'What is it? It must be terribly important.'

Mrs. Cole looked at her daughter. Yes, she probably should have known. *Could* have known. But thought became anger, and Mrs. Cole began to breathe deeply. She stared at her daughter.

'Well?' said Jane.

'You've—done—everything, havent you?'

'Oh, now really. What is this, anyway? *What* have I done?'

'I say, you've done everything. Haven't you?'

'I heard you say it. First time. Be a little more specific. *What* everything?'

'Who is a boy named Roddy?'

'Oh.'

'Yes. Oh.'

'I see. I suppose Laura Wilton's been over here in my absence.'

'I haven't seen Laura Wilton,' said Mrs. Cole.

'You must have. No one else here knows I know this boy.' Then: 'Oh, *no! Oh* no. You wouldn't open, you wouldn't open a letter. Oh, oh. You did. Oh, what disgusting—Dis*gus*ting.' Jane stood up.

'*Sit* down. I want to have this out with you before your father comes home.'

'I'd rather not be in the same room with you.'

'Well, you'll just have to. Or perhaps you'd rather have your father here, too.'

'I suppose you've showed him the letter.'

'No, I haven't. I want to know all about this. Who is this boy?'

'What good will it do you to know that? I won't tell you anything about him.'

'I know quite a little about him right this minute. And I know quite a lot about you.'

'Well, aren't you pleased with yourself? Especially the way you found out. Now may I have the letter? Maybe you'd like to know I came home early because I was expecting a letter.'

'No letter came. This one was post-marked March twenty-eighth.' Mrs. Cole paused. 'I think it was the twenty-eighth. It could have been the twenty-sixth or the twenty-ninth.''

'That's funny. That's really funny. That was the first letter he ever wrote me. That's why I kept it. You should have seen some of the others, if you liked that so much. How did you happen to find this one?'

'I thought I'd surprise you. I knew you were having trouble with your radio, so I sent for the repair man, and when he came he said he'd have to take it away with him, and that's how I found this letter.'

'But that doesn't explain how you happened to read it.'

'I won't try to explain that.'

'No, dear. You can't. You never can, as long as you live. Well, what are you going to do? Have me put in a home for delinquent girls or something?'

'Hiding a letter in a radio.'

'It wasn't a very good place, was it? Well, I still say, what are you going to do? Besides tell Father.'

'That's just it. You know I couldn't.'

'Oh-ho. You could do anything,' said Jane. 'But I wonder what he'll think when you tell him how you found out. He'll love that. It's the kind of thing that he'd die rather than do. Die.'

'Well, we'll have to take this up again, because there he is now.'

Neither the mother or her daughter could come to a decision about leaving the room, and then there was Mr. Cole, hair in disarray from the wind, a thick-knitted wool scarf sticking out from under his upturned coat collar, two tennis racquets under his arm, white flannels turned up at the cuffs, shoes stained from an En-Tout-Cas court. He was smiling.

'I beat Harry Young in straight sets,' he said. 'Seven-five, six-two. Six-*two*. And I've never beaten him before in my life. Oh, was he burned up! And the worst loser.' Mr. Cole dropped into a chair. 'He was feeling very cocky, so he said before we started, "Jim. I'll give you a break. I'll give you three games a set." Well, of course he's usually been giving me one game. And beating me. Maybe once in a while I'll take a seven-fiver, but I've never beaten him; that is, I've never left the court a winner. But to-day, I don't know, I was so damn mad when the so-and-so gave me three games a set, I said, "For how much?" He said, "Oh, the usual five bucks." "Make it ten," I said. He laughed. Didn't want to take my money. That kind of thing. By the way, Janie, ring for Joseph, will you, please? I feel a Tom Collins coming on.'

Jane reached behind her and pushed a button.

'I—' Mr. Cole began. 'Say, what's the matter? Have my girls been battling again? What is it this time?'

Mrs. Cole said nothing. Jane said nothing. Then Mrs. Cole stood up. 'You'll have to excuse me, please,' she said, and went up the stairs.

'Oh, now, what's the matter? You tell me, Janie? . . . Uh, Joseph, I'd like a Tom Collins. Janie, how about something for you?'

'No, thanks.'

'Yes, sir,' said Joseph, and went out. Jane left too. She ran up the stairs and went to her mother's room.

'Mother.' Her mother was lying on the bed.

'What?' said Mrs. Cole.

'Mother, can't we tell him it's about money, or something?'

Mrs. Cole put her handkerchief to her eyes. 'Yes, we'll have to. Oh, come here. Janie.'

CHAPTER 32

No Sooner Said

The last drawer of the file coasted back on its ball bearings and settled in place with a slight thump. Miss Ross pushed the button lock and turned the key, which locked all the drawers in the file at one turn. She went to her desk and took out her purse and a folded towel. Mr. Jay stared straight ahead, holding his hand to his forehead like an Indian shading his eyes from the sun, and at the same time resting his head in that hand. He heard Miss Ross's footsteps going down the hall, and a few minutes later he heard her coming back. She put her purse on the desk, folded the towel again and put it in the drawer of the desk, and went to the water-cooler, to one side of which was a mirror, to the other side a clothes tree. There were two hats on the clothes tree—Miss Ross's was a Juliet cap, white, but to make it modern there was a two-inch thick woollen pigtail in the middle; and the other hat was Mr. Jay's, a three-dollar straw number with a plain black band. Reaching for her cap, Miss Ross, more concerned with her face in the mirror, knocked Mr. Jay's hat to the floor. It gave forth a couple of hollow sounds before settling flat.

'Oh, I beg your pardon! I knocked your hat off.'

'That's all right,' said Mr. Jay. 'That hat's had plenty of knocking around.'

'But look what I *did*. It's chipped.'

'No, you didn't do that. That was there before.'

'Are you positive? No. There, right there.' She stooped over a second time, this time picking up a fragment of straw hat. 'Here's a piece of straw, so I must have. I must of done it. How much was it?'

'Oh. A little chip off it? What's that? I've got my money's worth out of that lid.'

'No, but I think in view of the fact that it was my carelessness plus my vanity. If I hadn't been so vain as to look at myself in the mirror instead of paying attention to what I was doing. Let me pay *part* of a new hat. I'd really feel much better about the whole matter.'

'Nope. No thanks. I wouldn't think of it, Miss Ross.'

'Well, if you want to be *gallant*, Mr. Jay. But I *am* very sorry. Why? What are you smiling about?'

'I was just thinking, here we've been in the same office—you came here right after the first of the year—and this is the first time we ever had any conversation outside of business.'

'Yes, that's correct,' said Miss Ross.

'Go on.'

'What do you mean, go on?'

'Well, there was something in the way you said that that made me think you were going to say something else.'

'Maybe I was, or at least thinking something else. But perhaps I better not.'

'Go ahead.'

'Well, frankly, Mr. Jay, the people in this office don't seem over-enthusiastic about me, as a person.'

'Why, Miss *Ross*? I happen to know from Mr. McDowell himself, he happened to say the other day, he said, "That Ross girl gets more work done than any other girl in the office," and he mentioned, he said about how you caught on so quickly. He said you have a postively photographic memory. You know—being able to remember everything on one of those cards, just from one look.'

'Oh, that. That's a minor accomplishment. I could always do that. When I went to Evander, I never had to study hard. That's just a thing that's born in you.'

'Have a cigarette?'

'Yes, thank you. I guess it's all right after hours.'

'Yes, the least they can do is let us smoke if they make us work overtime. Here, I'll light it for you.'

'Thank you.' She took off her hat again and ruffled her hair, and sat on top of a desk. 'How long have you been here, Mr. Jay?'

'Seven and a half years.'

'I see you're a member of Phi Beta Kappa.'

'Oh, yes. For what it's worth. I don't know why I wear the damn thing. I guess it's the only thing that makes my wife give me credit for having any brains.'

'Oh, are you married?'

'Don't I look it? I'll be married eleven years next October. We have two children, two girls. One just eight and the other going in five.'

'Oh, really?'

'Yes, two little girls. What about you? Are you married?'

'Not me. I've never been specially urged.'

'I don't believe that.'

'Well, it's sad but true, Mr. Jay. Oh, I know a lot of young dopes, they get hot pants—I beg your pardon.'

Mr. Jay laughed. 'Don't tell *me*. *I* know.'

'Oh, but think of me using an expression like that I mean, the first time.'

'Well, what the hell, it's the truth, isn't it? It's true, and they want to get married on twenty-five dollars a week. By God, if my girls want to get married, they'll have to bring around a couple of men that can support them. Of course by the time they're ready to *get* married, maybe there won't be any marriage.'

'You sound like my brother. Are you a Communist?'

'Communist? Me? That's a lifework. To be a member of the party—'

'I know. I get it from Mortie all the time. His idea of Utopia would be an income of, say, hundred bucks a week so he could go around and agitate. Agitate. He's right, of course, but it just doesn't work out that way.'

'Well, I wish him luck. But if he's sincere, you tell him not to get married.'

'Apropos of marriage, what made you think I might be?'

'Well, we had a girl here, the girl that had your job before you came, and none of us knew she was married, but about two or three months after she quit she had a baby, and her husband didn't even have a job. Maybe you heard the other girls mention her. Miss Gallon.'

'No, I never heard of her. The other girls! I've been here since January and there isn't one of them ever so much as asked me to have lunch with her. I don't mean pay for it; I just mean have it together, Dutch. What's the matter with me?'

'You're too pretty.'

'No, it isn't that. I know what it is, all right. Miss Kelly. I've seen her letters. The worst speller I ever saw, but I guess I know how she holds her position.'

'I guess we all do, more or less.'

'Yes. And that Simpson dame. It's a very personal thing, but somebody oughta give her a bath. Her *neck* is dirty. And that dope that has the desk next to mine. Schmidt. Huh. The others I don't come in contact with so very much. Oh, I can't wait to get out of this place. I've been looking for another position for weeks. But don't say anything, Mr. Jay.'

'Certainly not.'

'This is the first human conversation I've had since I came here. Well—in a way. It depends on what you call human.'

'I know what you mean.'

'No, you don't. You couldn't possibly. The conversation I have reference to didn't take place in the office.'

'But I'll bet I know,' said Mr. Jay.

'No you don't.'

'Was it with Mr. McDowell?'

'Yes. How did you know?' said Miss Ross.

'I know the signs. First he waits till Kelly goes out to lunch, and then he comes out and looks around the office and pretends he picks a girl at random. Then he says, "Uh, Miss Ross, can you take dictation?" And of course you say you can, and he says he has a letter he wants to get off right away. Remember?'

'*Do* I!'

'Then the next sign is when he tells me what a good worker you are. Listen, I've been here over seven years.'

'Well, all I can say is I'm glad I started looking for another job.'

'Did he accidentally take you home?'

'About as accidental as—as if he sent me a memo saying, "Be in the car or else," ' she said.

'Another cigarette?'

'No, thanks. I have to be going.'

'Will you do me a favour?'

'Of course.'

'Don't quit this job. I mean before you quit, let me know. Sometimes I get fed up here, too.'

'Why? The girls making passes at you, Mr. Jay? Oh, I'm sorry I said that, really I am.'

'It's all right.' There was a silence.

'Why don't you do the rest of that to-morrow? Do you live uptown?'

'All the *way* uptown,' said Mr. Jay.

'Well—do you want to walk part of the way? I feel like walking.'

'No sooner said than done,' said Mr. Jay.

CHAPTER 33

Good-Bye, Herman

Miller was putting his key in the lock. He had two afternoon papers folded under one arm, and a package—two dress shirts which he had picked up at the laundry because he was going out that night. Just when the ridges of the key were fitting properly, the door was swung open and it was his wife. She was frowning. 'Hello,' he said.

She held up her finger. 'Come in the bedroom,' she said. She was distressed about something. Throwing his hat on a chair in the foyer, he followed her to the bedroom. She turned and faced him as he put down his bundle and began taking off his coat.

'What's up?' he said.

'There's a man in there. He came to see you. He's been here for an hour and he's driving me crazy.'

'Who is he? What's it all about?'

'He's from Lancaster, and he said he was a friend of your father's.'

'Well, has he been causing any trouble?'

'His name is Wasserfogel, or something like that.'

'Oh, hell. I know. Herman Wasservogel. He was my father's barber. I knew he was coming. I just forgot to tell you.''

'Oh, you did. Well, thanks for a lovely hour. Hereafter, when you're expecting somebody, I wish you'd let me know beforehand. I tried to reach you at the office. Where were you? I tried everywhere I could think of. You don't know what it is to suddenly have a perfectly strange man—'

'I'm sorry, darling. I just forgot. I'll go in.'

He went to the living-room, and there sat a little old man. In his lap was a small package, round which he had wrapped his hands. He was looking down at the package, and there was a faint smile on his face, which Miller knew to be the man's customary expression. His feet, in high, black shoes, were flat on the floor and parallel with each other, and Miller guessed that this was the way the little old man had been sitting ever since he first arrived.

'Herman, how are you? I'm sorry I'm late.'

'Oh, that's all right. How are you, Paul?'

'Fine. You're looking fine, Herman. I got your letter and I forgot to tell Elsie. I guess you know each other by now,' he said as Elsie came into the room and sat down. 'My wife, Elsie, this is Herman Wasservogel, an old friend of mine.'

'Pleased to meet you,' said Herman.

Elsie lit a cigarette.

'How about a drink, Herman? A little schnapps? Glass of beer?'

'No thank you, Paul. I just came; I wanted to bring this here. I just thought maybe you would want it.'

'I was sorry I didn't see you when I was home for the funeral, but you know how it is. It's such a big family, I never got around to the shop.'

'Henry was in. I shaved him three times.'

'Yes, Henry was there longer then I was. I was only there overnight. I had to come right back to New York after the funeral. Sure you won't have a beer?'

'No, I just wanted to bring this in to give to you.' Herman stood up and handed the little package to Paul.

'Gee, thanks, a lot, Herman.'

'What's that? Mr. Wasserfogel wouldn't show it to me. It's all very mysterious.' Elsie spoke without looking at Herman, not even when she mentioned his name.

"Oh, he probably thought I'd told you.'

Herman stood while Paul undid the package, revealing a shaving mug. 'This was my father's. Herman shaved him every day of his life, I guess.'

'Well, not every day. The Daddy didn't start shaving till he was I guess eighteen years old, and he used to go away a lot. But I guess I shave him more than all the other barbers put together.'

'Damn right you did. Dad always swore by you, Herman.'

'Yes, I guess that's right,' said Herman.

'See, Elsie?' said Paul, holding up the mug. He read the gold lettering: ' "J. D. Miller, M.D." '

'Mm. Why do you get it? You're not the oldest boy. Henry's older than you,' said Elsie.

Herman looked at her and then at Paul. He frowned a little.

'Paul, will you give me a favour? I don't want Henry to know it that I gave you this mug. After the Daddy died, I said, "which one will I give the mug to?" Henry was entitled to it, being the oldest and all. In a way he should have got it. But not saying anything against Henry—well, I don't know.'

'Mr. Wasservogel liked you better than he did Henry, isn't that it, Mr. Wasservogel?' said Elsie.

'Oh, well,' said Herman.

'Don't you worry, Herman, I'll keep quiet about it. I never see Henry anyway,' said Paul.

'The brush I didn't bring. Doc needed a new one this long time, and I used to say to him, "Doc, are you so poor yet you won't even buy a new shaving brush?" "I am," he'd say to me. "Well," I said, "I'll give you one out of my own pocket for a gift." "You do," he'd say, "and I'll stop coming here. I'll go to the hotel." Only joking, we were, Mrs. Miller. The Doc was always saying he'd stop coming and go to the hotel, but I knew better. He was always making out like my razors needed sharpening, or I ought to get new lights for my shop, or I was shaving him too close. Complain, complain, complain. Then around the first of last year I noticed how he'd come in, and all he'd say was, "Hello, Herman. Once over, not too close," and that's all he'd say. I knew he was a sick man. He knew it, too.'

'Yes, you're right,' said Paul. 'When'd you get in, Herman?'

'Just to-day. I came by bus.'

'When are you going back? I'd like to see some more of you before you go away. Elsie and I, we're going out tonight, but tomorrow night—'

'Not tomorrow night. Tomorrow night is Hazel's,' said Elsie.

'Oh, I don't have to go to that,' said Paul. 'Where are you stopping, Herman?'

'Well, to tell you the truth, I ain't stopping. I'm going back to Lancaster this evening.'

'Why, no! You can't. You just got here. You ought to stick around, see the sights. Come down to my office and I'll show you Wall Street.'

'I guess I know enough about Wall Street; all I want to know. If it wasn't for Wall Street, I wouldn't be barbering. No. Thanks very much, Paul, but I got to get back. Got to open the shop in the morning. I only have this relief man for one day. Young Joe Meyers. He's a barber now.'

'Well, what the hell? Keep him on for another day or two. I'll pay him. You've got to stick around. How long is it since you've been in New York?'

'Nineteen years last March I was here, when young Hermie went to France with the Army.'

'Herman had a son. He was killed in the war.'

'He'd be forty years old, a grown man,' said Herman. 'No. Thank you, Paul, but I think I better be going. I wanted to take a walk down to where the bus leaves from. I didn't get my walk in to-day yet, and that will give me the chance to see New York City.'

'Oh, come on, Herman.'

'Don't be so insistent, Paul. You can see Mr. Wasservogel wants to go back to Lancaster. I'll leave you alone for a few minutes. I've got to start dressing. But not too long, Paul. We've got to go all the way down to Ninth Street. Good-bye, Mr. Wasservogel. I hope we'll see you again sometime. And thank you for bringing Paul the cup. It was very sweet of you.'

'Oh, that's all right, Mrs. Miller.'

'Well, I really must go,' said Elsie.

'I'll be in in a minute,' said Paul. 'Herman, you sure you won't change your mind?'

'No, Paul. Thank you, but I have the shop to think of. And you better go in and wash up, or you'll catch the dickens.'

Paul tried a laugh. 'Oh, Elsie isn't always like that. She's just fidgety to-day. You know how women get.'

'Oh, sure, Paul. She's a nice girl. Very pretty-looking. Well.'

'If you change your mind—'

'Nope.'

'We're in the phone book.'

'Nope.'

'Well, just remember, if you *do* change your mind; and I really don't know how to thank you, Herman. You know I mean it, how much I appreciate this.'

'Well, your Dad was always good to me. So were you, Paul. Only don't tell Henry.'

'That's a promise, Herman. Good-bye, Herman. Good luck, and I hope I'll see you soon. I may get down to Lancaster this fall, and I'll surely look you up this time.'

'Mm. Well, *auf Wiedersehen*, Paul.'

'*Auf Wiedersehen*, Herman.'

Paul watched Herman going the short distance to the elevator. He pushed the button, waited a few seconds until the elevator got there, and then he got in without looking back. 'Good-bye, Herman,' Paul called, but he was sure Herman did not hear him.

CHAPTER 34

Give and Take

The door was opened and in came a woman in her late forties. She was carrying a cheap brief-case from which the varnish was peeling. She leaned forward with the weight of her front, although she was not exceptionally heavy behind. She wore silver-rimmed spectacles which made her eyes seem weak, until you really saw them, and then they were strong, bright, brown. She closed the door quietly, making a full half-turn in closing it. She was frowning a little, the way people sometimes do when they are trying not to make any noise. She went through the little foyer and came into the living-room and said 'Oh!' in a shrill voice, and put her hand approximately over her heart and laughed. 'Tommy. What are you doing up so early?'

'Hello, Mom,' he said, very friendly. 'I'm doing a little work on the claws.' He looked at her—their eyes met—and then he went on filing his fingernails. He was wearing a blue pin-stripe suit, rather tight for his fat body. His legs were crossed. He was somewhere between twenty-five and thirty years old, and he had white, shiny skin, and as he filed his nails, four white, strong teeth clamped over his lower lip. 'What's with you, Mom? How was school?'

'It's always the same. After the first year. And you know how long I've been at it.' She took off her hat and put it on one of those little pedestals in the closet in the foyer. It was a hat that could just as well have been thrown on the floor. 'What got you up so early? It's only a little after four.'

'I couldn't sleep,' said Tommy. 'I just couldn't pound out any more after—oh, ten this morning. I didn't get up then. I stayed in the hay till around twelve-thirty, but then I thought, "I'll get up," So I did.'

'Did you have any breakfast?'

'No scoff. Just a little mocha-java-coffee.'

'And you've been in all this time?' said Mom.

'Well, no I went out and shot a little game of pool and bought the aptanoon papers. Came home. Read the papers. Made a few phone calls. Then I remembered shooting pool how the claws looked. I don't know, Mom. I always look at other guys' fingernails to see if they got—you know—Burns Brothers. But my own, I don't hardly ever look at them.'

'Don't hardly.'

'Seldom.'

Mom sat down comfortably and without grace, and began taking school papers out of the brief-case. 'You're not broke, by any chance? That isn't why you stayed here till I came here?'

'Mom, I am. Last night I went out with Joey Forbstein, and there's a great student of the dollar. We went to a couple places, and every time a cheque came around, Joey recognised somebody that he thought he could put the touch on. So he'd get up and leave me with the bruise. Maybe he put the touch on these guys, but if he did, I never saw any of the gelt. He'd come back and I didn't want to ask him how he did, becuss that would look like I wanted him to pay the cheque. So.'

'Why do you go out with people like that? For somebody that knows a lot about human nature!'

'That's it! Now Joey, for instance. Last night cost me—I mean extra, on account of Joey—about fifteen clams. Well, Joey's promoting a benefit for some cops up in Westchester some place. I go out with him. He rounds up maybe a half a dozen names. They promise to show at this benefit. What happens? Maybe four of them show. They got gold badges from the cops. Joey gets whatever he gets, but knowing Joey, I'd say the cops better bring their pistols when Joey gets to adding up the take. So Joey always does all right on the financial end. Comes away with five hundred dollars, say. I watch when this beneift is put on, and I know exactly when to go to Joey and say, "Joey, I need a hunnerd and twenty-fi dollars." Joey always overestimates what he's going to rob these cops of, so he gives me one two five. I do know human nature, Mom, because for instance if I ask Joe for one hundred, he'll say fifty. But one two five sounds like I needed one two five, and he lets me have it.'

'And how do you pay him back? You don't.'

'In favours, Mom. It's give and take. Don't you see that? I wouldn't think of taking that kind of money from Joey if I didn't know I could pay him back. Not in cash, necessarily. But I know people that sooner or later Joey has to get to. He *hass* to. Where could Joey get a pair of fight tickets at the last minute for nothing? Nowhere in the City of New York. But I just happen to know the right people. What if Joey has some enterprise that he has to see, like somebody in the cops? I mean something legitimate, of course, but a lot of times time counts. For a nickel or a dime, the price of two phone calls, I save him endless bother. So in about two weeks I'm good for a hunnerd and twenty-fi dollars from Joey alone. When the time comes, he'll be around to ask his favour, and that means we're square. That is to *say*, Mom, on an investment of fifteen dollars, I get back one two five. Then I can pay you back if you need it.'

'I only hope I don't need it. I can give you twenty-five dollars now.'

'Make it twenty, Mom. Twenty is enough. To-night I'll only need hat-check money, a taxi maybe. Tomorrow I have a dinner at the Astor to go to. Little Artie McFadden is putting on a dinner, and I got him a couple full-page ads for his programme. My end ought to be twenty-fi dollars, and I know Artie's good for it.'

'I'll have to give you a cheque,' said Mom.

'A cheque's fine, Mom. And a quarter to get uptown. I kept looking at my fingernails shooting pool, and I didn't win a game.'

Mom folded the papers and got up and went to the desk and wrote out a cheque. Tommy stood beside her with one hand on her shoulder. 'Where the dough department is concerned, you're O.K., Mom,' he said. 'You're a fast man with a buck.' She finished writing the cheque and handed it to him with her left hand. She kept looking at the inkwell.

'Tommy,' she said, still looking at the inkwell.

'What, Mom?'

'Nothing,' she said.

He stood there reading the cheque, holding it in both hands. 'Oh, I know,' he said. 'But one of these days I'll hit.' Then he went out, and the bow on his hatband was on the wrong side of his head.

CHAPTER 35

Peggy

Aren't they sweet together, those two? Look at them. *Look*. Did you see? He just kissed her on the ear, right out in front of everybody. Now, I don't care what you say, those two. If I ever saw two people. You know, it makes me want to get up and give them a push and say, 'Go on, go on, you two. Get married and be happy.' It really does. They're made for each other. You know, they come here for dinner every night, or at least every night I've been here this year. Every single time I've been here for dinner, here they were. And always like this. Now watch them when they dance. They're getting up to dance. You're sitting in a bad place to see them at the table, but now you'll be able to see them.

She's good, isn't she? She used to dance professionally, you know. . . . Oh, yes. When she first came back from Hollywood—they were stinking to her out there. She came back, and right away—John Powers. She had this money, of course, but as she said to me, 'If I can possibly help it, I'm going to touch as little of that money as I possibly can.' I guess she thought everybody *knew* about it, but only the Coast crowd and a few here in New York. I happened to know about it, but a lot of people didn't, and I admitted her. She had enough so she could—you know, travel. She didn't have to work, but right away she got this job modelling for John Powers. She got lots of work, because she's got that kind of figure, and her face, it's that sort of not-quite-homely that's rather cute. It gets them. I've seen her at parties with the absolutely prettiest girls in New York. I remember a party at the Casino several years ago—Brownie and that crowd gave it—and I swear to you, and nothing against *her*, far from it, she was the unprettiest girl at the party. But oh-ho-ho! All those men, artists, accustomed to seeing the real so-called beauties, they flocked around her like—anything. And the other girls were *furious!* Livid! That's the trouble. She isn't really popular with most of the girls, and I don't think it's fair, because she has a lot of likeable qualities, but you know how girls are. How many popular girls with men are really sincerely liked by other women?

That, of course, that's what happened in Hollywood. She went out there from some night club in, I think Chicago. Sigmund Bernette was in Chicago; I think it was for some kind of a Legion of Decency convention about two years ago. I *know* that, because I was with Bernette then, and I remember—oh, God, what a time. I was sort of in charge of fashion stills for the magazines in the East, and we got this memo saying the heat was on and lay off sexy pictures of our stars. Then Bernette went to Chicago and gave the speech of his life, telling how Bernette Pictures would co-operate to the fullest degree, and any suggestions, et cetera. You may not believe it just to look at Bernette, but when he gets up there.

So of course he went to this night club where she was dancing, and to make a long story short, inside of a week little Peggy was on the Chief. Well, he signed her up to a long-term contract, but without options. I think three years, at seven-fifty a week. Well, of course, that wasn't known right away. She had an agent, and the agent would pick up her cheque every week. But she not only didn't get in any picture, but there was no publicity on her. She wasn't even announced for a picture. What a life! Beautifully dressed and, as I say, quite attractive. She'd got to the Vendome one day and the Derby the next, and then the Vendome and then the Derby. Always got a good table. But always with the same two or three girls, and never any men. Oh, Bernette. He's too smart for that. I've seen Bernette go into the Vendome while she was there and bow to the girl with her and pretend he didn't even know Peggy. In fact, I'm pretty sure I saw him being introduced to her a couple of times. A lot of men of course tried to move in, but I will say for Peggy, she handled them beautifully. That's another thing about Bernette. He doesn't trust anybody. For a while he'd let her go out with this little pansy in the music department. He was a beautiful dancer. But one night Bernette happened to get a load of Peggy doing a rumba with Jackie, and from then on. See what I mean? Isn't she marvellous? She's really primitive.

Well, that was her life. Car, clothes, money—and nothing to do but be there for Bernette. Then she took sick and he sent her to the desert, and of course the doctor had to be one of those handsome

young California Nordics. Bernette was *furious!* Livid. But there
wasn't much he could do, in a way, I mean, she had this wonderful
contract and—oh, perhaps two years to run. So what he did, he
got to her agent and told him, he said sure, he knew the contract
would be tough to break in a court of law, but he told this agent,
he said, 'You have a lot of other clients, and I imagine some of
them would like to work on this lot, but if you're going to be tough
about Peggy's contract, you might just as well forget there is any
such studio as the Bernette.' So of course the agent hemmed and
hawed, and the result was Peggy settled for one year's salary in
cash. And the ironic thing was I heard several times how smart
Bernette was in getting rid of deadwood, settling contracts with
people that were drawing salary but not doing anything.

She came back with this money, and I admire her; she went right
to work, and in no time this young Williamson is carrying the torch,
and I hear when he's twenty-five, he comes into something like four
million dollars from his grandmother. Of course he hasn't a brain
in his head, but he *is* nice-looking, and I imagine—well, Peggy's no
gold-digger or she could have made it unpleasant for Mr. Bernette,
but then what if she had and there'd had been all that publicity?
Williamson would have known all about it, instead of which all he
knows is he has a very attractive girl, who makes a good thing with
a respectable job, and is good fun and doesn't try to take him for
any money. Get the cheque and we'll stop and say hello to them
on the way out. I'd just like to hear what on earth they talk about.

CHAPTER 36

Straight Pool

I'll shoot you fifty points if you spot me ten balls. Isn't that a laugh? You spotting me. Snowball! Rack 'em up for straight pool. *I'll play it safe.*

It sure is a laugh, you spotting me, when I used to beat you fifty to thirty-five. For a while there—*I'll play the four-ball, cross sides*—for a while there I could beat you fifty to thirty-five without any trouble, but now I'm lucky if I can beat you with you spotting me fifty or forty. *Eleven-ball. Your shot, and there they are, all open for you.* You know, I'm not making any alibi, Jack, but this is the first time I've had a cue in my hand in over a month. Oh, geez, way over a month. I bet it's two months. I had to practically pack up a suitcase and join the Army or something to get out to-night. Mae and one of her crying spells again. Damn it, Jack—*oh, nice shot, atta working in there*—you know I'm not a hard guy to get along with. At least I don't think I am, but Mae gets these crying spells, and honest to God, I can't stay in the house another minute. And then if I say I'm going out, even if it's only for a pack of cigarettes, why, she suddenly all of a sudden stops crying and sits there looking at me, not saying a word, and it's worse than her crying. I don't know what makes her do that. If I stay, she cries all the time I'm there, and if I make a move to go out of the house—honest, I'm afraid to leave her alone. When she gets in one of these spells, she's liable to do anything, so I very seldom leave. But I can stand only so much. I'm only human, just like anybody else, and you go around fixing refrigerators all day long, getting up and sitting down and answering dumb questions and any man would want some peace when he gets home. But not me. I mean, do I get it? No. I come home and it's an even chance she's going to have a crying spell. I never can tell how it's going to be till I'm home a while, and then all of a sudden she's liable to get up from the table and be gone a half an hour, and I eat by myself and finally I have to do the dishes. And when I go to the bedroom, it's always the same story. She's lying there on the bed and when I come in the room she won't even look at me. She says, 'Did you do the dishes?' and I say, 'Yes,' and she says I shouldn't of. Then I tell her if she feels lousy she ought to go to bed, but I know damn well it isn't that she feels sick or anything. I mean there's nothing wrong with her. I had her go to the doctor to see if there was anything really wrong with her, but there wasn't. She had an aunt that died of cancer, and I thought maybe she was afraid of that, but no. She was O.K., according to the doctor.

That was a tough one to miss, Jack. Play the ten, in the side. Now the one-ball in the corner. That makes it ten to four this frame, and look at that break shot. Hey, Snowball, rack 'em up. I'll play it off the pile . . . Kee-ripes! What a miss! There you are, all yours.

So after she went to see the doctor and he said there was nothing wrong, I thought maybe it was just something that would wear off. You know how women are. They get these funny ideas in their heads and all they need is a little attention. So I stayed home a lot and took her to the pictures and I didn't go out of the house except to go to work, and it looked for a while as if she was all right. So one night I said I was going down and shoot a game of pool. 'Who with?' she said. And I said I didn't know, just going down to the Olympic and see if there was anybody there. 'No, you're not,' she said. 'You're going down there and talk about me. You're going to talk about me with Jack McMorrow,' she said. 'No, I wasn't,' I told her. I said maybe I'd shoot a game with you, but I said I wasn't going to talk about her to you, and that was the last time I was down here. I guess that must of been close to two months ago.

Nice run, boy. I don't see how you missed that one. It was dead for the corner. You're not giving me any breaks, are you? . . . Well, there's my high run. Three balls. You'll be out in five frames the way I'm playing.

Well, when I got home that night, the last time I was down here, the first thing she wanted to know was did I talk to you about her, and I told her I didn't even see you. She has some kind of fear about us talking about her, I guess. It must of been that, because every time since then, every time I wanted to come down here she'd put on that stare act and I'd be afraid to leave her.

Nice shot.

I'd be afraid to leave her on account of I didn't know what would

happen while I was gone. She was nuts on the subject of you. Not
about you, exactly, but about us taking about her. Jack McMorrow!
Jack McMorrow! For some reason I can't fathom out she had this
idea that when you and me get together we'd always talk about
her. She'd say, 'I know men. They always talk about girls that
way.' I said to her, 'Listen,' I said, 'a man doesn't go to a poolroom
to talk about his wife. At least I don't,' I said. I said, 'I go to a
poolroom to shoot pool.' But I couldn't convince her.

Well, you left me safe enough. Play the five.

Well, I decided I had to humour her. There was something wrong
that she wouldn't tell me about, and I decided to humour her for
a while and maybe it'd come out all right. She was always talking
about you, always you, and you were the one she had this idea
about, so I said to her, I told her I wouldn't see you any more. I
said I'd stop getting down to the Olympic, and she knew I wouldn't
see you anywhere else, and that made her feel all right, I think,
because the crying spells slackened off and stopped altogether. So
she seemed to be all right again and when I had to go to Waterbury,
Connecticut, two weeks ago, to attend the funeral of my aunt, I
asked her if she wanted to go along but she said no, and then I
said I wouldn't go, and she said she was all right, and she sounded
all right, so I went to Waterbury to this funeral and stayed overnight. Well, I guess that's where I made my mistake. I shouldn't
of left her alone overnight. When I came back from Waterbury, I
could see she was all upset and nervous, and she had one of her
crying spells and so on, and then the day before yesterday I came
home and she was cockeyed drunk with a bottle of gin. I never saw
her so drunk. We had a big fight and all. A hell of a fight, and
yesterday she didn't get up for breakfast, and last night when I
came home from work she wouldn't say a word. And then to-night
when I came home, the same story over again. Cockeyed again.
'What's the idea!' I said, and we had it out hot and heavy, but she
didn't want me to leave, so I said I'd leave all right, and she was
lucky if I came back. I got the hell out of the house as sore as a
boil. I guess I oughtn't to be talking about her like this, especially
to you, because you're the one she thinks is always talking about
her, but I have to talk to somebody. I think I'll go to Brooklyn and
get drunk. How about it? . . .

'What's the matter? You quitting? . . . Oh! If I'd of known you
had a date, we could of made it twenty-five points. You're ahead

anyhow, and I don't feel like shooting much. Guess I'll go to Brooklyn. My brother just got a gallon of apple. . . .

CHAPTER 37

The Doctor's Son

My father came home at four o'clock one morning in the fall of 1918, and plumped down on a couch in the living-room. He did not get awake until he heard the noise of us getting breakfast and getting ready to go to school, which had not yet closed down. When he got awake he went out front and shut off the engine of the car, which had been running while he slept, and then he went to bed and stayed, sleeping for nearly two days. Up to that morning he had been going for nearly three days with no more than two hours' sleep at a stretch.

There were two ways to get sleep. At first he would get it by going to his office, locking the rear office door, and stretching out on the floor or on the operating table. He would put a revolver on the floor beside him or in the tray that was bracketed to the operating table. He had to have a revolver, because here and there among the people who would come to his office, there would be a wild man or woman, threatening him, shouting that they would not leave until he left with them, and that if their baby died they would come back and kill him. The revolver, lying on the desk, kept the more violent patients from becoming too violent, but it really did no good so far as my father's sleep was concerned; not even a doctor who had kept going for days on coffee and quinine would use a revolver on an Italian who had just come from a bedroom where the last of five children was being strangled by influenza. So my father, with a great deal of profanity, would make it plain to the Italian that he was not being intimidated, but would go, and go without sleep.

There was one other way of getting sleep. We owned the building in which he had his office, so my father made an arrangement with one of the tenants, a painter and paper-hanger, so he could sleep in the room where the man stored rolls of wallpaper. This was a good arrangement, but by the time he had thought of it, my father's strength temporarily gave out and he had to come home and go to bed.

Meanwhile there was his practice, which normally was about forty patients a day, including office calls and operations, but which he had lost count of since the epidemic had become really bad. Ordinarily if he had been ill his practice would have been taken over by one of the young physicians; but now every young doctor was as busy as the older men. Italians who knew me would even ask me to prescibe for their children, simply because I was the son of Mister Doctor Malloy. Young general practitioners who would have had to depend upon friends of their families and fraternal orders and accidents and gonorrhoea for their start, were seeing—hardly more than seeing—more patients in a day than in normal times they could have hoped to see in a month.

The mines closed down almost with the first whiff of influenza. Men who for years had been drilling rock and had chronic miner's asthma never had a chance against the mysterious new disease; and even younger men were keeling over, so the coal companies had to shut down the mines, leaving only maintenance men, such as pump men, in charge. Then the Commonwealth of Pennsylvania closed down the schools and churches, and forbade all congregating. If you wanted an ice cream soda you had to have it put in a cardboard container; you couldn't have it at the fountain in a glass. We were glad when school closed, because it meant a holiday, and the epidemic had touched very few of us. We lived in Gibbsville; it was in the tiny mining villages—'patches'—that the epidemic was felt immediately.

The State stepped in, and when a doctor got sick or exhausted so he literally couldn't hold his head up any longer, they would send a young man from the graduating class of one of the Philadelphia medical schools to take over the older man's practice. This was how Doctor Myers came to our town. I was looking at the pictures of the war in the *Review of Reviews*, my father's favourite magazine, when the doorbell rang and I answered it. The young man looked like the young men who came to our door during the summer selling magazines. He was wearing a short coat with a sheepskin collar, which I recognised as an S.A.T.C. issue coat.

'Is this Doctor Malloy's residence?' he said.

'Yes.'

'Well, I'm Mr Myers from the University.'

'Oh, I said. 'My father's expecting you.' I told my father, and he said: 'Well, why didn't you bring him right up?'

Dr Myers went to my father's bedroom and they talked, and then the maid told me my father wanted to speak to me. When I went to the bedroom I could see my father and Dr Myers were getting along nicely. That was natural: my father and Dr Myers were University men, which meant the University of Pennsylvania; and University men shared a contempt for men who had studied at Hahnemann or Jefferson or Medico-Chi. Myers was not an M.D., but my father called him Doctor, and as I had been brought up to tip my hat to a doctor as I did to a priest, I called him Doctor too, although Dr Myers made me feel like a lumberjack; I was so much bigger and obviously stronger than he. I was fifteen years old.

'Dr Myers, this is my boy James,' my father said, and without waiting for either of us to acknowledge the introduction, he went on: 'Dr Myers will be taking over my practice for the time being and you're to help him. Take him down to Hendricks' drug store and introduce him to Mr Hendricks. Go over the names of our patients and help him arrange some kind of a schedule. Dr Myers doesn't drive a car, you'll drive for him. Now your mother and I think the rest of the children ought to be on the farm, so you take them there in the big Buick and then bring it back and have it overhauled. Leave the little Buick where it is, and you use the Ford. You'll understand, Doctor, when you see our roads. If you want any money your mother'll give it to you. And no cigarettes, d'you understand?' Then he handed Dr Myers a batch of prescription blanks, upon which were lists of patients to be seen, and said good-bye and lay back on his pillow for more sleep.

Dr Myers was almost tiny, and that was the reason I could forgive him for not being in the Army. His hair was so light that you could hardly see his little moustache. In conversation between sentences his nostrils would twitch and like all doctors he had acquired a posed gesture which was becoming habitual. His was to stroke the skin in front of his right ear with his forefinger. He did that now downstairs in the hall. 'Well . . . I'll just take a walk back to the hotel and wait till you get back from the farm. That suit you, James?' It did, and he left and I performed the various chores my father had ordered, and then I went to the hotel in the Ford and picked up Dr Myers.

He was catlike and dignified when he jumped in the car. 'Well, here's a list of names. Where do you think we ought to go first? Here's a couple of prescription blanks with only four names apiece. Let's clean them up first.'

'Well, I don't know about that, Doctor. Each one of those names means at least twenty patients. For instance Kelly's. That's a saloon, and there'll be a lot of people waiting. They all meet there and wait for my father. Maybe we'd better go to some single calls first.'

'O.K., James. Here's a list.' He handed it to me. 'Oh, your father said something about going to Collieryville to see a family named Evans.'

I laughed. 'Which Evans? There's seventy-five thousand Evanses in Collieryville. Evan Evans. William W. Evans. Davis W. Evans. Davis W. Evans, Junior. David Evans?'

'David Evans sounds like it. The way your father spoke they were particular friends of his.'

'David Evans,' I said. 'Well—he didn't say who's sick there, did he?'

'No. I don't think anybody. He just suggested we drop in to see if they're all well.'

I was relieved, because I was in love with Edith Evans. She was nearly two years older than I, but I liked girls a little older. I looked at his list and said: 'I think the best idea is to go there first and then go around to see some of the single cases in Collieryville.' He was ready to do anything I suggested. He was affable and trying to make me feel that we were pals, but I could tell he was nervous, and I had sense enough to know that he had better look at some flu before tackling one of those groups at the saloons.

We drove to Collieryville to the David Evans home. Mr Evans was district superintendent of one of the largest mining corporations, and therefore Collieryville's third citizen. He would not be there all the time, because he was a good man and due for promotion to a bigger district, but so long as he was there he was ranked with the leading doctor and the leading lawyer. After him came the Irish priest, the cashier of the larger bank (of which the doctor or the lawyer or the superintendent of the mines is president), the brewer, and the leading merchant. David Evans had been born in Collieryville, the son of a superintendent, and was popular, a thirty-second degree Mason, a graduate of Lehigh, and a friend of my father's.

They would see each other less than ten times a year, but they would go hunting rabbit and quail and pheasant together every autumn and always exchanged expensive Christmas gifts. When my mother had large parties she would invite Mrs Evans, but the two women were not close friends. Mrs Evans was a Collieryville girl, half Polish, and my mother had gone to an expensive school and spoke French, and played bridge long before Mrs Evans had learned to play '500'. The Evanses had two children: Edith, my girl, and Rebecca, who was about five.

The Evans Cadillac, which was owned by the coal company, was standing in front of the Evans house, which also was owned by the coal company. I called to the driver, who was sitting behind the steering wheel, hunched up in a sheepskin coat and with a chequered cap pulled down over his eyes. 'What's the matter Pete?' I called. 'Can't the company get rid of that old Caddy?'

'Go on wid you,' said Pete. 'What's the wrong wid the doctorin' business? I notice Mike Malloy ain't got nothin' better than Buicks.'

'I'll have you fired, you round-headed son of a bitch,' I said. 'Where's the big lad?'

'Up Mike's. Where'd you t'ink he is?'

I parked the Ford and Dr Myers and I went to the door and were let in by the pretty Polish maid. Mr Evans came out of his den, wearing a raccoon coat and carrying his hat. I introduced Dr Myers. 'How do you do, sir,' he said. 'Dr Malloy just asked me to step in and see if everything was all right with your family.'

'Oh, fine,' said Mr Evans. 'Tell the dad that was very thoughtful, James, and thank you too, Doctor. We're all O.K. here, thank the Lord, but while you're here I'd like to have you meet Mrs Evans. Adele!'

Mrs Evans called from upstairs that she would be right down. While we waited in the den Mr Evans offered Dr Myers a cigar, which was declined. Dr Myers, I could see preferred to sit, because Mr Evans was so large that he had to look up to him. While Mr Evans questioned him about his knowledge of the anthracite region, Dr Myers spoke with a barely discernible pleasant hostility which was lost on Mr Evans, the simplest of men. Mr Evans appeared in a house dress. She looked at me shyly, as she always did. She always embarrassed me, because when I went in a room where she was sitting she would rise to shake hands, and I would feel like telling her to sit down. She was in her middle thirties and still pretty, with

rosy cheeks and pale blue eyes and nothing 'foreign' looking about
her except her high cheek bones and the lines of her eyebrows,
which looked as though they had been drawn with crayon. She
shook hands with Dr Myers and then clasped her hands in front of
her and looked at Mr Evans when he spoke, and then at Dr Myers
and then at me, smiling and hanging on Mr Evans' words. He was
used to that. He gave her a half smile without looking at her and
suggested we come back for dinner, which in Collieryville was at
noon. Dr Myers asked me if we would be in Collieryville at that
time, and I said we would, so we accepted his invitation. Mr Evans
said: 'That's fine. Sorry I won't be here, but I have to go to Wilkes-
Barre right away.' He looked at his watch. 'By George! By now I
ought to be half-way there.' He grabbed his hat and kissed his wife
and left.

When he had gone Mrs Evans glanced at me and smiled and
then said: 'Edith will be glad to see you, James.'

'Oh, I'll bet she will,' I said. 'Where's she been keeping herself
anyway?'

'Oh, around the house. She's my eldest,' she said to Dr Myers.
'Seventeen.'

'Seventeen?' he repeated. 'You have a daughter seventeen? I can
hardly believe it, Mrs Evans. Nobody would ever think you had a
daughter seventeen.' His voice was a polite protest, but there was
nothing protesting in what he saw in Mrs Evans. I looked at her
myself now, thinking of her for the first time as someone besides
Edith's mother. . . . No, I couldn't see her. We left to make some
calls, promising to be back at twelve-thirty.

Our first call was on a family named Loughran, who lived in a
neat two-story house near the Collieryville railroad station. Dr
Myers went in. He came out in less than two minutes, followed by
Mr Loughran. Loughran walked over to me. 'You,' he said. 'Ain't
we good enough for your dad no more? What kind of a thing is this
he does be sending us?'

'My father is sick in bed, just like everybody else, Mr Loughran.
This is the doctor that is taking all his calls till he gets better.'

'It is, is it? So that's what we get, and doctorin' with Mike Malloy
sincet he come from college, and always paid the day after payday.
Well, young man, take this back to Mike Malloy. You tell him for
me if my woman pulls through it'll be no thanks to him. And if she
don't pull through, and dies, I'll come right down to your old man's

office and kill him wid a rock. Now you and this one get the hell outa here before I lose my patience.'

We drove away. The other calls we made were less difficult, although I noticed that when he was leaving one or two houses the people, who were accustomed to my father's quick, brusque calls, would stare at Dr Myers' back. He stayed too long, and probably was too sympathetic. We returned to the Evans home.

Mrs Evans had changed her dress to one that I thought was a little too dressy for the occasion. She asked us if we wanted 'a little wine', which we didn't, and Dr Myers was walking around with his hands in his trousers pockets, telling Mrs Evans what a comfortable place this was, when Edith appeared. I loved Edith, but the only times I ever saw her were at dancing school, to which she would come every Saturday afternoon. She was quite small, but long since her legs had begun to take shape and she had breasts. It was her father, I guess, who would not let her put her hair up; she often told me he was very strict and I knew that he was making her stay in Collieryville High School a year longer than was necessary because he thought her too young to go away. Edith called me Jimmy—one of the few who did. When we danced together at dancing school she scarcely spoke at all. I suspected her of regarding me as very young. All the little kids at dancing school called me James, and the oldest girls called me sarcastic. 'James Malloy,' they would say, 'you think you're sarcastic. You think you're clever, but you're not. I consider the source of that remark.' The remark might be that I had heard that Wallace Reid was waiting for that girl to grow up—and so was I. But I never said things like that to Edith. I would say: 'How's everything out in the metropolis of Collieryville?' and she would say they were all right. It was no use trying to be sarcastic or clever with Edith, and no use trying to be romantic. One time I offered her the carnation that we had to wear at dancing school, and she refused it because the pin might tear her dress. It was useless to try to be dirty with her; there was no novelty in it for a girl who had gone to Collieryville High. I told her one story, and she said her grandmother fell out of the cradle laughing at that one.

When Edith came in she took a quick look at Dr Myers which made me slightly jealous. He turned and smiled at her, and his nostrils began to twitch. Mrs Evans rubbed her hands together nervously, and it was plain to see that she was not sure how to introduce Dr Myers. Before she had a chance to make any mistakes I shook hands with Edith and she said, 'Oh, hello, Jimmy,' in a very offhand way, and I said: 'Edith, this is Dr Myers.'

'How do you do?' said Edith.

'How are you?' said the doctor.

'Oh, very well, thank you,' Edith said, and realised that it wasn't quite the thing to say.

'Well,' said Mrs Evans. 'I don't know if you gentlemen want to wash up. Jimmy, you know where the bathroom is.' It was the first time she had called me Jimmy. I glanced at her curiously and then the doctor and I went to wash our hands. Upstairs he said: 'That your girl, James?'

'Oh, no,' I said. 'We're good friends. She isn't that kind.'

'What kind? I didn't mean anything.' He was amused.

'Well, I didn't know what you meant.'

'Edith certainly looks like her mother,' he said.

'Oh, I don't think so,' I said, not really giving it a thought, but I was annoyed by the idea of talking about Edith in the bathroom. We came downstairs.

Dinner was a typical meal of that part of the country: sauerkraut and pork and some stuff called nep, which was nothing but dough, and mashed potatoes and lima beans, coffee, tea, and two kinds of pie, and you were expected to take both kinds. It was a meal I liked, and ate a lot. Mrs Evans got some courage from somewhere and was now talkative, now quiet, addressing most of her remarks to Dr Myers and then turning to me. Edith kept looking at her and then turning to the doctor. She paid no attention to me except when I had something to say. Rebecca, whose table manners were being neglected, had nothing to contribute except to stick out her plate and say: 'More mash potatoes with butter on.'

'Say please,' said Edith, but Rebecca only looked at her with the scornful blankness of five.

After dinner we went to the den and Dr Myers and I smoked. I noticed he did not sit down; he was actually a little taller than Edith, and just about the same height as her mother. He walked around the room, standing in front of enlarged snapshots of long-deceased setter dogs, one of which my father had given Mr Evans. Edith watched him and her mother and said nothing but just before we were getting ready to leave Mrs Evans caught Edith staring at her and they exchanged mysterious glances. Edith looked defiant and Mrs Evans seemed puzzled and somehow alarmed. I could not figure it out.

II

In the afternoon Dr Myers decided he would like to go to one of the patches where the practice of medicine was wholesale, so I suggested Kelly's. Kelly's was the only saloon in a patch of about one hundred families, mostly Irish, and all except one family were Catholics. In the spring they have processions in honour of the Blessed Virgin at Kelly's patch, and a priest carries the Blessed Sacrament the length of the patch, in the open air, to the public school grounds, where they hold Benediction. The houses are older and stauncher than in most patches, and they look like pictures of Ireland, except that there are no thatched roofs. Most patches were simply unbroken rows of company houses, made of slatty wood, but Kelly's had more ground between the houses and grass for the goats and cows to feed on, and the houses had plastered walls. Kelly's saloon was frequented by the whole patch because it was the post office substation, and it had a good reputation. For many years it had the only telephone in the patch.

Mr Kelly was standing on the stoop in front of the saloon when I swung the Ford around. He took his pipe out of his mouth when he recognised the Ford, and then frowned slightly when he saw that my father was not with me. He came to my side of the car. 'Where's dad? Does he be down wid it now himself?'

'No,' I said. 'He's just tired out and is getting some sleep. This is Dr Myers that's taking his place till he gets better.'

Mr Kelly spat some tobacco juice on the ground and took a wad of tobacco out of his mouth. He was a white-haired, sickly man of middle age. 'I'm glad to make your acquaintance,' he said.

'How do you do, sir?' said Dr Myers.

'I guess James here told you what to be expecting?'

'Well, more or less,' said Dr Myers. 'Nice country out here. This is the nicest I've seen.'

'Yes, all right I guess, but there does be a lot of sickness now. I guess you better wait a minute here till I have a few words with them inside there. I have to keep them orderly, y'understand.'

He went in and we could hear his loud voice: ' . . . young Malloy said his dad is seriously ill . . . great expense out of his own pocket

secured a famous young specialist from Philadelphee so as to not
have the people of the patch without a medical man . . . And any
lug of a lunkhead that don't stay in line will have me to answer to
. . .' Mr Kelly then made the people line up and he came to the
door and asked Dr Myers to step in.

There were about thirty women in the saloon as Mr Kelly guided
Dr Myers to an oilcloth-covered table. One Irishman took a
contemptuous look at Dr Myers and said: 'Jesus, Mary and Joseph,'
and walked out, sneering at me before he closed the door. The
others probably doubted that the doctor was a famous specialist,
but they had not had a doctor in two or three days. Two others
left quietly but the rest remained. 'I guess we're ready, Mr Kelly,'
said Dr Myers.

Most of the people were Irish, but there were a few Hunkies in
the patch, although not enough to warrant Mr Kelly's learning any
of their languages as the Irish had had to do in certain other
patches. It was easy enough to deal with the Irish: a woman would
come to the table and describe for Dr Myers the symptoms of her
sick man and kids in language that was painfully polite. My father
had trained them to use terms like 'bowel movement' instead of
those that came more quickly to mind. After a few such encounters
and wasting a lot of time, Dr Myers more or less got the swing of
prescribing for absent patients. I stood leaning against the bar,
taking down the names of patients I didn't know by sight, and
wishing I could have a cigarette, but that was out of the question
because Mr Kelly did not approve of cigarettes and might have
told my father. I was standing there when the first of the Hunkie
women had her turn. She was a worried-looking woman who even
I could see was pregnant and had been many times before, judging
by her breasts. She had on a white knitted cap and a black silk
shirtwaist—nothing underneath—and a nondescript skirt. She was
wearing a man's overcoat and a pair of Pacs, which are short rubber
boots that men wear in the mines. When Dr Myers spoke to her
she became voluble in her own tongue. Mr Kelly interrupted: 'Wait
a minute, wait a minute,' he said. 'You sick?'

'No, no. No me sick. Man sick.' She lapsed again into her own
language.

'She has a kid can speak English,' said Mr Kelly. 'Hey, you.
Leetle girl Mary, you daughter, her sick?' He made so-high with
his hand. The woman caught on.

'Mary. Sick. Yah, Mary sick.' She beamed.

Mr Kelly looked at the line of patients and spoke to a woman. 'Mame,' he said. 'You live near this lady. How many has she got sick?'

Mame said: 'Well, there's the man for one. Dyin' from the way they was carryin' on yesterday and the day before. I ain't seen none of the kids. There's four little girls and they ain't been out of the house for a couple of days. And no wonder they're sick, runnin' around wild widout no—'

'Never mind about that, now,' said Mr Kelly. 'I guess, Doctor, the only thing for you to do is to go to this woman's house and take a look at them.'

The woman Mame said: 'To be sure, and ain't that nice? Dya hear that everybody? Payin' a personal visit to the likes of that but the decent people take what they get. A fine how-do-ya-do.'

'You'll take what you get in the shape of a puck in the nose,' said Mr Kelly. 'A fine way you do be talkin' wid the poor dumb Hunkie not knowing how to talk good enough to say what's the matter wid her gang. So keep your two cents out of this, Mame Brannigan, and get back into line.'

Mame made a noise with her mouth, but she got back into line. Dr Myers got through the rest pretty well, except for another Hunkie who spoke some English but knew no euphemisms. Mr Kelly finally told her to use monosyllables, which embarrassed Dr Myers because there were some Irishwomen still in line. But 'We can't be wasting no time on politeness,' said Mr Kelly. 'This here's a doctor's office now.' Finally all the patients except the Hunkie woman were seen to.

Mr Kelly said: 'Well, Doctor, bein's this is your first visit here you gotta take a little something on the house. Would you care for a brandy?'

'Why, yes, that'd be fine,' said the doctor.

'James, what about you? A sass?'

'Yes, thank you,' I said. A sass was a sarsaparilla.

Mr Kelly opened a closet at the back of the bar and brought out a bottle. He set it on the bar and told the doctor to help himself. The doctor poured himself a drink and Mr Kelly poured one and handed it to the Hunkie woman. 'There y'are, Mary,' he said. 'Put hair on your chest.' He winked at the doctor.

'Not joining us, Mr Kelly?' said the doctor.

Mr Kelly smiled. 'Ask James there. No, I never drink! Not a drop. Handle too much of it. Why, if I took a short beer every time I was asked to, I'd be drunk three-quarters of the time. And another advantage is when this here Pro'bition goes into effect I won't miss it. Except financially. Well, I'll take a bottle of temperance just to be sociable.' He opened a bottle of ginger ale and took half a glassful. The Hunkie woman raised her glass and said something that sounded more like a prayer than a toast, and put her whole mouth around the mouth of the glass and drank. She was happy and grateful. Dr Myers wanted to buy another round, but Mr Kelly said his money was no good there that day; if he wanted another drink he was to help himself. The doctor did not want another, but he said he would like to buy one for the Hunkie woman, and Mr Kelly permitted him to pay for it, then we said goodbye to Mr Kelly and departed, the Hunkie woman getting in the car timidly, but once in the car her bottom was so large that the doctor had to stand on the running board until we reached her house.

A herd of goats in various stages of parturition gave us the razz when we stopped at the house. The ground around the house had a goaty odour because the wire which was supposed to keep them out was torn in several places. The yard was full of old wash-boilers and rubber boots, tin cans and the framework of an abandoned baby carriage. The house was a one and a half story building. we walked around to the back door, as the front door is reversed for the use of the priest when he comes on sick calls. The Hunkie woman seemed happier and encouraged and prattled away as we followed her into the house, the doctor carefully picking his way through stuff in the yard.

The woman hung up her coat and hat on a couple of pegs on the kitchen wall, from which also hung a lunch can and a tin coffee bottle, the can suspended on a thick black strap, and the bottle on a braided black cord. A miner's cap with a safety lamp and a dozen buttons of the United Mine Workers of America was on another peg, and in a pile on the floor were dirty overalls and jumper and shirt. The woman sat down on a backless kitchen chair and hurriedly removed her boots, which left her barefoot. There was an awful stink of cabbage and dirty feet in the house, and I began to feel nauseated as I watched the woman flopping around, putting a kettle on the stove and starting the fire, which she indicated she wanted to do before going to look at the sick. Her breasts swung to and fro and her large hips jounced up and down, and the doctor smirked at these things, knowing that I was watching, but not knowing that I was trying to think of the skinniest girl I knew, and in the presence of so much woman I was sorry for all past thoughts or desires. Finally the woman led the way to the front of the house. In one of the two front rooms was an old-fashioned bed. The windows were curtained, but when our eyes became accustomed to the darkness we could see four children lying on the bed. The youngest and oldest were lying together. The oldest, a girl about five years old, was only half covered by the torn quilt that covered the others. The baby coughed as we came in. The other two were sound asleep. The half-covered little girl got awake, or opened her eyes and looked at the ceiling. She had a half-sneering look about her nose and mouth, and her eyes were expressionless. Dr Myers leaned over her and so did her mother, speaking to the girl, but the girl apparently made no sense even in the Hunkie language. She sounded as though she were trying to clear her throat of phlegm. The doctor turned to me and said dramatically: 'James, take this woman out and get her to boil more water, and go to the car and get your father's instrument case.' I grabbed the woman's arm and pulled her to the kitchen and made signs for her to boil the water, then I went out to the Ford and wrestled with the lid of the rear compartment, wondering what the hell Myers wanted with the instrument case, wondering whether he himself knew what he wanted with it. At last I yanked the lid open and was walking back with the leather case in my hand when I heard a loud scream. It sounded more deliberate than wild, it started so low and suddenly went so high. I hurried back to the bedroom and saw Dr Myers trying to pull the heavy woman away from her daughter. He was not strong enough for her, but he kept pulling and there were tears in his eyes: 'Come away, God damn it! Come away from her, you God damn fool!' He turned to me for help and said: 'Oh, Jesus, James, this is awful. The little girl just died. Keep away from her. She had diphtheria!'

'I couldn't open the back of the car,' I said.

'Oh, it wasn't your fault. Even a tracheotomy wouldn't have saved her, the poor little thing. But we've got to do something for these others. The baby has plenty of spots, and I haven't even looked at the other two.' The other two had been awakened by their mother's screams and were sitting up and crying, not very

loud. The woman had the dead girl in her arms. She did not need
the English language to know that the child was dead. She was
rocking her back and forth and kissing her and looking up at us
with fat streams of tears running from her eyes. She would stop
crying for a second, but would start again, crying with her mouth
open and the tears, unheeded, sliding in over her upper lip.

Dr Myers took some coins from his pocket and tried to make
friends with the in-between kids, but they did not know what money
was, so I left him to go in to see how the man was. I walked across
the hall to the other bedroom and pulled up the curtains. The man
was lying in his underwear; gaunt, bearded, and dead.

I knew he was dead, but I said: 'Hyuh, John, hyuh.' The sound
of my voice made me feel silly, then sacrilegious, and then I had
to vomit. I had seen men brought in from railroad wrecks and mine
explosions and other violent-accident cases, but I had been prepared
for them if only by the sound of an ambulance bell. This was
different. Dr Myers heard me being sick and came in. I was crying.
He took a few seconds to see that the man was dead and then he
took me by the arm and said: 'That's all right, kid. Come out in
the air.' He led me outside into the cold afternoon and I felt better
and hungry.

He let go of my arm. 'Listen,' he said. 'As soon as you feel well
enough, take the car and go to the hospital. The first thing you do
there is get them to give you twenty thousand units of antitoxin,
and while you're doing that tell them to send an ambulance out
here right away. Don't go near anybody if you can help it except
a doctor.' He paused. 'You'd better find out about an undertaker.'

'You'll need more than twenty thousand units of antitoxin,' I
said. I had had that much in my own back when I was eight years
old.

'Oh, no. You didn't understand me. The antitoxin's for you. You
tell whoever's in charge at the hospital how many are sick out here,
and they'll know what to send.'

'What about you?'

'Oh, I'll stay here and go back in the ambulance. Don't worry
about me. I want to stay here and do what I can for these kids.' I
suddenly had a lot of respect for him. I got into the Ford and drove
away. Doctor's cars carried cardboard signs which said By Order
State Department of Health, which gave them the right to break
speed laws, and I broke them on my way to the hospital. I pulled

in at the *porte-cochère* and met Dr Kleiber, a friend of my father's, and told him everything. He gave me antitoxin. He smiled when I mentioned getting an undertaker. 'Lucky if they get a wooden rough box, even, James. These people aren't patients of Daddy's, are they, James?'

'No.'

'Well then, I guess maybe we have to send an Army doctor. I'm full up so I haven't a minute except for Daddy's patients. Now go home and I'll take care of everything. You'll be stiff in the back and you want a rest. Good-bye now.' So I drove home and went to bed.

III

I was stiff the next morning from the antitoxin, but it had not been so bad as the other time I had taken it, and I was able to pick up Dr Myers at the hotel. 'I feel pretty damn useless, not being able to drive a car,' he said. 'But I never had much chance to learn. My mother never had enough money to get one. You know that joke: we can't afford a Ford.'

'Oh, well,' I said, 'in Philadelphia you don't need one. They're a nuisance in the city.'

'All the same I'd like to have one. I guess I'll have to when I start practising. Well, where to first?' We outlined a schedule, and for the next couple of days we were on the go almost continually. We hardly noticed how the character of the region was changed. There was little traffic in the streets, but the few cars tore madly. Most of them were Cadillacs: black, company-owned Cadillacs which were at the disposal of young men like Dr Myers and the two drunken Gibbsville doctors who did not own cars; and grey Cadillacs from the USAAC base in Allentown, which took officers of the Army Medical Corps around to the emergency hospitals. At night the officers would use the cars for their fun, and there were a few scandals. One of my friends, a Boy Scout who was acting as errand boy—'courier', he called himself—at one of the hospitals, swore he witnessed an entire assignation between an Army major and a local girl who was a clerk in the hospital office. One officer was rumoured to be homo-sexual and had to be sent elsewhere. Opinion among us boys was divided: some said he was taken away and shot, some said he was sent to Leavenworth, others said he was dishonourably discharged. The ambulances were being driven by members of the militia, who wore uniforms resembling those of the marine corps. The militia was made up of young men who were exempt from active service. They had to make one ambulance driver give up his job, because he would drive as fast as the ambulance would go even when he was only going to a drug store for a carton of soap. Another volunteer driver made so much noise with the ambulance bell that the sick persons inside would be worse off than if they had walked. The women of wealth who could drive their own cars drove them, fetching and carrying blankets and cots, towels and cotton, but their husbands made some of the women stop because of the dangers of influenza and Army medical officers. Mrs Barlow, the leader of society, did not stop, and her husband knew better than to try to insist. She was charming and stylish and looked very English in her Red Cross canteen division uniform. She assumed charge of the emergency hospital in the armoury and bossed the Catholic sisters and the graduate nurses around and made them like it. Her husband gave money and continued to ride a sorrel hunter about the countryside. The rector of the Second Presbyterian Church appeared before the Board of Health and demanded that the nuns be taken out of the hospitals on the ground that they were baptizing men and women who were about to die, without ascertaining whether they were Catholics or Protestants. The *Standard* had a story on the front page which accused unnamed undertakers of profiteering on 'rough boxes', charging as much for pine board boxes as they had for mahogany caskets before the epidemic.

Dr Myers at first wore a mask over his nose and mouth when making calls, and so did I, but the gauze stuck to my lips and I stopped wearing it and so did the doctor. It was too much of a nuisance to put them on and take them off every time we would go to a place like Kelly's, and also it was rather insulting to walk in on a group of people with a mask on your face when nobody in the group was wearing one. I was very healthy and was always glad to go in with the doctor because it gave me something to do. Of course I could have cleaned spark plugs or shot some air into the tyres while waiting for the doctor, but I hated to monkey around the car almost as much as I liked to drive it.

In a few days Dr Myers had begun to acquire some standing among the patients, and he became more confident. One time after

coming from my father's bedroom he got in the car with some
prescriptions in his hand and we started out. To himself he said,
looking up from a prescription: 'Digitalis . . . now I wonder?' I
turned suddenly, because it was the first time in my life I had
heard anyone criticize a prescription of my father's. 'Oh, I'm sorry,
Jimmy,' he said.

'You better not ever let him hear you say anything about his
prescriptions.'

'Yes, I know. He doesn't want anyone to argue with him. He
doesn't think I'm seeing as many people as I should.'

'What does he expect?' I said.

'Oh, he isn't unreasonable, but he doesn't want his patients to
think he's neglecting them. By the way, he wants us to stop in at
the Evanses in Collieryville. The David Evanses. Mrs Evans phoned
and said their maid is sick.'

'That's O.K. with me,' I said.

'I thought it would be,' he said.

Collieryville seemed strange with the streets so deserted as on
some new kind of holiday. The miners did not work on holydays of
obligation, and the miners would get dressed and stand around in
front of poolrooms and saloons, but now they were not standing
around, and there was none of the activity of a working day, when
coal wagons and trucks rumble through the town, and ten-horse
teams, guided by the shouted 'gee' and 'haw' of the driver, would
pull loads of timber through the streets on the way to the mines.
Collieryville, a town of about four thousand persons, was quiet as
though the people were afraid to come out in the cold November
grey.

We were driving along the main street when I saw Edith. She
was coming out of the P.O.S. of A. Hall, which was a poolroom on
the first floor and had lodge rooms on the two upper stories. It was
being used as an emergency hospital. I pulled up at the curb and
called to Edith. 'Come on, I'll give you a ride home,' I said.

'Can't. I have to get some things at the drug store,' she said.

'Well, we're going to your house anyway. I'll see you there,' I
said.

We drove to the Evans house and I told the doctor I would wait
outside until Edith came. She appeared in about five minutes and
I told her to sit in the car and talk to me. She said she would.

'Well, I'm a nurse, Jimmy,' she said.

'Yes, you are,' I said scornfully. 'That's probably how your maid got sick.'

'What!'

'Why, you hanging around at the P.O.S. of A. Hall is probably the way your maid got sick. You probably brought home the flu—'

'Oh, my God!' she said. She was nervous and pale. She suddenly jumped out of the car and I followed her. She swung open the front door and ran towards the kitchen, and I was glad she did; for although I followed her to the kitchen, I caught a glimpse of Mrs Evans and Dr Myers in Mr Evans's den. Through the half-closed doors I could see they were kissing.

I didn't stop, I know, although I felt that I had slowed up. I followed Edith into the kitchen and saw that she was half crying, shaking her hands up and down. I couldn't tell whether she had seen what I had seen, but something was wrong that she knew about. I blurted out, 'Don't go in your father's den,' and was immediately sorry I had said it; but then I saw that she had guessed. She looked weak and took hold of my arms; not looking at me, not even speaking to me, she said: 'Oh, my God, now it's him. Oh, why didn't I come home with you? Sarah isn't sick at all. That was just an excuse to get that Myers to come here.' She bit her lip and squeezed my arms. 'Jimmy, you mustn't ever let on. Promise me.'

'I give you my word of honour,' I said. 'God can strike me dead if I ever say anything.'

Edith kissed me, then she called out: 'Hey, where is everybody?' She whispered to me: 'Pretend you're chasing me like as if I pulled your necktie.'

'Let go!' I yelled, as loud as I could. Then we left the kitchen, and Edith would pull my necktie at every step.

Mrs Evans came out of the den. 'Here, what's going on here?'

'I'm after your daughter for pulling my tie,' I said.

'Now, Edith, be a good girl and don't fight with James. I don't understand what's the matter with you two. You usedn't to ever fight, and now you fight like cats and dogs. You oughtn't to. It's not nice.'

'Oh—' Edith said, and then she burst into tears and went upstairs.

I was genuinely surprised, and said: 'I'm sorry, Mrs Evans, we were only fooling.'

'Oh, it's not your fault, James. She feels nervous anyhow and I

guess the running was too much for her.' She looked at the doctor
as if to imply that it was something he would understand.

'I guess I'll go out and sit in the car,' I said.

'I'll be right out,' said the doctor.

I sat in the car and smoked, now and then looking at the second-
floor window where I knew Edith's room was, but Edith did not
come to the window and in about twenty minutes the doctor came
out.

'The maid wasn't sick after all,' he said. 'It was Mrs Evans. She
has a slight cold but she didn't want to worry your father. I guess
she thought if she said she was sick, your father'd come out himself.'

'Uh-huh,' I said. 'Where to now?'

'Oh, that Polish saloon out near the big coal banks.'

'You mean Wisniewski's,' I said.

IV

Doctor Myers must have known I suspected him, and he might
even have suspected that I had *seen* him kissing Mrs Evans. I was
not very good at hiding my likes and dislikes, and I began to dislike
him, but I tried not to show it. I didn't care, for he might have
told my father I was unsatisfactory, and my father would have
given me hell. Or if I had told my father what I'd seen, he'd have
given Dr Myers a terrible beating. My father never drank or
smoked, and he was a good, savage amateur boxer, with no scruples
against punching anyone smaller than himself. Less than a year
before all this took place my father had been stopped by a traffic
policeman while he was hurrying to an 'OBS'. The policeman knew
my father's car, and could have guessed why he was in a hurry,
but he stopped him. My father got out of the car, walked to the
front of it, and in the middle of a fairly busy intersection he took a
crack at the policeman and broke his jaw. Then he got back and
drove around the unconscious policeman and on to the confinement
case. It cost my father nearly a thousand dollars; the policeman's
friends and my father's enemies said: 'God damn Mike Malloy, he
ought to be put in gaol.' But my father was a staunch Republican
and he got away with it.

I thought of this now and I thought of what my father would
have done to Dr Myers if he found out. Not only would he have

beaten him up, bit I am sure he would have used his influence at
the University to keep Myers from getting his degree.

So I hid, as well as I could, my dislike for Dr Myers, and the
next day, when we stopped at my home, I·was glad I did. My
father had invented a signal system to save time. Whenever there
was a white slip stuck in the window at home or at the office, that
meant he was to stop and pick up a message. This day the message
in the window read: 'Mrs David Evans, Collieryville.'

Dr Myers looked at it and showed it to me. 'Well, on to Collieryville,' he said.

'O.K., but would you mind waiting a second? I want to see my
mother.'

He was slightly suspicious. 'You don't need any money, do you?
I have some.'

'No, I just wanted to see if she would get my father to let me
have the car to-night.' So I went in and telephoned to the Evanses.
I got Edith on the phone and told her that her mother had sent for
Dr Myers.

'I know,' she said. 'I knew she would. She didn't get up this
morning, and she's faking sick.'

'Well, when we get there you go upstairs with the doctor, and if
he wants you to leave the bedroom, you'll have to leave, but tell
your mother you'll be right outside, see?'

'O.K.,' said Edith.

I returned to the car. 'How'd you make out?' said Dr Myers.

'She thinks she can get him to let me have it,' I said, meaning
that my father would let me have the car.

When we arrived at the Evans house I had an inspiration. I
didn't want him to suspect that we had any plan in regard to him,
so I told him I was going in with him to apologize to Edith for our
fight of the day before. There was the chance that Edith would fail
to follow my advice and would come downstairs, but there was the
equally good chance that she would stay upstairs.

The plan worked. In some respects Edith was dumb, but not in
this. Dr Myers stayed upstairs scarcely five minutes, but it was
another five before Edith came down. Dr Myers had gone out to
wait in the Ford.

Edith appeared. 'Oh, Jimmy, you're so nice to me, and I'm often
mean to you. Why is that?'

'Because I love you.' I kissed her and she kissed me.

'Listen, if my dad ever finds this out he'll kill her. It's funny, you and me. I mean if you ever told me a dirty story, like about *you* know—people—'

'I did once.'

'Did you? I mustn't have been listening. Anyhow it's funny to think of you and me, and I'm older than you, but we know something that fellows and girls of our age, they only guess at.'

'Oh, I've known about it a long time, ever since I went to sisters' school.'

'And I guess from your father's doctor books. But this isn't the same when it's your own mother, and I bet this isn't the first time. My dad must have suspicions, because why didn't he send me away to boarding school this year?' I graduated from high last year. I bet he wanted me to be here to keep an eye on her.'

'Who was the other man?'

'Oh, I can't tell you. Nobody you know. Anyhow, I'm not sure, so I wouldn't tell you. Listen, Jimmy, promise to telephone me every time before he comes here. If I'm not here I'll be at the Bordelman's or at the Haltensteins', or if not there, the Callaways'. I'll stay home as much as I can, though. How long is he going to be around here, that doctor?'

'Lord knows,' I said.

'Oh, I hope he goes. Now give me a good-bye kiss, Jimmy, and then you have to go.' I kissed her. 'I'm worse than she is,' she said.

'No, you're not,' I said. 'You're the most darling girl there is. Good-bye, Ede,' I said.

Dr Myers was rubbing the skin in front of his ear when I came out. 'Well, did you kiss and make up?'

'Oh, we don't go in for that mushy stuff,' I said.

'Well, you will,' he said. 'Well . . . on to Wizziski's.'

'It's a good thing you're not going to be around here long,' I said.

'Why? Why do you say that?'

'Because you couldn't be in business or practice medicine without learning Hunkie names. If you stayed around here you'd have to be able to pronounce them and spell them.' I started the car. I was glad to talk. 'But I tell you where you'd have trouble. That's in the patches where they're all Irish with twenty or thirty cousins living in the same patch and all with the same name.'

'Oh, come on.'

'Well, it isn't as bad as it used to be,' I said. 'But my father told me about one time he went to Mass at Forganville, about fifteen miles from here, where they used to be all Irish. Now it's half Polack. Anyhow my father said the priest read the list of those that gave to the monthly collection, and the list was like this: John J. Coyle, $5; Jack Coyle, $2; Johnny Coyle, $2; J. J. Coyle, $5; Big John Coyle, $5; Mrs John Coyle the saloon keeper's widow, $10; the Widow Coyle, $2. And then a lot of other Coyles.'

He did not quite believe this, but he thought it was a good story, and we talked about college—my father had told me I could go to Oxford or Trinity College, Dublin, if I promised to study medicine—until we reached Wisniewski's.

This was a saloon in a newer patch than Kelly's. It was entirely surrounded by mine shafts and breakers and railroads and mule yards, a flat area broken only by culm banks until half a mile away there was a steep, partly wooded hill which was not safe to walk on because it was all undermined and cave-ins occurred so frequently that they did not bother to build fences around them. The houses were the same height as in Kelly's patch, but they were built in blocks of four and six houses each. Technically Wisniewski's saloon was not in the patch; that is, it was not on company ground, but at a crossroads at one end of the rows of houses. It was an old stone house which had been a tavern in the days of the King's Highway. Now it was a beery-smelling place with a tall bar and no tables or chairs. It was crowded, but still it had a deserted appearance. The reason was that there was no one behind the bar, and no cigars or cartons of chewing tobacco on the back bar. The only decorations were a calendar from which the October leaf had not been torn, depicting a voluptuous woman stretched out on a divan, and an Old Overbolt sign, hanging askew on the toilet door.

The men and women recognized Dr Myers and me, and made a lane for us to pass through. Wisniewski himself was sick in bed, and everybody understood that the doctor would see him first, before prescribing for the mob in the bar-room.

Dr Myers and I went to Wisniewski's room, which was on the first floor. Wisniewski was an affable man, between forty and fifty, with a Teutonic hair-cut that never needed brushing. His body under the covers made big lumps. He was shaking hands with another Polack whose name was Stiney. He said to us: 'Oh, hyuh, Cheem, hyuh, Cheem. Hyuh, Doc.'

'Hyuh, Steve,' I said. 'Yoksheemosh?'

'Oh, fine dandy. How's yaself? How's Poppa? You tell Poppa what he needs is lay off this here booze.' He roared at this joke. 'Ya, you tell him I said so, lay off this booze.' He looked around at the others in the room, and they all laughed, because my father used to pretend that he was going to have Steve's saloon closed by the County. 'You wanna drink, Cheem?' he asked, and reached under the bed and pulled out a bottle. I reached for it, and he pulled the bottle away. 'Na na na na na. Poppa close up my place wit' the County, I give you a drink. Ya know, miners drink here, but no minors under eighteen, hey?' He passed the bottle around, and all the other men in the room took swigs.

Dr Myers was horrified. 'You oughtn't to do that. You'll give the others the flu.'

'Too late now, Doc,' he said. 'T'ree bottle now already.'

'You lose all your customers, Steve,' I said.

'How ya figure dat out?' said Steve. 'Dis flu make me die, dis bottle make dem die. Fwit! Me and my customers all togeder in hell, so I open a place in hell. Fwit!'

'Well, anyhow, how are you feeling?' said the doctor. He placed a thermometer under Steve's arm. The others and Steve were silent until the temperature had been taken. 'Hm,' said Dr Myers. He frowned at the thermometer.

''M gonna die, huh, Doc?' said Steve.

'Well, maybe not, but you—' he stopped talking. The door opened and there was a blast of sweaty air from the bar-room, and Mr Evans stood in the doorway, his hand on the knob. I felt weak.

'Dr Myers, I'd like to see you a minute please,' said Mr Evans.

'Hyuh, Meester Ivvins,' called Steve. Evans is one name which is consistently pronounced the same by the Irish, Slavs, Germans, and even the Portugese and Negroes in the anthracite.

'Hello, Steve, I see you're drunk,' said Mr Evans.

'Not yet, Meester Ivvins. Wanna drink?'

'No, thanks. Doctor, will you step outside with me?'

Dr Myers stalled. 'I haven't prescribed for this man, Mr Evans. If you'll wait?'

'My God, man! I can't wait. It's about my wife. I want to know about her.'

'What about her?' asked the doctor.

'For God's sake,' cried Mr Evans. 'She's sick, isn't she? Aren't you attending her, or don't you remember your patients?'

I sighed, and Dr Myers sighed louder. 'Oh,' he said. 'You certainly—frightened me, Mr Evans. I was afraid something had happened. Why, you have no need to worry, sir. She has hardly any temperature. A very slight cold, and she did just the sensible thing by going to bed. Probably be up in a day or two.'

'Well, why didn't you say so?' Mr Evans sat down. 'Go ahead, then, finish with Steve. I'll wait till you get through. I'm sorry if I seemed rude, but I was worried. You see I just heard from my timber boss that he saw Dr Malloy's car in front of my house, and I called up and found out that Mrs Evans was sick in bed, and my daughter sounded so excited I thought it must be serious. I'll take a drink now, Steve.'

'Better not drink out of that bottle, Mr Evans,' said the doctor, who was sitting on the edge of the bed, writing a prescription.

'Oh, hell, it won't hurt me. So anyhow, where was I? Oh, yes. Well, I went home and found Mrs Evans in bed and she seemed very pale, so I wanted to be sure it wasn't flu. I found out you were headed this way so I came right out to ask if you wouldn't come back and take another look. That's good liquor, Steve. I'll buy a case of that.' He raised the bottle to his lips again.

'I give you a case, Meester Ivvins. Glad to give you a case any time,' said Steve.

'All right, we'll call it a Christmas present,' said Mr Evans. 'Thanks very much.' He was sweating, and he opened his raccoon coat. He took another drink, then he handed the bottle to Stiney. 'Well, James, I hear you and Edith were at it again.'

'Oh, it was just in fun. You know. Pulling my tie,' I said.

'Well, don't let her get fresh with you,' he said. 'You have to keep these women in their place." He punched me playfully. 'Doctor, I wonder if you could come to the house now and make sure everything's all right.'

'I would gladly, Mr Evans, but there's all that crowd in the bar-room, and frankly, Mrs Evans isn't what you'd call a sick woman, so my duty as a—physician is right here. I'll be only too glad to come if you'd like to wait.'

The Hunkies, hearing the Super talked to in this manner, probably expected Meester Ivvins to get up and belt the doctor across the face, but he only said: 'Well, if you sure an hour couldn't make any difference.'

'Couldn't possibly, Mr Evans,' said Dr Myers.

He finished with Steve and told him to stop drinking and take his medicine, then he turned to leave. Steve reached under his pillow and drew out a bundle of money. He peeled off a fifty-dollar bill and handed it to the doctor.

'Oh, no, thanks,' said Dr Myers. 'Dr Malloy will send you a bill.'

'Aw, don't worry about him, eh, Cheem? I always pay him firs' the mont, eh, Cheem? Naw, Doc, dis for you. Go have a good time. Gt twenty-five woman, maybe get drunk wit' boilo.' I could imagine Dr Myers drinking boilo, which is hot moonshine. I nudged him, and he took the money and we went to the bar-room.

I carried the chair and table and set them in place, and the Hunkies lined up docilely. Mr Evans waited in Steve's room, taking a swig out of the bottle now and then until Dr Myers had finished with the crowd. It was the same as usual. It was impractical to get detailed descriptions from each patient, so the flu doctors would ask each person three or four questions and then pretend to prescribe for each case individually. Actually they gave the same prescription to almost all the patients, not only to save time, but because drug supplies in the village and city pharmacies were inadequate, and it was physically impossible for druggists to meet the demand. They would make up large batches of each doctors standard prescription and dole out boxes and bottles as the patrons presented their prescriptions.

It took about two hours to dispose of the crowd at Steve's. Mr Evans told Doctor Myers to come in the Cadillac because it was faster than the Ford—which I denied. I followed in the Ford and got to the Evans house about three minutes after the Cadillac. Edith met me at the door. 'Oh, what a scare!' she said.

'If you think you were scared, what about me?' I said. I told her how I had felt when her father appeared at Steve's. 'Your father phoned and wants you to take that Myers home,' she said, when I had finished.

'Did he say why?' I asked.

'No, he just said you weren't to make any more calls this afternoon.'

'I wonder why.'

'I hope it hasn't got anything to do with him and my mother,' she said.

'How could it? Only four people know about it. He couldn't guess

it, and nobody will tell him. Maybe he's got up and wants me to
drive for him.'

'Maybe . . . I can't think. I'm afraid of them up there. Oh, I
hope he goes away.' I kissed her, and she pushed me away. 'You're
a bad actor, James Malloy. You're bad enough now, but wait till
you grow up.'

'What do you mean grow up? I'm almost six feet.'

'But you're only a kid. I'm seventeen, and you're only fifteen.'

'I'll be in my seventeenth year soon.' We heard footsteps on the
stairs, and Dr Myers voice:' . . . absolutely nothing to worry about.
I'll come in again to-morrow. Good-bye, Mr Evans. Good-bye,
Edith. Ready, Jim?'

I gave him my father's message and we drove home fast. When
we got there one of the Buicks was in front of the house, and we
went in the living room.

'Well, Dr Myers,' my father said. 'Back in harness again. Fit as
a fiddle, and I want to thank you for the splendid attention you've
given my practice. I don't know what my patients would have done
without you.'

'Oh, it's been a privilege, Doctor. I'd like to be able to tell you
how much I've appreciated working for you. I wouldn't have missed
it for the world. I think I'd like to serve my internship in a place
like this.'

'Well, I'm glad to hear it. I'm chief of staff at our hospital, and
I'm sorry I can't offer you something here, but you ought to try
some place like Scranton General. Get the benefit of these mining
cases. God damn interesting fractures, by the way. I trephined a
man, forty-eight years old—all right James, I'll call you when I
need you.' I left the room and they talked for half an hour, and
then my father called me. 'Dr Myers wants to say good-bye.'

'I couldn't leave without saying good-bye to my partner,' said
the doctor. 'And by the way, Dr Malloy, I think I ought to give
part of this cheque to James. He did half the work.'

'If he did I'll see that he gets his share. James knows that. He
wants one of these God damn raccoon coats. When I was a boy
the only people that wore them drove hearses. Well—' My father
indicated that it was time for the doctor and me to shake hands.

'Quite a grip James has,' said the doctor.

'Perfect hands for a surgeon. Wasted, though,' my father said.
'Probably send him to some God damn agricultural school and

make a farmer out of him. I want him to go to Dublin, then Vienna. That's where the surgeons are. Dublin and Vienna. Well, if you ever meet Dr Deaver tell him I won't be able to come down for the Wednesday clinics till this damn thing is over. Good luck, Doctor.'

'Thank you, many thanks, Dr Malloy.'

'James will drive you to the hotel.'

I took him to the hotel and we shook hands. 'If you ever want a place to stay in Philadelphia you're always welcome at my house.' He gave me the address of a fraternity house. 'Say good-bye to the Evanses for me, will you, Jim?'

'Sure,' I said, and left.

My father was standing on the porch, waiting impatiently. 'We'll use the Buick,' he said. 'That Ford probably isn't worth the powder to blow it to hell after you've been using it. Do you really want one of those livery stable coats?'

'Sure I do.'

'All right. Now, ah, drive to Kelly's.' We drove to Kelly's, where there was an ovation, not too loud, because there were one or two in the crowd on whom my father was liable to turn and say: 'You, ya son of a bitch, you haven't paid me a cent since last February. What are you cheering for?' We paid a few personal visits in the patch. At one of them my father slapped a pretty Irish girl's bottom; at another he gave a little boy a dollar and told him to stop picking his nose; at another he sent me for the priest, and when I came back he had gone on foot to two other houses, and was waiting for me at the second. 'What the hell kept you? Go to Terry Loughran's, unless the skunk got another doctor.'

'He probably did,' I said jovially. 'He probably got Lucas.'

'*Dr*. Lucas. Dr Lucashinsky. Ivan the Terrible. Well, if he got Lucas it serves him right. Go to Hartenstein's.'

We drove until one o'clock the next morning, taking coffee now and then, and once we stopped for a fried-egg sandwich. Twice I very nearly fell asleep while driving. The second time I awoke to hear my father saying: ' . . . And my God! To think that a son of mine would rather rot in a dirty stinking newspaper office than do this. Why, I do more good and make more money in twenty minutes in the operating room than you'll be able to make the first three years you're out of college. If you *go* to college. Don't drive so fast!'

It was like that for the next two days. I slept when he allowed me to. We were out late at night and out again early in the morning.

We drove fast, and a couple of times I bounded along corduroy roads with tanks of oxygen (my father was one of the first, if not the first, to use oxygen in pneumonia) ready to blow me to hell. I developed a fine cigarette cough, but my father kept quiet about it, because I was not taking quinine, and he was. We got on each other's nerves and had one terrible scene. He became angered by my driving and punched me on the shoulder. I stopped the car and took a tyre iron from the floor of the car.

'Now just try that again,' I said.

He did not move from the back seat. 'Get back in this car.' And I got back. But that night we got home fairly early and the next morning, when he had to go out at four o'clock, he drove the car himself and let me sleep. I was beginning to miss Dr Myers. It was about eight o'clock when I came down for breakfast, and I saw my father sitting in the living-room, looking very tired, staring straight ahead, his arms lying on the arms of the chair. I said hello, but he did not answer.

My mother brought me my breakfast. 'Did you speak to your father?'

'Oh, I said hello, but he's in a stupor or something. I'm getting sick of all this.'

'Hold your tongue. Your father has good reason to be unhappy this morning. He just lost one of the dearest friends he had in the world. Mr Evans.'

'Mr. Evans!' I said. 'When'd he die?'

'At about four o'clock this morning. They called your father but he died before he got there. Poor Mrs. Evans—'

'What did he die of? The flu?'

'Yes.' I thought of the bottle that he had shared with Steve and the other Hunkies, and Mrs. Evans's illness, and Dr. Myers. It was all mixed up in my mind. 'Now you be careful how you behave with your father to-day,' my mother said.

I called up Edith, but she would not come to the phone. I wrote her a note, and drove to Collieryville with some flowers, but she would not see me.

Even after the epidemic died down and the schools were reopened she would not see me. Then she went away to school and did not come home for the Easter holidays, and in May or June I fell in love with another girl and was surprised, but only surprised, when Edith eloped. Now I never can remember her married name.

Sermons
and
Soda-Water

Contents

Foreword to

Sermons and Soda Water

I am perfectly well aware that each of these three novellas could have been made into a full-length, 350-page-or-more, novel, and since the question is bound to come up, I shall try to answer it in advance: why did I choose the shorter form? The first, and probably the best, answer is that I wrote them this way because I wanted to. It is the answer that other authors will understand. However, I had reasons other than that. The form is one I like in spite of its un-popularity. Edith Wharton, Thomas Mann, Ernest Hemingway, Carl Van Vechten, David Garnett and James Hilton are among the few who have used the form successfully, but how few they are when you consider how many full-length novels are published in any one year, and the authors I have mentioned cover roughly fifty years. The resistance to the novella form comes from the non-professional public, the men and women who want their money's worth when they buy a book, and whose first test of a book is its avoirdupois. I don't quarrel with that right; the buyer of a book may set up any test or standard, or none at all. It is, of course, too bad that he must miss some good writing through the hefting test. I trust—but not too confidently —that a vast number of people will forget to weigh these small volumes.

I have another reason for publishing these stories in the novella form: I want to get it all down on paper while I can. I am now fifty-five years old and I have lived with as well as in the Twentieth Century from its earliest days. The United States in this Century is what I know, and it is my business to write about it to the best of my ability, with the sometimes special knowledge I have. The Twenties, the Thirties, and the Forties are already history, but I cannot be content to leave their story in the hands of the historians and the editors of picture books. I want to record the way people talked and thought and felt, and to do it with complete honesty and variety. I have done that in these three novellas, within, of course, the limits of my own observations. I have written these novellas from memory, with a minimum of research, which is one reason why the novella is the right form. I am working on a big novel that will take two years' research—reading, correspondence, travel—but it is my practice to be writing while I am doing research, and by the time I am ready to start writing the longer book, I may well have written two shorter ones. It will take me two years to *write* the longer book, and at fifty-five I have no right to waste time. Two years' research could mean a lot of wasted time while I wait for answers to letters and go on trips and yield to reading distractions that have nothing to do with the material I need for my longer, longest novel. That one *will* pass the hefting test, if it comes to pass.

I dedicate these books to my wife, Katharine Barnes O'Hara, and to my daughter, Wylie Delaney O'Hara, who sustain me.

John O'Hara

Spring 1960
Princeton, New Jersey

I

The Girl on the Baggage Truck
the beautiful movie star who
didn't get what she wanted
'Rich and Beautiful People,
and some who are less rich
and less beautiful, and
some who are outright heels.
The sex is rough,
the taste bittersweet;
it is all 100 proof O'Hara.'

San Francisco Chronicle

CHAPTER 1

The Girl on the Baggage Truck

When I was first starting out in New York I wrote quite a few
obituaries of men who were presumably in good health, but who
were no longer young. It was the custom on the paper where I
worked that a reporter who had no other assignment was given this
task, which most reporters found a chore but that I rather enjoyed.
The assistant day city editor would tell you to prepare an obit on
some reasonably prominent citizen, you would go to the office
library and get out the folder of the citizen's clippings, and for
the remainder of the afternoon you would read the clippings and
appropriate reference books, and reconstruct a life from the available facts, keeping it down to forty lines or whatever length the
subject's prominence had earned. It was good experience. One time
I had to look up Jack Smedley, one of the richest oil men in the
United States, and I discovered that his folder was so slim that you
could have mailed it for the price of a two-cent stamp; while a
Bronx politician of almost the same name had six bulging folders
that cluttered up my desk. Later, when the two men died, the rich
man was a Page One story all over the world, and the Bronx
politician got thirty lines halfway down the column on the obituary
page. You got what in more recent times was called a sense of
values.

It was through an advance obituary assignment that I first
learned that Thomas Rodney Hunterden was born in my home
town. I have never known that, and my ignorance was certainly
shared by most of my fellow townsmen. The baseball players,
concert singers, vaudeville performers, Grade B Wall Street figures,
clergymen, army officers, gangsters, and other minor celebrities who
were natives or onetime residents of the town were always claimed
with varying degrees of civic pride. The people in my home town
not only remembered its former residents; they also clung to the

memory of the famous visitors to the place—Theodore Roosevelt, John Philip Sousa, Colonel William F. Cody, Ruth St. Denis and Ted Shawn, Ignace Paderewski, Harry DeWolf Hopper, E. H. Sothern and Julia Marlowe, the Borax 20–Mule Team, a stuffed whale on exhibition in a railway coach, the dirigible *Shenandoah*, two reigning Imperial Potentates of the Ancient Arabic Order of the Nobles of the Mystic Shrine, James J. Corbett, Arthur Guy Empey, Leopold Stokowski and the Philadelphia Orchestra, Paul Whiteman and His Orchestra, Billy Sunday, Dr. Frank Buchman, Dr. Russell H. Conwell, and William Jennings Bryan, to name a few who had passed through or over the town. The people of my town were as quick with reminiscences of a suffragan bishop who lived in New England as they were with stories about a whoremaster who operated in Atlantic City, and it just was not in character for them to forget Thomas Rodney Hunterden.

The next time I was home on vacation I had a beer with an old-time newspaper man who knew everything about everybody. 'Claude, did you ever hear of Thomas R. Hunterden?' I asked.

'Thomas Rodney Hunterden, d, *e*, n? Sure. Why?'

'Did you ever know him?'

'How would I know *him*?'

'Because he was born in Gibbsville, and he's about your age.'

Claude shook his head. 'He wasn't born in Gibbsville. I'd know it if he was,' said Claude quietly.

'I could take some money away from you on that,' I said.

'I'll bet you a new hat.'

'No, no bet. I *know*.'

It was afternoon, and the public library was open till nine in the evening, so we had a few more beers and then went to look up Thomas R. Hunterden in *Who's Who in America*. My friend Claude Emerson, who was half Pilgrim stock and half Pennsylvania Dutch, was so miserable at being caught in an error that we went back to the speak-easy and drank more beer, but he was not so talkative. Several weeks after I returned to New York a note came from Claude.

Dear Jim:

If Thomas R. Hunterden claims to have been born in Gibbsville, the man is a liar. I spent an entire day at the Court House in among the birth and tax records. No one named Hunterden was ever born in Lantenengo County since records have been kept, nor has anyone paid taxes under that name. You have aroused my curiosity. Wish I could track this down. If you get the opportunity to interview Hunterden, would be much obliged to hear what you learn.

Yours sincerely,
Claude Emerson

The opportunity to interview Thomas R. Hunterden was a long time coming. I was fired from the paper and it was several months before I got a job as a press agent for a movie company. My interest in Hunterden was non-existent until one morning when I was at Grand Central Terminal, meeting the Twentieth Century Limited. Charlotte Sears, who was one of my employer's not-quite-top stars, was coming in on the Century, and I was there to handle the reporters and photographers. There were three photographers and a reporter from the *Morning Telegraph* and we were a little group down on the platform, conspicuous only because the photographers had their cameras out and camera cases hanging from their shoulders. The fellow from the New York Central press department came to me with the information that the car in which Charlotte had a drawing-room would be at a point farther up the platform, and our group accordingly moved on.

I noticed casually that a tall gentleman in a Chesterfield and carrying a silver-mounted walking stick was standing at approximately the point toward which we were headed. He paid no attention to our group until he saw the cameras, then there was no mistaking his reaction for anything but panic. He saw the cameras, he put a yellow-gloved hand to his face, and he quickly walked—almost ran—past us and up the ramp and out of sight. I vaguely recogised him as a man whose photographs I had seen but whom I had not seen in person. In a minute or two the Century pulled in and I had other things to think about than a man who did not want his picture taken. I had my job to do.

I reintroduced myself to Charlotte Sears, whom I had met on previous occasions, and we posed her sitting on a baggage truck with her legs crossed and an inch or two of silk-stockinged thigh showing. The little man from the *Telegraph* asked her the usual questions about the purpose of her visit, the future of talking pictures, the rumored romance with an actor who everyone in the industry knew was a drug addict and a homosexual, and the chance of her doing a stage play. The photographers and reporter finished their jobs and Chottie Sears and I were alone. 'I have a limousine to take you to the hotel,' I said.

'I think I'm being met,' she said.

'I'm afraid not,' I said, guessing. 'I think the photographers frightened him away.'

'Mr Hunterden? Oh, Lord, of course,' she said. 'But he *was* here?' I immediately identified Hunterden as the man with the cane.

'Yes, he was here,' I said. 'But as soon as he saw those cameras . . .'

'Of course, I should have warned him. All right, Jim, will you take me to the hotel? Have you had your breakfast?'

'I had a cup of coffee,' I said.

'That's all I've had. Have breakfast with me.'

On our way to the hotel I told her about the interviews we had scheduled for her and the public appearances she was expected to make. 'I hope you haven't booked me for any evening engagements,' she said. 'If you have, that's your hard luck.'

"A charity ball,' I said. 'At the Astor.'

She shook her head. 'Nothing in the evening. Tell Joe Finston I have other plans.'

'*You* tell him.'

'All right, I'll tell him. And believe me, when Finston knows who the plans are with, he won't raise any objections. Well, *you* know. You saw him at the station. To think how close he came to getting his picture in the papers. That was a narrow escape. I should have warned him. Do you know him, I mean personally?'

'No, I've never met him.'

'He hates reporters and those people. He has a positive aversion to them. Are you married, Jim?'

'No.'

'I know you weren't the last time I was here, but things happen fast in this life. Why I asked is, while I'm in town will you do the honors? Take me out and so forth?'

'That's no hardship, and it's what I'm paid for anyway.'

"The only trouble is, you'll have to sort of stand by. I won't know when I'll need you.'

'I could guess that,' I said.

She took a bath while breakfast was on the way to her suite and
I was disposing of the telephone calls from high school interviewers,
jewelry salesmen and furriers. 'No call from that certain party?' she
said.

'Not unless he was pretending to be from New Utrecht High,' I
said. 'Or maybe he was the man just in from Amsterdam. I don't
know his voice.'

"You don't have to know his voice,' she said. 'The manner gives
him away. He's used to giving orders.'

"So I'd infer, although I have nothing to do with the stock
market. Eat your breakfast. It's a cold and wintry day.'

'I wish he'd call, damn it.'

'He will. Have some coffee.'

'What do you know about his wife?'

'Mrs Thomas Rodney Hunterden, a name on the society pages.
A doer of good works, I gather. That's all. I could look her up if
you want me to.'

'No, I just thought you might have some information offhand.'

'I don't get around in those circles,' I said.

'You and me both,' said Chottie. 'The way I was brought up,
anybody that finished high school is in society.'

'Oh, come on,' I said.

'Really,' she said. 'I can do simple arithmetic and I read a lot,
but that's the extent of my culture. And travel. It's a good thing I
liked to travel or I'd have been bored to death by the time I was
twelve. But I liked it. Split weeks in Shamokin and Gibbsville, P.A.'

'Be careful. That's where I come from.'

'Shamokin?' she said. 'The Majestic Theatre.'

'No, Gibbsville.'

'The Globe. I played the Globe in vaudeville, twice, and I did a
split week in Gibbsville with a road company of *The Last of Mrs
Cheyney*. You didn't happen to catch me in that, did you?'

'I'd left there by then,' I said. I do not know why I refrained
from mentioning Gibbsville as the birthplace of her Mr Hunterden.
I think it was because she was upset about the photographers at
Grand Central and nervous about the telephone call that had not
yet come.

'I was young for the part,' she said. 'But I was glad to get the
job. I had to get out of New York. I don't mean I had to because
I was forced to or anything like that, but there was a young polo

player in love with me. A strong infatuation, call it. He was a nice kid, but a kid. His parents made life very difficult for me.'

'Threatened you?'

'Anything but. They belonged to the school that thinks a young man ought to sow his wild oats, and I was his wild oats. Tame wild oats. I didn't have a bad reputation, and they sort of approved of me as Junior's girl friend, just as long as I didn't show any signs of wanting to marry him. Oh, I visited them and I went for a cruise on their yacht. But then I began to ask myself, what was I? What was I getting out of it? I was a combination of nursemaid and mistress. It was a dandy arrangement—for them and for Junior. Then I began to get sore. I hate being a chump. Other girls I knew would have taken him for plenty. They figured I was just too nice to be that kind of a girl. So I got out of New York.'

'But why? There's something missing here.'

'Because I was beginning to get a little stuck on the kid and there was no future in it. I wasn't in love with him, but he had charm and I wasn't going out with anyone else, so I began to get stuck on him. But two weeks on the road and he was nothing to me, nothing.' She had a sip of coffee. 'When I'm on the road I'm a great sightseer. I go for walks. Other people on the bill, or in the company, they travel all over the country, thousands of miles, and all they ever see is the inside of one theatre after another. All they ever read is *Billboard* and *Zit's*. Maybe the *Racing Form* and the *Christian Science Monitor*. But they never read the local papers, or books or magazines. Some of them don't even bother to read their notices, because half the time the hick critics are on the take from the local theatre manager. Those that aren't, they pan everything. We got one notice on *Mrs Cheyney* that didn't even know Freddie Lonsdale was an Englishman. What a business!' The telephone rang. It was Joe Finston, welcoming the star to New York and inquiring whether she was being well taken care of.

She hung up. 'Joe Finston. That heel. Last year he'd have been here in person, but the grosses are down on my last two pictures, so he uses the telephone. This call was to soften me up. He'll be nice to me because he wants to talk me out of my contract, but fat chance he has. I have three more years to go, raises every year automatically. The only way I'll let him out of the contract is if he pays me one hundred per cent of what the contract calls for.'

'You know what he'll do, don't you?'

'Sure. Put me in one stinker after another till I holler for help. But it won't work with me. I'll be on the set and made up at six o'clock every morning. I'll go on location to Patagonia. I know all the tricks. Stills that make me look fifty years old. But I worked a lot harder for sixty dollars a week than I do now for six thousand. Finston doesn't know that. Finston isn't show business. He's a picture-business nephew. He doesn't realise that it would be cheaper to settle the contract for a hundred per cent on the dollar now than put me in four or five stinkers.'

'Would you settle now?'

'Did he tell you to ask me that?'

'No.'

'Then I'll tell you, yes. I'd settle now, this minute. Do you know how much I have coming to me on the contract? Only $1,488,000. That's forty weeks left of this year, and three more years with raises. If you figure interest, that's over a million and a half. I won't get it. He won't settle. But he'd be much smarter if he did, because if you put a star in a stinker you have a bigger stinker than if you had no star.'

'You said it. Would you quit the movies if you got all that money at once?'

'Nobody ever quits the movies, Jim. They go into enforced retirement. The talkies killed off those that couldn't read lines or had voices that wouldn't record. But they didn't quit. A queen doesn't—what's the word?'

'Abdicate?'

'Abdicate. And that's the way you're treated while you're a star. Like a queen. Bring in those grosses, and you're treated like royalty. Begin to slip a little, and choose the nearest exit. But that isn't abdicating. That's escaping from the angry mob. I'll do what others have done. I'll take the money and come back here and wait for a good play. The difference is, if you have a flop on Broadway, it doesn't count against you the next time out. And if I happen to get a hit on Broadway, the next time I go to Hollywood I'll start at ten thousand! And maybe Joe Finston will be the one who pays it. Wouldn't that be nice?'

'It sure would.' I got up and looked at the scrambled eggs that were being kept warm over an alcohol burner. 'You sure you won't have some solid food?'

'All right,' she said.

I started to dish out the eggs and the telephone rang. 'You want me to go in the other room?' I asked.

'I'll go.'

We both guessed it was Hunterden, and we were right. She went to the bedroom and was gone about fifteen minutes. When she came back she was calm and self-possessed. Whatever had been said on the telephone, her composure was now that of a star. I dished out the eggs again and she ate a big breakfast, speaking very little. 'I was hungry,' she said. 'I want to go to the theatre every night I'm in town. Will you arrange for the tickets? I may not *get* there every night, but when I can't, you take some friend of yours. Here.' She handed me a $100 bill.

'What's this for? I'll get the tickets from a scalper and have them put on your hotel bill.'

'Your expenses.'

'I put in an expense account at the office.'

'I'm trying to give you a little present, you idiot,' she said.

'Oh. Well, thanks. I can use it. Thanks very much.'

'I should thank you. You got me through a difficult two hours. Imagine what I'd have been like, missing him at the station and then sitting here fidgeting."

'You go for this guy in a great big way, don't you?'

'I guess I do. Why else would I give a darn? Why else would I keep all my evenings free?'

All this was thirty years ago, as remote-seeming to many people today as the Gay Nineties had seemed to me. New York now is as different from New York then as New York then was from London. The one pervasive factor in all our lives was Prohibition, which made lawbreakers of us all and gave a subtly conspiratorial, arcane touch to the simple act of dining out. Even that was phony, for there were only a few speakeasies which you could not talk your way into, where you had to be known. Indeed, it is harder to get a table at the best restaurants today than it was to gain admittance to the illegal cafés of those days. The other pervading factor, whose influence has been exaggerated in retrospect, was the national greed, the easy dollar in the stock market. But Prohibition, with the speakeasy, and the stock market, with the lucky dollar, facilitated romances like that between Charlotte Sears and Thomas R. Hunterden. Men like Hunterden have always had mistresses like

Chottie Sears, but the speakeasy made it all so much simpler and the stock market paid the bills.

In the beginning I mentioned an oil millionaire whose newspaper clippings failed to fill a single folder. That was not true of Thomas R. Hunterden. His record filled three or four folders, and when I visited the library of the newspaper from which I had been fired, and checked what I had read, I now noticed that not a single clipping was dated prior to 1917.. According to the other information available, Hunterden was in his early forties when the United States entered the war. His age had kept him out of the army draft, but there was no mention of any war activity whatever, either in his clippings or in the standard reference books of the period. In his brief *Who's Who* sketch he stated that he was born in Gibbsville, Pa., on April 2, 1876, and educated in 'public schools' but did not say where; and there was no mention of his parents, a most unusual oversight if it was an oversight. The next item stated that he married Alice Longstreet in 1919. If there were any children they were not mentioned. After that followed a list of corporations of which he was board chairman: American Industrial Corporation, British-American Transportation, Throhu Petroleum, Omega Development. and Omega Holding. He then listed his clubs: the New York Yacht, the Bankers, and several golf and yacht clubs in Florida and South America. The only address he gave was his office on Lower Broadway. The Social Register provided one additional bit of information: Alice Longstreet was not her maiden name. She had been married to a man named Longstreet and her maiden name was Alice Boyd.

I then looked up all the Longstreet clippings and I found what I wanted. In 1918 Forrest Longstreet committed suicide by jumping from a window in his office in the financial district. Surviving were his wife, the former Alice Boyd, and two daughters. Longstreet had been quite a fellow. In the clippings he was often described as the sportsman-financier, prominent clubman, big-game hunter, aeronaut, foxhunter, and so on. He had played football at Harvard and had once set a record for driving his racing car from Rome to Paris. The newspaper photographs of him showed a handsome man with think blonde hair and eyebrows, a black moustache, and white even teeth. The pictures confirmed my guess that he had been a wild man. It was not a particularly shrewd guess; the clippings gave the clues. Sporting accidents, expeditions into Africa, a suit for breach of promise, a swimming race from the Battery to Bedloe's Island. I was too young and too deep in the Pennsylvania mountains to have heard of Longstreet, but now he interested me as much as Hunterden, and I knew that in finding out about the one I would be learning about the other.

I had a speakeasy friend named Charley Ellis, who was my age and who was my principal connection with New York society, as I was his with the Broadway-theatre-newspaper world. Charley had a job that he did not take very seriously, and he was easily persuaded to have me to lunch at his club.

'Why the sudden interest in old Forrest Longstreet?' he asked, when I began to question him. 'Not that he was so very old. I guess he'd be about fifty-five or—six if he'd lived. He was a friend of my old man's.'

'Did you know him yourself?'

'Oh, sure. He used to take me for rides in his car. He had a car called a Blitzen-Benz. We'd go like hell out the Vanderbilt Parkway and on the way back he'd give me cigarettes. Now that I think of it, I guess he was my godfather. Yes, he was.'

'Why did he do the dry dive?'

'What's this for? You're not going to put it in the paper, are you?'

'What paper? I don't work for a paper any more.'

'No, but you might again. This has to be under the hat.'

'It will be.'

'Well, Forrie Longstreet was mixed up in some very suspicious stock promotion, and when he killed himself his family gave out the story that he did it for the insurance. The insurance was supposed to pay back his friends that went in on the stock deal. Actually, they were paid back by other members of his family. He blew all his own money, but the Longstreets still had plenty and they came through. My old man collected something, I know.'

'What about his wife?'

'What about her?'

'Well, how did he leave her fixed?'

'Oh. Well, it didn't really matter, I guess. She married a fellow called Hunterden, supposed to be in the chips.'

'Which one don't you like? Hunterden, or Longstreet's widow? You're holding out on me.'

'I know I am, Jim. I don't know what you want this information for, and I liked Forrie Longstreet. Let him rest in peace.'

'I think Hunterden is a phony. I know he is, in some things, and I want to find out how much of a phony. I have no intention of writing an exposè, or giving it to the papers, but I've had my curiosity aroused. He's having an affair with Charlotte Sears, and I like her. It's none of my business. She's a big girl now and not a great friend of mine, but she's on the up-and-up. I did a little digging on Hunterden and I happened to come across Longstreet's name.'

'Charlotte Sears is much too good for him, but as you say, if she's having an affair with him, what business of ours is it to interfere?'

'Not interfere, but be ready when the roof caves in. She trusts me, and she's a good egg. Would you like to meet her? I'm taking her to the theatre tonight. Meet us at Tony's, twelve o'clock.'

'I've met her. She was going around with Junior Williamson a couple of years ago. Not that she'd remember me, but I'd like to see her again.'

We said no more about Forrest Longstreet or Thomas Hunterden. Late that night Charlotte Sears and I went to Tony's, a speakeasy that was a meeting place for theatrical and literary people, and Charley Ellis joined us. He was too polite to remind her that they had met in the past, but she remembered him and he was pleased. 'What's Junior up to these days?' she asked.

'Oh, he's talking about going into politics.'

'Is that his idea, or his wife's?'

'His, I guess. He doesn't know what to do with himself.'

'I guess when you have as much money as he has, it gets to be a problem. You don't feel like making any more money, and if you're in love with your wife, you don't go on the make. At least not yet. But he will. There isn't much there, you know. This may sound like sour grapes, but Junior's a mama's boy.'

'That's no secret,' said Charley Ellis.

'Maybe not, but it's the secret of his charm.'

'How could it be?'

'A man wouldn't understand that, Mr Ellis. As soon as a girl discovers that Junior's a mama's boy, every girl thinks she's going to be the real mama.'

'A strange way to look at it.'

'You're talking to somebody that learned it through experience. Oh, well, he was a nice kid and I guess he always will be. The women will vote for him. Once. What's he going to run for? Governor?'

'He hadn't said, but I doubt if he'd run for governor.'

She laughed. 'I could defeat him.'

'You'd run against him?'

'Hell, no. I'd support him. The minute I opened my mouth the Democrats would thank me for saving them the trouble. Can you imagine the horror at Republican headquarters if I came out for Junior?'

'You should have been a politican,' said Charley.

'Should have been? I am, every day of my life. Ask Jim. In our business Al Smith wouldn't last a minute. By the way, Jim, Joe Finston is taking me to lunch tomorrow, apropos of nothing at all.'

Two acting couples invited themselves to our table and in a little while we all went to the Central Park Casino. Before saying goodnight Charley Ellis asked me to meet him for lunch the next day, and I said I would be glad to.

'That was fun last night,' said Charley Ellis, at lunch.

'Yes, we didn't get home till after seven. We went to Harlem.'

'I have to go through the motions of holding down my job,' he said. 'She's a good egg, Charlotte Sears. Confusing, though. I kept thinking she was still carrying the torch for Junior Williamson.'

'Maybe she is.'

'She's wasting her time. I didn't want to say anything, but Junior has his next wife all picked out already. Sears is right. There isn't much there. I like Sears.'

'Yes, I can tell you do. Why don't you grab her away from Hunterden?'

'Somebody ought to. Hunterden is bad business.'

'Take her away from him. She liked you. She said so.'

He smiled. 'She said so to me while I was dancing with her. As a matter of fact, Jim, and very much *entre nous*, I'm seeing her tonight.'

'Good work,' I said. 'Fast work, too.'

'Well, I thought it was worth a try. Maybe she just wants to talk about Junior, but we'll get on other subjects.'

'I'm sure you will. I wonder what she plans to tell Hunterden,' I said. 'You know, I never got the feeling that she was in love with Hunterden as much as she was afraid of him.'

'He's bad business. And you want to hear about Forrie Longstreet. He didn't kill himself over money.'

'You more or less implied there was another reason.'

'It was his wife. Forrie was a wild man. Cars and airplanes and all that. But he was crazy about Aunt Alice. We weren't related, but when I was a kid I called her Aunt Alice. Absolutely devoted to her, Forrie was. And apparently she was in love with him till this Hunterden guy came along. Hunterden went to Forrie with a business proposition that looked like easy money, just for the use of Forrie's name, and that's how Hunterden met Alice. Forrie lost his dough, his good name, and his wife, all to the same guy. My old man told me Alice didn't even wait six months before she married Hunterden. But I guess she's paying for it.'

'How so?'

'Everybody dropped her like a hotcake. My mother wouldn't have her in the house, even before she married Hunterden. My mother of course was one of those that knew what was going on between Alice and Hunterden, and I gather she had a talk with her, but Alice wouldn't listen. You think you come from a small town, but what you may not realise is that there's a very small town right here in New York, composed of people like my mother and father. They never see anyone outside their own group and have no desire to, and believe me, the gate was closed on Alice Longstreet. The portcullis is lowered and the bridge over the moat has been raised, permanently.'

'I see her name in the paper all the time.'

'Yes, and you should hear my mother on the subject. "Alice still doing public penance, I see." That's what Mother says about Alice and her charities.'

'How do the boys downtown feel about Hunterden?'

'Depends on what boys you're talking about. My old man and his friends give him the cut direct, and any time they hear he's in anything, they stay out of it.'

'How did he get in all those clubs?'

'There's a funny thing about clubs. If the right people put you up, a lot of members hesitate to blackball you. The members figure that a man's sponsors must have their own good reasons for putting him up, and the members are inclined to respect those reasons, even in a case like Hunterden's. And there are some clubs he'll never get in.'

'This one, for instance?'

'Oh, hell, this isn't what it used to be. I mean it isn't as hard to get in. There was a time when all the members knew each other. Now as I look around I don't even know all the guys my own age. This is where Forrie Longstreet used to hang out. I'll take you upstairs and show you some pictures of him.'

'I've seen some. He was a dashing figure.'

'In everything he did. He belonged in another age, when all gentlemen carried swords.'

'I don't know, Charley. In Walpole's time fellows like Longstreet got into debt and had to do business with guys like Hunterden.'

'So they did, but the Hunterdens never met the Longstreets' wives.'

'I wonder.'

'Well, maybe they did,' said Charley Ellis. 'You *like* to think things were better long ago.'

'Better for whom?' I said. 'Two hundred years ago I wouldn't be sitting here with you.'

'If you say that, you know more about your family two hundred years ago than I do about mine. I'm not an ancestry snob, Jim. Maybe you are, but I'm not. My objection to Hunterden isn't based on who his grandfather was. Neither was my father's or mother's. It's what Hunterden himself was. And is. I consider Charlotte Sears more of a lady for dropping Junior Williamson than I do Alice Longstreet for marrying Hunterden. When I was in prep school I remember seeing pictures of Charlotte Sears, before she had a reputation as a movie actress. Around the same time Alice, Aunt Alice Longstreet, was a beautiful lady who was a friend of my mother's. But now Charlotte Sears is the beautiful lady, and Alice Hunterden is a social climber, trying to climb back. And having hard going.'

'Very instructive conversation,' I said. 'And that isn't sarcasm.'

'A little sarcasm. You know, Jim, people from your side of town, they choose to think that all the snobbery is concentrated in people like my mother and father. But all my father and mother want to do is see their friends and mind their own business. That's the way they like to live, and since they can afford it, that's the way they do live. And incidentally, money has very little to do with it. I know damn well my old man has friends that don't make as much money as you do. But they *are* his *friends*. Whereas, on Broadway, and the

Hollywood people, a big star doesn't want to be seen with anyone that isn't just as big a star or a little bigger. And among those people there's nothing worse than a has-been. With my father and mother there is no such thing as a has-been.' He smiled to himself.

'What?' I said.

'I said to the old man this morning that I'd been out with Charlotte Sears last night. "Tell me about her," he said. "What's she like?" He's never met her, but he's seen her movies and plays, and he was really interested. But he doesn't want to know her any better, and neither would my mother. That isn't snobbishness, but you might think it is, and I guess Charlotte would too. You're the snob of us two.'

'Why do you say that? It may be true,' I said.

'One night when you took me to that place called Dave's Blue Room.'

'I remember,' I said.

'We sat down at a table, a booth, and you knew everybody there. They all said hello to you and they gave me the cold stare till you introduced me. "Charley Ellis, of the *Daily News*." Then they relaxed.'

'Why was I a snob? Maybe they were, but why was I?'

'Because you were embarrassed in your own crowd, to be seen with somebody that wasn't a member of the crowd. You had to explain who I was. If you hadn't been a snob, you'd have just introduced me as Charley Ellis, or even Charley Ellis, customer's man at Willetts & Ellis.'

'You're right,' I said.

'Well, Charley Ellis, customer's man, has to make a few phone calls, but if you'd like to hang around for a while I'll play you some pool.'

'Thanks, but I'm going up to see La Sears. She has a fan-magazine interview at four o'clock. Any message for her?'

'Just that I'm looking forward to seeing her tonight.'

Chottie's maid let me in and I had a half-hour wait before Chottie turned up. It was immediately apparent that her luncheon with Joe Finston had not gone well. 'Do you know a good cheap gangster that's looking for a night's work?' she said.

'I know several. Your candidate's Finston?'

'Who else? He offered me a picture that's been turned down by everybody on the lot, and of course when I said no, he said he was going to offer it to me by registered letter, and then if I turned it down he'd put me on suspension.'

'That's what you pay an agent for.'

'I know, but my agent is on the Coast and this little maneuver is all Finston's, in New York. Oh, I'll figure out something, but this heel, this nephew, Finston, he's doing all he can to spoil my visit. He wants to get out of the contract and then show his uncles what a smart boy he is. To show you how cheap he is, he said if he wanted to, he could legally notify me in New York, today, and if I refused to do the picture, I'd not only go on suspension. I'd even have to pay all my expenses while I'm here.'

'Well, from what I know of him, he'd do it.'

'Jim, you stay out of it. I know you're on my side, but I don't want you to lose your job on account of me.'

'Finston won't fire me, not right away. He wants to get some personal publicity in the New York papers and he's convinced I'm the one that can get it for him. Chottie, I haven't been with the company very long, and you have, but I know something you may not know.'

'What's that?'

'Finston has his eye on the Coast. He'd do anything to get in the production end. But his uncles don't want any part of him out there. They don't even like it when he takes trips out there. Don't forget, it's his mother that's a Rosenbaum, not his father. The Rosenbaum brothers want to keep Joe Finston here in the home office, as far away from production as he can get.'

'I knew some of this, but not all. I didn't know he was trying to get into production.'

'Oh, yes. When he was in college he wanted to be a writer. He told me that himself. He wants to fire all the writers on the Coast and get all new ones. Also directors. He thinks he knows about directing.'

'He couldn't direct a blind man across the street.'

'I'm sure of it. Well, if I were you, I'd stall him till you go back. Let him say or do anything he pleases. Then when you get back to the Coast, go see Morris Rosenbaum and tell him you understand Finston is getting ready to take over production. If he recovers from his stroke, you tell him you heard a lot of rumors to that effect while you were here. In fact, you say to Morris you got that impression because Finston wanted you to star in this turkey and tried to talk you into it all the time you were in New York.'

'I think I'll marry you, Jim.'

'Just the way I am? I ought to go out and buy a few things. And you have a date tonight with a friend of mine.'

'Well, he asked me. And you didn't.'

'I didn't, because it's my job to take you out, and I do it on company money. I don't mean anything to you, Chottie, so don't pretend I do.'

'Truthfully, you never did before, but this trip—I don't know. I never knew you before. I'll break the date with Ellis?'

'Oh, no. You keep the date with Ellis.'

'Will you meet us later?'

'No.'

'Well then, don't be jealous of Ellis. Jealous of Ellis! Well listen to the girl.'

I decided to catch her off balance. 'Where is Hunterden?'

'Hunterden? Why?'

'Okay, it's none of my business.'

'No, it isn't,' she said haughtily, so haughtily that I guessed something had gone wrong.

'Sorry I mentioned it,' I said. 'Now about this dame that's coming to interview you. She's new, but watch her. She's meek and mild, and asks innocuous questions, but she's out to make a score and we've had a little trouble with her. She doesn't write the usual fan-magazine slop.'

'Everybody's out to make a score, in one way or another. I wish I had six children and lived in Chillicothe. Any Chillicothe, just so it wasn't New York or Hollywood.'

'You've seen all those towns, but you never lived in them, and you never could.'

'Don't be hard on me, Jim. I don't know where I'm at. If you want to know the truth, I'm scared.'

'Of what?'

'Hunterden. Ellis. Finston. Junior Williamson. Oh, *he* phoned. He saw in the paper I was in town, and he quote just called up to chat unquote. So don't you add to my troubles, please. On the train East I had everything all worked out so neatly. Hunterden would meet me and we'd see each other and maybe get a few things settled. But he ran away from the photographers. And then I met

your friend Ellis and I liked him, but he's on the make. Not that I
blame him, but there I go with Junior again, only this time his
name is Ellis. And I'm scared of Finston. He has a mean little face
and I don't think it's going to be easy to fight him.' She stopped.
'I'm ashamed of myself, Jim. I tried flirting with him, but he wasn't
having any. Ashamed and scared. An ugly little man like that ought
to be easy to handle, but he just looked at me like I was another
man. No, not like another man. He wouldn't have the guts to look
at another man with such contempt. Do you know what he said? I
can hardly repeat it.'

'Don't if you don't want to.'

'There we were in the middle of Sardi's and I was trying to use
my feminine wiles, hating it but acting. And he said, "Any time
you want to put your clothes back on, let's talk contract." '

'Did you have any answer to that?'

'Yes, I said I hoped he got a good look because the only way he
ever would be in his imagination. That's when I wished I
could mention Hunterden's name, but how can I? I haven't seen
Hunterden since I've been in New York. If you were a woman
you'd know what I'm going through with Finston and Hunterden.
Slapped in my famous teeth by a little horror I wouldn't even step
on, and given the absent treatment by a big shot. And what's in
between? An ex-college boy on the make, your friend Ellis. Don't
be hard on me, Jim. I'm scared.'

'I'll get you out of this interview.'

'Can you? I couldn't face a tough dame this afternoon.'

'You go downstairs and wait in the limousine. I'll wait till she
gets here and tell her you're launching a battleship, or something.
I'll get rid of her. I suggest you go for a drive through the Park
and come back in about an hour.'

'I don't want to be alone,' she said. 'Please, Jim. You get rid of
her and then come down and go for a drive with me.'

'Well then, park the car up Fifth Avenue and I'll join you as
soon as I can.'

I was not in love with Chottie and I never could be. She was a
public person and I had already observed that a public person
could only be in love with another public person; in Chottie's case
another star, a famous young heir, a mysterious but nonetheless
public figure like Hunterden. And yet as I made my way to the
limousine, and as we drove through the Park and over to Riverside

Drive, I wanted to protect her, to keep her from injury, to shield her from roughness. In the Park she reached over and took my hand.

'What are you thinking about, Jim?'

'You.'

'I thought so,' she said. She did not go on, and neither did I. If I told her that I wanted to protect her, I would be taking away her strongest protection, which was her belief in her own toughness. I saw her clearly as something gay and fragile that could be hurt and even destroyed, but she was as proud of her independent spirit as she was of her beauty and talent. I let her think whatever she was thinking, and for the remainder of the ride she encouraged me to talk about myself and jobs I had had. Back at the hotel entrance she said, before getting out of the car: 'Do you want to keep the car?'

'You mean, don't come up,' I said.

'That's what I mean. Don't come up. This would be a very bad time to start anything, if we ever are.'

'And if we don't now, we probably never will,' I said.

'Probably,' she said. 'I'll give you a wonderful kiss and you'll always know we could have.'

'If you give me a wonderful kiss, we will,' I said.

'Yes, I guess so. Then no kiss, but when you get old and think back on your girls, I give you permission to include me. We just as good as. Thank you, Jim.'

She left me, and I found that the factual part of my mind was busy wondering how old she was. Until that moment she had been among those actresses whose beauty and fame, while they last, make them impervious to questions as to their real names and real ages. But we had come very close to making love, and she herself had been the one to mention age. It was on her mind, and now it was on mine. Until then I would have accepted any age under thirty as a true one for her. With some sense of treacherous guilt I told the driver to take me to my newspaper alma mater, and I passed the next two hours in the files.

Allowing for margins of error, I found that she was no less than thirty-five, and quite possibly thirty-eight. Shows and plays she had been in, the kind of roles she had played, established her age within those three years. My first thought when I considered her age was

that at the time that I was begging my father to buy me an air
rifle, Charlotte Sears had her name in lights in Herald Square.

In the morning I was at my desk, doing my routine chores that
consisted of making up small items for the movie news column, and
I was summoned to Joe Finston's office. I went upstairs and waited
to be admitted.

'Hello, Jim,' he said. 'Sit down. Two things. First, I'd like you
to look over this and see if there's a story in it. It's about me when
I was managing a theatre out in Rockaway. It has some amusing
stuff in it about how I started in the industry. Don't read it now.
I just sort of batted it out because I thought it'd be kind of amusing.
The other matter is this Sears dame. We're getting ready to give
her the old heave-ho. The key cities are howling bloody murder
over her last two pictures and I got nothing but telegrams from all
over the country. 'Don't give us any more Sears pictures,' is what
they unanimously agree. I don't know what those production guys
can be thinking of. I think some of them get softening of the brain
from that California sunshine. I can tell you, from my experience
as an exhibitor, this dame is costing us. You should see what her
last two or three did, the grosses.'

'Well, two costume pictures in a row,' I said.

'Costume pictures are all right if they make money, but they
don't with her in them. What I want you to do, I don't want this
dame to have a line, not a line, as long as she's in New York.
Cancel all interviews and don't give out any releases on her. I don't
care if she climbs the Statue of Liberty, marries the Prince of Wales,
she gets no publicity through this office. If you want to plant it that
she's on the way out, the gossip writers are all friends of yours.'

'Whatever you say, Joe. But I can't ask the gossip writers for any
more favors just now. They're laying off the Hunterden story.'

'What Hunterden story? Thomas R. Hunterden?'

'Yes, and Sears.'

'Our Sears? Charlotte Sears and Hunterden? I don't know about
that story. You have to enlighten me.'

'Well, now you've got *me* confused. I thought she was all set here
because she's Hunterden's girl friend.'

'The first I knew about it,' said Finston. 'Where did you hear it
from?'

'I didn't *hear* it. He was there to meet her at the station, the day she came in. And he called her up while I was with her at the hotel. He's married, but I don't know why the gossip writers don't hint at it.'

'You saw him at the station?'

'Did I? You should have seen him scatter when he saw those photographers.'

'You positively couldn't be mistaken?'

'Not a chance. Thomas R. Hunterden was born in my home town, Gibbsville, P A. Look him up.'

'Does she admit it, Sears? I mean about being his girl friend?'

'Oh, sure. She has nothing to lose.'

Finston removed his glasses and chewed on the tortoise shell. 'Then it's true, eh?'

'What?'

'Well, you hear things and half the time you don't pay any attention, the rumors and gossip you hear.' He was trying to lie his way out of his ignorance of the Hunterden-Sears affair, and doing it so badly that I was almost embarrassed for him. He looked at his watch, and I knew he was reckoning the time on the Pacific Coast. 'Tell you what you do, Jim, you read that material I gave you and let me know what you think of it. I'll let you know later about the Sears publicity. I still want to think it over a while longer.'

'Whatever you say, Joe.' I went out, and I stood a moment to light a cigarette near his secretary's desk. Finston's voice came through the intercom.

'Get me Mr Morrie in Hollywood,' he said. 'Home, if he isn't at the studio.'

I could have been quietly noble about what I had done for Chottie Sears, but she needed some good news and I had it for her. It amused her, too, that I had accidentally but quite truthfully been able to make use of the two men who were giving her the most trouble, to play them against each other without telling a lie. 'You know who would have enjoyed this was my grandfather, Pat Somerville,' she said. 'Did you ever hear of Pat Somerville? An old-time song-and-dance man. And playwright. He wrote dozens of plays and acted in many of them. A good Mick, like yourself, and it was always a feast or a famine for him and my grandmother. Unfortunately it was all famine by the time I came along, and I never got the benefit of any of the feast. But my mother had a lot

of wonderful stories about him. One day they'd be putting on the
ritz with servants and horses, and the next day men would come
and start moving the furniture out of the house.' She paused and
studied a diamond ring she was wearing. 'My mother used to tell
me those stories, but she had more spunk than I have. My
father—they had an act together—lit out and left her stranded in
Pittsburgh without a nickel and she never heard from him again.
He took all their money and her diamond ring. In those days
show people used to put their money in diamonds when they were
working, and of course hock them when there was a long layoff.
They boarded me in a house in Brooklyn in those days, so I could
go to school. She got back to New York and partnered up with
another man and went out again doing the same act. All she said
to me was that my father was taken sick with consumption and in
a sanitarium. Being a show-business kid, I'd often heard of that.
TB was very common among show people, and I guess I cried a
little but my father had never been much to me. Or me to him. My
mother'd make him come to see me in Brooklyn when they'd lay
off during the summer, but he never tried to pretend that I didn't
bore him. And the three of us never lived together after I was about
eight years old. I was taking violin lessons and it used to drive him
crazy when I'd practice, so they always lived in a hotel and I went
on boarding in Brooklyn.

'Finally, when I finished eighth grade my mother and her partner
got William K. Frobisher to write them a new act that I could be
in. Songs, dances and witty sayings, and me on my fiddle doing a
toe dance. Damn near ruined my legs, that toe-work. Thank God
I gave *that* up in time.'

'What was the name of the act? Did your mother marry her new
partner?'

'The original name of the act was Dowd and Somerville. My real
name is Catherine Dowd. Then the new act was Snow and Somerville *introducing* Charlotte Sears. Sears was the name of a face powder
my mother used, and Charlotte—just a fancier name than
Catherine, and there were thirty-five thousand Kitties, so I became
Charlotte Sears. Society people ask me if I have relations in Boston,
and out in the sticks they ask me how's Mr Roebuck. But I was
named after a face powder and a famous empress. Who went nuts,
didn't she?'

'Yes, I think so.'

'Well, I can sympathise with her, the last couple of days. But I feel better now, temporarily,' she said. 'Anyway, Jim, the story of my life isn't very interesting, but I left out what I really started to tell you. I don't want to be poor. *I* don't want to be stranded in Pittsburgh. I haven't got as much spunk as my mother. Not that I *am* poor. When I began earning my own living at fifteen, I saved something out of every week's pay. I never missed a week. Never. No matter where I was, I'd go to the post office and send back a money order, even if it was only two or three dollars. There was a bank here that show people used to use for that. So I'm not poor. But it isn't only the money. It's something else. All the years I've been in show business, every new job paid me more money than the last one. I've never taken a cut, and I've never taken a job that didn't pay me more than I'd been getting. That's why I'll fight Finston. It isn't only Finston I'm fighting. It's—oh, hell, you know what it is. Do I have to say it?'

'No.'

'Do you know the picture I turned down? Do you know the story?'

'No, I haven't seen the script.'

'I play the mother of a seventeen-year-old girl. That is, I would if I took the picture. I could very easily have a daughter seventeen, but I'm not going to let fifty million people see me playing a mother to a seventeen-year-old girl that everybody knows is twenty-two. Jean Raleigh. I'm not going to play Jean Raleigh's mother, because then the public will think I must be over forty, and I'm not. I may not have ten years to go before I'm forty, but I'm not there yet. And regardless of how old I am, your friend Ellis doesn't think I'm so old. And Junior Williamson called again today. He won't take no for an answer, that one. You know, it's almost as if he were taking advantage of me.'

'How so?'

'This way. He's very anxious to see me and I've told him absolutely no. But he's not going to give up. He told me so. Well, last night Ellis took me to that speakeasy on 49th Street, Jack and Charlie's. I'd never been there before, and who should be there but Mr Thomas R. Hunterden? He was with two other men.'

'Did you speak to him?'

'No. But he kept looking at me and at Ellis, and he didn't like it a bit that I was with Ellis. Ellis and I had a quick dinner and left

to go to the theatre and Hunterden was still there with the two
men. Well, what I'm getting at is, what if I showed up there again
tonight, this time with Junior Williamson? Or tomorrow night? Or
every night?'

'Why hasn't Hunterden got in touch with you?'

She did not immediately answer me. 'You risked your job for me,
so I'll tell you,' she said. 'But this is between you and me and
nobody else.'

'All right,' I said.

'The reason he hasn't *seen* me is because he can't. He's in the
middle of the biggest deal he ever made. One of the men he was
with last night was an Englishman, and the other one I guess was
a Turk. He wore a fez, so I guess he was a Turk. Hunterden told
me yesterday that there were some men in town that he was going
to have to be with until they left. In fact, he said he wasn't going
to let them out of his sight. I thought he was lying, but I guess
those were the men.'

'Sounds like it,' I said. 'Then he still loves you?'

'Love? Hunterden would choke on that word. A man like
Hunterden doesn't think about love, although I shouldn't complain.
It's a long time since I've said it and meant it. Jim, maybe you'll
be famous some day and then you'll understand certain things.'

'What would I be famous for?'

'Writing, maybe. You have something, or I wouldn't be attracted
to you. Politics, maybe. Or you might be head of a studio.'

'Well, what is it that I'll understand that I don't understand
now?'

'Two people like Hunterden and me. We're very much alike. I
don't know anything about him—that is, the kind of things I told
you about myself. I've only known him less than a year. He came
out to the Coast and I met him and I fell for him. Not love. And
not just sex. I didn't even know who he was, but naturally he had
to be *somebody*, to be invited to Morrie Rosenbaum's to dinner. I
guessed that much about him. I didn't sit near him at dinner, but
after dinner he sat with me and the first thing he asked me took
me completely by surprise. He said, "Miss Sears, if you owned the
Rosenbaum Studio, what other company would you like to merge
with?" I said I wouldn't merge with any, not if merging meant
equal partnership. I said I'd go into competition with one particular
studio and drive them out of business, and then buy them out

cheap. "How would you do that?" he said. And I told him I'd steal their biggest stars and best directors. He asked me how I'd do that and I said if he'd give me the Rosenbaum Studio and plenty of money I'd show him how. Well, he wanted to know how I'd go about getting a certain star. I won't tell you her name. Miss Smith. How would I go about getting Miss Smith, who was under contract to a certain other studio? I said in that particular case I wouldn't go after Miss Smith herself, I'd go after a certain cameraman. It isn't so much that he's one of the famous cameramen, but if Miss Smith ever made a picture without him, she'd soon find out that fifty per cent of her success in pictures is due to him. She'd see herself photographed by someone else, and she'd follow the cameraman as soon as she could.

' "Very interesting," he said. Then he wanted to know who I'd keep if I suddenly got control of the company, and I said in other words he wanted to know who I'd fire. "Not quite," he said. So I told him I'd keep Morrie Rosenbaum, because he was more interested in making pictures than in the stock market.

'Then he made his first personal remark. He said, "You know, Miss Sears, there's enough for everybody in this business, but if you and I had known each other ten years ago, we could have had most of it."

'And I said, "Well Mr Huntington, let's take what's left." I thought his name was Huntington.

' "No," he said. 'Let's take our share, and then look into other possibilities, and see what we have ten years from *now*." That particular moment was when Ruth Rosenbaum decided everybody ought to play poker. It was all right. I won about two thousand dollars, but I didn't see Hunterden alone till four or five days later. A Sunday noon. He came to my house unannounced, without calling up in advance. He came down to the pool, where I was reading the Sunday papers, and he said, "Am I too late for breakfast, or too early for lunch?" He stayed till Tuesday afternoon, and then he had to go back to New York. Incidentally, Wednesday or Thursday of that week I saw in the trade papers that Guy Smallwood had just signed a new contract with the Rosenbaum Studio. He was the cameraman. You can guess who the star was.'

'Oh, sure. She's with us now.'

'And getting a picture I wanted to do.'

'But I'm surprised that Morrie Rosenbaum didn't know about you and Hunterden.'

'We never went out together in Hollywood, and the few times we went to speakeasies in New York, other people were along with us. Hunterden has a deadhead that works for him, and if anybody saw the four of us out together they wouldn't know whether I was with Hunterden or his straight man.'

'You started to tell me you and Hunterden are very much alike, then you got sidetracked.'

'We are. If I were a man I'd be the same way with Charlotte Sears as he is. I understand where I fit into his life and where I don't. In fact, I don't have to be a man to understand all this. If I were on the crest of the wave, I might be treating Hunterden the way he's treating me. But I'm not on the crest of the wave. I have things worrying me, and when that happens I'm not as sure of myself. No spunk. I'm best at figuring things out when the heats not on me. Hunterden has this big business proposition bothering him, and he doesn't want to be bothered with a woman too till it's all settled.' She smiled. 'I wish you were just a moron. Then you could make love to me and I could forget about Hunterden. But if you were a moron I wouldn't want you to make love to me.'

'I'm very close to making love to you right this minute.'

'I know, and it's exciting. But we better not, Jim.'

'If it means so little, why not? Who'd know?'

'I would. The next man that I let make love to me—you don't know what I'm like. I try to run your life, I'm jealous.'

'You're not with Hunterden.'

'No, because I'm afraid of him. There ought to be another word for love, for people like Hunterden and me. Attraction. Respect. Success. I'm successful, a star. He respects that in me and we're attracted to each other. I know he's a big shot, a star in his own line. So there's a strong attraction that leads to sex. Well, I won't knock sex. I've had affairs that were nothing else and I've stayed up all night waiting for that phone to ring, just like anybody else. But with Hunterden—if I'd refused him on the sexual side, he wouldn't have bothered with me any more, but sleeping with me wasn't all he wanted. I suppose you might say I'm like one of his businesses, but I'm more than that to him and yet it isn't love.

'I don't know about love, anyway, Jim. I've been in love, all the symptoms. Happiness and thrills and desperation. Once I had them change my bookings so I could be on the bill with a magician I was in love with. Oh, he was a bad man, too.'

'Did he want to saw you in half?'

'You think you're joking, but he gave me a beating one Saturday night in Baltimore that I never thought I'd make the Monday matinée in Philly. I had to wear black tulle over my arms and shoulders, and I had a mouse under my eye that I had to have leeches for. I was doing a single and up to the last minute I wasn't sure I could go on. But then I saw him grinning at me and I said to myself, "You so-and-so, you go out there and wow them, and that'll show him." I did, too, although I was half dead.'

'No spunk, eh?' I said.

'Oh, I'll fight. By no spunk I mean I don't have the endurance that my mother had. The long pull, as they say down in Wall Street.'

'I think you underestimate yourself all around,' I said.

'Not to hear me talk about what a success I am,' she said. 'Well, a week from now and I'll be getting off the train at Pasadena, with a lot of new clothes and probably a whole trunkful of new headaches. I have two more days in New York.'

'How do you figure that?'

'I'm going away for the weekend. To Long Island,' she said. She waited for me to say something, but I remained silent. 'You won't ask me where?'

'It's none of my business,' I said. I could not keep the huffiness out of my tone, and she laughed.

'I like to tease you,' she said.

'In more ways than one,' I said.

'Oh, now that's not fair. I didn't tease you the other way, and I could have.'

'You didn't do so well with Finston,' I said, knowing as I said it that it was a cruel and vicious thing to say; but I had no control over, no knowledge of the depth of, the frustration I felt.

She looked at me very calmly. 'After that remark you can't stay here any longer,' she, the movie queen, said.

I got my hat and coat out of the foyer closet and went down the hall and pushed the button for the elevator. I put on my coat and watched the indicator as the elevator climbed and then began its descent. It was two or three stories above me when I heard her voice. 'Jim? Come on back.'

I went back and she was holding the door open for me. She closed it behind me and stood leaning against it. We looked at each other and then as naturally as we breathed we embraced, and I kissed her. She reached back her hand and turned the deadlatch. 'It's what you want, isn't it?' she said.

'Very much,' I said.

'Then I do too,' she said.

I had seen, as a hundred million others had seen, the outlines of her body many times, but the extraordinary beauty of it as I saw her in the next few minutes was beyond my past imaginings. There was no bad disposition or sorrow in her love-making; she was pleased and she was happy to be pleasing. I think she was glad to be friends again, to heal the hurt I had inflicted on her and to do so by an ultimate generous act of her own, without waiting for me to express my regret, without pausing to forgive.

I was young, not inexperienced, but young, and my experience counted for little in this new lesson. I was learning for the first time that a woman could be gracious in a calculated act of love, that she could deny the pleasure to many who wanted it, who even wanted to trade love for it, but that she could make a present of pleasure and of the honor of her trust without asking for promises or tokens. Both of us knew that this would not happen again, and that her earlier warning to the next man who might make love to her did not now apply. I had enjoyed what she gave, she had enjoyed the giving. She lit a cigarette for me and asked me if I wanted to sleep, and as she sat on the edge of the bed she seemed reluctant to get dressed again.

'Don't you want to go to sleep?' I said.

'Oh, no. But you can. I'll let you sleep for a half an hour.' She took my cigarette and inhaled once, then put it out in the ash tray. 'I'll remember this when you're famous,' she said.

'I'll have you to the White House,' I said.

She shook her head. 'No, this is just between us, you and me. You did a lot for me out of niceness, and I couldn't let you think I was a teaser.'

'I didn't think that.'

'You might have. You did. You thought I was teasing you about the weekend, and I guess I was. Yes, I was. I didn't think I was, but I was. Don't be stubborn, Jim. Ask me where I'm going.'

'Where are you?'

'The Williamsons'.'

'The father and mother's?'

'No, Junior's house. His wife invited me.'

'I didn't know you knew her.'

'I don't. At least I've never met her. Have you met her?'

'Hell, no. Or him either. I don't know those people. I only know Ellis through a speakeasy that's open in the morning.'

'From something Ellis told me, Junior's wife is quite desperate. And she's pretty clever, too. Junior has his next wife picked out, according to Ellis, and the present one I *think* would like me to break that up. She knows I had an affair with Junior, and I guess she thinks the next Mrs Williamson won't like it a bit if I show up again. You're not listening. Go to sleep.'

'I heard every word you said,' I said, and then I dozed off.

It was dark and the traffic sounds of early evening in New York—the beep horns, the protesting second speeds of the buses, and the cab starters' whistles—brought me back to consciousness. Charlotte Sears in negligee and panties, was sitting at her dressing-table. 'You rejoining the party?' she said.

'Where's your maid?'

'She'll be here in a little while. I couldn't hide anything from her, so I don't try. I had your suit pressed.'

'Have I got a date with you tonight?'

'Well, I have theatre tickets and I have no other date.'

'Fine.'

'You can do me a great favor, if you will. Have you got a car?'

'No.'

'Well, will you hire one and drive me out to the Williamsons' tomorrow afternoon?'

'Sure.'

'She offered to send a car for me, but I want to do it my way. If I feel like getting the hell out of there, will you come out and rescue me?'

'Of course.'

'Hunterden phoned while you were asleep.'

'I thought I heard you talking.'

'You didn't hear a thing. You were really out. Anyway, he wants to see me Sunday night, in town, so even if I don't call you before then, will you come out and get me Sunday afternoon?'

'Sure.'

'Finston has lost,' she said.

'Good work. Did you find that out from Hunterden?'

'I sure did. Morrie called Hunterden from the Coast and said he had good news for him. The Studio was giving me the lead in *Rhapsody on Broadway*, a musical that I'm dying to do. Morrie giggled and said he just thought Hunterden would like to know. Hunterden was taken completely by surprise, but he wasn't annoyed. In fact he was pleased. But the man that really swung the whole thing—little old you.'

'Great,' I said. 'Tomorrow I'll watch Mr Finston crawl.'

'I'm going to do something worse. I'm not going to answer the phone when he rings. I'll let him hang for a week. But doesn't that please you, how it worked out?'

'It certainly does.'

'And yesterday I was down at the bottom of the bottomless pit. Do you like champagne?'

'Not much.'

'But let's have some tonight, even if we don't drink it all.'

'Company money,' I said.

'What kind of a car would you like? I mean to own?'

'Don't buy me a car, Chottie. It'd be a waste of money.'

'All right, then, not a car, but I'm going to give you something. You wouldn't wear a diamond ring, would you?'

'No.'

'How about a trip to Europe?'

'Well, it would be fun to go as a passenger. I've been to Europe, but I worked my way.'

'The *Ile de France?* Would you like that?'

'Who wouldn't?'

'You decide when you want to go, and the boat, and I'll pay your fare both ways and all your hotel and travel expenses for a month. Can you get a leave of absence?'

'I don't know, but it won't make the slightest difference. I'll just go.'

'Just tell me when, and the trip is yours.'

'Thank you.'

We had dinner at Jack and Charlie's. It was a small room, low-ceilinged, and no table would seat more than six comfortably, but it was the best speakeasy in New York; the food was excellent, and there were many rumors to explain the high quality of the liquor, the recurring one being that certain highly placed financiers had got Andrew Mellon to allow the Bermuda rumrunners to slip through the Coast Guard patrols. Everything was expensive, and I seldom went there when I was not spending company money.

'Over in the corner, the table that's hidden by the bar,' said Charlotte Sears.

'Who?' I said.

'Hunterden and the Turk and the Englishman. Now he sees me.' She bowed. 'Might as well speak to him if Morrie knows about us. He's coming over.'

Thomas Rodney Hunterden, expensively tailored in a black suit and wearing a black silk necktie with a smoked pearl stickpin, shook hands with Chottie. 'How do you do, Miss Sears,' he said.

'Hello, Mr Hunterden. I saw you here last night but you didn't recognise me. Will you join us? This is Mr Malloy, of our publicity department.'

'Could I sit with you for a minute?' He included me in the question, but he did not wait for my answer.

'I've seen you before, haven't I, Mr Malloy?'

'Well, I get around,' I said.

'What part of the country do you come from?' he said.

'I come from a place called Gibbsville, Pennsylvania.'

'Oh, yes. In the coal regions.'

'Oh, you've heard of it?'

'I was born there, but I left when I was very young.'

'You two were born in the same town?' said Chottie.

'But I persuaded my parents to take me away when I was two years old,' he said. It was not very funny, but it was a remark that put me in my place. 'I saw your picture in the paper, Miss Sears. Will you be in town long?'

'Leaving for the Coast Monday.'

'Well, I hope we run across each other again. Nice to see you. I have a very good friend in your organization, Mr Malloy. remember me to him if you see him.'

'Who's that, and I will?'

'Morrie Rosenbaum. have to get back to my friends.' He rejoined the Turk and the Englishman.

'Dying to know who you were,' said Chottie.

'And to make sure I didn't get any ideas. he has a very good friend in my organization.'

She patted my knee. 'Don't let him annoy you. After all, two hours ago.'

'What do you think kept me from telling him to go to hell?'

'Me.'

'True,' I said.

'You can be as independent as you please, but I can't.'

'But you are.'

'No, I'm not. I cheated with you, Jim, but he's my big moment. He always will be. We didn't find a word to use instead of love, but whatever it is, that describes it. And it's the same with him. He had to know who you were.'

'Why not call it love, Chottie? Nobody's going to fine you for misusing the word.'

'You get over love. I won't get over this.'

'Then you're worse than in love.'

'Oh, I know that. That's what I've been trying to tell you.'

'I'm a very unimportant guy,' I said. 'He didn't have to threaten me by telling me what good pals he is with M.R.'

'He shouldn't have done that, but he couldn't help it. And don't forget, Jim. His instinctive jealousy was right. Where were you and I two hours ago? The man is no fool.'

'I never thought of it that way.'

'The same instinct that made him pick me out at Ruth and Morrie's dinner party. He said to me one time, the secret of his success was to find out everything he could about, well, about a business. Get all the facts, and then play his hunches, even when the facts seemed to lead in another direction. Just now he followed a hunch. Maybe I was sitting too close to you, or enjoying myself too much. But he had a hunch, and he was right. Although he'll never know he was right.'

'Yes, but maybe he'd be jealous of anybody.'

'He wasn't jealous of Ellis. There goes that rhyme again. He saw me with Ellis, but he didn't come to the table. He had no hunch about Ellis, and he did about you. Give him credit.' She paused. 'Also, I don't like to say this, but watch your step. I'm going to lie to him when he asks me about you, but he may not believe me, although he'll pretend he does. And he might make up some other excuse to have you fired.'

'Oh, he wouldn't do that to another Gibbsville boy,' I said.

Abruptly Hunterden rose and came over to our table again. 'Have you and Mr Malloy been to the Florence Club, the Chez Florence? I'm taking my friends there later if you'd care to join us. About two o'clock? It doesn't start till late, or is that no news to Mr Malloy?'

'I've been there quite a few times,' I said.

'Miss Sears?'

'All right, fine,' she said.

'I see you're just finishing dinner, so I infer you're going to the theatre. Two o'clock, then? Splendid.' He went back to his table.

'Well, that was pretty smart,' I said.

'Why?'

'Don't you get it? We go to the theatre and we get out after eleven, probably go some place for a drink, meet him at two, and stay under his watchful eye till four or five. The whole evening taken care of, in case I get any ideas. That was damned smart. And at five o'clock tomorrow morning, or whenever, he'll deposit me right at my door, in his beautiful big Rolls-Royce.'

'How do you know he has a Rolls?'

'There's one parked outside, so I guess it's his.'

'It is. I recognised the chauffeur.'

I had failed to anticipate the degree of Hunterden's strategy. At the Florence Club he and his companions were with three show girls from Mr Ziegfeld's production. The Turk did not drink, but the Englishman and I drank a lot, while Hunterden nursed a high-ball until about half-past four. Hunterden then made his excuses and departed with Chottie, and the Turk, the Englishman, and I were left with the show girls and Hunterden's Rolls. The girl who got me was as sore as hell, as she might well have been, to have had such an unprofitable evening, but at least I got four hours' sleep before going to the office.

I telephoned Chottie. 'Do you still want me to drive you out to Long Island?'

'Why? You're not running out on me, are you?'

I laughed. 'You're a fine one to be talking about running out. Is everything okay?'

'Blissful,' she said, and she meant it. 'Will you call for me around five-thirty?'

'Yes. What am I supposed to be, I mean am I your brother or cousin? In case I have to act a part at Mrs Williamson's.'

'You be a devoted admirer that likes to do things for me. That's real type-casting.'

'It's a part I like to play, Chottie,' I said. I liked this woman in a way and to a degree that probably only another man would understand, although it was a woman—she herself—who had come closest to putting it into words when she declared that you get over love, but you don't get over 'this.'

I drew some expense money and went up to Columbus Circle and picked out a second-hand Duesenberg S-J, which was on sale for $18,000. It was a phaeton with a tonneau windshield. 'I want to hire it for the weekend,' I said.

'Not a chance,' the salesman said.

'Don't be so hasty,' I said. 'I want to hire it, and I don't want to pay you a nickel.' I introduced myself and told the man that I was squiring Miss Charlotte Sears around Long Island society, and if he didn't want the publicity, I'd just as soon give it to another car. He said he'd have to talk to the manager.

'Get me a picture I can blow up and put in my window, and the car is yours,' the manager said. 'With Miss Sears at the wheel, of course.'

'Of course,' I said.

I then got my coonskin coat out of hock and Charlotte Sears and devoted friend drove out to the Williamsons' in style. The Williamson butler was not impressed, but Mrs Williamson was. 'What a beautiful car,' she said. 'Did you drive from California?'

'It isn't my car,' said Chottie.

'It's yours, Mr Malloy?'

'For the time being,' I said.

'I've never driven one,' said Mrs Williamson, wistfully. 'Are you in a terrible hurry? Couldn't the three of us . . . ?'

The butler removed Chottie's luggage and we went for a ride out the North Country Road. Polly Williamson took the wheel, and she was a good driver. On the stretch past the Hutton place she hit ninety m.p.h., and after we turned around she took the same stretch at slightly more than a hundred. Her delight was simple and disarming. 'I've never done that before in my life. What a wonderful car. Thank you, Mr Malloy.' She herself was simple and disarming, unlike the person I had expected her to be. She was not pretty by the standards of the three girls I had seen the night before; but she had a good figure and legs, and if her hands had not been strong we would have landed in a ditch. The Duesenberg was not a woman's car, and I guessed that Polly Williamson was accustomed to handling big Irish hunters.

She was wearing a checked suit and was hatless, and her blond hair was in disarray from the spin. When we got out of the car at her house she patted the door and smiled. 'Can you come in and have a drink?' she said.

'Thanks, but I have to be on my way,' I said.

'I hope I didn't make you late. If you're going to be in the neighborhood why don't you come in Sunday afternoon? Don't call or anything, just come if you can.'

I almost hated to leave, and Polly Williamson, by her unexpected friendliness, had made me feel I was welcome to stay. She was in her middle twenties, the age of most of the girls I was taking out at that period of my life. She had two small children, and I knew that she was having trouble with her husband. But where I had been led to expect a neurotic, jealous woman, I could see only a young wife who was making an effort to save her marriage by resorting to the kind of intrigue that I was sure was new to her. I do not wish to imply that I saw her as a simple, suburban housewife; the butler wore silver-buttoned livery; the Junior Williamsons' house was only the second largest on the estate, perhaps a quarter-mile distant from the main house whose chimneys and roofs we could see above the trees on a hilltop; and while we were saying goodbye a toothless little man in breeches and buttoned canvas puttees rode past us on a lathery gelding, leading another horse with the stirrup irons tucked up, on his way to the stables. The little man tipped his cap to Polly Williamson. 'Just back, Peter?' she said.

'Yes ma'am, just these five or ten minutes,' he said, without halting.

'My husband and a friend of his,' said Polly Williamson. 'They must have stopped in at the big house, but you sure you can't wait to meet them?'

'Afraid not, but thanks very much, and Chottie, see you Sunday if not before?'

Chottie Sears was grinning at me and my not well-hidden admiration of her hostess. 'I hope you can make it Sunday,' she said.

'I'll try,' I said, and put the Duesenberg in gear. I had plans for the weekend; I was not going to waste the Duesenberg; but I drove away reluctantly. I suppose that at that period I was about as fancy-free as it is possible for a man to be, which in my case, however, meant also that I was ready to fall in love with almost any attractive girl. There was an element of pity in my admiration of Polly Williamson, and that element nullified what would otherwise have been the awesome effect of her possessions.

I took the Port Washington ferry and spent Friday and Saturday nights with friends in Connecticut. At noon on Sunday, while we were having breakfast, I was called to the telephone. It was, of course, Chottie Sears. 'Duty calls,' she said.

'How's it going?' I said.

'Not so good. Can you get here around five? They're having some people in and I have to stay for that, but I want to be ready to go any time. I'll be packed and everything, so we can leave here before eight. You don't have to play any part. Polly Williamson knows who you are. We've gotten to be friends. Her whole plan collapsed last night after dinner. Junior got plastered and he and his lady friend disappeared about eleven and never came back. We'll see how things are at lunch, but as of now this marriage is a fiasco, and for her sake I'm sorry. She wanted to make it go, but he's a silly, spoiled brat. Wait till you see what took him away from Polly.'

The other guests had not arrived when I got to the Williamsons' house, and without prior information I could not have guessed that all was not serene. Junior Williamson, dressed for town in a blue suit, black shoes, and stiff collar, pretended to me that I had cost him money he could not afford. 'My wife wants a Duesenberg just like yours,' he said.

'She can have mine, because it isn't mine. I rented it,' I said.

'Isn't it a new car?'

'No, it's second-hand. They want eighteen thousand for it.'

'That's quite a come-down from the original price, isn't it? Don't they sell for over twenty thousand?'

'Around twenty-two, I think,' I said.

'That's a lot of money. I'm in favor of renting cars. I always do when I go abroad.'

'Yes, but if people like you don't buy those cars, they'll stop making them,' I said.

'No, not really. There'll always be guys like Thomas R. Hunterden to buy them. You know, Thomas R. Hunterden, the holding-company guy?'

'He's coming here this afternoon,' said Polly Williamson.

'That's what made me think of him,' said Williamson. 'Somebody told me he kept a Rolls in New York, one in London, and one in Paris. And they're not rented.'

'Well, I suppose a fellow like that can make sixty thousand dollars in one day,' I said.

'Easily, but think of the upkeep. My father and I together, I think there are about eighteen cars on this place, with the two small trucks. A ton-and-a-half Dodge truck and a Ford. That may seem like a lot, but we have a full-time mechanic, an absolute genius with cars, and we get a good discount on gasoline and oil, quantity buying. It probably doesn't cost us as much to keep a Pierce-Arrow going as it does some fellow that has one Chevrolet. And I'll bet you—no. I was going to exaggerate. I was about to say we could run our whole garage on what a fellow like Hunterden spends for three cars in three cities. I was thinking about three chauffeurs, garage bills, and so forth. I suppose the actual outlay is less for Hunterden, but our cars are always in use. That's where the big difference is. Every car on this place is in actual use. My mother, my father. My wife. Taking one of the children to school. Servants to church. Marketing. Actually, if we had room in the garage, my father was thinking of buying a horse van *as an economy*. He gets awfully tired of paying a fellow in Roslyn every month for vanning. Five dollars a head, just from here to Meadow Brook.'

The fascinating thing about Williamson's monologue was his taking for granted that I shared his problem: I was in his house, I had his highball in my hand, and I therefore was a sympathetic listener. I had once experienced the same blind, uncomplimentary acceptance when I was sent to interview a Princeton professor who had won a prize for some scholarly research in Sanskrit. Both Williamson and the professor assumed, without the courtesy of inquiring into my interests and my ignorance, that their language was also mine. Williamson had paid no attention to my remark that I was renting a second-hand car, other than to assume that my reason for renting a second-hand car would be the same as his for hiring cars in Europe. If his wife had not been present I would have made a burlesque of his father's persecution by the Roslyn horse-vanner, but I did not want to add to her troubles. I also did not want to kid this humorless man into giving me a punch in the nose. He glowed with health and strength; in the downward turn of the corners of his eyes there were warnings of a bad temper, and he had the meaty hands of a former oarsman. Four—six—eight years of rowing gives them a good fist that they keep all their lives.

Williamson was ready to change the subject, and did. 'It's been awfully nice having Chottie here again,' he said. 'Chottie, you mustn't ignore us the way you've been doing.'

'Hollywood isn't exactly around the corner, Junior,' said Chottie Sears.

'I know, but don't you have to come to New York a lot?' he said.

'Not often enough,' said Chottie.

'Why can't they make their pictures just as well in New York? I read an article not so long ago, about making movies over in Long Island City. Ever since the talkies they have to film everything inside a studio, it said. So the California sunshine isn't an advantage any more.'

'Real estate,' said Chottie. 'The picture companies have a lot of money tied up in real estate.'

'California bores me,' said Williamson. 'That everlasting sunshine.'

'Go there during the rainy season,' said Chottie.

'The what? I didn't know it ever rained there. But I suppose it must sometime.'

I was beginning to understand Williamson and his attraction for women. In ten minutes he had proved to me that he was one of the stupidest men I had ever met, but the society girl and the movie queen watched every move he made and attended every trivial word. He would take a sip of his drink, and they would watch the elevation of the glass, the lowering of it, and then their gaze would go back on his face. His wife had hardly spoken a word since my arrival, and I noticed for the first time a phenomenon of her attentiveness: when Williamson was speaking, she would look at his mouth, and her lips would move in a barely discernible, unconscious forming of his words. Polly Williamson was a rich girl in her own right, from a family as rich as the Williamsons, and was therefore not dazzled as Chottie Sears might be by the Williamson fortune. In an otherwise masculine face Williamson had a feminine, cupid's-bow mouth, and I now recalled Chottie's remark about his being a mama's boy. He was indeed a mama's boy, with the mouth of a pubert and the appetites of a man; the brainless cruelty of a child, and the strength to arouse in a woman an urgent need to give him pleasure. With the addition of my own observations I agreed with Chottie's epithet. Williamson also had a rather musical voice, not at all unpleasant, and he spoke in the accent of his class. He would pronounce third and bird as though they rhymed with an r-less beard. Polly Williamson's pronunciations were identical with his and her voice was nicely modulated, so that in the present company the Williamsons' accent and voices were harmonious, while Chottie Sears, deep-voiced and with a smoothed-over Brooklyn enunciation, and I, with a harsh voice and an Eastern Pennsylvania twang, were two soloists against a duet. Our voices, our accents, and we ourselves were out of place in this house, in this room. I cannot say whether I became conscious of our vocal sounds first and of Polly Williamson's silent lip-moving second or that the order of observation was reversed. But my more vivid recollection is of Polly Williamson's lips. Chottie Sears, experienced in turning on and simulating facial expressions, gave no indication of her thoughts while Williamson boldy dismissed the telephone calls he had been making since Chottie's arrival in New York. He correctly assumed that she would play his game in spite of his having shown a preference for another woman the night before.

Williamson was a study of an arrogant aristocrat at work. He represented strength and vitality, three or four generations of careful breeding (with some rather distinguished citizens in his blood lines), and great wealth. He had begun to serve on many boards of trustees that governed the policies of philanthropies and cultural activity of the city and the nation, which had been preceded by his earlier participation in polo and fox-hunting committees and his support of Yale athletics. I had no doubt that he sincerely believed that a seat in the House, to be followed by a seat in the Senate, a Cabinet office and an ambassadorship in London or Paris, all would and should be his. As these things raced through my mind I looked over at Polly Williamson and wanted to tell her that her marriage was safe temporarily: Williamson would not ask for a divorce until his maiden political campaign was over. But I also would have had to tell her that in the event of his defeat (which I regarded as certain), the marriage was finished.

At that point we were joined by a tall, handsome woman of about twenty-eight. I looked at Chottie Sears, who gave me a quick pair of nods, and glanced from the newcomer to Williamson. This, she was telling me, would be the next Mrs Williamson. Her name, as

she was introduced, was Mrs Underwood; her first name, as she
was greeted by the Williamsons, was Eunice.

Eunice Underwood was actually not very tall and not very handsome, but she had chic in abundance. She wore a small black hat
with a rhinestone pin on the left side, and as she entered the room
she slipped off her mink coat and handed it to a maid, revealing a
black satin dress, of which the fringed skirt was cut on the bias.
The dress had long, close-fitting sleeves that came down over her
wrists. She wore sheer black stockings and black suede shoes that
had rhinestone buckles that matched her ornament on her hat.
From a platinum chain around her neck hung a large diamond. Two
words came to mind: the word dramatic, and the word mistress. I
suppose the first word made her costume a success, even though I
would not tell her so; and I suppose the second word was in my
mind before I saw her, although I might have had the same verbal
association without advance preparation. She was black, white, and
sleek. Her hard, high little breasts pointed forward against her shiny
satin. I had seen breasts like them on an expensive whore; all nipple
and little flesh.

She went up to our hostess and said 'Hello, Polly,' but did not
kiss her or shake hands.

'Hello, Eunice,' said Polly Williamson.

'Hello, there,' said Junior Williamson, exuberantly.

She reached out and smoothed down his necktie. 'Hello,' she
said. 'Hello, Miss Sears.' She then was silent while I was being
introduced, but she looked at me and my readymade suit during
the utterance of our names, and I was out of her life before she said
'Howja do.' She immediately turned away from me and handed
Williamson an ivory cigarette holder into which he fitted a cigarette
from his own case. I suspected that she had made him change to
her brand, since there was no discussion over that. She put the
holder in her mouth and Williamson lit the cigarette.

'Have you got crowds more people coming, Polly?' she said.

'Between thirty and forty.'

'Oh, well, that's not so bad. I'll be able to find a place to sit with
only that many.'

'Wouldn't some nice gentleman give you a seat?' said Chottie
Sears. Polly Williamson suppressed a smile.

'They're not as polite here as I'm sure they must be in Hollywood,' said Eunice Underwood. 'That reminds me, not that I've

seen many films, but I don't think I've ever seen anyone sitting down in one. They're all so busy shooting at each other or throwing pie in each other's faces.'

'A lot of them do sit down, though,' said Chottie Sears. 'There's a trick to it. We call them prat-falls.'

'Do you know where your prat is, Eunice?' said Williamson, laughing.

'I can imagine. Where did *you* learn where it is? From Miss Sears?'

Williamson laughed again.

'Steady, girl,' said Chottie Sears.

'You two,' said Williamson, laughing. 'I swear.'

A group of six men and women now entered. Three of the men and one of the women were slightly tight, and Eunice Underwood slowly moved away to a chair in a far corner of the room. 'Hey, Eunice,' said one of the men.

'Stay where you are, Billy. Don't come over and bother me. You spray people when you're plastered.'

'We could do with a little spraying around here,' said the woman who was tight, and whom I took to be Billy's wife. A maid brought in a trayful of drinks which apparently had been ordered by the new guests on arrival. The butler stood in the doorway and watched the drinks being served, and then disappeared. Almost immediately another group of six arrived and among them was Charley Ellis.

'Have you been here all weekend?' he said.

'No, I just got here a little while ago,' I said.

'I hear there was a bit of a *crise* last night. I thought you might be able to tell me about it.'

'Can't tell you a thing,' I said. 'I was on the other side of Long Island Sound.'

'I'll be back after I've said hello,' he said. He left me and kissed Polly Williamson and shook hands with Chottie Sears.

Eunice Underwood called to him: 'Charles, come here and sit with me a minute.'

'I'll sit with you,' said one of the other men.

'I didn't ask you, I asked Mr Charles Ellis.'

'I'm giving you your last chance,' said the man.

'Is that a threat or a promise?' said Eunice Underwood. 'Polly, if I were you I'd tell McDonald to dilute the drinks.'

'Oh, I don't think so, Eunice,' said Polly Williamson.

'Well, in that case I'm going to have to get tight in self-defense. Junior, get me a martini in a champagne glass, please.'

'How'd it be if I got you champagne in a martini glass?' said Williamson, laughing.

'Oh, don't be the life of the party,' said Eunice.

Charley Ellis rejoined me. 'Where is *Mister* Underwood?' I asked. 'Or isn't there any?'

'Eunice's husband? He's feeding the fishes. He got drowned in Bermuda a couple of years ago.'

'Oh, that's why she's all in black?'

'No, I don't think that has anything to do with it. She didn't waste many tears on him. Not that he would have on her.'

'Has she got a lot of dough?'

'Well, she has enough. But let's just say that if she hooks Junior she'll change her scale of living, not downward.'

'Where is she from? She wasn't one of this crowd originally, was she?'

'No, she's from Brooklyn. Her father was a minister.'

'Oh, she wants to be a nun,' I said.

'I hadn't heard *that*,' said Charley. 'But I'm told she's tried everything else, and believe me, if she doesn't get Junior she's going to have to change her scene of operations.'

'Not very popular?'

'Well, not with the women. Decidedly not with the women. Most of these people have known each other all their lives. Some of them were engaged to be married and married somebody else, but it's a closed corporation, and Eunice, the complete outsider, married Buddy Underwood and played it straight for a while. But she was in too much of a hurry. You can't hurry these people. They've been together too long.'

'What was she in a hurry to do?'

'Oh, I suppose get rid of Buddy and make a better marriage. If she'd stuck by Buddy, who wasn't much good, she'd have gotten ahead faster. But instead she went after the men. She's a good rider, and she used that, and she's quite a good tennis player.'

'She doesn't look the athletic type.'

'She is, though. Don't let that slinky get-up fool you. She rides sidesaddle, and in a top hat and skirt she's even more impressive than she is today. Plenty of guts, too. And knows she's hated. Junior is sort of her last chance, and she knows that. If she doesn't land

him, she knows she'll have to clear out. She gets invited everywhere
because nobody wants to snub the next Mrs Junior Williamson,
but this is the ninth inning, two out, nobody on base, and she's at
bat. A scratch single isn't going to do it for her. She has to knock
one out of the ball park.'

'Why is she after you?'

'After me? She isn't after me. Polly's my cousin, and Eunice
would like to line up a few of Polly's relations on her side. She isn't
after anybody but Junior, and everybody in this room knows it.
That's why I asked you about last night. If she had an open spat
with Polly, that would cook her goose for fair, because Junior doesn't
want to be hurried. Don't forget, old Mr Williamson and Mrs
Williamson are still very much alive. Junior takes Eunice to their
house every chance he gets, but the old boy and Mrs Williamson
like Polly and they're crazy about those grandchildren.'

'Why would Thomas R. Hunterden be invited here this
afternoon?'

'I didn't know he was. That'll be a new face, and you don't see
many of them in this house. He'd never be asked to the big house,
so I guess Junior invited him.'

'Why not Polly?'

'Well, anything's possible. Let's see if Alice comes with him. If
she does, then it just means that Alice and one of her hospitals has
been working on Junior and one of his hospitals. I don't know. You
see anybody you'd like to make a play for?'

'Yes. Your cousin.'

He shook his head. 'No. Anything's possible, but I wouldn't like
to see you make a play for Polly now. If a son of a bitch like
Hunterden wants to, that's different. But not a friend of mine. If
on the other hand she ever gets a divorce from Junior, I'll be as
helpful as I can.'

'Thanks,' I said. 'I could go for her.'

'I think she's about the best we have to offer, and I'd like to see
her shake loose from Junior, but she isn't ready to give up. See
anybody else?'

'The blonde in the blue tweed suit.'

'Mary Day? Can be had. The coast is absolutely clear, there.
Billy's forever on the make for Eunice and it makes Mary sore as
a wet hen. Hey, Mary.'

The girl called Mary Day sauntered over.

'Here's a friend of mine that thinks you're pretty darn attractive.'

'Why shouldn't he? I think he is, too. And a stranger in our midst. Where are you from?'

'He's a Pennsylvania boy,' said Charley Ellis.

'Oh, God. Another Biddle?'

'No, I'm one of the anthracite Malloys.'

'Oh, Scranton. I was in a wedding there once and I never saw people drink so much—except here, of course. But somehow it shocked me to see out-of-town people do it. Maybe you were at the wedding. It was—'

'I'm not from Scranton. I'm from Gibbsville.'

'Oh, Gibbsville. Well, I know a girl that lives *there*. Caroline Walker, married to somebody called English. I spent one god-awful year at Bryn Mawr and she was one of the few bright spots. How is she?'

'Well, I saw her the last time I was home. She was looking well.'

'She invited me to her wedding and I invited her to mine. End of correspondence, but I liked her. She was very nice to me. You give her my love when you see her. Mary Patterson. Can you remember that?'

'Mary Patterson. Sure. I'll remember.'

'Are you visiting Charley? I didn't see you at lunch, did I?'

'I'm squiring Charlotte Sears.'

'Oh, I want to hear all about her. Is it true that she's going to break up this thing between Junior and Eunice? I *may* have had one too many cocktails, don't you think? I shouldn't drink on Sunday. He who drinks on the Sabbath will live to fight some more. What did you say your name was?'

'James Malloy.'

'It won't stick. I've forgotten it already,' she said. She was sitting on a sofa between Charley Ellis and me, holding her cocktail glass in both hands. 'What did you say it was again? Spell it.'

'M, a, l, l, o, y.'

'Mallory.'

'No, there's no r in it.'

'Like oysters.'

'Yes. I'm out of season.'

'I don't think you are. I think you're very much *in* season, and if you want to know the truth, so am I. You wouldn't like to take me out of here, would you, Mr Mallory?'

'Where would you like to go?'

'I don't know. I'm open to suggestion.'

'I'd love to take you anywhere, if we can be back here by eight o'clock.'

'Oh, I don't think we would be. I really don't think we would. In other words, you're spoken for?'

'Not exactly spoken for, but I'm here to drive Miss Sears back to New York.'

'Too bad. Or maybe not. Now this old gossip won't have any sleuth. Except that he did hear me proposition you.'

'Am I the old gossip?' said Charley Ellis.

'What is sleuth?'

'I thought you were a friend of Caroline's. Sleuth is gossip. An old Bryn Mawr word for gossip. Talk-gossip. But Charley Ellis is a talker-gossip. If you want to know anything about anybody here, ask Charley. Isn't that right, Charley?'

'Just about,' said Charley Ellis, not at all offended.

'*But*—if you want to know everything about *Charley*, you have to ask *me*. That's right, too, isn't it, Charley?'

'Just about.'

'Ask him something about me,' said Mary Day.

'Anything at all?' I said.

'Anything.'

'All right,' I said. 'Has she had her appendix out?'

She laughed. 'Go ahead answer him. I want to see what you say. You're in a spot. You don't know whether to be chivalrous or truthful. Go on, Charley, answer his question.'

'You answered it for me,' said Charley. 'I didn't have to say a word—and I still haven't. So stop calling me a gossip, Mary. You get a few too many drinks in you and talk too much, and then you accuse other people of gossiping.'

Mary Day turned to me. 'Ask me whether *he's* had *his* appendix out? The answer is yes. And have you had yours out, Mr Mallory?'

'You're not going to find out as easily as that.'

'Well said, Jim,' said Charley.

'Has Charlotte Sears had hers out?' said Mary Day. '*Why, look at him! He's blushing!* I took him completely by surprise.'

'I wouldn't know,' I said.

'Oh, come on, it's too late. You got as red as a beet. Why, Mr

Mallory. And you're the one that started this whole thing about appendixes. That's rich.'

'You jump to conclusions, Mrs Day,' I said.

She was staring at Chottie Sears, who was sitting between two men, laughing with them and enjoying their admiration. 'Some women just have it, that's all,' said Mary Day. 'I wonder if she ever got tight over some damn man.' She got to her feet and slowly, rather shyly, joined Chottie and her admirers.

'She's a swell girl till she drinks, and then—bang! No inhibitions. Says anything that comes into her head, no matter who gets hurt in the process.' He was trying, I knew, to avoid the topic of Chottie Sears and me, but he believed Mary Day had made a discovery and he was resentful of it. He had his masculine pride, and I was his successful, deceitful rival.

'Well, as she herself said, she oughtn't to drink on Sunday,' I said.

'Or between Sundays. She does most of her damage on Sunday, because there are more people around. But Sunday isn't the only time she drinks too much. She's another of those girls around here that set their caps for Junior, and who got him? Her best friend, Polly. I know what fixed that, too. Mary gave up everybody else for Junior, wouldn't even let people cut in at dances. No dates with anyone else, and behaving like an engaged girl, although Junior was going his merry way. And as against that possessiveness, there in the background, so to speak, was Polly Smithfield, the logical one, waiting to be asked. And she got asked and Mary didn't. That was some wedding. Mary the maid of honor instead of the bride, eyes red going up the aisle. Tight as a tick at the reception, and eloped with Billy Day the next week. She was back here and settled down before Polly and Junior got back from their wedding trip.'

'Day isn't so much, is he?'

'He never used to be, but Junior has helped him along and he's doing very well. He has a seat on the Stock Exchange that I understand Junior put up the money for, and downtown Billy's known as Junior's man. Considering what he would have been without Junior's help, that's nice going.

'You know, when you have forty or fifty million behind you, that money does double service. Triple. Quadruple. For instance, McDonald isn't just a butler. He's Junior Williamson's butler, with forty million behind him. Junior Williamson's tailor isn't just a tailor. He has a forty-million-dollar customer. And downtown, Billy Day is Junior's man and that much closer to the money, even if he never gets his hand on it. I could probably get Junior's business. Polly's my cousin. But I think Polly wants Billy to have it, and in any case I wouldn't want to be known as Junior's man. Or anybody else's. When my father dies . . .' He cut himself off.

'What?'

He shook his head. 'Don't know you well enough, Jim,' he said, with finality. 'If I talk about it, I won't do it.'

'You wouldn't tell me if I guessed, would you?'

'No, but I'd be interested to hear your guess.'

'You want to write,' I said.

'Well, it's an interesting guess,' said Charley Ellis.

'You're probably not kidding your father one bit.'

'Probably not. But time is on his side. The longer he lives, the better the chances that I'll give up any crazy ideas I have.'

'Why don't you just up and go?'

'The time to do that was when I graduated from college, and never to have gone downtown at all. That was *my* mistake and where the old man was clever. Hell, look at the guys in this room. At least half of them wish they were doing something else. I could tell you about most of them. Eddie Patterson wishes he could be a guide in Canada. Mike Bell should have been a vet. He studied it at Cornell, but now he's a big trader in oil stocks.'

'I always wanted to be something else, too,' I said.

'You did? What?'

'A millionaire.'

Charley smiled. 'Do you mean a million a year, or a million all told?'

'I wasn't greedy. At least, not till you said a million a year.'

'There are both kinds of millionaire in this room. See if you can tell them apart.'

'I guess I couldn't.'

'No, I don't think you could, just by looking. Mike Bell probably has a million-dollar income, and Billy Day probably has around a million capital.'

'But why does a guy like Bell give up what he wants to do when he has all that money?'

'It's the system, my boy. Or what I call the system, and you know the old saying. ".Don't buck the system or you're liable to

gum the works." Mike went to St Mark's and then his father
allowed him to go to Cornell and study animal husbandry. Then
when he graduated, Mr Bell told Mike he needed him downtown,
just about the way my old man did me. 'You start going downtown,
you get a lowly job as a runner or something, and you want to earn
a promotion to prove that you could do it if you wanted to. So you
earn that promotion and they give you some responsibility, which
you have to fulfil. Pride. Meanwhile you're having a very pleasant
time. You have lunch with your friends, go to parties, come out
here weekends, get married, start having children. You're in the
system. You're part of it. And what you wanted to be, or do, that
becomes your hobby. In Mike's case, he's an amateur vet. You see,
Jim, the best of these guys would have been good at something else.
The others, let's not worry about them. They're the Billy Days.'

'And what about the Junior Williamsons?'

'How many are there? Not more than half a dozen. Let's not
worry about them, either. They're the royalty, and the others are
the nobility, the peerage.'

'Where are the commoners?'

'Well, there aren't any, not in this group. Not really *in* this group,
Eunice is one, and the only way she'll be anything else is by
becoming Junior's wife.'

'What if I married Polly Williamson?' I said.

'Well, you wouldn't marry her unless you were in love with her
and she was in love with you, and we'd know that. You'd get credit
for marrying her in spite of her dough and not because of it. But
you could never look at another woman, not even flirt a little. You
couldn't start spending her money on yourself. You'd have to get
something to do that her money wouldn't help you with. *And* if
Polly had an affair with another guy, you'd take the rap. It would
all come back to your marrying her for her money. And I wouldn't
be surprised if that's why Polly wants to save her marriage. She's
a very intelligent girl, and she knows there aren't many Junior
Williamsons around.'

'This is all based on the assumption that I'd give a damn what
people said about me.'

'Of course it is.'

'Well, I don't.'

'Well you damn soon would, my friend,' he said. 'Where are you
and Polly going to live? Here? Then you'd be surrounded by Polly's

friends. Gibbsville, Pennsylvania? I'll bet your friends would be tougher on you than Long Island. You may think you wouldn't give a damn about Polly's friends or your friends, but people is what people have to live with. And if you're surrounded by hostile people, your friends or Polly's or strangers, your marriage wouldn't last. Oh, just coming in. A perfect example of the commoner.

'I resent that,' I said.

'No you don't,' said Charley Ellis.

The newcomer was Thomas Rodney Hunterden, dressed for the Scottish moors in August in a tweed jacket and matching plus-threes, tab garters, and fringed-tongue brogues. 'Lord Plush-bottom,' I said. There were others in the room similarly dressed, but the stiffness had not gone out of Hunterden's suit and shoes, nor out of him.

'New York Yacht Club tie,' said Charley.

Hunterden made straight for Polly Williamson.

'No Alice,' said Charley.

Most of the men showed that they had met Hunterden or recognised his name, but the only woman who greeted him with any informality was Chottie Sears. To my astonishment Junior Williamson took Hunterden's arm and steered him among the men and women, taking care of the introductions. 'Mr Ellis, and Mr Malloy,' said Williamson.

'Mr Ellis,' said Hunterden. 'Mr Malloy, I've had the pleasure. Did you get home safely the other night, Malloy?'

'Yes, did you?'

His quick anger was beautifully controlled. 'Quite safely.'

'Hunterden, what will you drink?' said Williamson.

'Sherry, please.'

Williamson nodded to McDonald. 'Damned sensible, I must say, I ought to stick to sherry. I hate the damn stuff,' said Williamson.

'Do you? I don't. I like a glass of sherry at this time of day,' said Hunterden.

'I don't even like it in soup. I come of a long line of whiskey drinkers, myself,' said Williamson. He again took Hunterden's arm, and said: 'Well, have you thought that over?' He piloted Hunterden away from everyone else and the two men sat off by themselves, engaged in private conversation. If I was curious, I was no more so than the other men in the room, who were curious and baffled.

'Be interesting to watch the stock ticker tomorrow morning,' said

Charley Ellis. 'I predict a steady rise in Omega Development. That's one of Hunterden's companies. It'll go up a couple of points between opening bell and twelve-thirty. It'll remain steady while these boys are exchanging information at lunch, and then it'll begin to drop off a little because nobody's going to be able to find out a damn thing and the timid ones will take a quick profit. Would you like to make a few dollars, Jim? I'll put in an order for you first thing in the morning, and sell out at twelve noon.'

'Do you know how much money I have in the bank?'

'None, the way you say it.'

'None.'

'Well, I'd lend you some but not to play the market on a tip I gave you.'

'Thanks very much, Charley,' I said. 'I've never been in the stock market, so I didn't lose anything when the crash came.'

'Well, that put you on even terms with a lot of guys that had been in it,' he said. 'At least we found out that Hunterden isn't here on Polly's invitation, and frankly I'm relieved.'

'So am I,' I said. 'They're still gabbing away. Williamson and Hunterden.'

'I'm going to see what I can find out from Polly,' he said. 'Very little, I'm sure, but I'll have a try at it.'

The party had grown in size, but there was no individual or group that I felt would welcome my presence, so I waited alone while Charley Ellis spoke to his cousin. She laughed at something he said and shook her head, shrugged her shoulders. Then she stopped smiling and looked over at me and was confused to see me looking at her. Charley Ellis rejoined me.

'Couldn't get a thing out of her,' he said.

'I know. So you changed the subject and told her I liked her.'

'Yes,' he said.

'But she didn't want to sit with us.'

'That's exactly right. Can you read lips?'

'No. I almost wish you hadn't said anything about me.'

'Would you like to hear what she said? It was nice,' he said.

'Sure, of course I would.'

'She said she met you at exactly the wrong time. From that I infer that any other time would have been the right time.'

'Excuse me,' I said. On an impulse I got up and went to Polly

Williamson, who was talking with a man and woman. 'May I see you a minute, please?'

We stood alone. 'Charley told me what you said.'

She nodded quickly.

'I have to tell you this. It may be the wrong time, Mrs Williamson, and it may not last, and I know I'll never see you again. But I love you, and whenever I think of you I'll love you.'

She turned away. 'I know, I know. Thank you for saying it. It was dear of you.'

I left her then and went back to Charley. 'You see,' he said. 'I couldn't have done that.'

'You don't know what I did.'

'Yes, I do, Jim. You told her you love her.'

'Yes, God damn it, I did.'

'Did she thank you? If she didn't, I do, for her.'

'Yes, she thanked me. Mrs Williamson.' I laughed. 'I don't know her well enough to call her Polly, but I had to tell her I love her. How did you know what I was saying?'

'What else would take possession of a man so completely? What else would you have to say to her that was so urgent? And—what else could make her look the way she did when she was first married to Junior? Oh, that was a damn nice thing to do, to make her feel love again. The existence of it, the urgency of it, and the niceness. How long since any two people in this room had a moment like that? Or ever will? You know who I wish *I* could say that to, don't you? You must know.'

'No, I don't,' I said.

'To *her!* To Polly! I've never loved anybody but my first cousin, and I never will. But it isn't because we're first cousins that I haven't told her so.'

'Why haven't you?'

'Well, yes, it is because we're first cousins. Closer than friends. Different from brother and sister. But she'd be shocked and frightened if she ever knew what it really is. It happens, and it works out, but when I was eighteen and she was fourteen I was ashamed because she was so young. And then when we got older she fell in love with Junior. So I've never told her. But now you see why I understand how you feel. You can't have her either.' He smiled. 'It seems to me we have a lot in common. I haven't slept with Chottie Sears, and you haven't slept with Mary Day, and I'd like to sleep with Chottie and you'd like to sleep with Mary. And neither of us will ever get anywhere with Polly. I've got drunk with friends of mine on less excuse than that. Shall we just quietly start putting it away, beginning with two double Scotches?'

'I'll have a double Scotch with you, but I have an eighteen-thousand-dollar car and a two-million-dollar movie queen to deliver safely. If you're going to be in New York tonight, I'll meet you anywhere you say.'

'I think this would be a good night to get drunk. Don't you? How about if I go in with you and Chottie?'

'That would be fine. We drop her at the hotel, put the car in the garage, and start out at Dan's.' I stood up. 'I'll go over and speak to our friend.'

Chottie made room for me beside her on the sofa. 'Are you about ready to go?' she said.

'Entirely up to you,' I said. 'You don't mind if Charley Ellis rides in with us, do you?'

'Not a bit. Love to have him. How soon will you be ready to go?'

'I'm ready whenever you are. I've had all I want of this party, and if I stay much longer I'll only get too plastered to drive.'

'You're not plastered now, are you? That's a big drink you have, Jim. And I noticed you jumping up and down and whispering things to Polly. Tell me if you're tight, because I'm scared to death to drive with anybody's had too much.'

'No, I'm not tight. But in another hour I might be.'

'You don't seem tight, but . . .'

'But what?'

'Well—just suddenly springing to your feet and taking Polly off to one side. You were like a wild man. What made you do that? Whatever you said, it had a big effect on her. First I thought she was going to cry, and then instead of that she turned all smiles. And you hardly know her.'

'I told her her slip was showing.'

'But it isn't. No, you didn't tell her any such thing. You sure you're not tight?'

'I'm not tight, and I won't take any more till I deliver you at the hotel.' I placed my glass on the table in front of us, and she crooked her finger at Hunterden. He said something to Williamson and then came over to Chottie.

'Did you signal me?' said Hunterden.

She made sure that no one was listening, and said: 'Can I drive in with you?'

It was obviously an interference with his schedule. 'I understood this fellow was to take you in.'

'She thinks this fellow is stewed,' I said. 'Where do you get that this-fellow stuff, Hunterden?'

'Jim,' said Chottie. 'Please?'

'Hunterden, you're a phony. You don't even tell the truth about where you were born. Where *were* you born, anyway? Not Gibbsville, P. A. I know that much. And don't this-fellow me. Nobody ever heard of you in Gibbsville and your name isn't even in the Court House records.'

'There's no doubt about it. He is stewed,' said Hunterden. 'You drive in with me and I'll take care of this nobody tomorrow. One phone call, Malloy.'

'Save your crooked nickel. I won't show up at the God damn office.' I now knew I was tight; I had not known it before.

'Was your father a doctor?' said Hunterden.

'Yes, my father was a doctor.'

'I thought so. I didn't like *him*, either.'

'But I'll bet you never told him. If you had, you wouldn't be here.' .

He turned to Chottie. 'This fellow is trying to create a scene, and I don't want a scene here, now.'

'Well, let's not have one. Take me out of here and stop arguing,' she said. 'Jim, I don't think I'll ever forgive you for this. You're just impossible. I don't know what ever came over you all of a sudden.'

'I'm not used to good booze,' I said.

'Come on,' said Hunterden. He put his hand under her elbow and they went to speak to Polly Williamson. She turned and said something to McDonald, and I guess he got her luggage from upstairs. Charley Ellis came and sat with me.

'What was that all about?' he said.

'I told him off, and it was damn unsatisfactory. I didn't tell him half the things I wanted to.'

'Are you plastered?'

'I didn't think so, but I guess I am.'

'Can you drive?'

'Oh, I think I can drive. I'm not that kind of tight. I just want to tell people off, and I'd like to give that Hunterden a crack in the jaw.'

'He's twice your age and you have fifteen pounds on him. Don't do that. Don't spoil Polly's miserable party.'

'I won't.'

'There's something brewing between Junior and Hunterden, and you could spoil it and Junior would blame Polly.'

'Oh, I realise that.'

'We'll give them a chance to leave, and then you and I can go. I'll drive.'

'All right.'

He studied my face. 'What came over you?'

'What ever possessed me? I'm like Mrs Day. I shouldn't drink on Sunday, I guess.

Thirty years later I remember most of that spring as well as I do some things that happened a month ago. In this morning's paper they treated Charlotte Sears rather well. She did not make Page One, but they gave her two-column top heads in the *Trib* and the *Times*, called her an 'early Academy Award winner' who had come out of retirement in 1958 to win a nomination for best supporting actress as the mother superior in the Joseph S. Finston production, *Benediction at Dawn*. She was described as the last member of a theatrical family that had been prominent in vaudeville during the Nineteenth Century, who had become an outstanding success in the so-called drawing-room comedies of the Twenties and Thirties. Her career, it said, was abruptly terminated in 1930, when an automobile in which she was riding was struck by a train at a grade crossing in Roslyn, Long Island, and she received facial injuries that disfigured her and forced her into a long retirement. In the same accident, Thomas R. Hunterdon, in whose car Miss Sears was riding, was fatally injured. Hunterden, a stock promoter (it said), was facing indictment on six counts of fraudulent conversion and other charges. His tangled financial affairs resulted in court action over a period of three years, and his manipulations were instrumental in bringing about the creation of the Securities Exchange Act of 1934. Hunterden, a native of Gibbsville, Pa., was a somewhat mysterious, publicity-shy figure who had made a fortune through speculations during the First World War. Later he sought to gain control of motion picture companies and at the time of his

death he had failed in a last-minute attempt to enlist the financial
support of a syndicate headed by Ethridge B. Williamson, Jr.
During the investigation of Hunterden's financial affairs Miss Sears
was questioned by the district attorney in an effort to locate securities worth more than $2,000,000 which could not be accounted for,
but no charges were made against her . . .

I remembered that. I went to the hospital every afternoon and
read the morning and afternoon papers to her. I would sit by the
window so that I could see the print; she would not allow the
electric light to be turned on. There were dressings on her nose and
chin, and her arm was in a cast.

She had other visitors besides me. Polly Williamson came in at
least twice a week. Morrie Rosenbaum made a special trip from the
Coast to tell her not to worry. She could have had more visitors,
but we three were the only ones she wanted to see. When Morrie
Rosenbaum heard that she was going to be questioned about the
missing bonds, he telephoned me from Hollywood. 'Mally,' he said
(at $125 a week I did not rate a correct pronunciation), 'Miss Sears
don't have none of them hot bonds. I stake my life on it. So I got
her a lawyer. Not my lawyer. I got her Percy Goodfellow. You
know who *he* is? Lawyer to the biggest firms in Wall Street. Bishops
he has for clients. The very picture of integrity and a God damn
shrewd man. I told him I want him there every minute they're
asking her questions.'

'Yes sir,' I said.

'Oh, why am I telling you? Because you go to hospital and tell
her she don't see no district attorney without Goodfellow being
there every single minute. You understand? She can't talk to me
over the phone, you understand, so you give her my instructions.
You tell that little lady we don't want her worrying about a thing.
Mally?'

'Yes sir?'

'Tell her love from Ruthie and Morrie. Ruthie is Mrs Rosenbaum,
my wife.' He then hung up.

I was never there when Polly Williamson came to see her, but I
always knew when she had been there, and not only by the flowers
that she continued to bring on every visit. She would stay only ten
minutes—a total of twenty minutes a week—but Chottie would
always have something to say about her. 'It took me a couple of
weeks before I got over something,' said Chottie.

'What was that?'

'Wishing she wouldn't come. I didn't want her coming here because she felt guilty, because if I hadn't gone to her place this never would of happened. I didn't want you coming for that reason, either. But with you—well, maybe you had another reason.'

'I did blame myself,' I said. 'It was the first thing I thought of when I read about it. If I hadn't got drunk—'

'I know. But you had a man-and-woman reason for coming. I'm in your memory-book. And you're in mine, too, Jim.'

'I hope so.'

'But Polly doesn't blame herself. I don't think she ever did. She comes here because the night before it happened, when Junior went off with the Underwood dame, Polly knew I was mad as hell at Junior being so insulting. So crude. He was crude. But now when Polly comes to see me, she only stays ten minutes, but she always makes me feel that if she were here instead of me, she'd want me to visit her. Do you see what I mean? She'd *want* me to come. And I've never had another girl that was that kind of a friend. Even if I look like Lon Chaney when I get out of here, it won't all be a total loss.'

Another time she said: 'Polly was here earlier this afternoon. She came today instead of tomorrow because Etty, the boy, has to go and have his tonsils out tomorrow, poor kid. A wonderful mother, that Polly. But am I glad I don't have children. If I'd of married any of those hambo boy friends of mine—present company excepted—I'd of wanted children. But if I had a son or a daughter waiting for me to get out of here, I just couldn't face them. The first time they'd see me with my face all banged up. I read something one time about Helen of Troy, if she had a nose that was different by a fraction of an inch, it would have changed the history of the world. Well, mine's going to be different, but it sure as hell isn't going to change the history of the world.'

My reading to her was usually confined to the theatrical and movie news and reviews, book reviews, the gossip columns, the principal news stories, and occasionally the sail-and-arrive items on the society pages. 'Ah, Eunice Underwood sailed yesterday in the *Ile de France*, to be gone a year,' I said.

'No matter how I look when I get out of here, I'll have a better figure than she ever had,' she said. 'I had a lovely figure.'

'And still have.'

'I wonder what I'll do about that? Oh, I guess I'll find somebody.'
She was depressed.

'They're all the same from the top row in the balcony,' she said.
'They're all the same with a bag over their heads. I saw a comedy
bit in a two-reeler one time. The comic, I forget who it was, he sees
this girl in a one-piece bathing suit, great figure, and he follows her
up the beach and tries to pick her up. Then when she turns around
she has a face like Bull Montana. The comic did a Bobby Vernon
grando and ran. I don't think it's as funny now as I did when I
saw it. Now don't give me false encouragement.'

'How do you know I was going to give you any?'

'Because I can see you, even if you can't see me. And you were
going to say something encouraging. Don't. They're gonna do what
they can, the doctors. I'll have a different nose, and they've got this
wire in my jaw. I'll be able to put make-up over the scar in my
cheek. I was thinking of changing my name and starting out playing
character bits, but everybody'd know it was me. That'd be too good
a story for you boys in publicity.'

'It would get around, even if we laid off.'

'Yes, and the last thing I want is stuff about brave little Charlotte
Sears. If I have to be brave I don't want to be brave in public.'

'You have spunk, just like your mother.'

'That's one satisfaction. I'm beginning to get over my inferiority
complex about her. But I'm only—well, I'm under forty, and I
hope and pray I find a good man. God protect me from gigolos.
God keep me from paying a man to sleep with me.'

She in her wisdom had thought it all out, the danger she faced
that had been my secret worry for her. We both knew actresses
who kept gigolos, and we knew that the gigolos laughed at them
and that some of the actresses even made cruel jokes at themselves.

'You have plenty of money,' I said. 'Look around and get something to do.'

'Don't think I haven't thought about that. I could be an agent. I
know this business cold, and I have the contacts. A lot of things I
could do, like being a script girl. Wardrobe. But I was a star, and
I don't need the money. I've been trying to think what I could do
out of show business entirely. I wish I'd gone to high school, then
I could go to college and study to be a doctor. I guess I'll get over
that as soon as I get out of here, but it was one idea I had. Open

a shop, but I'd soon get tired of that. Interior decorator. Doesn't interest me.'

'Charity work,' I suggested.

'No, I'm too accustomed to making my own living. I have to do something I'll be paid for, even if it isn't much at first. By the way, Jim. You're still going to take that trip to Europe.'

'No.'

'Yes. I didn't mention it before because I needed you here. But in another three or four weeks I'll be going back to the Coast.'

'I don't want to go to Europe. As soon as you leave I'm quitting Rosenbaums'. I start a new job the first of August. Second-string dramatic critic. It's a job I want. Pretty good pay, and time to start writing a novel.'

'Morrie's paying my bills here, you know, so it isn't a question of money.'

'Be honest, Chottie.'

'Well, I'll tell you. Morrie is paying all my bills and I'm letting him do that. He really wants to, and I want him to. It makes him feel good, he and Ruthie. But of course I'm through at the Studio. I'm going to sell my house and have that money for capital. The money I've invested will keep me the rest of my life, not in luxury, but comfortably. I'll get a little house out in the Brentwood section for me and my maid, and I'll live quietly out there. Morrie told me I'd never have to worry about money, and he's one that keeps his word. Well, if he gives me as much every year as I have been getting every week, finances won't worry me. Morrie says he'll figure out a way to keep me on the payroll. Story department, most likely. He knows I'm a great reader, and if I give them one story idea a year, like suggesting a magazine serial they ought to buy, I'll be earning my pay.'

'You certainly will.'

'There's one thing I've always been interested in and it's why I always used to go for walks. Remember me telling you I used to go for those long walks when I was on the road? You know, in most towns I played, if you walk steadily for fifteen-twenty minutes, you're out of the business section and you start getting in the residential.'

'It's only about a hundred-yard dash where I come from.'

'Yes, it varies with the size of the town. But when you get out of the built-up section, you come to the thing that interested me the most. Hold on to your seat.'

'I'm holding on.'

'Flowers. I love flowers. I used to ask the stagehands who had the best gardens in every town I went to. The wise-guys used to ask me if I meant beer gardens. Sometimes I'd take the trolley to look at a garden, if it was too far out to walk. If there was a real famous one, big, I'd even take a taxi. I have over a hundred books on flowers and gardening. You know, Polly Williamson I discovered knows a lot about flowers, but I have to admit, I know more. You know, most flowers have at least two names. Different names in different countries, like larkspur for delphinium, bachelor's button for cornflower. That's in addition to the Latin names. I never got as far as Latin, so I don't know many Latin names, but I guess I've learned about fifty, the more common flowers. Our California flowers—' She halted. 'That's enough of that. When I start talking about our California flowers. Do you know who loved flowers?'

'Who?'

'Loved flowers, and had a great knowledge of them. Tom Hunterden. A discovery we both made by accident. One day he was at my house and he got up and walked over slowly toward one of my rose bushes. "What's the matter?" I said. "Do you see a snake?" Up where my house is we get rattlers. "No," he said. "This is a hybrid tea rose, and I've been thinking of putting them in at home." We didn't spend *all* our time talking about picture business, Jim. Even if you didn't like him, he was a fascinating man.'

'Why were you afraid of him? You told me once you were.'

'I wasn't afraid of him. But he inspired fear in me. It wasn't only the fear of losing him. It was just fear, Jim. A lot of times just thinking about him would make me afraid of something, I didn't know what. He believed in hunches himself, and hunches are nothing but intuition. I had the same thing after I got to know him. Not hunches. But intuitive fear.'

'A premonition?'

'Yes, I guess it was, considering what happened. When I came to New York this last time, when he didn't meet me at the station, I was upset but I was relieved. I thought maybe he and I were through and I'd get over this fear I had. I was glad to make love with you, because that showed me that I wasn't hypnotised by Hunterden. But I guess maybe I was hypnotised by him, if you

remember later that night. By the way, did you sleep with that
show girl?'

'No.'

'She was a real gold-digger. She was a Ziegfeld edition of Eunice
Underwood. That's one thing nobody could ever say about me.
Will you write to me, answer my letters if I write to you?'

By agreement I did not see her off when she left the hospital,
and I did not know the condition of her face. She took the less
fashionable trains, and had reservations under fictitious names.
Ruth Rosenbaum met her in Los Angeles and helped her to find
the house in Brentwood that she bought as Catherine Dowd. With
make-up to cover the scar, she did not look too awful unless you
remembered the original, but in the new house she had no photographs of herself before the accident, and she was gradually trying
to get used to the new face and the old name. All this I learned in
her occasional, chatty letters, which came less frequently as time
went on. Brentwood was not fancy enough for the movie stars who
were buying and building in Beverly Hills, although Greta Garbo
lived not far from Chottie's house. 'She vants to be alone and so
do I,' wrote Chottie, 'but I really am. I went shopping in Santa
Monica and nobody recognised me. I have not got up nerve enough
to shop in Beverly but I will.'

Then one day, about a year after the accident, she wrote that she
had bought a greenhouse, which she was calling Dowd & Company,
and her letters became few and far between. We exchanged Christmas cards, but I stopped hearing from her until 1934, when my
novel was published and she sent me some California reviews. She
had bought a copy of the book but had not had a chance to read
it but would read it before I got to California, which she knew
would be as soon as she had read that I had signed with Paramount.

I drove out to have dinner at her house and I realised on the
way that I had never seen her face after the accident. I found her
house with some difficulty. The place was surrounded by an eight-
foot hedge that gave her complete privacy, and since I knew I was
to be the only guest for dinner, I parked my car in the short
driveway and rang the front doorbell.

She opened it herself, swung it wide and stood smiling.

'Would you have recognised me?' she said.

'Not immediately, not unless you spoke.' I kissed her and she
hugged me.

'You don't have to be careful what you say. I'm all right. It's so good to see you again. You're older, and more attractive that way. You've been married and divorced, and you've written a fine book, and what kind of a deal did you make at Paramount?'

'One of those seven-year option things. I signed the first contract they offered me because I wanted to get out of New York. How is Dowd & Company?'

'Doing very well. It was tough in the beginning, but I survived the first year, and the second year I just about broke even on the business, and now there's a lot of real-estate activity in this section and that means business for us.'

'Us? You have a partner?'

'You'll meet him.' She nodded without looking at me. 'I found somebody.'

'That's the best news, Chottie.'

She nodded again. 'Yes. I did the other, though. What I was afraid I'd do, out of loneliness and desperation. He wasn't a gigolo with patent-leather hair. He was a young writer, very unsuccessful *and*, I found out, not very talented. I had a hard time getting rid of him.'

'How did you?'

'I gave him money to go to Mexico.'

'That doesn't always work.'

'Not if you have no one else, but now I have someone else.'

'Tell me about him.'

'Oh, I will. He's married, of course. Separated from his wife. He's fifty, has two grown children that live with her, down in Whittier. That's on the other side of Los Angeles. He's a landscape architect and that's how I met him.'

'And what of the future?'

'His wife won't give him a divorce till the daughter gets married, but that will be in June, when she finishes college. Then we have over a year to wait, but what's a year? The wife is as anxious to get out of it as he is, but not before the girl is married off. He has a room over in Santa Monica. Most of his work is around here. Brentwood Heights. Beverly. Bel-Air. He isn't really my partner yet, but I don't know what I'd do without him. I couldn't.'

We had a good dinner, starting, as Californians do, with a salad, and we talked without pause until nine-thirty, when the doorbell rang. 'That's Lou. On the dot. By the way, he knows about you and our one matinée, so don't mind if he sizes you up.'

Louis Grafmiller was a stocky, sunburned man with close cropped iron-gray hair. 'Hello, Catherine,' he said, and kissed her on the lips. He shook hands with me and it was a firm handshake.

'Glad to know you, Mr Malloy,' he said. 'This girl is always singing your praises.'

'Well, she's just finished singing some of yours,' I said.

'Have a drink, Lou?'

'Oh, a glass of wine, maybe. Some of that Chianti? You just get in from the East?'

'Monday.'

'Your first visit to California, Catherine said.'

'Yes, I'd never been west of the Mississippi before.'

'It's a big country, and a good country. People don't realise how big or how good. They ought to get around more and see what they have before they turn it over to the Communists. I know I didn't vote to take it away from Wall Street just to hand it over to those other bastards.'

I had a quick revelation of what he would do to Chottie's gigolo writer if he ever showed up again. She was well protected now.

'I understand your book is a big success. Do you know Ernest Hemingway?'

'No.'

'I like his kind of writing. Catherine gave me your book but I haven't started it yet.'

'Are you going to write another, Jim?' asked Chottie.

'Yes, when I go back. I don't think I'll stay out here past the first option.'

'Don't you like California?' he smiled.

'Not yet. I don't dislike it yet, either. But I'll never be a Californian.'

'That's what I said twenty-five years ago, but I'm still here. There are only two states that have everything. California, and Pennsylvania.'

'I'm from Pennsylvania.'

'I know. So am I. Pittsburgh. You're from the other end of the state. I have cousins in Reading.'

Now slowly I was conscious of Chottie's changed face as she listened to our conversation; it was very right that her face should be different when she herself was so different as well. Her face, her name, and the domesticity were all new to me. I was still very fond of what I could remember, but when I left her house she shook hands with me, did not kiss me, and we were both reconciled to the finality of the farewell. Grafmiller walked with me to my car and gave me directions for getting back to Hollywood, and I could not help thinking that he had likewise directed Chottie, but not in the way I was headed. We did not bother to shake hands. Neither of us regarded the introduction as a true meeting, and we paid this silent respect to our harmless mutual animosity.

I never heard from her after that night, although I often went to Hollywood to work on movie scripts. Once on an impulse I looked up Grafmiller in the telephone book and his address was the same as the house where I had met him, hers. Then I heard somewhere that he had died, but the information came long after his death and I did not write to Chottie. She was swallowed up in the anonymity of former movie stars living in Los Angeles—the easiest way for a former movie star to become obscure —until Joe Finston put her in *Benediction at Dawn*. In today's obituaries there is mention of Louis Grafmiller, but not a word about their greenhouse, and for some reason or other that pleased me. On the same page there was an obituary of a man who had once won the 500 mile race at Indianapolis but who died while playing shuffleboard at St Petersburg, Florida.

I close this reminiscence with one more fact. Thomas Rodney Hunterden was born Thomas Robert Huntzinger in Gibbsville, Pa. I have no idea why he disliked my father, and I am long past caring.

II

Imagine Kissing Pete
the couples who are intoxicated
by marriage on the rocks
'The History of a young man who
discovered sex belatedly,
and the history of the Girl
who married him on the
rebound . . . of lust and love,
of ecstasy and tragedy and
tedium . . . but always with
an eye for the truth.'

St. Louis Post-Dispatch

CHAPTER 2

Imagine Kissing Pete

To those who knew the bride and groom, the marriage of Bobbie Hammersmith and Pete McCrea was the surprise of the year. As late as April of '29 Bobbie was still engaged to a fellow who lived in Greenwich, Connecticut, and she had told friends that the wedding would take place in September. But the engagement was broken and in a matter of weeks the invitations went out for her June wedding to Pete. One of the most frequently uttered comments was that Bobbie was not giving herself much opportunity to change her mind again. The comment was doubly cruel, since it carried the implication that if she gave herself time to think, Pete McCrea would not be her ideal choice. It was not only that she was marrying Pete on the rebound; she seemed to be going out of her way to find someone who was so unlike her other beaus that the contrast was unavoidable. And it was.

I was working in New York and Pete wrote to ask me to be an usher. Pete and I had grown up together, played together as children, and gone to dancing school and to the same parties. But we had never been close friends and when Pete and I went away to our seperate prep schools and, later, Pete to Princeton and I to work, we drifted into that relationship of young men who had known each other all their lives without creating anything that was enduring or warm. As a matter of fact, I had never in my life received a written communication from Pete McCrea, and his handwriting on the envelope was new to me, as mine in my reply was to him. He mentioned who the best man and the other ushers would be—all Gibbsville boys—and this somewhat pathetic commentary on his four years in prep school and four years in college made an appeal to home town and boyhood loyalty that I could not reject. I had some extra days coming to me at the office, and so I told Pete I would be honored to be one of his ushers. My next step was to talk to a Gibbsville girl who lived in New York, a friend of Bobbie Hammersmith's. I took her to dinner at an Italian speakeasy where my credit was good, and she gave me what information she had. She was to be a bridesmaid.

'Bobbie isn't saying a word,' said Kitty Clark. 'That is, nothing about the inner turmoil. Nothing *intime*. Whatever happened happened the last time she was in New York, four or five weeks ago. All she'd tell me was that Johnny White was impossible. Impossible. Well, he'd been very possible all last summer and fall.'

'What kind of a guy was he?' I asked.

'Oh—*attractive*,' she said. 'Sort of wild, I guess, but not a roué. Maybe he is a roué, but I'd say more just wild. I honestly don't know a thing about it, but it wouldn't surprise me if Bobbie was ready to settle down, and he wasn't. She was probably more in love with him than he was with her.'

'I doubt that. She wouldn't turn around and marry Pete if she were still in love with this White guy.'

'Oh, *wouldn't* she? Oh, are you ever wrong there. If she wanted to thumb her nose at Johnny, I can't think of a better way. Poor Pete. You know *Pete*. Ichabod McCrea. Remember when Mrs McCrea made us stop calling him Ichabod? Lord and Taylor! She went to see my mother and I guess all the other mothers and said it just had to stop. Bad enough calling her little Angus by such a common nickname as Pete. But calling a boy Ichabod. I don't suppose Pete ever knew his mother went around like that.'

'Yes he did. It embarrassed him. It always embarrassed him when Mrs McCrea did those things.'

'Yes, she was uncanny. I can remember when I was going to have a party, practically before I'd made out the list Mrs McCrea would call Mother to be sure Pete wasn't left out. Not that I ever would have left him out. We all always had the same kids to our parties. But Mrs McCrea wasn't leaving anything to chance. I'm dying to hear what she has to say about this marriage. I'll bet she doesn't like it, but I'll bet she's in fear and trembling in case Bobbie changes her mind again. Ichabod McCrea and Bobbie Hammersmith. Beauty and the beast. And actually he's not even a beast. It would be better if he were. She's the third of our old bunch to get married, but much as I hate to say it, I'll bet she'll be the first to get a divorce. Imagine *kissing* Pete, let alone any of the rest of it.'

The wedding was on a Saturday afternoon; four o'clock in Trinity

Church, and the reception at the country club. It had been two years since I last saw Bobbie Hammersmith and she was now twenty-two, but she could have passed for much more than that. She was the only girl in her crowd who had not bobbed her hair, which was jet-black and which she always wore with plaited buns over the ears. Except in the summer her skin was like Chinese white and it was always easy to pick her out first in group photographs; her eyes large dark dots, quite far apart, and her lips small but prominent in the whiteness of her face beneath the two small dots of her nose. In summer, with a tan, she reminded many non-operagoers of Carmen. She was a striking beauty, although it took two years' absence from her for me to realise it. In the theatre they have an expression, 'walked through the part,' which means that an actress played a role without giving it much of herself. Bobbie walked through the part of bride-to-be. A great deal of social activity was concentrated in the three days—Thursday, Friday, and Saturday—up to and including the wedding reception; but Bobbie walked through the part. Today, thirty years later, it would be assumed that she had been taking tranquilisers, but this was 1929.

Barbara Hammersmith had never been anything but a pretty child; if she had ever been homely it must have been when she was a small baby, when I was not bothering to look at her. We—Pete McCrea and the other boys—were two, three, four years older than Bobbie, but when she was fifteen or sixteen she began to pass among us, from boy to boy, trying one and then another, causing several fist fights, and half promising but never delivering anything more than the 'soul kisses' that were all we really expected. By the time she was eighteen she had been in and out of love with all of us with the solitary exception of Pete McCrea. When she broke off with a boy, she would also make up with the girl he had temporarily deserted for Bobbie, and all the girls came to understand that every boy in the crowd had to go through a love affair with her. Consequently Bobbie was popular; the boys remembered her kisses, the girls forgave her because the boys had been returned virtually intact. We used the word hectic a lot in those days; Kitty Clark explained the short duration of Bobbie's love affairs by observing that being in love with Bobbie was too hectic for most boys. It was also true that it was not hectic enough. The boys agreed that Bobbie was a hot little number, but none of us could claim that she was not a virgin. At eighteen Bobbie entered a personal middle age, and

for the big social occasions her beaus came from out-of-town. She
was also busy at the college proms and football games, as far west
as Ann Arbor, as far north as Brunswick, Maine. I was working on
the Gibbsville paper during some of those years, the only boy in
our crowd who was not away at college, and I remember Ann
Arbor because Bobbie went there wearing a Delta Tau Delta pin
and came back wearing the somewhat larger Psi U. 'Now don't you
say anything in front of Mother,' she said. 'She thinks they're both
the same.'

We played auction bridge, the social occupation in towns like
ours, and Bobbie and I were assimilated into an older crowd: the
younger married set and the youngest of the couples who were in
their thirties. We played for prizes—flasks, cigarette lighters, vanity
cases, cartons of cigarettes—and there was a party at someone's
house every week. The hostess of the evening usually asked me to
stop for Bobbie, and I saw her often. Her father and mother would
be reading the evening paper and sewing when I arrived to pick
up Bobbie. Philip Hammersmith was not a native of Gibbsville, but
he had lived there long enough to have gone to the Mexican Border
in 1916 with the Gibbsville company of mounted engineers, and he
had gone to France with them, returning as a first lieutenant and
with the Croix de Guerre with palm. He was one of the best golfers
in the club, and everyone said he was making money hand-over-
fist as an independent coal operator. He wore steel-rim glasses and
he had almost completely gray hair, cut short. He inspired trust
and confidence. He was slow-moving, taller than six feet, and always
thought before speaking. His wife, a Gibbsville girl, was related, as
she said, to half the town; a lively little woman who took her
husband's arm even if they were walking only two doors away. I
always used to feel that whatever he may have wanted out of life,
yet unattained or unattainable, she had just what she wanted: a
good husband, a nice home, and a pretty daughter who would not
long remain unmarried. At home in the evening, and whenever I
saw him on the street, Mr Hammersmith was wearing a dark-gray
worsted suit, cut loose and with a soft roll to the lapel; black knit
four-in-hand necktie; white shirt; heavy gray woolen socks, and
thick-soled brogues. This costume, completely unadorned—he wore
a wrist watch—was what he always wore except for formal
occasions, and the year-to-year sameness of his attire constituted
his only known eccentricity. He was on the board of the second

most conservative bank, the trustees of Gibbsville Hospital, the armory board, the Y.M.C.A., and the Gibbsville and Lantenengo country clubs. Nevertheless I sensed that that was not all there was to Philip Hammersmith, that the care he put into the creation of the general picture of himself—hard work, quiet clothes, thoughtful manner, conventional associations—was done with a purpose that was not necessarily sinister but was extraordinarily private. It delighted me to discover, one night while waiting for Bobbie, that he knew more about what was going on than most of us suspected he would know. 'Jimmy, you know Ed Charney, of course,' he said.

I knew Ed Charney, the principal bootlegger in the area. 'Yes, I know him pretty well,' I said.

'Then do you happen to know if there's any truth to what I heard? I heard that his wife is threatening to divorce him.'

'I doubt it. They're Catholics.'

'Do you know her?'

'Yes. I went to Sisters' school with her.'

'Oh, then maybe you can tell me something else. I've heard that she's the real brains of those two.'

'She quit school after eighth grade, so I don't know about that. I don't remember her being particularly bright. She's about my age but she was two grades behind me.'

'I see. And you think their religion will keep them from getting a divorce?'

'Yes, I do. I don't often see Ed at Mass, but I know he carries rosary beads. And she's at the eleven o'clock Mass every Sunday, all dolled up.'

This conversation was explained when Repeal came and with it public knowledge that Ed Charney had been quietly buying bank stock, one of several moves he had made in the direction of respectability. But the chief interest to me at the time Mr Hammersmith and I talked was in the fact that he knew anything at all about the Charneys. It was so unlike him even to mention Ed Charney's name.

To get back to the weekend of Bobbie Hammersmith's wedding: it was throughout that weekend that I first saw Bobbie have what we called that faraway look, that another generation called Cloud 90. If you happened to catch her at the right moment, you would see her smiling up at Pete in a way that must have been reassuring to Mrs McCrea and to Mrs Hammersmith, but I also caught her at several wrong moments and I saw something I had never seen before: a resemblance to her father that was a subtler thing than the mere duplication of such features as mouth, nose, and set of the eyes. It was almost the same thing I have mentioned in describing Philip Hammersmith; the wish yet unattained or unattainable. However, the pre-nuptial parties and the wedding and reception went off without a hitch, or so I believed until the day after the wedding.

Kitty Clark and I were on the same train going back to New York and I made some comment about the exceptional sobriety of the ushers and how everything had gone according to plan. 'Amazing, considering,' said Kitty.

'Considering what?'

'That there was almost no wedding at all,' she said. 'You must promise word of honor, Jimmy, or I won't tell you.'

'I promise. Word of honor.'

'Well, after Mrs McCrea's very-dull-I-must-say luncheon, when we all left to go to Bobbie's? A little after two o'clock?'

'Yes.'

'Bobbie asked me if I'd go across the street to our house and put in a long-distance call to Johnny White. I said I couldn't do that, and what on earth was she thinking of. And Bobbie said, "You're my oldest and best friend. The least you can do is make this one last effort, to keep me from ruining my life." So I gave in and I dashed over to our house and called Johnny. He was out and they didn't know where he could be reached or what time he was coming home. So I left my name. *My* name, not Bobbie's. Six o'clock, at the reception, I was dancing with—I was dancing with *you*.'

'When the waiter said you were wanted on the phone.'

'It was Johnny. He'd been sailing and just got in. I made up some story about why I'd called him, but he didn't swallow it. "*You* didn't call me," he said. "*Bobbie* did." Well of course I wouldn't admit that. By that time she was married, and if her life was already ruined it would be a darned sight more ruined if I let him talk to her. Which he wanted to do. Then he tried to pump me. Where were they going on their wedding trip? I said nobody knew, which was a barefaced lie. I knew they were going to Bermuda. Known it since Thursday. But I wouldn't tell Johnny . . . I don't like him a bit after yesterday. I'd thought he was attractive, and he *is*, but he's got a mean streak that I never knew before. Feature this, if

you will. When he realised I wasn't going to get Bobbie to come to
the phone, or give him any information, he said, "Well, no use
wasting a long-distance call. What are you doing next weekend?
How about coming out here?" "I'm not that hard up," I said, and
banged down the receiver. I hope I shattered his eardrum.'

I saw Pete and Bobbie McCrea when I went home the following
Christmas. They were living in a small house on Twin Oaks Road,
a recent real-estate development that had been instantly successful
with the sons and daughters of the big two-and three-servant
mansions. They were not going to any of the holiday dances; Bobbie
was expecting a baby in April or early May.

'You're not losing any time,' I said.

'I don't want to lose any time,' said Bobbie. 'I want to have a
lot of children. Pete's an only child and so am I, and we don't think
it's fair, if you can afford to have more.'

'If we can afford it. The way that stock market is going, we'll be
lucky to pay for this one,' said Pete.

'Oh, don't start on that, Pete. That's all Father talks about,' said
Bobbie. 'My father *was* hit pretty hard, but I wish he didn't have
to keep talking about it all the time. Everybody's in the same boat.'

'No they're not. *We're* on a *raft*.'

'I asked you, please, Pete. Jimmy didn't come here to listen to
our financial woes. Do you see much of Kitty? I've owed her a letter
for ages.'

'No, I haven't seen her since last summer, we went out a few
times,' I said.

'Kitty went to New York to try to rope in a millionaire. She isn't
going to waste her time on Jim.'

'That's not what she went to New York for at all. And as far as
wasting her time on Jim, Jim may not want to waste his time on
her.' She smiled. 'Have you got a girl, Jim?'

'Not really.'

'Wise. Very wise,' said Pete McCrea.

'I don't know how wise. It's just that I have a hell of a hard time
supporting myself, without trying to support a wife, too,' I said.

'Why I understood you were selling articles to magazines, and
going around with all the big shots.'

'I've had four jobs in two years, and the jobs didn't last very
long. If things get any tougher I may have to come back here. At
least I'll have a place to sleep and something to eat.'

'But I see your name in magazines,' said Pete. 'I don't always read your articles, but they must pay you well.'

'They don't. At least I can't live on the magazine pieces without a steady job. Excuse me, Bobbie. Now you're getting *my* financial woes.'

'She'll listen to yours. It's mine she doesn't want to hear about.'

'That's because I know about ours. I'm never allowed to forget them,' said Bobbie. 'Are you going to all the parties?'

'Yes, stag. I have to bum rides. I haven't got a car.'

'We resigned from the club,' said Pete.

'Well we didn't *have* to do that,' said Bobbie. 'Father was going to give it to us for a Christmas present. And you have your job.'

'We'll see how much longer I have it. Is that the last of the gin?'

'Yes.'

Pete rose. 'I'll be back.'

'Don't buy any more for me,' I said.

'You flatter yourself,' he said. 'I wasn't only getting it for you.' He put on his hat and coat. 'No funny business while I'm gone. I remember you two.'

He kept a silly grin on his face while saying the ugly things, but the grin was not genuine and the ugly things were.

'I don't know what's the matter with him,' said Bobbie. 'Oh, I do, but why talk about it?'

'He's only kidding.'

'You know better than that. He says worse things, much worse, and I'm only hoping they don't get back to Father. Father has enough on his mind. I thought if I had this baby right away it would—you know—give Pete confidence. But it's had just the opposite effect. He says it isn't his child. *Isn't his child!* Oh, I married him out of spite. I'm sure Kitty must have told you that. But it *is* his child, I swear it, Jim. It couldn't be anybody else's.'

'I guess it's the old inferiority complex,' I said.

'The first month we were married—Pete was a virgin—and I admit it, I wasn't. I stayed with two boys before I was married. But I was certainly not pregnant when I married Pete, and the first few weeks he was loving and sweet, and grateful. But then something happened to him, and he made a pass at I-won't-say-who. It was more than a pass. It was quite a serious thing. I might as well tell you. It was Phyllis. We were all at a picnic at the Dam and several people got pretty tight, Pete among them. And there's no other word for it, he tried to rape Phyllis. Tore her bathing suit and slapped her and did other things. She got away from him and ran back to the cottage without anyone seeing her. Luckily Joe didn't see her or I'm sure he'd have killed Pete. You know, Joe's strong as an ox and terribly jealous. I found out about it from Phyllis herself. She came here the next day and told me. She said she wasn't going to say anything to Joe, but that we mustn't invite her to our house and she wasn't going to invite us to hers.'

'I'm certainly glad Joe didn't hear about it. He would do something drastic,' I said. 'But didn't he notice that you two weren't going to his house, and they to yours? It's a pretty small group.'

She looked at me steadily. 'We haven't been going anywhere. My excuse is that I'm pregnant, but the truth is, we're not being asked. It didn't end with Phyllis, Jim. One night at a dinner party Mary Lander just slapped his face, in front of everybody. Everybody laughed and thought Pete must have said something, but it wasn't something he'd said. He'd taken her hand and put it—you know. This is *Pete! Ichabod!* Did you ever know any of this about him?'

'You mean have I heard any of this? No.'

'No, I didn't mean that. I meant, did he go around making passes and I never happened to hear about it?'

'No. When we'd talk dirty he'd say, "Why don't you fellows get your minds above your belts?" '

'I wish your father were still alive. I'd go see him and try to get some advice. I wouldn't think of going to Dr English.'

'Well, you're not the one that needs a doctor. Could you get Pete to go to one? He's a patient of Dr English's, isn't he?'

'Yes, but so is Mrs McCrea, and Pete would never confide in Dr English.'

'Or anyone else at this stage, I guess,' I said. 'I'm not much help, am I?'

'Oh, I didn't expect you to have a solution. You know, Jim, I wish you would come back to Gibbsville. Other girls in our crowd have often said it was nice to have you to talk to. Of course you were a very bad boy, too, but a lot of us miss you.'

'That's nice to hear, Bobbie. Thank you. I may be back, if I don't soon make a go of it in New York. I won't have any choice.'

During that Christmas visit I heard other stories about Pete McCrea. In general they were told as plain gossip, but two or three times there was a hint of a lack of sympathy for Bobbie. 'She knew

what she was doing . . . she made her bed . . .' And while there was
no lack of righteous indignation over Pete's behavior, he had
changed in six months from a semi-comic figure to an unpleasant
man, but a man nevertheless. In half a year he had lost most of his
old friends; they all said, 'You've never seen such a change come
over anybody in all your life,' but when they remembered to call
him Ichabod it was only to emphasise the change.

Bobbie's baby was born in April, but lived only a few weeks.
'She was determined to have that baby,' Kitty Clark told me. 'She
had to prove to Pete that it was anyway *conceived* after she married
him. But it must have taken all her strength to hold on to it that
long. All her strength *and* the baby's. Now would be a good time
for her to divorce him. She can't go on like that.'

But there was no divorce, and Bobbie was pregnant again when
I saw her at Christmas, 1930. They no longer lived in the Twin
Oaks Road house, and her father and mother had given up their
house on Lantenengo Street. The Hammersmiths were living in an
apartment on Market Street, and Bobbie and Pete were living with
Mrs McCrea. 'Temporarily, till Pete decides whether to take this
job in Tulsa, Oklahoma,' said Bobbie.

'Who do you think you're kidding?' said Pete. 'It isn't a question
of me deciding. It's a cousin of mine deciding if he'll take me on.
And why the hell should he?'

'Well, you've had several years' banking experience,' she said.

'Yes. And if I was so good, why did the bank let me go? Jim
knows all this. What else have you heard about us, Jim? Did you
hear Bobbie was divorcing me?'

'It doesn't look that way from here,' I said.

'You mean because she's pregnant? That's elementary biology,
and God knows you're acquainted with the facts of life. But if you
want to be polite, all right. Pretend you didn't hear she was getting
a divorce. You might as well pretend Mr and Mrs Hammersmith
are still living on Lantenengo Street. If they were, Bobbie'd have
got her divorce.'

'Everybody tells me what I *was* going to do or *am* going to do,'
said Bobbie. 'Nobody ever consults me.'

'I suppose that's a crack at my mother.'

'Oh, for Christ's sake, Pete, lay off, at least while I'm here,' I
said.

'Why? You like to think of yourself as an old friend of the family,

so you might as well get a true picture. When you get married, if
you ever do, I'll come and see you, and maybe your wife will cry
on my shoulder.' He got up and left the house.

'Well, it's just like a year ago,' said Bobbie. 'When you came to
call on us last Christmas?'

'Where will he go now?'

'Oh, there are several places where he can charge drinks. They
all think Mrs McCrea has plenty of money, but they're due for a
rude awakening. She's living on capital, but she's not going to sell
any bonds to pay his liquor bills.'

'Then maybe *he's* due for a rude awakening.'

'Any awakening would be better than the last three months, since
the bank fired him. He sits here all day long, then after Mrs McCrea
goes to bed he goes to one of his speakeasies.' She sat up straighter.
'He has a lady friend. Or have you heard?'

'No.'

'Yes. He graduated from making passes at all my friends. He had
to. We were never invited anywhere. Yes, he has a girl friend. Do
you remember Muriel Nierhaus?'

'The chiropractor's wife. Sure. Big fat Muriel Minzer till she
married Nierhaus, then we used to say he gave her some adjustments. Where is Nierhaus?'

'Oh, he's opened several offices. Very prosperous. He divorced
her but she gets alimony. She's Pete's girl friend. Muriel Minzer is
Angus McCrea's girl friend.'

'You don't seem too displeased,' I said.

'Would you be, if you were in my position?'

'I guess I know what you mean. But—well, nothing.'

'But why don't I get a divorce?' She shook her head. 'A spite
marriage is a terrible thing to do to anybody. If I hadn't deliberately
selected Pete out of all the boys I knew, he'd have gone on till Mrs
McCrea picked out somebody for him, and it would almost have
had to be the female counterpart of Pete. A girl like—oh—Florence.
Florence Temple.'

'Florence Temple, with her cello. Exactly right.'

'But I did that awful thing to Pete, and the first few weeks of
marriage were just too much for him. He went haywire. I'd slept
with two boys before I was married, so it wasn't as much of a shock
to me. But Pete almost wore me out. And such adoration, I can't
tell you. Then when we came back from Bermuda he began to see

all the other girls he'd known all his life, and he'd ask me about
them. It was as though he'd never seen them before, in a way. In
other ways, it was as though he'd just been waiting all his life to
start ripping their clothes off. He was dangerous, Jim. He really
was. I could almost tell who would be next by the questions he'd
ask. Before we'd go to a party, he'd say. "Who's going to be there
tonight?" And I'd say I thought the usual crowd. Then he'd rattle
off the list of names of our friends, and leave out one name. That
was supposed to fool me, but it didn't for long. The name he left
out, that girl was almost sure to be in for a bad time.'

'And now it's all concentrated on Muriel Minzer?'

'As far as I know.'

'Well, that's a break for you, *and* the other girls. Did you ever
talk to him about the passes he made at the others?'

'Oh, how could we avoid it? Whoever it was, she was always
"that little whore." '

'Did he ever get anywhere with any of them?'

She nodded. 'One, but I won't tell you who. There was one girl
that didn't stop him, and when that happened he wanted me to
sleep with her husband.'

'Swap, eh?'

'Yes. But I said I wasn't interested. Pete wanted to know why
not? Why wouldn't I? And I almost told him. The boy was one of
the two boys I'd stayed with before I was married—oh, when I was
seventeen. And he never told anybody and neither have I, or ever
will.'

'You mean one of our old crowd actually did get somewhere with
you, Bobbie?'

'One did. But don't try to guess. It won't do you any good to
guess, because I'd never, never tell.'

'Well, whichever one it was, he's the best liar I ever knew. And
I guess the nicest guy in our whole crowd. You know, Bobbie, the
whole damn bunch are going to get credit now for being as honor-
able as one guy.'

'You were all nice, even if you all did talk too much. If it had
been you, you would have lied, too.'

'No, I don't think I would have.'

'You lied about Kitty. Ha ha ha. You didn't know I knew about
you and Kitty. I knew it the next day. The very next day. If you
don't believe me, I'll tell you where it happened and how it

happened, and all about it. That was the great bond we had in common. You and Kitty, and I and this other boy.'

'Then Kitty's a gentleman, because she never told me a word about you.'

'I kissed every boy in our crowd except Pete, and I necked, heavy-necked two, as you well know, and stayed with one.'

'The questions is, did you stay with the other one that you heavy-necked with?'

'You'll never know, Jim, and please don't try to find out.'

'I won't, but I won't be able to stop theorising,' I said.

We knew everything, everything there was to know. We were so far removed from the technical innocence of eighteen, sixteen, nineteen. I was a man of the world, and Bobbie was indeed a woman, who had borne a child and lived with a husband who had come the most recently to the knowledge we had acquired, but was already the most intricately involved in the complications of sex. We—Bobbie and I—could discuss him and still remain outside the problems of Pete McCrea. We could almost remain outside our own problems. We knew so much, and since what we knew seemed to be all there was to know, we were shock-proof. We had come to our maturity and our knowledgeability during the long decade of cynicism that was usually dismissed as 'a cynical disregard of the law of the land,' but that was something else, something deeper. The law had been passed with a 'noble' but nevertheless cynical disregard of men's right to drink. It was a law that had been imposed on some who took pleasure in drinking by some who did not. And when the law was an instant failure, it was not admitted to be a failure by those who had imposed it. They fought to retain the law in spite of its immediate failure and its proliferating corruption, and they fought as hard as they would have for a law that had been an immediate success. They gained no recruits to their own way; they had only deserters, who were not brave deserters but furtive ones; there was no honest mutiny but only grumbling and small disobediences. And we grew up listening to the grumbling, watching the small disobediences; laughing along when the grumbling was intentionally funny, imitating the small disobediences in other ways besides the customs of drinking. It was not only a cynical disregard for a law of the land; the law was eventually changed. Prohibition, the zealots' attempt to force total abstinence on a temperate nation, made liars of a hundred million men and cheats of their children; the West Point cadets who cheated in examinations, the basketball players who connived with gamblers, the thousands of uncaught cheats in the high schools and colleges. We had grown up and away from our earlier esteem of God and country and valor, and had matured at a moment when riches were vanishing for reasons that we could not understand. We were the losing, not the lost, generation. We could not blame Pete McCrea's troubles—and Bobbie's—on the Southern Baptists and the Northern Methodists. Since we knew everything, we knew that Pete's sudden release from twenty years of frustrations had turned him loose in a world filled with women. But Bobbie and I sat there in her mother-in-law's house, breaking several laws of possession, purchase, transportation and consumption of liquor, and with great calmness discussing the destruction of two lives—one of them hers—and the loss of her father's fortune, the depletion of her mother-in-law's, the allure of a chiropractor's divorcée, and our own promiscuity. We knew everything, but we were incapable of recognizing the meaning of our complacency.

I was wearing my dinner jacket, and someone was going to pick me up and take me to a dinner dance at the club. 'Who's stopping for you?' said Bobbie.

'It depends. Either Joe or Frank. Depends on whether they go in Joe's car or Frank's. I'm to be ready when they blow their horn.'

'Do me a favor, Jim. Make them come in. Pretend you don't hear the horn.'

'If it's Joe, he's liable to drive off without me. You know Joe if he's had a few too many.'

In a few minutes there was a blast of a two-tone horn, repeated. 'That's Joe's car,' said Bobbie. 'You'd better go.' She went to the hall with me and I kissed her cheek. The front door swung open and it was Joe Whipple.

'Hello, Bobbie,' he said.

'Hello, Joe. Won't you all come in? Haven't you got time for one drink?' She was trying not to sound suppliant, but Joe was not deceived.

'Just you and Jim here?' he said.

'Yes. Pete went out a little while ago.'

'I'll see what the others say,' said Joe. He left to speak to the three in the sedan, and obviously he was not immediately persuasive, but they came in with him. They would not let Bobbie take their coats, but they were nice to her and with the first sips of our drinks we were all six almost back in the days when Bobbie Hammersmith's house was where so many of our parties started from. Then we heard the front door thumping shut and Pete McCrea looked in.

There were sounds of hello, but he stared at us over his horn-rims and said to Bobbie: 'You didn't have to invite me, but you could have told me.' He turned and again the front door thumped.

'Get dressed and come with us,' said Joe Whipple.

'I can't do that,' said Bobbie.

'She can't, Joe,' said Phyllis Whipple. 'That would only make more trouble.'

'What trouble? She's going to have to sit here alone till he comes home. She might as well be with us,' said Joe.

'Anyway, I haven't got a dress that fits,' said Bobbie. 'But thanks for asking me.'

'I won't have you sitting here—'

'Now don't make matters worse, Joe, for heaven's sake,' said his wife.

'I could lend you a dress, Bobbie, but I think Phyllis is right,' said Mary Lander. 'Whatever *you* want to do.'

'*Want* to do! That's not the question,' said Bobbie. 'Go on before I change my mind. Thanks, everybody. Frank, you haven't said a word.'

'Nothing much for me to say,' said Frank Lander. But as far as I was concerned he, and Bobbie herself, had said more than anyone else. I caught her looking at me quickly.

'Well, all right, then,' said Joe. 'I'm outnumbered. Or outpersuaded or something.'

I was the last to say goodbye, and I whispered to Bobbie: 'Frank, eh?'

'You're only guessing,' she said. 'Goodnight, Jim.' Whatever they would be after we left, her eyes were brighter than they had been in years. She had very nearly gone to a party, and for a minute or two she had been part of it.

I sat in the back seat with Phyllis Whipple and Frank Lander. 'If you'd had any sense you'd know there'd be a letdown,' said Phyllis.

'Oh, drop it,' said Joe.

'It might have been worth it, though, Phyllis,' said Mary Lander. 'How long is it since she's seen anybody but that old battle-ax, Mrs

McCrea? God, I hate to think what it must be like, living in that house with Mrs McCrea.'

'I'm sure it would have been a *lot* easier if Bobbie'd come with us,' said Phyllis. 'That would have fixed things just right with Mrs McCrea. She's just the type that wants Bobbie to go out and have a good time. Especially without Pete. You forget how the old lady used to call up all the mothers as soon as she heard there was a party planned. What Joe did was cruel because it was so downright stupid. Thoughtless. Like getting her all excited and then leaving her hung up.'

'You've had too much to drink,' said Joe.

'*I* have?'

'Yes, you don't say things like that in front of a bachelor,' said Joe.

'Who's—oh, Jim? It is to laugh. Did I shock you, Jim?'

'Not a bit. I didn't know what you meant. Did you say something risqué?'

'My husband thinks I did.'

'Went right over my head,' I said. 'I'm innocent about such things.'

'So's your old man,' said Joe.

'Do you think she should have come with us, Frank?' I said.

'Why ask me? No. I'm with Phyllis. What's the percentage for Bobbie? You saw that son of a bitch in the doorway, and you know damn well when he gets home from Muriel Nierhaus's, he's going to raise hell with Bobbie.'

'Then Bobbie had nothing to lose,' said Joe. 'If Pete's going to raise hell with her, anyway, she might as well have come with us.'

'How does he raise hell with her?' I said.

No one said anything.

'Do you know, Phyllis?' I said.

'What?' said Phyllis.

'Oh, come on. You heard me,' I said. 'Mary?'

'I'm sure I don't know.'

'Oh, nuts,' I said.

'Go ahead, tell him,' said Frank Lander.

'Nobody ever knew for sure,' said Phyllis, quietly.

'That's not true. Caroline English, for one. She knew for sure.'

Phyllis spoke: 'A few weeks before Bobbie had her baby she rang Caroline's doorbell in the middle of the night and asked Caroline if she could stay there. Naturally Caroline said yes, and she saw that Bobbie had nothing but a coat over her nightgown and had bruises all over her arms and shoulders. Julian was away, a lucky break because he'd have gone over and had a fight with Pete. As it was, Caroline made Bobbie have Dr English come out and have a look at her, and nothing more was said. I mean it, it was kept secret from everybody, especially Mr Hammersmith. But the story got out somehow. Not widespread, but we all heard about it.'

'We don't want it to get back to Mr Hammersmith,' said Mary Lander.

'He knows,' said Frank Lander.

'You keep saying that, but I don't believe he does,' said Mary.

'I don't either,' said Joe Whipple. 'Pete wouldn't be alive today if Phil Hammersmith knew.'

'That's where I think you're wrong,' said Phyllis. 'Mr Hammersmith might want to kill Pete, but killing him is another matter. And what earthly good would it do? The Hammersmiths have lost every penny, so I'm told, and at least with Pete still alive, Mrs McCrea supports Bobbie. Barely. But they have food and a roof over their heads.'

'Phil Hammersmith knows the whole damn story, you can bet anything on that. And it's why he's an old man all of a sudden. Have you seen him this trip, Jim?' said Frank Lander.

'I haven't seen him since the wedding.'

'Oh, well—' said Mary.

'You won't—' said Joe.

'You won't recognise him,' said Frank Lander. 'He's bent over—'

'They say he's had a stroke,' said Phyllis Whipple.

'And on top of everything else he got a lot of people sore at him by selling his bank stock to Ed Charney,' said Joe. 'Well, not a lot of people, but some that could have helped him. My old man, to name one. And I don't think that was so hot. Phil Hammersmith was a carpetbagger himself, and damn lucky to be in the bank. Then to sell his stock to a lousy stinking bootlegger . . . You should hear Harry Reilly on the subject.'

'I don't want to hear Harry Reilly on any subject,' said Frank Lander. 'Cheap Irish Mick.'

'I don't like him any better than you do, Frank, but call him something else,' I said.

'I'm sorry, Jim. I didn't mean that,' said Frank Lander.

'No. It just slipped out,' I said.

'I apologise,' said Frank Lander.

'Oh, all right.'

'Don't be sensitive, Jim,' said Mary.

'Stay out of it, Mary,' said Frank Lander.

'*Everybody* calm down,' said Joe. 'Everybody knows that Harry Reilly is a cheap Irish Mick, and nobody knows it better than Jim, an Irish Mick but not a cheap one. So shut the hell up, everybody.'

'Another country heard from,' said Phyllis.

'Now *you*, for Christ's sake,' said Joe. 'Who has the quart?'

'I have my quart,' said Frank Lander.

'I have mine,' I said.

'I asked who has mine. Phyllis?'

'When we get to the club, time enough,' said Phyllis.

'Hand it over,' said Joe.

'Three quarts of whiskey between five people. I'd like to know how we're going to get home tonight,' said Mary Lander.

'Drunk as a monkey, if you really want to know,' said Joe. 'Tight as a nun's.'

'Well, at least we're off the subject of Bobbie and Pete,' said Phyllis.

'I'm not. I was coming back to it. Phyllis. The quart,' said Joe.

'No,' said Phyllis.

'Here,' I said. 'And remember where it came from.' I handed him my bottle.

Joe took a swig in the corner of his mouth, swerving the car only slightly. 'Thanks,' he said, and returned the bottle. 'Now, Mary, if you'll light me a cigarette like a dear little second cousin.'

'Once removed,' said Mary Lander.

'Once removed, and therefore related to Bobbie through her mother.'

'No, *you* are but I'm not,' said Mary Lander.

'Well, you're in it some way, through me. Now for the benefit of those who are not related to Bobbie or Mrs Hammersmith, or Mary or me. Permit me to give you a little family history that will enlighten you on several points.'

'Is this going to be about Mr Hammersmith?' said Phyllis. 'I don't think you'd better tell that.'

'You're related only by marriage, so kindly keep your trap shut. If I want to tell it, I can.'

'Everybody remember that I asked him not to,' said Phyllis.

'Don't tell it, Joe, whatever it is,' said Mary Lander.

'Yeah, what's the percentage?' said Frank Lander. 'They have enough trouble without digging up past history.'

'Oh, you're so noble, Lander,' said Joe. 'You fool nobody.'

'If you're going to tell the story, go ahead, but stop insulting Frank,' said Mary Lander.

'We'll be at the club before he gets started,' said Phyllis.

'Then we'll sit there till I finish. Anyway, it doesn't take that long. So, to begin at the beginning. Phil Hammersmith. Phil Hammersmith came here before the war, just out of Lehigh.'

'You're not even telling it right,' said Phyllis.

'Phyllis is right. I'm screwing up my own story. Well, I'll begin again. Phil Hammersmith graduated from Lehigh, then a few years *later* he came to Gibbsville.'

'That's better,' said Phyllis.

'The local Lehigh contingent all knew him. He'd played lacrosse and he was a Sigma Nu around the time Mr Chew was there. So he already had friends in Gibbsville.'

'Now you're on the right track,' said Phyllis.

'Thank you, love,' said Joe.

'Where was he from originally?' I asked.

'Don't ask questions, Jim. It only throws me. He was from some place in New Jersey. So anyway he arrived in Gibbsville and got a job with the Coal & Iron Company. He was a civil engineer, and he had the job when he arrived. That is, he didn't come here looking for a job. He was hired before he got here.'

'You've made that plain,' said Phyllis.

'Well, it's important,' said Joe.

'Yes, but you don't have to say the same thing over and over again,' said Phyllis.

'Yes I do. Anyway, apparently the Coal & Iron people hired him on the strength of his record at Lehigh, plus asking a few questions of the local Lehigh contingent, that knew him, *plus* a very good recommendation he'd had from some firm in Bethlehem. Where he'd worked after getting out of college. But after he'd been here a while, and was getting along all right at the Coal & Iron, one day a construction engineer from New York arrived to talk business at the C. & I. Building. They took him down-cellar to the drafting-room and who should he see but Phil Hammersmith. But apparently

Phil didn't see him. Well, the New York guy was a real wet smack, because he tattled on Phil.

'Old Mr Duncan was general superintendent then and he sent for Phil. Was it true that Phil had once worked in South America, and if so, why hadn't he mentioned it when he applied for a job? Phil gave him the obvious answer. "Because if I had, you wouldn't have hired me." "Not necessarily," said Mr Duncan. "We might have accepted your explanation." "You say that now, but I tried telling the truth and I couldn't get a job." "Well, tell me the truth now," said Mr Duncan. "All right," said Phil. So he told Mr Duncan what had happened.

'He was working in South America. Peru, I think. Or maybe Bolivia. In the jungle. And the one thing they didn't want the natives, the Indians, to get hold of was firearms. But one night he caught a native carrying an armful of rifles from the shanty, and when Phil yelled at him, the native, ran, and Phil shot him. Killed him. The next day one of the other engineers was found with his throat cut. And the day after that the native chief came and called on the head man of the construction outfit. Either the Indians thought they'd killed the man that had killed their boy, or they didn't much care. But the chief told the white boss that the next time an Indian was killed, two white men would be killed. And not just killed. Tortured. Well, there were four or maybe five engineers, including Phil and the boss. The only white men in an area as big as Pennsylvania, and I guess they weighed their chances and being mathematicians, the odds didn't look so hot. So they quit. No hero stuff. They just quit. Except Phil. He was fired. The boss blamed Phil for everything and in his report to the New York office he put in a lot of stuff that just about fixed Phil for good. The boss, of course, was the same man that spotted Phil at the C. & I. drafting-room.'

'You told it very well,' said Phyllis.

'So any time you think of Phil Hammersmith killing Pete McCrea, it wouldn't be the first time,' said Joe.

'And the war,' I said. 'He probably killed a few Germans.'

'On the other hand, he never got over blaming himself for the other engineer's getting his throat cut,' said Joe. 'This is all the straight dope. Mr Duncan to my old man.'

We were used to engineers, their travels and adventures in far-off places, but engineers came and went and only a few became

fixtures in our life. Phil Hammersmith's story was all new to Mary
and Frank and me, and in the cold moonlight, as we sat in a
heated automobile in a snow-covered parking area of a Pennsylvania
country club, Joe Whipple had taken us to a dark South American
jungle, given us a touch of fear, and in a few minutes covered Phil
Hammersmith in mystery and then removed the mystery.

'Tell us more about Mr Hammersmith,' said Mary Lander.

Mary Lander. I had not had time to realise the inference that
must accompany my guess that Frank Lander was the one boy in
our crowd who had stayed with Bobbie. Mary Lander was the only
girl who had not fought off Pete McCrea. She was the last girl I
would have suspected of staying with Pete, and yet the one that
surprised me the least. She had always been the girl our mothers
liked us to take out, a kind of mothers' ideal for their sons, and
possibly even for themselves. Mary Morgan Lander was the third
generation of a family that had always been in the grocery business,
the only store in the county that sold caviar and English biscuits
and Sportsmen's Bracer chocolate, as well as the most expensive
domestic items of fruit, vegetables, and tinned goods. Her brother
Llewellyn Morgan still scooped out dried prunes and operated the
rotary ham slicer, but no one seriously believed that all the Morgan
money came from the store. Lew Morgan taught Sunday School
in the Methodist Episcopal Church and played basketball at the
Y.M.C.A., but he had been to Blair Academy and Princeton, and
his father had owned one of the first Pierce-Arrows in Gibbsville.
Mary had been unfairly judged a teaser, in previous years. She was
not a teaser, but a girl who would kiss a boy and allow him to
wander all over her body so long as he did not touch bare skin.
Nothing surprised me about Mary. It was in character for her to
have slapped Pete McCrea at a dinner party, and then to have let
him stay with her and to have discussed with him a swap of
husbands and wives. No casual dirty remark ever passed unnoticed
by Mary; when someone made a slip we would all turn to see how
Mary was taking it, and without fail she had heard it, understood
it, and taken a pious attitude. But in our crowd she was the one
person most conscious of sex and scatology. She was the only one
of whom I would say she had a dirty mind, but I kept that observation to myself along with my theory that she hated Frank Lander.
My theory, based on no information whatever, was that marriage

and Frank Lander had not been enough for her and that Pete
McCrea had become attractive to her because he was so awful.

'There's no more to tell,' said Joe Whipple. We got out of the
car and Mary took Joe's arm, and her evening was predictable:
fathers and uncles and older brothers would cut in on her, and
older women would comment as they always did that Mary Lander
was *such* a sensible girl, *so* considerate of her elders, a *wonderful* wife
to Frank. And we of her own age would dance with her because
under cover of the dancing crowd Mary would wrap both legs
around our right legs with a promise that had fooled us for years.
Quiet little Mary Lander, climbing up a boy's leg but never forgetting to smile her Dr Lyons smile at old Mrs Ginyan and old Mr
Heff. And yet through some mental process that I did not take time
to scrutinise, I was less annoyed with Mary than I had been since
we were children. I was determined not to dance with her, and I
did not, but my special knowledge about her and Pete McCrea
reduced her power to allure. Bobbie had married Pete McCrea and
she was still attractive in spite of it; but Mary's seductiveness
vanished with the revelation that she had picked Pete as her lover,
if only for once, twice, or how many times. I had never laughed at
Mary before, but now she was the fool, not we, not I.

I got quite plastered at the dance, and so did a lot of other people.
On the way home we sang a little—'Body and Soul' was the song,
but Phyllis was the only one who could sing the middle part
truly—and Frank Lander tried to tell about an incident in the
smoking-room, where Julian English apparently had thrown a drink
in Harry Reilly's face. It did not seem worth making a fuss about,
and Frank never finished his story. Mary Lander attacked me: 'You
never danced with me, not once,' she said.

'I didn't?'

'No, you didn't, and you know you didn't,' she said. 'And you
always do.'

'Well, this time I guess I didn't.'

'Well, *why* didnt you?'

'Because he didn't want to,' said Frank Lander. 'You're making
a fool of yourself. I should think you'd have more pride.'

'Yeah, why don't you have more pride, Mary?' said Joe Whipple.
'You'd think it was an honor to dance with this Malloy guy.'

'It is,' I said.

'That's it. You're getting so conceited,' said Mary. 'Well, I'm sure I didn't have to sit any out.'

'Then why all the fuss?' said Frank Lander.

'Such popularity must be deserved,' I said, quoting an advertising slogan.

'Whose? Mary's or yours?' said Phyllis.

'Well, I was thinking of Mary's, but now that you mention it . . .' I said.

'How many times did he dance with *you*, Phyllis?' said Joe.

'Three or four,' said Phyllis.

'In that case, Frank, Jim has insulted your wife. I don't see any other way out of it. You have to at least slap his face. Shall I stop the car?'

'My little trouble-maker,' said Phyllis.

'Come on, let's have a fight,' said Joe. 'Go ahead, Frank. Give him a punch in the nose.'

'Yeah, like you did at the Dam, Frank,' I said.

'Oh, God. I remember that awful night,' said Phyllis. 'What did you fight over?'

'Bobbie,' I said.

'Bobbie was the cause of *more* fights,' said Mary Lander.

'Well, we don't need her to fight over now. We have you,' said Joe. 'Your honor's been attacked and your husband wants to defend it. The same as I would if Malloy hadn't danced with *my* wife. It's a good thing you danced with Phyllis, Malloy, or you and I'd get out of this car and start slugging.'

'Why did you fight over Bobbie? I don't remember that,' said Mary.

'Because she came to the picnic with Jim and then went off necking with Frank,' said Phyllis. 'I remember the whole thing.'

'Stop *talking* about fighting and let's *fight*,' said Joe.

'All right, stop the car,' I said.

'Now you're talking,' said Joe.

'Don't be ridiculous,' said Phyllis.

'Oh, shut up,' said Joe. He pulled up on the side of the road. 'I'll referee.' He got out of the car, and so did Frank and I and Phyllis. 'All right, put up your dukes.' We did so, moved around a bit in the snow and slush. 'Go on, mix it,' said Joe, whereupon Frank rushed me and hit me on the left cheek. All blows were directed at the head, since all three of us were armored in coonskin coats. 'That was a good one, Frank, Now go get him, Jim.' I swung my right hand and caught Frank's left eye, and at that moment we were all splashed by slush, taken completely by surprise as Phyllis, whom we had forgotten, drove the car away.

'That bitch!' said Joe. He ran to the car and got hold of a door handle but she increased her speed and he fell in the snow. 'God damn that bitch, I should have known she was up to something. Now what? Let's try to bum a ride.' The fight, such as it was, was over, and we tried to flag down cars on their way home from the dance. We recognised many of them, but not one would stop.

'Well, thanks to you, we've got a nice three-mile walk to Swedish Haven,' said Frank Lander.

'Oh, she'll be back,' said Joe.

'I'll bet you five bucks she's not,' I said.

'Well, I won't bet, but I'll be damned if I'm going to walk three miles. I'm just going to wait till we can bum a ride.'

'If you don't keep moving you'll freeze,' said Frank.

'We're nearer the club than we are Swedish Haven. Let's go back there,' I said.

'And have my old man see me?' said Joe.

'Your old man went home hours ago,' I said.

'Well, somebody'll see me,' said Joe.

'Listen, half the club's seen you already, and they wouldn't even stop,' I said.

'Who has a cigarette?' said Joe.

'Don't give him one,' said Frank.

'I have no intention of giving him one,' I said. 'Let's go back to the club. My feet are soaking wet.'

'So are mine,' said Frank. We were wearing pumps, and our feet had been wet since we got out of the car.

'That damn Phyllis, she knows I just got over a cold,' said Joe.

'Maybe that's why she did it,' I said. 'It'd serve you right if you got pneumonia.'

We began to walk in the middle of the road, in the direction of the clubhouse, which we could see, warm and comfortable on top of a distant plateau. 'That old place never looked so good,' said Joe. 'Let's spend the night there.'

'The rooms are all taken. The orchestra's staying there,' I said.

We walked about a mile, our feet getting sorer at every step, and the combination of exhaustion and the amount we had had to drink made even grumbling an effort. Then a Dodge touring car, becurtained, stopped about fifty yards from us and a spotlight was turned on each of our faces. A man in a short overcoat and fur-lined cap came toward us. He was a State Highway patrolman. 'What happened to you fellows?' he said. 'You have a wreck?'

'I married one,' said Joe.

'Oh, a weisscrackah,' said the patrolman, a Pennsylvania Dutchman. 'Where's your car?'

'We got out to take a leak and my wife drove off with it,' said Joe.

'You from the dance at the gulf club?'

'Yes,' said Joe. 'How about giving us a lift?'

'Let me see you' driwah's license,' said the cop.

Joe took out his billfold and handed over the license. 'So? From Lantenengo Street yet? All right, get in. Whereabouts you want to go to?'

'The country club,' said Joe.

'The hell with that,' said Frank. 'Let's go on to Gibbsville.'

'This aint no taxi service,' said the cop. 'And I aint taking you to no Gippsfille. I'm on my way to my substation. Swedish Haven. You can phone there for a taxi. Privileged characters, you think you are. A bunch of drunks, you ask me.'

I had to go back to New York on the morning train and the events of the next few days, so far as they concerned Joe and Phyllis Whipple and Frank and Mary Lander, were obscured by the suicide, a day or two later, of Julian English, the man who had thrown a drink at Harry Reilly. The domestic crisis of the Whipples and the Landers and even the McCreas seemed very unimportant. And yet when I heard about English, who had not been getting along with his wife, I wondered about my own friends, people my own age but not so very much younger than Julian and Caroline English. English had danced with Phyllis and Mary that night, and now he was dead. I knew very little about the causes of the difficulties between him and Caroline, but they could have been no worse than the problems that existed in Bobbie's marriage and that threatened the marriage of Frank and Mary Lander. I was shocked and saddened by the English suicide; he was an attractive man whose shortcomings seemed out of proportion to the magnitude of killing himself. He had not been a friend of mine, only an acquaint-ance with whom I had had many drinks and played some golf; but friends of mine, my closest friends in the world, boys-now-men like myself, were at the beginning of the same kind of life and doing the same kind of thing that for Julian English ended in a sealed-up garage with a motor running. I hated what I thought those next few days and weeks. There is nothing young about killing oneself, no matter when it happens, and I hated this being deprived of the sweetness of youth. And that was what it was, that was what was happening to us. I, and I think the others, had looked upon our squabbles as unpleasant incidents but belonging to our youth. Now they were plainly recognisable as symptoms of life without youth, without youth's excuses or youth's recoverability. I wanted to love someone, and during the next year or two I confused the desperate need for love with love itself. I had put a hopeless love out of my life; but that is not part of this story, except to state it and thus to show that I knew what I was looking for.

2.

When you have grown up with someone it is much easier to fill in gaps of five years, ten years, in which you do not see him, than to supply those early years in the life of a friend you meet in maturity. I do not know why this is so, unless it is a mere matter of insufficient time. With the friends of later life you may exchange boyhood stories that seem worth telling, but boyhood is not all stories. It is mostly not stories, but day-to-day, unepisodic living. And most of us are too polite to burden our later-life friends with unexciting anecdotes about people they will never meet. (Likewise we hope they will not burden us.) But it is easy to bring old friends up to date in your mental dossiers by the addition of a few vital facts. Have they stayed married? Have they had many more children? Have they made money or lost it? Usually the basic facts will do, and then you tell yourself that Joe Whipple is still Joe Whipple, plus two sons, a new house, a hundred thousand dollars, forty pounds, bifocals, fat in the neck, and a new concern for the state of the nation.

Such additions I made to my friends' dossiers as I heard about them from time to time; by letters from them, conversations with my mother, an occasional newspaper clipping. I received these facts with joy for the happy news, sorrow for the sad, and immediately went about my business, which was far removed from any business of theirs. I seldom went back to Gibbsville during the Thirties—mine and the century's—and when I did I stayed only long enough to stand at a grave, to toast a bride, to spend a few minutes beside a sickbed. In my brief encounters with my old friends I got no information about Bobbie and Pete McCrea, and only after I had returned to New York or California would I remember that I had intended to inquire about them.

There is, of course, some significance in the fact that no one volunteered information about Bobbie and Pete. It was that they had disappeared. They continued to live in Gibbsville, but in parts of the town that were out of the way for their old friends. There is no town so small that that cannot happen, and Gibbsville, a third-class city, was large enough to have all the grades of poverty and wealth and the many half grades in between, in which $10 a month in the husband's income could make a difference in the kind and location of the house in which he lived. No one had volunteered any information about Bobbie and Pete, and I had not remembered to inquire. In five years I had had no new facts about them, none whatever, and their disappearance from my ken might have continued but for a broken shoelace.

I was in Gibbsville for a funeral, and the year was 1938. I had broken a shoelace, it was evening and the stores were closed, and I was about to drive back to New York. The only place open that might have shoelaces was a poolroom that in my youth had had a two-chair bootblack stand. The poolroom was in a shabby section near the railroad stations and a couple of cheap hotels, four or five saloons, an automobile tire agency, a barber shop, and a quick-lunch counter. I opened the poolroom door, saw that the bootblack's chairs were still there, and said to the man behind the cigar counter: 'Have you got any shoelaces?'

'Sorry I can't help you, Jim,' said the man. He was wearing an eyeshade, but as soon as he spoke I recognised Pete McCrea.

'Pete, for God's sake,' I said. We shook hands.

'I thought you might be in town for the funeral,' he said. 'I should have gone, too, I guess, but I decided I wouldn't. It was nice of you to make the trip.'

'Well, you know. He was a friend of my father's. Do you own this place?'

'I run it. I have a silent partner, Bill Charney. You remember

Ed Charney? His younger brother. I don't know where to send you
to get a shoelace.'

'The hell with the shoelace. How's Bobbie?'

'Oh, Bobbie's fine. *You* know. A lot of changes, but this is better
than nothing. Why don't you call her up? She'd love to hear from
you. We're living out on Mill Street, but we have a phone. Call her
up and say hello. The number is 3385-J. If you have time maybe
you could go see her. I have to stay here till I close up at one
o'clock, but she's home.'

'What number on Mill Street? You call her up and tell her I'm
coming? Is that all right?'

'Hell, yes.'

Someone thumped the butt of a cue on the floor and called out:
'Rack 'em up, Pete?'

'I have to be here. You go on out and I'll call her up,' he said.
'Keep your shirt on,' he said to the pool player, then to me: 'It's
402 Mill Street, across from the open hearth, second house from
the corner. I guess I won't see you again, but I'm glad we had a
minute. You're looking very well.' I could not force a comment on
his appearance. His nose was red and larger, his eyes watery, the
dewlaps sagging, and he was wearing a blue denim work shirt with
a dirty leather bow tie.

'Think I could get in the Ivy Club if I went back to Princeton?'
he said. 'I didn't make it the first time around, but now I'm a big
shot. So long, Jim. Nice to've seen you.'

The open hearth had long since gone the way of all the mill
equipment; the mill itself had been inactive for years, and as a
residential area the mill section was only about a grade and a half
above the poorest Negro slums. But in front of most of the houses
in the McCreas' row there were cared-for plots; there always had
been, even when the mill was running and the air was full of smoke
and acid. It was an Irish and Polish neighborhood, but knowledge
of that fact did not keep me from locking all the doors of my car.
The residents of the neighborhood would not have touched my
father's car, but this was not his car and I was not he.

The door of Number 402 opened as soon as I closed my car door.
Bobbie waited for me to lock up and when I got to the porch, she
said: '*Jim*. Jim, Jim, Jim. How nice. I'm so glad to see you.' She
quickly closed the door behind me and then kissed me. 'Give me a
real kiss and a real hug. I didn't dare while the door was open.' I

kissed her and held her for a moment and then she said: 'Hey, I guess we'd better cut this out.'

'Yes,' I said. 'It's nice, though.'

'Haven't done that since we were—God!' She stood away and looked at me. 'You could lose some weight, but you're not so bad. How about a bottle of beer? Or would you rather have some cheap whiskey?'

'What are you drinking?'

'Cheap whiskey, but I'm used to it,' she said.

'Let's both have some cheap whiskey,' I said.

'Straight? With Water? Or how?'

'Oh, a small slug of whiskey and a large slug of water in it. I'm driving back to New York tonight.'

She went to the kitchen and prepared the drinks. I recognised some of the furniture from the Hammersmith and McCrea houses. 'Brought together by a shoestring,' she said. 'Here's to it. How do I look?'

'If you want my frank and candid opinion, good enough to go right upstairs and make up for the time we lost. Pete won't be home till one o'clock.'

'If then,' she said. 'Don't think I wouldn't, but it's too soon after my baby. Didn't Pete tell you I finally produced a healthy son?'

'No.'

'You'll hear him in a little while. We have a daughter, two years old, and now a son. Angus McCrea, Junior. Seven pounds two ounces at birth.'

'Good for you,' I said.

'Not so damn good for me, but it's over, and he's healthy.'

'And what about your mother and father?' I said.

'Oh, poor Jim. You didn't know? Obviously you didn't, and you're going to be so sorry you asked. Daddy committed suicide two years ago. He shot himself. And Mother's in Swedish Haven.' Swedish Haven was local lore for the insane asylum. 'I'm sorry I had to tell you.'

'God, why won't they lay off you?' I said.

'Who is they? Oh, you mean just—life?'

'Yes.'

'I don't know, Jim,' she said. 'I've had about as much as I can stand, or so I keep telling myself. But I must be awfully tough, because there's always something else, and I go right on. Will you let me complain for just a minute, and then I'll stop? The only one of the old crowd I ever see is Phyllis. She comes out and never forgets to bring a bottle, so we get tight together. But some things we don't discuss, Phyllis and I. Pete is a closed subject.'

'What's he up to?'

'Oh, he has his women. I don't even know who they are any more, and couldn't care less. Just as long as he doesn't catch a disease. I told him that, so he's been careful about it.' She sat up straight. 'I haven't been the soul of purity, either, but it's Pete's son. Both children are Pete's. But I haven't been withering on the vine.'

'Why should you?'

'That's what *I* said. Why should I have nothing? Nothing? The children are mine, and I love them, but I need more than that, Jim. Children don't love you back. All they do is depend on you to feed them and wash them and all the rest of it. But after they're in bed for the night —I never know whether Pete will be home at two o'clock or not at all. So I've had two tawdry romances, I guess you'd call them. Not you, but Mrs McCrea would.'

'Where is dear Mrs McCrea?'

'She's living in Jenkintown, with an old maid sister. Thank heaven they can't afford carfare, so I'm spared that.'

'Who are your gentlemen friends?'

'Well, the first was when we were living on the East Side. A gentleman by the name of Bill Charney. Yes, Ed's brother and Pete's partner. I was crazy about him. Not for one single minute in love with him, but I never even thought about love with him. He wanted to marry me, too, but I was a nasty little snob. I *couldn't* marry Bill Charney, Jim. I just couldn't. So he married a nice little Irish girl and they're living on Lantenengo Street in the house that used to belong to old Mr Duncan. And I'm holding court on Mill Street, thirty dollars a month rent.'

'Do you want some money?'

'Will you give me two hundred dollars?'

'More than that, if you want it.'

'No, I'd just like to have two hundred dollars to hide, to keep in case of emergency.'

'In case of emergency, you can always send me a telegram in care of my publisher.' I gave her $200.

'Thank you. Now I have some money. For the last five or six

years I haven't had any money of my own. You don't care how I spend this, do you?'

'As long as you spend it on yourself.'

'I've gotten so stingy I probably won't spend any of it. But this is wonderful. Now I can read the ads and say to myself I could have some expensive lingerie. I think I will get a permanent, next month.'

'Is that when you'll be back in circulation again?'

'Good guess. Yes, about a month,' she said. 'But not the same man. I didn't tell you about the second one. You don't know him. He came here after you left Gibbsville. His name is McCormick and he went to Princeton with Pete. They sat next to each other in a lot of classes, McC, McC, and he was sent here to do some kind of an advertising survey and ran into Pete. They'd never been exactly what you'd call pals, but they *knew* each other and Mac took one look and sized up the situation and—well, I thought, why not? He wasn't as exciting as Mr Charney, but at one time I would have married him. *If* he'd asked me. He doesn't live here any more.'

'But you've got the next one picked out?'

'No, but I know there will be a next one. Why lie to myself? And why lie to you? I don't think I ever have.'

'Do you ever see Frank?'

'Frank? Frank Lander? What made you think of him?'

'Bobbie,' I said.

'Oh, of course. That was a guess of yours, a long time ago,' she said. 'No, I never see Frank.' She was smoking a cigarette, and sitting erect with her elbow on the arm of her chair, holding the cigarette high and with style. If her next words had been 'Jeeves, have the black Rolls brought round at four o'clock' she would not have been more naturally grand. But her next words were: 'I haven't even thought about Frank. There was another boy, Johnny White, the one I was engaged to. *Engaged to*. That close to spending the rest of my life with him—or at least part of it. But because he wanted me to go away with him before we were married, I broke the engagement and married Pete.'

'Is that all it was? That he wanted you to go away with him?'

'That's really all it was. I got huffy and said he couldn't really love me if he wanted to take that risk. Not that we hadn't been taking risks, but a pre-marital trip, that was something else again. My five men, Jim. Frank. Johnny. Bill and Mac. And Pete.'

'Why didn't you and Frank ever get engaged?'

'I wonder. I *have* thought about *that*, so I was wrong when I said I never think of Frank. But Frank in the old days, not Frank now. What may have happened was that Frank was the only boy I'd gone all the way with, and then I got scared because I didn't want to give up the fun, popularity, good times. Jim, I have a confession to make. About you.'

'Oh?'

'I told Frank I'd stayed with you. He wouldn't believe he was my first and he kept harping on it, so I really got rid of Frank by telling him you were the first.'

'Why me?'

'Because the first time I ever stayed with Frank, or anybody, it was at a picnic at the Dam, and I'd gone to the picnic with you. So you were the logical one.'

'Did you tell him that night?'

'No. Later. Days later. But you had a fight with him that night, and the fight made it all the more convincing.'

'Well, thanks, little pal,' I said.

'Oh, you don't care, do you?'

'No, not really.'

'You had Kitty, after all,' she said. 'Do you ever see Kitty?'

'No. Kitty lives in Cedarhurst and they keep to themselves, Cedarhurst people.'

'What was your wife like?'

'She was nice. Pretty. Wanted to be an actress. I still see her once in a while, I like her, and always will, but if ever there were two people that shouldn't have got married . . .'

'I can name two others,' said Bobbie.

'You and Pete. But you've stuck to him.'

'Don't be polite. I'm stuck with him. Can you imagine what Pete would be like if I left him?'

'Well, to be brutally frank, what's he like anyway? You don't have to go on paying for a dirty trick the rest of your life.'

'It wasn't just a dirty trick. It would have been a dirty trick if I'd walked out on him the day we were getting married. But I went through with it, and that made it more than a dirty trick. I *should have* walked out on him, the day we got married. I even tried. And he'd have recovered—then. Don't forget, Pete McCrea was used to dirty tricks being played on him, and he might have got over it if

I'd left him at the church. But once I'd married him, he became a different person, took himself much more seriously, and so did everyone else. They began to dislike him, but that was better than being laughed at.' She sipped her drink.

'Well, who did it? I did. Your little pal,' she said. 'How about some more cheap whiskey?'

'No thanks, but you go ahead,' I said.

'The first time I ever knew there *was* a Mill Street was the day we rented this house,' she said, as she poured herself a drink. 'I'd never been out this way before.'

'You couldn't have lived here when the mill was operating. The noise and the smoke.'

'I can live anywhere,' she said. 'So can anyone else. And don't be too surprised if you find us back on Lantenengo. Do you know the big thing nowadays? Slot machines and the numbers racket. Pete wants to get into The Numbers, but he hasn't decided how to go about it. Bill Charney is the kingpin in the county, although not the real head. It's run by a syndicate in Jersey City.'

'Don't let him do it, Bobbie,' I said. 'Really don't.'

'Why not? He's practically in it already. He has slot machines in the poolroom, and that's where people call up to find out what number won today. He might as well be in it.'

'No.'

'It's the only way Pete will ever have any money, and if he ever gets his hands on some money, maybe he'll divorce me. Then I could take the children and go away somewhere. California.'

'That's a different story. If you're planning it that way. But stay out of The Numbers if you ever have any idea of remaining respectable. You cant just go in for a few years and then quit.'

'Respectable? Do you think my son's going to be able to get into Princeton? His father is the proprietor of a poolroom, and they're going to know that when Angus gets older. Pete will never be anything else. He's found his niche. But if I took the children to California they might have a chance. And *I* might have a chance, before it's too late. It's our only hope, Jim. Phyllis agrees with me.'

I realised that I would be arguing against a hope and a dream, and if she had that much left, and only that much, I had no right to argue. She very nearly followed my thinking. 'It's what I live on, Jim,' she said. 'That—and this'. She held up her glass. 'And a little admiration. A little—admiration. Phyllis wants to give me a trip to New York. Would you take us to "21" and those places?'

. 'Sure.'

'Could you get someone for Phyllis?'

'I think so. Sure. Joe wouldn't go on this trip?'

'And give up a chance to be with Mary Lander?'

'So now it's Joe and Mary?'

'Oh, that's old hat in Gibbsville. They don't even pretend otherwise.'

'And Frank? What about him?'

'Frank is the forgotten man. If there were any justice he ought to pair off with Phyllis, but they don't like each other. Phyllis calls Frank a wishy-washy namby-pamby, and Frank calls Phyllis a drunken trouble-maker. We've all grown up, Jim. Oh, haven't we just? Joe doesn't like Phyllis to visit me because Mary says all we do is gossip. Although how she'd know *what* we do . . .'

'They were all at the funeral, and I thought what a dull, stuffy little group they've become,' I said.

'But that's what they are,' said Bobbie. 'Very stuffy and very dull. What else is there for them to do? If I were still back there with them I'd be just as bad. Maybe worse. In a way, you know, Pete McCrea has turned out to be the most interesting man in our old crowd, present company excepted. Joe was a very handsome young man and so was Frank, and their families had lots of money and all the rest of it. But you saw Joe and Frank today. I haven't seen them lately, but Joe looks like a professional wrestler and I remember how hairy he was, all over his chest and back and his arms and legs. And Frank just the opposite, skin like a girl's and slender, but now we could almost call *him* Ichabod. He looks like a cranky schoolteacher, and his glasses make him look like an owl. Mary, of course, beautifully dressed I'm sure, and not looking a day older.'

'Several days older, but damn good-looking,' I said.

A baby cried and Bobbie made no move. 'That's my daughter. Teething. Now she'll wake up my son and you're in for a lot of howling.' The son began to cry, and Bobbie excused herself. She came back in a few minutes with the infant in her arms. 'It's against my rules to pick them up, but I wanted to show him to you. Isn't he an ugly little creature? The answer is yes.' She took him away and returned with the daughter. 'She's begun to have a face.'

'Yes, I can see that. Your face, for which she can be thankful.'

'Yes, I wouldn't want a girl to look like Pete. It doesn't matter so much with a boy.' She took the girl away and when she rejoined me she refilled her glass.

'Are you sorry you didn't have children?' she said.

'Not the way it turned out, I'm not,' I said.

'These two haven't had much of a start in life, the poor little things. They haven't even been christened. Do you know why? There was nobody we could ask to be their godfathers.' Her eyes filled with tears. 'That was when I really saw what we'd come to.'

'Bobbie, I've got a four-hour drive ahead of me, so I think I'd better get started.'

'Four hours to New York? In that car?'

'I'm going to stop and have a sandwich halfway.'

'I could give you a sandwich and make some coffee.'

'I don't want it now, thanks.'

We looked at each other. 'I'd like to show how much I appreciate your coming out to see me,' she said. 'But it's probably just as well I can't. But I'll be all right in New York, Jim. That is, if I ever get there. I won't believe that, either, till I'm on the train.'

If she came to New York I did not know about it, and during the war years Bobbie and her problems receded from my interest. I heard that Pete was working in a defense plant, from which I inferred that he had not made the grade in the numbers racket. Frank Lander was in the Navy, Joe Whipple in the War Production Board, and by the time the war was over I discovered that so many other people and things had taken the place of Gibbsville in my thoughts that I had almost no active curiosity about the friends of my youth. I had even had a turnover in my New York friendships. I had married again, I was working hard, and most of my social life originated with my wife's friends. I was making, for me, quite a lot of money, and I was a middle-aged man whose physician had made some honest, unequivocal remarks about my life expectancy. It took a little time and one illness to make me realise that if I wanted to see my child grow to maturity, I had to retire from night life. It was not nearly so difficult as I had always anticipated it would be.

After I became reconciled to middle age and the quieter life I made another discovery: that the sweetness of my early youth was a persistent and enduring thing, so long as I kept it at the distance of years. Moments would come back to me, of love and excitement and music and laughter that filled my breast as they had thirty years earlier. It was not nostalgia, which only means homesickness, nor was it a wish to be living that excitement again. It was a splendid contentment with the knowledge that once I had felt those things so deeply and well that the throbbing urging of George Gershwin's 'Do It Again' could evoke the original sensation and the pictures that went with it: a tea dance at the club and a girl in a long black satin dress and my furious jealousy of a fellow who wore a yellow foulard tie. I wanted none of it ever again, but all I had I wanted to keep. I could remember precisely the tone in which her brother had said to her: 'Are you coming or aren't you?' and the sounds of his galoshes after she said: 'I'm going home with Mr Malloy.' They were the things I knew before we knew everything, and, I suppose, before we began to learn. There was always a girl, and nearly always there was music; if the Gershwin tune belonged to that girl, a Romberg tune belonged to another and 'When Hearts Are Young' became a personal anthem, enduringly sweet and safe from all harm, among the protected memories. In middle age I was proud to have lived according to my emotions at the right time, and content to live that way vicariously and at a distance. I had missed almost nothing, escaped very little, and at fifty I had begun to devote my energy and time to the last, simple but big task of putting it all down as well as I knew how.

In the midst of putting it all down, as novels and short stories and plays, I would sometimes think of Bobbie McCrea and the dinginess of her history. But as the reader will presently learn, the 'they'—life—that had once made me cry out in anger, were not through with her yet. (Of course 'they' are never through with anyone while he still lives, and we are not concerned here with the laws of compensation that seem to test us, giving us just enough strength to carry us in another trial.) I like to think that Bobbie got enough pleasure out of a pair of nylons, a permanent wave, a bottle of Phyllis Whipple's whiskey, to recharge the brightness in her. As we again take up her story I promise the reader a happy ending, if only because I want it that way. It happens also to be the true ending. . . .

Pete McCrea did not lose his job at the end of the war. His Princeton degree helped there. He had gone into the plant, which specialised in aluminum extrusion, as a manual laborer, but his

IBM card revealed that he had taken psychology courses in college, and he was transferred to Personnel. It seemed an odd choice, but it is not hard to imagine that Pete was better fitted by his experience as a poolroom proprietor than as a two-year student of psychology. At least he spoke both languages, he liked the work, and in 1945 he was not bumped by a returning veteran.

Fair Grounds, the town in which the plant was situated, was only three miles from Gibbsville. For nearly a hundred years it had been the trading center for the Pennsylvania Dutch farmers in the area, and its attractions had been Becker's general store, the Fair Grounds Bank, the freight office of the Reading Railway, the Fair Grounds Hotel, and five Protestant churches. Clerks at Becker's and at the bank and the Reading, and bartenders at the hotel and the pastors of the churches, all had to speak Pennsylvania Dutch. English was desirable but not a requirement. The town was kept scrubbed, dusted and painted, and until the erection of the aluminum plant, jobs and trades were kept in the same families. An engineman's son worked as water-boy until he was old enough to take the examinations for brakeman; a master mechanic would give his boy calipers for Christmas. There were men and women in Fair Grounds who visited Gibbsville only to serve on juries or to undergo surgery at the Gibbsville Hospital. There were some men and women who had never been to Gibbsville at all and regarded Gibbsville as some Gibbsville citizens regarded Paris, France. That was the pre-aluminum Fair Grounds.

To this town in 1941 went Pete and Bobbie McCrea. They rented a house no larger than the house on Mill Street but cleaner and in better repair. Their landlord and his wife went to live with his mother-in-law, and collected the $50 legally frozen monthly rent and $50 side payment for the use of the radio and the gas stove. But in spite of under-the-table and black-market prices Pete and Bobbie McCrea were financially better off than they had been since their marriage, and nylons at black-market prices were preferable to the no nylons she had had on Mill Street. The job, and the fact that he continued to hold it, restored some respectability to Pete, and they discussed rejoining the club. 'Don't try it, I warn you,' said Phyllis Whipple. 'The club isn't run by your friends any more. Now it's been taken over by people that couldn't have got in ten years ago.'

'Well, we'd have needed all our old friends to go to bat for us,

and I guess some would think twice about it,' said Pete. 'So we'll
do our drinking at the Tavern.'

The Dan Patch Tavern, which was a new name for the renovated
Fair Grounds Hotel bar, was busy all day and all night, and it was
one of the places where Pete could take pleasure in his revived
respectability. It was also one of the places where Bobbie could
count on getting that little admiration that she needed to live on.
On the day of Pearl Harbor she was only thirty-four years old and
at the time of the Japanese, surrender she was only thirty-eight.
She was accorded admiration in abundance. Some afternoons just
before the shift changed she would walk the three blocks to the
Tavern and wait for Pete. The bartender on duty would say 'Hi,
Bobbie,' and bring her currently favorite drink to her booth. Sometimes there would be four men sitting with her when Pete arrived
from the plant; she was never alone for long. If one man tried to
persuade her to leave, and became annoyingly insistent, the
bartenders came to her rescue. The bartenders and the proprietor
knew that in her way Bobbie was as profitable as the juke box. She
was an attraction. She was a good-looking broad who was not a
whore or a falling-down lush, and all her drinks were paid for. She
was the Tavern's favorite customer, male or female, and if she had
given the matter any thought she could have been declared in. All
she wanted in return was a steady supply of Camels and protection
from being mauled. The owner of the Tavern. Rudy Schau, was
the only one who was aware that Bobbie and Pete had once lived
on Lantenengo Street in Gibbsville, but far from being impressed
by their background, he had a German opinion of aristocrats who
had lost standing. He was actively suspicious of Bobbie in the
beginning, but in time he came to accept her as a wife whose
independence he could not condone and a good-looking woman
whose morals he had not been able to condemn. And she was good
for business. Beer business was good, but at Bobbie's table nobody
drank beer, and the real profit was in the hard stuff.

In the Fair Grounds of the pre-aluminum days Bobbie would
have had few women friends. No decent woman would have gone
to a saloon every day—or any day. She most likely would have
received warnings from the Ku Klux Klan, which was concerned
with personal conduct in a town that had only a dozen Catholic
families, no Negroes and no Jews. But when the aluminum plant
(which was called simply The Aluminum or The Loomy) went

into war production the population of Fair Grounds immediately doubled and the solid Protestant character of the town was changed in a month. Eight hundred new people came to town and they lived in apartments in a town where there were no apartments: in rooms in private houses, in garages and old stables, in rented rooms and haylofts out in the farming area. The newcomers wasted no time with complaints of double-rent, inadequate heating, holes in the roof, insufficient sanitation. The town was no longer scrubbed, dusted or painted, and thousands of man-hours were lost while a new shift waited for the old to vacate parking space in the streets of the town. Bobbie and Pete were among the lucky early ones: they had a house. That fact of itself gave Bobbie some distinction. The house had two rooms and kitchen on the first floor, three rooms and bath on the second, and it had a cellar and an attic. In the identical houses on both sides there were a total of four families and six roomers. As a member of Personnel it was one of Pete's duties to find housing for workers, but Bobbie would have no roomers. 'The money wouldn't do us much good, so let's live like human beings,' she said.

'You mean there's nothing to buy with the money,' said Pete. 'But we could save it.'

'If we had it, we'd spend it. You've never saved a cent in your life and neither have I. If you're thinking of the children's education, buy some more war bonds and have it taken out of your pay. But I'm not going to share my bathroom with a lot of dirty men. I'd have to do all the extra work, not you.'

'You could make a lot of money doing their laundry. Fifty cents a shirt.'

'Are you serious?'

'No.'

'It's a good thing you're not, because I could tell you how else I could make a lot more money.'

'Yes, a lot more,' said Pete.

'Well, then, keep your ideas to yourself. I won't have boarders and I won't do laundry for fifty cents a shirt. That's final.'

And so Bobbie had her house, she got the admiration she needed, and she achieved a moderate popularity among the women of her neighborhood by little friendly acts that came spontaneously out of her friendly nature. There was a dinginess to the new phase: the house was not much, the men who admired her and the women who welcomed her help were the ill-advantaged, the cheap, the vulgar, and sometimes the evil. But the next step down from Mill Street would have been hopeless degradation, and the next step up, Fair Grounds, was at least up. She was envied for her dingy house, and when Pete called her the Queen of the Klondike she was not altogether displeased. There was envy in the epithet, and in the envy was the first sign of respect he had shown her in ten years. He had never suspected her of an affair with Mac McCormick, and if he had suspected her during her infatuation with Bill Charney he had been afraid to make an accusation; afraid to anticipate his own feelings in the event that Charney would give him a job in The Numbers. When Charney brought in a Pole from Detroit for the job Pete had wanted, Pete accepted $1,000 for his share of the poolroom and felt only grateful relief. Charney did not always buy out his partners, and Pete refused to wonder if the money and the easy dissolution of the partnership had been paid for by Bobbie. It was not a question he wanted to raise, and when the war in Europe created jobs at Fair Grounds he believed that his luck had begun to change.

Whatever the state of Pete's luck, the pace of his marriage had begun to change. The pace of his marriage—and not his alone—was set by the time he spent at home and what he did during that time. For ten years he had spent little more time at home than was necessary for sleeping and eating. He could not sit still in the same room with Bobbie, and even after the children were born he did not like to have her present during the times he would play with them. He would arrive in a hurry to have his supper, and in a short time he would get out of the house, to be with a girl, to go back to work at the poolroom. He was most conscious of time when he was near Bobbie; everywhere else he moved slowly, spoke deliberately, answered hesitantly. But after the move to Fair Grounds he spent more time in the house, with the children, with Bobbie. He would sit in the front room, doing paper work from the plant, while Bobbie sewed. At the Tavern he would say to Bobbie: 'It's time we were getting home.' He no longer darted in and out of the house and ate his meals rapidly and in silence.

He had a new girl. Martha—'Martie'—Klinger was a typist at the plant, a Fair Grounds woman whose husband was in the Coast Guard at Lewes, Delaware. She was Bobbie's age and likewise had two children. She retained a young prettiness in the now round face and her figure had not quite reached the stage of plumpness. Sometimes when she moved an arm the flesh of her breast seemed to go all the way up to her neckline, and she had been one of the inspirations for a plant memo to women employees, suggesting that tight sweaters and tight slacks were out of place in wartime industry. Pete brought her to the Tavern one day after work, and she never took her eyes off Bobbie. She looked up and down, up and down, with her mouth half open as though she were listening to Bobbie through her lips. She showed no animosity of a defensive nature and was not openly possessive of Pete, but Bobbie knew on sight that she was Pete's new girl. After several sessions at the Tavern Bobbie could tell which of the men had already slept with Martie and which of them were likely to again. It was impossible to be jealous of Martie, but it was just as impossible not to feel superior to her. Pete, the somewhat changed Pete, kept up the absurd pretense that Martie was just a girl from the plant whom he happened to bring along for a drink, and there was no unpleasantness until one evening Martie said: 'Jesus, I gotta go or I won't get any supper.'

'Come on back to our house and have supper with us,' said Pete. 'That's okay by you, isn't it, Bobbie?'

'No, it isn't,' said Bobbie.

'Rudy'll give us a steak and we can cook it at home,' said Pete.

'I said no,' said Bobbie, and offered no explanation.

'I'll see you all tomorrow,' said Martie. 'Goodnight, people.'

'Why wouldn't you let her come home with us? I could have got a steak from Rudy. And Martie's a hell of a good cook.'

'When we can afford a cook I may hire her,' said Bobbie.

'Oh, that's what it is. The old snob department.'

'That's exactly what it is.'

'We're not in any position—'

'*You're* not.'

'*We're* not. If I can't have my friends to my house,' he said, but did not know how to finish.

'It's funny that she's the first one you ever asked. Don't forget what I told you about having boarders, and fifty cents a shirt. You keep your damn Marties out of my house. If you don't, I'll get a job and you'll be just another boarder yourself.'

'Oh, why are you making such a stink about Martie?'

'Come *off* it, Pete, for heaven's *sake.*'

The next statement, he knew, would have to be a stupidly trans-
parent lie or an admission, so he made no statement. If there had
to be a showdown he preferred to avert it until the woman in
question was someone more entertaining than Martie Klinger. And
he liked the status quo.

They both liked the status quo. They had hated each other, their
house, the dinginess of their existence on Mill Street. When the fire
whistle blew it was within the hearing of Mill Street and of
Lantenengo Street; rain from the same shower fell on Mill Street
and on Lantenengo Street; Mill Street and Lantenengo Street read
the same Gibbsville newspaper at the same time every evening. And
the items of their proximity only made the nearness worse, the
remoteness of Mill Street from Lantenengo more vexatious. But
Fair Grounds was a new town, where they had gone knowing
literally nobody. They had spending money, a desirable house, the
respectability of a white-collar job, and the restored confidence in
a superiority to their neighbors that they had not allowed themselves
to feel on Mill Street. In the Dan Patch Tavern they would let
things slip out that would have been meaningless on Mill Street,
where their neighbors' daily concern was a loaf of bread and a
bottle of milk. 'Pete, did you know Jimmy Stewart, the movie actor?'
'No, he was several classes behind me, but he was in my club.'
'Bobbie, what's it like on one of them yachts?' 'I've only been on
one, but it was fun while it lasted.' They could talk now about
past pleasures and luxuries without being contradicted by their
surroundings, and their new friends at the Tavern had no knowledge
of the decade of dinginess that lay between that past and this
present. If their new friends also guessed that Pete McCrea was
carrying on with Martie Klinger, that very fact made Bobbie more
credibly and genuinely the woman who had once cruised in yacht.
They would have approved Bobbie's reason for not wanting Martie
Klinger as a guest at supper, as they would have fiercely resented
Pete's reference to Bobbie as the Queen of the Klondike. Uninten-
tionally they were creating a symbol of order that they wanted in
their lives as much as Bobbie needed admiration, and if the symbol
and the admiration were slightly ersatz, what, in war years, was
not?

There was no one among the Tavern friends whom Bobbie
desired to make love with. 'I'd give a week's pay to get in bed with
you, Bobbie,' said one of them.

'Fifty-two weeks' pay, did you say?' said Bobbie.

'No dame is worth fifty-two weeks' pay,' said the man, a foreman named Dick Hartenstein.

'Oh, I don't know. In fifty-two weeks you make what?'

'A little over nine thousand. Nine gees, about.'

'A lot of women can get that, Dick. I've heard of women getting a diamond necklace for just one night, and they cost a lot more than nine thousand dollars.'

'Well, I tell you, Bobbie, if I ever hit the crap game for nine gees I'd seriously consider it, but not a year's pay that I worked for.'

'You're not romantic enough for me. Sorry.'

'Supposing I did hit the crap game and put nine gees on the table in front of you? Would you and me go to bed?'

'No.'

'No, I guess not. If I asked you a question would you give me a truthful answer? No. You wouldn't.'

'Why should I?'

'Yeah, why should you? I was gonna ask you, what does it take to get you in bed with a guy?'

'I'm a married woman.'

'I skipped all that part, Bobbie. You'd go, if it was the right guy.'

'You could get to be an awful nuisance, Dick. You're not far from it right this minute.'

'I apologise.'

'In fact, why don't you take your drink and stand at the bar?'

'What are you sore at? You get propositioned all the time.'

'Yes, but you're too persistent, and you're a bore. The others don't keep asking questions when I tell them no. Go on, now, or I'll tell Rudy to keep you out of here.'

'You know what you are?'

'Rudy! Will you come here, please?' she called. 'All right, Dick. What am I? Say it in front of Rudy.'

Rudy Schau made his way around from the bar. 'What can I do for you, Bobbie?'

'I think Dick is getting ready to call me a nasty name.'

'He won't,' said Rudy Schau. He had the build of a man who had handled beer kegs all his life and he was now ready to squeeze the wind out of Hartenstein. 'Apolochise to Bobbie and get the hell outa my place. And don't forget you got a forty-dollar tab here. You won't get a drink nowheres else in tahn.'

'I'll pay my God damn tab,' said Hartenstein.

'That you owe me. Bobbie you owe an apolochy.'

'I apologise,' said Hartenstein. He was immediately clipped behind the ear, and sunk to the floor.

'I never like that son of a bitch,' said Rudy Schau. He looked down at the unconscious Hartenstein and very deliberately kicked him in the ribs.

'Oh, *don't*, Rudy,' said Bobbie. '*Please* don't.'

Others in the bar, which was now half filled, stood waiting for Rudy's next kick, and some of them looked at each other and then at Rudy, and they were ready to rush him. Bobbie stood up quickly. 'Don't, Rudy,' she said.

'All right. I learned him. Joe, throw the son of a bitch out,' said Rudy. Then suddenly he wheeled and grabbed a man by the belt and lifted him off the floor, holding him tight against his body with one hand and making a hammer of his other hand. 'You, you son of a bitch, you was gonna go after me, you was, yeah? Well, go ahead. Let's see you, you son of a bitch. You son of a bitch, I break you in pieces.' He let go and the man retreated out of range of Rudy's fist. 'Pay your bill and don't come back. Don't ever show your face in my place again. And any other son of a bitch was gonna gang me. You gonna gang Rudy, hey? I kill any two of you.' Two of the men picked Hartenstein off the floor before the bartender got to him. 'Them two, they paid up, Joe?'

'In the clear, Rudy,' said the bartender.

'You two. Don't come back,' said Rudy.

'Don't worry. We won't,' they said.

Rudy stood at Bobbie's table. 'Okay if I sit down with you, Bobbie?'

'Of course,' said Bobbie.

'Joe, a beer, please, hey? Bobbie, you ready?'

'Not yet, thanks,' she said.

Rudy mopped his forehead with a handkerchief. 'You don't have to take it from these bums,' said Rudy. 'Any time any them get fresh, you tell me. You're what keeps this place decent, Bobbie. I know. As soon as you go home it's a pigpen. I get sick of hearing them, some of the women as bad as the men. Draft-dotchers. Essengial industry! Draft-dotchers. A bunch of 4-F draft-dotchers. I like to hear what your Daddy would say about them.'

'Did you know him, my father?'

'Know? I was in his platoon. Second platoon, C Company. I went over with him and come back with him. Phil Hammersmith.'

'I never knew that.'

Rudy chuckled. 'Sure. Some of these 4-F draft-dotchers from outa town, they think I'm a Nazi because I never learn to speak good English, but my Daddy didn't speak no English at all and he was born out in the Walley. My old woman says put my dischartch papers up over the back-bar. I say what for? So's to make the good impression on a bunch of draft-dotchers? Corporal Rudolph W. Schau. Your Daddy was a good man and a good soldier.'

'Why didn't you ever tell me you knew him?'

'Oh, I don't know, Bobbie. I wasn't gonna tell you now, but I did. It don't pay to be a talker in my business. A listener, not a talker.'

'You didn't approve of me, did you?'

'I'm a saloonkeeper. A person comes to my—'

'You didn't approve of me. Don't dodge the issue.'

'Well, your Daddy wouldn't of liked you coming to a saloon that often. But times change, and you're better off here than the other joints.'

'I hope you don't *mind* my coming here.'

'Listen, you come here as much as you want.'

'Try and stop me,' she said, smiling.

Pete joined them. 'What happened to Dick Hartenstein?' he said.

'The same as will happen to anybody gets fresh with your wife,' said Rudy, and got up and left them.

'There could be a hell of a stink about this. Rudy could lose his license if the Company wanted to press the point.'

'Well, you just see that he doesn't,' said Bobbie.

'Maybe it isn't such a good idea, your coming here so often.'

'Maybe. On the other hand, maybe it's a wonderful idea. I happen to think it's a wonderful idea, so I'm going to keep on coming. If *you* want to go to one of the other places, that's all right. But I like Rudy's. I like it better than ever, now.'

No action was taken against Rudy Schau, and Bobbie visited the Tavern as frequently as ever. Hartenstein was an unpopular foreman and the women said he got what had been coming to him for a long time. Bobbie's friends were pleased that their new symbol had such a forthright defender. It was even said that Bobbie had saved Hartenstein from a worse beating, a rumor that added to the respect she was given by the men and the women.

The McCrea children were not being brought up according to Lantenengo Street standards. On the three or four afternoons a week that Bobbie went to the Tavern she would take her son and daughter to a neighbor's yard. On the other afternoons the neighbors' children would play in her yard. During bad weather and the worst of the winter the McCreas' house was in more frequent service as a nursery, since some of the neighbors were living in one-or two-room apartments. But none of the children, the McCreas' or the neighbors', had individual supervision. Children who had learned to walk were separated from those who were still crawling, on the proven theory that the crawling children were still defenseless against the whimsical cruelties of the older ones. Otherwise there was no distinction, and all the children were toughened early in life, as most of their parents had been. 'I guess it's all right,' Pete once said to Bobbie. 'But I hate to think what they'll be like when they got older. Little gangsters.'

'Well, that was never your trouble, God knows,' said Bobbie. 'And I'm no shining example of having a nannie take care of me. Do you remember my nannie?'

'Vaguely.'

' "Let's go and see the horsies," she'd say. And we'd go to Mr Duncan's stable and I'd come home covered with scratches from the stable cat. And I guess Patrick was covered with scratches from my nannie. Affectionate scratches, of course. Do you remember Mr Duncan's Patrick?'

'Sure.'

'He must have been quite a man. Phyllis used to go there with her nannie, too. But the cat liked Phyllis.'

'I'm not suggesting that we have a nannie.'

'No. You're suggesting that I stay away from the Tavern.'

'In the afternoon.'

'The afternoon is the only time the mothers will watch each other's children, except in rare cases. Our kids are all right. I'm with them all day most of the time, and we're home every evening, seven nights a week.'

'What else is there to do?'

'Well, for instance once a month we could go to a movie.'

'Where? Gibbsville?'

'Yes. Two gallons of gas at the most.'

'Are you getting the itch to move back to Gibbsville?'

'Not at all. Are you?'

'Hell, no.'

'We could get some high school kid to watch the children. I'd just like to have a change once in a while.'

'All right. The next time there's something good at the Globe.'

Their first trip to the Globe was their last. They saw no one they knew in the theatre or in the bar of the John Gibb Hotel, and when they came home the high school kid was naked in bed with a man Pete recognised from the plant. 'Get out of here,' said Pete.

'Is she your kid, McCrea?'

'No, she's not my kid. But did you ever hear of statutory rape?'

'Rape? This kid? I had to wait downstairs, for God's sake. She took on three other guys tonight. Ten bucks a crack.'

The girl put on her clothes in sullen silence. She never spoke except to say to the man: 'Do you have a room some place?'

'Well,' said Pete, when they had gone. 'Where did you get her from? The Junior League?'

'If you'd stared at her any more you'd have had to pay ten dollars too.'

'For sixteen she had quite a shape.'

'She won't have it much longer.'

'You got an eyeful, too, don't pretend you didn't.'

'Well, at least she won't get pregnant that way. And she *will* get *rich*,' said Bobbie.

Pete laughed. 'It was really quite funny. Where *did* you get her?'

'If you want her name and telephone number, I have it downstairs. I got her through one of the neighbors. She certainly got the word around quickly enough, where she'd be. There's the doorbell. Another customer?'

Pete went downstairs and informed the stranger at the door that he had the wrong address.

'Another customer, and I think he had two guys with him in the car. Seventy dollars she was going to make tonight. I guess I'm supposed to report this at the plant. We have a sort of a V-D file of known prostitutes. We sic the law on them before they infect the whole outfit, and I'll bet this little character—'

'Good heavens, yes. I must burn everything. Bed linen. Towels. Why that little bitch. Now I'm getting sore.' She collected the linen and took it downstairs and to the trash burner in the yard. When she returned Pete was in bed, staring at the ceiling. 'I'm going to sleep in the other room,' she said.

'What's the matter?'

'I didn't like that tonight. I don't want to sleep with you.'

'Oh, all right then, go to hell,' said Pete.

She made up one of the beds in the adjoining room. He came and sat on the edge of her bed in the dark. 'Go away, Pete,' she said.

'Why?'

'Oh, all right, I'll *tell* you why. Tonight made me think of the time you wanted to exchange with Mary and Frank. That's all I've been able to think of.'

'That's all passed, Bobbie. I'm not like that any more.'

'You would have got in bed with that girl. I saw you.'

'Then, I'll tell you something. You would have got in bed with that man. I saw you, too. You were excited.'

'How could I help being excited, so suddenly come upon something like that. But I was disgusted, too. And still am. Please go away and let me try to get some sleep.'

She did not sleep until first light, and when the alarm clock sounded she prepared his and the children's breakfast. She was tired and nervous throughout the day. She could not go to the Tavern because it was her turn to watch neighbors' children, and Pete telephoned and said bluntly that he would not be home for supper, offering no excuse. He got home after eleven that night, slightly drunk and with lipstick on his neck.

'Who was it? Martie?' said Bobbie.

'What difference does it make who it was? I've been trying to give up other women, but you're no help.'

'I have no patience with that kind of an excuse. It's easy enough to blame me. Remember, Pete, I can pick up a man just as easily as you can make a date with Martie.'

'I know you can, and you probably will.'

It was the last year of the war, and she had remained faithful to Pete throughout the life of their son Angus. A week later she resumed her affair with Bill Charney. 'You never forgot me,' he said. 'I never forgot you, either, Bobbie. I heard about you and Pete living in Fair Grounds. You know a couple times I took my car and dro' past your house to see which one it was. I didn't know,

maybe you'd be sitting out on the front porch and if you saw me,
you know. Maybe we just say hello and pass the time of day. But
I didn't think no such thing, to tell you the God's honest truth. I
got nothing against my wife, only she makes me weary. The house
and the kids, she got me going to Mass every Sunday, all like that.
But I ain't built that way, Bobbie. I'm the next thing to a hood,
and you got that side of you, too. I'll make you any price you say,
the other jerks you slept with, they never saw that side of you. You
know, you hear a lot about love, Bobbie, but I guess I came closer
to it with you than any other woman I ever knew. I never forgot
you any more than you ever forgot me. It's what they call a mutual
attraction. Like you know one person has it for another person.'

'I know.'

'I don't see how we stood it as long as we did. Be honest, now,
didn't you often wish it was me instead of some other guy?'

'Yes.'

'All right, I'll be honest with you. Many's the time in bed with
my wife I used to say to myself, "Peggy, you oughta take lessons
from Bobbie McCrea." But who can give lessons, huh? If you don't
have the mutual attraction, you're nothin'. How do you think I
look?' He slapped his belly. 'You know I weigh the same as I used
to weigh? You look good. You put on a little. What? Maybe six
pounds?'

'Seven or eight.'

'But you got it distributed. In another year Peggy's gonna weigh
a hundred and fifty pounds, and I told her, I said either she took
some of that off or I'd get another girl. Her height, you know. She
can't get away with that much weight. I eat everything, but I do
a lot of walking and standing. I guess I use up a lot of excess
energy. Feel them muscles. Punch me in the belly. I got no fat on
me anywhere, Bobbie. For my age I'm a perfect physical specimen.
I could get any amount of insurance if I got out of The Numbers.
But nobody's gonna knock me off so why do I want insurance? I
may even give up The Numbers one of these days. I got a couple
of things lined up, strictly, strictly legitimate, and when my kids
are ready to go away to school, I may just give up The Numbers.
For a price, naturally.'

'That brings up a point.'

'You need money? How much do you want? It's yours. I *mean*
like ten, fifteen gees.'

'No, no money. But everybody knows you now. Where can we meet?'

'What's the matter with here? I told you, I own this hotel.'

'But I can't just come and go. People know me, too. I have an idea, though.'

'What?'

'Buy a motel.'

'Buy a motel. You know, that thought crossed me a year ago, but you know what I found out? They don't make money. You'd think they would, but those that come out ahead, you be surprised how little they make.'

'There's one near Swedish Haven. It's only about a mile from my house.'

'We want a big bed, not them twin beds. I tell you what I could do. I could rent one of the units by the month and move my own furniture in. How would that suit you?'

'I'd like it better if you owned the place.'

'Blackmail? Is that what you're thinking about? Who'd blackmail me, Bobbie? Or my girl? I'm still a hood in the eyes of some people.'

There was no set arrangement for their meetings. Bill Charney postponed the purchase of the motel until she understood he had no intention of buying it or of making any other arrangement that implied permanence. At first she resented his procrastination, but she discovered that she preferred his way; he would telephone her, she would telephone him whenever desire became urgent, and sometimes they would be together within an hour of the telephone call. They spaced out their meetings so that each one produced novelty and excitement, and a year passed and another and Bobbie passed the afternoon of her fortieth birthday with him.

It was characteristic of their relationship that she did not tell him it was her birthday. He always spoke of his wife and children and his business enterprises, but he did not notice that she never spoke of her home life. He was a completely egocentric man, equally admiring of his star sapphire ring on his strong short-fingered hand and of her slender waist, which in his egocentricity became his possession. Inevitably, because of the nature of his business, he had a reputation for being close-mouthed, but alone with Bobbie he talked freely. 'You know, Bobbie, I laid a friend of yours?'

'Was it fun?'

'Aren't you gonna ask me who?'

'You'll tell me.'

'At least I guess she's a friend of yours. Mary Lander.'

'She used to be a friend of mine. I haven't seen her in years.'

'Yeah. While her husband was in the service. Frank.'

'You're so busy, with all your women.'

'There's seven days in the week, honey, and it don't take up too much of your time. This didn't last very long, anyway. Five, maybe six times I slept with her. I took her to New York twice, that is I met her there. The other times in her house. You know, she's a neighbor of mine.'

'And very neighborly.'

'Yeah, that's how it started. She come to my house to collect for something, some war drive, and Peggy said I took care of all them things so when I got home I made out a cheque and took it over to the Landers' and inside of fifteen minutes—less than that—we were necking all over the parlor. Hell, I knew the minute she opened the door—'

'One of those mutual attractions?'

'Yeah, sure. I gave her the cheque and she said, "I don't know how to thank you," and I said if she had a couple of minutes I'd show her how. "Oh, Mr Charney," but she didn't tell me to get out, so I knew I was in.'

'What ever broke up this romance?'

'Her. She had some guy in Washington, D.C., she was thinking of marrying, and when I finally got it out of her who the guy was, I powdered out. Joe Whipple. I gotta do business with Joe. We got a home-loan proposition that we're ready to go with any day, and this was three years ago when Joe and I were just talking about it, what they call the talking stage.'

'So you're the one that broke it off, not Mary.'

'If a guy's looking at you across a desk and thinking you're laying his girl, you stand to get a screwing from that guy. Not that I don't trust Joe, because I do.'

'Do you trust Mary?'

'I wondered about that, if she'd blab to Joe. A dame like Mary Lander, is she gonna tell the guy she's thinking of marrying that she's been laying a hood like me? No. By the way, she's queer. She told me she'd go for a girl.'

'I'm surprised she hasn't already.'

'Maybe she has. I couldn't find out. I always try to find out.'

'You never asked me.'

'I knew you wouldn't. But a dame like Mary, as soon as she opened the door I knew I was in, but then the next thing is you find out what else she'll go for. In her case, the works, as long as it isn't gonna get around. I guess I always figured her right. I have to figure all angles, men *and* women. That's where my brother Ed was stupid. I used to say to him, find out what kind of a broad a guy goes for before you declare him in. Ed used to say all he had to do was play a game of cards with a guy. But according to my theory, everybody goes into a card game prepared. Both eyes open. But not a guy going after a broad. You find out more from broads, like take for instance Mary. Now I know Frank is married to a dame that is screwing his best friend, laid a hood like me, and will go for a girl. You think I'd ever depend on Frank Lander? No. And Joe Whipple. Married to a lush, and sleeping with his best friend's wife, Mary.'

'Then you wouldn't depend on Joe, either?'

'Yes, I would. Women don't bother him. He don't care if his wife is a lush, he'll get his nooky from his best friend's wife, he *isn't* going to marry her because that was three-four years ago, and he's tough about everybody. His wife, his dame, his best friend, *and* the United States government. Because I tell you something, if we ever get going on the home-loan proposition, don't think Joe didn't use his job in Washington every chance he got. The partnership is gonna be me and Joe Whipple, because he's just as tough as I am. And one fine day he'll fall over dead from not taking care of himself, and I'll be the main guy. You know the only thing I don't like about you, Bobbie, is the booze. If you'd lay off the sauce for a year I'd get rid of Peggy, and you and I could get married. But booze is women's weakness like women are men's weakness.'

'Men are women's weakness.'

'No, you're wrong. Men don't make women talk, men don't make women lose their looks, and women can give up men for a hell of a long time, but a female lush is the worst kind of a lush.'

'Am I a lush?'

'You have a couple drinks every day, don't you?'

'Yes.'

'Then you're on the way. Maybe you only take three-four drinks a day now, but five years from now three or four drinks will get you stewed, so you'll be stewed every day. That's a lush. Peggy eats like a God damn pig, but if she ever started drinking, I'd kick her out. Fortunately her old man died with the D.T.'s, so she afraid of it.'

'Would you mind getting me a nice double Scotch with a little water?'

'Why should I mind?' He grinned from back molar to back molar. 'When you got a little load on, you forget home and mother.' He got her the drink, she took it in her right hand and slowly poured it down his furry chest. He jumped when the icy drink touched him.

'Thank you so much,' she said. 'Been a very pleasant afternoon, but the party's over.'

'You sore at me?'

'Yes, I am. I don't like being called a lush, and I certainly don't like you to think I'd make a good substitute for Peggy.'

'You *are* sore.'

'Yes.'

The children did not know it was her birthday, but when Pete came home he handed her two parcels. 'For me?' she said.

'Not very much imagination, but I didn't have a chance to go to Gibbsville,' he said.

One package contained half a dozen nylons, the other a bottle of Chanel Number 5. 'Thank you. Just what I wanted. I really did.'

He suddenly began to cry, and rushed out of the room.

'Why is Daddy crying?' said their daughter.

'Because it's my birthday and he did a very sweet thing.'

'Why should he cry?' said their son. He was nine years old, the daughter eleven.

'Because he's sentimental,' said the daughter.

'And it's a very nice thing to be,' said Bobbie.

'Aren't you going to go to him?'

'Not quite yet. In a minute. Angus, will you go down to the drug store and get a quart of ice cream? Here's a dollar, and you and your sister may keep the change, divided.'

'What flavor?' said the boy.

'Vanilla and strawberry, or whatever else they have.'

Pete returned. 'Kids gone to bed?'

'I sent them for some ice cream.'

'Did they see me bawling?'

'Yes, and I think it did them good. Marjorie understood it. Angus was a little mystified. But it was good for both of them.'

'Marjorie understood it? Did you?'

'She said it was because you were sentimental.'

He shook his head. 'I don't know if you'd call it sentimental. I just couldn't help thinking you were forty years old. Forty. You forty. Bobbie Hammersmith. And all we've been through, and what I've done to you. I know why you married me, Bobbie, but why did you stick it out?'

'Because I married you.'

'Yes. Because you married Ichabod. You know, I wasn't in love with you when we were first married. You thought I was, but I wasn't. It was wonderful, being in bed with you and watching you walking around without any clothes on. Taking a bath. But it was too much for me and that's what started me making passes at everybody. And underneath it all I knew damn well why you married me and I hated you. You were making a fool of me and I kept waiting for you to say this farce was over. If you had, I'd have killed you.'

'And I guess rightly.'

'And all the later stuff. Running a poolroom and living on Mill Street. I blamed all of that on you. But things are better now since we moved here. Aren't they?'

'Yes, much better, as far as the way we live—'

'That's all I meant. If we didn't have Lantenengo Street and Princeton and those things to look back on, this wouldn't be a bad life for two ordinary people.'

'It's not bad,' she said.

'It's still pretty bad, but that's because we once had it better. Here's what I want to say. Any time you want to walk out on me, I won't make any fuss. You can have the children, and I won't fight about it. That's my birthday present to you, before it's too late. And I have no plans for myself. I'm not trying to get out of this marriage, but you're forty now and you're entitled to whatever is left.'

'Thank you, Pete. I have nobody that wants to marry me.'

'Well, maybe not. But you may have, sometime. I love you now, Bobbie, and I never used to. I guess you can't love anybody else while you have no self-respect. When the war was over I was sure I'd get the bounce at the plant, but they like me there, they've kept me on, and that one promotion. We'll never be back on Lantenengo Street, but I think I can count on a job here maybe the rest of my life. In a couple of years we can move to a nicer house.'

'I'd rather buy this and fix it up a little. It's a better-built house than the ones they're putting up over on Fair Grounds Heights.'

'Well, I'm glad you like it too,' he said. 'The other thing, that we hardly ever talk about. In fact never talk about. Only fight about sometimes. I'll try, Bobbie. I've been trying.'

'I know you have.'

'Well—how about you trying, too?'

'I did.'

'But not lately. I'm not going to ask you who or when or any of that, but why is it you're faithful to me while I'm chasing after other women, and then when I'm faithful to you, you have somebody else? You're forty now and I'm forty-four. Let's see how long we can go without cheating?'

'You don't mean put a time limit on it, or put up a trophy, like an endurance contest? That's the way it sounds. We both have bad habits, Pete.'

'Yes, and I'm the worst. But break it off, Bobbie, whoever it is. Will you please? If it's somebody you're not going to marry, and that's what you said, I've—well, it's a long time since I've cheated, and I like it much better this way. Will you stop seeing this other guy?'

'All right. As a matter of fact I *have* stopped, but don't ask me how long ago.'

'I won't ask you anything. And if you fall in love with somebody and want to marry him—'

'And he wants to marry me.'

'And he wants to marry you, I'll bow out.' He leaned down and kissed her cheek. 'I know you better than you think I do, Bobbie.'

'That's an irritating statement to make to any woman.'

'I guess it is, but not the way I meant it.'

Now that is as far as I need go in the story of Pete and Bobbie McCrea. I promised a happy ending, which I shall come to in a moment. We have left Pete and Bobbie in 1947, on Bobbie's fortieth birthday. During the next thirteen years I saw them twice. On one occasion my wife and I spent the night with them in their house in

Fair Grounds, which was painted, scrubbed and dusted like the Fair Grounds houses of old. My wife went to bed early, and Pete and Bobbie and I talked until past midnight, and then Pete retired and Bobbie and I continued our conversation until three in the morning. Twice she emptied our ash trays of cigarette butts, and we drank a drip-flask of coffee. It seemed to me that she was so thorough in her description of their life because she felt that the dinginess would vanish if she once succeeded in exposing it. But as we were leaving in the morning I was not so sure that it had vanished. My wife said to me: 'Did she get it all out of her system?'

'Get what out of her system?'

'I don't know, but I don't think she did, entirely.'

'That would be asking too much,' I said. 'But I guess she's happy.'

'Content, but not happy,' said my wife. 'But the children are what interested me. The girl is going to be attractive in a few more years, but that boy! You didn't talk to him, but do you know about him? He's fourteen, and he's already passed his senior mathematics. He's *finished* the work that the high school seniors are supposed to be taking. The principal is trying to arrange correspondence courses for him. He's the brightest student they ever had in Fair Grounds High School, ever, and all the scientific men at the aluminum plant know about him. And he's a good-looking boy. too.'

'Bobbie didn't tell me any of this.'

'And I'll bet I know why. He's their future. With you she wanted to get rid of the past. She adores this boy, adores him. That part's almost terrifying.'

'Not to me,' I said, 'It's the best thing that could have happened to her, and to Pete. The only thing that's terrifying is that they could have ruined it. And believe me, they could have.'

In 1960, then, I saw Pete and Bobbie again. They invited me, of all their old friends, to go with them to the Princeton commencement. Angus McCrea, Junior, led his class, was awarded the mathematics prize, the physics prize, the Eubank Prize for scholarship, and some other honors that I am sure are listed in the program. I could not read the program because I was crying most of the time. Pete would lean forward in his chair, listening to the things that were being said about his son, but in an attitude that would have been more suitable to a man who was listening to a pronouncement

of sentence. Bobbie sat erect and smiling, but every once in a while
I could hear her whisper, 'Oh, God. Oh, God.'

There, I guess, is our happy ending.

III

We're Friends Again
the big shuffle in which the right
wife doesn't always come up on top
'The ways of the rich,
the seemingly cold women
who are really passionate
to the point of abandon, the
conviction that most people
get a raw deal in love.'

New York Herald Tribune

CHAPTER 3

We're Friends Again

I know of no quiet quite like that of a men's club at about half past nine on a summer Sunday evening. The stillness is a denial of the meaning and purpose of a club, and as you go from empty room to empty room and hear nothing but the ticking of clocks and your own heel taps on the rugless floor, you think of the membership present and past; the charming, dull, distinguished, vulgar, jolly, bibulous men who have selected this place and its company as a refuge from all other places and all other company. For that is what a club is, and to be alone in it is wrong. And at half past nine on a summer Sunday evening you are quite likely to be alone. The old men who live there have retired for the night, sure that if they die before morning they will be discovered by a chambermaid, and that if they survive this night they will have another day in which their loneliness will be broken by the lunch crowd, the cocktail crowd, and the presence of a few men in the diningroom in the evening. But on a summer Sunday evening the old men are better off in their rooms, with their personal possessions, their framed photographs and trophies of accomplishment and favourite books. The lounge, the library, the billiard and card rooms have a deathly emptiness on summer Sunday evenings, and the old men need no additional reminder of emptiness or death.

It is always dark in my club at half past nine in the evening, and darker than ever on Sunday in summer, when only the fewest possible lights are left burning. If you go to the bar the bartender slowly folds his newspaper, which he has been reading by the light from the back bar, takes off his glasses, says 'Good evening', and unconsciously looks up at the clock to see how much longer he must stay. Downstairs another club servant is sitting at the telephone switchboard. There is the spitting buzz of an incoming call and he says, 'Devening, St. James Club? . . . No, sir he isn't . . . No sir, no message for you . . . Mr. Crankshaw went to bed about an hour ago. Orders not to disturb him, sir . . . You're welcome. Goodnight' The switchboard buzzes, the loudest, the only noise in the club, until the man pulls out the plug and the weight pulls the cord back into place, and then it is quiet again.

I had been a member of the St. James for about ten years, but I could not recall ever having been there on a Sunday until this night a year or so ago. I was summoned on the golf course by an urgent message to call the New York operator, which I did immediately. 'Jim, I'm sorry to louse up your golf, but can you get a train in to New York? I don't advise driving. The traffic is terrible.'

'There's a train that will get me to Penn Station about eight-thirty,' I said. 'But what's this all about?'

The man I was speaking to was Charles Ellis, one of my best friends.

'Charley? What's it all *about*?' I repeated.

'Nancy died this afternoon. She had a stroke after lunch.'

'Oh, no. Charley, I can't tell you—'

'I know, and thanks. Are you still a member at the St. James?'

'Yes, why?'

'Will you meet me there? I'll tell you why when I see you.'

'Of course. What time will you get there?'

'As soon after eight-thirty as I can.'

For a little while the stillness of the club was a relief from the noise and unpleasantness of the train, which was filled with men and women and children who had presumably been enjoying themselves under the Long Island sun but were now beginning to suffer from it, and if not from the damage to their skin, from the debilitating effects of too much picnic food and canned beer. At Jamaica there was an angry scramble as we changed trains, and all the way from Jamaica to Penn Station five men fought over some fishing tackle on the car platform while three young men with thick thatches and blue jeans tormented two pansies in imitation Italian silk suits.

The bartender gave me some cold cuts and bread and cheese and made me some instant coffee. 'How late do you work, Fred?' I said.

'Sundays I'm off at ten,' he said, looking at the clock for the fifth or sixth time. 'Don't seem worth the while, does it?'

'I'm expecting a friend, he's not a member.'

'Then if I was you I'd make sure Roland knows about it. He's just as liable to fall asleep. You know, asleep at the switchboard?

You heard the old saying, asleep at the switch. That fellow can go to sleep with his eyes open.'

'I've already spoken to him,' I said. I wandered about in the lounge and the library, not to be out of earshot when Charley Ellis arrived. As all the clocks in the club struck ten Fred came to me, dressed for the street, and said: 'Can I get you anything before I go?'

'Can you let me have a bottle of Scotch?'

'I can do that, and a bowl of ice. You want soda, Mr. Malloy?'

'Just the Scotch and the ice, thanks.'

'About the only place you can drink it is in your room, if you want water with it. I have to close up the bar.'

'It's all right if we sit here, isn't it?'

'Jesus, if you *want* to,' said Fred.

At that moment Charles Ellis arrived, escorted by Roland.

'Oh, it's Mr. Ellis,' said Fred. 'Remember me? Fred, from the Racquet Club?'

'Yes, hello, Fred. Is this where you are now?'

'Six and a half years,' said Fred.

'Thanks very much, Fred,' I said. 'Goodnight.'

'I'll bring you the bottle,' said Fred.

'I don't want a drink, if that's what you mean,' said Charles Ellis. 'Unless *you've* fallen off the wagon.'

'Then never mind, thanks, Fred. Goodnight.'

Fred left, and I switched on some lights in the lounge.

'You saddled with that bore?' said Charley.

'I don't see much of him,' I said.

'I'm sorry I'm so late. I got here as soon as I could. I called this number but it didn't answer.'

'That's all right. I guess Roland had the buzzer turned off.'

'Hell of an imposition, taking you away from golf and so forth. How is Kay?'

'Very distressed, naturally. She said to give you her love.'

'I almost asked her to come in with you.'

'She almost came,' I said. 'But she has her grand-children coming tomorrow.'

He was silent, obviously wondering where to begin.

'Take your time,' I said.

He looked up at me and smiled. 'Thanks.' He reached over and patted my knee. 'Thanks for everything, Jim.'

'Well, what the hell?'

'First, why did I want to see you here? Because I didn't want to ask you to come to the apartment, and I didn't want to go to the Racquet Club.'

'I figured something like that.'

'How did it happen, and all that? Nancy and I were spending the weekend at her uncle's. We went out to dinner last night, and when we came home she said she had a headache, so I gave her some aspirin. This morning she still had the headache and I asked her if she wanted me to send for a doctor, but she didn't. She said she hadn't slept very well, and I probably should have called the doctor, but I didn't. Then there were four guests for lunch and I didn't have a chance to speak to her. In fact the last thing I said to her was before lunch, I told her that if she didn't feel better after lunch, she should make her excuses and lie down. And that's what she did. She excused herself, shook her head to me not to follow her, and about twenty minutes later the maid came and told us she was dead. Found her lying on the bathroom floor. I can't believe it. I can't be devoid of feeling, but I just can't believe it.'

'Did the doctor give you anything?'

'You mean sedative? Tranquilizers? No, I haven't needed anything. I guess I must be in some sort of shock.'

'Where are the children?'

'Well, of course Mike is in Germany, still in the Army. And I finally located Janey about an hour ago, at a house in Surrey where she's spending the weekend. She's been abroad all summer. She's flying home tomorrow and Mike has applied for leave. The Army or the Red Cross or somebody will fly him home in time for the funeral' He paused.

'Wednesday morning at eleven o'clock. Church of the Epiphany, on York Avenue. I decided Wednesday so that Mike could be here, in case there's any hitch.' He looked about him. 'You couldn't ask for a gloomier place than this, could you?'

'No, it's certainly appropriate.'

'Well, what do I do now, Jim? You've been through it.'

'Yes, I've been through it. The answer is, you're going to be so damn busy with details the next few weeks that you won't have too much time to know what hit you. You're going to find out how really nice people can be. Maybe you haven't thought about that lately, but you're going to find out. You're also going to find out that some people are shits. Real shits. I'll give you the two worst. The old friend that won't make any effort at all except maybe to send you a telegram, if that. You'll be shocked by that, so you ought to be prepared for it, I mean very close friends, guys and women you grew up with that just won't come near you. Then there's the second type, just as bad. He'll write you a letter in a week or two, and it'll be all about himself. How sad *he* is, how well he knew Nancy, how much he appreciated her, and rather strongly implying that *you* didn't know her true worth as well as he did. You'll read one of those letters and reread it, and if you do what I did, you'll throw it in the wastebasket. But the next time you see the son of a bitch, he'll say, "Hey, Ellis, I wrote you a letter. Didn't you ever get it?" So be prepared for those two. But against them, the nice people. The *kind* people, Charley, sometimes where you'd least expect it. A guy that I thought was about as cold a fish as there is in the world, he turned out to have more real heart than almost anybody. In my book he can never do another wrong thing. The third group I haven't mentioned. The lushes. But they're obvious and you can either put up with them or brush them off. The only advice I can give you—keep busy. Don't take any more time off from your work than you absolutely have to.'

'And when will it really hit me?'

'I don't know when, but I know how. Suddenly, and for no apparent reason. When your guard is down. You'll be in a subway, or walking along the street, not any favourite street full of memories, but any anonymous street. Or in a cab. And the whole God damn thing will come down on you and you'll be weeping before you know it. That's where nobody can help you, because it's unpredictable and you'll be alone. It'll only happen when you're relaxed and defenseless. But you're not relaxed, really. It's just that you're weak, *been* weakened without realising what it's taken out of you. Emotional exhaustion, I guess it is. Then there are two other things, but I won't talk about them now. They may not happen to you, and I've told you enough.'

'Thanks, Jim.'

'Charley, you know what let's do? Let's go for a walk. We won't run into anybody.'

'Yes. Nothing against your club, but I think I've had it here.'

So the two of us went for a not too brisk walk, down Fifth Avenue, up Fifth Avenue, and to the door of Charley's apartment house.

The doorman saluted him and said: 'Sorry fur yur trouble, Mr. Ellis. A foine lovely woman, none foiner.'

I happened, and only happened, to be looking at Charley as the doorman spoke. He nodded at the doorman but did not speak. I took his arm and led him to the elevator. 'Mr. Ellis's apartment,' I said, and frowned the elevator man into silence. He understood.

We got off at Charley's floor, the only apartment on that floor, and he went to the livingroom and sat down and wept without covering his face. I stayed in the foyer. Five minutes passed and then he said: 'Okay, Jim. I'm okay now. What can I give you? Ginger ale? Coke? Glass of milk?'

'A ginger ale.'

'It hit me sooner than we expected,' he said. 'Do you know what it was? Or what I think it was? It was the doorman saying nice things, and he didn't really know her at all. He's only been here a few weeks. He doesn't know either of us very well. Why don't you stay here tonight, instead of going back to that God damn dreary place?'

'I will if you'll go to bed. And don't worry, you'll sleep.'

'Will I?'

'Yes, you'll sleep tonight. Twenty blocks to a mile, we walked damn near four miles, I make it. Take a lukewarm tub and hit the sack. I'll read for a while and I'll be in Mike's room. Goodnight, Charley.'

'Goodnight, Jim. Thanks again.'

One afternoon in 1937 I was having breakfast in my apartment in East Fifty-fifth Street. I had worked the night before until dawn, as was my custom, and I was smoking my third cigarette and starting on my second quart of coffee when the house phone rang. Charley Ellis was in the vestibule. I let him in and he shook his head at me in my pajamas, unshaven, and with the coffee and newspapers beside my chair. 'La Vie de Bohème,' he said.

'That's right,' I said. 'Come on out, Mimi, and stop that damn coughing.'

Charley looked at me with genuine alarm. 'You haven't got a dame here, have you? I'm sorry if—'

'No dame.'

'I don't want to interrupt anything.'

'I wouldn't have let you in,' I said. 'But I've just been reading about you, so maybe I would have. Curiosity. Who is Nancy Preswell?'

'Oh, you saw that, did you? Well, she's the wife of a guy named Jack Preswell.'

'All right, who is *Jack* Preswell?' I said. 'Besides being the husband of a girl named Nancy Preswell.'

'Well, you've met him. With me. Do you remember a guy that we went to the ball game with a couple of years ago?'

'I do indeed. I remember everything about him but his name. A very handsome guy, a little on the short side. Boyish-looking. And now I know who she is because I've seen them together, but I never could remember his name. Not that it mattered. He didn't remember me at all, but she's quite a beauty. Not *quite* a beauty. She *is* a beauty. And you're the home-wrecker.'

'According to Maury Paul I am, if you believe what he writes.'

'He's often right, you know,' I said. 'He had me in his column one time with a woman I'd never met, but I met her a year or so later and he turned out to be a very good prophet. So it's only your word against his.'

'I didn't come here to be insulted,' he said, taking a chair.

'Well, what did you come here for? I haven't seen or heard from you in God knows how long.' It always took a little while for Charley Ellis to get started on personal matters, and if I didn't talk a lot or kid him, he would sometimes go away without saying what he had intended to say. 'Now I understand *why*, of course, but I gather Mrs. Preswell hasn't even gone to Reno yet.'

'If you'll lay off this heavy-handed joshing, I guess you'd call it, I'd like to talk seriously for a minute.'

'All right. Have a cup of coffee, or do you want a drink? If you want a drink, you know where it is.'

'I don't want anything but your respectful attention and maybe some sound advice. What I really want is someone to talk to, to talk things out with.'

Charley Ellis was about thirty-three years old then, and not a young thirty-three. He had stayed single because he had been in love with his first cousin, a lovely girl who was the wife of Junior Williamson, Ethridge B. Williamson, Junior; he had wanted to write, and instead had gone to work for his father's firm, Willetts & Ellis. His father knew about the second frustation, but I was now

more convinced than ever that I was the only person to whom
Charley had confided both.

'You may be right, you know,' he said. 'I probably am the home-
wrecker. At least a good case could be made out against me. Nancy
and Jack never have got along very well, and made no secret of the
fact. But I guess I'm the first one that shall we say took advantage
of the situation. They had a couple of trial separations but they
always went back together until I happened to come into the picture
during the last one.'

'But you're not blaming yourself or anything like that, I hope.'

'Not one bit. That's a form of boasting, or so it always seemed
to me.'

'And to me, too. That's why I'm glad you're not doing the *mea
culpa* act.'

'Oh, hell no. I didn't create the situation,' he said.

'Do you know who did?'

'Yes, I do,' said Charley. 'Franklin D. Roosevelt, your great pal.'

'Yeah. The inventor of bubonic plague and the common cold,
and now the louser-up of the Preswell marriage. You've been
spending too much time at Willetts & Ellis. You ought to come up
for air.'

'You were bound to say something like that, but it happens to
be a fact. Preswell was one of the bright young boys that went to
Washington five years ago, and that didn't sit too well with Nancy
or her family. Then two years ago Preswell himself saw the light
and got out, but he'd made a lot of enemies while he was defending
Roosevelt, and he came back to New York hating everybody. He
said to me one time, "They call me a traitor to my class, like the
Glamour Boy himself, but my class has been a traitor to me.' He
used to go around telling everybody that they ought to be grateful
to him, that he and Roosevelt were holding the line for the American
system. But then when he quit, he was just as violent against
Roosevelt as anybody, but nobody would listen. He'd been so God
damn arrogant when he was *with* Roosevelt, said a lot of personal
things, so nobody cared whose side he was on. And of course he
began to take it out on Nancy.'

'What does this gentleman do for a living?'

'He *was* with Carson, Cass & Devereux, but they don't want him
back. That's just the point. Nobody wants him.'

'Was he a good lawyer?'

'Well, *Harvard Law Review*, assistant editor, I think. I don't really know how good a lawyer he was. With a firm like Carson, Cass, you don't get any of the big stuff till you've been there quite a while. He has nothing to worry about financially. His father left him very well fixed and Nancy has money of her own. Her father was, or *is* Alexander McMinnies, Delaware Zinc.'

'Oh, that old crook.'

'Why do you say that? You don't know whether he's a crook or a philanthropist.'

'He could be both, but even if he is your girl's father, Charley, you know damn well what he is. I'll bet the boys at Carson, Cass have sat up many a night trying to keep him out of prison.'

'And succeeded, in spite of Roosevelt and Homer S. Cummings.'

'Those things take time,' I said.

'Get your facts right. Mr. McMinnies won in the Supreme Court. Unless you were looking forward to the day when Franklin D. decides to abolish the courts and all the rest of that stuff. Which is coming, I have very little doubt.'

'You don't really think that, but you have proved beyond a doubt that Roosevelt loused up Preswell's marriage. Aren't you grateful?'

'You're a tricky bastard.'

'It's so easy with you guys. You have a monomania about Roosevelt.'

'Monophobia.'

'No, wise guy. Monophobia means fear of being alone. So much for you and your four years at the Porcellian.'

'I could correct you on that four years, but I have to spoil your good time.'

'All right, we're even,' I said. 'What's on your mind, Charley?'

'Yes, we can't even have a casual conversation without getting into politics,' he said. 'Can we forget about politics?'

'Sure, I like to rib you, but what's on your mind? Nancy Preswell, obviously.'

He was smoking a cigarette, and rubbing the ashes from the glowing end into the ash tray as they formed, turning the cigarette in his fingers. And not looking at *me*. 'Jim, I read a short story of yours a few months ago. Nancy read it, too. She liked it, and she said she'd like to meet you. It was that story about two people at a skiing place.'

'Oh, yes. "Telemark".'

'That's the one,' he said. 'They agree to get married even though they weren't in love. Was that based on your own experience—if you don't mind my asking?'

'No. I was in love when I got married, we both were. But it didn't last. No, that story was invention on my part. Well, not all invention. What is? When I was in Florida two years ago I saw this couple always together and always talking so earnestly, so seriously, and I began to wonder what they were talking about. So I thought about them, forgot them, and remembered them again and changed the locale to a skiing place, and that was the story.'

'Nancy liked the story, but she didn't agree with you. You seemed to imply that they *should* have gotten married.'

'Yes, I believe that, and they did.'

'That's what Nancy didn't agree with. She said they were both willing to face the fact that they weren't in love, but where they were dishonest was in thinking they could make a go of it without being in love.'

'I didn't imply that they'd make a go of it,' I said. 'But it seemed to me they had a chance. Which is as much as any two people have.'

'I didn't get that, and neither did Nancy. We both thought you were practically saying that this was as good a start as two people could have.'

'So far, so good, but that's *all* I implied.'

'Do you think they *really* had a chance? Nancy says no. That marriage hasn't any chance without love, and not too much of a chance with it.'

'Well, what do you think? How do you feel about it?'

'I wasn't ready for that question.'

'I know damn well you weren't, Charley, and that's what's eating you. It may also be what's eating Nancy. Does she know you were in love with Polly Williamson?'

'Never. You're the only one that knows that. But here I am, thirty-three, Jim. Why can't I get rid of something that never *was* anything?'

'Go to Polly and tell her that you've always been in love with her, and can't be in love with anyone else.'

'I'm afraid to,' he said, and smiled. 'Maybe I'm afraid she'll say she feels the same way, and divorce Junior.'

'Well, that's not true. She doesn't feel the same way, or you'd have found out before this. But if you admit to yourself that you're afraid, then I think you don't really love Polly as much as you think you do, or like to think you do. I was in love with Polly for one afternoon, and I told her so. I mean it, every word of it. But every now and then I see her with Williamson and I thank God she had some sense. A girl with less sense might conceivably have divorced Williamson and married me, and how long would that have lasted? Polly is Williamson's wife, prick though he may be. And if she wants Williamson, she certainly doesn't want me, and probably not you. Has Polly ever stepped out on her own?'

'I think she did, with a guy from Boston. An older guy, I don't think you'd even know his name. A widower, about forty-five. Not a playboy type at all. Very serious-minded. Just right for Polly. You know, Polly has her limitations when it comes to a sense of humour, the lighter side. She was born here, but her father and mother both came from Boston and she's always been more of a Boston type than New York. Flowers and music and the children. But she does her own work in the garden, and she often goes to concerts by herself. What I'm saying is, no *chi-chi*. She's a good athlete, but there again it isn't what you might call public sport. The contest is always between her and the game itself, and the things she's best at are games like golf or trapshooting. Skiing. Figure-skating. Polly damn near doesn't need anyone else to enjoy herself. And God knows she never needed me.' He paused. 'Did you ever hear her play the piano?'

'No.'

'She's good. You know, Chopin. Rachmaninoff. Tschaikovsky.'

'Charley, I just discovered something about you,' I said.

'What?'

'*You're* a Bostonian.'

'Maybe.'

'The admiring way you talk about Polly, and of course you're a first cousin. Isn't it practically a tradition in Boston that you fall in love with your first cousin?'

'It's been known to happen, but I assure you, it had nothing to do with my falling in love with Polly.'

'Do you mind if I take issue with you on that point? I have a theory that it had a *lot* to do with your falling in love with Polly, and that your present love affair, with Nancy, is your New York side.'

He laughed. 'Oh, God. How facile, and how stupid . . . I take back stupid, but you're wrong.'

'Why am I wrong? You haven't given the theory any thought. And I have, while listening to you. You'd better give it some thought, and decide whether you want to be a New Yorker or a Bostonian.'

'Or you might be wrong and I won't have to make the choice.'

'Yes, but don't reject my theory out of hand. You're a loner. You wanted to be a writer. You're conventional, as witness working in the family firm against your will, but doing very well I understand. And you were talking about yourself as much as you were about Polly.'

'Not at all. I was a great team-sport guy. Football in school, and rowing in college.'

'Rowing. The obvious joke. Did you ever meet that Saltonstall fellow that rowed Number 5?'

'I know the joke, and it was never very funny to us. A Yale joke. Or more likely Princeton.' He seemed to ignore me for a moment. He sat staring at his outstretched foot, his elbow on the arm of his chair, his cheek resting on the two first fingers of his left hand while the other two fingers were curled under the palm. 'And yet, you may have a point,' he said, judicially. 'You just may have a point. Dr. Jekyll and Mr. Hyde. Larry Lowell and Jimmy Walker. Waldo Emerson and Walter Winchell. This conversation may be the turning point of my whole life, and I'll owe it all to you, you analytical son of a bitch.'

'That's the thanks I get. Watery compliments.'

He rose. 'Gotta go,' he said.

'How come you're uptown at this hour?'

'I took the afternoon off,' he said. 'I have a perfectly legitimate reason for being uptown, but I know your nasty mind. Will you be in town next week? How about dinner Tuesday?'

'Tuesday, no. Wednesday, yes.'

'All right, Wednesday. Shall we pick you up here? I'd like Nancy to see the squalor you live in.'

'Others have found it to have a certain Old World charm,' I said. 'All right, Mimi. You can come out now.'

'Listen, don't have any Mimi here Wednesday, will you, please?'

'That's why I said Wednesday instead of Tuesday.'

'Degrading. And not even very instructive,' he said.

'Not if you don't want to learn.'

My apartment was actually a comfortable, fairly expensively furnished two rooms and bath, which was cleaned daily by a coloured woman who worked full-time elsewhere in the building. But Charley Ellis's first remark when he arrived with Nancy Preswell was: 'Why look, he's had the place all spruced up. Is all this new?'

'All goes back to Sloane's in the morning,' I said. 'How do you do, Mrs. Preswell?'

'Wait a minute. You haven't been introduced,' said Charley. 'You could have put me in a hell of a spot. What if this hadn't been Mrs. Preswell?' He was in high good humour, determined to make this a pleasant evening.

'I often wish I weren't,' she said, without bitterness, but as her first words to me they were an indication that she knew Charley confided in me. 'By the way, how do you do?'

'I've often seen you. Well, pretty often,' I said.

'And always pretty,' said Charley.

I looked at him and then at her: 'You've done wonders with this guy. I hardly recognise the old clod.' My remark pleased her, and she smiled affectionately at Charley. 'Gallantry yet,' I said.

'It was always there,' said Charley. 'It just took the right person to bring it out.'

'I like your apartment, Mr. Malloy. Is this where you do all your writing?'

'Most of it. Practically all of it.'

'Oh, you type your stories?' she said looking at my typewriter. 'But don't you write them in longhand first?'

'No. I don't even write letters in longhand.'

'Love letters?'

'I type them,' I said.

'And mimeographs them,' said Charley. 'Shall we have a free drink here, saving me two and a quarter?'

'The market closed firm, but have you ever noticed that Charley hates to part with a buck?'

'No, that's not fair,' said Nancy Preswell.

'Or true. What's the name of that friend of yours, that writes the Broadway stories?'

'Mark Hellinger?'

'Hellinger. Right. I thought he was going to have a stroke that night when I paid a cheque at "21".'

'I very nearly had one myself.'

'No, now that isn't fair,' said Nancy Preswell.

'I'm softening him up for later,' I said.

We had some drinks and conversation, during which Nancy slowly walked around, looking at my bookshelves and pictures. 'I gather you don't like anything very modern,' she said.

'Not in this room. Some abstract paintings in the bathroom.'

'May I see your bedroom?'

'Believe me, that's the best offer he's had today,' said Charley.

'A four-poster,' she said.

'Early Wanamaker,' I said. '*Circa* 1930.'

'All you need is a rag rug and a cat curled up on it. I like it. That's not your father, is it?'

'My grandfather. Practically everything in this room is a copy of stuff I remember from when I was a kid. I depended entirely on their taste.'

'But you bought it all yourself, so it's your taste, too,' said Nancy Preswell. 'Very interesting, and very revealing, considering what some of the critics say about your writings.'

'What does it reveal to you?' I said.

'That basically you're very conventional.'

'I could have told you that,' I said.

'Yes, but I probably wouldn't have believed you if I hadn't seen your apartment.'

'I think I ought to tell you, though. I went through an all-modernistic phase when I lived in the Village.'

'Why are you for Roosevelt?' she said.

'No! Not tonight, please,' said Charley.

'You shouldn't be, you know,' she persisted.

'Shall we not argue about it? I'm for him, and you're not, and that's where we'd be if we argued till tomorrow morning,' I said.

'Except that I think I could convince you. You don't know my husband, do you? I know you've met him, but you've never talked with him about Roosevelt.'

'When was *he* most convincing?' I said. 'When he was with him, or against him?'

'He was never in the least convincing when he was for him. And he's not very convincing now. But as a writer you should be able to disregard a lot of things he says and go beneath the surface. Then you'd see what a man like Roosevelt can do to an idealist. And my husband *was* an idealist.'

'Don't look at me. I'm not saying a word,' said Charley.

'I do look at you, for corroboration. Jack *was* an idealist. You may not have liked him, but you have to admit that.'

'Yes, he was,' said Charley.

'And so were you. But Jack did something about it. You played it safe.'

'Jim is wondering why I'm not taking this big. The reason is we've had it out before,' said Charley.

'Many times,' said Nancy Preswell. 'And probably will again.'

'But not tonight, shall we?' said Charley Ellis.

'I hate Mr. Roosevelt,' she said. 'And I can't stand it when a writer that I think is good is *for* him. I'm one of those people that think he ought to be assassinated, and I just hope somebody else does it, not my poor, drunken disillusioned husband.'

'Is he liable to, your husband?' I said.

'I don't suppose there's any real danger of it. But it's what he thinks of day and night. I don't want you to think I love my husband. I haven't for years. But Jack Preswell was an idealist, and Roosevelt turned him into a fanatic.'

'He might have been a fanatical idealist.'

'He *was!* Four years ago, that's what he was. But there's nothing left now but the fanaticism. Don't you see that, Mr. Malloy? Mr. Roosevelt took away his ideals.'

'How are you on ideals, Mrs. Preswell?'

'If that's supposed to be a crusher, it isn't . . . I have a few, but they're not in any danger from—that awful man. Now I've said enough, and you probably don't want to have dinner with us.'

'Yes, I would. You're a very attractive girl.'

'As long as I don't say what I think? That's insulting, and now I'm not sure *I* want to have dinner with *you*.'

There was a silence, broken by Charley: 'Well, what shall we do? Toss a coin? Heads we dine together, tails we separate.'

'I'll agree to an armistice if Mr. Malloy will.'

'All right,' I said. 'Let's go. Maybe if we have a change of scenery . . .'

'I promise I'll be just as stupid as you want me to be,' said Nancy Preswell.

There was not another word about politics all evening and at
eleven o'clock we took a taxi to a theatre where I was to meet an
actress friend of mine, Julianna Moore, the female heavy in an
English mystery play. Julie was about thirty, a girl who had been
prematurely starred after one early success, and had never again
found the right play. Her father was a history professor at Yale,
and Julie was a well-educated girl whom I had first known in our
Greenwich Village days. We had been lovers then, briefly, but now
she was a friend of my ex-wife's and the mistress of a scenic designer.

Nancy Preswell began with compliments to Julie, ticking off six
plays in which Julie had appeared.

'You must go to the theatre all the time, to have seen some of
those sad little turkeys,' said Julie.

'I go a lot,' said Nancy.

'Did you ever do any acting?'

'*Did* I? "Shall I speak ill of him that is my husband?/Ah, poor
my lord, what tongue shall smooth thy name . . . " '

' "When I, thy three-hours wife, have mangled it?" Where and
when did you do Juliet?' said Julie.

'At Foxcroft.'

'I'll bet you were a very pretty Juliet,' said Julie.

'Thank you. If I was, that says it all. I was cured.'

'Well, I was the kind of ham that never was cured, if you don't
mind a very small joke . . . I always thought it would have been
fun to go to Foxcroft. All that riding and drilling.'

'Where *did* you go?'

'A Sacred Heart school in Noroton, Connecticut, then two years
at Vassar.'

'Where did you go to school, Charley?' I said.

'I don't know. Where did you?' he said.

'Oh, a Sacred Heart school in Noroton, Connecticut. Then two
years at Foxcroft,' I said.

'Too tarribly fonny, jost too tarribly fonny,' said Julie.

'That's her Mickey Rooney imitation. Now do Lionel Barrymore,'
I said.

'Too tarribly fonny, jost too tarribly fonny,' said Julie.

'Isn't she good?' I said. 'Now do Katharine Hepburn.'

'Who?' said Julie.

'She's run out of imitations,' I said.

We went to '21,' the 18 Club, La Rue, and El Morocco. We all had had a lot to drink, and Julie, who had played two performances that day, had soon caught up with the rest of us by drinking double Scotches. 'Now the big question is, the all-important question—*is*,' said Julie.

'What is the big question, Julie dear?' said Nancy.

'Ah, you like me, don't you? I like you too,' said Julie. 'I like Charley, too. And I used to like Jim, didn't I, Jim?'

'Used to, but not any more.'

'Correct. Jim is a rat. Aren't you, Jim?'

'Of course he's a rat,' said Nancy. 'He's a Franklin D. Roosevelt rat.'

'I'm a Franklin D. Roosevelt rat. You be careful what you say,' said Julie.

'The hell with that. What was the big question?' said Charley.

'*My* big question?' said Julie.

'Yes,' said Charley.

'I didn't know I had one. Oh, yes. The big *question. Is.* Do we go to Harlem and I can't go on tomorrow night and I give my under-study a break. *Or. Or.* Do I go home to my trundle bed—and you stay out of it, Jim. You're a rat. I mean stay out of my trundle. Nevermore, quoth the raven. Well, what did my understudy ever do for me? So I guess we better go home. Right?'

'Yeah. I haven't got an understudy,' said Charley. He signaled for the check.

'Jim, why are you such a rat? If you weren't such a rat. But that's what you are, a rat,' said Julie.

'Pretend I'm not a rat.'

'How can I pretend a thing like that? I'm the most promising thirty-year-old ingénue there is, but I can't pretend you're not a rat. Because that's what you are. Your ex-wife is my best friend, so what else are you but a rat? Isn't that logical, Jim? Do you remember Bank Street? That was before you were a rat.'

'No, I was a rat then, Julie.'

'No. No, you weren't. If you were a rat then, you wouldn't be one now. That's logical.'

'But he's not a bad rat,' said Nancy.

'Oh, there you're wrong. If he was a good little rat I'd take him home with me. But I don't want a rat in my house.'

'Then you come to my house,' I said.

'All right,' said Julie. 'That solves everything. I don't know *why* I didn't think of that before. Remember Bank Street, Jim?'

'Sure.'

She stood up. '*Good*night, Nancy. *Good*night, Charley.' On her feet she became dignified, the star. She held her mink so that it showed her to best advantage and to the captains who said, 'Goodnight, Miss Moore,' she nodded and smiled. In the taxi she was ready to be kissed. 'Ah, Jim, what a Christ-awful life, isn't it? You won't tell Ken, will you?'

'No. I won't tell anybody.'

'Just don't tell Ken. I don't want him to think I care that much. He's giving me a bad time. Kiss me, Jim. Tell me I'm nicer than Nancy.'

'You're much nicer than Nancy. Or anybody else.'

She smiled. 'You're a rat, Jim, but you're a nice old rat. It's all right if I call you a rat, isn't it? Who the hell is she to say you aren't a bad rat? She's not in our game, is she?'

'No.'

'We don't have to let her in our game. But *he* does, the poor son of a bitch.'

When she saw my bedroom she said: 'Good Lord, Jim, I feel pregnant already. That's where Grandpa and Grandma begat. Isn't it? I hope *we* don't beget.'

I was still asleep when she left, and on my desk there was a note from her:

Dear Rat:

You didn't use to snore on Bank Street. Am going home to finish my sleep. It is eight-fifteen and you seem good for many more hours. I had a lovely time and have the hangover to prove it. Want to be home in case K. calls as he said he would. In any case we are better off than Nancy and Charles. Are they headed for trouble!!!

Love,

J.

P.S.: The well-appointed bachelor's apartment has a supply of extra toothbrushes. My mouth tastes like the inside of the motorman's glove. Ugh!!!

J.

The motorman's glove. Passé collegiate slang of the previous decade, when the word whereupon was stuck into every sentence and uzza-mattera-fact and wet-smack and swell caught on and held on. I read Julie's note a couple of times, and 'the motorman's glove' brought to mind two lines from *Don Juan* that had seemed strangely out of character for Byron:

Let us have wine and women, mirth and laughter, Sermons and soda-water the day after.

The mirth and laughter, the wine and women were not out of character, but there was something very vulgar about Byron's taking soda-water for a hangover as I took Eno's fruit salts. An aristocrat, more than a century dead, and a man I disliked as cordially as if he were still alive. But he had said it all, more than a hundred years ago. I made a note to buy a copy of *Don Juan* and send it, with that passage marked, to Julie. At that moment, though, I was trying to figure out what she meant by Nancy and Charley, headed for trouble. There was trouble already, and more to come.

I waited until four o'clock and then telephoned Julie. 'It's the rat,' I said. 'How are you feeling?'

'I'll live. I'll be able to go on tonight. Actually, I'm feeling much better than I have any right to, considering the amount I drank. I went home and took a bath and fiddled around till Ken called—'

'He called, did he?'

'Yes. There isn't going to be anything in the columns about you and me, is there?'

'My guess is a qualified no. If we went out again tonight there would be, but—'

'But we're not going out again tonight,' she said. 'I don't have to tell you that last night was a lapse.'

'You don't have to, but you did,' I said.

'Now don't get huffy,' she said. 'It wouldn't have happened with anyone else, and it wouldn't have happened with you if it hadn't been for the old days on Bank Street.'

'I know that, Julie, and I'm not even calling you for another date. I want to know what you meant by—I have your note here—Nancy and Charley headed for trouble. Was something said? Did something happen that I missed?'

'Oh, God, I have to think. It seems to me I wrote that ages ago. And it was only this morning. Is it important? I could call you back?'

'Not important.'

'*I* know. I know what it was. Is Nancy's husband a man named Jack Preswell?'

'Yes.'

'Well, he was at Morocco last night. Standing at the bar all alone and just staring at us. Staring, staring, staring. I used to know him when I was a prom-trotter, back in the paleolithic age.'

'How did you happen to see him and we didn't?'

'Because I was facing that way and you weren't,' she said. 'Maybe I should have said something. Maybe I did.'

'No, you didn't.'

'I don't think I did. No, I guess I didn't, because now I remember thinking that I wasn't positively sure it was he. But when you and I left I caught a glimpse of him, and it was. If anybody was tighter than we were, he was. His eyes were just barely open, and he was holding himself up by the elbows. I'll bet he didn't last another ten minutes.'

'Well, just about,' I said.

'What do you mean?'

'Have you seen the early editions of the afternoon papers?'

'No. I don't get the afternoon papers here.'

'Preswell was hit by a taxi at 54th and Lexington. Fractured his skull and died before the ambulance got there. According to the cops he just missed being hit by a northbound cab, and then walked in front of a southbound. Four or five witnesses said the hack driver was not at fault, which is another way of saying Preswell was blind drunk.'

'Well, I guess I could almost swear to that, but I'm glad I don't have to. I won't, will I?'

'Not a chance. He wasn't with us, and none of us ever spoke to him. The *Times* and the *Trib* will print the bare facts and people can draw their own conclusions. The *News* and the *Mirror* will play it up tonight, but it's only a one-day story. However, there is one tabloid angle. If the *Mirror* or the *News* finds out that Nancy was in Morocco with Charley—well, they could do something with that.'

'And would you and I get in the papers?'

'Well, if I were the city editor of the *News* or the *Mirror*, and a prominent actress and an obscure author—'

'Oh, Lord. And I told Ken I went straight home from the theatre. Jim, you know a lot of those press people . . .'

'Julie, if they find out, your picture's going to be in the tabloids. I couldn't prevent that.'

'And they *are* going to find out, aren't they?'

'The only straight answer is yes. You spoke to a lot of people as we were leaving. Waiter captains. People at the tables. If you can think of a story to tell Ken, I'll back you up. But maybe the best thing is to tell him the truth, up to a certain point.'

'He'll supply the rest, after that certain point. He knows about Bank Street.'

'That was eight years ago. Can't you have an evening out with an old friend?'

'Would you believe that line?'

'No,' I said. 'But I have a very suspicious nature.'

'You're a blind man trusting a boy scout compared to Ken. He didn't believe me when I told him I went straight home from the theatre. But in the absence of proof—now he's got his proof.'

'Well, then have a date with me tonight. Make the son of a bitch good and jealous.'

'I'm almost tempted. When will we know about the *News* and the *Mirror?*'

'Oh, around nine o'clock tonight.'

'You'll see them when they come out, before I can. If they mention me, will you stop for me at the theatre? That isn't much of an offer, Jim, but for old time's sake?'

'And if you're not mentioned, you have a date with Ken?'

'Yes,' she said.

'All right. You understand, of course, this is something I wouldn't do for just anybody, take second best.'

'I understand exactly why you're doing it, and so do you,' she said.

'I detect the sound of *double entendre*.'

'Well, that's how I meant it. You're being nice, but you also know that nice little rats get a piece of candy. And don't make the obvious remark about piece of what. Seriously, Jim, I can count on you, can't I?'

'I would say that you are one of the few that can always count on me, Julie. For whatever that's worth.'

'Right now, a great deal.'

'Well, I wish you luck, even though I'll be the loser in the deal.'

'You didn't lose anything last night. And I may have lost a husband. He was talking that way today.'

'Do you want to marry him?'

'Yes, I do. Very much. Too much. So much that all he ever sees is my phony indifference. Too smart for my own good, I am. Jim, ought I to call Nancy Preswell, or write her a note?'

'A note would be better, I think.'

'Yes, I do, too.'

'I've been calling Charley all afternoon, and nobody knows where he is. But he'll be around when he wants to see me.'

'It's a hateful thing for me to say, but in a way he's stuck, isn't he?'

'He wants to be.'

'He's still stuck,' said Julie.

At about eleven-twenty I was standing with the backstage doorman, who was saying goodnight to the actors and actresses as they left the theatre. 'Miss Moore's always one of the last to leave,' he said. 'We us'ally break about five to eleven, but tonight she's later than us'al. I told her you was here. I told her myself.'

'That's all right,' I said.

'She dresses with Miss Van, one flight up. I'll just go tell her you're here.'

'No. No thanks. Don't worry her,' I said.

'She's us'ally one of the last out, but I don't know what's keeping her tonight.'

'Making herself look pretty,' I said.

'She's a good little actress. You know, they had to change the curtain calls so she could take a bow by herself.'

There were footsteps on the winding iron stairway, the cautious, high-heeled footsteps of all actresses descending all backstage stairways, but these were made by Julie. She did not make any sign of recognition of me but took my arm. 'Goodnight, Mike,' she said.

'Goodnight, Miss Moore. See you tomorrow. Have a good time,' said the doorman.

'Let's go where we won't see anybody. Have you got the papers? I don't mind being seen with you, Jim, but I don't want to be seen crying. As soon as Mike said "Mr. Malloy," I knew. Tomorrow the press agent will thank me for the publicity break. Irony.'

I took her to a small bar in the New Yorker Hotel, and she read the *News* and the *Mirror*. The *Mirror* had quite a vicious little story by a man named Walter Herbert, describing the gay foursome and the solitary man at the bar of El Morocco, and leaving the unmistakable inference that Jack Preswell had stumbled out into the night and thrown himself in front of a taxi. The *News*, in a story that had two by-lines, flatly said that Preswell had gone to the night club in an attempt to effect a reconciliation with his wife, who was constantly in the company of Charles Ellis, multi-millionaire stockbroker and former Harvard oarsman, and onetime close friend of the dead man. The *Mirror* ran a one-column cut of Julie, an old photograph from the White Studios; the *News* had a more recent picture of her in the décolleté costume she wore in the play. There was a wedding picture of Preswell and Nancy in the *News*, which also came up with a manly picture of Charley Ellis in shorts, shirt, and socks, holding an oar. There was no picture of me, and in both papers the textual mention of Julie and me was almost identical: Julie was the beautiful young actress, I was the sensational young novelist.

'Were we as gay as they say we were? I guess we were,' said Julie.

'The implication is, that's what happens to society people when they mix with people like you and me.'

'Exactly. They only got what they deserved. By the way, what did they get, besides a little notoriety? I'm beginning to feel sorry for Preswell. I lose possible husband, but it must hurt to be hit by a taxi, even if you do die right away.'

'You're taking it very well,' I said.

'I thought Ken might show up, if only to demand an explanation. He loves to demand explanations. Have you talked to Ellis?'

'No. I'd like to know if there's anything in that *News* story, about Preswell and the reconciliation. I doubt it, and nobody will sue, but either the *News* has a very good rewrite man or they may have something. If it's something dreamed up by the rewrite man he ought to get a bonus, because he's taken a not very good story and dramatised the whole scene at Morocco.'

'Thank goodness for one thing. They left my father and mother out of it,' she said. 'Poor Daddy. He groans. He comes to see me in all my plays, and then takes me to one side and asks if it's absolutely necessary to wear such low-cut dresses, or do I always *have* to be unfaithful to my husband? He told Thornton Wilder I'd

have been just right for the girl in *Our Town*. Can you imagine how
I'd have had to hunch over to play a fourteen-year-old?'

We were silent for a moment and then suddenly she said: 'Oh,
the hell with it. Let's go to "21"?'

'I'll take you to "21", but no night clubs.'

'I want to go to El Morocco and the Stork Club.'

'No, you can't do it.'

'I'm not in mourning.'

'I used to be a press agent, Julie. If you want to thumb your
nose at Ken, okay. But if you go to El Morocco tonight, you're
asking for the worst kind of publicity. Capitalizing on those stories
in the *News* and *Mirror*. You're better than that.'

'Oh, the hell I am.'

'Well, you used to be.'

'The hell with what I used to be. I was a star, too, but now I'm
just a sexy walk-on. And a quick lay, for somebody that calls me
up after eight years. Why *did* you take me out last night?'

'Because you're a lady, and so is Nancy.'

'Oh, it was Nancy you were trying to impress? I wish I'd known
that.'

'I have no desire to impress Nancy. I merely thought you'd get
along with her and she with you.'

'Why? Because she did Juliet at Foxcroft?'

'Oh, balls, Julie.'

'Would you say that to Nancy?'

'If she annoyed me as much as you do, yes, I would. If you'll
shut up for a minute. I'll tell you something. I don't like Nancy. I
think she's a bitch. But I like Charley.'

'Why do you like Charley? He's not your type. As soon as you
make a little money you want to join the Racquet Club and all the
rest of that crap. That apartment, for God's sake! And those guns.
You're not Ernest Hemingway. Would you know how to fire a gun?'

'If I had one right now I'd show you.'

'When did you get to be such pals with Charley Ellis?'

'I was hoping you'd get around to that. I knew him before I
knew you, before I ever wrote anything. As to the armament, the
shotguns belonged to my old man, including one that he gave me
when I was fourteen. I do admit I bought the rifle four years ago.
As to the apartment—well, you liked it last night. If you want to
feel guilty about it, go ahead. But you said yourself it was a damned

sight more comfortable than that studio couch on Bank Street. What do you want to do? Do you want to go to "21" and have something to eat, or shall I take you home?' I looked at my watch.

'It isn't too late to get another girl, is it?'

'That's exactly what I was thinking.'

'Some girl from one of the night clubs?'

'Yes.'

'I thought they only went out with musicians and gangsters.'

'That's what you thought, and you go on thinking it. Do you want to go to "21"?'

'How late can you get one of those girls?'

'Two-thirty, if I'm lucky.'

'You mean if you call up now and make the date?'

'Yes.'

'You're a big liar, Jim. They have a two o'clock show that lasts an hour, so you can call this girl any time between now and two o'clock, and you won't meet her till after three. I know the whole routine. A boy in our play is married to one of them.'

'The girl I had in mind isn't a show girl and she isn't in the line. She does a speciality.'

She put her chin in her hand and her elbow on the table, in mock close attention. '*Tell* me about her specialty, Jim. Is it something I should learn? Or does one have to be double-jointed?'

'You want to go to "21"?'

'I'm dying to go to "21",' she said.

'Well, why didn't you say so?'

'Because you're such a grump, and I had to get a lot of things out of my system.'

We used each other for a couple of weeks in a synthetic romance that served well in place of the real thing; and we were conscientious about maintaining the rules and customs of the genuine. We saw only each other and formed habits: the same taxi driver from the theatre, the same tables in restaurants, exchanges of small presents and courtesies; and we spoke of the wonder of our second chance at love. It was easy to love Julie. After the first few days and nights she seemed to have put aside her disappointment as easily as I was overcoming my chronic loneliness. We slept at my apartment nearly every night, and when she stayed at hers we would talk on the telephone until there was nothing more to say. We worried about each other: I, when the closing notice was put up at her theatre, and she when a story of mine was rejected. A couple of weeks became a couple of months and our romance was duly noted in the gossip columns: we were sizzling, we were hunting a preacher. 'Would you ever go back to the Church?' she said, when it was printed that we were going to marry.

'I doubt it. Would you?'

'If Daddy wanted me to get married in the Church, I would.'

'We've never talked about this.'

'You mean about marriage?'

'*Or* the Church. Do you want to talk about marriage?'

'Yes, I have a few things I want to say. I love you, Jim, and you love me. But we ought to wait a long time before we do anything about getting married. If I'm married in the Church I'm going to stick to it.'

'You wouldn't have with Ken.'

'No, but he never was a Catholic. If I married you, in the Church, I'd want a nuptial Mass and you'd have to go to confession and the works. With a Protestant—Ken—I couldn't have had a nuptial Mass and I'd have been half-hearted about the whole thing. But marrying you would be like going back to the Church automatically. I consider you a Catholic.'

'Do you consider yourself a Catholic?'

'Yes. I never go to Mass, and I haven't made my Easter duty since I was nineteen, but it's got me. I'm a Catholic.'

'It's gone from me, Julie. The priests have ruined it for me.'

'They've almost ruined it for me, but not quite. I don't listen to the priests. I can't tell that in confession, but that's why I stay away. Well, one of the reasons. I don't believe that going to bed with you is a sin.'

'The priests do.'

'Let them. They'll never be told unless I marry a Catholic and go to confession. That's why I say we ought to wait a long time. I'm thinking of myself. If I marry a Catholic, I'll be a Catholic. If I don't I'll be whatever I am. A non-practicing member of the faithful. I'll never be anything else.'

'Well, neither will I. But I'm a heretic on too many counts, and the priests aren't going to accept me on my terms. It wouldn't be the Church if they did. It would be a new organization called the Malloyists.'

'I'll be a Malloyist until we get married.'

'There's one thing, Julie. If you get pregnant, what?'

'If I get pregnant, I'll ask you to marry me. I've had two abortions, but the father wasn't a Catholic. It was Ken. I paid for the abortions myself and never told him I was pregnant. I didn't want to have a baby. I wanted to be a star. But if I ever get pregnant by you, I'll tell you, and I hope you'll marry me.'

'I will.'

'However, I've been very, very careful except for that first night.'

I have never been sure what that conversation did to us. I have often thought that we were all right so long as we felt a future together without getting down to plans, without putting conditional restrictions on ourselves, without specifying matters of time or event. It is also quite possible that the affection and passion that we identified as love was affection and passion and tenderness, but whatever sweetness we could add to the relationship, we could not add love, which is never superimposed. In any event, Julie stayed away one night and did not answer her telephone, and the next day I was having my coffee and she let herself in.

'Hello,' I said.

'I'm sorry, Jim.'

'I suppose you came to get your things,' I said. I took a sip of coffee and lit a cigarette.

'Not only to get my things.'

'You know, the awful thing is, you look so God damn—oh, nuts.' She was wearing a blue linen dress that was as plain as a Chinese sheath, but there was more underneath that dress than Chinese girls have, and I was never to have it again. Someone else had been having it only hours ago.

'All right,' I said. 'Get your things.'

'Aren't you going to let me say thank-you for what we had?'

'Yes, and I thank you, Julie. But I can't be nice about last night and all this morning.' I took another sip of coffee and another drag on my cigarette, and she put her hand to her face and walked swiftly out of the room. I waited a while, then got up and went to the bedroom. She was lying face down on my unmade bed and she was crying.

'You'll wrinkle your dress,' I said.

'The hell with my dress,' she said, and slowly turned and sat up. 'Jim.' She held out her arms.

'Oh, no,' I said.

'I couldn't help it. He came to the theatre.'

'Oh, hell, I don't want to hear about that.'

'I promised him I wouldn't see you again, but I had to come here.'

'No you didn't, Julie. I could have sent you your things. It would have been much better if you'd just sent me a telegram.'

'Put your arms around me.'

'Oh, now that isn't like you. What the hell do you think I am? I've had about two hours' sleep. I'm on the ragged edge, but you don't have to do that to me.'

She stood up and slipped her dress over her head, and took off her underclothes. 'Can I make up for last night?' she said. 'I'll never see you again. Will you put your arms around me now?'

'I wish I could say no, but I wanted you the minute I saw you.'

'I know. That's why you wouldn't look at me, isn't it?'

'Yes.'

She was smiling, and she could well afford to, with the pride she had in her breasts. 'How do you want to remember me? I'll be whatever you want.'

'What is this, a performance?'

'Of course. A farewell performance. Command, too. You don't want me as a virgin, do you?'

'No.'

'No, that would take too much imagination on *your* part. But I could be one if that's what you want. But you don't. You'd much rather remember me as a slut, wouldn't you?'

'Not a slut, Julie. But not a virgin. Virgins aren't very expert.'

'You'd rather remember me as an expert. A whore. Then you'll be able to forget me and you won't have to forgive me. All right.'

She knew things I had never told her and there was no love in the love-making, but when she was dressed again and had her bag packed she stood in the bedroom doorway. 'Jim?'

'What?'

'I'm not like that,' she said. 'Don't remember me that way, please?'

'I hope I don't remember you at all.'

'I love him. I'm going to marry him.'

'You do that, Julie.'

'Haven't you got one nice thing to say before I go?'

I thought of some cruel things and I must have smiled at the thought of them, because she began to smile too. But I shook my head and she shrugged her shoulders and turned and left. The hall door closed and I looked at it, and then I saw that the key was being pushed under it. Twenty-three crowded years later I still remember the angle of that key as it lay on the dark-green carpet. My passion was spent, but I was not calm of mind; by accident the key was pointed toward me, and I thought of the swords at a court-martial. I was being resentenced to the old frenetic loneliness that none of us would admit to, but that governed our habits and our lives.

In that state of mind I made a block rejection of a thousand men and women whom I did not want to see, and reduced my friendships to the five or ten, the three or five, and finally the only person I felt like talking to. And that was how I got back in the lives of Charley Ellis and Nancy McMinnes Preswell Ellis.

They had been married about a month, and I was not sure they would be back from their wedding trip, but I got Charley at his office and he said he had started work again that week. He would stop in and have a drink on his way home.

'Gosh, the last time I was in this apartment—' he said, and it was not necessary to go on.

'You ended up getting married, and I damn near did myself.'

'To Julie Murphy?'

'Close. Julianna Moore. In fact, your coming here rounds out a circle, for me. She ditched me today.'

'Are you low on account of it?'

'Yes, so tell me about you and Nancy. I saw the announcement of your wedding, in the papers.'

'That's all there was. We didn't send out any others.'

'You lose a lot of loot that way,' I said.

'I know, but there were other considerations. We wanted people to forget us in a hurry, so Nancy's mother sent short announcements to the *Tribune* and the *Sun*. You can imagine we'd had our fill of the newspapers when Preswell was killed.'

'I don't have to imagine. It was the start of my romance, the one that just ended.' I told him what had happened, a recital which I managed to keep down to about fifteen minutes. I lied a little at the end: 'So this morning she called me up and said she'd gone back to her friend Mr. Kenneth Kenworthy.'

'Well, you might say our last meeting here did end in two marriages,' said Charley.

'If he marries her. He's been married three times and if she marries him she's going to have to support herself. He has big alimony to pay. I hope they do get married. Selfishly. I don't want any more, synthetic romances. They're just as wearing as the real thing, and as Sam Hoffenstein says, what do you get yet?'

'Everything, if it turns out all right. You remember Nancy and her theory that nobody should get married without love, the real thing? That story of yours we talked about—"Telemark"?'

'Yes.'

'Well, to be blunt about it, I really forced Nancy to marry me. All that notoriety—I put it to her that if she didn't marry me, *I'd* look like a shitheel. So on that basis—'

'Oh, come on.'

'It's true. That's why she took the chance. But what was true then isn't true now. I want you to be the twenty-fifth to know. We're having a child.'

'She never had any by Preswell?'

'No, and she wanted one, but his chemistry was all wrong. We expect ours in March or April.'

'Congratulations.'

'Thank you. Needless to say, I'm an altogether different person.'

'You mean you have morning sickness?'

'I mean just the opposite. I'm practically on the wagon, for one thing, and for the first time in my life I'm thinking about someone besides myself. Get married, Malloy, and have a baby right away.'

'I *like* to think about myself,' I said.

'That's bullshit, and it's a pose. All this crazy life you lead, I think you're about the lonesomest son of a bitch I know.'

I bowed my head and wept. 'You shouldn't have said that,' I said. 'I wish you'd go.'

'I'm sorry, Jim. I'll go. But why don't you drop in after dinner if you feel like it?'

'Thanks,' I said, and he left.

He had taken me completely unawares. His new happiness and my new misery and all that the day had taken out of me made me susceptible of even the slightest touch of pity or kindness. I stopped bawling after two minutes, and then I began again, but during the second attack I succumbed to brain fag and fell asleep. I slept about three hours and was awakened by the telephone.

'This is Nancy Ellis. I hope you're coming up, we're expecting you. I'll bet you haven't had your dinner. Tell me the truth?'

'As a matter of fact, I was asleep.'

'Well, how about some lamb chops? Do you like them black on the outside and pink on the inside? And have you any pet aversions in the vegetable line?'

'Brussels sprouts. But do you mean to say you haven't had your dinner?'

'We've had ours, but I can cook. Half an hour?'

It was a pleasant suburban evening in a triplex apartment in East Seventy-first Street, with one of the most beautiful women in New York cooking my supper and serving it; and it was apparent from their avoidance of all intimate topics that they had decided how they would treat me. At ten-thirty Nancy went to bed, at eleven Charley went to see how she was, and at eleven-thirty I said goodnight. I went home and slept for ten hours. Had it not been for Nancy and Charley Ellis I would have gone on a ten-day drunk. But during those ten days I met a fine girl, and in December of that year we were married and we stayed married for sixteen years, until she died. As the Irish would say, she died on me, and it was the only unkind thing she ever did to anyone.

The way things tie up, one with another, is likely to go unnoticed unless a lawyer or a writer calls our attention to it. And sometimes both the writer and the lawyer have some difficulty in holding things together. But if they are men of purpose they can manage, and fortunately for writers they are not governed by rules of evidence or the whims of the court. The whim of the reader in all that need concern a writer, and even that should not concern him unduly; Byron, Scott, Milton and Shakespeare, who have been quoted in this chronicle, are past caring what use I make of their words, and at the appointed time I shall join them and the other millions of writers who have said their little say and then become forever silent—and in the public domain. I shall join them with all due respect, but at the first sign of a patronising manner I shall say. 'My dear sir, when you were drinking it up at the Mermaid Tavern, did you ever have the potman bring a telephone to your table?'

I belonged to the era of the telephone at the tavern table, and
the thirty-foot extension cord that enabled the tycoon to talk and
walk, and to buy and sell and connive and seduce at long distances.
It is an era already gone, and I may live to see the new one, in
which extra-sensory perception combines with transistors, enabling
the tycoon to dipense with the old-fashioned cord and *think* his way
into new power and new beds. I may see the new era, but I won't
belong to it. The writer of those days to come will be able to tune
in on the voice of Lincoln at Gettysburg and hear the clanking of
pewter mugs at the Mermaid, but he will never know the feeling
of accomplishment that comes with the successful changing of a
typewriter ribbon. A writer belongs to his time, and mine is past.
In the days or years that remain to me, I shall entertain myself in
contemplation of my time and be fascinated by the way things tie
up, one with another.

I was in Boston for the tryout of a play I had written, and Charley
Ellis's father had sent me a guest card to his club. 'The old man
said to tell you to keep your ears open and be sure and bring back
any risqué stories you hear.'

'At the Somerset Club?'

'The best. Where those old boys get them, I don't know, but
that's where they tell them.'

I used the introduction only once, when I went for a walk to get
away from my play and everyone concerned with it. I stood at the
window and looked out at the Beacon Street traffic, read a newspaper, and wandered to a small room to write a note to Mr. Ellis.
There was only one other man in the room, and he looked up and
half nodded as I came in, then resumed his letter-writing. A few
minutes later there was a small angry spatter and I saw that a book
of matches had exploded in the man's hand. '*Son* of a *bitch!*' he said.

His left hand was burned and he stared at it with loathing.

'Put some butter on it,' I said.

'What?'

'I said, put some butter on it.'

'I've heard of tea, but never butter.'

'You can put butter on right away, but you have to wait for the
water to boil before you have tea.'

'What's it supposed to do?'

'Never mind that now. Just put it on. I've used it. It works.'

He got up and disappeared. He came back in about ten minutes. 'You know, it feels much better. I'd never heard of butter, but the man in the kitchen had.'

'It's probably an old Irish remedy,' I said.

'Are you Irish?'

'Yes. With the name Malloy. I couldn't be anything else.'

'Howdia do. My name is Hackley. Thanks very much. I wonder what it does, butter?'

'It does something for the skin. I guess it's the same principle as any of the greasy things.'

'Of course. And it's cooling. It's such a stupid accident. I thought I closed the cover, but I guess I didn't'. He hesitated. 'Are you stopping here?'

'No, staying at the Ritz, but I have a guest card from Mr. Ellis in New York.'

'Oh, of course. Where did you know *him*?'

'His son is a friend of mine.'

'You're a friend of Charley's? I see. He's had another child, I believe. A daughter, this time.'

'Yes. They wanted a daughter. I'm one of the god-fathers of the boy.'

'Oh, then you know him very well.'

'Very,' I said.

'I see. At Harvard?'

'No, after college. Around New York.'

'Oh, yes. Yes,' he said. Then: 'Oh, *I* know who you are. You're the playwright. Why, I saw your play night before last.'

'That wasn't a very good night to see it,' I said.

'Oh, I didn't think it was so bad. Was I right in thinking that one fellow had trouble remembering his lines? The bartender?'

'Indeed you were.'

'But aside from that, I enjoyed the play. Had a few good chuckles. That what-was-she, a chorus girl? They do talk that way, don't they? It's just that, uh, when you hear them saying those things in front of an audience. Especially a Boston audience. You know how we are. Or do you? We look about to see how the others are taking it. Tell me, Mr. Malloy, which do you prefer? Writing books, or writing for the stage?'

'At the moment, books.'

'Well, of course with an actor who doesn't remember lines. A friend of mine in New York knows you. She sent me two of your books. I think one was your first and the other was your second.'

'Oh? Who was that?'

'Polly Williamson is her name.'

So here he was, the serious-minded widower who had been Polly Williamson's only lover. 'That was damn nice of Polly. She's a swell girl.'

'You *like* Polly. So do I. Never see her, but she's a darn nice girl and I hear from her now and again. Very musical, and I like music. Occasionally she'll send me a book she thinks I ought to read. I don't always like what she likes, and she knows I won't, but she does it to stimulate me, you know.'

I had an almost ungovernable temptation to say something coarse. Worse than coarse. Intimate and anatomical and in the realm of stimulation, about Polly in bed. Naturally he misread my hesitation. 'However,' he said. 'I enjoyed your first book very much. The second, not quite as much. So you're James J. Malloy?'

'No, I'm not James J. Malloy. I'm James Malloy, but my middle initial isn't J.'

'I beg your pardon. I've always thought it was James J.'

'People do. Every Irishman has to be James J. or John J.'

'No. There was John L. Sullivan,' said Hackley.

'Oh, but he came from Boston.'

'Indeed he did. But then there was James J. Wadsworth. I know he wasn't Irish.'

'No, but he was sort of a friend of Al Smith's.'

'*Was he really*? I didn't know that. Was—he—really? Could you by any chance be thinking of his father, James *W.* Wadsworth?'

'I am. Of course I am. The senator, James *W.* Wadsworth.'

'Perfectly natural mistake,' said Hackley. 'Well, I have to be on my way, but it's been nice to've had this chat with you. And thank you for the first-aid. I'll remember butter next time I set myself on fire.'

On the evening of the next day I was standing in the lobby of the theatre, chatting with the press agent of the show and vainly hoping to overhear some comment that would tell me in ten magic words how to make the play a success. It was the second intermission. A hand lightly touched my elbow and I turned and saw Polly Williamson. 'Do you remember me?' she said.

'Of course I remember you. I told you once I'd never forget you.'

Then I saw, standing with but behind her, Mr. Hackley, and I was sorry I was quite so demonstrative. 'Hello, Mr. Hackley. How's the hand?'

He held it up. 'Still have it, thanks to you.'

'Just so you can applaud long and loud.'

'The bartender fellow is better tonight, don't you think?'

'Much better,' I said. 'I'm glad you can sit through it a second time.'

'He has no choice,' said Polly Williamson.

'I hadn't, either,' said Hackley. 'I'll have you know this lady came all the way from New York just to see your play.'

'You did, Polly?'

'Well, yes. But I don't know that I ought to tell you why.'

'Why did you?' I said.

'Well, I read excerpts from some of the reviews, and I was afraid it wouldn't reach New York.'

'We've tightened it up a little since opening night. I think the plan is now to take it to Philadelphia. But it was awfully nice of you to come.'

'I wouldn't have missed it. I'm one of your greatest fans, and I like to tell people I knew you when.'

'Well, I like to tell people I know you.'

'I suppose you're terribly busy after the show,' said Hackley.

'Not so busy that I couldn't have a drink with Polly and you, if that's what you had in mind.'

They waited for me in the Ritz Bar. Two tweedy women were sitting with them, but they got up and left before I reached the table. 'I didn't mean to drive your friends away,' I said.

'They're afraid of you. Frightened to death,' said Hackley.

'They're pretty frightening themselves,' I said, angrily.

'They are, but before you say any more I must warn you, one of them is *my* cousin *and* Charley Ellis's cousin,' said Polly Williamson.

'They thought your play was frightful,' said Hackley.

'Which should assure its success,' said Polly. 'Maisie, my cousin, goes to every play that comes to Boston and she hasn't liked anything since I don't know when.'

'*The Jest*, with Lionel and Jack Barrymore, I think was the last thing she really liked. And not so much the play as Jack Barrymore.'

'I don't think she'd *really* like John Barrymore,' I said.

'Oh, but you're wrong. She met him, and she does,' said Hackley.

It seemed to me during the hour or more that we sat there that he exerted a power over Polly that was effortless on his part and unresisted by her. He never allowed himself to stay out of the conversation, and Polly never finished a conversational paragraph that he chose to interrupt. I was now sure that their affair was still active, in Boston. She had occasion to remark that he never went to New York, which led me to believe that the affair was conducted entirely on his home ground, on his terms, and at as well as for his pleasure. I learned that he lived somewhere in the neighborhood—two or three minutes' walk from the hotel; and that she always stayed with an aunt who lived on the other side of the Public Garden. Since they had not the slightest reason to suspect that I knew any more about them than they had told me, they unconsciously showed the whole pattern of their affair. It was a complete reversal of the usual procedure, in which the Boston man goes to New York to be naughty. Polly went to Boston under the most respectable auspices and with the most innocent excuses—and as though she were returning home to sin. (I did not pass that judgment on her.) Williamson was an ebullient, arrogant boor; Hackley was a Bostonian, who shared her love of music, painting, and flowers; and whatever they did in bed, it was almost certainly totally different from whatever she did with Williamson, which was not hard to guess at. I do know that in the dimly lighted bar of the hotel she seemed more genuinely at home and at ease than in her own house or at the New York parties where I would see her, with the odd difference that in Boston she was willingly under the domination of a somewhat epicene aesthete, while in New York she quietly but, over the years, noticeably resisted Williamson's habit of taking control of people's lives. After fifteen years of marriage to Williamson she was regarded in New York as a separate and individual woman, who owed less and less to her position as the wife of a spectacular millionaire. But none of that was discernible to me in her relations with Hackley. She did what he wanted to do, and in so doing she completed the picture of her that Charley Ellis had given me. In that picture, her man was missing. But now I saw that Hackley, not the absent Williamson, was her man.

It was hardly a new idea, that the lover was more husband than the husband; but I had never seen a case in which geography, or a city's way of life, had been so influential. Polly not only returned to Hackley; she returned to Boston and the way of life that suited

her best and that Hackley represented. There was even something
appropriately austere about her going back to New York and Williamson. Since divorce was undesirable, with Williamson, the multi-
millionaire, she was making-do. The whole thing delighted me. It
is always a pleasure to discover that someone you like and have
underestimated on the side of simplicity turns out to be intricate
and therefore worthy of your original interest. (Intricacy in someone
you never liked is, of course, just another reason for disliking him.)

'I have to go upstairs now and start working on the third act.' I
said.

'Oh, I hope we didn't keep you,' said Hackley.

'You did, and I'm very glad you did. The director and the
manager have had an hour to disagree with each other. Now I'll
go in and no matter what I say, one of them will be on my side
and the other will be left out in the cold. That's why I prefer writing
books, Mr. Hackley . . . Polly, it's been very nice to've seen you
again. Spread the good word when you go back. Tell everybody it's
a great play.'

'Not great, but it's good,' said Polly. 'When will you be back in
New York?'

'Leaving tomorrow afternoon.'

'So am I. Maybe I'll see you on the train.'

There was a situation in my play that plainly needed something
to justify a long continuing affair, something other than an arbitrary
statement of love. In the elevator it came to me: it was Polly's
compromise. In continuing her affair with Hackley, Polly—and the
woman in my play—would be able to make a bad marriage appear
to be a good one. The character in the play was a movie actress,
and if Polly saw the play again she never would recognise herself.
The director, the manager, and I agreed that we would leave the
play as-is in Boston, and open with the new material in Philadelphia. Only three members of the cast were affected by the new
material, and they were quick studies. One of them was Julianna
Moore.

I had said to my wife: 'Would you object if I had Julie read for
the part?'

'No. You know what I'd object to,' she said.

'Well, it won't happen. There won't be any flare-up. Kenworthy
is doing the sets, and they seem to be making a go of it.'

There was no flare-up. Julie worked hard and well and got good

notices in Boston, and I got used to having her around. I suppose
that if she had come to my room in the middle of the night, my
good intentions would have vanished. But we had discussed that.
'If people that have slept together can never again work together,'
she said, 'then the theatre might as well fold up. They'd never be
able to cast a play on Broadway. And as to Hollywood . . .'

'Well, if you get too attractive, I'll send for my wife,' I said.

'You won't have to. Ken will be there most of the time,' she said.
'Anyway, Jim give me credit for some intelligence. I know you
thought this all out and talked it over with your wife. Well, *I* talked
it over with Ken, too. He hates you, but he respects you.'

'Then we're in business,' I said, and that was really all there was
to it. I made most of my comments to the actors through the
director, and Julie was not the kind of woman or actress who would
use acquaintance with the author to gain that little edge.

Polly Williamson was at the Back Bay station and we got a table
for two in the diner. 'Do you think Mr. Willkie has a chance?' she
said.

'I think he did have, but not now. Roosevelt was so sure he was
a shoo-in that he wasn't going to campaign, and that was when
Willkie had his chance. But luckily I was able to persuade the
President to make some speeches.'

'You did?'

'Not really,' I said. 'But I did have a talk with Tim Cochran in
August, and I told him that Roosevelt was losing the election. I
was very emphatic. And then one of the polls came out and showed
I was right.'

'Are you a New Dealer? I suppose you are.'

'All the way.'

'Did you ever know Jack Preswell? I know you know Nancy,
Nancy Ellis, but did you know her first husband?'

'I once went to a baseball game with him, that's all.'

'That's a tragic story. You know how he was killed and all that,
I'm sure, but the real tragedy happened several years before. Jack
was a brilliant student in Law School and something of an idealist.
He had a job with Carson, Cass & Devereux, but he quit it to get
into the New Deal. I probably shouldn't be saying this . . .'

'You can say anything to me.'

'Well, I *want* to. Nancy is married to my cousin and I know you and he are very good friends, but all is far from well there, you know.'

'No, I didnt know. I haven't seen them lately.'

'Nancy and her father hounded Jack Preswell. They were very contemptuous of his ideals, and when he went to Washington Nancy wouldn't go with him. She said it would be a repudiation of everything she believed in and her father believed in and everything Jack's *family* believed in. As a woman I think Nancy was just looking for an excuse. Nancy is *so* beautiful and has been told so *so* many times that she'd much rather be admired for her brains. Consequently she can be very intolerant of other people's ideas, and she made Jack's life a hell. Not that Jack was any rose. I didn't agree with him, but he had a perfect right to count on Nancy's support, and he never got it. Not even when he got out of the New Deal. She should have stuck by him, at least publicly.'

'Yes, as it turned out, Preswell became as anti-New Deal as she was, or Old Man McMinnies. I knew a little about this, Polly.'

'Well, did I tell it fairly? I don't think you could have known much of it, because she was at her worst in front of his friends. She's a very destructive girl, and now she's up to the same old tricks with Charley. You don't know *that*, do you?'

'No.'

'She's gotten Charley into America First. You knew that?'

'No, I didn't.'

'Yes. And even my husband, as conservative as he is, and his father, they've stayed out of it. What's the use of isolationism now, when we're practically in it already? I agree with you, I think Roosevelt's going to win, although I just can't vote for him. But he'll get in and then it's only a question of another *Lusitania*, and we'll be in it too. So I don't see the practical value of America First. We ought to be getting stronger and stronger and the main reason I won't vote for Mr. Roosevelt is that he's such a hypocrite. He won't come out and honestly say that we're headed toward war.'

'A little thing about neutrality and the head of the United States government.'

'Oh, come. Do you think Hitler and Mussolini are hoping for a last-minute change of heart? Roosevelt should be uniting the country instead of playing politics. This nonsense about helping the democracies is sheer hypocrisy. There is no France, there's only England.'

'You're very fiery, Polly.'

'Yes. We have two English children staying with us. Their father was drowned coming back from Dunkerque. Nancy has Charley convinced that their presence in our house is a violation of neutrality. She said it wouldn't be fashionable to have two German children. When have I ever given a darn about fashion? That really burned me up.'

I became crafty. 'How do they feel about this in Boston? What does Mr. Hackley think?'

'Ham? The disappointment of his life was being turned down, by the American Field Service. He'd have been wonderful, too. Speaks French, German, and Italian, and has motored through all of Europe. He'd make a wonderful spy.'

'They'd soon catch on to him.'

'Why?'

'If he burnt his hand, he'd say "Son of a bitch," and they'd know right away he was an American.'

'Oh, yes.' She smiled. 'He told me about that. He's nice, don't you think?'

She was so nearly convincingly matter-of-fact. 'Yes. He and I'd never be friends, but of his type I like him. Solid Boston.'

'I don't know,' she said. 'Charley's almost that, and you and he have been friends quite a long time. Poor Charley. I don't know what I hope. Oh, I do. I want him to be happy with Nancy. I just hate to see what I used to like in him being poisoned and ruined by that girl.'

'And you think it is?'

'The Charley Ellis I used to know would have two English children staying with him, and he'd probably be in the Field Service, if not actually in the British army.'

'Well, my wife and I haven't taken any English children, and I'm not in the Field Service, so I can't speak. However, I'm in agreement with you in theory about the war. And in sentiment.'

'Look up Charley after your play opens. Talk to him.'

'Do you think I'd get anywhere in opposition to Nancy?'

'Well, you can have a try at it,' she said.

I did have a try at it, after my play opened to restrained enthusiasm and several severe critical notices. Charley and I had lunch one Saturday and very nearly his opening remark was: 'I hear you caught up with Polly and her bosom companion!'

I was shocked by the unmistakable intent of the phrase. 'Yes, in Boston,' I said.

'Where else? He never leaves there. She nips up there every few weeks and comes home full of sweetness and light, fooling absolutely no one. Except herself. Thank God I didn't go to Oxford.'

'Why?'

'Well, you saw Hackley. He went to Oxford—after Harvard, of course.'

'You sound as if you had a beef against Harvard, too.'

'There are plenty of things I don't like about it, beginning with der Fuehrer, the one in the White House,' he said. 'Polly fill you up with sweetness and light, and tell you how distressed she was over Nancy and me?'

'No, we had my play to talk about,' I said.

'Well, she's been sounding off. She's imported a couple of English kids and gives money to all the British causes. She'd have done better to have a kid by Hackley, but maybe they don't *do* that.'

'What the hell's the matter with you, Charley? If I or anyone else had said these things about Polly a few years ago, you'd have been at their throat.'

'That was before she began saying things about Nancy, things that were absolutely untrue, and for no reason except that Nancy has never gone in for all that phony Thoreau stuff. Nature-lover stuff. You know, I think Polly has had us all fooled from 'way back. You fell for it, and so did I, but I wouldn't be surprised if she'd been screwing Hackley all her life. One of those children that Junior thinks is his, *could* very well be Hackley's. The boy.'

'Well, I wouldn't know anything about that. I've never seen their children. But what turned you against Polly? Not the possibility of her having had a child by Hackley.'

'I've already told you. She's one of those outdoor-girl types that simply can't tolerate a pretty woman. And she's subtle, I'll give her that. She puts on this act of long-suffering faithful wife, while Junior goes on the make, and of course meanwhile Polly is getting hers in Boston.'

'But you say not getting away with it.'

'She got away with it for a long time, but people aren't that stupid. Even Junior Williamson isn't that stupid. He told Nancy that he's known about it for years, but as long as she didn't interfere with his life, he might as well stay married to her. Considering the

nice stories Polly spread about Preswell and Nancy, I think Nancy
showed considerable restraint in not making any cracks about
Hackley and Polly's son. Nancy has her faults, but she wouldn't
hurt an innocent kid.'

The revised portraits of Junior Williamson, tolerating his wife's
infidelity for years, and of Nancy Ellis, withholding gossip to protect
a blameless child, were hard to get accustomed to. I did not try
very hard. I was so astonished to see what a chump Nancy had
made of my old friend, and so aggrieved by its effect on him, that
I cut short our meeting and went home. Three or four months
later the war news was briefly interrupted to make room for the
announcement that Mrs. Ethridge Williamson, Jr., had established
residence in Reno, Nevada. 'A good day's work, Nancy,' I said
aloud. Much less surprising a few months later, was the news item
that Mrs. Smithfield Williamson, former wife of Ethridge Williamson, Jr., millionaire sportsman and financier, had married
Hamilton Hackley, prominent Boston art and music patron, in
Beverly, Massachusetts. The inevitable third marriage did not take
place until the summer of 1942, when Lieutenant Commander Williamson, USNR, married Ensign Cecilia G. Reifsnyder, of the
Women Accepted for Volunteer Emergency Service, in Washington,
D.C. It seemed appropriate that the best man was Lieutenant
Charles Ellis, USNR. The bride's only attendant was her sister,
Miss Belinda Reifsnyder, of Catasauqua, Pennsylvania. I gave that
six months, and it lasted twice that long.

My war record adds up to a big, fat nothing, but for a time I was
a member of an Inverness-and-poniard organization, our elaborate
nickname for cloak-and-dagger. In Washington I moved about from
'Q' Building to the Brewery to South Agriculture and houses that
were only street addresses. One day in 1943 I was on my way out
of 'Q' after an infuriatingly frustrating meeting with an advertising-
man-turned-spy, a name-dropper who often got his names a little
bit wrong. In the corridor a man fell in step with me and addressed
me by my code nickname, which was Doc. 'Do I know you?' I said.

'The name is Ham,' said Hackley.

'We can't be too careful,' I said.

'Well, we can't, as a matter of fact, but you can relax. I called
you Doc, didn't I?' He smiled and I noticed that he needed dental
work on the lower incisors. He had grown a rather thick moustache,

and he had let his hair go untrimmed. 'Come have dinner with Polly and me.'

'I can think of nothing I'd rather do,' I said.

'Irritating bastard, isn't he?' he said, tossing his head backward to indicate the office I had just left.

'The worst. The cheap, pompous worst,' I said.

'One wonders, one wonders,' said Hackley.

We got a taxi and went to a house in Georgetown. 'Not ours,' said Hackley. 'A short-term loan from some friends.'

Polly was a trifle thick through the middle and she had the beginnings of a double chin, but her eyes were clear and smiling and she was fitting into the description of happy matron.

'You're not at all surprised to see me,' I said.

'No. I knew you were in the organization. Charley told me you'd turn up one of these days.'

'Charley Who?'

'Heavens, have you forgotten all your old friends? Charley Ellis. Your friend and my cousin.'

'I thought he was at CINCPAC.'

'He's back and forth,' she said. She put her hand on her husband's arm. 'I wish this man got back as often. Would you like to see Charley? He's not far from here.'

'Yes, but not just now. Later. I gather you're living in Boston?'

'Yes. My son is at Noble's and my daughter is still home with me. How is your lovely wife? I hear nothing but the most wonderful things about her. Aren't we lucky? Really, aren't we?'

'We are that,' I said. Hackley had not said a word. He smoked his cigarette in a slow movement that reminded me of the royal wave. I remembered the first time I had seen him and Polly together, when he would tack on his own thought to everything she said. 'Are you still with us?' I said.

'Oh, very much so,' he said.

'Can you tell Jim what you've been doing?'

'Well, now that's very indiscreet, Polly. Naturally he infers that I've told you, and he could report me for that. And should,' said Hackley. 'However, I think he can be trusted. He and I dislike the same man, and that's a great bond.'

'And we like the same woman,' I said.

'Thank you,' said Polly.

'I've been in occupied territory,' said Hackley. 'Hence the hirsute adornment, the neglected teeth. I can't get my teeth fixed because I'm going back, and the Gestapo would take one look at the inside of my mouth and ask me where I'd happened to run across an American dentist. Hard question to answer. So I've been sitting here literally sucking on a hollow tooth. Yes, I'm still with you.'

'I wish I were with *you*—not very much, but a little.'

'You almost were, but you failed the first requirement. I had to have someone that speaks nearly perfect French, and you took Spanish.'

'I'm highly complimented that you thought of me at all. I wish I did speak French.'

'Yes, the other stuff you could have learned, as I had to. But without the French it was no go. French French. Not New Orleans or New Hampshire.'

'Do you go in by parachute—excuse me, I shouldn't ask that.'

'You wouldn't have got an answer,' said Hackley. He rose. 'I wonder if you two would excuse me for about an hour? I'd like to have a bath and five minutes' shut-eye.'

As soon as he left us Polly ceased to be the happy matron. 'He's exhausted. I wish they wouldn't send him back. He's over fifty, you know. I wish they'd take me, but do you know why they won't? The most complicated reasoning. The French would think I was a German agent, planted in France to spy on the Resistance. And the Germans would know I was English or American, because I don't speak German. But imagine the French thinking I was a German. My coloring of course, and I *am* getting a bit dumpy.'

'Where are your English children?'

'One died of leukemia, and their mother asked to have the other sent back, which was done. John Winant helped there. The child *is* better off with her mother, and the mother is too, I'm sure.'

'Ham wants to go back, of course,' I said.

'I wonder if he really does. Every time he goes back, his chances—and the Germans are desperate since we invaded Italy. It's young men's work, but a man of Ham's age attracts less attention. Young men are getting scarcer in France. Oh, I'm worried and I can't pretend I'm not. I can to Ham, but that's because I have to. But you saw how exhausted he is, and he's had—'

'Don't tell me. You were going to tell me how long he's been home. Don't I don't want to have that kind of information.'

'Oh, I understand. There's so little I want to talk about that I'm permitted to. Well, Charley Ellis is a safe subject. Shall I ask him to come over after dinner?'

'First, brief me on Charley and Nancy. I haven't seen him for at least a year.'

'Nancy is living in New York, or you could be very sure I'd never see Charley. I didn't want to ever again. It was Nancy that stirred up the trouble between Junior and me, and I'm very grateful to her now but I wasn't then. Junior'd had lady friends, one after another, for years and years, and if he'd been a different sort of man it would have been humiliating. But as Charley pointed out to me, oh, twenty years ago, there are only about half a dozen Junior Williamsons in this country, and they make their own rules. So, in order to survive, I made mine, too. I really led a double life, the one as Mrs. Ethridge Williamson, Junior, and the other, obviously, as Ham's mistress. You knew that, didn't you?'

'Well, yes.'

'I didn't take anything away from Junior that he wanted. Or withhold anything. And several times over the years I did stop seeing Ham, when Junior would be going through one of his periods of domesticity. I was always taken in by that, and Junior can be an attractive man. To women. He has no men friends, do you realise that? He always has some today, or somebody that he has to see a lot of because of business or one of his pet projects. But he has no real men friends. Women of all ages, shapes, and sizes and, I wouldn't be surprised, colors. He married that Wave, and the next thing I heard was she caught him in bed with her sister. Why not? One meant as much to him as the other, and I'm told they were both pretty. That would be enough for Junior. A stroke of luck, actually. He's paying off the one he married. A million, I hear. And she's not going to say anything about her sister. What will those girls do with a million dollars? And think how much more they would have asked for if they'd ever been to the house on Long Island. But I understand he never took her there. That's what he considers home, you know. Christmas trees, and all the servants' children singing carols, and the parents lining up for their Christmas cheques. But the Wave was never invited. Oh, well, he's now an aide to an admiral, which should make life interesting.'

'Having your commanding officer toady to you?'

'That, yes. But being able to pretend that you're just an ordinary commander, or maybe he's a captain now, but taking orders and

so on. An admiral that would have him for an aide is the kind
that's feathering his nest for the future, so I don't imagine Junior
has any really unpleasant chores.'

'Neither has the admiral. He's chair-borne at Pearl.'

'Yes, Charley implied as much. I've talked too much about
Junior, and you want to know about Charley and Nancy. Well,
Nancy stirred up the trouble. I never would have denied that I was
seeing Ham, if Junior'd asked me, but that isn't what he asked me.
He asked me if Ham were the father of our son, and I felt so sick
at my stomach that I went right upstairs and packed a bag and
took the next train to Boston, not saying a single word. When I got
to my aunt's house, Junior was already there. He'd flown in his
own plane. He said, "I asked you a question, and I want an answer.
Entitled to an answer." So I said, "The answer to the question is
no, and I never want to say another word to you." Nor have I. If
he was entitled to ask the question, which I don't concede, he was
entitled to my answer. He got it, and all communication between
us since then has been through the lawyers.'

'What about Nancy, though?'

'Oh, bold as brass, she told people that she thought my son's
father was Ham. Which shows how well she doesn't know old Mr.
Williamson. The boy looks exactly like his grandfather, even walks
like him. But she also didn't know that Mr. Williamson is devoted
to the boy, wouldn't speak to Junior for over a year, and worst of
all, from Mr. Williamson's point of view, I have my son twelve
months of the year at school in Boston, so his grandfather has to
come to Boston to see him. I refuse to take him to Long Island.
And Mr. Williamson says I'm perfectly right, after Junior's nasty
doubts. Doubts? Accusations.'

'But you and Charley made it up,' I said.

'Yes and no. Oh, we're friends again, but it'll never be what it
used to be. Shall I tell you about it? You may be able to write it
in a story sometime.'

'Tell me about it.'

'Charley was getting ready to ship out, his first trip to the Pacific,
and he wrote me a letter. I won't show it to you. It's too long and
too—private. But the gist of it was that if anything happened to him,
he didn't want me to remember him unkindly. Then he proceeded to
tell me some things that he'd said about me, that I hadn't heard,
and believe me, Jim, if I'd ever heard them I'd have remembered

him *very* unkindly. He put it all down, though, and then said, "I do not believe there is a word of truth in any of these things." Then he went on to say that our friendship had meant so much to him and so forth.'

'It does, too, Polly,' I said.

'Oh, James Malloy, you're dissembling. You know what he really said, don't you?'

'You're dissembling, too. I know what he used to feel.'

'*I* never did. I always thought he was being extra kind to an awkward younger cousin,' she said. 'And he never liked Junior. Well, since you've guessed, or always knew, you strange Irishman, I'll tell you the rest. I wrote to him and told him our friendship was just where it had always been, and that I admired him for being so candid. That I was hurt by the things he had said, but that his first loyalty was to Nancy. That I never wanted to see Nancy again, and that therefore I probably would never see him. But since we lived such different lives, in different cities, I probably wouldn't see him anyway, in war or peace.'

'But you did see him.'

'Yes. We're friends again. I've seen him here in Washington. We have tea together now and then. To some extent it's a repetition of my trips to Boston to see Ham. Needless to say, with one great difference. I never have been attracted to Charley that way. But I'm his double life, and the piquancy, such as it is, comes from the fact that Nancy doesn't know we see each other. Two middle-aged cousins, more and more like the people that come to my aunt's house in Louisburg Square.'

'Do you remember the time we came down from Boston?'

'Had dinner on the train. Of course.'

'You said then, and I quote, that all was far from well between Nancy and Charley.'

She nodded. 'It straightened itself out. It wasn't any third party or anything of that kind. It was Nancy reshaping Charley to her own ways, and Charley putting up a fight. But she has succeeded. She won. Except for one thing that she could never understand.'

'Which is?'

'That Charley and I like to have tea together. If she found out, and tried to stop it, that's the one way she'd lose Charley. So she mustn't find out. You see, Jim, I don't want Charley, as a lover or as a husband. I have my husband and he was my lover, too. As far as I'm concerned, Charley is first, last and always a cousin. A dear one, that I hope to be having tea with when we're in our seventies. But that's all. And that's really what Charley wants, too, but God pity Nancy if she tries to deprive him of that.'

For a little while neither of us spoke, and then she said something that showed her astuteness. 'I'll give you his number, but let's not see him tonight. He doesn't like to be discussed, and if he came over tonight he'd know he had been.'

'You're right,' I said. 'Polly, why did you divorce Williamson?'

'You're not satisfied with the reason I gave you?'

'It would be a good enough reason for some women, but not for you.'

She looked at me and said nothing, but she was disturbed. She fingered her circle of pearls, picked up her drink and put it down without taking a sip.

'Never mind,' I said. 'I withdraw the question.'

'No. No, don't. You gave me confidence one day when I needed it. The second time I ever saw you. I'll tell you.'

'Not if it's an ordeal,' I said.

'It's finding the words,' she said. 'The day Junior asked me point-blank if he was the father of my son, I had just learned that I was pregnant again. By him, of course. One of his periods of domesticity. So I had an abortion, something I'd sworn I'd never do, and I've never been pregnant since. I had to have a hysterectomy, and Ham and I did want a child. You see, I couldn't answer your question without telling you the rest of it.'

After the war my wife and I saw the Ellises punctiliously twice every winter; they would take us to dinner and the theatre, we would take them. Dinner was always in a restaurant, where conversation makes itself, and in the theatre it was not necessary. Charley and I, on our own, lunched together every Saturday at his club or mine, with intervals of four months during the warm weather and time out for vacations in Florida or the Caribbean. Every five years on Charley's birthday they had a dance in the ballroom of one of the hotels, and I usually had a party to mark the occasion of a new book or play. We had other friends, and so had the Ellises, and the two couples had these semi-annual evenings together only because not to do so would have been to call pointed attention to the fact that the only friendship was that of Charley and me. Our wives, for example, after an early exchange of lunches never had lunch together again; and if circumstance put me alone with Nancy, I had nothing to say. In the years of our acquaintance she had swung from America First to Adlai Stevenson, while I was swinging the other way. She used the word valid to describe everything but an Easter bonnet, another favorite word of hers was denigrate, and still another was challenge. When my wife died Nancy wrote me a note in which she 'questioned the validity of it all' and told me to 'face the challenge.' When I married again she said I had made the only valid decision by 'facing up to the challenge of a new life.' I had ceased to be one of the authors she admired, and in my old place she had put Kafka, Kierkegaard, Rilke, and Camus. I sent her a copy of Kilmer to make her velar collection complete, but she did not think it was comical or cute.

Charley and I had arrived at a political rapprochement: he conceded that some of the New Deal had turned out well, I admitted that Roosevelt had been something less than a god. Consequently our conversations at lunch were literally what the doctor ordered for men of our age. To match my Pennsylvania reminiscences he provided anecdotes about the rich, but to him they were not the rich. They were his friends and enemies, neighbors and relatives, and it was a good thing to hear about them as such. Charley Ellis had observed well and he remembered, and partly because he was polite, partly because he had abandoned the thought of writing as a career, he gave me the kind of information I liked to hear.

We seldom mentioned Nancy and even less frequently, Polly. If he continued to have tea with her, he did not say so. But one day in the late Forties we were having lunch at his club and he bowed to a carefully dressed man who limped on a cane and wore a patch over his left eye. He was about sixty years old. 'One of your boys,' said Charley.

'You mean Irish?'

'Oh, no. I meant O.S.S.'

'He must have been good. The Médaille Militaire. That's one they don't hand out for traveling on the French Line.'

'A friend of Ham Hackley's. He told me how Hackley died.'

All I knew was that Hackley had never come back from France after my evening with him in Washington. 'How did he?' I said.

'The Germans caught him with a wad of plastic and a fuse wire in his pocket. He knew what he was in for, so he took one of those pills.'

'An "L" pill,' I said.

'Whatever it is that takes about a half a minute. You didn't know that about Ham?'

'I honestly didn't.'

'That guy, the one I just spoke to, was in the same operation. He blew up whatever they were supposed to blow up, but he stayed too close and lost his eye and smashed up his leg. You wouldn't think there was that much guts there, would you? He knew he couldn't get very far, but he set off the damn plastic and hit the dirt.' Charley laughed. 'Do you know what he told us? He said, "I huddled up and put my hands over my crotch, so I lost an eye. But I saved everything else." We got him talking at a club dinner this winter.'

'I wish I'd been here.'

'Not this club. This was at the annual dinner of my club at Harvard. He was a classmate of Ham's. I don't usually go back, but I did this year.'

'Did you see Polly?'

'Yes, I went and had tea with her. Very pleasant. Her boy gets out of Harvard this year. Daughter's married.'

'We got an announcement. What does Polly do with her time?'

'Oh, why, I don't know. She always has plenty of things to do in Boston. A girl like Polly, with all her interests, she'd keep herself very busy. I must say she's putting on a little weight.'

'What would she be now?'

'How old? Polly is forty-one, I think.'

'Still young. Young enough to marry again.'

'I doubt if she will,' said Charley. 'I doubt it very much. Boston isn't like New York, you know. In New York a woman hates to go to a party without a man, but in Boston a woman like Polly goes to a party by herself and goes home by herself and thinks nothing of it.'

'Nevertheless she ought to have a husband. She's got a good thirty years ahead of her. She ought to marry if only for companionship.'

'Companionship? Companionship is as hard to find as love. More so. Love can sneak up on you, but when you're looking for companionship you shop around.'

'Maybe that's what Polly's doing, having a look at the field.'

'Maybe. There's one hell of a lot of money that goes with her, and she's not going to marry a fortune-hunter. Oh, I guess Polly can take care of herself.'

'Just out of curiosity, how *much* money is there?'

'How much money? Well, when Polly's father died, old Mr. Smithfield, he left five million to Harvard, and another million to a couple of New York hospitals, and a hundred thousand here and a hundred thousand there. I happen to know that he believed in tithes. All his life he gave a tenth of his income to charity. So if he followed that principle in his will, he was worth around seventy million gross. I don't know the taxes on that much money, but after taxes it all went to Polly. In addition, Ham Hackley left her all his money, which was nothing like Cousin Simon Smithfield's, but a tidy sum nonetheless. I also know that when Polly divorced Junior Williamson, old Mr. Williamson changed his will to make sure that the grandchildren would each get one-third, the same as Junior. That was quite a blow to Junior. So all in all, Polly's in a very enviable position, financially.'

'Good God,' I said. 'It embarrasses me.'

'Why you?'

'Don't you remember that day I told her I loved her?'

'Oh, yes. Well, she took that as a compliment, not as a business proposition. She's never forgotten it, either.'

'Well, I hope Polly holds on to her good sense. When I was a movie press agent I made a great discovery that would have been very valuable to a fortune-hunter. And in fact a few of them had discovered it for themselves. Big stars, beautiful and rich, would come to New York and half the time they had no one to take them out. They depended on guys in the publicity department. I never would have had to work for a living.'

'How long could you have stood that?'

'Oh, a year, probably. Long enough to get tired of a Rolls and charge accounts at the bespoke tailors. Then I suppose I'd have read a book and wished I'd written it. I knew a fellow that married a movie star and did all that, and he wasn't just a gigolo. He'd taught English at Yale. He took this doll for God knows how much, then she gave him the bounce and now he's living in Mexico. He'd had a succession of fifteen-year-old wives. Once every two or three years he comes to New York for a week. He subsists entirely on steak and whiskey. One meal a day, a steak, and all the whiskey he can drink. He's had a stroke and he knows he's going to die. I could have been that. In fact, I don't like to think how close I came.'

'I don't see you as Gauguin.'

'Listen, Gauguin wasn't unhappy. He was doing what he wanted to do. I don't see myself as Gauguin either. What I don't like to think of is how close I came to being my friend that married the movie actress. That I could have been.'

'No, you were never really close. You were no closer than I was to marrying Polly. You thought about it, just as I did about marrying Polly. But I wasn't meant to marry Polly, and you weren't meant to steal money from a movie actress and go on the beach in Mexico.'

'Go on the beach? Why did you say that?'

'It slipped. I knew the fellow you're talking about. Henry Root?'

'Yes.'

'Before he taught at Yale he had the great distinction of teaching me at Groton. You know why he *stopped* teaching at Yale? Bad cheques. Not just bouncing cheques. Forgeries. There was one for a thousand dollars signed Ethridge B. Williamson, Junior. That did it. He had Junior's signature to copy from, but that wasn't the way Junior signed his cheques. He always signed E. B. Williamson J R, so his cheques wouldn't be confused with his father's, which had Ethridge written out. Henry was a charming, facile bum, and a crook. You may have been a bum, but you were never a crook. Were you?'

'No, I guess I wasn't. I never cheated in an exam, and the only money I ever stole was from my mother's pocket-book. And got caught, every time. My mother always knew how much was in her purse.'

'Now let me ask you something else. Do you think Henry Root would ever have been a friend of Polly's? As good a friend, say, as you are?'

'Well—I'd say no.'

'And you'd be right. When she was Polly Smithfield he'd always give her a rush at the dances, and it was an understood thing that Junior and I would always cut in. I don't think we have to worry about Polly and fortune-hunters, or you about how close you came to being Henry Root. I don't even worry about how close that damn story of yours came to keeping Nancy from marrying me.'

'Oh, that story. "Christiana". No. "Telemark." That was it, "Telemark." '

'You don't even remember your own titles, but that was the one.'

'I may not remember the title, but the point of the story was that two people could take a chance on marriage without love.'

'Yes, and Nancy was so convinced that you were wrong that she had it on her mind. You damn near ruined my life, Malloy.'

'No, I didn't.'

'No, you didn't. My life was decided for me by Preswell, when he walked in front of that taxi.'

I knew this man so well, and with his permission, but I had never heard him make such an outright declaration of love for his wife, and on my way home I realised that until then I had not known him at all. It was not a discovery to cause me dismay. What did he know about me? What, really, can any of us know about any of us, and why must we make such a thing of loneliness when it is the final condition of us all? And where would love be without it?

HENRY CECIL OMNIBUS

BROTHERS IN LAW is about Roger Thursby, called to the bar and promptly plunged into practice. He finds himself pitch-forked into a court without the most shadowy notion of his brief; knowing that he must get to his feet and address the Judge, but not having the slightest idea what he is to say. This funny, wise, sympathetic book must obviously be read and studied intently by all law students. But to the reader whose knowledge of law is the average man's *Brothers in Law* should prove exhilarating.

'Full of charm and humour, I think it is the best Henry Cecil yet.'
P. G. Wodehouse

FRIENDS AT COURT, like *Brothers in Law*, is extremely funny.

'No one has ever caught more precisely or wittily the atmosphere of litigation.' *Cyril Hare* (*Judge Gordon Clark*) in the *Daily Telegraph.*

SETTLED OUT OF COURT, which had a successful run as a West End play, is recommended reading for all law-makers, law-breakers and law abiders. Mr. Cecil has a persuasive way of presenting the most outrageously improbable situations, and getting away with them by dazzling entertaining dialogue.

THE VICTOR CANNING OMNIBUS

THE PYTHON PROJECT is Victor Canning's most exciting thriller. The trail leads through Paris, Florence and Rome, to the sandy shores of North Africa.

'Canning in great form . . .' *Evening Standard*

'Beyond praise for inventiveness and wit . . .' *Punch*

A DELIVERY OF FURIES – Keith Marchant is a tough, free-wheeling ex-R.A.F. pilot who makes a precarious living transporting shady cargoes around the world. His plan is a bold one; he will hijack a cargo of six Hawker Sea Fury fighters on the high seas and deliver them to the sun-drenched Caribbean port of Acaibo, headquarters of Angelo Libertad, the fanatical Guevara-type leader of an island revolution, but he becomes caught up in the ruthless intrigue behind the revolution. Readers will enjoy this famous novel.

'**THE MELTING MAN** is well up to Mr. Canning's high standard of exuberant ingenuity, with the usual seafaring finale.' *Daily Telegraph*

'No one thrills like Canning can – and does.' *Yorkshire Post*

Mr. Canning is a professional thriller writer of high competence.' *Times Literary Supplement*

CHRISTOPHER LANDON
OMNIBUS

ICE COLD IN ALEX – The thought of ice-cold lager, as served in Alexandria, haunted Captain Anson living on whisky – and his nerves – in doomed Tobruk. It became an obsession when he, his sergeant-major and two nurses set out in the ambulance Katy to break through Rommel's encircling panzers. Their desperate journey ran full tilt into action, excitement, personal drama – and Captain Zimmerman, who claimed to be a South African . . .

'The tension of this nighmare drive will grip you.'
Manchester Evening News

'Finely imagined, finely told.' *Birmingham Post*

'Wholly realistic and believable.' *Guardian*

DEAD MEN RISE UP NEVER is a novel of suspense with a dramatic courtroom twist and a tense finale aboard a sardine trawler off the coast of Spain.

THE SHADOW OF TIME – Anger, love and, above all, fear – these are the emotions that drive the characters in *The Shadow of Time* to their various fates. Christopher Landon is a master of suspence, and he keeps the reader on tenterhooks until the very end.

ANDREW GARVE OMNIBUS

MURDER IN MOSCOW – Verney had been sent to Moscow to report on changes in the Russian scene. When the leader of a British peace delegation is murdered, Verney discovers only too quickly the sort of changes that have occurred; the authorities produce a pseudo-criminal – and Verney soon sees why the truth doesn't make a scrap of difference.

'Convincing and fascinating.' *Illustrated London News*

'An authentic peek behind the curtain.' *New Statesman*

THE ASHES OF LODA – This is the story, told at a gripping pace, of how a man struggled single-handed and in alien surroundings to uncover events, intrigues and passions long buried in the 'ashes of Loda' – and of what he found.

THE CUCKOO LINE AFFAIR – When a highly respected citizen is accused by a pretty girl of assaulting her in a train, and two unimpeachable witnesses say they saw him do it, his position is serious. The incident was only the beginning of troubles for Edward Latimer, sixtyish, lovable and slightly quaint, on a journey to the Essex village of Steepleford by the ancient single-track railway known locally as the Cuckoo Line.

Andrew Garve is undoubtedly one of the most successful writers of detective-thrillers to emerge since the war. This is largely due to the vivid atmosphere he evokes from the varied and authentic backgrounds against which he sets his stories.